MISTRUNNER
BOOK 2

MISTRUNNER

BOOK 2

NICHOLAS SEARCY

Podium

All rights reserved. No part of this publication may be reproduced, stored in a retrieval system, or transmitted in any form or by any means electronic, mechanical, photocopying, recording, or otherwise without prior written permission from Podium Publishing.

This is a work of fiction. Names, characters, places, and incidents are either products of the author's imagination or used fictitiously. Any resemblance to actual events, locales, or persons, living, dead, or undead, is entirely coincidental.

Copyright © 2024 by Nicholas Searcy

Cover design by Pius Bak

ISBN: 978-1-0394-5023-3

Published in 2024 by Podium Publishing, ULC
www.podiumaudio.com

MISTRUNNER
BOOK 2

CHAPTER ONE

CLEANING UP

I gave everything to him, but he never saw me as anything but a subordinate. Instead, he gave the greatest treasure in our world to a child.

—Nora Lancaster

I awoke to the sound of birds chirping, and it took me a moment to remember how dire my situation was. But once that realization set in, I couldn't stop myself from recounting the events of the previous few days. My uncle—along with everyone in Mobile—was dead, and I was all alone in the world. Certainly, Pick had survived, but I hardly counted him. Despite the fact that he had recently saved my life, I knew he was next to useless in a fight. If I was going to survive—or more importantly, get my revenge—I would only be able to rely on myself. So, with that in mind, I navigated through my interface to bring up my status. When I did, the effects of the previous day's efforts were on display:

NAME	Mirabelle Lisa Braddock
CLASS	MISTRUNNER
LEVEL	10 (0%)
CONSTITUTION	38/80
MIND	35/80
MIST	34/80
SKILLS	5/7

SKILL NAME	Skill Tier	Modifiers	Abilities
CYBERNETIC MASTERY	Tier 1 (0%)	100% Efficiency	6 Cybernetic Slots
COMBAT	Tier 1 (0%)	+50% Damage (All) +50% Speed (Melee) +50% Accuracy (All) +25% Range (Firearms) +50% Reload Speed (Firearms)	Empowered Shot (D) Double Shot (E) Combination Punch (D) Pummel (E) Engage (E) Disengage (F) Mark Target (F) Barrage (F)
INFILTRATION	Tier 1 (0%)	+15% Effectiveness (Stealth)	Stealth (E) Camouflage (E) Deception (E) Mimic (E) Observation (D)
MISTRUNNER	Tier 1 (0%)	+25% Speed (Misthack) +25% Processing Speed (Mistwalk) +50% Strength (Mistwall) +50% Breach Range	Mistwalk (D) Misthack (D) Mistwall (C) System Redirect (F) Disable Cybernetics (F) Overcharge (E)
FIELDCRAFT	Tier 1 (0%)	+25% Combat Effectiveness	Triage (D) Basic Explosives Handling (D) Combat Focus (C) Pain Tolerance (D) Resistance (E) Foraging (E) Improvisation (D) Regeneration (D)
OPEN			
OPEN			

I could scarcely count the number of ways I had improved. Not only had my modifiers seen marked gains, but I'd also opened up two new skill slots, as well. That left me with an infinite number of possibilities. On top of that, all my skills had evolved, as well. I hadn't even put any of them to the test, but I felt like a changed person.

It only took one look down at my limp hand for me to realize that some of those changes were less beneficial than others. From my Triage ability, I knew that if I didn't find treatment soon, I would lose the appendage. It probably wouldn't be the end of the world or anything—I could always get a cybernetic limb that would probably be an upgrade—but I hated the idea of being forced to waste one of my slots on something like that. If I was going to get cybernetics, I wanted it to be a choice, rather than a necessity. But as I had recently discovered, I couldn't count on always getting what I wanted.

Otherwise, my uncle and everyone else wouldn't be dead.

With a sigh, I decided to delve into my new skill trees. First up was the generically named [Combat] that had been the result of a fusion between [Firearms] and [Close Quarters Combat]:

Tree	Combat: Tier 1 (0%) +50% Damage (All) +50% Speed (Melee) +50% Accuracy (All) +25% Range (Firearms) +50% Reload Speed (Firearms)			
Branch	Small Arms: Tier 0 (0%)	Heavy Weaponry: Tier 0 (0%)	Melee: Tier 0 (0%)	Movement: Tier 0 (0%)
Tier 1	+25% Damage	+50% Damage	+15% Speed	+5% Movement
Tier 2	+25% Range	+15% Range	+25% Damage	+25% Jump Height
Tier 3	Ability: Explosive Shot	Ability: Shatter Shot	Ability: Riposte	Ability: Double Jump
Tier 4	+25% Accuracy	+50% Rate of Fire	+25% Accuracy	+15% Movement
Tier 5	Ability: Multishot	Ability: Instant Reload	Ability: Execute	Ability: Teleport

The skill tree was a lot simpler than the ones it had replaced, but it was also a good deal stronger. Not only were the modifiers far better, but my focus immediately settled on the various abilities in the higher tiers. Some, like Teleport and Instant Reload were self-explanatory, but others were a mystery that I would have to unravel when I reached Tier 5. And considering that it had taken me the better part of three years' worth of focused training to reach Tier 5 in the previous trees, I suspected it would take me far longer to do the same with the new skill trees. However, I liked the idea of having those abilities dangling just out of reach; they were great as distractions and even better as motivators to keep moving forward.

After spending a few minutes inspecting the [Combat] tree, I moved my focus to the next one on my list, which was [Infiltration]. It was the result of [Spycraft] and [Stealth Operations] merging into one skill, and given that they'd always had some overlap between them, I felt that it was the most predictable fusion of them all. I opened the tree:

Tree	Infiltration: Tier 1 (0%) +15% Effectiveness (Stealth)			
Branch	Spycraft: Tier 0 (0%)	Stealth: Tier 0 (0%)	Deception: Tier 0 (0%)	Sensory Input: Tier 0 (0%)
Tier 1	+15% Effectiveness (Deception)	+15% Effectiveness (Stealth Abilities)	+15% Effectiveness (Deception)	+25% Effectiveness (Observation)
Tier 2	+15% Effectiveness (Deception)	+25% Effectiveness (Stealth Abilities)	+15% Effectiveness (Mimic)	+25% Effectiveness (Observation)
Tier 3	Ability: Charisma	Ability: Distraction	Ability: Bluff	Ability: Sense Deception
Tier 4	+15% Effectiveness (Charisma)	+15% Effectiveness (Stealth Abilities)	+25% Effectiveness (Bluff)	+15% Effectiveness (Sense Deception)
Tier 5	Ability: Interrogate	Ability: Vanish	Ability: Chameleon	Ability: True Sight

The modifiers dealt almost exclusively with enhancing my abilities with Stealth and Deception, but I was also very happy to see that Observation was in for quite a boost to its effectiveness. And some of the abilities looked very interesting—specifically Chameleon and Vanish. The others were a little too vague for me to get excited about.

After I'd thoroughly studied that tree, I moved on to the next, which was [Mistrunner].

Tree	Mistrunner: Tier 1 (0%) +25% Speed (Misthack) +25% Processing Speed (Mistwalk) +50% Strength (Mistwall) +50% Breach Range			
Branch	Misthack: Tier 0 (0%)	Mistwalk: Tier 0 (0%)	Mistwall: Tier 0 (0%)	Combat: Tier 0 (0%)
Tier 1	+15% Speed (Misthack)	+25% Infiltration Stability	+15% System Defense	+5% Damage (All)
Tier 2	+15% Ghost Strength	+25% Processing Speed (Mistwalk)	+25% System Defense	+5% Damage (All)
Tier 3	Ability: Surge	Ability: Rewind	Ability: Backlash	+5% Damage (All)
Tier 4	+25% Ghost Stability	+25% Processing Speed (Mistwalk)	C-Grade System Defense	+5% Damage (All)
Tier 5	Ability: Plague	Ability: Skeleton Key	Ability: Mental Fortress	Ability: Assassinate

It was probably the most familiar of the four trees, and most of its modifiers dealt with enhancing Misthack, Mistwalk, or Mistwall. However, I was also pleased to note that it had a combat branch, as well, which culminated in the Assassinate ability. It seemed that my class, which shared a name with the tree, was about far more than merely infiltrating various systems. If I'd had any doubts about my choice before, they quickly dissipated as I studied my new skills.

Finally, I moved on to the evolution of what I thought of as my most useful skill, [Fieldcraft], which had evolved from [Combat Utility]. I already knew that it was a unique skill that had come from my uncle's experiences, and because of that, I treasured it even more than I had in the past. It was his legacy, and one I fully intended to live up to. I examined the tree:

Tree	**Fieldcraft: Tier 1 (0%)** +25% Combat Effectiveness			
Branch	Medic: Tier 0 (0%)	Survival: Tier 0 (0%)	Communication: Tier 0 (0%)	Utility: Tier 0 (0%)
Tier 1	+50% Effectiveness (Triage)	+25% Less Food/Water Required	Ability: Universal Language	+25% Effectiveness (Combat Focus)
Tier 2	+50% Recovery Speed	+25% Less Sleep Required	Ability: Share Map	+25% Effectiveness (Regeneration)
Tier 3	Ability: Stabilize	Ability: Bastion	Ability: Waypoint	Ability: Ignore Injury
Tier 4	+25% Medication Effectiveness	+50% Endurance	Ability: Combat Map	+25% Explosives Yield
Tier 5	Ability: Mend	Ability: Tinkering	Ability: Secure Connection	Ability: Focused Will

    Like was the case with [Combat Utility], it didn't look like a particularly flashy tree. Some of the abilities, like Stabilize, Mend, and the entirety of the Communication branch appeared downright mundane. But that assessment was based purely on their names. From experience, I knew just how deceptive that could be. I fully expected [Fieldcraft] to become even more useful than its predecessor.

    Just as I started to ponder my two empty skill slots, I heard Pick stir. I looked over to see him grimace as he sat up. Clearly, he wasn't used to roughing it.

    "Tough night?" I asked, summoning a bottle of water from my arsenal implant.

    Nodding as he took it from me, he said, "You could say that. I don't know how you do it."

    Pick was one of the few people who knew that I'd spent the previous few weeks away from civilization. For most, that would have been completely unconscionable, but for me, it seemed almost commonplace. Certainly, I knew that the wilderness was a dangerous place, but I was confident enough in my skills that I didn't question my ability to survive. Of course, that had been one of the driving forces behind my uncle's decision to train me.

For a few minutes, neither of us said anything while we broke our fast on ration bars and bottled water. However, the reality of our situation certainly hung over us like a thundercloud. We were all alone, in the wilderness, and we'd completely lost our respective support systems. It would've been easy to let panic overtake us, and I could tell that Pick wasn't far off from doing just that.

"What are we going to do?" he asked.

"I'm going back to Nova," I said. "After I kill the rest of the Enforcers in the area, of course."

Not only were they responsible for killing everyone I knew or cared about, but my previous experiences told me that they were just bags of Mist waiting to add to my levels. If I stuck around and killed every one of them, there was every chance I might reach level eleven.

"Are you serious?" he asked, his eyes wide.

"Of course. Why wouldn't I be?"

"Because! You can't just . . . I mean . . . Those are people!" he insisted.

"They're enemies," I said. "And we're supposed to kill enemies."

It sounded harsh, even to me, but I reasoned that was just the old Mirabelle asserting herself. The one who hadn't just experienced loss on such a grand scale. The new me, she didn't mind a little murder, so long as she got her revenge. In a lot of ways, that new attitude brought me closer to my uncle. He'd done much the same thing just after the Initialization, and as far as I knew, he'd never really stopped.

Still, I knew everyone wouldn't think like that. Pick might've been a familiar acquaintance, but he clearly wasn't ready to participate in my planned revenge. So, I said, "You don't have to help. I can do this on my own."

"What about your hand?" he asked.

I looked down at the useless appendage. The tendons had been completely severed, and I knew that if I didn't get treatment soon, I'd lose it. Already, the health indicator on my HUD, which presented itself as a silhouette in varying colors, sported a dark-red hand. That, as well as my Triage ability, told me that I'd reached dire straits.

I shrugged. "Can't get it fixed till we get to Nova," I said. "And I'm not going to leave and then come back. So, I need to kill these assholes before I head to the city."

It was a simple, logical solution, but I knew there were plenty of risks involved. Not only would I run the risk of death or discovery as I waged my war against the Enforcers still in the area, but the longer I put off getting my hand fixed, the worse it was going to be. Still, I didn't care. I'd already killed almost a hundred Enforcers, but I still felt like the job was only half-finished. I was, in a word, unsatisfied.

I glanced back at Pick, who was looking at me like I'd lost my mind. "Where do you live, anyway?" I asked. I didn't really intend to help him get back to wherever he'd come from, but it seemed like a pertinent question.

He looked away. "Me and Remy, we lived in *The Jitterbug*," he said. "Usually, we'd stay in a town or something, but that ship was the only place that ever felt like home."

"What happened to it?" I asked.

"They blew it up," he said. "Just before the bombardment started. Remy and me, we were fixing some of the damage from when that condor attacked, and . . . they were on us before either of us knew what was going on. I tried sending a distress signal, but they took us before I could get to the comms. I think that's the only reason we survived when everyone else died. They got us before the attack, took us back to their temporary base. After that, they bombed the hell out of Mobile. I've never seen anything like it. I knew the moment those cannons started going off that nobody was going to survive."

"When did they get my uncle?" I asked.

He looked away, and I could see the moisture in his eyes. "He was hurt bad," Pick said. "One of his arms was just gone, and his leg didn't work. But he came at them, then. I couldn't even follow what was going on. He killed a hundred of them. Maybe more. But then . . . then they caught him with some kind of trap. Even after that, he didn't go down until they'd hacked him to pieces. And the last I saw of him before they took Remy and me down to the basement of that building was him . . . his . . . head on that pike. He was still alive. I know 'cause he followed me with his eyes. I don't know when he finally died, but we were down there for almost two weeks before you came."

"And Remy? How did he die?" I asked.

"T-they tortured us," he said. "They wanted to know about some fancy Nexus Implant. I didn't know what they were talking about, but they didn't care. Remy, he wasn't . . . up for the torture. One day, when they threw him in there with me, h-he . . . he didn't get back up. He just didn't get back up."

"Pick, listen . . ."

"Don't call me that," he said, looking up. He had a shell-shocked look about him. "Just Patrick now."

I understood the sentiment. Pick—or Pickle—had been the name of a child, and after what he'd just been through, he didn't really qualify for that designation anymore. I hated that he'd lost his innocence, and my heart went out to him, but there wasn't much room in my head for anything but vengeance. So, I just nodded, saying, "Fair enough, Patrick. Do you want to come with me when I head to Nova?"

He shrugged. "Where else am I supposed to go?" he asked.

Where, indeed?

Like me, he didn't really have a home anymore. But unlike me, he didn't have the tools or the skills to survive on his own. I would help him, so long as it didn't derail my mission, but the moment he slowed me down too much, I'd have to cut him loose. I couldn't allow myself to worry about anything but the path before me. If I concerned myself with his well-being, I wouldn't see the dangers ahead.

"Alright, then," I stated, trying my best to sound confident. In charge. My uncle always did that. "Like I said before, I'm going to spend the next day or so hunting Enforcers. After that, we'll head toward Nova. In the meantime, try to think about what you want to do."

"What do you mean?" he asked.

"You're a pilot with no ship," I said, taking a bite of my ration bar. "Seems to throw a bit of a monkey wrench into your future plans, I would think. So, what's your plan for when we get to Nova? You mentioned a [Cybernetic Engineer] skill, right? Did you get it?"

He nodded. "Soon as we got back, the Wraith . . . Jeremiah, he gave it to me," Patrick answered. "But I don't know how to train it."

"We'll worry about that when we get to Nova," I said. "Apprentice you to someone in the Garden or something. I'm sure they'll trip all over themselves to get someone with the actual skill."

I knew that many of the cybernetic engineers in Nova City had related skills, like [Medicine] or [Cybernetic Repair], but few could live up to their titles via an actual skill. In a lot of ways, it reminded me of my own class choice. In the city, most warriors were known as Operators, and I knew based on the requirements that few would have qualified for the actual class. The same went for my own class, {Mistrunner}; as far as I knew, there were only a handful of people in the whole world who had the skill slots to meet the requirements, much less the very specific skills to do so. I felt almost certain that I was, if not unique on Earth, then at least very rare.

But before we got to Patrick and his fate, we needed to get back to Nova City.

Even before that, though, I had some hunting to do. So, after letting the conversation peter out, I spent quite some time checking my equipment. I was beginning to run low on ammunition—especially for my rifle—but I felt like I would have enough to see me through. I'd never want to tackle a Rift so poorly equipped, but it would be enough to take care of a few Enforcers.

However, the real issues were with all my other supplies. My medical kit had been decimated, and aside from some antiseptic swabs and bandages, it was almost completely empty. By contrast, my food situation was decent, and I had enough ration bars to last for at least a few more weeks. Water was a little scarcer, but now that I was in familiar territory, gathering more shouldn't prove to be much of an issue.

Looming large in my arsenal implant were the Rift Shards, though. There were almost a hundred of the smallest variety, twenty-five or so of the midsize ones, and, of course, the large one. I had no real notion of what any of it was worth, but my uncle had intimated that they were exceedingly valuable. Once I got to Nova and headed to the Bazaar, I hoped that I could turn my spoils into enough capital to wage my war on Nora and whoever else had been responsible for the decimation of Mobile.

For the next hour or so, I went through the equipment I'd pilfered from the Enforcers I'd already killed, and I was happy to find that some of the ammunition would work for my Kicker. They weren't the high-quality rounds I was used to, but they would do in a pinch—especially with all the extra modifiers I had gained.

None of the other stuff I found was very useful, so I left it piled in the corner. That's when Patrick stepped up, asking, "Is that stuff valuable?"

I shrugged. "Maybe? It's probably not worthless," I said. "But I don't have room for all of it in my arsenal implant."

"Do you want me to carry it?" he asked.

"Uh . . . like, in a backpack or something?" I asked. Then, I remembered that he'd summoned an information chip back in the basement where I'd found him, which hinted that he had access to something like an arsenal implant himself.

He said, "I have a cargo implant. It's part of my skill."

"The [Pilot] skill?" I asked, narrowing my eyes. "Or was it from something else?"

"Um . . . I don't really have a [Pilot] skill, exactly," he said. "More of a [Smuggler] skill, you know?"

"And the third skill?" I asked. I already knew he was Tier 3, so with [Smuggler] and [Cybernetic Engineer], he had to have one other skill.

"It's called [Gunfighter]," he said, looking a little embarrassed. "Most of it's pistol stuff, but there's some . . . uh . . . other abilities that go with it. I haven't had much chance to work on it, though, because it's new."

That explained how he'd managed to stagger the Banshee leader. He must've had a few modifiers that, while they didn't give him enough power to actually kill her, gave him enough oomph behind his shots to stun her. That, in turn, had allowed me to use Empowered Shot to end the threat.

"Good," I said. "You're going to need it. But to answer your question, sure. I don't know how much you can hold, but take as much as you can. While I'm gone, try not to get in trouble, yeah?"

"O-okay . . ."

Clearly, he didn't like the idea of being left alone, but he didn't want to go into battle, either. So, I said, "And Patrick? Thanks. You saved my life, and I won't forget that anytime soon."

It was as much to bolster his confidence as it was to express my gratitude. Either way, what followed was an awkward silence, and I couldn't get out of that ruined church quickly enough.

And with my exit, the hunt began.

CHAPTER TWO

DISAPPOINTMENT

When I was little, I thought I was destined for adventure, like in the cartoons I used to watch. However, as the years ticked by and I progressed into adulthood, I realized that I wasn't even the main character in my own story. I was just a henchwoman. A nameless mook meant to take orders and hope for the best. That is a disappointing thing, that recognition that you're not special, and it can drive a woman down a dark road.

—Nora Lancaster

I left the fallen church behind, eager to wreak havoc on the Enforcers who were still in the area. However, I didn't let my eagerness override my caution, and I employed all the wilderness-survival skills I had learned from Jorge. I was like a ghost, leaving no tracks or trail behind. Jorge would have been proud.

I gave a mental shake of my head, realizing that that wasn't terribly accurate. The leader of the Amigos had been a harsh taskmaster, and regardless of how well I learned his lessons, he almost never offered a word of praise. In that respect, he was much like my uncle. When I accomplished a task or mastered a skill, they would be right there behind me, pointing to the next hill I was supposed to climb. It had instilled in me a propensity to never be satisfied because there was always another obstacle to overcome. Another skill to learn. Another enemy to defeat.

With that in mind, I redoubled my focus, paying attention to my surroundings like I never had before. As I did, focused on Stealth and Camouflage, pulling up their descriptions:

Stealth (E)—Manipulate Mist to fade into the background.

I knew from experience that the ability was activated, meaning that I had to think about using it. Camouflage, by comparison, was the opposite. I could turn it off if I wanted to, but otherwise, it always gave a passive modifier to my ability to hide. That hadn't always been the case, but I'd progressed the ability far enough to fundamentally change its nature.

Either way, I used both abilities as I traversed the wilderness, skirting alongside a poorly maintained road as I made my way toward what was left of Mobile. Soon, I started seeing abandoned buildings; most were barely standing, and more than a few had succumbed to the passage of time, crumbling altogether. Still others had been reduced to their foundations. In any case, they provided plenty of cover as I slowly approached the point where I expected to find the ring of sniper's nests that surrounded the destroyed city.

I still had a few of them marked on my map, but when I checked those positions, I found nothing but more obviously empty and abandoned buildings. However, I wasn't going to let that dissuade me, so I veered off course and swung around in a wide circle so I could approach one of the buildings from the rear. Once I reached the back wall, I wasted no time before leaping to an open window. Once upon a time, it had probably held glass, but it was long since gone, making for a perfect entrance.

With a silent exhale, I pulled myself up with one arm, and I cursed my useless hand. It had only gotten worse throughout the night, as evidenced by the ominous red indicator on my HUD's health silhouette, and I knew that if I didn't receive medical attention soon, I was going to lose it entirely. It wouldn't be the end of the world or anything; after all, many people willingly removed limbs in order to replace them with cybernetics. But I was still very much attached to my flesh and blood, and I would do everything in my power to keep my original parts.

Of course, there was still room for enhancements like subdermal armor, but without my uncle's deep pockets, that could very well be out of my price range. I had the Rift Shards still in my possession, but I had no idea what they were really worth. For all I knew, I couldn't even sell them. That was a concern for another day, though. For now, I had a sniper's nest to investigate.

Slowly, I crept through the building, checking each of the rooms until I was satisfied the entire floor was unoccupied. Then, I moved up to the third and top level, finding much the same thing. There was evidence that people had been there, but everything I found suggested that they'd been gone for a while.

My anger roiled beneath the surface of my calm exterior. I wanted—no, I needed—to kill someone. To make the Enforcers pay. I had already taken out quite a few of them before I'd hit the base the day before, but those kills felt hollow. Even killing the beautiful, blonde leader left me completely unsatisfied.

Finding nothing of note in the building, I moved to the next sniper's nest. Then the next after that. Still, I found nothing. The Enforcers, it seemed, had decided to vacate the area. So, after steadily searching the outer bands of the ruined city, I cautiously approached the walled town. It remained much the same as when I'd left it, all crumbling buildings, burned-out husks of vehicles, and rubble. But my approach did net me a sighting of a squad of Enforcers.

There were three of them. Two were plainly guards, but the other was kneeling next to a downed drone. I silently approached, drawing close enough to hear their whispered conversation.

"This place gives me the fucking creeps," said one of the guards. He turned his head to look at the kneeling drone technician, asking, "You 'bout done back there, Sheila?"

"Workin' on it, man," she muttered, not bothering to look up from her task. "This thing's barely functional."

"Typical," said the other guard. "They send us in after all the action, leaving us to fight some fucking assassin. Meanwhile, we've got to make do with shitty equipment."

The first guard responded, "Same old thing. The higher-ranked squads get all the glory of taking out a high-tiered threat, and we get stuck with guard duty. Makes me wish I would've gone into the private sector instead of joining the Enforcers, you know? My uncle lives out west, and they don't have to deal with people like that Wraith asshole. Or whoever came in and blew up the fucking base."

"I heard it was a whole squad," said the second guard. I crept to the side, staying hidden behind a pile of rubble. As I did so, I exchanged my rifle for one of my daggers. I had no idea if there were other squads in the area, so I needed to do things quietly. "Full-on ninjas and shit. With swords."

"It's always ninjas with you, Moore," was the first guard's chuckled response. "Too many cartoons, man."

"Just what I heard, Damien," the other man mumbled. I knelt only a couple of yards away, but none of them could see through the combination of my active Stealth and passive Camouflage. It would be different if they stared right at me or if I was out in the open, but the two guards were looking the other way. The technician, meanwhile, was wholly focused on her work. "You hear they took out Camilla? God, what a waste, right? She had a body like—"

"Just stop," said the kneeling technician. "I really don't want to hear you describe a dead woman's body."

"Just sayin' . . ."

"Not my type," said Damien, the first guard. He scanned the area as he spoke. "I like 'em natural. Like Pike back there."

"Gross," said Pike.

"Don't knock it till you try it, sweet—"

I'd had enough, as evidenced by the fact that I'd buried one of my nano-bladed daggers in his eye. A second later, and I'd thrust another dagger into Moore's exposed neck. I ripped it free, and I was rewarded with a gout of thick, red blood. Both guards were dead in the space of two seconds; neither had had any opportunity to call for help. It could have been faster, but I was hampered by my lack of a hand. Still, it felt good, watching them slump to the ground.

For a moment, Pike stared at the scene, wide-eyed and slack-jawed. However, it only took an instant before terror crashed through her surprise. She scrambled away, fumbling at her belt for a communicator. I had no intention of letting her call for help, so I darted forward, aiming a front kick at her chest that, when it connected, sent her sprawling. I was on top of her in a second, knocking the communicator away from her belt.

With my knee in her chest, I leaned forward and put the crackling blue edge of my knife to her throat. It was so sharp that just resting it there resulted in a thin line of blood. I whispered, "If you scream, I'll cut your throat down to your spine. If you try to get to that communicator, I'll do the same. But if you don't answer my questions, I'm going to really make you regret it. Got me?"

She did her best to nod without slitting her own throat, so I eased up a little. Not because I cared if she cut herself to pieces, but rather, because I didn't want her to die before I got my answers.

"First question," I said. "Where did all the Enforcers go?"

"W-we . . . we were ordered to pull out after the base was destroyed," she answered, her voice quivering in absolute terror. "None of us were top ranked in the first place, but the only thing that's left are the rookies and a few technicians like me." She took a deep breath and begged, "P-please don't kill me. I won't tell anybody anything. I'm just a tech—"

If I hadn't just discovered that people like her were responsible for the deaths of everyone I cared about, I might have been swayed. But every time I felt the tiniest bit of sympathy, my uncle's face flashed through my mind. Then, it was Jo. Her parents. Little Elie, who only wanted to heal people and eat mangoes. The Amigos. And a hundred other people who didn't deserve what the Enforcers had given them. With those images in my mind, my resolve hardened.

Over the next few minutes, I continued to question her. And during the course of that interrogation, I learned that once my uncle's death had been confirmed, the Enforcers' true elites had retreated back to Nova City, leaving the organization's lower-ranked members to manage the area. That certainly explained how I'd run through them so easily. They weren't quite the dregs—no Enforcer could be considered that—but they were far from the best the organization had to offer, either. Even the leader, whose name was Camilla Laster, had only just become a Banshee, and her ascension was rumored to have been less about her capability and more about whom she was sleeping with. Of course, I had no idea whether that was true, but the technician seemed to believe it.

Which made me rethink my victory, such as it was. Winning that fight had required Patrick's intervention, and even then, I'd barely managed to come out alive. Not only had my hand been rendered useless, but I'd been gutted, as well. The only reason I hadn't been entirely incapacitated was because of my various abilities. Without them, I would've already been dead.

And that was against their B team.

No, it was worse than that. I wasn't exactly sure how the Enforcers' organization was structured, but from what the technician told me, the force that had been left in Mobile after my uncle's death was the bottom of the barrel.

That made my path abundantly clear. If I was going to take on people that powerful, I couldn't stop improving. My uncle had once told me that I would always be training, in one respect or another, but while I interrogated that technician, I came to realize just how right he'd been.

Finally, after I didn't think I could get anything else out of her, I asked, "Who sent you?"

"What do you mean?" she asked, having relaxed a little since the beginning of the questioning. "We work for the Ruling Council of Nova City."

"Not the politicians," I said. I knew precisely how things worked in Nova City. The members of the Council were elected as figureheads, and they didn't do anything unless their masters told them to. According to my uncle, even those masters worked for the alien overlords who couldn't descend upon the planet for another seven years. I couldn't get to them, so I'd have to make do with the lackeys. "The real rulers of Nova. Who gave the Council their orders?"

"I . . . I don't know . . ."

I pressed my dagger against her slender throat. "You sure about that?" I asked.

"I . . . I don't know . . . I swear . . . I'm just a technician!" she sobbed, tears falling down her cheeks. "I don't know anything about the people in charge. I just get my orders, and I go do what I'm told."

"So, you were just following orders, huh?" I asked. "You're a technician, right? You had drones in the sky, didn't you? Or did you man one of the cannons that tore this town to pieces?" She didn't respond, so I hammered her forehead with the pommel of my knife. "Answer me!"

"I . . . I just . . . I was just following orders . . ."

"Orders," I growled. Again, I leaned close. "Your orders killed thousands of innocent people. You killed my friends. My only family. You might not have pulled the trigger. You might not have guided the plasma bombs. But you're complicit, same as the ones who did."

With that, I raked my dagger across her throat and watched as she bled out. I didn't look away until the life in her eyes had entirely faded.

And I felt nothing.

Just a pervasive numbness.

Rationally, I knew that she probably didn't deserve what I had just done. She was just a cog in the machine, a woman trying to make her way as best she could. She'd even chosen a noncombat career path, proving her intentions. But on the other hand, I just didn't care. She had contributed to so many deaths that her entire being was stained red with the blood of innocents. She was just doing a job. Following orders. But that didn't mean she wasn't complicit in the horrors she had facilitated.

Still, as righteous as my anger had been, I felt no satisfaction when she breathed her last gurgling breath. Just an exhaustion that I couldn't quite understand.

Mechanically, I retrieved everything of worth they had on them—including the drone, which barely fit in my arsenal implant—and set off back to the church. There was no point in continuing my search, what with the Enforcers already moving out of the area. I was in no position—mentally or physically—to fight the lot of them, so I had no choice but to give up my hunt. Before I left the corpses behind, I used Mimic to adopt the technician's identity.

Ultimately, it was all so disappointing.

In my head, I'd imagined myself as an avenging angel, doling out punishment and judgment in equal measure. What I got was the anticlimactic execution of a woman who was clearly in over her head. It left a bitter taste in my mouth that, even when I saw the church, still hadn't faded.

I circled the building, making certain that no one had found the place while I was away. The area was empty of threats, though, so I went inside. When I did, I found myself facing the barrel of a pistol.

"Knock it off," I said, slapping it away. "It's me. Mira."

"You don't look like you . . ."

"That's because I'm using an ability," I said. "It lets me take on the appearance of another person. I found and killed a drone technician, so I took her identity. The way I see it, there's no way I'm getting into Nova looking like myself. So, I snatched her uniform, too. When we get there, I'll just bluff my way through security. Once we're inside, I'll either go back to being me or adopt another identity."

"What about me?" Patrick asked. "And how can I be sure it's you?"

"Your name is Patrick," I said. "But until this morning, you went by Pick, which was what you used to call yourself as a child. Your mom called you Pickle, though. That enough? Or should I keep going?"

He sighed, obviously relaxing. "Fine," he said. "So, are we leaving, then? Or do you still have . . . stuff to do?"

"Nobody left to kill," I said. "Everyone that was left is leaving. By tomorrow morning, this place will be completely deserted."

I crossed the room and sat down. Then, I retrieved a couple of ration bars from my arsenal implant and tossed one Patrick's way. After ripping the packaging open with my teeth, I dug in. As I did, I said, "I think there was probably a uniform in the pile that would fit you. That, along with my stolen identity, should be enough to get us inside Nova. From there . . . Well, we'll see."

He sat next to me. "Do you want to talk about it?" Patrick asked.

I shook my head, saying, "Not even a little bit. I'm not really a talk-it-out kind of girl. More of a bury-everything-inside-until-it-eventually-explodes type. But thanks. I'll be fine."

"Can't be healthy."

I shrugged. "I've spent the last few years training to be a deadly warrior," I said. "Healthy was never part of the equation."

I took another bite, then continued, "Which reminds me. You're going to need some training with that pistol. While we're headed toward Nova, I'll help you as much as I can. It won't do much, but you might advance your skill."

"Oh. Thanks," he said. "I hope . . . Yeah . . . That makes sense. Thank you."

CHAPTER THREE

A LONG ROAD

My parents never wanted me. I know that because they told me so. Hundreds of times, and with such bitterness that I couldn't help but resent my own existence. And then Jeremiah came along, and suddenly, I felt like someone cared about me. But that wasn't true. He never cared. He just wanted to use me.

—Nora Lancaster

For the rest of the day, I busied myself with my puzzles, but I knew I'd have to get a new program soon because they were becoming so easy that I barely even had to concentrate in order to complete them. Patrick had it worse, though. He didn't have anything to distract him, so he tried to occupy his mind by going over the various pieces of equipment I had looted. There weren't any real surprises there, but I did pick up a few spare outfits. If I continued to run through clothing like I had during my training—or more accurately, during my tests—I'd have plenty of options for replacements.

About an hour after dark, I looked up to see Patrick staring out into space, which, given his mental state, I didn't think was a good sign. So, in order to distract him, I asked, "So, what kind of skills do you know about?"

"Huh?"

"Skills. I figure it's probably a good idea to know what's out there," I said. "And considering you're literally my only source of information right now, you're it. Know of any cool or essential skills?"

He shrugged. "Not really," he said. "Remy never really gave me a lot of choices, you know? It's not like I went to a skill shop and just picked things out. Not that we could ever afford anything like that."

"Skill shop?"

"Yeah. There's one in Atlanta," Patrick explained. "Another up north somewhere. Remy mentioned a city up there a few times, but we never went that far. He said it was a bad place."

"Huh," I breathed, wondering what constituted a "bad place" for the old smuggler. "Did he elaborate?"

Patrick shook his head, saying, "No. He only told me things he thought I needed to know. Always said he'd tell me more when I got older. Now, though . . ."

"Yeah. Jeremiah was the same way," I acknowledged. "So—skill shops? Have you been to one? Do you think they have one in the Bazaar?"

"I have no idea," Patrick answered. "I've never even been to the Bazaar. We couldn't afford the entry fee."

It was news to me that there even was an entry fee, but it made sense. The place had to be run by someone, and that someone needed to make a profit. That attitude was the driving force behind everything, at least as far as I could tell, so it made sense that the Bazaar followed that same mantra. But that threw a bit of a monkey wrench into my plans. If the Bazaar required an entry fee, I was screwed. My uncle might've been rich, but I was decidedly not. In fact, I only had a few hundred credits to my name, and I knew that wouldn't take me far.

"So? Skills? Know of anything good?" I asked.

Again, he shrugged. "Not really," he said. "Why?"

"Just making conversation," I lied. The reality was that I had two open skill slots, but I had no idea what to use them for. In fact, I didn't even know enough to make an educated guess, much less home in on the best combination. Not for the first time, I found myself missing Jeremiah's guidance. He'd been a taciturn man, and he'd often responded to questions by telling me to figure it out for myself, but he'd always steered me in the right direction on the important stuff. Now, I felt like I was adrift.

I wasn't ignorant of the fact that, for three years, I hadn't really had much in the way of agency when it came to the direction of my life. When I was in the thick of training, it was easy to accept. But now that I didn't have anyone telling me what to do or where to go, I was beginning to realize just how inadequate certain aspects of my training really had been. I could only think that Jeremiah had had some kind of plan to remedy that; we just never got the chance to get that far.

As it stood, I was little more than a weapon. And I needed to become something else. Something like what he'd been. I had no desire to run a criminal empire, but one thing Jeremiah had always had was a surety of purpose. He knew who he was and what he was meant to do.

And all I knew was that I wanted to kill Nora and anyone else who'd had a hand in the massacre of Mobile. Beyond that, I was a leaf in the wind.

That uncertainty extended to my two empty skill slots. I could only hope that when I did get to the Bazaar, where I hoped to meet with Dexter and Gala, the two alien shopkeepers I'd met before, perhaps they could offer some advice. I wasn't certain if I could trust them with information about my skills and abilities, but I also knew that, left to my own devices, I would almost certainly make all the wrong choices. I needed information, and they were the best source I could think of.

Besides, Dexter and Gala were aliens, and they couldn't do anything to really hurt me for another seven years. The same couldn't be said for their human counterparts on Earth. That, more than anything, made the decision for me.

"You don't have to distract me, you know," Patrick said, fiddling with a knife from the pile of loot he had sequestered in his storage implant. "I'm not going to break down again."

"It's okay."

"No, it's not," he said, looking up. When he did, I saw a gleam of determination in his eyes. "I'm going to pull my weight, Mira. I just needed a little while to adjust to . . . you know . . ."

"Me, too," I said.

"Yeah, but you adjusted by going out and killing people," he said, swallowing hard. "I did it by crying like a little baby. But I'll be fine. I'll do better."

"There's nothing wrong with crying," I said. "I can't count the number of times I cried just in the past two months."

It was true. There were times in the Rift, especially, when my frustrations had boiled over and the tears had come.

"You haven't cried about Jeremiah, though," he said. "I know you haven't."

"I don't . . ."

Suddenly, I realized that he was right. Everything had happened so fast, I'd never had the chance to process my emotions. Instead, I'd gone from one crisis to another, never stopping for more than a few minutes. And when I did stop, I'd always kept my mind occupied. Not that it mattered. I didn't have time to cry. Not now. Not when I had a job to do.

But before I knew what was happening, I felt tears flowing down my cheeks. I wiped them away, then hung my head, sobbing quietly. When I finally looked back up, Patrick said, "I'm sorry. I didn't mean to . . . you know . . ."

I wiped my eyes again. "You didn't do anything wrong," I said. "It's me. I just hate feeling so helpless."

"You? Helpless? I've never met anyone less helpless in my life," he said.

"Not like that. I mean, I can kill people just fine," I stated. "But I couldn't save any of those people. I couldn't help my uncle. And now I know that they were only after him because of me."

"What? Why would they want you?" Patrick asked.

I sighed. I needed to trust someone, and Patrick was my only real choice. Besides, he seemed solid enough. So, I chose to tell him what had prompted the attack. "They came to Mobile to get my uncle," I said. "I think it's been coming for a long time, but the only reason they came after him now was because, before, he'd had something they wanted. I guess they hoped they could take it from him somehow. I don't know. But he gave it to me, and I used it, so they didn't have any reason to keep him alive anymore."

"I think it's more complicated than that, Mira," he said. "You didn't see what I saw. It took hundreds of Enforcers to take him down. The whole city was destroyed, but he was only wounded. Even then, he almost killed them all. I think they didn't come after him because they were afraid. You probably don't realize, but your uncle, he was famous. Everybody who had even a little bit of power knew who he was. And not just around here. Everywhere. You don't go after somebody like that unless you know you can take him out."

I nodded, the tears still tracing lines down my cheeks. "Maybe," I said. Patrick might not have blamed me, but I knew that my guilt was at least somewhat justified. The timing alone suggested as much. But I also knew that I wasn't the real culprit. That was Nora. And whoever gave the order. So, I wasn't going to allow myself to wallow in self-pity and let my guilt derail me. Instead, I resolved to focus on walking the path I had chosen. Anything else would have been an insult to my uncle's memory.

I checked the time, then said, "Get some sleep. It's going to be an early morning."

He gave me a nod, but he didn't say anything else. Instead, he just extinguished the Mist lamp, turned over, and went to sleep. Despite his resolution not to cry, his soft sobs continued for a few more minutes until they were replaced by the even sound of his breathing. After that, I went back to my puzzles, losing myself in the program until, at last, I felt fatigue pushing me toward sleep.

When that happened, I flipped over to the Leviathan file Jeremiah had given me, then closed my eyes. I lay there for a long while, just basking in the sound of my favorite band while trying my best to remember my uncle's face. For some reason, as familiar as it was, the image in my mind had grown blurry. The defining features were all there, but it was almost like his death had robbed me of all the details that brought his face together.

Eventually, I fell asleep, only to wake up a few hours later when the sun shone through the cracks in the walls. For whatever reason, looking at that, I felt a little better about the world. Not good, mind you. But better. So, I rose, went outside to take care of some morning necessities, then returned a few minutes later to find Patrick finally stirring.

"Wakey, wakey," I said. "I want to get moving today."

"What's the rush?" he groaned.

"Uh..."

I held out my hand, letting it flop around grotesquely. It hurt a little, but most of it was mitigated by Pain Tolerance. Plus, it was funny watching him go pale.

"That is so gross."

"Yeah, well, I'd like to get it fixed before, you know, I have to lose my hand," I said. "So, no big deal, right? Take your sweet time."

"Fine," he muttered, pushing himself to his feet. "Just give me, like, ten minutes, okay?"

"You can have fifteen," I said, resolving to take the time to resplint and rebandage my hand after having removed the bindings while washing up with bottled water. It looked worse than before, but most of the pain had faded to a dull ache. I knew that was probably indicative of nerve damage, which wasn't a good sign, but I had no choice but to accept it and move on. Worrying about it wasn't going to make anything better. "But we eat on the road."

He shrugged, then went outside. I noticed that he had his pistol out, which was probably a good habit. If something attacked him out there, I might not be fast enough to save him.

About ten minutes later, he returned, saying, "I miss toilets."

"I miss the Dew Drop's breakfasts," I countered.

"And showers."

I gave myself a good sniff, then added, "Definitely showers."

Usually, I would've been very self-conscious to acknowledge my horrid stench around a boy, but Patrick just felt safe to me. I knew he wouldn't judge me for it any more than I would judge him. A rarity, I suspected.

"Alright—let's not leave anything behind," I said. After that, we gathered what little gear that Patrick hadn't stored way and, without any further ado, set off back toward Mobile. It might've been smarter to go cross-country, but I wanted to make sure that the Enforcers had indeed left the area. If they hadn't, I wasn't above picking a few more of them off.

However, when I entered the familiar territory of the outskirts of Mobile, I discovered that it was deserted. Still, with Patrick in tow, I carefully made my way toward the walled town, which I spent a while inspecting, as well. By the time I was satisfied that the Enforcers were gone, half the day had already passed us by. So, I handed Patrick one of my ration bars, and we went on our way.

It was toward the end of the day when we finally passed out of the old city's ruins and into the wilderness. It was just before dark when I found a viable building in which to camp. Once I had Patrick settled in, I scouted out the surrounding area, killing a couple of predators who thought they could get the jump on me. One was a wolf who sported a lower jaw entirely made of some gleaming metal, while the other was an enormous snake. I didn't have much trouble with either of them, and after they were dead, I dragged them a few miles away from our camp so as not to attract scavengers or other predators to where we would be sleeping. Then, I began the short trek back.

However, the moment the building came into view, I knew something was wrong. My first clue was the mook standing out front, a cigarette dangling from his lips and a curiously high-tech light machine gun in his hands.

I crept forward, and as I did, I noticed two others. One was armed with a rifle, and the other had a pair of submachine guns, one in either hand. Which marked him as the stupidest of the bunch. Likely, he meant to just spray bullets downrange, and he'd probably hit something by virtue of sheer volume.

Cigarette, which was what I'd decided to call him, banged on the building's wall, shouting, "Just come on out, kid. We ain't gonna hurt you none. All's we want is your stuff, see? Ain't worth your life, is it?"

Patrick responded with a resounding, "Fuck you!" that was punctuated with a gunshot. It missed punching a hole in Cigarette, but the wall wasn't so lucky.

"What the goddamn fuck, son?!" he roared. "You damn near got me!"

Of course, that had been the point, but I didn't say as much. Instead, as Cigarette continued to shout at Patrick, I slowly inched forward, activating Stealth as I did. I exchanged my Kicker, which had become increasingly frustrating to use due to my injured wrist, for my nano-bladed sword. Then, when I was right next to Stupid—or the man who fancied himself a dual wielder—I struck. His head detached from his shoulders with surprising ease.

But I didn't see it because I was already moving toward Rifle. Just as I came within a couple of yards, he turned to face me. His eyes widened, and he tried to bring his weapon around. But I wasn't going to allow that. With a quick strike, I knocked his rifle aside. Then, I swept my sword up at an angle, slicing right through his jaw and bisecting his head.

That's when Cigarette entered the battle.

His light machine gun thundered, but I'd never stopped moving. The earth erupted into a spray of dirt and natural detritus, but he couldn't move his weapon quickly enough to keep pace with me. However, it also meant that I had to keep going in the same direction because the moment I ran at him, he would fill me full of holes. I'd been there before, and I didn't want to repeat the experience. So, I dismissed my blade and summoned Ferdinand II.

But before I could take aim, four new gunshots joined the cacophony, and Cigarette's aim flew wide as he flailed in pain. The light machine gun fell from his grip, and he crashed into the ground, revealing Patrick's figure behind him.

He held his pistol in shaking hands, but his aim had been true. Cigarette was a goner. Still, I took one-handed aim at the man and put two more rounds in his head. Then, I did the same to the man whose head I'd bisected. The decapitated Stupid, I left alone. There were only a handful of people in the whole world who could survive being decapitated, and I didn't think I'd met one in the backwoods around Mobile.

But then again . . .

I walked over to the severed head and put one more bullet in it. Just in case.

Finally, I turned to Patrick, saying, "Never stop shooting until you know they're dead, okay?"

He nodded, though he looked like he was going to vomit.

"Here. We need to relocate," I said. "All that blood's going to attract predators."

"W-what kind of predators?" he muttered.

"The kind you don't want to meet in the middle of the night" was my response. "Now, c'mon. Let's get moving."

After that, we set off. Luckily, we found another building a few miles to the east, where we set up for the night. I had to forego my usual scouting of the surroundings, but there was nothing to be done. I was strong, but traipsing through the wilderness at night was a recipe for disaster.

However, I knew it was going to be a long night when I heard something rustling outside. Patrick, who'd already given up on sleep, looked as if he was going to say something, but I held my finger up to my lips and shook my head. I had no idea what was out there, but it didn't sound good.

And then I heard a sound that sent a chill up my spine.

A guttural barking filled the air, coming from a dozen different sources. I'd heard it before, and I knew precisely what it meant. The wildlings had found us.

CHAPTER FOUR

HAVEN

Praise is a funny thing. It's especially potent when you've spent most of your life devoid of any positive influences. And for me, the fact that it came from someone like Jeremiah made it doubly effective. For the longest time, I lived for those tiny acknowledgments that I was making progress.

—Nora Lancaster

"Upstairs!" I whispered to Patrick, nodding to the decrepit stairs leading to the next level. The building only had a pair of floors, but the steps looked solid enough to support his weight. "And be quiet!"

Patrick, for all the panic writ large on his face, immediately obeyed. Every step brought with it a creaking sound, but for now, they held. I knew that wouldn't last, though. So, once Patrick was safe on the second floor, I followed him up. My steps were light, but even that was almost too much for the ancient staircase. Still, I made it without incident, summoning my scattergun along the way.

It was large, bulky, and unwieldy, which would make it a pain to use one-handed. However, I had no better option for quickly dealing with the pack of wildlings. Besides, I had plenty of ammunition canisters for the weapon, while my stores of ammo for my Kicker had dwindled down to almost nothing. I had enough for one more battle, but even that would have to be a short one. So, resting the barrel of the scattergun on my forearm, I knelt at the top of the staircase, where I waited on the wildlings to make their appearance.

A few moments later, the heavy steel door, which bore a coat of thick oxidation, screeched open, admitting a long-limbed and misshapen humanoid form. She was naked, eschewing even the loincloths I'd seen on other wildlings, skeletally thin, and had gaunt, hollow features. However, her body was corded with ropy muscle, and her eyes glimmered with animalistic cunning as she searched the area.

Soon, another naked wildling—this one male—followed. Then another. And another after that. They kept piling into the building, one twitchy form at a time. Their movements were quick and jerky, reminding me of certain addicts I'd seen back in Nova, and they all sported sharp teeth that looked like they'd been filed to points. Perhaps they had grown that way, but it seemed artificial to me.

Which was altogether disturbing, not least because it suggested that they were far more intelligent than expected.

My fingers tightened on the grip of my scattergun, and I held my breath in the hope that they would give up the search. I didn't want to kill the unfortunate creatures, after all. They were only acting according to their nature. And more than anything, I just felt sorry for them. However, if push came to shove, I knew what choice I would make. My heart bled for them, but in the end, I was far more concerned with my own self-preservation.

The alpha wildling tilted her head to the ceiling, then sniffed the air. After that, she grunted a couple of times, getting the attention of the other dozen of her packmates. One snapped at another with a growl, but an additional bark from the alpha settled them down. Squatting, she leaned forward, her nose only inches from the floor, and she sniffed again. I wasn't blind to the fact that she was on top of the spot where Patrick had been standing.

I ground my teeth in frustration as the alpha followed our scent to the staircase. That's when she saw me and let out a screeching howl that got the attention of the rest of her pack. She wasted no time in rushing up the stairs, and the other wildlings followed on her heels. But they soon discovered the perils of weakened architecture when the staircase finally gave out beneath their feet.

The alpha leaped forward, her dirty, grimy, and thick-clawed fingers digging into the wooden platform only a foot in front of me, but the rest of the creatures tumbled to the ground. Most were unhurt, but none escaped completely unscathed. Not that I spared them any attention before rising to my feet and aiming a kick at the alpha's ascending face. She took it square in the jaw, and I was rewarded with an audible crack of a broken bone before she fell.

"What now?" Patrick muttered from a few feet behind me. I glanced back to see that he was clutching his pistol like his life depended on it. A good habit, as far as I was concerned, because his life might, indeed, depend on his proficiency with that weapon.

"Extermination," I said, my voice emotionless. Then, I took aim with my scattergun, activated Double Shot, then fired. A cone of dense lightning erupted from the barrel and spread across the unfortunate creatures. It pulsed with the effect of the ability, doubling the damage as it tore through them. Most were fried on the spot, but a few were sturdy enough that the scattergun, which had been intended as a nonlethal weapon, functioned as it was supposed to. So, I shot them again. And again. I emptied the entire cannister, not stopping until the creatures had been reduced to smoking husks.

"Fuck . . ."

"I know," I said. "I didn't want to. I just . . . I just didn't have a choice."

"I know, but . . . but it's not . . . It just doesn't feel right," he said. "They look like people."

"Because they are, Patrick," I said. "They've gone crazy or something, but most of them didn't start out any different than you or me. Just got unlucky when their Nexus Implants didn't take. Or maybe they never got them."

"Everyone gets a Nexus Implant," he said.

That's when I realized that I had no idea how the unaffiliated towns and villages got access to a Node in the first place. In Nova City, everyone just reported to the Dome when they turned sixteen. I'd preempted that by absorbing the Tier 7 Nexus Implant I'd gotten from my uncle, but others wouldn't be so lucky, would they? So, I asked Patrick about it.

"I got my implant in Atlanta," he said. "One of the black market Nodes. We snuck into the city, got the implant, then snuck back out. But most everybody else outside the megacities gets their implants from the traveling Nodes."

"Huh?"

"They just show up sometimes," he explained. "These big pillars of metal. Anywhere with more than a couple of Unawakened people, you know. Nobody really knows where they come from or where they go, but most everyone thinks they're just part of the system, you know? Still, some people that live near megacities prefer to head into town. It's supposed to increase your odds of getting a good tier. Remy said that was all bullshit, but . . . Well, it always made sense to me."

"Huh," I mumbled. "Interesting."

"So . . . what are we going to do about them?" he asked, nodding to the first floor, which was covered in charred wildlings.

"For now, nothing," I said. "We'll stay up here for the night. Then, we'll move on in the morning."

"Do you think that will be safe?"

I shrugged. "Probably not," I said, cradling my scattergun in the crook of my arm as I exchanged the spent cannister for another. "But if we have any other issues, I'll take care of it. I don't need as much sleep as you, and if we push, we can make it to Haven tomorrow. I'll rest there and hopefully get my wrist fixed."

I wasn't very hopeful on that last part, but I was trying my best to remain optimistic. The other alternative was to simply give in to the cynicism like my uncle had. And though it had served to keep him alive, I had known Jeremiah well enough to recognize that he was anything but happy. I knew just how easily I could follow him down that dark path, and I wanted to avoid it if I could.

I wasn't so naive as to think that I wouldn't come close, regardless. My quest for revenge wouldn't leave much room for a positive mindset. But I'd resolved to do what I could with what I had.

I nodded to a nearby corner, saying, "Get some sleep, Patrick. I'll keep you safe."

I could tell he wanted to argue, likely because he wanted to feel like he was pulling his own weight. However, the day had exhausted him, and that quickly overcame any arguments he might have made. So, he retreated to the indicated corner and curled up as best he could. I noticed that he kept his pistol close at hand, though.

What followed was a long night, throughout which various animals came to investigate the scorched wildlings. Most left once they realized that the meat had been burned so badly that it was inedible, but a few were still hungry enough to make a go of it. I tried my best to ignore the fact that I was watching the creatures eat what once were human beings, but more than a few times, I felt myself on the verge of vomiting. It was not a pleasant experience, and when the sun finally rose, I counted myself lucky to have kept my ration bars down.

Thankfully, most of the truly dangerous predators were nocturnal, so they fled back to their dens the moment the sky brightened. For his part, Patrick had a rough night, which he spent tossing and turning so much that I worried that he might alert the wildlife below. But the animals were either too engrossed in their free meals, or they simply didn't hear him. Either way, we were ignored.

Once I judged it safe, Patrick and I shared a meal of ration bars and bottled water before climbing down to the ground floor and continuing on our journey. Mostly, we kept to the wide roads that ran between Mobile and Nova; they weren't in a great state of repair, and some of them would have proven impassable by anything but heavy-duty trucks with plenty of ground clearance. But on foot, we had no difficulties.

Throughout that day, I had to fight off a few opportunistic animals, but none proved difficult enough to push me into getting really serious. I even let Patrick kill a wild pig that charged us; he performed well, and in his hands, the pistol packed a decent punch. I couldn't help but wonder what kind of modifiers his [Gunfighter] skill gave him, but I chose not to ask because I didn't think he'd tell me. Besides, even if he did, he'd probably expect his honesty to be reciprocated, and I had no intention of sharing the details of my skills with anyone. Even Patrick, who seemed earnest and honest to a fault.

We didn't make it to Haven that day. Or even the next. My concept of how far we had to go was skewed by the fact that I'd only made the trip between

Nova and Mobile a single time, and that had been in a vehicle. Also, I'd been so anxious and excited that I hadn't paid much attention to the passage of time. Couple that with the attack we had endured from the bandits, and it wasn't that surprising that it ended up taking far longer than I'd anticipated.

But at least we didn't run into any significant issues along the way.

At least, not until Haven finally came into sight. We'd left the main road behind a few hours before, taking the side path north. However, the first indication that something was wrong was that the path itself was lousy with tire tracks, telling me that a convoy had just passed through.

Kneeling, I studied the tracks until Patrick asked, "What do you think?"

Using the tracking skills I'd learned from Jorge, I'd already determined that the tread pattern was different from what I would expect from my uncle's convoys. More than that, I wasn't even sure those convoys were still going. After all, Jeremiah was dead, and I knew that he was the engine for the whole organization. Without him running the show, I'd fully expected everything to come to a screeching halt.

"I think it's either bandits or Enforcers," I said, pushing myself to my feet. I summoned my Kicker, then flipped the switch to reconfigure it into sniper mode. I glanced back at Patrick, adding, "You should go back to that house we saw about twenty minutes back. I'm going to check it out."

"I can help," he insisted.

"You'll just slow me down" was my response. And it was true. Without him tagging along, I could move far more quickly. And more importantly, I could use my various abilities to avoid detection. But as much as anything else, I just wanted to keep him out of harm's way. He was eager to prove his own worth, but the last thing I wanted was to lose him when we were so close to reaching our destination.

Again, he clearly wanted to argue, but he thought better of it. Probably because he still wasn't entirely comfortable with me after seeing some of my handiwork. Sometimes, it almost felt like he was going to open up, but then we'd get attacked by some creature, and it was like flipping a switch in his mind. I understood it, to a certain degree. After all, most of the time, I just looked like a petite young woman, but then he'd see just how much blood I had on my hands, and I think it reminded him of how dangerous I was.

It was regrettable. I did like him. But I also couldn't be bothered to look for ways to make him more comfortable. Either he'd get over it, or he wouldn't. It wasn't my problem to worry about.

Once I saw Patrick safely back to the building—which had probably been some sort of store, given its structure—I set off to follow the tracks. Mostly, I kept off the path itself. Instead, I trekked through the thick brush of what felt like a primordial forest. The vegetation was incredibly dense, but after spending so much time in the wilderness, I'd gained a sort of sixth sense for the traversal of such terrain.

Eventually, the concrete walls of Haven came into view, and just as I'd suspected, it was practically crawling with Enforcers. If there were less than two dozen of them, I would have been surprised, but I suspected the number was at least half again more than that. However, I was relieved to see that the way station's denizens were still alive, albeit cuffed and being readied for transport, likely back to Nova City.

My blood boiled.

I'd missed my chance to kill all the Enforcers back in Mobile, but it seemed that fate had given me the opportunity to rectify that cosmic mistake. So, I retreated to a particularly tall tree I'd seen on my way through the forest. Then, I laboriously climbed until I found myself peeking above the canopy. More importantly, I was given a great view of the way station.

Hooking a leg around a thick branch, I extended the arms of my weapon's built-in bipod, which I rested on the wooden surface. Then, I leaned forward, steadying myself with my injured arm. Without a hand with which to grip, I wouldn't be as steady as I might have liked, but it was the best I could do under the circumstances.

Finally, I activated Camouflage and Stealth before taking aim.

I spent a couple of minutes tracking from one target to the next in rapid succession until, at last, I felt confident in my firing pattern. Then, without any further hesitation, I embraced Empowered Shot, waited the requisite two seconds, and let loose. The first shot destroyed an Enforcer's chest. The second unempowered shot hit another in the head. Still another took out a third. Only then did they realize they were under attack.

The Enforcers scattered, taking cover behind walls and vehicles, but it did them no good. With my high vantage point, their cover was useless, and I continued to pick them off, one after the other until there were only a handful left.

That's when they finally pinpointed my location.

A hail of gunfire came my way, but I slipped from the branch, following the path I'd used to climb into my position. It could have gone more quickly if I'd had the use of both hands, but after stowing my weapon, I still managed the descent fairly well. By the time my boots thudded to the ground, only a few seconds had passed, and I quickly started to relocate. As I did, I once again focused on my Stealth ability, hoping it would be enough to keep me hidden.

I crept through the forest, and with Observation sharpening my senses, I knew precisely when the remaining Enforcers mustered enough courage to come after me. There were three of them left, and none of them made any efforts at stealth. Or they were simply unused to the wilderness, I amended. It was entirely possible that they just didn't spend much time outside the city.

Either way, it was child's play to track them, and it was even easier to avoid discovery.

Clearly, these weren't the best the Enforcers had to offer. They could have sent a thousand of these idiots after my uncle, and he wouldn't have gotten a scratch. But I knew I couldn't lose my focus, so I maintained my concentration as I crept forward, summoning my nano-bladed knife along the way.

The Enforcers had spread out a little, so I only had to wait a while for an appropriate moment to strike. When it came, I acted without hesitation, burying my blade in the base of the woman's skull. It rammed home with a visceral thunk, and she collapsed only an instant later.

I caught her, then guided her body to the ground before stalking my way toward the second. This one fell to a slashed throat, my knife cutting so deeply that I nearly severed his spine. The last fell almost as easily when I leaped from a branch and hammered my dagger home into the top of his skull. None of them ever even knew I was there, much less had any opportunity to defend themselves.

I spent the next couple of minutes gathering their equipment, which I shoved into my arsenal implant. There was just enough room, largely because I'd already used most of my rifle ammunition. It was a pity that the Enforcers' weapons used a completely different caliber. Otherwise, I'd have been able to easily restock.

Even so, I stockpiled a few of their rifles, as well as all the ammunition they'd carried on their persons, just in case I needed it in a pinch. Their weapons weren't nearly as high-quality as my Kicker, but beggars couldn't really be choosers. If it came down to it, I'd rather have a poor-quality weapon than nothing at all.

After that, I headed to the way station, where I saw a pair of familiar faces. Viola and Douglas looked much the same as the last time I had seen them, which was to say that she had an even darker complexion than I did, and he was still wearing that same wide-brimmed hat studded with alligator teeth. However, they had both clearly been on the wrong end of a beating, with Viola sporting a black eye while Douglas's jaw looked swollen.

Still, Viola smiled broadly when she saw me, saying, "I knew someone would come! Where's your uncle?"

Whatever good mood I'd managed to cobble together faded in that instant, and I just shook my head, saying, "He's not coming."

CHAPTER FIVE

BACK TO NOVA

I've always wanted to be strong. Growing up, I saw what happened to weak people. But I refused to let myself become one of them. Jeremiah gave me the opportunity to leave that fate behind, and I never looked back.

—Nora Lancaster

Telling Viola and Douglas about my uncle's fate was an exceedingly difficult thing. They reacted as well as could be expected, which was to say that Viola shed a few tears while Douglas struggled to remain stoic. It was an uncomfortable situation for me, so I quickly headed back to collect Patrick. I found him huddled in the corner of the building where I'd sent him, clutching the gun with white-knuckled hands. He'd obviously heard the battle, and I think he'd convinced himself that I'd already fallen. Thankfully, he had underestimated my prowess.

We returned to Haven, where we found that Viola and Douglas had already released the rest of the prisoners and organized them into groups. As I approached, I asked, "What's going on?"

"We can't stay here now," drawled Douglas. "The Enforcers will be back, and when they come, they'll come in force. We couldn't stand up to them before, and we won't be able to when they come back."

"Where are you going to go?" I asked.

"Some are going to Nova," Viola said. "We'll get them set up with jobs and the like. Others, they'll come with us up to Memphis."

I glanced around, and that's when I realized that Haven was populated by far more people than it had housed when we'd come through on my way out of Nova City. And they all looked terrible. Thin to the point of malnourishment, dirty, and with slumped shoulders, the people were clearly refugees of one sort or another.

"What's going on here?" I asked.

"Enforcers," Viola said. "They've been aggressively expanding Nova's influence lately. We weren't sure what was going on until you told us about Jeremiah. He was the only one keeping them in check. Now that he's gone, there's nobody to stop them from taking what they want."

I nodded, understanding exactly what she was talking about. After having seen what was going on in Bayou La Batre, I knew that there was plenty of wealth waiting to be harvested outside of the city. Before, I'd thought that the Enforcers just didn't want to rock the boat, but now, it was clear that the threat of my uncle's retribution had kept them from taking over. Now that he was gone, they were free to do what they wanted to do. The poor people of the free towns didn't stand a chance against high-tiered and well-trained soldiers.

"Any news of Bayou La Batre?" I asked.

"That old shrimpin' town?" asked Douglas. "No. Haven't heard anything from that neck of the woods. Not surprisin', though. We didn't even know about Mobile until you got here. Most of these people came from the towns closer to Nova."

"What are you going to do now?" asked Viola.

"I'm heading to Nova," I announced. "I just don't know exactly how I'm getting in."

"You could tag along with some of the refugees," Douglas said, taking off his hat and wiping his forearm across his forehead. He squinted in the direction of Nova City. As large as it was, the barest outline of the city was visible even this far away. It was like a mountain looming in the distance. "I'm not sure what you've got goin' on, but you feel like a Tier 2 at best, and a weak one at that. Now, I know that ain't true, so the way I figure it, you got somethin' to keep you hidden. Right?"

I nodded.

"So, here's what I suggest," he said. "You and your friend, you get all dirtied up and join the refugees. We already bribed the guard at the Green Gate, so shouldn't be any issues gettin' you inside, so long as you don't stand out too much."

"What do you have planned for when you get back inside?" asked Viola. "Please tell me you don't intend to take over your uncle's business."

I shook my head. "No" was my truthful answer. I had no desire to follow in Jeremiah's footsteps in that respect. But I also didn't want to go running my mouth about what I did have planned. For all I knew, Douglas and Viola had been complicit in my uncle's death. I didn't think it likely, but then again, I'd never expected Nora to turn traitor, either. So, it seemed smart to hold my cards close to my chest. I figured I could trust Patrick—at least for the most part—but everyone else, I would treat like strangers.

"Good," said Viola. "Girl like you, you'd get eaten alive."

I clenched my jaw, but I didn't respond. She had no idea what I was capable of. But then again, that wasn't that surprising, considering my age. It was probably difficult to imagine that, if I wanted to, I could kill every single person in that town without missing a beat. How they thought I'd managed to free them, I had no idea. Perhaps they just thought I was good with a rifle. Either way, her misconception was my gain.

"What d'ya say?" asked Douglas. "You in?"

"When do you plan to leave?" I asked.

"Soon," he said. "Before nightfall. We can't stay here any longer than that. The Enforcers already know we're here, so it's only a matter of time before they send another squad out this way. So long as we make it to the edge of the Dead Zone, they'll leave us be."

I shrugged. "Suits me just fine," I said.

After that, Patrick and I went inside one of the buildings and took a few minutes to eat. As I bit into a ration bar, he asked, "What are we going to do when we get inside the city?"

"I need to find a doctor," I said, holding up my splinted hand. "That's the first order of business. Then, I need to hit the Bazaar. You should probably come with me when I do. After that, I think we might want to part ways. I'll try to set you up with someone to—"

"Don't give me that shit, Mira," he said, and for the first time, it sounded like he had a little steel in his spine. "I know you're going to find out who's responsible for killing all those people back in Mobile. I have a stake in that, too, you know. My stepdad was one of the victims, remember? I want in."

I sighed. "And what do you offer?" I asked. "This isn't some game, Patrick. I'm going to kill a lot of people. Some of them are going to be really dangerous, too. Like, you remember that blonde woman you shot? She was midlevel, at best. The people I'm going after are much stronger than her. Some of that power might be political, but it's just as likely they'll be on my uncle's level. That's what I'm going up against, and I can't afford to drag around deadweight. I like you. I even trust you, mostly. But this isn't the kind of mission where I can afford to babysit you."

Indeed, the necessity to protect him had already shown its detriments during our trip from Mobile to Haven. If I'd been alone, I would've only been forced to fight a few times. But with Patrick along for the ride? The entire journey had been punctuated by one fight after another. In the wilderness, I could live with that. But in Nova City? My uncle hadn't explained exactly how powerful the people there were, but he'd intimated that they were not to be trifled with.

If I was going against those sorts of people, I couldn't afford any baggage.

"I have a [Smuggler] skill, which means I have a lot of useful abilities," he said.

"And what does that entail?" I asked. "What kind of abilities does it give you?"

"Mostly pilot stuff," he admitted. "But I have my [Gunfighter] abilities, too. And [Cybernetic Engineer]. I'm not saying I want to go out and fight with you or anything, but there's nothing that says I can't support you, right? What if your cybernetic implants get damaged? What are you going to do then? Go to some shady cyber-ripper or something? I can help you, Mira. I want to help you."

I sighed. He wasn't wrong. I was realistic enough to understand that my hand probably wasn't salvageable. I would try to get it fixed, but if push came to shove, I'd be forced to get a cybernetic one. And even the high-grade versions needed maintenance sometimes. Having a cybernetic engineer in my pocket could certainly come in handy. On top of that, I expected that I'd have to leave Nova City at some point, and when I did, having a pilot—or a [Smuggler]—to ferry me around would make things a lot easier.

And he'd already saved my life once. Without him, I'd have been either dead or subject to a slave implant, which was probably the worse of the two options. Patrick had proven his mettle, and I felt I owed it to him to give him a shot.

So, I said, "Fine. But the moment you aren't pulling your weight, I'll drop you. I can't let you drag me down."

He smiled and said, "Works for me. I can earn my keep."

After that, we finished our ration bars, then retreated into separate rooms to change into something more appropriate for refugees. Patrick's clothes were mostly fine; he hadn't changed since being taken captive, so he was pretty grimy. However, he did change his shirt for one that was a little less bloodstained. For my part, I donned the clothes I'd used for my disguise back in Bayou La Batre. They'd worked well back then, and I figured they'd do the trick now. However, I was a little distressed to find that the jeans were far tighter than they had been back then.

Was I getting fat? No. There was no way. But maybe I was finally growing into my figure. Or more likely, all the exercise I'd had in the year since I'd last worn the jeans had done my body good. Either way, they weren't so tight that I couldn't wear them, so I pushed it from my mind. Added to those jeans was a loose and ripped tee-shirt and a pair of sneakers, which completed the refugee look.

When I rejoined Patrick, I couldn't help but notice that his eyes lingered a bit on my backside, but I found that I didn't mind so much. Clearly, I'd never be a bombshell like Heather, my uncle's girlfriend, but I was okay with a little male attention.

Once outside, Patrick and I smeared dirt on our faces and clothes to sell the refugee look a little more, then headed over to where Viola and Douglas were organizing the others. They had been joined by another man, who stood by while everyone loaded into the back of a transport truck with huge, knobby tires.

I looked him up and down. He was tall, thin, and sported a cybernetic implant that coated his neck and much of his upper chest in black metal. I had no idea what it was for, but I couldn't help but think he'd left it exposed for a reason. Perhaps he liked the way it looked, as inexplicable as that preference was. After all, he left his shirt unbuttoned halfway down his torso in an effort to show it off. Some people might've been attracted to that sort of thing, but I certainly wasn't one of them.

As for his face, he had hollow cheeks and a long, thin nose, and his short hair came to a dramatic widow's peak. In short, the moment I laid eyes on him, I knew that he was a shady character.

"You two!" he shouted. "What the hell are you waitin' on? Get in the fuckin' truck!"

Viola looked like she was about to say something to the man, but I gave her a subtle shake of my head. If Metal Neck—yes, that was what I decided to call him—didn't know who we were, he couldn't betray us. I'd already activated Mimic, taking on the appearance and apparent tier of a woman I'd met back in Mobile. She was a couple of years older than me, and similar looking enough that we could have been siblings. Or at least cousins. More importantly, she was only a Tier 1, which I liked because it would cause everyone to underestimate me.

Metal Neck clearly did just that because, as Patrick and I joined the others in climbing into the truck, he looked us both over with a dismissive sneer. Once everyone was inside, I heard him tell Viola that he would take us into Nova City, but he didn't plan on doing any more runs. That made plenty of sense to me; if the Enforcers were out and about, it was probably smart to lie low.

Before long, we were rumbling along, and I found myself studying the other refugees. Most of them were Tier 2, but there were a fair few Tier 1s, as well. Patrick was one of only three Tier 3s, which meant that he was one of the more powerful people in the back of the truck. That was discounting Metal Neck up front, who was also Tier 3 and moved like he could handle himself at least a little, though.

The trip itself was mostly uneventful. There were no giant, mutated alligators to attack us, at least, and we made decent time, arriving at our destination a few hours later. I felt the truck pull to a stop, and then, after the lift shuddered, we were moving upward. Some of the refugees looked panicked, but I did my best to calm them.

"It's just an elevator," I said. "Nova's way up in the sky. This is just taking us up to the city."

That helped, but I could see in their eyes that some of them were still quite nervous. I couldn't really blame them, either. They'd lived their whole lives in the backcountry, and after everything they knew had been upended by the Enforcers, they were going to a completely unfamiliar place. In their shoes, I would have been nervous, too.

The elevator slowed to a stop, and a few moments later, the truck was moving again. With Observation on my side, I heard the exchange with the Enforcer on guard, and it was clear from that conversation that the man was on the take. He let the truck through without much issue.

However, it was a further ten minutes before we pulled to a stop.

"Alright!" yelled Metal Neck. "Everybody out! Let's get you all set up in your new life."

I followed the others out of the truck, and I was unsurprised to see that we were in Algiers. But what did surprise me was when Metal Neck started sorting people into groups. The young girls like me were all put into one group. The strong-looking boys were put into another. And anyone over the age of twenty-five was pushed into yet another cluster. When one of the older women complained, Metal Neck shut her up with a backhand.

I was about to respond when I noticed that the lot we were in was surrounded by men and women with guns. And all those weapons were trained in our direction.

"Now," said Metal Neck. "Some of you probably thought you were headed to a new, better life. And maybe that'll be true. Eventually. But for now? You're all going to be fitted with control implants and put to work in appropriate jobs. If you've got free skill slots, we'll provide you with something appropriate. Got me?"

A din of conversation and complaints erupted, but Metal Neck shut them up by yelling, "Rhetorical question, idiots! Marvin! Let's get those implants, yeah?"

As a short, pudgy man scurried forward from the shadows, I let out a sigh. I muttered, "Nothing is ever easy, is it?"

Then, I activated Engage and darted forward. I moved so quickly that Metal Neck didn't have even a second to respond, and by the time he realized what was going on, I had my nano-bladed knife to the underside of his chin. With a flick of my wrist, I could jam it up through his jaw and into his brain.

"What the . . ."

"Call off your guys," I growled. "Or you're done, you dumb mook."

He yelled out, "Don't shoot! Don't shoot, guys!"

"Good," I said. "Now, listen close. Did you do this on your own? Or did Viola and Douglas know about it? Tell the truth 'cause I'll know the difference."

"I . . . I didn't . . . I mean, I just thought . . . these people would have a better life . . . if I could give them jobs," he gibbered. I could see tears falling down his cheeks and snot running from his nose. "P-please . . . I didn't mean no harm . . ."

I rolled my eyes. "What do you have on you? Any credits?" I asked. His eyes widened, and I said, "Transfer them to me. Let's call it an idiot tax, yeah? Be an idiot, lose some money. Or we could do it the other way."

To punctuate my point, I pushed the knife up a little, drawing blood. A second later, a prompt to receive a transfer of a few thousand credits flashed across my HUD. I accepted it, then said, "Now, let's do this nice and slow, okay? You and me, we're going to get in that truck, and we're going to take all these nice people somewhere else, alright? And none of your mooks are going to follow, right?"

He muttered, "Y-yes, ma'am . . ."

"Good," I said. "Let's go, then."

After that, everyone climbed back into the truck. Some moved far more slowly than others, and I could see quite a few tear-stained faces. Patrick helped organize them, though, which just cemented my decision to keep him around. Once the refugees were back into place, Metal Neck and I got into the truck's cab, and soon, we were on our way. Once we were inside, I exchanged the knife for Ferdinand II, which I kept aimed at the mook's temple.

As we traversed the breadth of Algiers, we crossed a half dozen different gang territories, which meant that Metal Neck's mooks weren't likely to follow. Once I judged we were safe, I directed him to pull up next to an abandoned tenement. It was barely standing, but it would provide some shelter for the refugees.

At least until they figured out how to make their own way.

Once they were all unloaded, I told Metal Neck that if I saw him again, I wouldn't hesitate to put him down. He nodded enthusiastically and, after he got back into the truck, raced away.

Perhaps I should've just killed him, but the fact was that he didn't pose any real threat to me. He had no idea who I was, and as far as he knew, I was just someone who'd gotten the jump on him. At worst, he would think I was just another Operator with the ability to mask my tier. Either way, in a city as big as Nova, that little bit of information wasn't nearly enough to identify me.

Turning back to the group of refugees, I said, "Alright, then. That's my good deed for the day. You're on your own now. Welcome to Nova City, I guess."

Then, without another word, I turned away and strode off into the city. Patrick hurried to follow, but I didn't slow my pace. If he wanted to tag along, that was fine, but he needed to learn to keep up. As for the refugees, either they would make it or they wouldn't. Their fate wasn't my problem.

CHAPTER SIX

SQUIRREL

Sometimes, I wonder where I would have ended up if Jeremiah hadn't taken me into his organization. Dead, maybe. Or perhaps I would have gone down a different path and ended up in some high-end brothel on Bourbon Street. Or worse, in a place like El Paradiso in Algiers. I might have even been one of those dead-eyed farmers working in the Silos. Whatever the case, I would've been powerless. Inconsequential. He gave me the means to matter, and for that, I will always be grateful.

—Nora Lancaster

It felt like I'd never left. Everywhere I looked, there were familiar sights. But for some reason, it all seemed smaller. The megabuildings that housed most of the Garden's population still towered just as tall as ever, but they didn't seem nearly as oppressive. The same could be said for the flashing lights, holographic displays, and neon signs that had once so thoroughly fascinated me.

Mostly, though, it was the people I found disappointing. Those hollow expressions on the factory workers' faces, the defeated eyes of farmers, the twitchy, constantly roving attention of the so-called Operators—they all seemed like cardboard cutouts meant to represent real people. I knew that impression was a trick, that I was fooling myself so that I didn't have to care about their plight. However, I couldn't bring myself to overcome it.

After everything that had happened to me, their petty problems seemed so insignificant. While I had been balanced on the edge between life and death, these people had been trudging along, completely unaware that they were mere prisoners, slaves to a system that seemed hell-bent on keeping their necks beneath the boots of their oppressors. And none of them were fighting back.

None of them had rebelled. They were content in their drudgery. From my perspective, it was easy to hold them in contempt.

I knew it was a trap, though. Those people, as sad as their lives might be, were still people, and because of that, they were worthy of at least a modicum of respect. Still, it was difficult not to scream at the top of my lungs at how blind they all were. They couldn't see. They didn't know. And because of that, they would never escape.

"Where are we going?" asked Patrick, hurrying to keep up with me.

"Doctor," I said. "I need to get my hand checked out. I just hope I have enough credits."

Indeed, my funds were incredibly low. I had some things I could sell—notably, the Enforcers' equipment and the Rift Shards I'd mined in the Rift—but doing so would cause issues. The equipment was probably going to be the easiest to move. And I thought I had a plan for that. At worst, I could sell the weapons piecemeal to Operators who didn't care about their gear's origins.

The Rift Shards were different, though. They were not only rare, but I had quite a few of them, too. I'd already decided I wouldn't sell them until I'd talked to my uncle's friends in the Bazaar; the aliens weren't altogether trustworthy, but I felt that they were less likely to screw me over than Nova City's merchants—especially the ones that had enough funds on hand to buy my Shards. My uncle had always said that there was nothing more dishonest than a salesman, and I was of a mind to heed that advice.

"I have some money if you need it," Patrick offered.

A second later, a transfer of two thousand credits flashed across my HUD. I accepted it, saying, "Thanks. I'll get you back once we have a chance to sell some stuff."

He shrugged. "The way I see it, I owe you."

"I'll pay you back," I insisted, which just elicited another shrug. After that, I used a few hundred credits to hire an autotaxi, and we gradually made our way toward our destination, which was an untethered doctor in the western portion of the Garden. After being dropped off in the general area, we had to take a few back alleys to reach an unassuming bodega situated on the ground floor of one of the megabuildings. It was an unaffiliated space that had, only a few years before, been the site of a war between three different tribes. The three-way war had escalated to the point where they'd eventually killed one another off, and the building hadn't been nearly valuable enough for anyone else to move in and claim it. So, it remained neutral territory—one of the few such places in the Garden.

"You want to wait out here?" I asked.

Predictably, Patrick shook his head. He'd been attached to my hip ever since we'd left the refugees behind in Algiers, and I knew him well enough to see that he was terrified. Not surprising, considering that he wasn't exactly a city boy. Likely, the place seemed incredibly chaotic to his virgin eyes.

"Alright," I said. Then, I strode forward. I only got a few steps inside before I became aware of someone aiming a gun at me. I don't know if it was a shift in the air, an errant noise, or just intuition, but I could practically feel the situation shift a few notches closer to danger. I held up my hands, saying, "Just here to see Erlich. I don't want any trouble."

A moment later, a pair of figures stepped out from between the aisles containing all the worst and cheapest nano-wave food in the city. My taste buds rebelled at the mere thought of ingesting those horrible imitations of the real thing. I'd grown up eating the like, but in Mobile, my taste had been refined to the point where I didn't know if I could ever go back. In fact, I would rather eat the tasteless ration bars than put imitation jambalaya in my mouth ever again.

I glanced from one figure to the next. Their features were similar enough that I suspected that they were siblings. Pale skinned, with black hair and blue eyes ringed in dark makeup, the two were so androgynous that I couldn't determine their gender. Not that I was concerned enough to truly investigate. Male, female, or nonbinary, all I cared about were the pistols in their hands.

"We don't know you," one said.

The other added, "And we don't like people we don't know."

"Hard to make friends like that," I said.

"We have no use for friends."

"And friends have no use for us."

I tried not to roll my eyes at Dumb and Dumber. Clearly, they'd practiced their shtick, probably to get under people's skin and throw them off guard. I couldn't let it affect me, though. As much as I wanted to just put them on the ground—not for good, mind you—I didn't think Erlich would appreciate me beating up his guards. So, I chose a more pacifistic path.

"You point those guns at me, and I'm going to splatter the both of you across this store," I said. "Either let me through or tell me to run along. If it's the second one, I'll go in peace. But I won't stand here and watch your bad little . . . whatever it is you were doing there. So, what's it going to be?"

They stared at me like I'd just slapped them. Which, if I'm honest, I really wasn't far from doing. Either way, I added, "And keep in mind—this is me being diplomatic. Don't waste my time, and we won't have a problem."

Maybe I needed to rethink my definition of diplomacy, but in my defense, my uncle had never really covered that. Instead, he'd taught me how to kill and avoid being killed in turn. Speaking to annoying people had never been part of the curriculum. Thankfully, I was saved from making good on my promise when a voice crackled over an unseen speaker, saying, "Let her down, idiots.

She's a patient. Patients mean money. Or did you forget we're running a business here, dumbasses?"

"But—"

"She said—"

"Enough!" came through the speaker, causing a crackle of feedback.

Dumber—or was it Dumb? I had no idea. Either way, one of the two pointed to a corner, saying, "Stairs are over there."

I nodded, then strode forward. Patrick followed close on my heels, and I led him down one of the aisles to the indicated corner, where I found a wall bearing a multitude of shelves. I was just about to ask what I was supposed to do when the entire wall shuddered, then slid backward, revealing a staircase.

"Cool," Patrick muttered, and I couldn't help but agree.

Inside, the stairwell was lit by only a few flickering fluorescent bulbs, but there was plenty of illumination for me to see the autoturret hanging in one corner. Its telltale red eye told me that it was active. I took a moment to activate Misthack and change that. A moment or two later, the red light went dark.

With that done, we quickly descended the steel staircase, switching back a couple of times as it led us deep underground. Steam periodically erupted from the pipes lining the walls, but after having lived in the drainage tunnels beneath the city, I didn't find them that alarming. After three flights of stairs, we found ourselves facing a heavy steel door that looked like it would have been perfectly at home in a bank vault. Not that I'd ever been inside of a bank, but I'd seen plenty in old movies. Either way, it was thick and heavy, and it looked impenetrable even if it bore plenty of signs of oxidation.

"Do we . . . uh . . . knock?" asked Patrick.

I shrugged. Then with my good hand, I banged on the door. I might've used a little more strength than necessary because it resulted in a series of resounding bangs that sounded like the ringing of the world's largest bell.

"I'm comin'. I'm comin'. Hold your horses, you degenerates," came another crackling voice through a still-unseen speaker. I flared Observation, but I still couldn't find a source, which led me to believe it was probably an ability, and not a very useful one at that. Perhaps the good doctor had a Ventriloquism ability or something.

After a minute or so, the huge door trembled, then slid open. It only moved a couple of inches every few seconds, almost as if it hadn't been opened for quite some time. Whatever the case, it only took a further thirty seconds or so before we were standing face-to-face with Dr. Erlich von Hastings.

Or, as most of the Garden knew him, Squirrel.

And the name fit, too. He had the features of a rodent—narrow, watery eyes, a twitchy nose, and a mouth full of crooked teeth that I had the misfortune of seeing when he smiled broadly. He scratched his patchy beard, saying,

"Don't get many customers these days on account of that unfortunate incident back . . . Well, never mind that. What can I do you for?"

"Uh . . . what incident?" asked Patrick.

"Doesn't matter," Squirrel said. Then, his eyes found my splinted wrist. "Oh, that. Nasty injury there. Let's get you in here, yeah? Let Doc Erlich fix you right up."

He turned and scurried back inside, leaving a bewildered Patrick staring at me. "I feel like he's going to try to harvest our organs if we go in there," he muttered. "And I'm not sure he'd have the decency to kill us before it started."

"It'll be fine," I said, watching the doctor. The man was slightly built, and he wore a stained white coat over a mesh shirt and faux-leather shorts that were short enough to expose the vast majority of his skinny legs. Still, I said, "He's got a decent reputation."

That wasn't necessarily true. He'd helped people, sure, but he'd also botched a number of treatments, as well. For one, rumor said that he'd once tried his hand at installing a cybernetic arm, but he clearly had neither the knack nor the skill for it. The poor Operator had ended up getting fried the first time he tried to move it. But his skill didn't matter that much to me; all I needed was for him to fix a couple of tendons, and if he couldn't, then tell me the hand wasn't salvageable. Easy.

So, I boldly strode forward.

And I very much wished I hadn't. Not because I felt like I was in danger. Rather, because the room in which I found myself was absolutely disgusting. It was a mostly open space, lined with a few freestanding metal shelves. In one corner, there was a bare mattress that sported quite a few stains I didn't want to know any more about. In another, there was a pile of trash. And in another, a commode. The centerpiece of the room was an old, outdated exam chair.

"Pardon the mess, yeah," said the rat-faced Squirrel, hurrying to one of the shelves. "I don't get out none too much these days. Not since the incident, at least. Never mind that, though. Let's get that arm all fixed up."

As he spoke, he plucked various instruments from the shelves. None of them looked sanitary, making me rethink the entire visit. Still, a simple examination shouldn't be too dangerous, right?

I crossed the room, intending to sit in the chair, but Squirrel pulled me up short, saying, "You might not want to sit on that. It isn't . . . uh . . . sanitary."

That's when I noticed the packaging, which was easily recognizable as the sort that had once contained virtual reality chips. The plastic was scattered across the dirty floor, indicating that he'd been too eager to get at the contents to bother with throwing it in the trash pile. One and all, they portrayed lewd scenes, telling me precisely what Squirrel had been using the chair for. I suppose that, in his defense, the chair looked a lot cleaner than the mattress. If I was faced with the decision of where to experience my pornographic chips, the chair would've been my choice, as well. Not that I would've gone down that road in such a disgusting place, but Squirrel didn't seem to have many options, so who was I to judge?

Patrick seemed a lot less open-minded, and he wore his disgust in the expression on his face. I couldn't blame him, either.

"Here," Squirrel said, suddenly standing at my shoulder. "Hand me your hand." He let out a little giggle at the phrasing.

I held out my arm, but when his skin touched mine, I almost pulled away. His own hands were incredibly clammy and far colder than they should've been. I guess that was better than if they'd been warm, considering what I had just seen. Either way, I felt the Mist swirl a bit as he bent close to my wrist until his eyes were only an inch or so away. Clearly, he was examining the damage, and I held my breath as I waited for his diagnosis.

Finally, he pulled away, saying, "I might could fix it."

"Might?" I asked, pulling my hand away.

"Might. Fifty-fifty, I'd say," he said. "It's a tricky procedure. If you came to me right after it happened, it would've been closer to ninety-ten, but . . . well, the tendons have started to get used to being unattached. You've got some sort of self-healing ability, yeah? Well, that's a good thing and a bad thing, you know? Good because it'll keep you alive. Bad because sometimes things heal all wrong. That's what's happening in your wrist. To fix it, I'd have to undo all that healing, then put everything back together. Not an easy procedure."

I shook my head, saying, "Shit."

If I was honest, I'd expected as much. Even without the blaring red hand on the health-indicating silhouette on my HUD, my Triage ability gave me some insight into the state of my body. And when I hadn't been ignoring it, I'd discovered that things were not ideal. Hearing that fixing it would be a fifty-fifty proposition hemmed me in and effectively removed one of my choices. As it stood, my only real option was to replace the entire hand with a cybernetic implant.

I didn't want to. I had limited slots in my [Cybernetic Mastery] skill, and though I wasn't using the majority of them, I had plans to change that. Now, it seemed that I was going to have to alter those plans. It wasn't really the adjustment that I hated, but rather that the choice had been forced on me by circumstances. I had half a mind to simply hire Squirrel to do his best and let the chips fall where they may. But that was stupid, and I didn't have room in my life for that kind of idiocy. I needed to be cold. Calculating. I needed to be logical.

And logic said to just replace the hand.

While I'd been thinking things through, Squirrel had continued explaining the issue. However, I'd stopped listening to him, so I just interrupted his babbling by asking, "How much do I owe you for the consultation?"

"You don't want me to fix it?" he asked.

"I'm going to replace it," I stated. "Fifty percent chance of success isn't good enough."

"Well, that's disappointing," he muttered, his fingers twitching with what I assumed was anger. As he spoke, I scanned the area for any more autoturrets, and my search was rewarded a few seconds later when I saw one half-concealed behind one of the shelves. Once again, I activated Misthack and uploaded the same Ghost I'd used with the robots that had been guarding the Rift-mining operation. It went to sleep a moment later. "I guess time really is a circle, and events are destined to repeat themselves."

His accent was all over the place. One second, he spoke like a rustic rube, and the next, he seemed almost erudite. But one thread connected everything—he was obviously crazy. That, as much as the odds of it not working, had cemented my decision not to take advantage of the good doctor's services.

"I require you to transfer all your credits to me, please," he said. "Otherwise, my autoturrets will . . . Well, you know what they do, I'm sure."

I did, but I'd continued scanning the room, and I was fairly certain that I'd gotten them all. There had been two others in the corners, which was overkill for the size of the space. If I hadn't deactivated them, I was sure that even I, with all my advantages, would have been absolutely screwed. It was a good thing, then, that I'd been thinking ahead.

"Yeah, that's not happening," I said. Leisurely, I drew my sword from my arsenal implant, then placed it on his neck. "By all rights, I should just cut your head off."

I could see the concentration on his face as he tried to mentally activate the autoturrets, but it was quickly followed by disappointment. "W-what did you do?" he whined. "My babies! What did you do?!"

"They're just asleep," I said. "Now—you obviously deserve a bit of punishment, don't you think? Maybe I could cut off that little dink you like to tug on so much." As I spoke, I moved the nano-bladed sword down to point at his groin. I gave it a light poke, and he flinched away. "Nah—I'm not that cruel. How about this? You don't tell anybody about me or my friend over there, and we'll call it square."

"H-huh?" he breathed out, cocking his head to the side. "Wait. Yes! Yes, of course! My patients enjoy the strictest confidentiality. My lips are sealed, and—"

"You're overdoing it," I said. I held up a hand at about head height, saying, "You're up here." I lowered it to midtorso height, adding, "And I need you down here. Okay?"

"Down here," he said, ducking down to the appropriate height.

I rolled my eyes, wondering if he really was that stupid. Or maybe he was just terrified. Either way, it was annoying. "Whatever," I said, withdrawing my sword and stowing it away. "We're going now. Remember—not a word, right? Or I'll come back. You don't want me to come back, do you?"

"N-no! I mean . . . If you need a doctor, I would—"

"Patrick? C'mon," I said, interrupting him. My decision wasn't made on a whim. Squirrel wasn't exactly connected, and he looked far too paranoid to spread the news of this incident. In fact, I fully expected him to lock himself in his vault and go back to doing . . . whatever it was he'd been doing. Besides, I'd come to him for a reason, after all. He had a reputation as a capable doctor, but he'd made so many enemies that only the desperate made use of his services. I was banking on that, plus the intimidation factor, to keep him in line. But even if it didn't, he really didn't know much about me. I wasn't even wearing my own face.

Was it base sentimentality to keep him alive? I don't know. But I chose to look at it as the most pragmatic choice. If I killed everyone who tried to take advantage of me, then I'd leave a trail of bodies in my wake. Eventually, someone would notice. Or perhaps I just wasn't as comfortable with murder as I wanted to think I was.

Either way, I wasted no time before turning around and going back the way we had come. Next stop, the Bazaar. Hopefully, it would be a little more fruitful of a visit.

CHAPTER SEVEN

GUNTHER'S GUNS

I remember the first time someone told me that I didn't act like a girl. In some ways, I understood it. After all, I was never a dainty, pretty little thing. Instead, I gravitated toward more rough-and-tumble activities, eventually climbing onto the treadmill of lifting progressively heavier things. But back then, that accusation cut deep into my psyche, and for a while, I tried so hard to be what they wanted me to be. In the end, though, Jeremiah was the one who made me understand that there was no such thing as acting "like a girl." I was just me. And so long as I was happy with who I was, that was all that mattered.

—Nora Lancaster

Before we could go to the Bazaar, I needed to unload a few of the firearms we'd looted from the Enforcers. I had almost fifteen thousand credits to my name, but I had no concept of how much it would cost to enter the Bazaar. Given that I didn't want to visit the Dome and be found wanting for funds, I had decided to visit an arms dealer in the Garden. So, after using Mimic once again, this time to adopt the persona of a middle-aged woman I passed along the way, Patrick and I set off toward the monorail, which was the quickest and cheapest way to cross the city.

As we walked the streets, Patrick stared this way and that like a tourist, a label that wasn't that far off the mark. I nudged him with my elbow, and his attention jerked away from a holographic display of a half-clothed woman hawking some sort of energy drink. "Keep your eyes in your head," I scolded. "You're drawing attention."

"Oh," he breathed. "It's just all so . . . different."

I could sympathize. After spending so long in a backwater like Mobile, I found the constant barrage of lights, holographic displays, and sexual innuendo to be a little disconcerting, as well. The only difference was that, while he'd spent his life hopping from one tiny outpost to the next, I'd grown up around such things. Still, I had to concentrate to keep my mind focused on what was important.

Doing anything less in a place like Nova was the height of stupidity, and it was a good way to end up as a rapidly decomposing corpse in one of the alleys.

We passed by some notable landmarks, like the Emporium, which was the district's arena. In there, prospective fighters would be pitted against one another while spectators wagered on the outcome. I'd never been—Jeremiah had barely let me out of the apartment, much less taken me to such a den of iniquity—but I'd overheard plenty of stories at school. Even in fights that weren't supposed to be to the death, many of the fighters would end up dead. The gamblers wagered on that potential eventuality, as well.

In addition, there were plenty of shops that took up the bottom floors of the various megabuildings. In fact, most of the huge structures had their own economies based on barter as well as the exchange of credits. Some were controlled by guilds that specialized in certain goods, but others, like the building where I'd grown up, housed tribes like the Specters. It was almost like each building was a city unto itself.

Eventually, we found our way to one of the monorail stops, and we took the lift up to the platform. It was at least a couple hundred feet above the hover cars on the street below, and we only had to wait a few minutes before the series of boxy transports came into view. They would eventually make an entire loop around the district, stopping at various points along the way.

Patrick and I boarded alongside a few dozen other people and quickly found a pair of empty seats. As we did, I couldn't help but notice just how dejected most of the other passengers looked. It was expected, considering that the majority were wearing clothing appropriate for factory or farmwork, but it was still a bit jarring after spending so much time in Mobile.

Sure, the town had its own problems—most notably that it couldn't have existed without the constant influx of medicine and other essentials that my uncle had arranged—but the people certainly looked a lot happier. But then again, it had also lacked a lot of the characteristics people in the bigger city took for granted, like the multitude of entertainment options, the fashion scene, and the support system that came with having a permanent Node in the Dome.

Plus, Mobile had been far less secure. For all the issues I had with the Enforcers, they ensured that the people of Nova City never had to worry about the wildlife. Meanwhile, Mobile had been subjected to daily attacks from the local fauna; most of those attacks had been easily managed, largely due to the wall and the Amigos, but quite a few had stretched the town's resources to their limits. Nova, for all its problems, would never have to worry about that.

"Why are there no flying vehicles?" asked Patrick.

"Huh?" I asked, surfacing from my deep thoughts. "What was that?"

"Flying vehicles," he said. "There aren't any."

"Oh. In school, we learned that they were originally allowed," I said. "But it got too dangerous, so they limited it to hover cars and bikes. If anything but this monorail or the drones goes higher than a few dozen feet, the Enforcers will shoot it down. No questions. No polite requests to land. Just gone."

"Seems a little extreme," he mumbled.

I shrugged. "And what about your experiences with the Enforcers makes you expect anything else?" I asked. "Besides, before, it was pandemonium. People were crashing all the time. Lots of innocent people died."

"I . . . I guess that makes sense," he said. "Where are we going?"

"I already told you—to sell some stuff," I said.

"That's a what, not a where," he responded.

Sighing, I rolled my eyes and said, "Fine. We're going to Gunther's Guns. He's got a few locations throughout the city, but I wanted to go to the main branch."

"Why?" he asked.

"Because they don't ask questions there," I answered. "Plus, Gunther is kind of famous in the city. People treat him almost like they treated my uncle. I only met him once, but he talked to . . . my uncle like he was an equal. That tells me he can buy what we're selling without worrying about any sort of repercussions."

"That makes sense, I guess," he said.

"Glad you approve," I answered with a slight smile. Patrick was clearly out of his depth, but he'd gotten better over the past few days. Eventually, his mind would catch up to his circumstances, and he'd be able to start focusing on what he wanted to do with his life. For my part, I'd already given it some thought, but I didn't want to make any firm plans until I knew what kind of funds I had to work with. Sponsoring his development and training would not be a cheap prospect, and I refused to sacrifice my own quest for revenge in order to support him. If it came down to it, I would have no choice but to cut him loose, whether I liked having him around or not.

The cityscape whipped by as the monorail accelerated to a truly frightening speed. The lights and holographic displays blended together into a rainbow of colors, casting the city's blocky, modular buildings in an otherworldly glow. At times like that, it was easy to forget just how much pain, suffering, and oppression lay beneath the city's often breathtaking surface. Case in point, in the very car we occupied, a dusthead was slumped against one of the windows, drool tracing a line along the glass. A nearby man was ogling one of the scantily clad female passengers, his eyes telling a story of just what he'd like to do to her. Just as obviously, she was ignoring his gaze, probably hoping that he would lose interest before she left the relative safety of the cabin. Still another man was watching something lewd on his tablet while his hand found a home in his synth-leather pants.

I sighed. That was life in Nova City. There were miraculous things all around, but it was all coated in a layer of grime.

Idly, I used Misthack on the masturbator's tablet, uploading a Ghost that shut it down. Sadly, that didn't stop him. Instead, he shifted his gaze to the female passenger and resumed his self-gratification. All the while, he wore a broad grin that exposed his almost toothless mouth.

I shook my head and looked away. A couple of minutes later, the monorail pulled to a stop, and the ogled woman exited as quickly as she could. Thankfully, neither of her two admirers followed. The monorail remained at the platform for a few more minutes before it accelerated once again. Three stops later, we reached our destination and exited onto the platform.

Once we'd made it down to the street below, Patrick said, "I never knew Nova was this big."

"This is just one district," I said, striding down the street. "It's the biggest one, but Algiers isn't much smaller. Bywater is the second biggest, and then there are the upscale districts like King's Row. They have smaller populations but occupy almost as much space."

"How big is the whole city?" he asked, hurrying to catch up to me.

I shrugged. "The Garden's platform is about twenty miles across," I said. "There are six platforms, too. Seven if you count the Council District, but nobody lives there. And what you see on the surface is just the beginning. There are a few places that have whole communities living in the drainage tunnels. Though they've been living down there long enough that they're not really much different from the megabuildings where most everybody else lives."

"How many people live here?" he asked.

"A lot," I said. "Millions upon millions."

For the next fifteen minutes, we wove our way through the pedestrians that were either going to or coming from work. Meanwhile, the relative cleanliness of our surroundings improved. It happened gradually, so it wasn't that noticeable, but to me, it was a surefire sign that we were approaching the edge of the district. Sure enough, the ramp to the next platform soon came into view.

Like the one leading down from the Garden and into Algiers, it was a twisting spiral wide enough to accommodate fifteen hover cars traveling side by side. And I knew it wasn't the only point of entry; there were three others scattered along the edge of the platform. Unlike was the case with the border between Algiers and the Garden, the base of this ramp boasted an Enforcer checkpoint manned by dozens of black-clad soldiers, more drones than I could count, and a plethora of autoturrets. It would be suicide to try to force entry.

It was a good thing, then, that we had no reason to do so. Instead, we turned down the street and soon found ourselves before a squat, garishly painted structure. Atop that building, which covered at least an entire block, was a sign proclaiming that it was Gunther's Guns. Predictably, there was a holographic display of a barely clothed woman holding a light machine gun. Beside her was a similarly clad and sculpted man that reminded me of the covers of my collection of romance novels. Just looking at him brought a blush to my cheeks. Hopefully, my Mimic ability would mask it.

"Come on," I said, grabbing Patrick by the wrist and dragging him across the street and into the building. However, once we'd passed through the doors, a figure stepped in front of us. Then another. And another after that.

"Please cancel all active abilities," came a feminine voice. I looked up at the owner and saw a face that might've matched the pitch. However, the rest of the body was anything but feminine. In fact, it wasn't even human. Sure, there were two arms and two legs, a torso and a head. But instead of flesh, there was nothing but the bulky metal of cybernetics right up to the head, which was surprisingly pretty, blonde, and smiling.

"What the . . ."

I ignored Patrick's exclamation and focused on Misthack. I had already uploaded a Ghost and moved on to the next cyborg when I heard someone clear his throat. "Please don't deactivate my guards," came a rough voice over an unseen speaker.

"Deactivate?" said the female cyborg, though I wasn't certain if gender identity really mattered when all the relevant parts were mechanical. A cybernetic hand shot out, but I batted it away. "What'd you do, you little—"

"Stop, Dierdre," said the voice over the intercom. "Or she'll have to get serious. None of us wants that. Just let her in. I'll keep her in line myself."

"But Mr. Gunderson, you pay us to—"

"And, ma'am, I trust you'll remove the hostile program from their systems before you leave," the intercom said. "I would hate to have to debug them myself."

I narrowed my eyes and nodded. "Assuming everything goes the way I hope it does, meaning I don't have to . . . get serious, as you say, I can do that," I allowed.

The female cyborg, whose name was obviously Dierdre, stepped aside, but she continued to glare at me. The others did the same, but judging by Dierdre's attempt to grab me, I didn't have much to worry about from them. It wouldn't be easy, but so long as I kept my wits about me, I could probably survive long enough to get away. Still, their state was curious; I wondered how they'd managed to avoid the Singularity with so many cybernetics. Perhaps the secret was that they hadn't.

Either way, I pushed past them, dragging a stunned Patrick with me into the building. Soon, we found ourselves in an expansive lobby containing a host of archaic weaponry. Not only were there giant bronze cannons, but there were muskets, suits of armor, and long guns of every sort on display. There was even a giant monstrosity of a tank right in the middle of the room.

I'd been there before, so I'd expected the display; Patrick, however, had not, and his jaw dropped at the sight.

"It's always nice when someone appreciates my collection," a man said as he stepped out from behind the tank. He was short and stout and sported a long, braided beard. He was dressed in an honest-to-God leather suit, complete with a bolo tie and a wide-brimmed hat. At his waist was a revolver so big it would've made Ferdinand II question his adequacy. You know, if he weren't an inanimate object. The man looked at me, adding, "But you seem like you might have been here before, Mistrunner."

"Maybe I have, maybe I haven't," I said. "What does it matter?"

"Oh, it matters," the man said, hooking his thumbs onto his belt and taking a wide stance. "Those boys and girls out there, they cost me a fortune in cybernetics, not to mention top-flight installation. And then you come along and pick their defenses apart like it's nothing. What was that program you uploaded?"

"I call it *Time Bomb*," I said. It was a lie; in reality, I'd uploaded the *Sleep Mode* Ghost, but I hadn't activated it. "You can guess what it does. You know, if you don't play nice, I mean. Easily removed, though. And their defenses barely qualified for the name, Gunther."

"Ah, so you know me?"

"I know of you," I said, focusing on the man. He was at least a Tier 4. Maybe even a Tier 5, though I got the feeling that he wasn't as strong as my uncle. However, whatever he lacked in raw strength, he could probably make up for in sheer firepower. He was not a man to be trifled with. "Word is that you're an honest businessman who doesn't care too much about where things come from. You pay what something's worth. Not a credit more or less."

"Glad that my reputation is still intact," he said. After that, Gunther rolled his shoulders and said, "Alright, here's the deal. If you want to do business, I'm going to need you to drop that ability that's concealing your identity. I won't ask you to do it until we're out of sight and in a clean room, but after that, I have to insist."

"And if I don't do that?" I asked.

"Then we don't do business," he said. He held up a hand and with two fingers pointed down, mimed a person walking away. "You head on your merry little way, and I go back to running my business. No harm, no foul. But if you make me go through all the trouble of setting up a clean room and then refuse to drop the ability, well . . . then we're going to have some problems."

I didn't want to drop Mimic, but given Gunther's reputation, I didn't think he'd run his mouth all over town. Still, letting the ability fall away would feel almost like taking off a set of armor. Once my identity was exposed—and I had no illusions about whether or not he'd recognize me despite meeting me only a single time—I would be bare to the world. But who was to say that other arms dealers throughout the city would be any less insistent on knowing my real identity? And besides, my uncle had trusted Gunther, after a fashion. That had to count for something.

But then again, he'd trusted Nora, too, and look where that had gotten him.

"Time's tickin' away," he said, tapping his wrist.

Finally, I made a decision and said, "Fine. I'll deactivate the ability once we're in a clean room."

He clapped his hands together, saying, "Wonderful! Come with me, then."

With that, he turned around and strode through the lobby. There were a few people around, but they were too interested in the displays of weapons to pay any attention to us. Gunther led us through another set of doors, and I briefly got a glimpse of a warehouse full of rack after rack of weapons before he led us down another hall and into an unadorned office. Once we were inside, he pressed a couple of buttons on the wall, and I felt the Mist in the air agitate.

"There we go," he said. "Clean as a whistle. Nothing in, nothing out. Now, if you will, Miss . . ."

"Braddock," I said, deactivating my ability. My image shimmered, and I once again looked like myself. "Mira Braddock. I believe you knew my uncle."

Gunther gaped at me for a long moment before he gathered his wits and said, "Little Mirabelle. I haven't seen you since—"

"It's been almost six years," I said. "You came to our apartment to broker some sort of deal with my uncle. I disobeyed and came out of my room while you were there, and you gave me a practice pistol. A dainty little thing that my uncle threw away the moment you were gone. He said it was a girl gun. And I have to agree, Mr. Gunderson."

"He threw it away?" the man asked. "Seriously? That little gun was, ounce for ounce, one of the most powerful . . . You know what? Never mind." He shook his head. "I was sorry to hear about Jeremiah. He was a good man. Misunderstood, but still, he had a good heart."

"Wait, you know what happened to him?" Patrick asked, his first contribution to the discussion.

He nodded. "Everybody knows," the bearded man said. "They broadcast it throughout the city. Claimed it was one of the finest achievements since the city was founded. They called him a terrorist."

"That's ridiculous," I said.

"Not really," Gunther said. "Jeremiah was . . . Well, let's just say he was a complicated man, and from their perspective, he was indeed a criminal and a terrorist. But let's not talk about that. I'm sure you came here for a reason, right?"

"Right. I want to sell some weapons," I said.

"Where are they?" he asked. "I understand if—"

I nodded at Patrick, and he emptied out his storage. In seconds, stacks of guns, blades, and Enforcer uniforms were on the floor.

"What did you do?" Gunther asked, staring at the pile wide-eyed.

"My uncle was killed by Enforcers," I said. "You do the math."

He swallowed hard, then nodded. "Give me a couple of minutes to go through everything," he said. "I'll buy the guns, but I don't want anything to do with the uniforms."

"Even the Banshee suits?" I asked.

"They're called infiltration suits," he said. "They mask heat signature and provide a little protection against small arms and blades."

"But you don't want them," I said.

"I do not," he responded. "Too hot. Nobody would buy them when doing so would just paint a target on their back."

I shrugged. "Fair enough," I said. "Just let me know when you're done with the tally."

With that, I retreated to lean against the other wall. I crossed my arms as Patrick joined me. He said, "That took a lot of Mist, so I'm not going to be able to store anything else for a day or two. Not without an access point to shoulder the cost."

I glanced in his direction and noticed that he looked paler than usual. I could understand that; I'd only rarely been pushed to my limits in terms of Mist usage, but it was never a pleasant experience.

After a few minutes, Gunther rose from where he'd been examining the weapons and turned to me. He said, "I can give you forty-eight thousand for everything. It would be more, but I'm going to have to spend some credits to pay a contractor to remove the identifier beacons."

I nodded and accepted the resulting transfer. "Can I ask your advice on something?" I asked.

"Sure," he agreed.

"I need a cybernetic engineer," I said. "A good one, too. There was a woman my uncle hired, but I can't remember her name."

"Cirilla Montague," Gunther said. "Your uncle went through me to hire her. He couldn't set foot in King's Row without setting off every alarm in the district. But I do business with some of them."

"Cirilla Montague," I said. "Can you get in touch with her? I intend to buy some cybernetics, and I'm going to need someone trustworthy to install them. And, if you can suggest a venue, somewhere to have it done, that would help."

I knew it was a lot to ask, but I wanted to trust Gunther. The combination of his reputation and the fact that he had been on good terms with my uncle predisposed me to trusting him. Besides, I needed some guidance, and he was the only person I could think of that might help me.

"I could do that," he said. "But you'd better have a lot more credits than what I just transferred to you."

"I don't," I admitted. "But I will after a trip to the Bazaar."

He nodded, an avaricious gleam in his eye. "Interesting," Gunther said. "But I won't pry into your secrets. The rates will depend on what you need done, so I won't quote you anything right now. But here . . ."

A communication request popped up on my HUD. I accepted the contact.

"Give me a call once you're ready," he said. "I'll do what I can."

"Thanks," I said. "Guess we're done, then. I'll see myself out."

Gunther said, "Don't forget to remove that program from my people on your way out."

"I won't," I said, moving toward the door.

"And Mirabelle?"

"Yeah?" I asked, standing by the door.

"I'm sorry about your uncle," he stated. "Like I said, he was a good man, and his passing was a loss for all humanity."

"Thanks" was my only response, but in the back of my mind, I couldn't help but remember that he hadn't just passed. He had been taken. Murdered. Tortured and then displayed like a trophy. It only reminded me that I still had a job left to do.

CHAPTER EIGHT

BACK TO THE BAZAAR

Jeremiah dragged me out of the proverbial gutter, gave me a place to live, food to eat, and training most people like me could only dream about. So, when it came time to get my Nexus Implant, I expected that he had something special planned. Looking back, I now know that he had the ability to give me power on a level that would truly make a difference, but despite how much he talked about us being like family, his decision not to give me the means to truly shine was the only declaration that really mattered. I was just a worker drone to him. Another cog in his machine. To Jeremiah, I was not special.

—Nora Lancaster

On our way to the Dome, I resisted the urge to swing by our old megabuilding. I didn't dare go inside—for now, at least—but I still wanted to look at it. Maybe I would get a glimpse of the betrayer. I wasn't so naive as to think that Nora didn't have her own reasons for doing what she'd done. I was well aware that it probably made perfect sense to her. But simple awareness didn't mean I cared about her excuses. Nor would it change my mind about what I intended to do. It would have to wait, though. I wasn't ready.

Certainly, I could probably engage in an all-out assault. I might even be able to snipe her from afar. However, that wasn't good enough. Her actions had resulted in my uncle being ripped limb from limb; I couldn't do anything less for her, could I? Ever since I'd discovered her betrayal, I had been dreaming about how I would enact my revenge. And none of those plans were quick, either. So, there was no reason for me to go by the megabuilding. I didn't need to see her now. I'd get plenty of that in the near future.

So, as the monorail pulled to a stop at the platform closest to where I'd grown up, I remained in my seat next to Patrick. He'd been quiet since leaving Gunther's Guns, and I suspected that he was lost in thought. Everything was so new to him that I'd have been surprised if he wasn't a little overwhelmed. Still, I had some hope that he would quickly adjust to his new reality.

For my part, I knew that I just needed to keep moving. So long as I had a goal, I wouldn't have to think about what I'd lost, about all the people who'd died. Jo. Her parents. The Amigos. Jeremiah. The list went on and on, and if I let myself focus on that, I'd get lost in the weeds of my grief. So, my plan was to keep working toward my revenge, and hopefully, by the time Nora lay dead at my feet, I'd be in a healthier place. Until then, though, I would keep checking off boxes on my to-do list.

To that end, we rode the monorail all the way across town to the Dome. It was located in Bywater, which was a kind of buffer between the poorer districts like the Garden and the much more affluent platforms like King's Row. In addition to being the home of the Dome, it was also a mercantile paradise, with thousands of businesses headquartering there. A few people did still live there, but the number wasn't nearly as high as in the Garden or Algiers, largely because it was too expensive for the lower class and too low-class for the aristocratic elites. Even so, there were a few high-tiered craftsmen and moderately successful business owners that made their homes in the district.

However, the biggest and most important structure on the entire platform was the Dome. My uncle had once told me that it had been based on a structure from the old world, but back then, I'd only half believed him. Now, though, after having seen some of the ruins of that same civilization, I found it far more plausible.

As we exited the monorail, the Dome itself was visible, even from blocks away. And Patrick was suitably impressed when we finally found our way to the square surrounding it. The square was populated by statues meant to depict humanity's mythological deities, each of which had their arms stretched toward the sky in a worshipful posture. The first time I'd seen them, I'd thought them beautiful and elegant. Now, though? I saw them for what they really were: propaganda for what would become our alien overlords.

Patrick and I quickly traversed the square, and once we were inside the Dome, we found our way to the red-and-white obelisk that would connect to the Confluence that, in turn, would take us to the Bazaar. I didn't really understand what any of that meant, but I took it to mean that the obelisk had been made to harness some sort of convergence of Mist that would power our virtual transport to the Bazaar.

Or perhaps I was entirely wrong. I had no way of knowing and nobody to ask, so I decided to simply accept my ignorance until I could cure it. After waiting in line for a couple of minutes, Patrick and I stepped forward and laid our hands on the obelisk. Immediately, a message flashed across my HUD.

Transportation to Station 25116452351 (colloquially known as "The Bazaar") approved. Fee: 25,000 credits per entity transferred.

Fifty thousand credits. It wouldn't quite wipe me out, but it wouldn't leave me with much left over, either. Suddenly, I understood why so few people went to the Bazaar. If the price of entry was so high, only the wealthy could afford to even visit, which further limited the power of the populace. It was yet another layer of oppression, and upon realizing that, I ground my teeth in frustration. Even so, I approved the transfer, and a moment later, I felt a swirl of Mist drag me away. This time, I managed to stop myself from screaming, but I still let out a gasp of surprise as I was whisked away and up into the sky. A couple of seconds later, I passed through the upper atmosphere and into space. That lasted only a moment before I landed in one of the Bazaar's entry halls.

"I think I'm going to be sick," came Patrick's mutter from beside me.

I couldn't help but laugh.

He glared at me, saying, "You could've warned me."

"Sorry," I said. "I just . . . I said almost the exact same thing the first time I did it. But I screamed, too. So, you've got one up on me."

"Really?" he asked, clearly surprised. Did he think me entirely unflappable? Had he really put me on that much of a pedestal?

"Yeah. But it wasn't as bad this time," I said. Then, I gave him the rundown my uncle had given me. Some of it, like the existence of the liaisons who worked with the aliens, he knew. Other parts, like the nature of the Bazaar, he didn't. Either way, it only took a few minutes before he knew most of what I did, and we set off toward our first destination.

As we walked the halls, passing through cavernous rooms containing hundreds of stacked shops manned by various types of aliens, I couldn't help but think that everything felt bigger than it had before. Likely, my excitement during my first trip to the Bazaar had taken the edge off of the travel time through the Bazaar.

Eventually, after walking for what felt like miles—which made no sense; if there were miles' worth of corridors and rooms within the space station, the structure would be visible from Earth's surface—we found our way to our first stop: Gala's shop.

It wasn't so much that I wanted to buy some weapons. Rather, of the two merchants we'd visited the first time around, she was the one I felt most comfortable with. And I needed some advice before I could enact the rest of my plans. So, after climbing the stairs, I planted myself in front of the plasti-steel door and knocked. It slid open a second later, revealing Gala herself.

She was, for lack of a better way to categorize her, a minotaur, complete with sweeping horns, tawny fur, and a face that looked like it belonged on a cow. Her fur-covered body was muscular enough that it would've put Nora's to shame, and she wore a leather jerkin with matching pants. At her hip was Ferdinand II's predecessor—a giant revolver that was more cannon than handgun.

"Little Mirabelle!" the minotaur exclaimed. "I was worried about you! Come in. Come in."

She grabbed me by the shoulder and dragged me inside. A stunned Patrick received similar treatment with the other hand, and a moment later, the door slid shut behind them. Then, Gala wrapped me in her strong arms and hugged me tightly.

"You poor thing," she said. I could hear the sobbing in her trembling voice. "I thought you were gone, just like Jeremiah."

"I . . . I got out," I said.

After a few more seconds, she pushed me to arm's length and looked me up and down. "A little worse for wear, aren't you?"

"Uh . . . I guess? It's a disguise," I said. "And how are you touching me when I'm not really here?"

"You're not the only one with skills," she said with a crooked grin that exposed her flat teeth. "I'm so glad you made it. Like I said, I was worried about you."

"So, you heard about my uncle, too?"

"I did," she said. "It was all anyone was talking about up here for a few days. He made a lot of trouble for some of the . . . more involved parties. Most of them were glad to see him gone, I'm sorry to say. But he had friends up here, too. I'm sorry it happened. Such a terrible way to attack someone like him. They couldn't challenge him one-on-one, so they sent an army after him."

"After they bombarded the entire town with heavy munitions," I said. "They killed thousands of people just to hurt him enough that they could . . . do what they did."

"Shameful."

I shook my head, saying, "Yeah. But I'm not here to talk about my uncle. I need some help, Gala."

"With what?" she asked, glancing at Patrick, who'd remained silent during the entire exchange. "And who is this young man? I sense that he's more than he appears at first glance. Do you have some sort of smuggling skill, boy? If you do, I might be able to put you to work."

"Uh . . ."

"We'll cover Patrick later, Gala," I said. "What do you know about Rift Shards?"

"Not much to know," she said. "They're raw energy. Crystallized Mist that's used for all sorts of crafting and to power various machines. This station goes through them like you wouldn't believe. Why? Did you get your hands on one?"

"More than one," I said. "What would you say if I told you I had about a hundred small ones? Maybe as big as my finger?"

"I'd say that you and I could do some real business," she said.

"And if I said I had about two hundred that are a little bigger?" I asked.

"What did you do, girl? Rob a mining camp?" Gala asked.

"Something like that" was my response. "And have you ever seen one that's about the size of my head?"

"You completed a Rift, didn't you?" Gala guessed.

I didn't see any reason to lie, so I nodded before telling her the story of how I'd assaulted the mining camp before delving the Rift itself. At the end, I told her about how I'd killed all the remaining aliens.

"No wonder they were so upset," she said, shaking her head. "The Castorix tried to keep it quiet, but you know how it goes. The moment you try to keep something secret is when it gets out to everyone. So, they lost a Rift. Good. Their methods are barbaric."

"I agree," I said. "Anyway, I need to unload those Shards, and I want to use that money to upgrade my cybernetics. I also need to see about buying a couple of skills."

"No weapons?" she asked.

"Uh . . . that depends on how much I can get," I said. "My current weapons are fine. But I screwed up my hand, so I'm going to need some sort of an implant to make it functional again. And like I said, I need a couple of skills. Maybe some subdermal armor. I don't even know what's available, honestly. But if I have money left over, I'd like to upgrade my rifle and get something a little stronger, too."

"You unlocked the Heavy Weaponry branch of the [Firearms] tree, didn't you?" she asked.

"Something like that."

At that, she grinned, saying, "Then I've got the perfect weapon for you. It's a bit bulky, metaphorically speaking, and it'll stretch the limits of your arsenal implant. But you won't get anything that packs more of a punch."

"That sounds perfect," I said. "But I'm not sure I can afford it."

"You'll be able to," she said. "That haul of Lesser Rift Shards is probably worth at least a million credits. Maybe a little more. The bigger ones, which are usually just known as Rift Shards, are worth at least twice that. And the big one? That's what's usually known as a Greater Rift Shard. And it's worth many more times that to the right buyer."

"And you know the right buyer?" I asked.

She nodded. "I believe I do," she said. "But he's a bit prickly, so I'll need to do the talking."

"That's fine by me," I responded. Then, I glanced at Patrick, who seemed completely out of his depth. "Oh. I'm going to need a new pistol for him, too. And probably some kind of training manuals for [Cybernetic Engineer]."

"Shouldn't be an issue," the minotaur answer. "Now, c'mon. No time to waste."

With that, she pushed through me, showcasing that our earlier ability to touch wasn't going to be a constant, and opened the door. Soon, Patrick and I were struggling to keep up with her as she strode through the station. Fifteen minutes later, she led us to a barely visible side passage, and when we followed her inside, the decor changed considerably. Gone were the shining metallic surfaces and crisp glyphs. Instead, this tunnel looked almost natural.

"What is this?" I asked.

"This station is far more than you know, hon," said Gala. "There are parts of it that would blow your little mind if you saw it right now."

"My mind isn't little," I muttered.

"Sure it's not" was her response.

After a few twists and turns, we found our way to what looked like a medieval village, complete with stone huts, oddly colored trees, and even a few animals. Instead of being predominantly green, the vegetation was purple, and the animals looked almost like dogs, except that they had a few extra legs and eyes.

"Borack brought most of his extended family with him," Gala said as they walked through the village. "Paid through the nose for it, but as he specializes in Rift Shards, he can afford it. You're probably the first Earthlings to ever lay eyes on this village."

"Why does it look like this?" I asked.

"Meant to mimic his home world," she explained. "It's not perfect, but he says they got the gist of it right."

"I said it was passable, you old cow," came a growling voice from one of the huts. I looked over to see a man that looked like a curious amalgam of insect and human. He had all the right pieces—two arms, two legs, and a head—but he was far too thin, with oddly jointed legs and skin that looked more like segmented chitin. "And I meant that it was barely acceptable. What are you doing here, Gala? And why did you bring these primates to my door?"

"Good to see you, too," Gala muttered. "I brought Mira here because she has a cache of Rift Shards she wants to sell."

"Bah! Send her to Treyachian," Borack said, waving a taloned hand dismissively. "I've got all the Lesser Rift Shards I can use."

"She doesn't just have Lesser Shards, Bor," Gala said.

"So she has a few midgrade Shards? Big deal," he said.

"I have over two hundred midgrade Shards, a little more than a hundred Lesser Shards, and one Greater Rift Shard," I said, tiring of the back and forth. "And I'm looking to sell."

Borack focused on me, and I felt a tremor go up my spine. How that was possible when I technically wasn't there, I don't know. It might have even been only in my mind. Either way, I could practically feel the power wafting off of the insectoid man.

"That's quite a claim," Borack said. "What do you want for them?"

"Uh..."

Gala stepped up, saying, "I'll be acting as her intermediary, and I'll guarantee delivery of the items."

"Interesting," Borack said, steepling his long, thin, and rigid fingers. They clacked together, sounding like nothing so much as plastic slapping against plastic. "Very interesting. I couldn't do more than five million for the lot, though."

"Oh, c'mon, Bor," Gala said with a flat-toothed grin. "You think I was born last cycle? The Greater Shard alone is worth twice that much."

I sighed as the pair went back and forth over the next few minutes. It wasn't that I didn't care about dickering; I knew it was something I'd have to learn at some point. Rather, I was just eager to get going with my other tasks. After all, I couldn't get to what was really important until I'd taken care of myself and my gear.

Finally, after almost fifteen minutes, Gala struck a deal that would see me being paid almost fifteen million credits for my Rift Shards. Hopefully, that would be enough to pay for what I needed because I didn't think I'd be hitting another Rift anytime soon. Whatever money I made from here on out was going to have to be earned the old-fashioned way. Or stolen from my enemies. Probably the second one, if I was being honest with myself.

Still, Gala seemed happy with the result, but then again, so did Borack, who told me before we left that he would be happy to buy any Shards I found in the future. I responded that I would keep him in mind if I ran across any, and after I accepted the pending transfer of credits, we were on our way. If, for whatever reason, I didn't come up with the Shards, I would be sanctioned by the system. I wasn't sure exactly what that meant, but I could intuit that it wasn't anything good. So, I resolved to load them into one of the rapid-transference nodes as soon as I got back to Nova.

"Next stop, a skill repository," said Gala. "I trust you know where to find cybernetics on your own."

I nodded. "Thanks, Gala," I said. "Your help means more to me than you could know."

"I owe it to your uncle," she said. "He was a good man. Besides, I've got a soft spot for freshly initiated worlds."

CHAPTER NINE

GEARING UP

The day I started taking the bio-enhancers was a watershed moment for me. It was only a year after I got my Nexus Implant, and I'd already reached the potential of my constitution. And given that Jeremiah wouldn't let me leave the city to level, I was stuck. So, I progressed the only way I could, and I've never regretted it since.

—Nora Lancaster

We made for a mismatched trio as we traversed the city-sized space station called the Bazaar. A tawny-furred female minotaur, a stout young man with a square jaw and messy, blond hair, and me. And we got plenty of odd looks along the way, from both humans and aliens alike. I ignored them, largely because I didn't care what they thought of me. But there was also the simple fact that I couldn't really do anything about it, either. I felt naked without Mimic to hide behind. Whatever the case, we walked in silence until, almost thirty minutes later, we found our way to an almost deserted portion of the space station.

There were a few shops around, but most of the stacked cubes looked empty. When I asked Gala about it, she said, "They'll be occupied once the Integration begins in a few years. For now, there's not much reason for most merchants to hang around. There are better, more profitable places to set up shop. Of course, it might get even emptier if certain factions have their way."

"What do you mean?" I asked.

"Can't say much without getting sanctioned by the system, but suffice it to say that if humanity gets enslaved, there won't be much room for merchants like me," she said. "Likely, one or two factions will make an alliance so they can strip the planet down to its core. Everyone else will head toward greener pastures."

My uncle had mentioned that there were two types of aliens: those who wanted to exploit humanity for all we were worth, and another group who wanted to work with us. I didn't need any more lessons to understand that the former would almost always outnumber the latter. It was up to humanity to tip the balance, and according to my uncle, we'd already lost the fight before it even began. The liaisons on the ground had seen to that, paving the way for the oppression of the entire planet.

For my part, I had already witnessed our future firsthand. The way those people had been treated at the Rift, forced into a cycle of reward and punishment that had rendered them into unthinking slaves—it wasn't something I would soon forget. Nor would I ever let that happen to me or anyone else I cared about. I would rather die than submit to that sort of life.

Of course, when I asked Gala about the Castorix, she informed me that they were among the worst of the worst. However, they were in no way alone in their treatment of the natives, and they often allied themselves with more powerful forces with the same overall outlook. Still, it was somewhat comforting to hear that they were outliers; most aliens wouldn't take things quite so far.

But in the end, slavery was slavery, and I wouldn't be subjected to any of its many forms.

Finally, we reached our destination in one of the less-occupied clumps of shops, and when Gala knocked, the door opened, and we were greeted by a tiny green man. He had huge black eyes, a multitude of antennae in the place of hair, and a body no bigger than that of a child. He wore a silvery jumpsuit and a wide variety of jewelry.

It wasn't until he spoke that I began to reconsider my concept of genders because he wasn't a he at all. Rather, she was clearly female, at least by my understanding. Of course, there were plenty of people in Nova City who occupied some space in between, so it was entirely possible that she was nonbinary. Or agender. Perhaps her species didn't even have sexes. So, I decided to use gender-neutral pronouns until I knew better.

"Gala, darling!" said the green alien, throwing their arms out wide. "So good to see you! Oh, and you brought friends!"

Gala knelt and gave the other alien a hug, and I couldn't help but smile at the disparity between their sizes. After the hug, Gala stood and introduced Patrick and me to her friend, who was named Ana.

Ana wagged her finger at me, saying, "I know what you're thinking, young lady. Ana isn't an alien name, right? Well, you're completely correct!" They thrust one of their fingers to the sky; I noticed that there were four on each hand. "Ana is actually short for Anaseteramanimix, and even that is a quirk of the translation construct. The point is that being called Ana helps me fit in. I've been studying you aliens for decades, and I do believe I've begun to understand you."

"Uh . . . okay," I said.

"For instance," they said. "I am sure that you are wondering about my gender, are you not? Well, you needn't wonder for much longer because I am a female of my species. Of course, that's just for now. Which reminds me—do humans change sex based on their environment? I can never get a straight answer from the information circuit."

"Uh . . . no," I said. "Well, we sometimes change, but only if we want to, I guess."

Indeed, there was a woman who had worked for my uncle who'd been born male. The moment she'd saved up enough money, she'd gone to a specialized doctor and had that issue rectified. I'd never met anyone happier, so I guess the procedure was a success.

"Interesting," Ana said. "Well, come in. Come in!"

I glanced at Gala, who wore a giant bovine smile, and followed the little green alien into her shop. When I did, I was blown away by its decor. Excluding Borack's private village, the other shops I'd visited had been sleek and mostly without decoration. Ana's, though, looked like it belonged to the world's most vapid teenage girl. The color pink was definitely a theme, and there were posters of various boy bands all over the wall. I didn't know most of them, but the ones I did recognize produced just the sort of music I loathed. Nothing like Leviathan or Echo Chamber or any of the other bands I followed. My preferred artists had soul, and by comparison, the boy bands were as shallow as a mud puddle.

"Do you like my posters? I've spent years finding just the right ones!" Ana practically squealed. "I try to watch all the shows, too. And I even met one of the boys from Ticker Tape. Not Johnny, of course—I didn't get that lucky. But Liam was always my favorite anyway. Of course Ticker Tape is no Angel Wings, but a girl takes what she can get, if you know what I mean!"

"Uh . . . yeah . . ."

"Oh, but you're probably up to date on *Pirates of Santa Monica*, aren't you?" she went on. "With the way the Bazaar is positioned right now, I've missed the last three episodes, so I have no idea if Tate got with Alex! Ugh. I wish I could just go down there and—"

"Ana, we came to browse your wares," Gala said.

Ana blinked her enormous eyes. "Oh. Right. Sorry. I am such a ditz sometimes," she said. "But I see humans so infrequently. That's the downside to dealing in skills. Very few can afford my work."

"You make skills?" I asked.

"I do," she said. "But my true passion is great music. As soon as the Integration comes, I intend to go down to the surface and follow Angel Wings as they tour. I might even finance the whole thing! You know what, you could come with me. We could be best friends, and—"

"Ana . . ."

The green alien blinked her huge eyes at Gala's interruption, then shook her head. "Sorry, sorry. I get a little worked up," she said. "But here, let's take a look at what we have available. What kind of skill are you looking for?"

"I'm not sure," I said. "Can I just browse?"

She nodded, then pressed a button on the wall. Immediately, the posters disappeared, revealing rack after rack of skill crystals. They were all multifaceted crystals, identical in every way. Even the color—or the lack thereof—was the same for each and every one of them. That was outside of my expectations; when I'd absorbed my other skills, the crystals had all been different colors. So, I asked Ana about it.

"Amateurs," she scoffed. For the first time, her chipper tone had faded. "Some {Skillsmiths} like to code their skills in various colors. It's a waste of Mist and time, and I won't have it. My skills are pure and uncluttered."

I nodded. Each of the skills was identifiable by a small holographic label beneath the crystals, and I was blown away by the sheer variety on display. However, I also noticed that the vast majority of them overlapped with skills and abilities I already had. For instance, there was [Fighting Instinct], which, when I asked for an explanation, Ana described as remarkably similar to Combat Focus. There were many others there, as well, from [Rifles] to [Pugilism] and everything in between. Strangely, there were no skills that mimicked my Mistwalk ability, further cementing its value in my mind. Already, I'd seen that most people weren't prepared to combat it, and I hoped that would remain the case.

In addition to the more combat-focused skills, there were plenty that would grant abilities in various trades. There was [Construction], [Horticulture], [Mining], and [Hunting], and that was just the tip of the iceberg. In addition, I saw [Tailoring] and [Armor Smithing]. However, given that I had no intention of splitting attention between combat and crafting, I ignored most of those.

But the moment I laid eyes on [Acrobatics], I knew I had to have it. So, I asked Ana about it, and she said, "It doesn't grant any abilities. Nor will you see modifiers on your status. Instead, it drastically increases your proprioception. Likely. Skills can affect different people in different ways. It depends on suitability."

That was news to me, but I didn't want to inadvertently reveal any of my secrets. I suspected that getting eight abilities from a single skill, like I had with [Combat Utility], was a rarity. So, I changed the subject, saying, "Increased proprioception sounds really useful to me."

"It's a waste of a skill slot for most people," Gala interjected. "Think about it. Say you've only got one or two skill slots. If you're a warrior, are you going to take something like [Rifles] that can help you deal damage? Or are you going to go with something that lets you flip around?"

I nodded. That made sense. If I had to choose between [Acrobatics] and any of the skills with which I had started, it wouldn't have stood a chance. But now? [Combat] was so overpowered that it opened up room for a niche skill like [Acrobatics]. For most people, it would've been a silly choice, but I had seven skill slots. I had room to spare. So, I chose it.

I was similarly unconflicted about the next skill. The second I laid eyes on [Demolition], I had no desire at all to continue the search. Still, I asked Ana about it, and she said, "Good eye. It's another one that doesn't really come with any abilities. Pure modifiers. But they're strong. If you like explosions—"

"Who doesn't?" Gala interrupted with a wide grin.

"There's no substitute for a good [Demolition] skill," Ana went on. "I was lucky to have the opportunity to blueprint that one. Most explosives skills are either combat- or noncombat-focused. This one is a nice blend."

With that, my choices were made, and Ana stated a price. However, this time, it was Patrick who spoke up with an objection, saying, "Three million is practically robbery. There's no way we're paying that!"

Ana narrowed her eyes, saying, "Smuggler."

"Better believe it," he said. Then, to me, he added, "I have an ability that sometimes tells me when I'm being ripped off. It just triggered. This alien's trying to cheat us."

"Cheat you?!" screeched Ana. "I never! Three million was the starting point! That's how bargaining works, young man."

"We'll do a million," he said. "Not a credit more."

"I spent more than that on the blueprints!" she protested. "The best I could do is two. And that's barely enough to keep the carnagogs at bay!"

I had no idea what a carnagog was, but I still got the meaning. After that, she and Patrick continued to dicker back and forth until, at last, they settled at a million and a half credits. When it was finished, I'd half expected Ana to throw us out, but instead, she got my attention and said, "You'd better keep that one around. Handsome and a good trader. Such a great combination. I don't suppose he can sing, can he? He's not pretty enough to make it in a top-tier band like Angel Wings, but with his strong jaw, he could—"

"Ana!" Gala interrupted.

"Right," said the alien, a purple blush finding its way to her cheeks. "Sorry. I get a little worked up is all." Then, she looked at Patrick, saying, "Come look me up when the Integration starts. I might have a job for you."

"O-okay," Patrick said, having lost the air of confidence with which he'd negotiated. I expect that an ability might have been involved, the change was so dramatic.

I thanked Ana, promising to come back and visit her when I could, and then we left. As we walked, I used the Bazaar's interface, which had automatically hooked into my HUD, to set up a rapid transference of the skill crystals. It was expensive, but I hoped that my goods would be waiting for me when our consciousnesses returned to our bodies on the surface.

Eventually, we made our way to Dexter's shop, where I hoped to find a cybernetic solution to my injured hand. When we drew close, Gala left to go back to her own premises, saying that she and Dexter didn't get along. As she walked away, she said, "Don't forget to come back by, even if you don't have any credits to spend. I might have something for you."

We parted ways, and Patrick and I quickly made our way to Dexter's cube. The alien himself was unchanged, with his four arms, burgundy skin, and three legs. However, he seemed just as down about Jeremiah's death as Gala had been. After he offered his condolences, he led us inside and activated what he called a privacy net. Once that was in place, he asked, "What can I do for you?"

"I need a hand," I said, raising my left arm. "I also need some kind of subdermal armor."

"Budget?"

"Just tell me what you've got," I said. "I'll figure out the budget after that."

"Hmm," he said. "Well, you've got two options for defense. I have the Tak-Mura Kinetic Sheath. It doesn't offer much protection for blunt force, but it's amazingly resilient against penetrative attacks."

"And that's subdermal armor?" I asked.

"It is," he said. "Easy to install, too. No real surgery necessary. Just nineteen injections in the appropriate spots, and the Mist does the rest. No muss, no fuss. The other advantage is that it doesn't affect movement at all. Not like the metallic versions that increase weight and decrease flexibility. Even the top-tier ones make their users more like walking tanks."

That made sense to me. The people I had seen who'd used such armor weren't exactly quick on their feet.

"What's the other option?"

"Personalized shield," he said, crossing one set of his arms. "Implant on your back. When you activate it, it starts draining your Mist to create an almost impenetrable shield. This one's made by Erdogan Enterprises, so it's better than average, but even then, we're talking a few seconds of protection before it needs to recharge. But for those few seconds, you're looking at complete invulnerability."

"Downsides?" I asked. "Other than the Mist expenditure, I mean."

"If you use it, you probably won't be able to use any active skills or abilities afterward," he said. "It's a great way to escape death, but it's also a trade-off. Both options are almost entirely undetectable on your world, too."

"Oh? And the Sheath? Anything else I need to know about it?" I asked.

"It's upgradable," he said. "This is top-of-the-line stuff, so all you'd need to do is inject the right upgrade module, and you'll have stronger armor. Very expensive, though, and those sorts of things aren't available around here. It can also utilize boosters that will repair the armor."

I nodded. My uncle had mentioned boosters to me once or twice, so I knew that they were hypos that would inject condensed Mist into the body. He'd described them as a good way to recover expended Mist, but if they were also useful for regenerating the Sheath, that just made them that much more valuable. To date, I'd never even used one—mostly because, with my high Mist attribute, they weren't necessary—but I'd definitely have to buy some if I chose to use the Sheath.

"Which would you recommend?" I asked.

With one set of his arms still crossed, Dexter scratched the back of his head. "I'm not sure," he said. "Pros and cons with either choice. Invulnerability, even if it's limited, can be a powerful card to play. But the Sheath is more well-rounded. It really just depends on what you want."

"What about both?" I asked.

"Not possible," he said. "Unless you've got a Rank 3 or higher cybernetics skill, they'll draw too much power to coexist." '

"Rank?" I asked. "What would you call [Cybernetic Mastery]?"

"Rank 2," he said. "Impressive at your age. But not enough to run both of those implants. Sorry, kid. You're going to have to choose."

"Make it the Sheath, then," I said. The way I saw it, if my survival came down to a couple of seconds of invulnerability, I was probably going to die anyway. It was better to go with the option that would help me in a wider variety of scenarios. Still, it was a difficult choice. "What about the hand?"

"Depends on what you're looking for," he said. "I have hands that can transform into cannons, ones that can spout Mist blades, and ones that are virtually indistinguishable from flesh and blood. You need to tell me what you want, and I'll give you options."

I nodded. I'd already given it some thought during our journey from the ruins of Mobile, and I'd decided that, if possible, I would go with something as close to my old hand as possible. So, I told him as much, adding, "The less detectable, the better."

He scratched his chin, then asked, "You're a {Mistrunner} right?"

"What? How do you know that?" I demanded, my heart beating out of my chest as panic mounted.

He held up all four hands, saying, "Whoa, whoa! Don't get all worked up! It's part of my array, okay? I just use it so I can tailor my suggestions to the customer. I can't tell anybody about it, either. Not without significant sanctions. And we're under a privacy net, so even the system can't see what we're doing."

I wasn't sure if I believed him, but I also didn't think it mattered that much. There wasn't really anything I could do about it, especially if he already knew my secrets. Which he obviously did. "Is that why you steered me away from the heavier armor options?" I asked.

He nodded. "It is," he said. "Look—I'm on your side. Jeremiah was my friend. If you don't believe anything else I've said, believe that, okay?"

I glanced at Patrick, who looked like he wanted to be literally anywhere but in the same room with the pair of us. Then, I sighed, telling Dexter, "Yes. That's my class."

"Rare one," he said. "Ultrarare, even. I'm not sure I've ever met an actual {Mistrunner}. Makes a guy wonder what Jeremiah did to get you that class."

"What does it matter?" I asked. "How does that affect which hand I get?"

He didn't answer. Instead, he turned around, and when he did, the wall slid open to reveal a shelf full of cybernetic hands. Some were claws. Others were clearly cannons, like the one used by the giant I'd encountered only a few days after my Awakening. But Dexter went to one that looked strikingly similar to a real hand, albeit without skin. The muscles were black and striated, while the bones were a matte gray.

Dexter retrieved it, then held it up to me. "This is what's known as the Hand of God," he said.

"What? Why?" I asked. "It looks pretty ordinary to me."

"Oh, that's because it's supposed to," he said with a grin. "Nano-fiber muscles. Mist-infused titalumiron bones. It's stronger than any organic hand, provided that the owner has less than a three hundred Constitution attribute."

"Okay? It's a strong hand," I said. "What makes it special?"

He dug his fingers into the forearm, retrieving a cord. In a lot of ways, it looked similar to the one I could extract from my undamaged wrist. However, where my cord was an unexciting black, the one in the Hand of God was laced with gold. Dexter said, "This is why. Any connection made through this jack will be almost four times as fast as anything else on the market. On top of that, the hand is entirely undetectable by anything on your planet. Anything on mine, come to that. It's only when you get to the older sectors that you'll have any chance of it being detected. Even then, it would take specialized equipment."

"Interesting" was my response, but I was pretty much sold already.

"Self-repairing, too," he said. "Up to a point. If you get the thing crushed somehow, you'll need a good cybernetic engineer, but for anything you're likely to see in the next few years, it'll hold up."

"Well, that sounds perfect for me," I said, already seeing the possibilities. With my modifiers, my Mistwalk ability was already very fast. With that personal link, I could blaze through any defenses I might find. It almost felt like it had been tailor-made for me. "I think we have a winner."

"I don't know if Jeremiah told you, but he bought something that he intended to give you. Supposed to have been a birthday present, I believe," Dexter said, rubbing the back of his neck. "When you showed up today, I assumed you'd come to collect."

"What is it?" I asked.

"One second," he said. "Let me go fetch it."

With that, he pressed another button, and a different portion of the wall resolved itself into a door, through which he disappeared a moment later. A couple of minutes after that, he returned with a simple bracelet in one of his hands.

"This is a Kyrobe Cutter," he said, and a shimmering hologram appeared above the bracelet. It was long and sleek, and I didn't need him to tell me what I was looking at. I'd been studying hover bikes ever since I was twelve years old. However, this one was clearly far superior to the models I'd seen back on Earth. "Completely collapsible inside the bracelet, so you'll never be without a ride. D-grade durability. E-grade speed, which means it's probably faster than any Earth-made bike, and not by a little. And it has the added bonus of being a cybernetic, which means that it can be affected by some of your skills and abilities."

"I . . . I don't . . . I don't know what to say," I said.

"No thank-you necessary," Dexter responded. "Like I told you, Jeremiah was a friend, and this was a favor to him. So, no matter what else happens here, the Cutter is yours. Now, let's get down to it. I can't take less than eight million for the other implants."

"Bullshit," said Patrick, his first contribution to the conversation. And so, the dickering began, and in the end, we paid a little more than half of Dexter's initial asking price. Once all the agreements were signed and I'd set up the rapid transference, we said our goodbyes. And off we went back to Gala's shop. I couldn't help but wonder what she had in store for us.

CHAPTER TEN

WEAPONS

I knew the bio-enhancers came with plenty of downsides. Everyone does. The decreased life span alone was enough to scare most people off. But I would rather die a few decades early than spend another moment corralled by the arbitrary limits on my Constitution. So, the choice was an easy one, and I haven't looked back since.

—Nora Lancaster

As Patrick and I walked through the halls of the Bazaar, I had a hard time thinking of anything else but my upcoming upgrades. The Hand of God was likely the most useful addition to my arsenal, but I had to admit that I was far more excited about the Sheath. I'd been shot enough that I knew just how valuable such protection would likely prove to be.

But then there were my new skills. [Acrobatics] would probably change everything about how I moved, though I wasn't entirely sure what that would look like. On top of that, I knew that different skills presented themselves differently based on the individual. For instance, my uncle had seemed a little surprised that I'd gotten so many abilities from [Combat Utility]. So, there was every chance that Ana's assessment that the skill wouldn't result in any abilities was inaccurate. The same could be said for [Demolition], which probably excited me even more than acrobatics.

After all, I did enjoy blowing things up. I only regretted that I hadn't been the one to activate the detonator back in Mobile. However, there was plenty of time to rectify that regret, and I intended to put my new skill—along with my existing Basic Explosives Handling ability—to the test. First, though, I needed to return to Gala and improve the rest of my arsenal.

As much as I loved the Kicker, I had already begun to outgrow it. Even before obtaining my class, I'd noticed that my bullets were doing less and less damage. The sniper configuration was still strong, especially when paired with Empowered Shot, but the assault rifle mode had proven itself insufficient. Usually, that was a problem that could be solved by pumping my enemies with a few extra magazines of bullets, but as effective as that was, I knew it was less than ideal. The simple fact was that I needed an upgrade.

The problem was that I knew that, if I wanted anything more powerful than the Kicker, I'd have to give up on having two weapons in one gun. More than once, I'd exploited the rifle's ability to reconfigure itself, and I knew I'd miss it once it was gone. But that was the price I'd have to pay. As my uncle had once said, increased power often meant decreased versatility.

Besides, nestled in a corner of my arsenal implant was the Pulsar Class sniper rifle my uncle had bought for me. I'd barely even looked at it, much less used it in any significant situations; in fact, until recently, I couldn't do so. Before the acquisition of my class, if I'd have pulled the trigger, nothing would happen. However, I felt positive that with the evolution of my skills, I'd be fine now.

Which meant I needed a real assault rifle to replace the Kicker. Hopefully that was what Gala had in mind because I wasn't sure I could afford anything else. After all, I only had about nine million credits left. It was a lot of money, but I'd seen how much my current arsenal had cost. In addition to that, I had to pay for a new base of operations as well as for someone—hopefully Dr. Montague—to install my new cybernetics.

Not to mention the cost of ammunition. I couldn't be sure, but I felt that there was a good chance that my uncle had spent even more on ammunition over the past few years than he had on my weapons. And I was running low on basically everything, which meant I needed to restock.

So many expenses, and my revenue stream was all but dried up. If I was going to make things work, I'd need to change that, too. It was yet another item to add to my to-do list, which had grown to become almost overwhelming in length. So, I used the same philosophy I'd employed when my training got tough—one step at a time. One foot in front of the other. Eventually, I would get where I wanted to go. It was a fancy way of forcing myself to divide my tasks into smaller bites, but it worked for me.

As we made our way back to Gala's shop, I distracted myself with thoughts of my new hover bike. I'd wanted one for as long as I could remember, but my uncle had always steadfastly refused to get me one. The fact that he'd always intended to do so was so on point with his personality that it almost brought tears to my eyes. For all his rough exterior, he'd never really denied me anything

I truly wanted. In fact, he almost always went that extra mile, like he had with the Leviathan file I still frequently listened to. The hover bike was no different, especially in that it far exceeded my expectations. I'd have been happy with a run-of-the-mill version, but instead, I'd gotten something that I expected even those rich assholes in King's Row couldn't afford.

Once again, Jeremiah had come through. Even after he was gone, I was still standing on his shoulders.

I let out a sigh, which Patrick noticed. As we walked, he asked, "What's wrong? I thought you'd be excited about all of this."

"I am," I said.

"Doesn't seem like it" was his response. "I haven't seen you smile . . . well . . . not since everything happened."

"Not a lot to smile about," I said, though I really wanted to dispute that claim. Surely, I'd smiled about something, right? I felt confident that I had, but I couldn't really think of what might have prompted it. Still, if I'd have gotten such a windfall before losing everyone, I'd have been grinning ear to ear. In fact, I had done just that during my last trip to the Bazaar, which felt like an eternity ago.

"We're alive," he said. "And you've got a hover bike. That's enough for a little smile, I think."

"Agree to disagree on that one," I said.

Patrick just shook his head. I knew why he was frustrated; I must have made for dour company. But in my defense, I felt I'd earned my sour mood. By all rights, I should've been curled in a corner somewhere and bawling my eyes out. Instead, I just felt alternating degrees of angry and numb.

Over the next few minutes, I noticed plenty of men and women in high-collared suits. According to my uncle, most of them were liaisons to the aliens. They were the tools by which our world had been oppressed, and they were only the beginning. In less than seven years, even they would no longer be necessary. At that point, the aliens could descend in force and take a stronger hand in stripping away Earth's resources.

It was an unavoidable and bleak future.

Certainly, I'd discovered that not all aliens were so heavy-handed as the Castorix who'd been in charge of mining the Rift. But if alien nature was anything like human nature, I suspected that their tactics were common enough. Few would be constrained by something so meaningless as morality. To them, we were barely more than animals, and I felt certain that we would be treated as such.

Any urge to smile faded in the face of that, so by the time we reached Gala's cube-shaped shop, I was in a much worse mood than when we'd left Dexter's. Still, I tried to put on a brave face as she let us inside.

"Alright," Gala said once the doors were shut. "Let's get the awkward part out of the way. What's your budget, here?"

I glanced at Patrick, who looked like he was going to be sick. And I understood it. For someone whose path was defined, at least in part, by negotiation, coming right out with that kind of information probably felt like sacrilege. But I wanted to trust Gala. And besides, if she tried to cheat us, he would pick up on it.

"I've got about nine million left," I said. "But I want to keep at least half of that for when I get back planetside."

My reasoning was clear; I knew I'd have expenses when it came to setting myself up to exact revenge on Nora and anyone else who'd contributed to my uncle's demise. So, I wanted to save a good chunk of credits so I'd have a comfortable margin for error.

Gala scratched her tawny-furred chin, then said, "It's going to be close. Really close. But I think we can fit it all in. But first things first, I have something for you. Free of charge."

With that, she set a box on her counter. The box itself was silver and edged in black, with a strange symbol decorating the lid. Gala pressed a button, and with a hiss of escaping air, it opened to reveal a bundle of black fabric. With her thick fingers, she gingerly retrieved the bundle, then shook it out to reveal what looked like a unitard.

"Demas Infiltration Suit, mark eleven," she said. "Hooks right into your interface. Thermal dampening. D-grade armor rating. And a host of other features. It's the best infiltration suit you're likely to see."

I stared at the garment, unsure what to say. So, I focused on the description Gala sent over to my HUD.

Infiltration Suit (Mark XI)—Demas Armorworks
Thermal dampening
Armor (D)
Hydration conservation
Friction dampening
Automatic wound compression
Automatic repair (minor)
Automatic cleaning (lesser)

"I . . . what's this for?" I asked.

"Call it a graduation gift," Gala said. "Your uncle intended to give this to you when you went back to Nova City, but he never got the chance. So, it falls to me to make good. Cherish that suit because it's worth almost as much as your entire arsenal. It's military grade, which means it shouldn't even be available in this sector."

"Wow," I muttered, still staring at the garment in her hands. It was made of black fabric, and given its size, I could tell that it was almost assuredly formfitting. In fact, I was reminded of the infiltration suits I'd stolen from the Banshees. However, instead of being comprised only of skintight fabric, this suit also sported armored plates that would protect all my vital organs. They weren't thick, and I suspected that they wouldn't even be that noticeable once I was wearing the suit, but with it hanging loose, they were apparent. Over the next couple of minutes, Gala turned the suit inside out so I could see the subtle blue lines of the Mist conduits running along the inside. She also took a moment to explain the difference between the minor and lesser designations. Minor was the lowest ranking, meaning that the automatic-repair function was less powerful than the cleaning feature. Still, given how often I found myself out in the wilderness, I knew just how valuable they both were.

"Now," Gala said, clapping her huge hands. I felt certain that if we had been there in person, I'd have felt a gust of wind. She grinned, saying, "For the fun part. I've got choices for you."

"Okay? What kind of choices?" I asked.

"First," she answered. "I think it's time you upgraded your primary weapon. You aren't really a sniper like your uncle, so an assault rifle is probably where you should look. What kind of certifications do you have?"

"Uh . . . I'm not sure," I said. I'd seen various certifications on my skill trees, but none of them had ever been displayed on my status. Once I admitted as much to Gala, she walked me through changing that. When I did, I took a look at the full breadth of my status:

NAME	Mirabelle Lisa Braddock		
CLASS	MISTRUNNER		
LEVEL	10 (4%)		
CONSTITUTION	41/80		
MIND	37/80		
MIST	36/80		
SKILLS	5/7		
SKILL NAME	Skill Tier	Modifiers	Abilities
CYBERNETIC MASTERY	Tier 1 (3%)	100% Efficiency	6 Cybernetic Slots

COMBAT	Tier 1 (12%)	+50% Damage (All) +50% Speed (Melee) +50% Accuracy (All) +25% Range (Firearms) +50% Reload Speed (Firearms)	Empowered Shot (D) Double Shot (E) Combination Punch (D) Pummel (E) Engage (E) Disengage (F) Mark Target (F) Barrage (F)
INFILTRATION	Tier 1 (4%)	+15% Effectiveness (Stealth)	Stealth (E) Camouflage (E) Deception (E) Mimic (E) Observation (D)
MISTRUNNER	Tier 1 (2%)	+25% Speed (Misthack) +25% Processing Speed (Mistwalk) +50% Strength (Mistwall) +50% Breach Range	Mistwalk (D) Misthack (D) Mistwall (C) System Redirect (F) Disable Cybernetics (F) Overcharge (E)
FIELDCRAFT	Tier 1 (7%)	+25% Combat Effectiveness	Triage (D) Basic Explosives Handling (D) Combat Focus (C) Pain Tolerance (D) Resistance (E) Foraging (E) Improvisation (D) Regeneration (D)
OPEN			
OPEN			

I'd made a little progress, gaining a few attribute points as well as covering some ground in my skills' proficiencies. However, it seemed like it was less than it should have been. Since the last time I'd looked at my status, I'd been using my skills and abilities almost constantly. But I didn't have a lot to show for it. That, as much as anything, brought home the necessity for continued and focused training. Even though I'd finished the program my uncle had prescribed, that didn't mean I had leave to slack off. If I did, I would never see my abilities—or attributes—progress. Some might even regress.

Finding somewhere to train was yet another item to add to my list of things I needed to do when I got back to Earth. It kept getting longer, and I feared it would eventually become overwhelming. Sighing, I pushed those thoughts to the side and focused on the next step. Anything else, and I'd be buried under the weight of everything I needed to do.

To that end, I backtracked to the overall menu in my interface:

Select one:
Status
Skill trees
Certifications
Equipment
Conditions
Upgrade modules

It had taken a mental adjustment to get my certifications, equipment, and conditions on the list; before, it had only been my status and skill trees. But my interface, which was governed by my KIOI, was nothing if not adaptable, and it seemed that I'd only begun to tap into its abilities.

Under equipment, I'd found nothing but my clothes, which were labeled as refugee's rags (unranked), and the weapons in my arsenal implant. Everything was grayed out, though, probably because I wasn't really in my body. Back on Earth, I was wearing the same outfit I'd used to blend in with the other refugees, so the label seemed appropriate.

Moving on to conditions, I was unsurprised to see that my hand was listed as damaged. There were some minor injuries there, as well, like a pulled muscle in my back, a cracked rib, and a slight concussion, but none of them were severe enough to make it past my Pain Tolerance.

Finally, I drilled down into my certifications, finding:

Certifications:
Mundane weaponry
Plasma rifles

Energy pistols
Weapon modification
Energy blades
Heavy weapons
Explosive weapons
Grenades (basic)
Explosives (basic)

I explained my certifications to Gala, who seemed impressed when she said, "That's a good start. A very good start. And it's further along than I expected. Hmm."

She tapped her chin, obviously lost in thought. Then, she said, "I think you'd be okay with an R-14 Semiautomatic Plasma Rifle. It's a D-grade weapon, just like the Pulsar Class Kinetic Sniper your uncle gave you last time you were here. By the way, you should be able to use that now, in case you didn't know."

As she spoke, she retrieved a wicked-looking long gun from a case on the back shelf. It was a little shorter than my Kicker was in its assault rifle configuration, but the casing was a little bulkier. Holding it up for me to inspect, she added, "Doesn't use material rounds, either. Instead, it fires concentrated bolts of condensed and superheated Mist plasma. Expensive ammunition, but anything worth shooting usually is."

"Power?" I asked. "Compared to the Kicker, I mean."

"At least three times as lethal," she said. "There might be a couple thousand people on your planet who could even use this kind of weapon, and even fewer that could afford it. You're an intersection of both."

"Okay? What's the other option?" I asked.

"For your primary weapon? Anything else would be a waste of your skills," she said. "The choices come with your other weapon."

"Oh."

"Now, my initial idea was to just upgrade you to a new scattergun," she said. "Something that could really lay down the pain."

"I like that idea," I said.

"But then I saw that [Demolition] skill, and I thought of something else," she said. "So, I've got a couple of options here. First up is called the DR-4 EMG, affectionately known as the Dragon."

Again, she retrieved a new weapon from one of the cases behind her; I was beginning to suspect that there was some spatial trick at play because the weapon she presented didn't look like it would fit in the small space where it had been stored. It was at least four feet long, with a casing as big around as my waist and a corrugated barrel that gave it an incredibly aggressive look. She held it at her waist, reminding me of how Horace Lafontaine had used his minigun.

"This bad boy right here will spit fire and destroy anything you point him at," she said. "I've seen a {Commando} armed with one of these take out an entire Sciora tank division. Beautiful piece of weaponry."

"It shoots literal fire?" I asked.

"Mist-charged elemental rounds, technically," she said. "The ammunition is depleted caramnium, so when it hits, it penetrates deep. It's a weapon designed for maximum destruction."

"What's the downside?" I asked.

"None," she said. "Unless you're trying to go quiet, in which case he's definitely not the right man for the job. There's no masking a Dragon's roar. But I still think you should consider the next option, too."

"Alright," I said, glancing at Patrick. He was awestruck at the sight of the weapon, and I couldn't help but hope that whatever Gala suggested for him would be just as impressive. I didn't think I needed to go to any great lengths to gear him up—he wasn't going to be running around in the thick of things, after all—but as far as I was concerned, everyone needed a good weapon. And though the Enforcers' pistol was a solid option for most people, I wanted better for him.

By the time I looked back at Gala, she'd set the Dragon aside and replaced it with a stubby weapon that looked like Ferdinand II's bigger, stouter brother. It wasn't much shorter than the R-14 assault rifle, but the barrel looked wide enough that it could accommodate one of my grenades. In addition, instead of a traditional magazine, it sported a round cannister that could hold thirty oversize rounds.

"This is the Baat Mobile Artillery Platform," she said. "Like Ferdinand II, he can fire a wide variety of rounds. From gas cannisters to full kinetic ammunition, he's the tool for any job. But if I were you, I'd use him as my big gun."

"Huh?"

"Say you want to destroy a building, right?" said Gala. "You can waltz in there and plant a bunch of explosives. Slow, right? Or you can take aim with the BMAP from a few hundred yards away and lob fifteen rounds a second, each with enough explosive force to demolish a small ship, at it. Now, you won't quite get there for a while—you're going to have level that Heavy Weaponry ability a bit—but once you get there, you'll be a walking, talking artillery emplacement."

"And what makes this better than the Dragon?" I asked.

"Simple," she said. "It'll benefit from two sets of modifiers. [Demolition] and Heavy Weaponry. They compound, so you'll be punching well above your weight class."

I nodded along. It was good advice. The BMAP was definitely a niche weapon, but I could already think of a few situations where that kind of firepower would have been very helpful. Besides, what had happened to my uncle had opened my eyes to just how powerful artillery could be. And if I could mimic even a portion of that power with the help of the BMAP, the decision sort of made itself.

But the Dragon could fill that same niche, couldn't it? When I said as much to Gala, she just shook her bovine head, saying, "The Dragon's an antipersonnel weapon. The BMAP is for when you want to go completely scorched earth on whoever stands in your way. The biggest downside is that most people can't use the BMAP to its fullest potential. You can."

That sealed it for me, and I chose the BMAP.

"Okay, what about Patrick?" I asked.

"You don't have to do that, Mira," he said. "I'm fine with the pistol I got from the—"

I cut him off with a glare. "I know I don't have to," I said. "I want to. So let me do this."

Gala acted like she didn't see the exchange and pulled a weapon from a drawer beneath the counter. The pistol was tiny in her hand, but in mine or Patrick's it would look like a real cannon. But unlike Ferdinand II, it wasn't a revolver.

"Tergan Tactical Energy Pistol," Gala said. "I assume you have the certification necessary?"

Patrick nodded, his eyes never leaving the weapon. It was mostly matte black, but there were gold accents running along the grip and lacing the barrel.

"Good," she said. "Two modes. One is for stunning—use that at your own discretion because that setting is relative. It will directly attack the nervous system, which will subject the enemy to seizures. However, for any human with a Constitution less than twenty or so, it will cause permanent brain and nerve damage."

"Uh . . . okay," Patrick breathed.

"Second mode is lethal," she said. "It functions a lot like a handheld rail gun, propelling a projectile via opposing magnetic force. The ammunition is made from an incredibly dense alloy that is designed to splinter on contact, ripping through your enemy's body. It's not particularly effective against armor, but no pistol really is. I trust your skills will help with that."

He nodded.

"For the lot, I can take six million," Gala said. "That's with me throwing in enough ammunition to get you started. Same package I gave your uncle last time."

Patrick gave me a nod, telling me that his ability had indicated that she wasn't trying to rip us off, so I agreed to the deal. It was a little more than I had expected, but that shouldn't have been so surprising, given the firepower I was buying.

I remembered the boxes of ammunition, and I figured that would be enough to see me through for at least a few months. Unless I started a war, which probably wasn't that far off from what I had planned. Still, that didn't leave much for practice. I said as much to Gala, and she was ready with a solution.

"You're getting into the expensive stuff now," she said. "But you're not the first. Once you get settled in, contact me. I'll transfer a shipment of practice ammo. It won't be nearly as lethal as the real stuff, but it's fine for training."

Obviously, my issues weren't uncommon, which was a relief.

Finally, with all our shopping done, Patrick and I said our goodbyes to Gala and took our leave. When we got back to our bodies, I had a lot to do before I could enact my plan of revenge.

CHAPTER ELEVEN

FULL OF DANGERS

The first time Jeremiah gave me real responsibility, I was so blown away that I almost failed the mission. Until then, I had only ever been a follower, so the authority—even if it was borrowed—was intoxicating. And I wanted more.

—Nora Lancaster

When we reentered our bodies back on Earth, night had already fallen. The Dome was still crowded with people, though, so it took us almost two hours to make our way to the rapid-transference network, where we stood in line for another forty-five minutes before finally getting our turn. The clerk in charge was a prim woman in a cheap uniform that consisted of a businesslike skirt and a high-necked top. The whole getup reminded me of the Enforcers' dress uniforms, albeit of much lower-quality materials. Her blonde hair was held in a bun, and she looked at Patrick and me with obvious disdain.

"No begging," she said. Then, looking past us, she said, "Next."

"We're not here to beg," I said. "I have some pickups."

She looked down her nose at me, which made me want to punch her in the face. She was only Tier 2, and I knew good and well that she was probably from the Garden. So, she had no reason to feel superior to anyone. But a lot of people were like that, latching on to whatever they could to make their lives feel a little less hopeless. I understood it, but that didn't mean I had much patience for her attitude.

Thankfully, all I had to do was put my hand on the security terminal's reader, which pulled up my account. I'd already paid for the transference, so my gear should have long since arrived. Still, the woman said, "Don't make me call security, lady."

I ground my teeth together before saying, "Just look at your screen. I've already paid for—"

"I don't need to look at anything, you piece of trash," she spat. "Now go back to whatever gutter you crawled out of before I call security in."

"But—"

I felt a hand clamp down on my shoulder, and a voice said, "Is there a problem here?"

"Yeah," I growled, yanking away from the man who'd approached from behind. I turned toward him and immediately surmised that he was a security guard, as evidenced by his blue-and-white uniform. I'd seen plenty of them stationed around the Dome. "This lady won't give me my stuff."

"Is that so?" he asked. "And?"

"And if she'd just look at the stupid screen, she would see that I've already paid for the transfer," I spat. "I don't know what's so difficult about that."

The man, who had a huge jaw and watery eyes, glanced over my shoulder to the screen. Judging by the look of superiority on his face, I expected that he was doing so in order to prove me wrong. However, the moment his eyes found the display, his expression faded into embarrassment.

"Janet," he said. "Take the woman to one of the private rooms and give her the packages."

"But—"

"Now, Janet!" he barked. Then, to me, he said, "I'm sorry about that, ma'am. Janet's new."

As he spoke, the clerk stared at the screen, aghast at what she saw. She smoothed her skirt, then stepped out from behind the counter and asked me to follow her. I did, and we soon found our way to one of the side rooms that ringed the huge lobby that housed the rapid-transference network. Once inside, she asked us to wait while she had someone fetch our packages.

Once she left, shutting the door behind us, I muttered, "I should've punched her in her stupid face. Maybe she would've hopped to it then. Stupid people and their silly prejudices."

Of course, I knew it was partially my fault. After all, I was still wearing my refugee rags, which made me look like the lowest of the low. It was especially bad because I still wore the identity of a middle-aged, Tier 2 woman. To anyone who looked, I probably didn't seem like the kind of person who could afford the entry fee for the Bazaar, much less to have something shipped down via the rapid-transference network. That was my fault. I should have considered the implications of my disguise. I resolved to do better in the future.

Patrick tried to engage me in small talk, but my mind was going a thousand miles an hour as I made plans for everything I had to do. There was no time for idle chitchat. I didn't have room to relax. I needed to focus. Eventually, a pair of burly men in coveralls brought a series of crates into the room. After I inspected them to make sure everything was there, I asked Patrick to store them away.

"If this storage node wasn't here, I wouldn't be able to yet," he said pointing to a short pillar in the corner. I could feel the swirl of Mist around it, but it had a different flavor than normal. Beneath it was a platform that was raised a couple of inches off the ground. Over the next few minutes, we placed one crate after another onto the dais. Once everything was in place, he did something on the storage node, and the crates flashed away, presumably into his storage space.

"Convenient," I said.

"Yeah, if you're in one of these cities," he said. "But this is only the second time I've been able to use one."

"Oh" was my response. In some ways, Patrick was far more worldly than me. He'd been to a ton of different places. However, most of those locations were small towns like Mobile. His only foray into a real city was when he'd gone into Atlanta, and even that had been a quick trip.

Once everything was stored away, Patrick and I left the room behind and started back toward the monorail. As we did, I took in my surroundings with a curious mixture of awe and disgust. Nova City could be a beautiful place, and at night, that beauty was accentuated. With all the lights, and with everyone sporting the latest colorful and daring fashions, it was easy to overlook all the seedier parts. However, it only took a single closer look to see just how inaccurate that first impression really was.

Beneath that thin veneer of beauty, there was a city of grime, oppression, and violence. Anyone that looked happy was probably on something. It didn't matter if it was drugs, alcohol, sex, or something else—it was all just a facade meant to hide the city's real nature. So long as the populace was distracted, they were easy to control.

As I glanced at the city's other more affluent platforms in the distance, I found it ironic that even the so-called aristocracy were no different than their poorer counterparts. They still spent their lives trying to distract themselves from the reality of their situations. The vices of the rich might've been more expensive than those of the impoverished, but they served the same purpose. The only difference was that at least they didn't have to worry about where their next meal was coming from.

I shook my head as we climbed the stairs to the monorail platform. When we reached it, I tried not to look at the couple having sex on the park bench. They'd at least covered all the naughtiest bits with a long coat, but it wasn't difficult to figure out what they were doing. Patrick's jaw dropped as he stared at them, at least until I elbowed him in the ribs. That woke him up, and for the next few minutes, he pretended not to notice the pair. However, his reddened cheeks and furtive glances told a different story.

Thankfully, the monorail arrived shortly after we reached the platform, and we soon left the copulating couple behind. The trip through the city was uneventful, though I couldn't help but notice that we had picked up a tail. Two men had followed us from the Dome, probably tipped off by either Janet or the security guard that we were carrying a lot of wealth. That, coupled with our apparently low tiers, was an invitation to be robbed. Sometimes, having too much wealth was a sin, and there were plenty of desperate men and women who were willing to dole out judgment.

"When we get to the next stop, we're going to split up," I said, keeping my voice low. I would have used the communication function of my KIOI, but I knew just how easily those could be intercepted or tracked. It took a real idiot to do anything important via that kind of connection. There were ways to establish a more secure line, but I'd yet to take the time to do so with Patrick. Even then, security was relative. Either way, it was another oversight on my part, and as soon as I had some spare time, it was one I intended to remedy. "Head straight to Gunther's."

"What's going on?" he asked, turning toward me.

"Act normal," I said. "But there are a couple of guys who followed us here. I'm going to take care of it."

"Aren't there, like, police or something?" he asked.

"The Enforcers," I said. Perhaps things were different in other cities; in Mobile, the Amigos headed up something like a security force that kept people mostly in line. But even they didn't bother with anything but the worst of the worst crimes. For instance, the gangs there made a habit out of running protection rackets, and nobody had ever done anything about it. "And I don't think we want their attention right now."

"R-right," he said.

"Besides, I'm a hands-on kind of girl," I said. "Don't worry. They don't feel very strong. I'll take care of it."

I was still down a hand, but I didn't think I'd have any difficulty dealing with the pair of mooks. One was Tier 3, while the other was Tier 2, which meant that, unless they'd spent decades leveling and training, there was no way their attributes were anywhere close to comparable with mine. Even with my Awakening only being a few years old, I knew that my training had put me in a unique position. I was aware that I couldn't stand toe-to-toe with the city's elites—not unless I manipulated the circumstances perfectly—but I felt confident against common, everyday mooks like the ones who'd followed us from the Dome.

As the monorail tore across the city, passing back into the Garden, I surreptitiously studied the two men. Nothing about them suggested that they were anything but what they appeared to be, so by the time the monorail pulled into our stop, I felt pretty confident in taking them out.

Patrick and I disembarked, then descended the steps down to street level. There, we joined the tide of pedestrians as we made our way toward Gunther's Guns. It was only a handful of blocks away, so I knew that as soon as we turned off the main thoroughfare, the men would make their move. When they did, I'd be ready.

Finally, we reached the street in question, and I hissed, "Now! Go!"

Patrick took off, sprinting in the direction of Gunther's Guns while I took off in the opposite direction. To my dismay, one of the mooks followed me, while the other ran after Patrick. Cursing inwardly, I ducked down a nearby alley and hid behind a pile of foul-smelling refuse. The man was hot on my heels, and his boots splashed in a disgusting puddle as he followed me.

The alley was a dead end, so he knew he had me. I watched as a long blade erupted from his cybernetic forearm. He held it out in front of him, saying, "C'mon out, lady. All I want is your shit. We can be civil about this."

I knew that was a lie. Even if I gave him everything in my possession, he'd still kill me and sell my parts on the black market. In Nova City, a fresh, mostly intact body could net you a few thousand credits, so long as you knew where to go. Nobody was willing to leave that kind of wealth on the table. Nor did any self-respecting Operator make a habit out of leaving his victims alive—not unless he knew good and well that victim couldn't come back to hurt him sometime in the future. And this mook didn't know anything about me, so the logical course would be to simply kill me and move on.

Of course, even if I'd been as helpless as I seemed to be, he would have to be careful. There were ways to retrieve things from spatial implants, but they were expensive. Likely, he'd prefer it if I gave everything up before he did what he had to do.

Not that it mattered. He wouldn't survive more than a few more moments.

I summoned my nano-bladed sword from my arsenal implant, and when he was a few steps into the alley, I sprang into action. To his credit, he reacted quickly, but with his attributes, he had no way of keeping up with me as I leaped over the refuse pile, kicked off the wall, and brought my sword down on the crown of his head. When I landed, I yanked my sword free, and he collapsed to the ground. In the space of a second, he'd gone from aggressor to victim when I'd bisected his head. I stowed my weapon away a moment later.

After dragging him into the pile of garbage, I threw some errant boxes on top of him, then took off after Patrick, only to find that he'd made it to Gunther's. Of the other mook, there was no sign. I didn't like that. It felt sloppy. Who knew what the other would-be mugger would do once he discovered his partner's death? So, after questioning Patrick, I went back outside and hunted him down.

Luckily, it didn't take long. He was camped out under a bridge in a location that would allow him a good vantage point to see the comings and goings of the patrons of Gunther's Guns. He died with a knife in the base of his skull, and I quickly returned to Gunther's, where I found Patrick waiting for me.

"Did you find him?" he asked.

"I did," I said. "Now, let's go see if Gunther found our cybernetic engineer."

We only had to cross halfway through the armory that passed for the building's lobby before Gunther himself appeared. He looked much the same as he had before, though he'd changed his brown leather suit for a black one. Doubtless, he'd been warned of our arrival by his cyborg guards. I'd ignored them on my way in, but they'd clearly taken note of me.

"Good," he said. "You're back. I've had Cirilla cooling her heels for the past four hours. She's going to charge you for that."

"Oh," I said. "How much?"

He quoted me a price, and I just shook my head, saying, "It costs what it costs, I guess."

In reality, the price, which was a few hundred thousand credits, wasn't much compared to what I'd spent in the Bazaar, but that was more of a testament to how far a credit went on Earth than anything else. Certainly, the engineer didn't strike me as the type to give discounts. I transferred Gunther his fee, and he escorted us through the labyrinthine building until we finally reached a room that looked strikingly similar to the one where I'd had my first set of implants installed.

As Gunther had claimed, Cirilla Montague was already there, and she looked incredibly impatient. A stern-looking woman with chin-length pink hair, she might've been pretty if she didn't look like she'd just tasted something sour.

"Finally!" she hissed in a haughty tone. "When I agreed to—"

I initiated the transfer of funds, which cut her off. "That should take care of it," I said. I'd added a little extra for her trouble. Then, I turned to Patrick and asked, "You have enough Mist to pull everything out?"

"I should," he said. Then, one crate after another appeared at his feet. They were all metallic boxes trimmed in black, and each of them bore various glyphs that I took to be identifiers. It didn't take long before I'd found the ones for the cybernetics. Once that was taken care of, I explained to the engineer what I wanted.

"You don't need me for the Sheath," she said, her voice taking on a bit more humanity than before. Money, it seemed, solved a lot of personality problems.

"I know," I said. "But I'd appreciate it if you installed it for me anyway."

"Very well" was her response. "I will do the hand first. Then the Sheath. Finally, I will link the hover bike. Is there anything else?"

I shook my head, saying, "But I want you to explain what you're doing to Patrick. He'll be here while you work on me."

"What? Why?" she asked, glancing in my companion's direction. He'd already retrieved his new pistol, and he looked ready to use it if the situation called for action.

"First, to keep you in line," I said. "I don't think you'd do anything stupid, but I've been wrong about this kind of thing before. You make the wrong move, and Patrick will put one in your temple."

"That is wildly unnecessary, and I—"

"Second, he's got the skill," I said. "And I want him to start laying the groundwork for advancing it. To that end, I'd like to hire you past today. All I want is for you to take him as an apprentice. I'll pay you, and on top of that, you get someone to help you out. Seems like a win-win to me."

"This is very irregular," she said.

"I'm an irregular kind of person," I said. "But give it some thought. I won't force that part on you. Right now, what I need is for you to do what I've hired you to do. What comes next is up to you."

"Very well," she said. Then, she gestured to the shiny steel chair behind her. "Have a seat. This procedure requires you to be unconscious."

I had expected as much. Some of the minor procedures could be performed with the patient still conscious, but having a hand replaced wasn't one of them. That's why Patrick was there.

I followed her instructions, and a few moments later, she put me under via a few needles hidden in her cybernetic fingers. As she did so, she explained to Patrick what she was doing, but even as her explanation droned on, I felt the blackness of unconsciousness overtake me. When it did, I dreamed of my impending revenge.

CHAPTER TWELVE

EL PARADISO

Once, someone told me that the only constant is change. But I disagree because self-interest seems pretty damn constant to me. Nobody does anything out of the goodness of their heart. They always get something out of it. It was the same with Jeremiah. He never cared about me or anyone else. He just wanted another tool.

—Nora Lancaster

I awoke what felt like an instant later, but my HUD told me that almost four hours had passed. A few blinking alerts in the corner of my vision told me that I had unread notifications, so I mentally selected the first.

Cybernetic Appendage (Hand of God)—Fexura Corporation [D-grade] found. Would you like to activate? You have four (4) unused cybernetic slots.
[Yes] or [No]

I selected the affirmative option, then moved on to the next notification:

Subdermal Armor (Kinetic Sheath)—Tak-Mura Armorworks [D-grade] found. Would you like to activate? You have three (3) unused cybernetic slots.
[Yes] or [No]

Again, I selected the first option, and I felt a slight tingle across my skin. After that, I moved on to the third and final notification:

Collapsible Conveyance (Cutter Class)—Kyrobe Transport Conglomerate [D-grade] found. Would you like to activate? You have two (2) unused cybernetic slots.
[Yes] or [No]

Once again, I selected the affirmative option, and with my notifications out of the way, I sat up. As I did, another message flashed across my HUD, telling me that my KIOI was integrating the new cybernetics into my overall interface. I shook my head as a wave of disorientation swept through me, but it soon passed.

"Easy," said Patrick, reaching out to grip my upper arm. I reacted on instinct, and my new cybernetic hand darted out to clamp down on his wrist. I could feel that, with only a little more pressure, I could shatter his arm. I remembered myself after only a moment, and I released him with an apology. He said, "It's fine. I shouldn't have grabbed you."

"No," I mumbled. "I need to be more aware. It won't happen again."

"Same on my side" was his response.

To change the subject, I asked, "What happened to Miss Montague?"

"It's doctor," Patrick said. "She made that abundantly clear when I made the same mistake. Apparently, she's got some kind of medical skill, too. It's one of the reasons she's so highly sought after."

"Whatever," I said. "Did she agree to train you?" I asked, and he told me that she had. Then, I asked, "Did you set it up?"

He nodded. "I have to come to her office once a week" was his reply. "But ... uh ... She said I needed to get some new clothes first."

"What?" I asked. "Seriously?"

"Well, no," he said. "She actually said that if I come around looking like a dust fiend, she won't let me in the door. And she said she'd call the Enforcers. Apparently, they've got a much bigger presence in Lakeview where she works."

"That ... bitch."

"She's not wrong," he said. "If we're going to fit in in places like that, we need to look the part. You should have seen Remy when he got cleaned up. He always said that a good suit was like body armor in high society. Course, he still complained about it, but he had a whole different wardrobe for when he had to meet high-class clients."

"Whatever," I said. I hated the notion that anyone would judge me based on my appearance, but I knew good and well that that was how the world worked. It was human nature, and railing against it was pointless. Better to simply adapt and use that to my advantage. My training had taught me that if I looked similar to the people around me, they would be far more likely to accept me. By contrast, if I was different in any way—be it skin color, my hair style, or the way

I was dressed—they'd look at me with suspicion or, at the very least, interest. And given that I wanted to fly under the radar, that was counterproductive. The brief exchange had highlighted yet another issue—my wardrobe—and added another line to my increasingly longer list of things I had to do.

To distract myself, I held up my new hand. Aside from a barely visible seam about halfway up my forearm, it looked little different than my old hand. Dr. Montague had used top-quality Realskin. There were even calluses and wrinkles in all the right places. I touched my new index finger to my thumb, and I was surprised to find that it was tactilely identical to my old hand. That was expected; what good would a new hand be if I couldn't feel it? However, I also knew that there were no pain sensors, either, so I'd have to be careful with it.

"How does it feel?" asked Patrick.

"The same, mostly," I answered. "It's a little weird, though. Almost like the feelings are muted. Or like the senses are blurred."

"Dr. Montague mentioned that," he said. "For the next few weeks, the cybernetic will link to your nervous system. Until it finishes, you'll have a microsecond or so of lag."

"Oh," I said. "That makes sense, I guess."

In truth, I would've accepted just about anything if it meant I'd have the use of my hand again. I'd tried to ignore it during the trip from Mobile to Nova City, but even if it hadn't affected my combat abilities that much, it was still a huge loss. Now, I wouldn't have to worry about it.

"Wish I could test the subdermal sheath," I said.

"I could stab you," Patrick offered with a grin. His joke kind of took me by surprise, and I just stared at him for a moment before he coughed in embarrassment, saying, "Sorry. I didn't mean it like—"

"I know," I said. "I'm just a . . . I'm just a little slow right now. Effects of the anesthetic or something, I think." I gave him a smile of my own. "I think I'll pass on getting stabbed for now, though."

He gave a nervous laugh. Then, he said, "I saw her inject it, though. The Sheath, I mean. So, I know it's there."

I didn't need his reassurance. After all, my interface had finished with the integration of the various cybernetics, and it told me that my new subdermal sheath, which was labeled as armor on my HUD, was operating at one hundred percent integrity. I suspected that the integrity would decrease each time I took a hit. However, unless it was completely destroyed, it would utilize a trickle of my Mist to repair on its own—a process I could speed up by injecting condensed Mist via a booster. I'd bought a handful of them from Dex, but they were incredibly expensive, so even my funds wouldn't hold up to continued usage.

Then, my mind turned to the collapsible transport, which had its own heading in my interface. When I selected it, the action opened a window in my HUD showing a slowly rotating three-dimensional model of my new hover bike. It was sleek, with an elongated nose and a stocky backside. Three Mist vents ran along the bottom, and a seat that would accommodate two people sat atop the shiny black fuselage, which was trimmed in silver accents. In short, it was probably the coolest thing I had ever seen.

The only problem was that it would definitely stand out. There was no hiding that it was an incredibly expensive bike, and that, I knew, would bring all sorts of unwanted attention. Thieves, busybodies, information mongers, and everyone else in Nova City would take notice of that beautiful bike.

Thankfully, according to Dexter, it was equipped with a solution to that problem. As a cybernetic, it was considered a part of me. That meant that my skills worked on it, too. I could only hope there wouldn't be any problems applying Mimic to the bike. Otherwise, it would be too conspicuous to actually use.

I sat up, then swiveled to hang my legs off the elevated chair. A wave of dizziness swept through me, but I steadied myself with my hands. The new one found the surface of the bed an instant after my biological one, hammering home the issue with the lag. I'd just have to get used to it until my body acclimated to the new addition.

"Did you learn anything?" I asked, looking up at Patrick.

"I did," he said with a small smile. "There's a lot more to installing cybernetics than just hooking things up. But I've always liked putting things together. So . . ."

"So, the skill fits?" I asked.

"I think so," he said.

There were few things worse than getting a skill and finding that you were ill-suited to use it. Nova City was littered with people who'd taken big, fancy skills and then failed when trying to put them to use. Getting a skill wasn't a shortcut to power; you still had to put in a lot of work if you wanted to use it properly, and a lot of people just weren't cut out for that kind of commitment.

But there were just as many hard workers out there who never got the chance to be anything but drones, trudging back and forth to their meaningless jobs as they worked to enrich someone else. Meanwhile, the people at the top thought that they were somehow better than those at the bottom, just because they'd lucked into a higher tier or generational wealth. It was disgusting.

At first, I'd labored under the illusion that my Tier 7 Nexus Implant made me better than other people. However, being brought low by a Tier 2 Amigo had cured me of that assumption. In the end, my elevated tier made things easier, and it raised my ceiling, but if someone outworked me—be it in training or via gaining levels—that advantage would quickly be erased. I needed to keep that in mind if I was going to survive.

It took a few more minutes for me to steady myself, and when I did, Patrick and I stepped out of the room only to find one of the cyborgs waiting for us. "Dierdre, isn't it?" I asked, recognizing the mechanical woman's face.

"It is," said the hulking mass of metallic parts. I couldn't imagine what would push someone to replace the majority of their body with metal, but I didn't want to be rude by asking. She continued, "Follow me, please. Mr. Gunderson is waiting."

"Gunther Gunderson. Quite a name, isn't it?" I asked with a slight snicker.

Dierdre didn't answer. Instead, she turned on her mechanical heel and marched down the hall. Her heavy footsteps thudded against the tiles as we followed her through the maze of corridors until we reached an elevator, which took us to the top floor. When we exited, I couldn't help but gape at the room before me. Or rather, the decor.

Everything was covered in rich leather, dark wood, or shelves containing hundreds of ancient books. Throughout the room were the heads of various monsters. I recognized an enormous alligator, a bear with metallic tusks, and a stag that looked strikingly similar to the one I'd seen outside of Mobile so long ago. Its antlers were metal, and I could practically feel the Mist gathering between the multitude of prongs.

In the center of the room was Gunther himself, sitting behind a massive desk made of the same polished wood that seemed so prevalent in the office. Aside from the elevator, there was only one other door in the room, and I presumed that it led to his personal living quarters.

"All fixed up, I see," he said with a grin. He noticed that I was still looking at the stag, and as he rose from his chair, which looked like a leather-clad throne, he said, "Ah, took that buck a few years back. Found him just outside of what used to be Houston. He'd just killed a pack of wolves, so he was already wounded. Wouldn't have been able to take him, otherwise."

I didn't know if he wanted me to be impressed or not, but I found the idea a little sad. The buck I'd encountered hadn't been aggressive, so the notion of killing it just didn't sit right with me. Of course, if it was wounded, there was every chance that it had been a mercy killing, but knowing what I knew of Gunther, I suspected that wasn't really the case. After all, he obviously liked his trophies, and the buck made for an impressive one.

"Thank you for letting me use your facilities," I said. "I'll remember it."

As I spoke, I initiated the final transfer of credits, which he accepted. "Anything else I can do for you?" he asked.

"Now that you ask, I could use a few things," I said. Then, I sent a list to him, which he took a moment to peruse.

"I can do most of this," he said. "Where are you setting up?"

"I don't think that's in my best interests to reveal," I stated. "That's part of what I'll be paying for."

My intention was simple. I needed a home base, and I intended to find an appropriate space in Algiers. But with my needs being what they were, any building I chose would require significant alteration. For that, I had turned to Gunther, who had plenty of contacts. With his help, I felt like I could get what I needed—especially considering that I was willing to overpay. In the Bazaar, my wealth might've seemed very limited, but in a place like Algiers, it would stretch extremely far.

"I'll put some feelers out," he said. "I know a few people who can do what you need. I will require a finder's fee, though."

"Naturally," I said. Then, I sent a communication link to him. It wasn't secure, but it didn't need to be, considering the purpose. Nothing sensitive would be discussed over that connection, but it was necessary if he intended to contact me later. He accepted, and after a little more small talk, Patrick and I took our leave. The cyborg escorted us from the building, and we soon found ourselves outside.

"I'm exhausted," Patrick said.

I was, too, so I said, "I know a place we can stay, I think. They don't ask questions there, and they know better than to talk about their . . . uh . . . clientele."

"Sounds good," he said.

I was tempted to summon my hover bike, but I chose not to for a couple of reasons. First, I'd never actually driven one before, so I wasn't confident that I could do so without running into everything on the road. I felt that I could pick it up quickly, but I didn't want to chance it. Second, I still didn't know how it would interact with my skills and abilities, and the last thing I wanted was to summon a gleaming and obviously expensive bike in the middle of the street. I could've probably gotten around that by doing so in an alley or something, but even then, there might have been eyes on me. So, I decided that it would be smarter to test things out later, when I could guarantee my privacy.

Patrick and I crossed the street and quickly found our way to the monorail platform. Unlike was the case with our previous trip on the elevated train, we didn't pick up any followers. However, as the monorail approached the boundary between the platforms containing Algiers and the Garden, the passengers gained at every stop grew steadily seedier. Some were Garden residents who were going in to work the night shift at one of the factories, but others were people who lived in the poorest district. And it wasn't difficult to make that distinction. The Algiers natives were almost all dirty, their clothes were ragged, and they had a malnourished look about them. The people of the Garden weren't exactly prosperous, but by comparison, they were practically wealthy.

But the most telling characteristic was that, one and all, the Algiers residents wore the dead-eyed expressions of people who'd truly given up. They were just going through the motions because they didn't know what else to do.

After passing the forest of silos that gave the Garden its name, we reached the edge of the platform, and the monorail's track dipped in a steep decline that descended into Algiers. I held on as my stomach clenched, and I was reminded of flying in *The Jitterbug*. Patrick was unsurprisingly unaffected, adopting a bored expression as the monorail evened out and shot off toward our destination.

Finally, we reached the appropriate platform, and we exited alongside a trio of Algiers natives. A few minutes later, we were passing the various abandoned buildings, with their broken windows and dirty facades. Patrick stared as we passed a shantytown; the hovels were sturdy enough, with brick walls and corrugated metal roofs, but they would offer little in the way of comfort. The living conditions were bad enough that I found myself appreciating life in the mega-buildings of the Garden. I'd had it easy in my uncle's penthouse, but I'd always pitied the other residents. But their lives were immeasurably better than the lives of the people who made their homes in Algiers.

Eventually, we found our way to the building that was our goal, El Paradiso Hotel.

Its name was far grander than its reality, and it was a two-story compound of buildings that practically oozed corruption. I wasn't unaware of the place's reputation. Even with my sheltered upbringing, I'd heard of Algiers' most famous no-tell motel. Everyone had. In school, a few of my classmates had even bragged that they'd lost their virginity there.

If the Garden had Bourbon Street, then Algiers had El Paradiso Hotel. Both trafficked in sex work, but even Bourbon Street seemed high-class compared to the hotel before us. There were plenty of people around. Some were clearly prostitutes. Men and women, all dressed as provocatively as possible, loitered near the street. But even as they tried to look fetching, they wore the same expressions as everyone else in Algiers. Still, there were plenty of customers who were willing to ignore it.

Interspersed with those working men and women and their customers were couples who looked around in paranoia. El Paradiso didn't ask questions, and being in Algiers, there was no chance of anyone from the higher platforms being recognized. So, it was a popular destination for cheating spouses who didn't want to chance discovery at the more reputable hotels in the other districts.

I didn't care about any of that. What I did care about was that the hotel's owner, Big Carla, guaranteed the anonymity of her patrons, and she had the muscle to back it up. Even the Enforcers would tread lightly around her—not that they would give two shits about who was sleeping with whom.

"Uh . . . Mira . . ."

"Come on," I said, taking Patrick's hand and dragging him across the street. "Just don't look any of them in the eye. They'll take that as an invitation."

Predictably, more than a few of the prostitutes offered their services, but neither of us gave any indication that we were amenable to that sort of thing, so they quickly moved on to greener pastures. After running the gauntlet of sex workers, we entered the hotel's office, where we were greeted by a pair of mooks. One was a woman shorter than me, while the other was a man that looked so wide, I questioned whether or not he could fit through the door.

"Let them through," called someone from behind a plasti-glass barrier. The two mooks parted, and I got my first look of Big Carla. She was a blonde woman who could generously be called stout. Less generously, she might've been called fat. Sitting on a chair that I didn't envy, she asked, "What do you want? I don't recognize either of you."

"A room," I said. "For the night."

"Hmm, robbing the cradle, aren't you?" the woman giggled, reminding me that I was wearing the face of a middle-aged woman. I blushed as I realized what she meant; Patrick was only sixteen, while I looked to be in my midforties. And given where we were, she'd clearly made a connection neither of us had intended.

"Uh . . ."

She held up her pudgy hands, saying, "No judgment, girl. You get yours where you can, I say. Regular room is fifty. A good room is a hundred. And the honeymoon suite's one fifty."

"Um . . . what's the difference?" I asked.

"We clean the good rooms and the suite after every guest," she said. "The regulars only get cleaned once a week. Honeymoon suite's got a bigger bed and comes with a bottle of real imitation champagne."

"We'll take one of the good rooms," I said.

"Suit yourself," she said, sending a transfer request. I sent her the credits, and she handed me a key. "Enjoy yourself. The young ones are fun once you get 'em trained up a bit."

I blushed furiously, and I knew that Patrick's reaction wasn't much better. Either way, we couldn't get out of there quickly enough, and I was extremely aware of Carla's knowing gaze following us out the door.

We quickly found our way to the appropriate room, let ourselves inside, and at last, I let myself relax. It had been an extremely long day, and even though I wasn't physically all that tired, I was mentally exhausted. Patrick, though, was dead on his feet, and he wasted no time in collapsing on the heart-shaped bed.

Clearly, El Paradiso knew precisely what their rooms were being used for, and they'd steered right into it. But there was only one problem.

"Uh . . . there's only one bed," said Patrick, suddenly realizing what I'd already noticed.

I glanced at him, and we both blushed again.

"You sleep first," I said. "Go take a shower, though. I don't want you stinking up the bed."

CHAPTER THIRTEEN

HOME IS WHERE YOU STORE YOUR AMMO

I remember that first job like it was yesterday. I was so young. So naive. It was a simple task. We were just supposed to hijack a transport truck headed toward one of the higher platforms. We were massacred, and I was the only one to make it out alive. That should have been my first hint that he didn't care about any of us. But all I could feel was pride that I was the only one strong enough to walk out of that situation still breathing.

—Nora Lancaster

After showering and changing, Patrick slipped under the bed's blankets and promptly passed out. Using Misthack, I set a quick alarm on the door before heading to the bathroom myself. For the first time in a while, I let Mimic drop, and when I glanced into the smartmirror, I was more than a little alarmed at how exhausted I looked. There were heavy bags under my eyes, and my cheeks were a little hollow from how much weight I'd lost. Ration bars were great, but their bland taste meant that I only ate when I absolutely had to. Contrast that with how much I looked forward to the Dew Drop Inn's food, and it wasn't difficult to see why my caloric intake had seen a precipitous drop.

Besides, I hadn't really stopped moving for weeks. I hadn't rested. And I had killed more people than I wanted to count. That combination had robbed me of what innocence I'd managed to maintain as well as the comfortable body I had cultivated during my training. I'd never been fat, but now, my compact figure looked stringy with corded and lean muscle. It didn't bulge like Nora's had, but there was certainly power there.

I quickly undressed and hopped into the shower, where I spent quite a while just luxuriating under the steaming-hot water. My muscles unkinked, and for the first time in a while, I just relaxed. Even so, there was still a layer of tension that would take a lot more than a hot shower to banish; after all, I wasn't quite safe yet. Maybe I never would be again.

That was a depressing and troubling thought. Was I destined to go through the rest of my life always looking for the knife in my back? Or would I eventually find leave to let my guard down? Had my uncle? Was that why he hadn't seen Nora's betrayal coming? Or was trusting her a conscious choice, like the one I'd made when I'd let Patrick in? Or when I had chosen to trust Gunther or Gala? I wasn't sure if I wanted to let my paranoia infect every facet of my life. At some point, I needed to let some people close, didn't I?

My stomach twisted into knots as I considered my uncle thinking those same thoughts. Certainly, trust hadn't worked out well for him. Could I hope for any better? I didn't know, and I knew that figuring it out was the work of a lifetime.

Sighing, I reached out with a cupped hand and let the automated dispenser squirt some body wash into my hand. It was cheap stuff that went way too far with the floral scent, but given where I was, I didn't think I had any reason to expect anything different. So, using that soap, I spent the next fifteen minutes arduously scrubbing the filth of weeks' worth of travel from my body. By the time I'd finished, I felt like I'd been hit with a sandblaster, but at least I was clean.

As I activated the air-drying function, I found myself appreciating the fact that I was finally back in a civilized city. I would always cherish my time in Mobile—as well as the people I'd met there—but there were definite advantages to being back in Nova. Not only were the amenities vastly superior, but the city was host to a wide variety of other advantages. From fashion to equipment, and everything in between, it was one of the hubs of what was left of human civilization.

Once I was dry, I stepped out of the shower and glanced at my reflection in the mirror. I looked better without all the dried blood, dirt, and other various bits of filth I'd picked up along the way. My body had changed quite a bit during my training, and not only had I filled out in all the right places, but even after my recent trials and tribulations, I looked quite a bit healthier than when I'd first arrived in Mobile. At some point, I had left girlhood behind, and I'd run headfirst into maturity.

After looking at my hair, which had been put through the ringer over the past couple of months, I frowned in disgust. I'd gotten over my hatred of my wild, curly hair, but it was an unassailable truth that the lack of attention had left it looking pretty terrible. During my training, I'd spent plenty of time experimenting with various styles, but while I'd been on my mission, that attention had fallen by the wayside. That, coupled with a few close calls where a few patches had been ripped out by the roots, had left it lopsided.

Shaking my head, I pulled the self-styler out. However, the moment I looked at the helmetlike apparatus, I was assailed by grief. It had been a birthday gift from Jo. A thoughtful present that showed just how well she knew me. But now, she was gone. Dead like so many others. I would never be able to return the gesture with a gift of my own. Nor would we ever hang out and talk about boys. Or, as was often the case for her, girls. I would never get the chance to show her around Nova. Nor would she ever realize her dreams of finding what I suspected was a mythological safe haven in the mountains out west.

Before I could stop them, the tears began, and I sat on the closed commode, burying my face in my hands. Like that, I remained, weeping for all the people I'd lost. It was easy enough to ignore my grief when I had a task in front of me. I was well versed in putting one foot in front of the other. However, the moment I stopped, those emotions crept up and tackled me to the ground.

I don't know how long I sat there weeping, but it wasn't a short span of time. Eventually, though, I pushed everything to the side, put on some spare clothes—really, my only truly clean set—and forewent the self-styler, choosing to simply put my hair up. After all, I wasn't going out. I didn't need to impress anyone.

Except maybe Patrick.

He certainly had his strong points. He seemed kind. Loyal. And he definitely wasn't bad looking, with his stocky frame, strong jaw, and wavy blond hair. And blue eyes that were easy to get lost in.

"God," I muttered to myself, trying to wrangle my thoughts and emotions. It didn't matter if I found him attractive. Right now, he was off-limits. Maybe that would change sometime in the future, but we were both far too vulnerable to head down that road. Besides, he was too young. And too innocent.

But even as the thought crossed my mind, I knew that last part wasn't so true anymore. He might be a little naive and ignorant of how things worked in Nova City, but after everything he'd been through, I suspected that his innocence had gone the same way mine had. After all, he'd lost just as much as I had.

With a sigh, I took one last look at my reflection before padding out into the room. Patrick's even breathing told me that he was already asleep, so I set myself up in the room's lone chair, and I spent the next few hours going through my puzzle program. My progress was shockingly fast, and not for the first time, I thought that I would need to be replaced before long. Soon enough, I abandoned that program in favor of delving into the portion of my interface reserved for writing Ghosts.

I didn't have any ideas for anything new, so I just worked on some older projects for a while. It was soothing, in a way, fully concentrating on the mechanical tasks of slowly building and adjusting the complex programs. Some of it reminded me of the logic or number puzzles to which I'd grown accustomed, but mostly, it was an exercise in creativity, trying to balance the intended features with the Mist limits imposed by my skill's tier.

Once, my instructor, Helen Stone, had likened it to a combination of building an incredibly complex and layered electrical circuit with mathematical equations. Add in a little old-Earth programming for flavor, and you had a hint of how writing a Ghost worked. For me, though, it had always felt like building a pyramid. Of equations that were all dependent on the layers below. While trying to use materials that were ill-suited for the job at hand.

Okay—so it's not easy to explain how it all worked because a lot of it was facilitated by my skill; without it, I could have stared at that mass of numbers, glyphs, equations, and connections for years without gleaning even the slightest meaning. But with [Mistrunner] illuminating the entire process, it all somehow made sense. I didn't have much of a reason to wonder why. I just accepted it as it was. Perhaps one day I'd have the freedom to investigate that sort of thing, but for now, I had so many other things on my plate that I couldn't afford to let my focus waver.

Finally, the alarm I'd set went off in my interface, and I woke a bleary-eyed Patrick up. He was still half-asleep, but he didn't complain when I told him it was his turn to play watchman. We swapped places, and I couldn't help but smile a bit at how warm the bed was. I was asleep in minutes.

Six hours later, I awoke to the sound of the alarm once again going off in my head. For a few minutes, I lay there, my eyes still closed as I debated whether or not I wanted to actually get up. Finally, I pushed myself out of bed to find that Patrick had dozed off in the chair. My initial reaction was to berate him, but I chose not to. After everything we'd been through, I couldn't really blame him for succumbing to his exhaustion.

I rose from the bed, then shook him awake, and he blurted, "I'm awake! I was just resting my eyes!"

"Sure, sure," I said with a grin. "My uncle used to always say the same thing. C'mon and get dressed. I want something other than ration bars for breakfast."

After that, I went into the bathroom to both take care of my morning ablutions as well as for a little extra privacy. For the day, I chose a nondescript pair of jeans and a tee-shirt that was mostly clean. I wouldn't be turning any heads in an outfit like that, but that was probably for the best. I topped the outfit off with a pair of worn sneakers. My combat attire remained in a corner of my arsenal implant.

After I left the bathroom, Patrick took his turn, and about twenty minutes later, we were on our way. For the day, I'd adopted a new persona by using Mimic to copy the appearance of one of the less-outrageous prostitutes. Luckily, it didn't affect my outfit; I couldn't imagine walking around in those kinds of clothes. I'd have died of embarrassment.

In any case, we quickly found our way to the monorail, which took us back into the Garden, where I wasted no time in leading Patrick to my favorite restaurant, called the Fortuna Diner. In retrospect, it couldn't hold a candle to the Dew Drop Inn, but I had many fond memories of going there for Sunday breakfasts with Jeremiah.

The restaurant occupied a corner of one of the district's ubiquitous megabuildings, but unlike most businesses, it was only accessible from the street entrance. The interior reminded me of the diners I'd read about in stories from the pre-Initialization world, with various booths and a long bar. It was packed with patrons, but Patrick and I found a booth in one of the corners.

Breakfast went about how I'd expected it to, though the food was a lot worse than I remembered. I could only think that I'd gotten spoiled by my time in Mobile, where meals were comprised of fresh ingredients and prepared by Jo's parents, who were skilled cooks. The diner, for all it tried, could only dress the soy-based meat substitute and powdered eggs up so much. But Patrick and I both agreed that it was a lot better than a ration bar.

"What's the plan for today?" he asked, biting into a faux sausage.

"We need somewhere to set up shop," I said; normally I would have worried about being overheard, but the place was so busy that even with the help of Observation, I had difficulty picking out individual conversations. Besides, it wasn't like I expected anyone to be hunting me. I was just a normal person now. And I intended to use that anonymity to my advantage while it lasted. "I'm thinking Algiers. There are a lot of abandoned buildings there that might serve our purposes. Plus, nobody goes there unless they have to, so it shouldn't be hard to keep things under the radar."

"Oh," he said. "Makes sense."

After that, we spent the rest of our breakfast engaged in small talk before we made our way back to Algiers. As we rode the monorail, I accessed the city's intranet to look for potential headquarters, and it didn't take me long to find a few good candidates.

Unfortunately, the first two turned out to be complete busts. The first one was right next to one of the supply depots in the dock area, which meant that it was crawling with Enforcers. Given that I didn't want to wake up with a bunch of guns in my face, I didn't think that was a great place to set up shop. So, we moved on to the next, which was just about falling apart. The photos I'd seen on the intranet were, to put it mildly, horribly inaccurate and so generous as to be outright lies. So, it was with a bad attitude that we crossed the district to visit the last option on my list.

When we approached, I was initially disappointed in the size. At only two stories tall and about two thousand square feet, it was the smallest of the buildings on my short list. But once we got inside and looking around, I said, "This could work, I guess."

"What's that over there?" asked Patrick, pointing to a corner.

"I don't know," I said, approaching the seam in the floor. I knelt down and dusted it off, which revealed that the crack was part of a trapdoor. I quickly levered it open. Grinning at Patrick, I said, "Wish me luck."

Then, I hopped into the hole, landing a split second later. After retrieving a Mist lamp from my arsenal implant, I looked around. "Oh, this is nice. Very nice."

Initially, I'd expected an unmarked basement, but what I'd found was an entrance to a cavernous underground space that was at least a couple of hundred yards wide. I knew that a significant portion of Nova's population lived beneath the surface of the city; in the beginning, the people who'd eschewed surfac-living confined themselves to disused draining tunnels, but they'd long since begun to expand, carving enormous caverns into the city's various platforms. Colloquially, it was known as the Undercity, and locations of the access points were a closely guarded secret for those who knew of them.

I felt certain that this basement wasn't that, largely because I didn't see any other entrances or exits. Instead, I suspected that someone had built it for some nefarious purpose. Perhaps it had housed an illegal farm. Or maybe a dust-refinement operation. It might've even been an illegal warehouse, given its proximity to the city's exits. Whatever the case, I couldn't help but think that it made the property the perfect place to set up shop.

"What's down there?" asked Patrick, sticking his head down through the trapdoor.

"I think we've come home," I said. "This is perfect."

After that, I contacted the seller via the intranet and bought the property anonymously. At only two hundred thousand credits, it was far cheaper than it probably should have been, but the moment I transferred the fee, the electronic deed of ownership appeared in my interface.

With that out of the way, Patrick and I set up a rope for temporary access to the basement, and then we started unloading his implant. Before long, there was a small pile of crates taking up a corner of the sublevel. Rubbing my hands together, I considered summoning my hover bike and testing it out, but I held off. There were more important things to do first.

That in mind, I contacted Gunther, and he put me through to some discreet contractors who could set up proper security in the building above. A separate and far more expensive contractor would be used to modify the property appropriately. Once all of that was done, I sat down and looked around. By establishing a base of operations, I'd taken the first step in my quest for revenge.

And it felt good.

CHAPTER FOURTEEN

SETTLING IN

He taught me how to seize power, and yet, he was surprised when I turned that on him. He should have been proud I learned the lessons so well.

—Nora Lancaster

I knelt at the edge of the roof, looking across the street at the megabuilding I'd once called home. For three days, I'd remained in place, studying the comings and goings of my uncle's killer. I knew that Nora hadn't actually pulled the trigger. She hadn't been the one to personally torture him. However, she was ultimately responsible. Without her betrayal, none of it would have been possible.

I also knew that my uncle bore some of the blame himself. After all, he'd been a taciturn, immovable man who'd spent most of his life angering his enemies, contemporaries, and underlings alike. It was only fitting that someone had eventually turned on him. But that didn't mean I wasn't going to make them all pay, starting with Nora herself.

My reconnaissance hadn't told me much, save that she had taken up residence in Jeremiah's penthouse. I'd yet to see Heather, so I had no idea what had happened to her, and even though we'd never really gotten along, I feared the worst. She wasn't a bad person; she'd just chosen the wrong man to latch on to. I hoped that Nora had shown her mercy, though judging by what I'd seen over the past three days, I wasn't optimistic.

Finally, I got the alert I'd been waiting on, and I retreated from the edge of the building. At last, the hired contractors had finished with my new home, and I was eager to see the compound that would become my base of operations. I knew it had great potential, and I had sunk hundreds of thousands of credits into making it work. So, I was understandably excited to see the results of that investment.

With that in mind, I crossed the roof to the access door. When I'd first entered the building, I'd jacked in via the personal link in the Hand of God and used Mistwalk to fake my credentials. Now, the system saw me as an administrator, so I enjoyed full and unlimited access. All I had to do was go to a security terminal, and I could access the building's surveillance and security features. Not that it was useful for much aside from getting in and out; the megabuilding had no real value to me aside from its proximity to Nora's—and subsequently, the Specters'—territory.

If I'd wanted to, I could have killed Nora at any time. She was right there, acting as if she was completely untouchable. One Empowered Shot from my sniper rifle, and she would be thoroughly obliterated. I chose not to do so for three reasons. First—and most importantly—I knew that my uncle's demise hadn't come only at her hands. There were plenty of other people involved, and she was my only real link to her coconspirators. I had no intentions of ending my crusade with one dead body, so I had no choice but to use her to find the others.

But more personally, I wanted to make her suffer. A simple shot wasn't enough. Instead, I wanted to tear it all down, to bring everything she cared about crashing down around her. To do that, I would have to pick apart the entire organization. Meanwhile, I had a plan to make her losses more personal. Nora didn't care about much, but I knew her weak points as well as anyone. And I intended to attack them.

Finally, my uncle had taken great pains to teach me about actions and consequences. I needed to watch. I needed to learn. And I needed to plan. Otherwise, things might not work out like I wanted them to.

This wasn't some inconsequential mission to a backwater like Bayou La Batre. I didn't have a safety net waiting in the wings to pull me out if things got too hot. I was on my own, and while my vengeance was foremost on my mind, I had no intention of throwing my life away to get it. So, I'd resolved not to act until I was absolutely certain that things would go according to my plans. Anything else would be an insult to my uncle's memory.

Once I went through the door, I quickly descended the steps and found my way to the top floor. This megabuilding was designed slightly differently than the one where I'd grown up; instead of a single block, it had a hollow core, creating a courtyard of open air. The layers of various apartments occupied the outer perimeter, with a multitude of shops making a home along the edge of the open courtyard. Residents clogged the walkways. Some of them loitered in groups and looked like they were up to no good, but others were clearly occupied with one task or another as they traversed the ramps that connected the floors.

I knew there were some people who almost never left their buildings. After all, they were like cities unto themselves, with access to all the necessities. For a lot of residents, there just wasn't any reason to go elsewhere. Instead, they were happy occupying themselves with various virtual reality chips, the entertainment feeds, or with their preferred inebriant. They were sad people with sad lives, but I knew I didn't have any real call to judge them. The real world was a depressing place, so it was understandable that they'd retreated into fantasy, especially when it made their lives that much easier to bear.

Still, it was difficult not to feel a mixture of pity and revulsion when I saw those sorts of people, so I wasted no time lingering in the megabuilding. Instead, I headed straight to the elevator, which was a metal cage studded with various screens playing advertisements, most of which featured sexually suggestive material that still made me a little uncomfortable.

Once, Nora had explained it to me. In the old world, there had been a saying: sex sells. And given the greed of our rulers, who were in turn funneling a good portion of those credits back to their unseen alien overlords, selling was the name of the game. On top of that, it was a distraction. It was the same reason that pornography and prostitution were so well represented within Nova City. In fact, there were so many entertainment options that I found it difficult to believe that the average person couldn't see through the ruse. Entertained people—whether the source of that entertainment was sex, drugs, or virtual reality chips—were placid people. Why fight for a better life when you could go home and watch your favorite program? Or when your next hit of dust was waiting on you?

It was disgusting, how easily we'd let ourselves be subjugated by our own interests. In the past, wars had been fought over fewer rights. But now? We accepted our own oppression so readily, and in exchange, we got slightly better pornography.

Sighing as the elevator took me down a few dozen floors, I pushed those thoughts to the back of my mind. If I let myself focus on it, I knew I'd spiral. And that wasn't productive. After all, there wasn't anything I could do about any of it. There were plenty of people in Nova City screaming for the rest of the citizens to wake up, but that didn't do any good. It was a prison, but a comfortable one. And nobody wanted to risk their amenities or vices for a chance at freedom.

The elevator clanked to a stop, and the cage slid open to reveal a parking structure. Technically, I didn't need one, but it seemed the most appropriate place to summon my hover bike. Once I was sure there was no one around, I activated the cybernetic link, and the bike materialized before me.

It worked similarly to my arsenal implant, using Mist to access a quarantined section of quantum space where the bike was usually stored, but unlike my arsenal implant, the space was reserved for the Kyrobe Cutter. In its natural form, the Cutter was comprised of a sleek black fuselage that didn't look so dissimilar from the motorcycles I'd seen back in Mobile. However, it differed in a few key ways. First, instead of wheels, it had three Mist vents; each one was about eight inches in diameter and half as thick, held in place by metallic clamps. When I was riding it, those clamps would move up and down to account for steering. For propulsion, it had a Mist engine that could push it to speeds in excess of three hundred miles an hour. I hadn't had a chance to really let it loose yet—Nova City was far too cramped for that—but I'd spent a few hours putting it through its paces as I raced around Algiers. And I was more than impressed; even with Observation and the enhanced reaction times from my high Mind attribute, it was capable of pushing me to my limits.

However, while its performance was a cut above the rest, that wasn't what made it so much better than the other hover bikes I'd seen around Nova City. No—where it really showed its worth lay in the fact that it was categorized as and integrated like a normal cybernetic implant. It technically wasn't; I could take off the band that housed its quantum space if I wanted to, but my interface—or more importantly, my skills—didn't seem to care. As a result, when I used Mimic, I could extend that camouflage to the bike.

I did so, and its image shimmered. A moment later, it looked like a much cheaper, far older, and barely functional hover bike. It would retain its high performance, but it wouldn't draw anyone's attention.

Just like me.

The new appearance was boxy, a little rusted, and only had two Mist vents. But it had the same basic shape and size, so there were no issues as I straddled the seat, leaned forward, and took off.

The Mist engine hummed to life as I rocketed forward, twisting and turning as I descended the parking structure until, at last I burst forth into the street, cutting off a hover car in the process. The driver shouted at me, but I gave him the finger as I sped away.

I had to resist the urge to let out an excited shout as the bike accelerated; piloting the Cutter was everything I ever hoped it could be, and despite the grim thoughts that had followed me through the megabuilding, I couldn't keep the grin from spreading across my face. For the first time in my life, I felt free in a way I couldn't really explain. It wasn't just the speed, either. It was the knowledge that if I so desired, I could just head straight to one of Nova's gates, burst through the Enforcer-guarded barricades, and leave the city. I could go wherever I wanted, too. The Cutter wasn't subject to the same restrictions as most hover cars, and even when the Mist grew chaotic, it could still work—at least for a while. It would cost a fortune in Rift Shards, but I'd saved a few of them just in case. Nothing would constrain me. I could just leave my revenge plot behind. I could just live my life.

But would that make me any different from most of Nova City's citizens, who chose comfort over fighting for their rights? I knew it wasn't a one-to-one comparison, but to me, it felt similar. Either way, I knew I would never—could never—do that.

The possibility that I could was comforting, though.

I raced through the Garden, weaving in and out of traffic. The hover bike wasn't as fast as the monorail, but it did have the benefit of being completely under my control. Plus, the monorail followed a defined course, and there were no platforms near my destination. So, the bike was a better option.

Plus, you know—hover bike. How could I not want to play with it every chance I got?

Still, as fast as my form of conveyance was, Nova City was enormous, and it still took me about thirty minutes to reach the spiraling ramp that led down to Algiers. When I began my descent, my grin widened. The ramp itself was wide, and the gradient was fairly shallow; as a result, the spiral almost felt like a racetrack as I sped around it. By the time I reached the bottom, I was flush with excitement, and I had to resist the urge to head straight back up and do it again.

But I had other things on the agenda, so I pushed those thoughts to the side as I headed out into Algiers. The poorest district in Nova City was the same as always, meaning that the buildings looked half-abandoned, the people were malnourished, pale, and dejected, and the streets were scattered with random trash. There were no utility drones to clean this district, and the people didn't care enough not to use the sidewalks as dumpsters. It was a disgusting way to live, and it, along with the distinctive odor of the multiple factories' emissions, gave the whole district a very unpleasant atmosphere. I ignored it, though.

The hover bike got a few casual looks, some of which were predatory, but I didn't stop long enough to get into any trouble. Even the old and barely functional appearance of my bike caught attention in a place like Algiers.

Eventually, I made my way to my neighborhood. After pulling into an alley, I dismissed the bike and used Mimic to once again change my appearance. Before, I'd looked like a nondescript man with brown hair, but now, I used one of my old standbys—a middle-aged woman with short black hair. Once I'd adopted the new identity, I ran toward the other end of the alley, leaped over a fence, and used Stealth before creeping toward my property. It took me almost ten more minutes before I reached the building, and I knew I was probably being a bit paranoid. But I refused to make the same mistakes I'd made during my training.

Outwardly, the property itself looked much the same as it had when I'd first bought it. A square, two-story building without any windows. The whole lot looked abandoned, but with Observation, I could notice the slight distortions on the corners of the buildings. They were concealed cameras and autoturrets. If any unauthorized personnel came to visit, they'd get ripped to shreds.

I glanced up; the sun had already begun to set, so the lot was cast in deep shadow. Still, I decided to wait a few minutes until the sky darkened enough that my Stealth had a few more shadows with which to work. Once night had enveloped the area, I crept across the property and entered the building.

If the outside looked like an abandoned building, the first floor followed that same theme. Piles of detritus were deliberately placed throughout; if someone made it past the cameras or autoturrets, they'd be disappointed to find that the building was precisely what it appeared to be.

I crossed the lobby—I'd discovered that the building had once belonged to a shipping company—and entered a hall on the other side of the large room. Once inside, I quickly traced a path through the maze of corridors until I found a specific closet, which I entered. The moment the door closed behind me, I placed my hand on a seemingly innocuous piece of the wall. A light beep sounded, and the hidden elevator took me up to the next floor. When the door slid open again, I was greeted by a perfectly modern apartment. It was almost completely bare, but given that it took up the entire floor, there was enough space to accommodate almost two dozen people. As for the decor, it contained the bare essentials and not much else. In that respect, I had similar taste to my uncle, which shouldn't have been surprising.

Patrick, who was sitting on a couch and looking at something on his interface, looked up. I saw his hand creep toward the pistol at his hip before I said, "Canary-candy-three-four-seven."

He relaxed. "That's a different disguise," he said.

I dropped my ability, my appearance reverting back to normal. "I've used it before," I said, crossing the room to sit next to him. Finally, I let myself relax. I glanced at him, asking, "You studying?"

He nodded. "There's way more to cybernetic engineering than I expected" was his response. "Until I can pass Dr. Montague's tests, she won't even let me in the office."

"Shouldn't be that hard," I said. I'd had so much information crammed into my brain that learning a few textbooks' worth of material didn't seem all that difficult. "Besides, it'll probably help your Mind attribute, right?"

"I guess," he said. "Slow going, though. Did you find what you're looking for?"

I shook my head. "Still nothing," I answered. "But it's probably coming soon. I know she hasn't stopped."

"I guess" was his response. Despite wanting revenge, he wasn't quite as committed to vengeance as I was. He was still on board, but I could see Patrick's resolve chipping away by the day.

"Did they finish?" I asked.

"Earlier today," he answered. "Everything should be ready downstairs."

I grinned. "Fantastic," I said. "You want to come give it a whirl? Training can do a lot to take your mind off of things."

He shook his head. "I need to work on this material," Patrick said. He summoned a chip from his own implant, adding, "Which reminds me—Gunther sent this over."

"Nice," I said, taking the chip. I quickly slotted it into the port on my neck, and I was happy to see that it was the next stage of my puzzle program. Instead of the rudimentary AI creating puzzles for me to solve, I was expected to create puzzles for the AI to solve. The whole thing was meant to push my Mind attribute to the next level while preparing me to write more complicated Ghosts.

"That chip cost more than my gun," he muttered.

"That's because Dex had to special order it," I said. I'd had it sent to Gunther first so I didn't have to cross the city to pick it up at the Dome. "This kind of thing isn't normally available on quarantined worlds."

"I don't know if we should trust those aliens. They're just here to exploit us, right?"

We'd had the discussion before, and I knew we'd probably do it again. But I wasn't in the mood, so I just said, "I know it's not without dangers, but I've got to take a few risks if any of this is going to work." I sighed again, then added, "You sure you don't want to come with me? You're going to have to train with that pistol at some point."

"Tomorrow," Patrick said.

I shook my head, saying, "I'll hold you to it."

With that, I retreated to the elevator and mentally commanded it to take me down to the refurbished basement. It really was amazing what a little money and some men and women with the right skills could accomplish in a few days. I'd been skeptical the contractors could work so quickly, but they'd come through with everything they'd promised. And, according to Gunther, the people he'd hired would be completely discreet. Otherwise, they'd have to deal with him.

Nobody in Nova wanted that.

But then again, the same could have been said about my uncle, and see where that got him. Nobody was invincible. No reputation was unassailable. Earlier, I'd spent almost six hours going through the building's security terminals looking for weaknesses or hostile programs. I hadn't found anything, but I'd already resolved to continue my sweeps just in case.

You could never be too careful, after all.

But all thoughts of paranoia faded when the elevator reached its destination and the door slid open to reveal my new training hall.

I smiled broadly, mumbling, "I'm home."

CHAPTER FIFTEEN

A NEW ROUTINE

Trust is surprisingly easy to betray. When I first contacted the Enforcers, I thought Jeremiah would pop up out of nowhere and kill me. But he never knew. Not until the end. All because he trusted me. That was his only real mistake.

—Nora Lancaster

As I looked at my new training hall, I couldn't stop the grin from spreading across my face. The basement had already been huge, and judging by the secret tunnels the contractors had found, it had clearly been used as some sort of smuggling warehouse. What had happened to the previous occupants, I had no idea. But their loss was my gain.

The first thing I'd had the contractors do was to enlarge the room even further, and in every dimension. It was longer, deeper, and wider now—all to accommodate the training regimen I'd been working on. I had new skills to develop, and my growth had already stagnated. That wouldn't do, so I needed a place that could double as a gym as well as a shooting range.

The gym part was easy. It only took Gunther a day to get ahold of the strongest Mist shackles available. With those, my Constitution would be cut by at least ninety percent, meaning I would need far less equipment to get a good workout. With my Constitution being what it was, the amount of weight I'd have to lift would soon grow out of control. The shackles would keep that to a minimum. At the same time, it would allow me to continue my work on the obstacle course I'd had built.

Lining one entire side of the room—which was almost four hundred yards long—the course was a lot like the one I'd used in Mobile. However, it differed in a couple of key aspects. First, it was at least ten times longer than the old one, which would really let me work on my attributes as well as my skills. Second, it had a few new sections that were meant to train my [Acrobatics] skill. I was both dreading and looking forward to putting myself to the test.

As I continued scanning the new training hall, my eyes settled on a pair of doors on one side. In there, I would find an enormous stockpile of ammunition. The bulk of it was practice ammo, which was made from mundane materials. It was supposed to be the cheaper option, but even that had taken a good chunk of my net worth. A smaller portion of the stockpile was decidedly more expensive. My new weapons were powerful, but with that power came some stringent requirements for ammunition; the only way to meet those requirements was to spend lots and lots of credits. Thankfully, I had enough, but it just served to remind me that my windfall from selling the Rift Shards wouldn't last forever. Eventually, I would have to find some way to earn a living.

After crossing the hall and inspecting the storage rooms, I decided to take a look at the hall's other features, which were meant to turn it into a relatively safe gun range. I ran my hand along one of the walls, feeling the soft tingle of a Mist shield. The entire room was blanketed in the stuff. As a result, any errant shots would be mostly contained. Certainly, if I used my real ammunition, it wouldn't hold up, but that was what the practice ammo was for.

But what really got me excited was that I'd gone back to the Bazaar and bought a very advanced training system from Gala. It was powered by Rift Shards, so any time I used it, it would eat through my stores; however, the benefit was supposed to be off the charts. Basically, it hooked into my interface and read my skills. Once it did, it would create a course of Mist constructs designed to push me to my limits.

I was more than a little eager to test it out, but first, I needed to get a good workout in. So, I headed into one of the corners, where I found a small bathroom. After ducking inside, I quickly changed into my M11 infiltration suit. The first time I'd tried it on, I had been more than a little self-conscious about how it fit me like a second skin. The tight black material that made up the inner layer left almost nothing to the imagination.

Thin but hard pads covered my arms and legs, but my vitals were protected by slightly thicker armor. According to the manual, it would deflect pretty much any mundane weaponry. But it would only dissipate some of the force from anyone whose attacks were modified by skills. Still, it was far better than my usual tactic of running into battle wearing nothing but fatigues.

Besides, I had my subdermal Sheath for anything the M11 couldn't stop. It wasn't nearly as impenetrable as some of the heavier armors, but it made up for it by being a far higher grade than almost anything else I could have bought. In addition, it was repairable via a simple Mist injection, which, given how often I seemed to get shot, was probably a good thing. After all, it wasn't like I intended to slow down. If anything, the future would probably see me in even more dangerous situations. Hopefully, the combination of the M11 and the subdermal Sheath would serve to mitigate some of that damage.

The good thing was that if I didn't see the Sheath listed on my interface, I never would've even known it was there. As far as I could tell, it hadn't affected my agility at all, which was one of the biggest reasons I had chosen it.

I retrieved my nano-bladed sword from my arsenal implant and placed it onto my back. The M11 automatically grabbed it, securing it into place. My dagger came next, which I clipped to my waist. Finally, Ferdinand II found a home in a holster on the other hip.

It wasn't ideal, but given that my arsenal implant only held four quick-access weapon slots, it was necessary. After all, my other slots were occupied by my Pulsar sniper rifle, my R-14 assault rifle, the scattergun, and my heavy weapon, the BMAP. I'd briefly considered throwing the BMAP into the part of my arsenal implant usually reserved for supplies and ammunition, but I figured Ferdinand II shouldn't be that difficult to draw from the hip. Besides, I liked the comforting weight.

Once I made sure that all my weapons were loaded with practice ammo—the last thing I wanted was to blow a hole in my new training hall and bring the building down on my head—I stepped out of the bathroom and readied myself for a training session. Before I did that, though, I wanted to check my status. It had been a while, and I thought it might inform my training regimen if I used it as a baseline so I could compare later.

To that end, I focused on my overall status:

NAME	Mirabelle Lisa Braddock		
CLASS	MISTRUNNER		
LEVEL	10 (4%)		
CONSTITUTION	41/80		
MIND	38/80		
MIST	37/80		
SKILLS	7/7		
SKILL NAME	Skill Tier	Modifiers	Abilities
CYBERNETIC MASTERY	Tier 1 (5%)	100% Efficiency	6 Cybernetic Slots

COMBAT	Tier 1 (13%)	+50% Damage (All) +50% Speed (Melee) +50% Accuracy (All) +25% Range (Firearms) +50% Reload Speed (Firearms)	Empowered Shot (D) Double Shot (E) Combination Punch (D) Pummel (E) Engage (E) Disengage (F) Mark Target (F) Barrage (F)
INFILTRATION	Tier 1 (8%)	+15% Effectiveness (Stealth)	Stealth (E) Camouflage (E) Deception (E) Mimic (E) Observation (D)
MISTRUNNER	Tier 1 (3%)	+25% Speed (Misthack) +25% Processing Speed (Mistwalk) +50% Strength (Mistwall) +50% Breach Range	Mistwalk (D) Misthack (D) Mistwall (C) System Redirect (F) Disable Cybernetics (F) Overcharge (E)
FIELDCRAFT	Tier 1 (8%)	+25% Combat Effectiveness	Triage (D) Basic Explosives Handling (D) Combat Focus (C) Pain Tolerance (D) Resistance (E) Foraging (E) Improvisation (D) Regeneration (D)
DEMOLITION	Tier 1 (0%)	+15% Explosive Radius +5% Explosive Strength	Blast Shield (E)
ACROBATICS	Tier 1 (1%)	+35% Proprioception	Balance (E)

None of my skills had taken any huge jumps since the last time I'd checked, but that was expected, given that I hadn't really done anything. My surveillance activities and constant use of Mimic had progressed [Infiltration] a little, but the gains were negligible almost everywhere else. However, I had gotten a point in both the Mind and the Mist attributes, which was a nice surprise, especially when I wasn't actively training.

The biggest shock, though, was that my newest skills had come with powerful modifiers as well as abilities. Even at only Tier 1, [Demolition] modified my explosives by a significant amount. I hadn't had the opportunity to try any of it out yet, but I knew that the modifiers were strong. On top of that, I'd gotten an ability called Blast Shield.

Blast Shield (E)—Halve the damage you receive from your own explosions. Reduce the effect of others' explosions on your body by 10%.

Given that part of my kit was a gun that shot what amounted to miniature warheads, it wasn't difficult to see how necessary the new ability was for my future. Obviously, I wouldn't go setting off explosions at my feet or anything, but it was nice to know that I could still use the BMAP in an enclosed space without blowing myself up. Of course, according to Gala, doing that would probably bring a building down on top of me, so I'd definitely only use that as a last resort.

In any case, I moved on to [Acrobatics], which increased my proprioception by a flat thirty-five percent. I'd already seen some of the benefits, and I had to admit that I was pretty excited about the skill's future. Not only did I have unprecedented control over my body, but I felt like I could do gymnastics across a tightrope. I hoped that the obstacle course would put it to the test. If the skill had only come with the modifier, I'd have probably counted it as a win, but it had also come with an ability:

Balance (E)—For ten (10) seconds, increase your balance by 300%.

I'd already tried the ability out, and though it was powerful, I knew it was also extremely dangerous. The ability was Mist hungry, so over the ten seconds it was active, it drained over half of my Mist reserves. Normally, I didn't use that many abilities, and I rarely ran low on Mist. However, as my skills grew more advanced, I knew that would change. Balance was a hint of what the future held, and I needed to get used to keeping an eye on my Mist usage. To that end, I'd adjusted my HUD to give me a simple indicator of how much I had remaining, which I'd tucked away in the corner next to the icons meant to represent the weapons in my arsenal implant.

My other skills hadn't seen much in the way of increases, so I decided not to look at my skill trees. Perhaps I'd have something to admire in a few weeks, but for now, I needed to get down to the business of training.

Without any further hesitation, I clapped the manacles around my wrists, and immediately, I was beset by a sense of weakness. Suddenly, the weapons at my hips and the one on my back felt like deadweight. But that was as expected. The restraints cut my Constitution attribute down to only a few points, so I was even weaker than I'd been before my Awakening. Which was precisely the point. I wanted—no, I needed to push myself. Anything less than extreme measures would feel like I was cheating.

Briefly, I considered removing the weapons, at least for the first few times. But I'd gone so long relying on my arsenal implant, and I needed to grow accustomed to them being there. The last thing I needed was to have the hilt of my sword snag on something in the middle of a fight.

After stretching a little, I began a modified version of the physical training program I'd used back in Mobile. It was a high-tempo combination of running, doing calisthenics, and lifting weights, and after an hour of that, I felt like I'd been working out all day. That was the effect of the manacles, I was certain. Every minute would equate to ten, so long as I pushed myself to my limits.

Once I finished that portion, I set in on the obstacle course. And I was sorely disappointed with my performance. I'd had no idea how much I had been depending on my attributes to see me through. Even back in Mobile, when Nora had taken over my training, the manacles I'd used at that time were only a third as strong as the ones I now wore. So, it was all I could do to finish the course a single time. Each obstacle took me a subjective eternity to overcome. By the time I finished, I was drenched in sweat, and all I wanted was to lie down and rest.

But I kept going.

This time, I removed the manacles—I couldn't even use my weapons with deflated attributes—and set about completing the training program set by the artificial intelligence I'd bought. And it was grueling. Not as difficult as when my uncle had personally curated my training, but it was still difficult enough that, by the time I headed back upstairs, I was in a terrible mood.

It felt like I'd backslid. That was unacceptable, and I resolved to right the ship over the next few weeks.

When I got back upstairs, I found that Patrick was still engaged in learning the material given to him by Dr. Montague. So, as I flopped down on the couch, I got his attention and said, "We need to talk."

His eyes immediately found my skintight suit, which I studiously ignored. I didn't hate that he looked, even if it made me feel a little self-conscious. Okay, very self-conscious. I couldn't help but wonder if he liked what he saw. Perhaps

I could get him a matching suit so I could ogle him for a few minutes. That would put him in his place, wouldn't it?

"What's up?" Patrick asked.

"We need money," I said.

"Already? I thought you were, like, a millionaire."

"I was a millionaire. All this new stuff didn't come cheap" was my response. "So, I was thinking about my mission when I realized the answer was right in front of me. Nora took over the Specters, right? Well, I'd already planned to destabilize the tribe, but what if I just . . . hijacked and robbed them? There's money there. It won't be a ton, but it might be enough to keep the operation running."

"Okay? But what happens once we take her down?" he asked. "I know you talked about going after the other people involved, but as far as you've said, those are all superrich assholes in King's Row. Which we can't even get into, by the way."

"I don't know," I said. "I'm working on it. But there's a chance that we're going to have to leave Nova if we want to make any real money. Maybe I can find another Rift or something. The last one almost killed me, but I made millions off of it."

"Maybe," he responded, though I could tell he was less than enthusiastic about the prospect. "But what about the future? What are we going to do when the aliens come?"

"I . . . I don't know," I admitted. "But for right now, I want to take things one step at a time. Otherwise, we'll get lost."

"I guess that makes sense."

"It's okay if you don't like my plans, you know," I said. "That's the whole reason I wanted to talk. If you see anything wrong with what I want to do, I need you to let me know. Poke holes in my plans if you can. I'm not so fragile that I can't take criticism."

"Are you sure?" he asked.

"I'm sure."

"Okay, then your plan is stupid," he said. "Leaving Nova is a huge mistake. Every time you come in and out of the city, you're going to draw attention. And if someone realizes who you are, it's game over for us. So, unless you can guarantee a way back in where you don't trip every alarm in the city, it's better to just make do with what we can get while we focus on the actual mission."

"Wow, tell me how you really feel . . ."

He swallowed hard. "I'm not trying to be a jerk," he said. "I just know how hard it is to get in and out of these cities. The only reason we got in last time was because someone bribed one of those Enforcers at the gate. Otherwise, we'd have been scanned. And believe me, those scanners are powerful enough that they'd have cut right through both of our skills."

What he said made sense, but I was still a little annoyed. After all, the Rifts were ripe for the harvest. I just had to hit one, mine a few Shards, and I wouldn't have to worry about money anymore. However, that plan also came with a few issues—aside from Patrick's reservations. First, I had no idea where to even find another Rift. The one I'd delved before had closed right after I'd finished it. So, I couldn't go back there. And it wasn't as if there were maps. Second, I hadn't been exaggerating when I'd said the other one almost killed me. The fact that I'd kept going had been stupid and reckless, but I'd been so hell-bent on accomplishing my mission—and impressing my uncle—that I'd never truly considered abandoning it.

"Fine," I said. "We'll just make do."

After that, I told Patrick that I intended to head back to my perch so I could continue my surveillance. I needed to know everything there was to know about Nora's activities. And when the time was right, I would strike. Until then, I had plenty to keep me busy.

CHAPTER SIXTEEN

ELYSIUM

I never meant to hurt so many people, but any road to true power is littered with the corpses of the innocent. Jeremiah always said as much, but I never really believed him. I considered myself a good person, after all. I wouldn't be like him. I wouldn't sacrifice everyone for some personal vendetta. But that was then, and this is now. We're all destined to repeat the mistakes of our mentors.

—Nora Lancaster

I followed the two men, my feet silent and my presence muted by Stealth. It wasn't a perfect ability; if I moved too quickly or ran into something solid, I'd quickly be found out. But I'd been trained by some of the best, and I kept a constant watch on my surroundings. It helped that the two mooks—both members of my uncle's old tribe, though I didn't recognize either of them—were careless and inattentive. In their territory, they didn't have to look out for dangers, after all.

My uncle had built a strong organization, and even without his reputation hovering over them, they'd retained much of that power. As a result, they still controlled one of the biggest territories in the Garden. There were a half dozen other tribes that could boast a similar degree of influence, and even a few who towered over them, but in their territory, which ran from Sadie Street all the way to the edge of the platform, they were kings.

Of course, even kings could fall. History told us that much, at least. No one was invulnerable. I just had to wait for the right opportunity to make my mark.

My surveillance had been exhaustive, and over the past month, I'd mapped out most of the Specters' activities. From Nora herself, who rarely left the penthouse I'd once called home, to the street-level Operators who were the backbone of the organization, I had categorized their activities down to the finest detail.

And I was a little disappointed at how well things were being run.

Not that it was much of a surprise, really. Nora had always been competent, and once she'd stepped out of my uncle's shadow, that ability had been allowed to shine. If she hadn't been the person most responsible for my uncle's demise and the destruction of Mobile, I might've even been proud of her. As it was, though, I kept reminding myself just how much I hated her.

Sure, she probably had her reasons for betraying Jeremiah, but in the face of my grief, those excuses mattered very little. In short, I just didn't care. I had my mission, and nothing could derail my pursuit of vengeance.

Which was how I found myself following a pair of Nora's most inept mooks. They were low-level couriers tasked with delivering a package into another territory. I had no idea what was in that package, just that it was important enough to warrant a shadow.

I glanced at a hover van nearby, and I felt the Mist swirling around it. More, I could sense the connection between it and one of the men I'd been following. That surveillance van complicated things. I knew from previous experience, back when Jeremiah had been running things, that it was packed full of strong Operators armed with advanced weaponry. If there was even a hint of things going wrong, they'd flood out of the van and solve the problem. Viciously, and with the kind of extreme prejudice that would make an Enforcer proud.

Once, I had seen the aftermath of such an event. It had been an arms deal gone wrong, and the support team had reduced the entire area to little more than rubble. That portion of Algiers still hadn't been rebuilt because the supports were unstable. Such was the power they could bring to bear.

Maybe I could defeat them, but to what end? I didn't want to alarm Nora. Nor did I want to turn the Garden into a war zone. Not yet, at least. No—I had something else in mind. Something that would cause a lot more problems than a few dead mooks in an organization with a population numbering in the thousands.

So, I continued to follow the two men, well aware that the black hover van was only a couple of blocks behind me. All around, the glimmering lights of the Garden's trademark holographic displays lit the night, but I ignored them as I trailed after the pair of mooks. The two Specters looked nervous, like they knew precisely how valuable their cargo was. Likely, they were aware that they were being used as bait, too. After all, why hunt your enemies when you could coax them from the shadows?

Nora's organization obviously wanted the deal to go off without a hitch, but if it didn't, they could still come out as winners, so long as they could rid the

Garden of a few of their competitors. In that way, the support team could play the dual roles of both protector and avenger, depending on the circumstance.

But they couldn't account for me or my plan.

Slowly, we approached their destination, Bourbon Street. It didn't come as a surprise. During my reconnaissance, I'd discovered the details of the meeting, so I'd mentally prepared myself for the infamous area. The name was a bit of a misnomer because it encompassed multiple streets and spanned quite a few blocks' worth of territory. Instead of towering megabuildings, it was comprised of casinos, brothels, strip clubs, and dens of iniquity that could cater to just about any vice known to man. If the Garden was known for its holographic signs and blinking lights, then Bourbon Street was the purest form of that expression. Everywhere I looked were layer upon layer of the lights and displays, each one going past sexually suggestive and into downright pornographic.

The people were an equally interesting cross section. As was the case anywhere else in the Garden, there were plenty of Operators, but many of them swaggered around in a drunken stupor. Fights were almost as common as men and women engaged in various sexual acts. On Bourbon Street, shame and modesty were entirely alien concepts. The revealing attire favored by most of the patrons was further evidence that the area was just different. I'd never seen so much skin, and there were quite a few people walking around almost entirely naked. I could feel the heat rising in my cheeks as I stared at a particularly chiseled man being led along at the end of an actual leash.

I jerked my attention away and refocused on the mission. Thankfully, the two mooks had gotten a little sidetracked in their own task and currently had their noses pressed against a window as they watched a mostly naked woman twirling around a pole. After a few seconds, the screen went black, and a holographic display told them that if they wanted to see more, they'd have to come inside and pay the price.

The two Operators scoffed at that and wasted no more time before moving on. I followed dutifully, glad that nobody had noticed me. It wasn't that I wasn't curious about the infamous area, but as inexperienced as I was, it almost felt like I was drowning in a sea of nudity, sex, and fetishes. It didn't take long before I realized that I needed to walk before I even attempted to run.

Of course, I knew that it was yet another distraction meant to pull people's attention from how terrible their lives really were. Another drug to keep them placid and controlled. In that respect, Bourbon Street was no different than dust or the entertainment feeds. Or those pornographic chips that people like Squirrel seemed to like so much.

Even more, I knew that beneath the glitz and glamour of the holographic signs and perfect bodies of the ubiquitous prostitutes and entertainers was a level of oppression that was even more insidious than what was present in the rest of Nova City. How many of those perfect-looking men and women had been forced into their lives, either by circumstances or slave implants? How many of them had been pushed into taking the skills necessary for such a profession?

My stomach twisted into knots as I realized that it probably wasn't much different from the Rift-mining operation I'd dismantled back in the Dead Zone. It was one thing when the aliens were the ones who did it; I had no idea what kind of perspective drove them, and it was entirely possible that they saw us as animals in need of herding. But humans doing it to humans? That was infinitely worse.

I forced those thoughts to the back of my mind as I continued to follow the men, and I was unsurprised to see them turning a corner and heading toward what looked like a church. It had a tall steeple flanked by two smaller ones, with a plethora of arched windows and a couple of small domes in the back. In each of the arched windows were holograms depicting various dancing men and women, all of whom were as close to nude as they could be without actually being naked. The building was, I knew, a recreation of an old cathedral from the destroyed New Orleans, but its name was lost to history. My uncle probably would have known, but to the residents of Nova City, it was simply called Elysium.

Everyone in the Garden knew of Elysium. The club was neutral ground, protected by treaties as well as a veritable army of high-tiered security Operators. It was where the city's elites peacefully hashed out their differences.

And it represented my first real roadblock.

However, my preparations had been extensive, so once I was free of prying eyes, I let Stealth drop. With Mimic active, I'd adopted a well-selected persona as a Tier 3 Operator named Azalea. She was a little taller than me, but we shared a similar build. In addition, she wasn't equipped with any cybernetics. The similarities meant that Mimic didn't have to work quite as hard, and while I didn't think I'd soon run low on Mist, I didn't want to waste it when it wasn't necessary.

Most importantly, Azalea—who, by now, had probably been eaten by one of the alligators in the swamp below the city—enjoyed VIP access to Elysium. A good thing because, passing through its doors, I felt a slight tingle that I knew from experience would deactivate any stealth or camouflage abilities. Mimic was unaffected, though, so my disguise remained intact.

Like that, I stepped inside one of the most infamous places in Nova City. I ignored the trio of guards near the door, and once they saw the pendant I wore around my neck, their attention shifted to the other entrants. The pendant itself wasn't anything special—just a cross wrapped in silver wire—but it marked me as a VIP.

Elysium's lobby was a study in contrasts. The decor was decidedly classy, with high, vaulted ceilings and elaborate marble statues depicting perfectly proportioned people. However, everything else painted a wholly different picture. The thump of dance music rattled the walls, and multicolored lights illuminated the area. But what really sold the contrast were the people. Everyone was dressed in expensive clothing—the poor and destitute masses didn't get into Elysium, after all—but it all reminded me of my uncle's old territory. The people of his tribe had some money, but they spent it on the most frivolous things. Like leopard-print couches. Golden statues. Or sound systems that were clearly far too large for the confines of one of the megabuilding's cheaply appointed apartments. The same could be said for Elysium's patrons. I saw quite a few fur coats over otherwise naked torsos, plenty of faux-leather pants, and more jewelry than I'd seen in my entire lifetime. Metal glinted where teeth should be, and cybernetics gleamed like they'd just been polished.

I was reminded of my uncle's categorization of his people as ghetto rich. They had money, but they weren't wealthy, and they'd gone a little wild with their expenditures, like if you gave a child unfettered access to a candy shop. It was inevitable that they'd overdo it.

He had also gone on to explain that it wasn't their fault before going on a rant about generational wealth that ended with him cursing the people in charge of the city, but that wasn't that uncommon for him. Usually, Jeremiah had been a man of few words, but when he got worked up, he'd go on some truly epic rants.

I crossed the Elysium lobby, following the two mooks as surreptitiously as I could manage. However, when they went into the next area, which was a bar lined with private booths, I turned in the opposite direction. I knew where they were going, and it was impossible for me to follow. Not directly, at least.

Instead, I headed deeper into the club and, after skirting the huge dance floor in the next room, found my way to a set of stairs. They were guarded by one of Elysium's security personnel. I leaned against one of the walls and, as I looked out over the dance floor, activated Misthack. Once I found a likely victim in a great, hulking bastard with a pair of exposed cybernetic arms plated in gold, I bypassed his laughable security and uploaded a Ghost I'd been working on for the past few days.

After that, I only had to wait a few seconds before it took effect. The Ghost itself was mostly harmless, but it was designed to hijack a person's interface with the purpose of altering their brain chemistry in order to increase aggression. I called it *Rage*, and the few times I'd tested it out, it had definitely lived up to its name. This instance was no different.

As I waited for the Ghost to take effect, I deactivated the various cameras in the room. There were also a few autoturrets, so I put them to sleep, as well.

By the time I finished, *Rage* had done its thing, and the man had already gotten into a shoving match with another dancer. The other mook was busy trying to deescalate the situation, but Big Boy wasn't having it. With how much adrenaline he had coursing through his veins, it wasn't a surprise when the altercation became a full-on brawl. Predictably, the man who was guarding the stairs raced in to break it up, and I used that distraction to slip into the stairwell.

Thankfully, no one else had taken the stairs, so I didn't run into anyone as I climbed to the next floor, which contained more private rooms. Most of them were occupied, but as curious as I was about what was going on in there—whether they were home to illicit deals between rival tribes, private parties, or orgies—I wasn't there for them. Besides, I was on a schedule. So, I hurried through the halls wearing a haughty expression so none of the other passersby would bother me. Eventually, I found my destination, and after looking around, I knelt down, grabbing the panel I knew would be there.

It had cost me quite a bit of my remaining fortune to acquire detailed schematics of Elysium, but it had paid dividends when I'd discovered that it was riddled with secret passageways. Given the nature of the club, it wasn't a surprise, and more importantly, possession of those schematics allowed me to easily map out an appropriate route to my true goal.

Once I removed the panel, a small passage was revealed. It would require me to crawl, but I could easily fit. So, I slid inside, replacing the panel on my way. After that, I slowly followed my plans and found my way to the private room occupied by the two mooks I'd been following.

It was at that point I realized that I probably hadn't needed to follow them at all. I could have just posted up in the passage and waited on them to arrive. It would have been uncomfortable, but I could have dealt with that. Letting out a slight sigh, I shook my head and resolved to plan better in the future. I knew I couldn't think of everything, but I needed to be more thorough if I was ever going to accomplish my goals.

The corridor in which I'd positioned myself was little bigger than a ventilation shaft, but I knew it had a more nefarious purpose. The owner of Elysium—a man by the name of Clyde Baxter—had clearly built it so that he could spy on his patrons. To that end, the ceiling of each of the private rooms had a cleverly concealed hatch that functioned similarly to a two-way mirror. I could see down into the room—and more importantly, hear everything that was said—but when they looked up, they'd just see a coffered ceiling in gold and black. It was an ingenious design, and I wanted a similar setup in my base.

I passed quite a few rooms—in which there were various dealings, including yet more people having drunken or otherwise inebriated sex—but I ignored them. Instead, I kept going until I found my two mooks. It was just in time, too, because only a couple of minutes later—during which I preemptively broke through their defenses—another trio of two men and a woman entered the room.

Immediately, I identified them as Cyberdogs. No other tribe in Nova City wore their cybernetics with quite as much pride. One of them had even replaced much of his face with an unmoving chrome visage. Whatever their appearances, their presence was a perfect setup for my plan.

After exchanging greetings, the man with the metal face said, "You got the package?"

One of Nora's mooks slapped the case at his feet, answering, "Right here, chief. You got the—"

I didn't let him finish. Instead, I activated my Ghost, which I'd chosen to call *Tranquilizer*, and the two Specters immediately passed out. Chrome Dome—yes, I know that's not very creative, but I'll stand by it—reacted without hesitation, barking, "What the—"

I never let him finish, dropping through the panel. As I fell, I aimed a specially bought pistol at his head and squeezed the trigger. Once. Twice. Three times. Apparently, the metal wasn't bulletproof. Or even bullet resistant. Because it exploded in an eruption of metal, flesh, bone, and brains. In the space of a second, I'd put his two subordinates down, as well.

They slumped to the ground, but I didn't bother looting them. Instead, I bent down, putting the pistol in the first mook's hand before leaping back to the passage above. I climbed through, and once I was out of sight, I reactivated the camera I'd hacked right before my descent. Then, I retreated the way I'd come, finding no impediments on my way back to the dance floor.

On my way out, I saw a group of Cyberdogs—all high-tiered Operators—running into the club. I had to suppress a grin.

Finally, I'd started my private war, and nobody but me knew that the battle had even begun.

CHAPTER SEVENTEEN

AFTERMATH

I was always meant to be in charge. Even Jeremiah could see that. That's why he gave me as much authority as he did. But it was a backhanded thing, and I eventually saw becoming his second-in-command as the insult it was.

—Nora Lancaster

I couldn't keep the smile from my face as I left Elysium behind. With Observation pushing my senses, I could hear the panic in the club building to a crescendo. The bodies had been discovered, and hopefully, the deaths would be pinned on Nora's people. It wouldn't be enough to ignite a war, but it was only the first step in my plan. If things went well, it wouldn't be long before the Specters started to feel the pressure from the Garden's other dominant tribes.

I barely noticed the promiscuity of Bourbon Street's patrons and the sex workers who catered to them. Certainly, a few sights caught my eye, but it didn't take much willpower to jerk my attention back to what was important. I'd gotten out of Elysium unscathed and unnoticed, but I wasn't so foolish as to let my guard down until I was safe in my own compound. To that end, I slowly made my way through the borough, careful not to go too quickly, lest I look out of place. I even stopped a few times to ogle some men and women who were putting on a show in the windows of the various brothels; after all, while I might have been unused to such sights, the woman whose identity I had taken was not. And there was only one reason people came to Bourbon Street.

Still, I didn't linger for long, and eventually, I continued on my way. However, I almost stumbled when I recognized one of the women dancing in another nearby window. Heather looked as perfectly proportioned as ever, but having known her for years, it didn't take me long to notice the slight bags beneath her eyes, the drugged expression on her face, or the mechanical way she twirled around the pole.

Gone was the warm, loving aura of the woman I knew. Instead, she was just like all the others. Sure, there were plenty of men and women who enjoyed sex work. I knew that, even if I didn't quite understand it. However, there were far more who'd had it forced upon them, either by circumstance or more nefarious means. Heather clearly belonged to that second group, judging by her demeanor.

Most of the men surrounding her window didn't see it, but that was probably because they didn't want to infect their good times with an admission of the real cost of getting their thrills. Some of the women looked a little more sympathetic, but that might've been my own biases making themselves known. After all, if they objected to what they were seeing, they wouldn't have had their noses pressed to the glass. They wouldn't have been scurrying to get inside the brothel to hire Heather for a few minutes of fun.

I was already disgusted by much of what I'd seen on Bourbon Street, but seeing someone I knew being so thoroughly degraded only made things worse. There was a part of me that wanted to march into the brothel and rescue her. The place was named Heaven and Hell, as evidenced by the sign flashing above the door; it depicted a naked woman with angel wings on one side and a similarly beautiful woman with demon horns on the other. But going by what I saw from Heather, there was nothing heavenly about the brothel.

As much as I wanted to do something, I stopped myself. I wasn't some knight in shining armor, was I? And as far as I knew, she wasn't a damsel in distress. Perhaps she wanted to be there, and my impression of her expression was completely fabricated by my own biased mind. But even as that thought flitted across my brain, I knew it wasn't true. I knew Heather, and I could recognize that she'd been beaten down by the system. After all, that was what it had been designed to do.

I had no idea if she had a slave implant or if she had just been out of options after my uncle died, but it broke my heart to see her like that. Thankfully, her dance quickly ended, and she was replaced by another dead-eyed stripper—this one male. With a shake of my head, I marked the location in my mind. I couldn't help Heather right then, but I'd be back once things settled down.

Almost as if the world wanted to punctuate the thought, I noticed a few Cyberdogs rush through the crowd, and a moment later, gunshots rang through the night air. That was my cue to head out, and thankfully, I now had an excuse to make haste. Gunfights weren't exactly uncommon in the Garden—or the rest of Nova City, come to that—but it would take a real fool to stand around and spectate. So, Bourbon Street's visitors wasted no time in surging toward the edges of the borough as they looked to escape the impending carnage.

I followed the flow of the crowd, using my high Constitution and the enhanced proprioception that had come with [Acrobatics] to keep from being bowled over. Eventually, I reached one of the side streets that led away from the area. I ducked out of the main flow of pedestrians and, after sliding behind a dumpster, activated Stealth. Only then did I let myself relax.

I hadn't escaped—not exactly—but I had confidence in my abilities. With Stealth active, I didn't think I'd be discovered by some random mook. Of course, I was well aware that the ability wasn't infallible. It had failed before, and I knew it would fail again. However, if it came down to a fight, I had plenty of tools at my disposal.

After taking a few deep breaths, I followed the side street until I was well and truly out of Bourbon Street. A few scattered pedestrians passed me by, but they were easy enough to avoid, and I quickly found my way into the parking structure of a megabuilding, where I summoned my disguised Cutter and set off back to my headquarters in Algiers. Along the way, I saw a few fights between the Specters, identifiable by the blue armbands they habitually wore, and groups of Cyberdogs, which told me that news of what had happened in Elysium had already begun to spread. Still, a few fights weren't the war I wanted to start, so I knew I had plenty of work cut out for me. Even so, it was gratifying to see such quick results, even if I knew the tension would die down in a few days.

It took me almost an hour to reach Algiers, mostly because the streets were clogged with traffic. A few of them were even closed altogether as some of the fights that had broken out had drawn the attention of the Enforcers. Their response was as ruthless as it was effective.

The worst of it was when a group of Enforcers—at least a dozen of them—had subdued a much larger group of Cyberdogs and Specters, disarming and taking them prisoner. However, instead of arresting them, the Enforcers had lined them all up and executed them. When I passed them by, the Enforcers were laughing and chatting like it wasn't anything out of the ordinary.

Of course, I knew they acted that way because, for them, it was just another Friday night. It would have been so easy to just end them all, right then and there. They didn't even know I was there, much less how much firepower I could bring to bear. I could pull out the BMAP and just go to work. I had yet to really use it at full power; instead, I'd been limited to practice ammunition. But if what Gala had claimed was true, I could've wiped them from the face of the city with no more than a few shots.

Or, if I wanted to savor it, I could have used the Pulsar, my sniper rifle. Even Ferdinand II was on the table. The only strategy I wouldn't be comfortable using was to just attack them in melee, but even that might've been fine, considering the protection provided by my subdermal Sheath and my M11 infiltration suit. I hadn't put my defenses to the test, but I felt pretty confident that they would see me through.

With a little focus, I pushed those ideas out of my mind. It wasn't time to go all out. Besides, that platoon of Enforcers was only the tip of the iceberg. In minutes, they could have ten times as many fighters on the ground, and I wasn't so naive that I thought such a response wouldn't include a few real elites. I wasn't ready for that.

So, I kept going, ignoring the carnage all around me. However, I was a little distressed when I saw that the ramp down into Algiers was blocked off by a barricade of Enforcers. The barricade itself consisted of four personnel carriers stretching from end to end across the highway, meant to funnel any traffic into a small gap.

Each of the Enforcers was well armed with assault rifles and their standard-issue black-and-white body armor. One of the women wore a pair of green goggles that I knew were meant to see through abilities and skills like my Stealth or Mimic. And while I was fairly confident in Mimic's strength, I wasn't willing to put that to the test. For all I knew, that was alien tech on par with my weaponry, and I would have been stupid to chance it.

Shaking my head, I guided the hover bike around a corner and made my way to the second ramp, but I was unsurprised to discover that a similar barricade had been put into place. The third and final ramp was no different, which put me in a tight spot. As far as I could tell, I had three options.

First, I could go in, guns blazing, and force my way through. That had the added bonus of letting me kill quite a few Enforcers. More, it would be a black mark on the public's perception of their absolute authority. Enough of those, and people would stop listening when the Enforcers gave them orders. After all, as Jeremiah always said, strength was about perception. And that adage was even more true for the Enforcers, whose numbers were propped up by unremarkable Tier 2 and 3 fighters. Only the elites could boast more power, but those couldn't be everywhere all at once.

However, that strategy would also mean me stepping out of the shadows. Killing a few people here and there wasn't enough to gain even a modicum of attention in Nova City, but breaking through an Enforcer barricade? That would be different, and it wouldn't take long for them to start hunting me.

At that moment, my greatest strength was anonymity. Even if the Enforcers knew I existed, there was no reason for them to suspect that I was in the city. And showing them otherwise was a good way to get killed.

Or captured.

I didn't want either, so I moved on to the second option. I could just try to sneak through, relying on Mimic to keep my true identity hidden. I was still wearing the face of Azalea, the woman I'd killed for the Elysium VIP pendant, and I could easily change that by stealing someone else's identity. But what if the ability was insufficient? Then, I'd be back to option one, though with the added detriment of revealing one of my secrets.

That pushed me to the third option. Lying low for a couple of days. As much as I didn't want to do that, I was beginning to think that I didn't have much in the way of a choice. So, I turned the bike around and retreated farther into the Garden.

But I was distressed to find that things had just gotten worse. The Garden had broken out into a hundred small battles, each more vicious than the last. How close to boiling over had the tensions in the area really been, if my actions had sparked such a reaction? There was no way that I was completely responsible; something else was obviously at play.

I pushed past those questions, and as I traversed the district, I did my best to avoid the various battles. It wasn't easy, and it was slow going, but that allowed me to formulate a plan. So, I quickly made my way back to one of my old haunts on the edge of the district and soon descended beneath the surface of the city. Before long, I found myself in the familiar confines of the old, abandoned cistern I'd used as my temporary home before my Awakening.

I was unsurprised to find that it was little different from when I'd left. The sparse furniture I'd lugged down into the cistern was mostly rotted away by the dense humidity, but it was otherwise unchanged. Even the power coupling I'd used to gain access to the city's intranet was still there, though I didn't dare use it.

After all, I knew just how easy it was to track someone like that. No—it was better if I limited my contact with Nova City's intranet as much as possible.

I did chance a simple message to Patrick, though. It didn't contain any sensitive information, but I wanted to let him know that I was okay. With that done, I settled down to wait things out.

For three days, I remained in that cistern. Periodically, I'd head topside to investigate things, but the Enforcer presence only grew more pronounced—until, on the fourth day, they were just gone. Likely, they'd accomplished their goals and gone back to wherever they were headquartered. If I had to guess, the whole thing was just an excuse to show the Nova City citizens who was really in charge, but there was no way I could know for sure. It was just as likely that the wrong person had been slumming it on Bourbon Street, and they'd gotten killed. If it was one of the aristocrats from King's Row—or worse, someone deemed important by the city's ruling council—such a response from the Enforcers would make sense.

Not that it mattered to me, of course. Eventually, they'd all get theirs. I was just getting started, and by the time I was finished, none of that power structure would remain. But for now, I had to keep low.

Once I emerged from the cistern, I decided to chance a little surveillance. It'd been a while since I'd looked in on Nora, and I was eager to see what kind of response my actions had provoked. So, I soon found my way to her megabuilding. I had no intention of heading up to the penthouse, but I didn't really have to, either. Instead, my goal was a certain security terminal in an out-of-the-way corner of the building. I knew from experience that nobody who didn't need to went down there, so I would have plenty of opportunity to Mistwalk into the terminal's system and use it to surveil Nora's penthouse.

There were safeguards in place that were meant to stop such an intrusion, but they wouldn't be difficult to overcome for a true {Mistrunner} like me.

And as it turned out, the so-called security measures were even easier to bypass than I had expected. Likely, when my uncle had had them installed, he'd never envisioned a situation where he'd be targeted by someone like me. And even if he had been, he wasn't exactly the sort of guy who flew under the radar. If someone knew his plans and used that information to attack him, he'd just overcome the odds with sheer strength. It was the prerogative of a man who'd been at the top for so long that he had forgotten the value of subtlety.

Whatever the case, I'd soon infiltrated the system and used my access to take control of the cameras in Nora's penthouse. As the camera feeds were routed to my HUD, I felt a surge of anger; there Nora was, sitting on what had once been my couch. More, there were a few men and women I recognized sitting across from her.

First was Wash, an Operator who specialized in thievery. He was a short, barrel-chested man who was rumored to be one of the best burglars in the city. I'd never gotten to know him well because my uncle had only met with him on special occasions.

Second was Echo. She was more familiar to me because she had helped Jeremiah with the logistical side of running the tribe. He'd often said that without her, he could never have done anything. Tall and thin, with jet-black hair, she wasn't a combatant. Still, her sharp mind and top-notch organizational skills made her a threat.

Finally, there was Ashleigh, a brutish fighter who eschewed Nora's bio-enhancements in favor of a slew of cybernetics. If she wasn't on the verge of reaching the Singularity, I didn't know who was, and her body was covered in red-painted mechanical parts. I knew she wasn't quite as dangerous as Nora—not in a physical confrontation, at least—but she didn't lag too far behind.

That they were all there told me that the conspiracy to betray Jeremiah had been more widespread than I'd originally thought. It wasn't unexpected, though. I knew that Nora couldn't have taken control of the Specters without significant support from the people my uncle had once depended on so heavily.

I focused on the feed and listened to the audio. At first, there was nothing of real interest, but that was how most reconnaissance went. Hours of boredom for a kernel of relevant information. I didn't mind, though. I was used to it. And sequestered in one of the most secluded places in the building, I didn't think I had much chance of discovery. Besides, I had Stealth active; if anyone did decide to come by, I was well hidden.

Eventually, Nora broached the subject I'd been waiting for when she asked, "Do we know exactly what happened in Elysium yet?"

Echo shook her head. "Brock and Purnell maintained the same story," she said. "One moment, they were sitting in the private room, and the next, the representatives of the Cyberdogs were dead."

"What do you think happened?" asked Nora.

"Those idiots probably thought they could get one over on us," growled Asheligh, slapping one metal fist into a similarly metallic palm. "I told you we were losing control, but you said everything was fine. Let me whip 'em into shape, and I guarantee we'll be—"

"I disagree," Echo butted in. "It is far more likely we were set up."

"By some mystery person?" was Asheligh's dismissive response. "And how did they get away without anyone noticing, huh? More importantly, why would someone just leave the case? Do you know how much those chips were worth?"

"That's not the question we should be asking right now," interjected Wash. "What we need to know is what we're going to do now. The Cyberdogs are on the verge of declaring outright war."

"We can take them," Nora muttered.

"And? What about their allies?" asked Wash. "They're on good terms with half the other tribes in the Garden."

"I'll take care of it," Nora said. "I've got a meeting with Duke in a few days. We'll work it out. He doesn't want war any more than we do."

"Bad for business," Echo said.

But Asheligh shrugged her mechanical shoulders. "War sounds like a bit of fun to me," she said, but no one favored her with a response.

After that, they moved on to other matters. I kept listening until the end of the meeting, but I'd gotten what I needed. Nora and the Specters were on the back foot. My initial reaction was to simply sabotage her meeting with Duke, who was the leader of the Cyberdogs, but that was too straightforward to work the way I wanted it to. Still, it was nice to know that things were going according to plan.

Once the meeting broke up, I left the megabuilding and headed back to Algiers. Thankfully, the barricades that had guarded the ramps were gone, and my way was clear.

Or that's what I thought until pain exploded in my shoulder. I almost lost control of my bike as I skidded across the street and collided with the barrier meant to keep people from sliding off the side of the spiraling ramp, but I barely kept it on track. With my shoulder on fire, I glanced to my rear only to see a pair of Operators bearing down on me.

I had no idea who they were, and nothing I saw gave me a hint as to their identities. One thing was clear, though—they weren't there to take me prisoner.

CHAPTER EIGHTEEN

RUN AND GUN

When Jeremiah took Mira away, I got a taste of being in charge. When I spoke, people had to listen. I had the entire tribe at my disposal. However, it wasn't long until I realized how hollow my authority was. With Jeremiah looming over me, I would never be anything but an underling.

—Nora Lancaster

I leaned forward, accelerating as I descended along the curved ramp. The centrifugal force of my passage pressed against me, but I urged the hover bike to go faster as I wove in and out of the sparse traffic. I had no clue as to the identity of my attackers, but they were out for blood. More, they didn't seem to care who knew it or if any bystanders were hurt. Hammering that home, they continued to fire, their bullets filling the slower hover cars with holes. One—a small, compact thing that could only accommodate one passenger—slammed into the ramp's barricade, flipping over the rampart and sailing over the edge. Soon, it would find a home in the swamp below.

I pushed the bike to greater speeds, but I didn't leave them completely behind. I probably could have—after all, the Cutter was far and away more advanced than any other hover bike in the city—but I chose to string them along. In the past, I might've been worried about the bystanders who were caught between us, but those sorts of concerns had been discarded the moment I'd vowed my revenge. I knew there would be collateral damage, and I'd accepted it as the price of my vengeance.

Down and down we spiraled until, at last, I burst forth from the ramp and into Algiers. The streets were largely empty of other vehicles, but there were still plenty of other obstructions. Trash, discarded furniture, and the gutted skeletons of old hover cars abounded, but I deftly wove between them, maneuvering the hover bike with precision. My pursuers had little difficulty following, even taking the opportunity to aim a couple of extra shots at me.

They missed, the bullets thudding into a nearby derelict of a building, sending masonry and mortar misting into the air. I jerked the handlebars to the side, and the hover bike's inertia took it into a slide as I accelerated down another street, narrowly avoiding a pedestrian along the way. The gunmen followed, spraying more bullets in my direction and riddling that same pedestrian full of holes. I gritted my teeth in annoyance. I was willing to sacrifice innocents if it meant getting what I wanted, but what my pursuers were doing was just pointless.

I continued along, barreling through Algiers as I twisted and turned, always a single step ahead of them. Just far enough away that they couldn't reliably take me out, but not so far that they lost sight.

As I went, I rolled my shoulder. My Sheath, combined with the M11 infiltration suit, had prevented the bullet from penetrating, which meant that I'd only received a bruise. It was the first time I'd tested out my new defenses, and I had to admit that I was happy with their combined performance. Of course, I'd have preferred not to get shot at all, but if nothing else, my experiences had taught me that you couldn't always avoid danger. Sometimes, like was the case with the gunmen following me, it popped up out of nowhere. I could only prepare as best I could and hope it was enough to see me through.

In this instance, it was, but I knew that wouldn't always be true. I needed to continue my training and put myself so far ahead of my enemies that they couldn't dream of hurting me. But even that was a futile hope, given what had happened to my uncle. He'd been at the top of the mountain, and even he hadn't been untouchable. No one was.

Finally, after a few more minutes, I slowed my bike, letting my pursuers catch up. When they were in range, I leaped to my feet, balancing on the seat, and jumped toward one of the buildings that lined the street. As I did so, I dismissed the bike. Even as it dissipated into motes of Mist, I kicked off the building, drew my nano sword from the sheath on my back, and rocketed toward the first of the gunmen.

She was wearing a helmet, but judging by the skintight leather suit she wore, I could confidently say that she was female. It didn't matter, especially when my sword arced out. She tried to dodge by jerking the bike to the side, but she was too slow. The blade sliced through her neck without even a hint of resistance.

I hit the ground with a roll, drawing Ferdinand II from my hip as I found my feet. The other gunman had been lagging a bit behind the first, so he was just passing me by. I took aim and fired. Ferdinand II's issue took the hover bike in the Mist engine, and after a tiny series of subdued explosions that sounded like popping balloons, it slid out of control and into a wall. The rider was thrown free, and he went tumbling down the sidewalk until skidding to a stop twenty yards away.

I rolled my shoulders, holstering Ferdinand II and sheathing my blade in quick succession. Then, I drew my new rifle from my arsenal implant. The R-14's grip felt good in my hands as I brought the stock to my shoulder and advanced on the writhing man. He was tall—probably a few inches over six feet—and rangy. Wearing a leather jacket studded with metal rivets and a pair of ripped denim jeans, he looked little different from a thousand other Operators I'd seen in Nova City. I didn't see any visible cybernetics, but that didn't really tell me anything. After all, my own hand was indistinguishable from the real thing, and I knew it didn't cost that much to buy decent Realskin. So, I approached with caution, heel to toe, aiming down the sight, just like I'd been taught.

I needn't have bothered. When I reached the man and kicked him over onto his back, I saw that his face had taken the brunt of the impact. It looked like ground meat—bloody, raw, and hanging off his skull in ragged strips. The eye on that side of his face had been ripped free, and the other was wet with tears.

"Who are you?" I growled, stepping back so that he couldn't surprise me with a quick attack. I'd learned that lesson from one of the Amigos, and it wasn't one I would soon forget. "Why did you attack me?!"

He didn't answer, save for an agonized groan. I wasn't surprised. In addition to his shredded face, one of his shoulders had clearly been ripped out of its socket, and elsewhere on his body, there were bulges jutting out in all the wrong places and at all the wrong angles. I was no doctor, but it seemed that he'd suffered a series of compound fractures. Likely, he'd have to replace at least one leg with a cybernetic, lest he lose his mobility.

But that was assuming I let him live, which really wasn't in the cards. It was one thing to let some mook like the would-be slaver survive; it was something else entirely to leave an enemy like the gunman behind. After all, he'd already proven that he could get the drop on me, and if that bullet had been just a few inches up, he might've gotten me in the head, where all I had was my Sheath to protect me.

No—he was already dead. He just wasn't aware of it yet.

If I was going to get anything out of him, though, I was going to have to waste a few resources. So, I retrieved a med-hypo from my arsenal implant and, after kneeling next to him, jabbed it into his least injured arm. It discharged its payload with a pneumatic hiss, and the effect was almost immediate. As he visibly relaxed, I kept my weapon aimed at his head.

He coughed.

"Feeling better?" I asked nonchalantly.

"W-who are you . . . ?"

"You attacked me, remember?" I asked, but the question told me almost everything I needed to know. He had no idea who I was, which meant that he hadn't meant to attack me specifically. Instead, he and his partner had likely seen a lone woman on a hover bike and thought to take their chances. The attack had come when it had because the Enforcers had better things to do than worry about people in a place like Algiers. Or on the ramp leading down into the slum.

"I didn't mean . . . We didn't . . ."

He coughed again, and over the next few minutes, I got the story out of him. He was an unaffiliated Operator who was just trying to make a living. The fact that he had a hover bike of his own told me that he'd been moderately successful, too. Until he'd met me, of course.

After I'd gotten his story, I took aim with the R-14. It barked, and a moment later, his head exploded in a conflagration of superheated plasma that went on to tear an eight-inch-deep crater in the pavement below. The weapon was much more powerful than the Kicker had ever been, but that single shot had cost almost as much as an entire magazine of the Kicker's rounds.

I grimaced at the cost, but I knew it was unavoidable. These two mooks might have been low-level and comparatively powerless, but that wouldn't always be the case. After all, I'd already seen how ineffective my weaponry was against even a midtier Banshee. If I came up against someone with any real power or skill, I'd need all the advanced weapons I could get.

Shrugging, I set about looting the bodies. I didn't find anything of much worth, but one of the hover bikes had survived mostly intact. It was a low-quality thing—not nearly on par with my Cutter—but it was still worth enough that I refused to leave it behind. However, it was also paired to the woman I'd beheaded. So, leaning over it, I pulled the black-and-gold cord from my cybernetic wrist and connected to it.

The defenses were laughable, and I bypassed them in only a handful of seconds. Once I did, the bike's interface was open to me. Only a few moments later, and it was mine. So, after retrieving the cord and letting it slip back into my wrist, I mounted the bike and started it up. The Mist engine came alive with a hum and then I was off.

The trip back to my headquarters was unsurprisingly uneventful. Most of the people in Algiers were far too dejected and beaten down to try anything. Still, the brief encounter with the two would-be bandits had driven home the necessity for me to keep my wits about me. If they had been a little more powerful—or if I'd have had a few fewer advantages—I might not have survived. More than anything, it made me grateful for my infiltration suit and the Sheath beneath my skin.

Of course, it was also a reminder that Nova City was full of desperate people who would do just about anything to get ahead. As I pulled around to the back of my building, I mentally triggered a concealed entrance. The lot rumbled slightly, then the ground split into a pair of doors that slid open to reveal a ramp that led down into my basement. I never slowed, and before long, I was sliding to a stop in my expansive training area. The doors had already closed, and the holographic display that kept the entrance hidden had reactivated.

To my surprise, Patrick was already down there, and he was busy running through the pistol course. I watched as he moved from one station to the next, stopping only long enough to fill the targets full of holes. It brought back memories; after all, I'd repeatedly run a similar course during the first few months of my training back in Mobile.

When he noticed that I'd arrived, his training drew to a close, and he canceled the program. After that, he headed in my direction. The basement was almost two hundred yards long, so it took him a moment to reach me. When he did, he looked at my new hover bike and asked, "Uh . . . where did that come from?"

"Some mooks tried to jump me on the ramp between here and the Garden," I answered. "They didn't make it."

"What? Why?"

"Why did I kill them? Or why did they jump me?" I asked.

"Both?" was his slightly exasperated reply.

"Well, they attacked me because they wanted my stuff," I answered. "It happens. People around here are desperate, Patrick. Most of the major tribes steer clear of that kind of thing—too much risk because you never really know who you're attacking—but independents aren't so picky. As far as why I killed them, I would think that's obvious."

"You couldn't have let them live?"

"No."

"But—"

I cut him off, saying, "Look, Patrick. I know you're not as comfortable with this kind of thing as I am. I get that, and I actually like that about you. But when somebody attacks me, I can't afford to hesitate before putting them down. That's how people end up dead."

In truth, I probably should have killed Metal Neck, the guy who'd tried to sell the refugees into slavery when we'd first made it to Nova City. I also shouldn't have let Squirrel live. But neither of them really posed much of a threat to me, so I'd chosen to leave them with their lives. Even then, on more than one night, I'd found myself lying awake and wondering if I should go back and rectify the error. In the meantime, I'd resolved not to make that mistake again.

"Seems like it might be a slippery slope," he said. "Where do we draw the line?"

"At people trying to kill me," I said.

"What about people intending to kill you? Are we going to preemptively attack them?" he asked.

"Probably. That's kind of why I'm here," I said. "Revenge at all costs. No hesitation. No quarter. I told you that when you decided to come with me, Patrick."

Indeed, I had. Obviously, he had thought I'd compromise, but that was because he didn't really know me. Sure, he saw what I'd shown him, but he had no idea what kind of training I had been through. He didn't know how many people I'd already killed. And he certainly had no idea how many I intended to add to that total.

Some I would directly kill. Others might be caught in the cross fire. I didn't care. Every other concern paled next to making everyone who'd had a hand in my uncle's murder pay for what they had done.

"Fine."

"What? No more arguments?" I asked.

"Would it do any good?" was his responding question.

"No."

"Then, fine," he reiterated. "I'm not an idiot, Mira. I can recognize when I'm fighting a losing battle. Besides, in case you forgot, I lost someone, too. And I'm just as invested in this as you are. I'm here to support you, not be your conscience. So, this is the last time you'll hear me complaining about that kind of thing."

At that moment, I hated the way he looked at me. I'd seen the same thing when people looked at my uncle. They weren't just afraid. It was more than that. Like I was a lost cause, that I just wasn't worth the debate. But there was fear there, too, and plenty of it. I knew what he was thinking. What if he stepped out of line? Would I put him down, too? When it came to the path of revenge, there wasn't room for alliance or friendship. Only tools to be used.

"I won't kill people unless I have to," I said. "You know that, don't you?"

"Sure," he said, but his tone was noncommittal.

"Really. I won't," I reiterated. "But I can't let up. I have to keep pushing forward, Patrick. This is all I have."

He looked at me for a long moment, then said, "I get it. I'm . . . I'm going back upstairs. I need to study before I go to Dr. Montague's tomorrow."

I sighed, but I didn't stop him. I had no idea what to say. I didn't know how to convince him that I wasn't some emotionless murderer. I just didn't have a choice, and I desperately wanted him to understand that.

Soon, I found myself alone and wondering if I was following the right path. After all, there was nothing really keeping me in Nova City. Patrick and I could leave any time we wanted, and we could figure things out from there. With our skills, it wouldn't even be difficult to make a living.

But the moment that thought crossed my mind, I remembered my uncle's disembodied head. That, in turn, was followed by a memory of Nora's smiling face. He'd given her everything she had, and she'd repaid that act with betrayal. No—this wasn't something I could leave behind. I needed to see it through, else I would never forgive myself.

So, with that in mind, I crossed the basement to set up a new training program. Then, I loaded my various weapons with practice ammunition before slapping the restrictive Mist shackles on my wrists. Once I felt my attributes fade down to almost nothing, I started working my way through my training, pushing myself harder than I ever had before.

For some people, those doubts, brief though they were, might have derailed their plans. But for me? They served as a reminder that I couldn't let myself waver. I needed to be strong, lest I veer off course. I wouldn't allow myself to falter. I refused.

So, I trained.

In the back of my mind, I think I realized that it was as much to keep me from pondering the implications of my decisions as it was to actually improve. But it was easy to ignore those quiet whispers.

CHAPTER NINETEEN

BOILING OVER

Sometimes, I wonder if I would have made the same decisions if I'd had all the information. Would I have subjugated myself to Jeremiah if I knew he would never appreciate me? If I knew he would toss me aside like so much refuse? I don't know. And that is a disappointing realization.

—Nora Lancaster

I sat atop the building, my knees clutched to my chest as I stared at the columns of smoke twisting into the night sky. For the past few weeks, they had been a constant reminder that things in the Garden had reached a boiling point, that the tribes had gone to war. Old grudges, past disagreements, and simple greed had pushed them all into conflict. Some had made alliances, while others had fallen under a deluge of attacks from their opportunistic rivals. And I knew it was just the beginning. More would come. If the gangs refused to cooperate, I would just have to give them a little push.

At least it hadn't spilled over into Algiers, but that wasn't that surprising. After all, anything worth fighting over—like the docks—had already been claimed by the various corporations that controlled the city's economy. And their interests were protected by Enforcers or well-equipped private security. Any tribe that chose to attack them would have to commit the entirety of their resources to the endeavor, and even then, they might lose. For most, it just wasn't worth it.

It was a good thing I wasn't one of them, though. I didn't need to hold territory. I was free to strike, then melt into the shadows. I didn't have anything to protect. Even my headquarters held no attachment.

Of course, I wasn't the island I wanted to be. Not really. Never was that more apparent than when Patrick cleared his throat from behind me. I acted as if I didn't hear him, but he'd seen just how sharp my senses were, so he knew that I had. Still, he didn't point it out, instead choosing to climb up beside me.

He sat on the edge of the big aluminum duct, his legs hanging off and his elbows on his knees. For a while, we just sat there, both staring at the war zone that the Garden had become. It hadn't just affected the Operators, either. Civilians had already started retreating into Algiers, and I knew more would come. There were even rumors that some planned to create caravans that would take them to other cities.

Idly, I wondered if they knew just what sort of dangers such a trip might entail. I'd been out there. I had seen dinosaur-sized alligators and hordes of feral wildlings. If a hundred trucks set out from Nova, I'd be surprised if half of them reached their destinations.

But what was the alternative when their homes had become battlegrounds? When every indication was that it was going to get worse? They'd been shoved into a corner, and they didn't have any other choice but to flee. If my resolve hadn't been so firm, I might have wavered in my mission. As it was, I could only hope that they took the proper precautions and had enough protection to see them through. I couldn't afford anything else.

"What are you thinking?" asked Patrick, finally breaking the silence.

I didn't immediately answer. Instead, I thought about what I wanted to say. Patrick wasn't quite as hard-hearted as me, and there was every chance that he'd want to do something about the flood of refugees that would soon flee Nova City. And there was a part of me—a cold, nearly dead part, to be sure, but a part all the same—that agreed. Before my uncle's death, I probably would have been driven to help them. Now, though? I couldn't allow empathy to affect me.

"I need to go to Gunther's," I said.

"What? Why?" he asked. He glanced at the plumes of smoke rising into the sky. "Is that smart right now?"

"I've hit a roadblock," I answered. "And things in the Garden aren't going to get any better anytime soon."

Not if I had anything to say about it, at least. When I'd first set out on my road to revenge, I'd thought the journey would end when I took care of Nora. However, only a little thought told me that she was only partially responsible. She still needed to be punished, but the true culprits were in the Council District. Or in King's Row. So, I'd adjusted my plan accordingly. Glancing back at those columns of smoke, I couldn't help but wonder what my revenge would end up costing.

"What kind of roadblock?" he asked. "Can I help?"

"Just keep doing what you're doing," I said. "I don't know how much you can help here, but at some point, we're going to be leaving Nova. When we do, you're going to be the key to what comes next."

With that, my tolerance for conversation had been reached, and I slipped from the duct and quickly found the door down into the compound. It still didn't feel like home, but I didn't think it ever would. After all, I had no intention of staying in Nova City any longer than it took me to see my plan through. Until then, the headquarters would work just fine, but after that, I'd move on. There was no point in settling in. Besides, my uncle had settled into his life in Nova City. And that hadn't ended well for him.

I found my way into the kitchen, where I tossed some imitation-beef stew into the nano-wave. There was no joy in eating it; the chunks of faux meat were heavily seasoned soy cubes, and the overriding taste was salty. Not savory. Not hearty. Just salty. Still, it was filling, and it would give me plenty of calories for the day.

While I ate, Patrick came down from the roof, but he didn't try to continue our brief conversation. Instead, he went back to studying the cybernetic engineering programs I'd purchased for him. He also had some medical texts meant to bolster his knowledge, if not his skills. I hoped that it would give him all the tools he needed, but I knew it would be a long time before he could rival someone like Dr. Montague. Even so, it should be sufficient to advance his skill to the point where he could repair my cybernetics if they were damaged.

After I finished my meal, I went to my room—which was little more than a cubicle where I slept—and changed into my M11 infiltration suit. Getting shot in the shoulder a few weeks before hadn't even damaged it, which really drove home how advanced it was. I could only hope that it would hold up just as well when I faced real enemies.

Over that suit, I donned an old green jacket and a pair of loose jeans before putting on a pair of worn work boots. Then, I tucked my hair into a matching cap and activated Mimic, taking on the appearance of a Tier 2 woman I'd seen on the monorail a week before. Instantly, my features changed to that of a haggard blonde woman in her midtwenties. She wasn't pretty. Nor was she ugly. Thoroughly average, especially for someone who lived in the Garden. In that guise, I knew nobody would give me a second glance.

Once I was happy with my disguise, I left the compound without further delay. Not for the first time, I counted myself lucky to have found the building. It was nestled in one of the least prosperous parts of Nova City, which meant that I'd have to go a couple of blocks before I found an occupied building. Everything else was abandoned, and most were in such a state of disrepair that they weren't fit for habitation even by the city's transient population. Still, I was glad to have had the presence of mind to set up a series of cameras so that I could be certain of my privacy. I'd taken the time to connect them to my interface, so it only took a few seconds for me to check them to make sure that the coast was clear.

Most interfaces couldn't handle such a workload; instead, they were dependent on wired security terminals. But the KIOI was not a normal interface, especially when it was boosted by [Cybernetic Mastery], so it could do so with relative ease.

Once I had checked the cameras and was satisfied that no one was around, I summoned my Cutter. Because of Mimic, it materialized with the appearance of a much cheaper, far less mechanically sound bike. Even when I ran my hand along its fuselage, I couldn't tell that beneath that facade was a sleek machine that was far more advanced than any other hover bike I had seen in Nova City.

When I mounted it, I couldn't keep a slight smile from turning up the corners of my mouth as I heard the Mist engine hum to life. The bike lifted an inch or two before I grasped the handles, leaned forward, and shot down the road. In an instant, I was up to cruising speed, and it was all I could do to stop myself from laughing out loud.

Even with all the horrible things I'd had to endure, there was still a primal sort of joy to riding that hover bike. I wasn't sure if it was the sense of freedom, speed, or something else entirely, but I loved the bike even more than I'd expected to. It was a convenient way to get around the city; the Cutter's maneuverability made dodging the detritus and trash that littered Algiers's streets easy, and I used those traits to full effect as I traversed the cramped and cluttered streets on my way to the spiral ramp that led up to the Garden.

My path was unimpeded, and I reached my native district without issue. However, I pulled to a stop when I saw that one of the tribes—the Bengals, judging by the prominent purple and gold in their attire—had blocked the street. So, I quickly turned down a side street only to find that my detour was blocked, as well. Over the next few minutes, I found that the Bengals had enacted a blockade on the Cyberdogs' territory. That was fine by me; the more conflict there was between the various tribes, the better. The only problem was that I couldn't quickly reach Gunther's without going through them.

Of course, I could have just gone back to the monorail and bypassed them altogether, but as I saw it, I'd been presented with an opportunity to gain some experience and sow the seeds of chaos. So, I ducked into a narrow alley, dismissed my Cutter, then tied a blue armband around my upper arm before adjusting Mimic and adopting a new persona.

Then, I summoned my weapons, one by one, and inspected them. They were all in pristine condition, loaded and ready for war. So, I attached my nano-sword to my back, checked that Ferdinand II was clear on my hip, then retrieved my Pulsar sniper rifle from my arsenal implant.

With that done, I crept to the end of the alley and peeked out into the street. Two hundred yards away, I could see a series of old and rusted hover cars parked end to end, with only a small gap between them. A dozen Operators, all wearing the purple and gold of the Bengals, stood guard, turning anyone who tried to enter the territory away. Anyone who complained or argued got a bullet or a beating, and I couldn't really tell what prompted the difference.

Of course, it didn't really matter that they were clearly willing to use their power to bully civilians. But it helped steel my nerves as I took aim at the biggest of the bunch—a hulking, bearded man clad only in leather pants and a vest. One of his legs had been replaced by a crude cybernetic, but the rest of him looked human.

I took a breath, then embraced Empowered Shot. Two seconds later, I squeezed the trigger. A comparatively tiny ball of superheated plasma erupted from the barrel and tore through the air, faster than most people could perceive. Less than a millisecond later, it hit the big mook's chest, disintegrating his entire torso. As his lower half collapsed to the street, I was already taking aim at one of his fellows. This time, I didn't bother with Empowered Shot, but the lack didn't really affect the lethality of the shot because it tore through his chest, leaving only a gaping hole behind.

In the space of a few more seconds, I fired one shot after another, and before any of the Bengals had even pinpointed my location, half were dead. That's when they retreated behind their hover-car barricade.

That was fine, too.

I ducked behind the corner, stowing my Pulsar and replacing it with my BMAP. To date, I hadn't seen what it could really do. Instead, I'd trained with comparatively weak practice ammunition. Now, though, I was finally going to get the opportunity to put it through its paces. So, I knelt, brought the stock to my shoulder, and leaned out of cover.

In the blink of an eye, I fired three arcing shots, each one aimed at one of the cars.

I thought I knew what to expect. After all, Gala had described the weapon by talking about how it could demolish a building. Even so, I was taken aback by the potency of the series of explosions that tore the barricade apart. Everything within thirty yards of each eruption was swallowed in a ball of white-hot flames, and when they settled, there was nothing left but three overlapping craters.

I stared, open-mouthed and wide-eyed.

So I didn't even see the squad of Bengals bearing down on me. But that changed when a bullet hit my shoulder and sent me spinning to the ground. The sound of gunfire filled the air as I rolled to the side, taking cover behind a dumpster. Rolling my arm, I was once again thankful for the combination of my infiltration suit and the subdermal Sheath. Without it, that bullet would have torn through my shoulder like it was paper. But with it, I felt like it would only bruise.

"Did we get him?" came a ragged, yet feminine voice that I could only hear because I'd flared Observation.

"Ain't sure it was a him, Dee."

"What the hell did he use, anyway? A goddamn rocket launcher?" asked another.

"Couldn't see," said yet another.

While they were arguing, I dismissed my BMAP; it could have probably done the trick, but they were close enough that I didn't want to chance being swallowed by the resultant explosion. Even with the protection of Blast Shield, that would've been stupid. So, I exchanged the BMAP for the R-14 assault rifle. Out of force of habit, I checked again that it was loaded before leaning out, taking aim, and sending a three-shot burst downrange. The shots rang out in such rapid succession that it almost sounded like a single gunshot.

The weapon's payload was similar to that of the Pulsar, meaning that it didn't fire solid rounds. Instead, it fired Mist-infused plasma that tore into the first mook, doing more than enough damage to drop him before he even knew what was going on. Another burst took out a gangly woman with blonde hair who might've been pretty if not for her rangy limbs and awkward appearance. Her ragged scream was enough to identify her as Dee.

The Operators all scattered, but the R-14 was accurate and had a high rate of fire. They never stood a chance, and I grimly persisted, tearing them apart with one well-placed burst after another. In the space of ten seconds, they were all dead or dying. Another handful of seconds, and the night grew quiet, save for the fires still burning from the BMAP's brief bombardment.

I stood and looked around. It hadn't been more than a couple of minutes, and I had killed almost two dozen Operators. None had been the cream of the crop; in fact, I'd have been surprised if any of them had exceeded Tier 3, much less worked to get the most out of their potential. However, knowing that and seeing how quickly I could dismantle an entire squad of Operators was a sobering experience.

One thing was for certain, though—my new weapons had far exceeded my expectations. Gala had done right by me, and I suspected that I'd only scratched the surface of their potential. After all, despite my training, my skills had only experienced moderate gains. I intended to change that, though.

I quickly looted the mooks who'd attacked me, but I left the bodies of the Operators who'd manned the barricade untouched. The BMAP hadn't left a lot behind, and I wasn't going to dig through the charred corpses. In any case, I had plans to augment my funding, and it didn't include looting a few mooks who were so low-ranked within their organization that they'd been put on blockade duty. They were fine to intimidate a bunch of civilians, but against anyone who knew what they were doing? They were fodder, and they'd been equipped as such.

So, I once again summoned my Cutter, mounted it, and took off into the heart of the Garden. However, when I saw the barricade on the other side of the territory, I didn't slow. Instead, I summoned my BMAP, took aim at one side of the barricade, then let loose. I only fired one shot, but that was enough to kill half of the Operators and distract the others long enough for me to race through the gap and into the next territory.

However, I did slow just long enough that they could see the blue band around my upper arm. After all, what good was it to kill a few nameless mooks if I couldn't pin it on Nora and her Specters?

Once I got out of sight, I ripped the armband off and adopted a new persona—this one, a slight man with skin color similar to my own—and continued on toward Gunther's, content in the fact that I'd almost assuredly just caused quite a few problems for Nora.

CHAPTER TWENTY

NOTHING WORTHWHILE IS EVER FREE

After . . . I did what I did, I had to call in a lot of markers in order to take control of the Specters. Even then, my grip was tenuous at best. I'm not sure if it was worth it.

—Nora Lancaster

I switched identities twice more on my way to Gunther's Guns. No one had followed me, at least as far as I could tell, but I knew assuming things like that was a good way to get killed. So, every few blocks, I ducked into an alley before adopting a new persona. When I emerged, I was a new person altogether. By the time I reached my destination, I felt almost certain that I didn't have a tail. Even so, I swiftly turned down a new alley, activated Stealth, and waited a few minutes to make sure I hadn't been followed.

My efforts were proven unnecessary because, even twenty minutes later, I was all alone.

Once I'd established that I hadn't picked up a tail, I took on yet another persona—this one fairly close to my own appearance, though with much lighter skin and far straighter hair—before heading into the arms dealer's premises. The two cyborgs at the door—neither of which were Dierdre—didn't even glance at me on my way in, though I wasn't certain if that was because they still recognized me despite my usage of Mimic or if they just didn't see me as a threat. Either way, my entrance was unimpeded, and once I found my way to the familiar lobby-slash-armory, I sent a message to Gunther, telling him that I had arrived.

With that done, I took a moment to wander around and investigate the decor. There were a few others around, but none of them paid me any mind. I was more than okay with returning that favor. I didn't need to know them, and I certainly didn't want them knowing me. I was content in my anonymity, and not just because it was smart. I'd quickly come to realize that I just didn't like attention, especially from strangers.

I was busy inspecting a pair of dueling pistols hanging from the wall when Gunther approached, saying, "To what do I owe this pleasure?"

I was past questioning how he always recognized me. It had to be a skill. Or perhaps an item. Either way, it was a grim reminder that my own abilities weren't infallible. If he could see through Mimic, then others could, as well. Of course, Gunther had power on par with my uncle's, so I couldn't believe the situation would be a common one. Still, I needed to be on the lookout for people who might be able to see past my skills in deception.

"I need to talk business," I said without turning to look at him. "Can we go somewhere private?"

He nodded, saying, "Follow me."

As I did, I couldn't help but notice that he was once again wearing one of his leather suits. With Observation, I could tell it was the real stuff, too. None of that faux leather that was so common in the city. Not surprising, considering his penchant for hunting and his obvious wealth. Clearly, he had the resources to get as much leather as he wanted.

Over the next couple of minutes, I followed him through his compound and to an elevator that took us to his private office. Once we were inside, he gestured to an overstuffed couch, saying, "Have a seat. Want a drink?"

I shook my head. Even if alcohol wasn't practically useless on me, there was no way I would ever take a drink from someone I didn't trust. Which meant that I'd never take one from anybody. Maybe Patrick, but even that was stretching it. I'd heard too many stories about people who'd done so and lived to regret it. The last thing I needed was to take a sip from some unknown drink only to wake up with a slave implant and a new master who wanted to put me to work on Bourbon Street.

"Suit yourself," he said when I declined. Though he did cross the room to a bar, grab one of the crystal decanters, and pour himself a glass. Once that was done, he sat across from me and asked, "So, what can I do for you?"

"I need to get into Lakeview," I said.

"Why?" was his question.

"You really need to know that? Can you get me in or not?" I asked. I had no intention of revealing my plans to Gunther. For one, I was playing my cards close to my chest, and I knew that the more people who knew a secret, the more likely it was to get out. For another, I didn't altogether trust Gunther. He'd already sold information to me, and I couldn't help but imagine a situation where someone would pay to hear my secrets, as well. No—it was best if he didn't know.

"Maybe," he said. "But I need two things."

"What do you want?"

"First," Gunther said, holding up one finger. I noticed he had rings on each digit, excluding his thumbs, and they were all gaudy, shiny things. "I need to know that you're not going to turn the place into a war zone."

"Why would you think—"

"I'm not blind, girl," he said. "Nor am I stupid. You come here with an axe to grind, and suddenly your uncle's old tribe is at war with the Cyberdogs? This whole district is about to boil over, and I think you're the cause."

I embraced my arsenal implant, ready to arm myself in an instant. More, I was already probing Gunther's cyberdefenses. I withdrew my awareness the moment I saw how complex they were. He'd clearly taken precautions against people like me. Still, if he was a threat, I felt that a few rounds from my R-14 assault rifle would be enough to cut him down to size.

"Don't do anything stupid," he said. "You attack me, and you'll be dead before you reach the lobby."

"You sound pretty confident," I said.

"Because I am," he stated. Then, he smiled broadly, revealing a mouth full of gleaming teeth. One of those teeth was encased in gold. "Besides, we're friends right? No need for things to get violent."

"I'm not going there to start a war," I said. "But things might get messy."

"Messy, I can deal with," he said. "Disastrous might be a bigger problem."

"In and out," I said. "That's my goal. If I have my way, nobody will ever know I was even there." When he didn't immediately respond, I asked, "So, what's the second thing?"

He shook his head, then said, "A favor."

I raised a single eyebrow, asking, "What kind of favor?"

"Nothing outside your ability," he said. "I just need someone killed is all."

"What? Why?" I asked, a little taken aback. I was a killer; I knew that. But I wasn't an assassin, especially not one for hire. "And why me? You seem to have plenty of firepower at your disposal."

"The why is my business," Gunther said. "And my employees are well-known and ill-suited to the task. It requires subtlety, a trait sorely lacking in Dierdre and her people."

I nodded. That made some sense. Dierdre and the other cyborgs seemed perfectly capable of leveling a building, but a stealth mission probably wasn't really in the cards. For a man like Gunther, it was probably easier to hire that kind of job out, rather than nurture an assassin. My uncle had done something similar when he'd founded his tribe, though he'd been a little more hands-on than Gunther seemed to be.

"You say it's within the scope of my abilities," I said. "How do you know that?"

To answer that question, Gunther sent a parcel of information through our unsecured connection. When I opened it, an ability description came across my HUD:

True Sight (C)—Allows user to detect another's class, skills, abilities, and level. Viability based on Mind and Mist attributes.

My jaw dropped. That ability seemed incredibly useful, and I could already think of a hundred situations where it would have helped me out. My uncle had often said that information was a soldier's best weapon, and True Sight was the ultimate in information-gathering abilities. With it, I could have saved myself a ton of trouble.

"What skill is that ability from?" I asked.

He grinned. "Now, you don't really expect me to reveal that, do you?" he asked. "Suffice it to say that one of my skills makes me the best-informed person in any room. And with it, I can tell that you have everything you'll need to successfully complete the mission I have in mind. Kudos, by the way. You are very advanced, given your age. I look forward to seeing how powerful you can become. Of course, there's the caveat that you need to stay alive if you're going to realize said potential, but I'm sure Jeremiah taught you how to do just that. Combat capability is not just about skills and abilities, right? It's about knowledge. It's about training."

I couldn't really disagree with him.

"And if I do this, you'll get me into Lakeview?" I asked. "Quietly."

"That's the deal. Do you agree?" he asked, and I nodded. Then, as he handed me a chip, he went on, "Then here. Slot that. It has all the information you're going to need to do the job. Once it's done, I'll get you into Lakeview. But before you ascend to those lofty heights, you might want to invest in a new wardrobe."

I nodded. I already knew that I'd have to eventually go shopping, and it seemed that my lacking options had finally caught up to me. Lakeview was an affluent district, after all. If I went there in my normal clothes, I'd draw the wrong kind of attention. And given what I intended to do, that would derail my whole plan.

"I've already got some ideas for that," I said, slotting the chip in the side of my neck. Immediately, a file appeared on my HUD. First, there was a photo of a handsome man with slicked-back hair and a beard that had been cut into a series of lightning-bolt patterns. The file named him Alistair Wallace. "Anything I need to know? How quiet do I need to be? Or am I good to go loud?"

Another grin spread across Gunther's face, and he said, "More than a whisper, less than a shout, my dear. So long as there's no collateral damage, I will be satisfied. All I require is that you confirm the kill."

"Gotcha," I said, continuing to read the file. Alistair Wallace wasn't really anyone special—just a low-tiered arms dealer who moonlighted as a smuggler. I assumed that he'd either stolen from or taken some of Gunther's business. Either way, I didn't see anything that made me want to rethink the contract. Wallace wasn't out-and-out evil, but he definitely wasn't a good guy, either. According to the file, he was suspected of dropping at least a dozen bodies in the past few years, some of whom were civilians.

He was also complicit in human trafficking, which was enough of a decider all on its own. More, it reminded me that I needed to take some time to head to Bourbon Street and rescue Heather. She and I had never really gotten along, but it was mostly because, back then, I'd been a little brat who resented her for monopolizing my uncle's time. Now, though? I could recognize that she'd done everything she could to be my friend.

And now she was stuck in a seedy Bourbon Street brothel called Heaven and Hell. I couldn't in good conscience leave her there. By all rights, I should have already taken care of it. My only excuse was that I had a lot on my plate, and I just hadn't had time to do anything more than what I was doing.

I nodded to Gunther, saying, "I'll do it."

"Good, good. I knew you'd see it my way," he said. "While you work on that, I'll start putting together your new identity. I'm assuming that Mimic ability will let you take on any appearance?"

That last comment was less of a question and more of a not-so-subtle reminder that he knew all my secrets, right down to my ability names. I couldn't help but wonder where the limits of True Sight lay.

"So long as I meet them, yeah," I said. "But I can't just see them on a recording."

"That won't be a problem," he stated. He gestured to the door, adding, "Unless there's anything else?"

I shook my head and, without any further conversation, left the room. I remembered my way out, so it wasn't long before I'd left Gunther's Guns behind. My target's place of business was located on the other side of the Garden, so I wasted no time before ducking into an alley and summoning my Cutter. In moments, I was rocketing through the streets. This time, I didn't go through the blockade; I knew just how busy the area probably was after what I'd done, so I chose to skirt it instead.

Like that, I made my way across the platform, and within the hour—most of which was wasted with me stuck in traffic—I found the appropriate building. It was a three-story structure that sat on the corner of a lot that had once housed a megabuilding. That particular block had been clear for as long as I could remember, but its original purpose was made obvious by the former occupant's footprint. There were a dozen other buildings that had taken its place, one of which belonged to Alistair Wallace.

I was tempted to attack it head-on, just belting out a few dozen rounds from my BMAP with the intention of demolishing anything in the area. However, I knew just how much negative attention that would bring, so I decided to be a little less obvious about it.

During the course of my trip across the city, I'd gone back and forth about whether to leverage my [Mistrunner] talents to infiltrate the building, much as I had in the Tiger stronghold back in Mobile. That had the benefit of being about as quiet as an assassination could get. I could sneak in, set myself up in the appropriate place, and then assassinate the target before fleeing. All the while, no one had to know what had even happened.

But on the negative side, that option would be slow, and it could end up taking most of the night, probably stretching into early morning. I wasn't sure if I had time for that, considering how much I needed to get done.

The other alternative would see me setting up somewhere where I'd have a clear line of sight, waiting for Wallace to come out into the open, and disintegrating his torso with a well-placed sniper shot from my Pulsar. The disadvantage of that option was that, once the deed was done, there was every chance of pursuit. It was still unlikely to prove fruitful, given that I would set myself up a good distance away, but it was a risk.

However, it was one I was willing to take because I'd already decided to go with the second option. To that end, I quickly crossed the street and ducked into an alley before dismissing my bike. After that, I changed appearances and slipped back out into the flow of pedestrians. A couple of minutes later, I found my way to my destination.

The tenement wasn't quite as tall as a megabuilding, which meant that it probably didn't have the same levels of security. More importantly, so long as I got on the roof, I'd have a clear line of sight into Wallace's compound.

To that end, I quickly entered the building through the front door, ignoring the addicts who'd stationed themselves near the stairs. A couple of them noticed me, but none moved. I wouldn't have been surprised if they were just squatting in the lobby, which was dirty, unmanned, and poorly lit.

I crossed the lobby to the stairs, then commenced my climb. Every now and then, I ran into another addict or a descending resident, but nobody paid much attention to me. Why would they? I kept my head down, and I was dressed just like everyone else, so I looked like I belonged. That, as much as anything else, told me that, if I intended to head to the higher platforms, I needed a new wardrobe. Otherwise, I'd stick out like a sore thumb.

I reached the top of the stairs without issue, and soon, I burst through the door, finding myself on the roof. Studded with various ducts and air-conditioning units, the roof looked little different than any other I had seen. But I wasn't there for the decor; rather, all I cared about was its sight line, which, when I reached the edge, I confirmed was absolutely perfect.

Wallace's building was a good distance away—maybe a thousand yards—but with Observation and the powerful scope attached to the Pulsar, that distance would amount for nothing. So, after extending the bipod from the weapon's barrel, I set it on the ledge and took aim.

Like that, I waited, watching for my target to make an appearance. According to the file I'd been given, he usually left the office at around this time, so I only had to be patient. And as luck would have it, he made an appearance a little more than half an hour later.

He looked little different than he had in the photo. The same slicked-back hair, artfully arranged beard, and a shiny suit that made him look like he was trying way too hard. None of that mattered, though. All I needed was a clear shot and a positive identification. I had both.

So, I lined the reticle up with his chest, activated Empowered Shot, and two seconds later, squeezed the trigger. A millisecond later, his entire torso exploded into a fiery conflagration of superheated Mist, blood, and charred flesh. The two mooks that I took to be his bodyguards reacted quickly enough, but Wallace's torso was destroyed before they even knew what had happened. So, too little, too late.

My job was done.

Now, I just had to hope Gunther would hold up his end of the bargain. If he didn't, well, I had a lot of bullets. And I hadn't really seen what the BMAP could do to a building. Either way, I felt like I was making at least some progress. It was slower than I would've liked, but at least I was moving forward.

CHAPTER TWENTY-ONE

A DAY OFF

There is nothing better than physically dominating someone. Once the bio-enhancers took hold, I really came into my own, and the knowledge that I could wrestle just about anyone into submission really did a number on my self-confidence. I've been leaning on it ever since.

—Nora Lancaster

I sat beside Patrick, watching the city whip by as we rode the monorail to Bywater, which was home to the highest-class shops I was likely to be allowed into. It was where most of the Garden's corporate lackeys shopped for their knockoff suits and imitation accessories. For my part, I'd never put much stock in who made my clothes, but to the sorts of people who worked on the higher platforms, such things mattered a great deal.

And for good reason, too. It wasn't just vanity, though that did play a role. Nor was it a desire to delude themselves into believing that they were somehow better than the men and women who worked in the factories or Silos. That was a part of it, as well, but it wasn't the driving force behind their choice of clothing. Instead, the culprit was a simple desire to climb the ladder.

Everyone who went to work on one of the higher tiers had one thing in mind: advancement. They wanted to prove themselves to their middle managers, who were once right where they were, so they could get promoted. Some were even ignorant enough to believe they might one day climb to the top and rub shoulders with the city's real aristocracy. It was sheer idiocy born of powerful delusion, but thousands—if not millions—of people had been caught up in the idea that they could somehow overcome their humble origins through nothing more than hard work. What they never considered was that the system was designed to prevent just that from coming to pass; after all, why would the higher-ups create a hierarchy at all if they weren't going to protect it by any means possible?

So, it was with a twisting anxiety in my stomach that I watched the Garden pass me by as we headed to Bywater. The district where I'd been born and raised was almost unrecognizable, it was mired in so much conflict. Everywhere I looked, there was evidence of the ongoing tribal war. Plumes of smoke, dead bodies, and burned-out hulks that were once megabuildings abounded, and with those sights came a modicum of guilt. After all, I had provided the spark that had become the conflagration that had engulfed the district. Without my actions, everything would have continued on like normal.

Not that I let the guilt spread. I wouldn't allow it to become much more than an inkling. An errant thought. A slight tickle up my spine. It was easy to ignore my own culpability when I remembered my mission. Even easier when I thought of those automatons going about their lives like they were really living. For some, catching an errant bullet would be a godsend. At least, then, they wouldn't have to trudge through a life of misery while they pretended they weren't banging their heads against an immovable wall.

I did my best not to look upon them with disgust. Or with a sense of superiority. But I was just so disappointed that nobody else seemed to realize—or care—that they were being oppressed. That they were willingly subjugating themselves to people who just didn't deserve their obeisance. It was difficult to see that and not feel the winds of condescension pushing me into a mindset I didn't really want to foster.

Regardless, I knew things would get much worse before they got better. Soon enough, the tribal war that was only beginning would escalate. I intended to see to that. But until then, I'd let them all stew in their own hostilities while I focused on more important things—like making Nora pay. To that end, I was heading toward Bywater, which was what passed for a mercantile district. Not only did it house the Dome, which in turn provided access to the Bazaar, but there were hundreds, if not thousands of shops in the vicinity. Some sold clothing. Others, cybernetics that only a desperate idiot would put in their body. Still others sold delicacies or weapons and everything in between. My uncle had once called it the city's mecca of capitalism, whatever that meant.

My needs, though, were very specific. I needed a new wardrobe. Too many times, I'd been hampered by my limited clothing options. Mimic was great, and it let me assume just about any identity I wanted to take. However, it was limited to my own body; my clothes would always stay the same. So, even if I took the face of someone who had every reason to head up to Lakeview, I'd still stick out because of my clothes, which were limited to a few sets of fatigues, my infiltration suit, a full Enforcer's uniform I'd looted in Haven, and my well-worn refugee rags. None of those, save for the Enforcer's uniform, would get me into Lakeview. And I didn't want the hassle that came with wearing that.

So, I needed something more mundane. Something that would let me blend into the crowd of starry-eyed, would-be ladder climbers that would be headed from the Garden and into Lakeview. Delusional, the lot of them, but pretending to be one of them would be fantastic camouflage when I took the next step in my quest for revenge.

The other passengers on the monorail were an eclectic bunch. A few were obviously Operators, identifiable by their shifty eyes, visible cybernetics, and easy confidence. Others were the dead-eyed factory or Silo workers who were on their way to the mercantile district to spend some of their meager earnings. They weren't paid enough to provide for much of a surplus, but even the most frugal would have a little extra to spend on luxuries. Otherwise, how else were they supposed to remain docile and placated?

It was a simple cost-benefit equation. If a worker was happy so long as she got a new dress once in a while, it behooved the powers that be to give her just enough to give her access to that luxury. It was meant to be infrequent. The carrot for the delusional donkeys to chase. Sometimes, they'd be allowed a bite, but not too often, lest they get the wrong ideas about what they deserved.

The other way, which involved the proverbial stick to the aforementioned carrot, was simply less profitable. Punishing poor workers worked well enough, but it wasn't a long-term solution. As my uncle was fond of saying, you drew more flies with honey than with vinegar. It was true with insects, and the same held for the working population.

For my part, I saw the truth, though. All those rewards were blindfolds meant to keep people from seeing the world as it really was. I pitied them almost as much as I resented the fact that they didn't even try to see reality.

"You okay?" asked Patrick, dragging me from my thoughts. I turned to see that he'd cast a concerned expression in my direction.

"I'm fine," I said. "Why? Don't I seem fine?"

He shrugged. "It's just that a lot's happened lately" was his response. "I guess it just seems like you've got a lot on your shoulders. Like, when's the last time you did anything fun?"

"I blew up a roadblock yesterday," I said, forcing a grin I didn't really feel after my previous line of thought.

"That's not what I'm talking about, Mira, and I think you know that."

I sighed, letting the fake grin fade away. "I know" was my response. "But I really am fine, Pick. I mean, Patrick. I have a skill that helps with that kind of thing."

It was true. My Combat Focus wasn't merely limited to assisting me in battle. It also helped with the aftermath. In Mobile, there had been a few people who didn't have an ability like that. They couldn't handle the mental strain they'd been forced to endure in battle. My uncle had called it PTSD, but I'd never experienced anything like what those poor people lived with every day. And I had no desire to, either. I'd seen how debilitating it could be.

"What was the last time you did anything just for fun, though?" he asked. "Not for training. Not for your . . . you know . . . quest. Just something for you to relax."

I was about to answer, but then I realized that I hadn't really stopped moving forward since I'd boarded *The Jitterbug* months before. Back then, I'd been tasked with completing my last training mission, which had involved me dismantling an alien Rift-mining operation, then running the Rift myself. It had been a transformative experience, not least because of the wealth I'd managed to attain via that opportunity.

However, it brought up a comment my uncle had made during my training. I'd just finished my first mission, and he'd given me some time off, telling me that taking some time for relaxation is almost as important as the training itself. Sometimes, he'd said, we just need to recharge our batteries.

But out of all his lessons, I'd chosen not to take that one to heart. It just felt somehow disrespectful of his memory to take time off. It felt like a betrayal to relax when my every instinct told me to keep driving forward and overcome any obstacles that might present themselves before me. I knew it was a trap and that, eventually, I'd run out of steam. But I just couldn't stop. Not of my own accord.

"How about this? Let's do something fun today," he said.

I narrowed my eyes. "Like what?" I asked.

He shrugged. "I don't know. What do you do for fun?" was his response. "Besides blowing things up, I mean."

That brought a genuine smirk out of me. "I don't know," I admitted. "Normal stuff, I guess? I like music, and—"

"Everyone likes music," he teasingly interrupted. "What kind?"

"My favorite band is Leviathan," I said. "They're . . . I don't know if they have a presence outside of Nova, but . . . Well, here."

I pulled the chip containing the Leviathan file from my arsenal implant and handed it over. He slotted it into his own port and gave it a listen. After almost a minute, he said, "This is good."

"Just good?" I asked with a quirk of my eyebrow.

He shrugged and removed the chip from his port before handing it back. "It's good. I like it," he said.

"Be honest."

"Okay, so it's not really my thing," he said. "But I grew up listening to Remy's music, which was a lot . . . slower. And twangier. I guess it grew on me."

I shook my head, storing the chip back in my arsenal implant. "No culture," I muttered.

"What else do you like to do?" he asked, a hopeful tone in his voice.

Once again, I shrugged. I didn't really have a good answer. Before my training, I'd enjoyed many of the same things any fifteen-year-old girl liked. Mostly, I'd spent my time reading or watching various programs on the entertainment feeds. After I got to Mobile, though, my horizons had been expanded to include hanging out with Jo and her friends. I'd never really gotten close to any of the others, but on more than one occasion, Jo and I would just talk for hours. However, I didn't think that was what Patrick had in mind.

Other than that, almost all my time had been monopolized by training. In a way, my whole life had been about that, and I was beginning to realize just how one-dimensional of a person I really was. Maybe I always had been.

"I . . . I don't know," I admitted, defeat lacing my words.

Thankfully, Patrick was nothing if not supportive. "How about this? You said the Bywater district is like a big market, right?" he asked. "Usually, it's not so hard to find fun things to do in those kinds of places."

I looked up at him and gave him a shy smile. "And you're an expert in big-city living, all of a sudden?" I asked.

"Not quite" was his self-deprecating response. He returned my smile with one of his own, adding, "But I've been in a lot of towns. And what's a city if not a big town? Just trust me. Worst that can happen is we wander around for a bit."

I shrugged, but I was saved from the necessity of a response by the monorail coming to a stop. We'd finally reached Bywater, so we disembarked the elevated train and descended the platform. Unlike the Garden, there were no megabuildings in sight. Instead, there were smaller and far more numerous structures. Above everything loomed the Dome, which we intended to steer clear of.

We also avoided the street vendors that surrounded the place. Instead, we made our way to what passed for an upscale shop. The attendant gave us a derisive look, but she probably knew better than to turn her nose up at a potential customer, so after I spent a little time trying on various corporate-style outfits, we made our purchases and left the shop. Altogether, it felt less like a step along my path of revenge and more like a mundane shopping trip. Which it was. But it was also more, considering what I planned to do with those clothes.

As we left the shop behind, Patrick said, "I think I've got an idea where to go."

"What? How?" I asked.

"While you were trying clothes on, I asked one of the other customers," he said. "Nice guy. He's starting a new job next week, and he's buying some new uniforms. Anyway, he said that if you want to have fun, just head to this place called the French Quarter. Supposedly, it's named after some big attraction that used to be in the original city."

I had heard the name in passing, but I had certainly never visited. So, what I knew of the place was woefully sparse, which just highlighted all the gaps in my knowledge of the city. I'd led a sheltered existence where I rarely went anywhere but school or home, and now, I was paying for it with my ignorance.

"New Orleans," I said, desperately trying to prove that I wasn't entirely ignorant of my own city. "That was the name of the old city. It was completely destroyed by some flooding right after the Initialization started. A lot of the people here are descendants of the survivors. I guess they named different parts of Nova after the old city."

"Cool," he said. Then, he reached out and grabbed my hand. I had to actively suppress my urge to react violently to the sudden motion, but I managed it with only a slight grimace that Patrick didn't notice. He was too busy holding my hand, which was far more nerve-racking than I might've expected it to be. Suddenly, I could feel sweat trickling down my back as my stomach tied itself into a million knots. Thankfully, he was blissfully unaware of the anxiety rampaging through my mind as he dragged me down the sidewalk.

For our outing, I'd chosen not to bother with a disguise. There was a risk to it, but I surmised that few people from my old life would even recognize me. And there was almost no chance of running into Nora; she was too busy putting out fires in the Garden to make a shopping trip to Bywater. Besides, it wasn't like anyone really knew to look for me in Nova. For all I knew, anyone who cared thought I was dead. Nora included.

In any case, it sometimes felt nice to wear my own face for a change.

I caught up to Patrick so he wasn't dragging me along, and like that, we made our way down the sidewalk. There were plenty of other pedestrians, but for once, I wasn't really paying attention to them. Because Patrick was holding my hand, which seemed far more important than some random people I would never see again.

Eventually, he led us down a side street. Then another. All the while, neither of us really talked. It didn't seem necessary. Instead, we just enjoyed each other's presence until, at last, we reached our destination.

The street opened up into a wide square filled with hundreds of street performers. There were dancers, jugglers, and tumblers. Musicians, singers, and even an acting troupe who were putting on a play assisted by holographic special effects. My jaw dropped as I beheld the chaotic spectacle of so many people moving in so many different ways.

Patrick, who'd stopped, echoed my awe when he said, "Wow." He gathered himself, then added, "Here—let's go walk around. Should be fun, right?"

I nodded, and we headed into the fray. The place was incredibly crowded, but I didn't mind the other jostling pedestrians. Instead, the whole of my attention was on the performers. We passed by a man who was breathing fire, then a pair of female tumblers. I tried to donate a few credits to everyone I saw, but there were so many that I knew I missed a couple.

After about twenty minutes, we stumbled upon an artist who created holographic caricatures, and Patrick paid for one featuring the pair of us. The artist worked quickly, and before I knew it, he'd produced an animated holograph featuring cartoon versions of Patrick and me riding hover bikes together.

Looking at it, I couldn't keep a wide grin from spreading across my face. Patrick initiated a transfer of credits, and the artist handed him a pair of chips containing the caricatures. I bought the device meant to play them, and then we moved on to the next performers.

Over the course of the next few hours, we enjoyed everything the French Quarter had to offer, even buying a local treat called beignets. They were just hunks of fried dough covered in powdered sugar, but they were absolutely delicious. I wasn't certain if it was the company I kept or the beignets themselves.

Either way, by the time we finished our circuit by watching a trio of musicians perform, I had a warm, fuzzy feeling in the pit of my stomach. And as we left the French Quarter behind, I felt like I was walking on air. That lasted all the way through the monorail ride back to the Garden, which saw the pair of us still holding hands while our shoulders pressed against each other.

However, once we reached the stop closest to our headquarters in Algiers, reality reasserted itself. It was a good night, and I'd had fun, but it didn't do anything to allay my responsibilities.

Still, Patrick and I had something of an awkward moment when we reached our headquarters, and it became clear that he wanted something from me. Something I wasn't prepared to give.

So, I bade him good night with a simple hug, then retreated to my bedroom. As I did, I wondered if I'd made the wrong decision. I knew he wanted a kiss, at the very least. Maybe more. But my situation hadn't changed. I didn't have room in my life for boys. Not with my quest for revenge looming over everything. I hoped Patrick would understand that, that he'd know that it wasn't about him.

Whatever the case, I had other things to worry about than whatever was happening between Patrick and me.

CHAPTER TWENTY-TWO

YOU SCRATCH MY BACK

For the longest time, Jeremiah neglected the Specters. The moment he took Mira out of the city, everything else took a back seat to her training. And everyone noticed. Did he think they would be okay with that?

—Nora Lancaster

The next morning, I found myself standing in my room and looking at myself in the mirror. I had already activated Mimic, so I was wearing the identity of a Tier 3 woman with black hair and features that reminded me of Kimiko's. Suddenly, I thought of little Elie, the doctor's mango-loving granddaughter. One day, she might've looked similar to the face staring back at me in the mirror.

Not anymore, though. She was buried beneath a pile of rubble. She would never grow up, never become the healer she'd desperately wanted to be. That future had been stolen from her. And she wasn't the only one. How many children would never see the future they should've had? How many had died in Mobile? And for what? So they could kill my uncle? It wasn't just a waste. It was a terrible shame, and the more I thought about it, the more my path of revenge cemented itself in my mind.

I just had to keep moving forward.

I couldn't let myself get distracted. Not by Patrick and whatever might have waited after that wonderful night in the French Quarter. No—I needed to keep my eye on the prize. I needed to remember why I'd vowed vengeance in the first place. Seeing that face in the mirror—and the memory that had come with it—was a good reminder to not lose my way, regardless of how much I might've wanted to.

Still, I knew I wasn't a nun. I hadn't taken a vow of chastity. But any relationship with Patrick would likely become a distraction for both of us. I couldn't let that happen. Not when I'd already set everything in motion. Already, the city's various tribes were at one another's throats. A few more sparks, and the conflict would become a wildfire that spread far and wide throughout Nova City.

But first, I had something else that needed to be done.

That was why I was wearing a black, high-collared skirt suit cut in the same fashion I'd seen during my trips to the Bazaar. The style might have been similar, but the materials were clearly inferior. It was the uniform of an underling, which I hoped would help me avoid notice as I headed into Lakeview.

Thankfully, my Mimic ability didn't require me to fiddle with cosmetics or arrange my hair. The moment I'd activated it, my outward appearance had changed to reflect the visage of the woman whose appearance I had borrowed. It wasn't perfect. If anyone tried to grab the long, silky hair of the illusion, they'd grasp nothing but air. But it would do for the brief excursion I had planned. Either way, once I was dressed, I was finished getting ready. So, after one more look into the mirror—it wasn't a smartmirror; I didn't want to chance that kind of connection—I sighed and left the bathroom.

Predictably, Patrick was already awake, and when I entered the common area, he looked up with an expression of expectation on his face. He gave me a small smile and said, "Good morning. Hungry?"

I shook my head. I wanted nothing more than to just sit down and have breakfast with him. The night before had opened my eyes to how lonely I was. That bit of normalcy would go a long way to assuaging that sense of loneliness. But I had responsibilities, and I was terrified of complicating things between us.

Or maybe I just didn't want to let anyone else get close. I'd done that before, and that hadn't ended well for anyone. A memory of Jo's smiling face flashed in my mind, reminding me what had happened to everyone I cared about.

"I want to get this done," I said, and I had to keep myself from visibly flinching at his disappointment. "Sorry. Another time, maybe?"

"Yeah . . . sure."

I wanted to stay and explain things to him, to say something that made it all better, but the reality of the situation was that I had no clue what to say. I wasn't a social butterfly. I wasn't good with interpersonal relationships. Not like Jo had been. My talents lay elsewhere. So, all I could do was give him an awkward nod before leaving the room and heading down the stairs. After a few more seconds, I left the building behind as I headed toward the monorail.

I got a few curious glances along the way, but that was to be expected. It was rare for people dressed like me to head into Algiers. So, I did my best to ignore them as I covered the two blocks to the monorail platform, which I mounted without hesitation. As I went, I tried not to notice the haggard faces of the other people waiting for the train. They'd all gone way past desperate and into resignation, and I knew they weren't alone.

What would that feel like, to simply give up? In a way, letting go and following the current would offer some degree of freedom. Perhaps those people had realized the futility of fighting against the system. Maybe they knew just how trapped they were.

The monorail arrived, dragging me away from those thoughts, and I quickly boarded before finding a spot in the back. As I did, I could feel eyes following my passage, but I didn't let it affect me. After all, the face I was wearing was a pretty one, and a certain degree of attention was expected.

Besides, if things got out of hand, I had the tools to end any altercation in a hurry. Not that I wanted to go down that path, of course. Doing so would run the risk of derailing my day's plans, and I just couldn't stomach that. So, I did my best to be as unobtrusive as possible.

Fortunately, my admirers were content to watch, and even though it made me feel decidedly uncomfortable, I could appreciate that it didn't go any further than a few leering gazes. Eventually, the monorail reached my destination in the Garden, and I quickly extracted myself from the train, leaving the oglers behind. After only a few more minutes of travel, I found my way to one of the newer megabuildings in the district.

It was the home of Serena Liu, the woman whose identity I'd taken for the day. Gunther had paid her well to stay home, and I was meant to take her place. I had no intention of making an appearance at her job—which was an upscale boutique on the north side of the Lakeview district. Instead, I only wanted to use her credentials to get onto the platform. After that, I had another destination in mind.

I waited in front of the megabuilding for almost five minutes before I saw a sleek black hover car pull up. My interface told me it was the one I'd ordered while riding the monorail, and it would be my ride into Lakeview.

Once I showed the driver my credentials in the form of a metallic card stamped with an identifying number, I boarded the car, and we took off. The car itself was nothing special, just a typical taxi that had been dressed up a bit. But it was necessary because the residents of Lakeview wouldn't allow something so low-class as a monorail to enter their platform. After all, public transportation was for the poor, wasn't it? The rich had no need for it.

I sat back and tried to look relaxed, schooling my face to placidity. However, beneath that calm exterior, my entire body was tense and ready to explode into motion. I knew I was walking into enemy territory, and I needed to be ready to do whatever was necessary should I be found out.

After ten minutes, we finally reached the base of the ramp leading up to the ascended platform that housed the Lakeview district. It was a few hundred yards higher than the Garden's platform, which meant that not only would the residents look down on us socially, but they could do so literally, as well. And that alone was enough to get my blood boiling.

The hover car pulled to a stop at the checkpoint in front of the ramp, and the driver was approached by one Enforcer, while another gestured for me to roll down my window. I did, and he said, "Need your credential card, ma'am."

I handed over the metallic card, and the blond-haired, blue-eyed Enforcer used a device to scan it. It must have fed right into his interface because, a second later, he nodded and handed it back, saying, "You have a good day, ma'am."

While I'd been checked, the driver had undergone a similar inspection. However, the Enforcers hadn't been quite as polite. After all, he was just a driver. The identity I'd stolen was mired in the lower echelons of Lakeview society, but it still held a much higher position than that of a mere driver. Whatever the case, we were soon on our way, following the spiraling ramp up toward Lakeview. When we finally reached the top and I beheld the district's skyline, I couldn't contain a gasp.

It was beautiful.

The buildings were tall and sleek, made from gleaming steel and glass that glittered like crystal. There were trees lining the street and fountains at every intersection. And that was nothing compared to the people. They were all so clean. So happy. So healthy. Suddenly, I understood why there were people clamoring all over one another to be Lakeview's lackeys.

After having left Algiers earlier that morning, I couldn't help but compare the two populations. And on the heels of my surprise came anger, fast and hot and demanding that I do something to even the odds. A few well-placed bombs would be enough to bring Lakeview down to size, wouldn't it?

But no.

I wasn't there to fight a class war, was I? And even if I was, going off half-cocked was a perfect way to fail. Instead, I focused on what I needed to do. Maybe after I got my revenge, I would burn it all down.

The driver navigated to the destination I'd input upon hiring the car, and during that time, I continued to marvel at the sights. Everything was so much cleaner than in the Garden, and there seemed to be an Enforcer on every corner. However, instead of the grim-faced stoicism I was used to seeing, these men and women wore welcoming smiles. I even saw one laughing as he spoke to a resident with a small child—and she didn't look the least bit intimidated, either.

Clearly, the relationship between the Enforcers and the population was very different in the aristocratic districts than it was in the Garden or Algiers.

Eventually, the hover car pulled to a stop at our preordained destination. Before stepping out, I paid him and headed to a nearby café. It was a small building—only a single story, and with a smaller footprint than my own headquarters—but it was packed full of patrons. I stepped up to the door, which slid open with a hiss, and the smell of real coffee nearly knocked me down.

I'd gotten used to it in Mobile, but I hadn't had that delectable beverage since then. And I hadn't even realized just how much I'd missed it until I found myself standing in a line before a broad counter. Workers dressed not unlike me scurried here and there behind the counter, making the various drinks their customers ordered. When I reached the counter, I said, "Uh . . . a coffee, please?"

The barista looked at me like I was an idiot before asking me to be more specific. When I clearly didn't understand what she meant, she pointed to a sign on the wall behind her. On it were listed a hundred different kinds of coffee, from something called a caffè mocha to cappuccinos and everything in between. I had no idea what any of it was, so I just picked one at random.

"Uh . . . Americano," I said. "With sugar."

The girl—she probably wasn't more than sixteen years old—rolled her eyes and went to fill my order. A couple of minutes later, she returned. Using the pad on the counter, I paid, then took my steaming beverage to one of the tables outside, where I sat and began my vigil.

I sipped the drink as I watched the building across the street. It was three stories tall and, like most of the other buildings in Lakeview, looked like a work of art that married the concepts of beauty and function, especially when bathed in the morning sunlight, which somehow seemed brighter in Lakeview.

Was it? Or did it just seem that way because of all the glimmering buildings?

As I sat there watching the other building, I felt someone looking at me. A quick glance in the appropriate direction told me that, once again, I had picked up an admirer. This time, though, it was a handsome young man who'd probably spent more on his shoes than I had on my headquarters. He gave me a wide smile that I pretended not to notice. Hopefully, that would be enough to dissuade any further admiration.

It was less that I wasn't interested and more that I wasn't even wearing my own face. And I suspected that if I was, he wouldn't have been nearly so admiring. One look at my wild hair or the thin scars on my body, and he'd run away.

But then again, Patrick hadn't run away. Instead, he'd wanted to take things further. So, maybe I wasn't really being objective when it came to my own appearance.

Whatever the case, I didn't have time to indulge myself with my new admirer. Thankfully, he took the hint and headed off to greener pastures. Or maybe I had imagined the whole thing. Either way, I pushed that to the back of my mind as I focused on why I'd come to Lakeview in the first place.

I sat there for almost an hour as I waited for my target to appear, and when she did, I wasted no time in following her into the building. I ended up having to Misthack a few cameras along the way—I didn't want a record of my being there—but I eventually joined her in an elevator.

She was a tall, thin woman with stringy black hair. But I hadn't targeted her for her looks. Rather, she was on my radar for one simple reason: her lab manufactured the bio-enhancers that had given Nora the ability to exceed her potential.

And the moment we reached her lab, I erupted into motion, pushing her into the room and slamming her against the wall. Nearby glassware shook, and a few vials nearly fell from their shelves as I summoned my nano-bladed knife from my arsenal implant. For this trip, because I couldn't very well walk through Lakeview with Ferdinand II on my hip and a sword on my back, I'd changed my loadout a little, replacing my sniper rifle with my dagger and the BMAP with Ferdinand II.

I pressed the knife against her throat hard enough to draw a trickle of blood. I hissed, "Be calm and nobody has to get hurt here. If I get one whiff of the Enforcers, you're the first to die. Got it?"

She pressed her back against the wall, swallowing hard. "I . . . I understand," she said, her voice far higher pitched than I expected. "What do you want?"

I smiled. "Nothing much," I said, backing away to give her some room. We both knew it was a symbolic gesture; if I wanted to, I could kill her in a heartbeat, regardless of how much space was between us. "I just need to sabotage a shipment is all. I need you to do your science thing and either render it inert or, better yet, give it the opposite effect."

As I spoke, my eyes darted around the laboratory. It looked much as I expected it to, with a handful of workstations that had a variety of scientific equipment. In the corner, there was a large safe that, judging by the way it felt, probably held Rift Shards. Likely, the scientists incorporated them into the process of creating the bio-enhancers somehow.

It didn't matter. That wasn't why I was there. As much as I could use a few extra credits, I had a more important task in front of me. To that end, I waited for the scientist—whose name was Mia Salvatore—to answer.

For a long few seconds, she just stared at me like I'd grown a third eye. Then, a wry smile spread across her face. Shaking her head, she stepped farther into the room and grabbed a tissue from a dispenser at one of the workstations and pressed it to the small wound on her neck.

"Well?" I asked. "Can you do it? Or do I need to find someone else? Perhaps one of your coworkers?"

There were six other scientists that worked in the laboratory, but Mia was the only one who came in on her off days. So, isolating her had been easy, and that ease was why I had chosen her.

"Oh, I can do it," she said. "But not for free."

"How much?" I asked.

"Not money" was her response. "I need a little favor. You scratch my back, and I'll scratch yours."

I narrowed my eyes. That was outside the scope of my plans, but in some ways, it made things easier. So long as I could guarantee that Mia would hold up her end of the bargain, I could save some of my dwindling credits. Or given what I was asking, a lot of them.

"What do you need?"

"Not much," she said, leaning against the workstation. "I simply need you to thin the herd a bit. Get rid of my competition."

"Who do you want me to kill?" I asked.

"Kill? Goodness, no! I'm not a barbarian! I don't want you to kill anyone," she said. Then, as if she thought better of it, Mia added, "Or not my competitor, at least. Instead, I want you to humiliate her. To prove that she is unfit for promotion. Do that and I will sabotage whatever you'd like me to sabotage. And I will tell you right now, I'm the only one who can do what you're asking me to do. The others . . . They're a bit . . . Well, they're just not capable."

That tracked with what I'd learned of her. Mia Salvatore was a bit of a rising star within the Blue Epoch Corporation, and she'd managed a meteoric rise through the ranks via sheer competence. Her colleagues were not nearly so talented, and their positions only really existed because they'd latched on to her coattails. I wasn't entirely certain that they were all completely incapable of doing what I needed, but using Salvatore made everything that much easier.

Still, I took a few seconds to think about it. I had a feeling that her task would end up being far more complicated than I'd hoped, but that wasn't necessarily a bad thing. If I did what she asked, then we would be tied together. I'd have something to hold over her, should she balk at holding up her end of the deal. So long as I kept good records, it was safer this way than if I just paid her.

"And how do you propose I do this?" I asked.

"Have you ever heard of Biloxi?" she asked.

I shook my head. "Can't say I have."

"Oh, you're going to love it" was her response. "Sandy beaches, casinos, and a kelp-harvesting operation that's second to none. Said operation is headed up by one Calvin Kane, son of my rival, Aurelia Kane. Your job is to sabotage his operation. I don't care how, so long as the blame falls on him. When the Blue Epoch Corporation sees that, they will lay the blame on her shoulders. After all, she was the one who got him that position in the first place. She will be humiliated, and I will have one less competitor."

I sighed, but I nodded in agreement. It looked like I was leaving Nova City again. Hopefully, this time, I wouldn't be gone for three years.

CHAPTER TWENTY-THREE

ALL-NATURAL

Both of my parents were prostitutes on Bourbon Street, dead from dust overdoses before I was a teenager. I sometimes wonder which came first—the drugs or the path that led them to prostitution. Some people love that kind of life, but I don't think my parents were among that group.

—Nora Lancaster

Leaving Nova City wasn't as easy as heading from one district to another. There were rules about who could and could not leave. Most people didn't bother jumping through all the hoops, instead choosing just to stay in the city. After all, there was nothing out there but vicious wildlife, wildlings, and a few settlements that barely qualified as civilization, right? Most residents of Nova City—at least in the Garden or Algiers—were completely unaware that other cities even existed. So, they were trapped by both circumstance and ignorance.

I knew that because I'd been in a similar position before my uncle showed me that the world was much broader than I'd been taught in school.

In any case, there were two ways out of Nova City. The first method would involve me getting all the proper permits and submitting to the authority of the Enforcers. I was confident in my ability to mask my identity, and I suspected that nobody was even hunting me anyway, but I didn't really want to chance it.

The second way out was risky, as well, but in a completely different way. There were certain people who smuggled things in and out of Nova City all the time. My uncle had utilized their services on a multitude of occasions. He'd even given me instructions on how to find the right people who wouldn't ask too many questions. It was supposed to be relatively safe, at least according to Jeremiah.

But safe for my uncle wasn't necessarily safe for everyone else. Not only was he personally stronger than anyone else in the city, but he also had the benefit of his reputation backing him up. Everyone knew what happened to people who messed with Jeremiah. And that wasn't even considering that he'd had an entire tribe behind him, too.

I wouldn't have any of that. Certainly, I could take care of myself, but going the smuggler's route would put me on their home turf, where I would be at a disadvantage. And being a lone young woman, regardless of my relative power, would invite challenge from the wrong sorts of people. Still, it was the best of bad options, so after leaving the laboratory, I'd contacted Gunther to ask him to provide an introduction, which he had.

So, two days later, I found myself heading to a part of the Garden I'd never visited. In a lot of ways, it looked little different from the rest of the district. The same monstrous megabuildings dominated the area, and the people looked similar, as well. However, I wasn't there for what was on the surface. Instead, my destination was the Undercity.

To that end, once I'd found the right area, I made my way to a huge concrete trench that cut through the region. Nova City was subject to stringent climate controls, but from time to time, the city's climate managers would manufacture storms intended to wash the worst of the grime from the streets. All that water had to go somewhere, so Nova was crisscrossed with various trenches and drainage tunnels, many of which had been blocked off or repurposed for the Underground. Such was the case with the trench in front of me.

Much of the structure was still viable for its intended purpose, but the nearby access tunnel had been co-opted by a smuggler's group called the Nats. Like most tribal names, it was an unimaginative moniker derived from the tribe's defining characteristic—primarily, that its members were entirely free of cybernetics. In other words, wholly natural. They had Nexus Implants and skills, but that was where they drew the line. They didn't even have the common rudimentary interfaces that didn't require a version of [Cybernetic Interface], let alone anything as advanced as mine. As far as I knew, they had no real way to keep track of their own progression.

Truthfully, I would have preferred to go somewhere else, but the Nats asked the least number of questions. And they were actively hostile to both the Specters and the Enforcers, which meant that they were extremely unlikely to rat me out, even if they figured out who I was. Given my preference to avoid any extra scrutiny, they seemed like the best choice.

Plus, Gunther had vouched for them, which was beginning to mean something to me.

With a shake of my head, I crossed the busy street and hopped the barricade meant to prevent people from accidentally stumbling into the steep-sided trench. It barely slowed me down, and in the space of a second, I was sliding down the sloped, algae-coated sides. After another second, I got my feet under me and slid to a stop on a platform that housed the access tunnel that was my destination.

A pair of mooks—both male, though as different in stature as you could imagine, with one being tall and broad, while the other was short and even thinner than me—were stationed just inside the tunnel. Both were armed with assault rifles that looked fairly well-made, and they were wearing worn body armor.

The big one grunted, "Get outta here, street rat. Ain't nothin' in here for you."

"Not a street rat, you mook," I said. "I'm here to see Gavin. Gunther sent me."

His eyes narrowed under his heavy brow, but he didn't argue. Instead, he unclipped a communicator from his waist—it was a big, heavy box with a long antenna attached—and pressed a button before saying, "This is Big Chief. Got a street rat here says she was sent by Gunther. Wants to talk to the boss man. Over."

I recognized the communicator from a display I'd seen in Gunther's lobby, so I knew they were based on some pre-Initialization technology. However, I didn't know exactly how that kind of stuff worked. In any case, a moment later, the box crackled, and a tinny voice came through, "Send her in. Boss's expectin' her."

"Ten-four," the so-called Big Chief said.

After that, they let me inside, where I was met by a young man. He was small, scrawny, and a little sickly looking. However, he had a jittery demeanor that told me he was full of energy.

"Hey. I'm Leif," he said, raking a hand through his coppery hair. "I'm supposed to lead you inside."

I gestured for him to do just that and said, "Lead on, then."

He grinned, then said, "Follow me. If you don't think you can make a jump, just let me know, and I'll get a ladder."

Then, he took off at a light jog, and I followed. The concrete ground was slippery with water and slime, and the sides of the tunnel were lousy with various pipes, but that was to be expected. I'd spent some time in the tunnels beneath the city, so I'd known what I was in for. Still, it surprised me how adroitly Leif navigated the tunnels. His footing was sure, and he kept up a solid pace.

Then, we reached a gap in the tunnel, which he leaped without even slowing down. I followed, making the seven-foot jump with ease. Leif looked back in surprise, but he didn't slow. Like that we ran through the tunnels for another ten minutes, turning this way and that until I was completely lost. My map was useless underground, so I was at Leif's mercy. As we went, the air steadily grew more and more humid until it wasn't so different from what I'd felt back in Mobile.

Thankfully, we soon found our way to a massive underground cavern that was absolutely filled with people. It was laid out similarly to one of the megabuildings, with a bunch of cubicle-like domiciles lining the outer area and a more communal space in the middle. There were vendors hawking a variety of wares, from guns to mushrooms and everything in between, and the whole place was lit by strings of lights hung from the low ceiling.

There was no forgetting that we were under the city, but I supposed that was kind of the point. These people weren't part of Nova City. Not really. They were residents of the Underground.

I got a few curious looks as we made our way through the crowd, but no one barred our way. Eventually, we made it to a cubicle that was a bit bigger than most. Leif knocked on the door, and a few seconds later, a bearded bear of a man opened it. He didn't have bulging muscles like Nora or Simon, who'd been one of my hand-to-hand instructors. Instead, he was just a huge mass of flesh. He wasn't blubbery, and he had plenty of muscle, but most of that was buried beneath a layer of fat. Still, there was an aura of strength about him that I couldn't deny. I got the sense that he was a Tier 4. Not as powerful as Gunther or my uncle, but if he was well trained, he could definitely be a problem.

Leif said, "Boss man—I brought her, just like you said."

"So you did," the man rumbled. Judging by how much he matched the description Gunther had given me, I assumed he was Gavin Paulson, the man in charge of the Nats and the one who was going to help me get out of Nova City. Getting back in was another story, but I had a plan for that, too, even if I was less sure about the return trip. "Good job, kid." Then, to me, he said, "Come on in and we'll get you sorted right out."

I followed him into the domicile, and I was a little taken aback by what I saw. The room was decidedly normal, and it reminded me quite a bit of my uncle's old penthouse. The decor was different, and the whole place seemed a lot cozier. Probably because there were plenty of soft surfaces like blankets and pillows on the couches, but there was also quite a bit of pre-Initialization technology present. Like a huge television hanging from the wall, looking absolutely archaic to anyone who'd grown up with the modern screens of Nova City.

"I know it's a bit . . . outdated in here," said the man with a wide grin splitting his bearded face. "But it's home. Can I get you anything? Drink?"

I shook my head. "Just ready to get out of the city" was my response.

"You're not the only one," he said. "Lots of folks trying to escape the tribal wars up top."

I shrugged. That wasn't why I wanted to leave, but he didn't need to know that. If he wanted to believe I was a refugee, then so be it.

"You have any implants?" he asked, gesturing to one of the couches as he sat in another one. "Not that I'll refuse to help you if you do or anything. Just asking."

"A couple," I said, sitting across from him. The couch was soft and made of real leather, reminding me of Gunther's office. I raised my hand, then tapped my temple. "Hand and interface. Why?"

He didn't need to know about my Sheath or my arsenal implant. The way I saw it, he likely already knew I wasn't completely natural, so denying it would've probably gotten me into hot water. I'd rather reveal a little information if it kept him from asking more questions.

He shrugged his massive shoulders. "Just asking," he said. "Doesn't it make you feel . . . less human? Like you're one step away from being a robot?"

"Not really," I said. "I like having the use of my hand, and this was the only way I could get that."

"Fair enough. Some of my people have more extreme views, though," he said. "So, don't just assume all Nats are as accepting as me. Some would kill you on sight if they knew you had an ounce of tech in your body. If we could get away with yanking out our Nexus Implants, we would."

"You ever been outside?" I asked.

"Can't say I have" was his response. "Not much call to leave the city."

"So, you've never seen a wildling?"

He shook his head.

"Count yourself lucky, then," I said. "There are packs of them. Hundreds strong, all roving around like animals. They'll attack anything. They'll eat anything. The only thing keeping most of us from becoming like that is the fact that we have our Nexus Implants. So, remember that when you start talking about getting rid of them."

He leaned forward, fixing me with an inscrutable gaze. After a few seconds, he said, "You're more than you seem, aren't you? Sometimes, I wish I had one of those fancy interfaces. Maybe then I could tell what makes you so different."

If I'd been wearing my own face instead of one I'd stolen from some random woman on the street, he might've recognized me for what I was. But to all outward appearances, I was just a normal Tier 3 woman. A little haggard. A bit rough around the edges, maybe. But normal. Just the sort of person who might think she could handle life outside the city, but not one so powerful that she could get out without help.

"Life can be a mystery," I said, refusing to back down. In a moment, I could have my pistol out and a round in the air. I wasn't afraid of him, and what's more, I think he knew it. After all, anyone who came recommended by Gunther was unlikely to be simple, so there was no reason for me to pretend otherwise.

Suddenly, he let out a bellowing laugh as he leaned back. For a few moments, his barrel chest heaved with genuine mirth until, at last, he said, "Oh, that's a good one. I like you. No wonder Gunther vouched for you."

"Can you get me out of the city?" I asked, tiring of his games. I wasn't there to impress him. I just wanted him to perform a service. I'd already transferred the fee to Gunther, and if I got what I needed, he would then pay Gavin in goods. Everything had already been arranged. I just needed the big man to hold up his end of the bargain.

"Of course," he said. "We're leaving in a few minutes. Just waiting on the others."

"Others?" I asked.

"There are only a few thousand," he stated. "Most of them former slaves who've escaped their bonds. Nasty implants, those. Worse than most. Most of our income comes from removing them."

"Really?" I asked. That was news to me. As far as I knew, if someone received a slave implant, their life as a free person was over. They were literally incapable of refusing commands from their masters. But I supposed that there had to be some cases where people needed them removed. And that wasn't the sort of thing you went to a cybernetic engineer for. Most would hijack the implant for their own benefit. Or sell the slaves to someone who would. It seemed that was where the Nats stepped in.

"So surprised," he said, shaking his head. "I don't know what you've heard about us, but we're not all degenerates. Some of us truly want to help others. And the money from reselling those implants helps."

I nodded. Nobody ever did anything out of the goodness of their heart. There was always some sort of angle, a way for them to exploit the situation for their own gain. That the Nats were profiting didn't negate the good they did, but it did nullify some of that altruistic aura.

"Well, time to go," he said, pushing himself to his feet with a grunt. "Follow me."

I rose and followed him out of the domicile and through the common area. We didn't have to walk far until we reached a side tunnel, which went on for a few hundred yards before opening up into another cavernous room. This one was packed full of people, as well, but they were markedly different from the residents of the Underground. No—with their lusterless eyes, sunken cheeks, and ragged clothes, these were the refugees who wanted to escape Nova City.

Gavin gestured with one meaty paw, saying, "Well, join your people."

I nodded to him, then did just that, mingling with the group. Each and every one of them smelled of desperation, body odor, and sometimes worse things. I tried to ignore it. Not because I had a sensitive stomach, but because they were the victims of my actions. I'd lit the fire that acted as the spark that started the tribal war. These people's lives had been upended because of me.

Did I feel guilty? Sure. A little. But I didn't regret it. I had always known there would be some degree of collateral damage in the pursuit of my revenge, and I'd long steeled my heart against letting it affect me. However, no one in my position could look at those pitiful creatures and feel anything but guilt. It was inevitable.

After a few more minutes, someone yelled for everyone to quiet down. The crowd did just that, so we had little trouble hearing when a woman said, "We're going to lead you down in fives. When you go, don't try to help. It'll just make this more difficult. So, just go limp and we'll take care of the rest."

Everyone murmured, but no one complained. After that, they started taking people away. Because the group was so big, it took quite a while for them to reach me. When they did, I followed a woman through a side tunnel for a few hundred feet until we reached a huge grate. There were a dozen men and women there, all wearing harnesses and hooked to a series of cables. Outside, I could see one of the huge pillars that supported the city.

A man approached me, then held out his hand. It was gnarled and the fingers looked crooked, as if they'd been broken a few times. "I'm Tam," he said with a crooked smile that creased his already wrinkled face. He was older—probably in his fifties—but his exposed arms revealed corded muscle and skin that looked like cured leather. "You're going to be with me, then. You ready to get hooked in?"

I gave him a dubious look, but I said, "I guess I don't have much of a choice. Let's do this."

"No name, huh? Probably for the best," he said, reaching out and wrapping a harness around me. He'd clearly done it hundreds—if not thousands—of times before, so he was done in moments. Then, he directed me to hook my harness to his via a series of clips. There seemed to be a lot of them, but I supposed that redundancy was probably a good thing in this kind of situation. In any case, I was soon strapped to him like a human backpack.

Once we were hooked together, with my back to his, he once again asked if I was ready. When I said I was, he started forward, reminding me to stay limp. I forced my body to do just that, and before I knew it, we were through the grate and clinging to a rope stretched along the underside of the city platform.

Then I looked down.

I think that's when I really started to wonder if I'd made a mistake.

CHAPTER TWENTY-FOUR

THE BAYOU

Regret is a funny thing. It's not a constant, but when that feeling comes for you, it hits like a sledgehammer. Lately, it feels like it's happening more and more, and I wonder if I might have been better off just swallowing my pride and enjoying the position I had.

—Nora Lancaster

"What the—"

My assault rifle, which I'd loaded into one of the quick-access weapon slots in my arsenal implant, was in my hand before I finished the exclamation. But even then, I wasn't quick enough to bring it to bear before I felt a pair of talons tear into my shoulder. For a moment, I was weightless as it tried to lift me free, but the bird wasn't strong enough to handle our collective weight. So, after only a second of furiously flapping wings, it released us.

I fell, and for the briefest of instants, I thought I was about to plummet to my death. But then the harness tightened, and the ropes snapped taut as we were jerked to a stop. Tam let out a grunt of pain, and I nearly dropped my rifle.

But I was made of stronger stuff than that. My training pushed at my mind as I raised my weapon, took aim, and fired. The R-14 barked three times in quick succession, and the resultant blobs of plasma tore through the air. When they hit the bird, which was some hawklike variant, sleek and swift with an eight-foot wingspan and metallic claws, it burst into an explosion of feathers, blood, and charred flesh.

It was too bad, then, that the hawk wasn't alone.

Looking down, I saw a swirling miasma of feathers and sharp talons. The flock of raptors looked like a solid thing, seething as its components reacted to the loss of one of their own.

"Uh . . . we've got a problem, Tam!" I shouted over the sudden screeching. "Head back!"

"Can't," he growled, climbing hand over hand back to the underside of the platform. We'd fallen almost a dozen feet before our momentum had been arrested by the ropes, so I was more than a little impressed that he had the strength to haul us both up. However, I was even more surprised to see that the grate through which we'd left the Underground had been closed and reinforced, likely to keep the hawks from getting inside.

"Shit," I muttered, going over my options. The BMAP would do little good against a flock of birds. Sure, when it hit one, it would do some damage, but its relatively slow-moving projectiles were ill-suited to the task of assaulting multiple fast-moving targets. For the first time, I found myself regretting my choice to eschew the Dragon, which was an antipersonnel weapon perfectly suited for the exact situation in which I'd found myself, in favor of the mobile artillery platform.

But right then, regret wouldn't do me any good, so I moved on to other options. Obviously, my nano-bladed dagger and sword were out of the question. If those birds got close, then I would be ripped to shreds. My Constitution had progressed past the human limits, but these monstrous birds were far too fast for me.

My assault rifle was another option, but anything more than a three-round burst would overheat and distort the barrel. The Pulsar was even less suited for the occasion, and while I could easily explode a hawk every second, there were hundreds of the things down there. By the time I made a dent in that flock, they'd have long since murdered Tam and me.

So, my only real option was the scattergun. Luckily, I'd given it one of the quick-access slots, so it only took a moment to exchange my R-14 for the stubby weapon. When I did, I made sure it had plenty of ammunition before taking aim. The birds were still too far away, but I wanted to be ready.

Tam was on the verge of panic, muttering to himself unintelligibly. Or maybe he was praying. Either way, it was getting on my nerves, so as I aimed down my weapon's sights, I said, "Shut up, Tam. We're fine. Just hold on tight."

"W-what . . ."

It was at that moment that the birds chose to attack. The flock raced upward as if they'd caught an updraft, and when the first few got within ten yards, I opened fire. Lightning erupted from my scattergun in a wide cone, arcing from one hawk to the next and electrocuting the little monsters. One by one, they fell from the sky; it was more than a thousand feet to the bayou far below, but I knew they wouldn't recover before hitting the ground.

And I felt certain that they wouldn't survive. Even if they did, they'd be too injured to pose much of a threat, and they'd probably end up as prey for other creatures who called the swamp home.

As devastating as that arc of lightning was, it wasn't enough. The cone was only about ten feet wide, but it carved a corridor through the ascending birds. Still, the moment the pulse faded, they flooded back in. I shot again, and the hawks closed in around us. I heard Tam scream, and suddenly, we were falling again.

I continued to fire until the rope snapped taut, jerking us to a stop. The sounds of a hundred bird cries coupled with the hissing boom of my scatter-gun's report filled the air. The smell of charred feathers and cooking meat surrounded me, but I continued to fire, one shot after another, until the cannister ran dry. The moment I started to exchange it for another, more birds swooped in, tearing at me with their vicious metal claws.

The infiltration suit combined with my Sheath to protect my vitals, but it didn't take the birds long to target my relatively unprotected face. Panic rose in my chest. My heart pounded. And all I wanted to do was flail to keep those vicious, stabbing beaks and metallic claws from my head. I forced myself to follow the procedure I'd repeated thousands of times before, slamming the new cannister into place before opening fire once again.

The birds fried, falling from the sky in droves.

But there were always more. For a subjective eternity, my world was nothing but feathers, talons, and pain, but I persisted because any other option would see me dead. After all, the most powerful motivator is simple survival.

Finally, when I was on my second-to-last cannister, the air cleared, and the few remaining birds glided away.

I sighed, hanging limp. I could feel that my face and hands were a mass of scratches, but I hoped none of them were serious. Thankfully, the Sheath protected my entire body, which had kept the talons from doing more than superficial damage. Still, I could feel that it had been pushed to the limits of what it could do. No single strike was enough to strain the subdermal armor, but after being subjected to hundreds of strikes from the ripping talons, it was on the verge of giving in. Thankfully, it would slowly syphon Mist to repair itself.

"You okay back there, Tam?" I asked.

There was no answer. "Tam?"

I knew he was dead before I turned my head, but even that slim preparation wasn't enough to keep me from vomiting. I couldn't get a good look, but from what I could see, it looked like his face had been ripped off. And I was fairly certain that most of the rest of his body had received similar treatment. After all, he didn't have high-grade armor to protect him.

Shaking my head, I tried to shift around, but I quickly realized that I was hampered by the harness that had been designed to keep us back-to-back. That's when I realized that if I wanted to get out of this mess, I would either need help, or I was going to have to unhook myself.

Even as I moved, the rope attaching us to the platform above twisted until I was facing the grate. There was a man standing there, staring at me with wide eyes.

"Help me!" I yelled across the twenty-foot expanse.

He shook his head, then backed away. As he went, I could see the fear in his eyes. And I knew it wasn't just directed at the birds. Instead, he was terrified of me, too. After all, the birds were scary enough, but I'd just killed dozens of them. Maybe hundreds. I was probably much more frightening.

Briefly, I pointed my weapon in his direction, but he'd already retreated out of sight. I swore in frustration, imagining all the things I'd like to do to the coward. But inwardly, I didn't really blame him; he was just afraid, and he wanted to stay alive. The seeds of empathy did little to assuage my anger, though.

I took a deep breath, calming myself as I thought through the problem. But I already knew how to solve it. I just didn't want to do it.

Of course, the situation didn't care about my hesitation, and it soon lit a fire under me in the form of a fraying rope. The moment I saw it, I knew it wouldn't hold the combined weight of Tam and me for very much longer. So, if I wanted to avoid a fall of more than a thousand feet, I needed to move.

After taking another deep, calming breath, I reached down and unhooked my harness. As I did, I grabbed hold of Tam's, and once I felt myself come free, I flipped around and started to climb.

With my [Acrobatics] skill, combined with my high Constitution attribute, I had little trouble clamoring over him and grabbing hold of the rope. A moment later, I was climbing hand over hand until I reached the underside of the platform. When I did, I grasped the handholds Tam had intended to use to make his way to the pylon that held the platform aloft. They were little more than iron pitons drilled into the concrete, but they were just big enough that I could wrap my fingers around them. The rope it had once held had already been sliced to ribbons, and I knew it would snap the moment I gave it my weight.

Swinging like a monkey, I made my way to the enormous concrete platform, and I soon found my next major obstacle. I wasn't sure if one of the pitons had fallen out or if there had been something else planned for the last ten feet, but there was a definite gap between me and the pylon.

"Crap," I muttered.

I couldn't go back. And I only had one option going forward. So, I ground my teeth together in frustration before I started swinging back and forth. When I'd gained enough momentum, I waited until I reached the apex of my swing and let go. My stomach dropped as I sailed through the open air, and for a single moment, I was sure I'd come up short.

I'd fall to the swamp below. Just like the hawks.

But then I realized that I had the opposite problem. I'd aimed too high. My swing had been too forceful. As a result, I slammed into the pylon five feet above the first piton. The air left my lungs in a rush, and a tinge of panic colored my thoughts. Still, I kept my wits about me as I began to fall.

After spending quite some time on the obstacle course, I'd grown accustomed to using my latest ability. So, it was almost subconscious when I activated Balance. Immediately, I knew the precise location of every inch of my body. More, that knowledge came with increased coordination, and I had no trouble at all grabbing the handhold that would have assuredly evaded my grasp without the ability pushing my proprioception and balance to superhuman levels.

I released the ability before it could completely drain my Mist, but even that brief activation had taken half my reserves. It was an ability that was intended for short-term use and, even then, only in emergencies. Still, as much as I'd wanted to save it, I knew that it had been a necessary expenditure.

I hung there for a few seconds before beginning the arduous climb down. I went one piton at a time, like I was descending the world's most awkward ladder—which was precisely what those crude handholds had been intended for. As I climbed down, I couldn't help but feel a surge of respect for the late Tam; if everything had gone to plan, he would have made the descent with me on his back. Likely, he was extremely specialized, but even so, I was impressed.

The descent took forever, and as I drew closer to the ground, I saw that a crowd of people were gathered at the bottom of the pylon. They were clearly the men and women who had preceded me, and when I finally reached the bottom, I was beset by questions.

I ignored them all. Instead, I summoned my Cutter, not even bothering to extend my Mimic skill to disguise it. In seconds, I was mounted up and speeding away, leaving a trail of swampy water in my wake.

My actions had made a lot of noise, and I knew that it wouldn't be long before the Enforcers responded. Perhaps they'd only send a drone, or maybe they had some sort of flying vehicles they could use around the underside of the city. Either way, I had no desire to find out. So, I put on as much speed as I could until I'd left the city behind.

When I looked back, the huge structure still loomed over me, but that would be true for miles more. In fact, Nova was so big that it could be seen halfway to Mobile, if only as a vague outline on the horizon.

After making certain that I hadn't been followed, I resumed my journey. Soon, I found the remnants of an old highway, which I followed for another few miles before coming across a mostly intact building. I dismounted and dismissed my Cutter before summoning my assault rifle. Thus armed, I approached the building and spent a few minutes clearing it of any threats. With Observation constantly running, I felt certain that it was empty, but still, I didn't want to take any chances. Once I was satisfied that the building was free of previous occupation, I set about the task of treating my wounds.

It had taken me over an hour to descend the pylon, and in that time, the blood had dried on my face. So, I took great care in cleaning the cuts before applying a foam bandage to the worst of them. Hopefully, that would prevent them from scarring, but even if it didn't, I felt confident that any scars would be shallow and hardly noticed.

So, that taken care of, I settled down to eat and rest. It was still only midafternoon, but a thunderstorm had begun. So, I chose to wait it out in the relative shelter of the abandoned building.

Leaning back against one of the walls, I found myself replaying the day's events in my mind. Could I have prevented Tam's death? No. He was ill-equipped to deal with even one of the hawks, much less a flock. However, I still wished he wouldn't have died.

Sighing, I wondered if Patrick was okay. He was probably at Dr. Montague's office, learning how to be a cybernetic engineer. According to him, he was already making great progress, which was faster than I'd expected. Of course, that was probably selling him short. After all, he was driven, talented, and unafraid of hard work. He'd proven that more than once. So, his progress shouldn't have been surprising.

Not for the first time, I found my mind drifting to the future. Things were coming to a head in Nova City. I still had a long way to go, but my plan's progress made it clear that I'd be finished in the city sooner rather than later. What would happen after that? I had no idea. But I couldn't deny that I hoped Patrick would be part of that future.

I spent a while just sitting there and thinking. An unfortunate side effect of tending to all the irons I had in the fire was that I rarely had time to just sit and let my mind wander. I was always planning one thing or another or worrying about the plans I'd made the day before. That didn't lend itself well to introspection.

But now? Alone in the wilderness, there was precious little else to do. Inevitably, my mind went to Nora's betrayal. Why had she done it? My uncle had treated her like family. I had treated her like a favorite aunt. Or a big sister. And yet, she'd betrayed Jeremiah. She had betrayed me. Was the allure of power really so strong? Or did she have another reason? What wasn't I seeing?

Those thoughts dominated my mind until, at last, I found myself drifting off to sleep. It was well into the night, and I hadn't made much progress in finding answers. I suspected that would be the case until I finally confronted Nora. But that was for the future. For now, I just needed to keep pushing forward until that confrontation could take place on my terms.

My sleep was blessedly dreamless, and I awoke to the incessant sound of my KIOI's alarm. So, I quickly rose, took care of my morning ablutions, and ate. When I got around to checking my wounds, I was unsurprised to find that they'd largely healed. Another day, and they would fade away to almost nothing. A day more, and there would only be unblemished skin.

Stretching a bit, I worked the kinks out of my muscles before heading back outside, where I summoned my Cutter and resumed my journey east. I didn't take the same roads I'd used on the trip back from Mobile, instead skewing a bit more south as I made my way toward the destination specified by Mia Salvatore, the woman who'd set me on the mission to undermine her rival's position within their company.

Finally, after most of the day had passed, I found what I was looking for.

Biloxi loomed before me, a strange mixture of Nova City and Bayou La Batre.

CHAPTER TWENTY-FIVE

BILOXI

I'm surrounded by incompetent people. One thing after another, everything has gone wrong since the moment I took over the Specters. Sometimes, I wonder why anyone ever bothers to be in charge.

—Nora Lancaster

I sat on my hover bike, one foot on the ground as I studied the town in the distance. It had some of the trappings of Nova, especially when it came to the atmosphere. It lacked the lewd holographic displays, but it was still bedecked in neon lighting, a feature that was even more prominent in the waning light of dusk. However, there were also clear signs of it being a frontier city. While some of the buildings were made of the same concrete, steel, and glass that I had grown accustomed to in Nova, there were plenty that had been constructed from wood, as well. In addition, there were some holdovers from the pre-Initialization era, looking entirely out of place amid the newer structures.

But more incongruous than those aged buildings were the ships moored right off the coast. Part of that incongruity lay in the fact that the only ships I'd ever seen had been back in Bayou La Batre; those had been created for a specific purpose, and they'd borne the characteristics of working toward that goal. With long arms, copious netting, and patched hulls, they had been working vessels. The ones off the coast of Biloxi were different in almost every way.

For one, they were much larger, resembling buildings themselves. The closest one was at least two hundred yards long, and its first deck soared almost a hundred feet from the surface of the water below. One deck after another rose from there, making it look like the slightest wind would see it tipping over to spill its inhabitants into the sea.

And there were a lot of them, too. Some of the people scurried across the deck, clearly engaged in one task or another, but plenty of others—the bulk, in fact—were mired in leisure. Wearing high-necked suits that were ill-suited to the weather, they sipped amber liquid from fluted glasses and dined on tiny hors d'oeuvres. With Observation active, I could just make out their smug, smiling faces as well as the haughty sneers they directed at the white-clad workers.

That first ship wasn't the only one, either. There were almost a dozen of them lined up along the coast. Judging by how little they moved, I could surmise that they'd been affixed to the seabed in some manner, though I couldn't quite understand the reasoning behind doing that. However, it didn't take me long to come to the same conclusion I'd discovered when confronted by the excesses of the rich: they did it because they could.

A half mile from the coast, I saw the telltale blue shimmer of a Mist shield, telling me that the area was at least nominally protected from the vicious marine life. Even as the sun set, I continued my study of Biloxi, and eventually, my gaze settled on a set of scaffolding suspended over a few square miles of the ocean. It was likewise protected by a Mist shield, but judging by how bright the shimmering blue barrier was, I surmised that it was far more potent than the one that protected the ships.

As night fell, the scaffolding lit up, revealing the sight of hundreds of people scurrying along the latticework. Some of them wore huge yellow exosuits as they hauled ropes that descended into the sea. Eventually, I saw the fruits of their labor in a huge basketful of some red, leafy substance, which a few laborers quickly hauled to the edge of the latticework where they loaded it into a flat-bottomed barge.

That, I knew, was the whole reason Biloxi existed. My contact, Mia Salvatore, had told me that the kelp was crucial to Blue Epoch's bioengineered enhancement supplements. She'd also provided a long and boring explanation about what role it played, but I'd never cared about that kind of thing. All that mattered was that I knew it was incredibly important—enough so that any interruption in the supply would have far-reaching and serious consequences.

Which was precisely why I was there.

Calvin Kane was the man who'd been put in charge of the operation, and if he failed to deliver in any way, not only would he suffer serious repercussions, but his mother, who'd gotten him the job in the first place, would also bear the ultimate shame of costing the company time and money.

It was one of those things that made so little sense to me. These affluent people, who'd been given everything in life, never understood that, to the masters they served, they were no different than the men and women who worked the Garden's Silos or Algiers's factories. They were only important inasmuch as they provided value to the company. The moment that value was compromised, they became expendable. It was an impersonal, cruel way of treating people, and most of Nova's de facto aristocracy failed to see that, in that respect, they were no different from those they considered their inferiors.

Everyone who was part of the system was subject to its harsh reality. Even the ones at the top were incapable of escaping that simple fact.

Night fell as I continued to study Biloxi, and I saw that it had a significant nightlife. The town itself was home to enough bars, clubs, and brothels to rival anywhere in Nova City, save for Bourbon Street itself. Sure, it was all stratified by perceived class, with the workers having their own establishments to patronize; the buttoned-up elites did, too, and the two didn't intermingle. Finally, I saw a serious security presence, which boded well for my plan for entry.

I remained there for hours more until I was satisfied that I'd seen what the town had to offer. Certainly, I didn't know everything. But my reconnaissance as well as the research I'd done before leaving Nova had given me a decent overview of what to expect. Now, I just needed to wait for the right moment before I could head into the town, find my mark, and execute my plan.

With that in mind, I turned around and retreated a few more miles to an abandoned building I'd marked along the way. Dismissing the hover bike, I ranged through the surrounding area until I felt sure that it was free of any predators, then headed inside the building. It had once been a store of some sort, with covered fueling stations in front, but it was long since abandoned. The interior of the building was empty, save for some overturned shelves and a few scattered plastic bottles. Vegetation grew out from the windows, covering half the floor, and I found a few bones and piles of dried excrement that suggested that the building had once been home to some sort of animal. It was long abandoned, though.

I hopped over a counter and headed into the back of the building where I found the remains of an old walk-in freezer. The door was still capable of closing, so I hoped it would be safe for the night. Once I'd gotten inside, I shut the door behind me. Grabbing a Mist lamp from my storage, I looked around; the interior of the freezer was as I'd expected. Rotten wooden crates decorated metal shelving, but the former contents had long since surrendered to the passage of time.

I was thankful for that because, if it hadn't already rotted away completely, the smell would likely have made the place uninhabitable, even for a single night. Though I'd slept in worse.

Whatever the case, I was grateful that I didn't have to make that call, and once I was certain that the area was secure, I allowed myself to relax. After eating a ration bar and once again lamenting the lack of decent food, I inspected my wounds. Most of them had already scabbed over, and due to my Regeneration and the benefits of my Triage ability, coupled with my high Constitution attribute, I knew they'd be completely healed by morning.

That was a relief. I knew I could cover them up with Mimic, but the last thing I wanted was to start a new mission already wounded. My plan didn't involve much in the way of fighting, but given my history, I didn't discount the possibility that things would end in battle. So, I needed to be at my best.

I spent the next few hours doing some calisthenics meant to help me maintain the gains I'd made over the last few weeks. It also served to loosen my muscles, which provided some relief. Traveling through the wilderness, especially after a fight like I'd experienced beneath the platform, was tense work, and I needed to stretch out.

After that, I spent a further couple of hours working on my Ghosts. I'd finished a few new ones of late, but they weren't perfect. So, I tinkered with them, trying to eliminate any weaknesses. I loved writing Ghosts, but editing them was the height of tedium. However, it was a necessary part of the process that I had little choice but to embrace. The alternative was to arm myself with buggy weapons that only sometimes did what they were supposed to do. And given my penchant for life-and-death situations, that just wasn't acceptable.

Finally, I found a corner of the refrigerator, curled up with a pillow and blanket I'd bought in Nova, and went to sleep. That night was blessedly dreamless, and I awoke the next morning to the internal sound of my HUD's alarm going off. With a mental flick, I turned it off and groaned as I pushed myself to my feet.

After taking some time to dress myself in one of the Banshee uniforms I'd looted back in Mobile, I activated Mimic to subtly change my features to those belonging to an Enforcer who'd been one of my first victims after the city's fall. The woman had possessed a build similar to mine, and her skin color was only a shade or two lighter. However, her features were completely different, with thin lips, almond-shaped eyes, and a perky, upturned nose. Objectively speaking, she was a very pretty woman, though when I'd used her visage back in Nova, I'd discovered that I vastly preferred my own face.

I also took a few minutes to use my selfstyler to straighten my hair. I hated how rough it was on my hair almost as much as I hated how it felt—like I was discarding some piece integral to who I was. It was silly, and I often complained about my wild hair, but it had become a part of how I saw myself. However, in this case, straightening it was necessary. Mimic was a strong ability, but it worked best when I made some effort to ease the transition. Trying to rely on the ability when my hair was so different from the original's would result in similar problems to if I tried to adopt the look of someone who was a lot bigger or smaller in stature. It would work, but the results wouldn't be nearly as seamless as they could've been.

Once all of that was done, I retrieved a collapsible mirror from my storage, unfolded it, and inspected the results. The person staring back at me was unrecognizable from my usual reflection. She had features similar to Kimiko's, but perfected by fortunate genetics, surgery, or some aspect of Mist. Either way, the woman whose face I'd stolen was a real knockout, which was a necessary facet of my plan.

After making sure that my disguise was as perfect as I could manage, I left the freezer and headed outside, where I summoned my hover bike. A moment later, I'd mounted up and was on my way back to Biloxi. The morning air hung heavy with humidity, and dense fog blanketed the area. However, with Observation, it was no real detriment to my passage, and I made good time on my way to the town I'd spent hours observing the day before.

Soon, it came into sight, the glimmering neon lights diffused by the copious fog and casting the area in an eerie glow. I didn't slow until I found my way to the front gate. It was constructed similarly to the gates of Nova City in that it was manned by a host of armed and armored Operators. They wore uniforms, but they weren't clad in the black and white of Enforcers. Instead, their clothing was dark blue with gold accents—the colors of Blue Epoch. I slowed to a stop and dismounted my hover bike, which was in its original undisguised appearance. I needed it to sell the guards on my importance.

I strode confidently forward, homing in on someone that looked important. He was a tall man, with heavy shoulders, a cybernetic hand, and a hook-nosed face. One of his eyes had also been replaced, and it gleamed red in the morning sun. He had a pistol at his hip and, like the other guards, a rifle clutched across his chest. As I stopped in front of him, I threw one of my hips out wide and rested a hand on Ferdinand II's grip—a subtle hint that I had no issues with forcing my way in, if necessary.

Someone nearby whispered, "Banshee," only audible because of Observation.

"Enforcer," said the man before me, his voice completely incongruent with his brutish appearance. I'd expected a deep tone, but instead, I got something better categorized as a tenor. "What brings you to Biloxi?"

"Business," I said, ignoring the oddity of his voice. "Is there an issue?"

"I . . . uh . . . I need to see some ID," he said. I saw the white of his knuckles as he gave his rifle a death grip. Tiny beads of sweat had appeared on his forehead, as well, though that could've been due to the humidity. I suspected he was just nervous.

I narrowed my eyes as if considering punishing him for his impudence. But then, I gave him a warm smile. "Of course you do," I said. Then, I rolled up my sleeve, revealing a symbol that had been tattooed on my inner wrist. The guard retrieved a pistol-shaped device that reminded me of a med-hypo from his belt, then pointed it at the tattoo. A moment later, a tiny web of light swept over it. His eyes took on that glassy appearance that told me he was looking at something on his HUD. "Everything in order?"

A second later, he shook his head, saying, "Yes, ma'am. Everything's fine. How long will you be staying in Biloxi?"

I flashed him another smile before saying, "Until the job's done. You know how it is."

He gave me a nervous grin of his own, then nodded. "Yeah. Ain't that the truth," he said. "Alright, head on in. Don't forget to check out when you leave."

"Will do."

With my entry assured, I turned my back on him and remounted my hover bike. A second later, I accelerated past him and into Biloxi. All the while, my appreciation for Gunther grew; the tattoo had come from him, and though it was temporary, he'd claimed that it was completely foolproof in a town like Biloxi. It'd be a different story in Nova City, where they'd have access to Enforcer records, but out on the frontier, security was a good deal lighter. It also helped that Biloxi wasn't an Enforcer outpost. Rather, the Operators were all private security, and so, they didn't have the technology to pierce through the ruse.

With that, the first step was complete. I was in. But as I'd learned back in Bayou La Batre, getting in was the easy part. Actually accomplishing the mission was where things got tricky. However, I believed that I had learned quite a few lessons since that disastrous mission. I was a different person, and what's more, I had far more information on my side. Back then, I'd gone in mostly blind, but now, I knew the lay of the land and exactly what I needed to do to accomplish my goal and had a good plan for how I would go about doing just that.

Still, I knew that the moment I grew complacent, the second I thought I was prepared—that was when something unexpected would rear its ugly head and knock me for a loop. So, I kept my head on a swivel as I headed toward my destination on the edge of the water.

The hotel was very different from my previous experiences with that sort of thing. It didn't have the rustic charm of somewhere like the Dew Drop Inn, and it certainly was a good deal nicer—and more importantly, cleaner—than El Paradiso back in Algiers. Coming in at six stories of gleaming glass and steel, the Calgary Hotel would have looked completely at home somewhere like Lakeview. It had the same general aesthetic, and what's more, the clientele were similarly polished, stylish, and carried themselves with that same air of superiority I'd seen in Nova's more affluent districts.

However, even they gave an inward cringe at seeing a Banshee in their midst.

It seemed that even among the rich, the Banshees were feared. That suited me just fine because it kept them from looking at me too closely as I pulled to a stop and stored my hover bike away. I knew it would create a bit of a stir, but that was the point. Anyone who possessed such a vehicle would be instantly categorized as someone important, which was part of my disguise.

With that, I strode up the handful of steps and through the front door of the Calgary. No one tried to stop me. No one dared impede a Banshee. It was a nice change of pace from my experiences in Nova City, where my every move was watched, weighed, and followed by curious onlookers, self-styled bandits, or creepy oglers.

A brave doorman stepped forward, asking, "Can I help . . . ?"

I swept past him with my head held high. The woman I was pretending to be wouldn't bother with someone like that. Instead, I walked straight to the front desk, which was made from soulless wood trimmed in bright silver. A crest adorned the front, but I paid it no heed. Logos didn't matter to me nor the woman I was pretending to be.

"I require your best-appointed room," I said to the stunned clerk. She was a pretty blonde with her hair in a braid. A similarly attractive man stood nearby. "Now."

"Uh . . ."

"Is there a problem?" I asked.

As if coming out of a daze, she shook her head, saying, "N-no. No, ma'am! Right away."

A few moments later, she was handing over a ring that would act as a key for the duration of my stay. I paid the fee, adding a little extra for the girl, then headed to my room. As I stepped into the elevator that would take me to the penthouse suite, I was elated at how easily everything had come together. No one had stopped me. Nobody had questioned my identity. They'd all just accepted that I was who I was pretending to be.

It was a good start, but I knew it was only the beginning.

CHAPTER TWENTY-SIX

SETTING THE HOOK

On the surface of it, Jeremiah shouldn't have been that difficult to track. But he flitted around like a shadow, rarely ever staying in one place for long enough to pin him down. With me feeding them real-time information, it became a lot easier. For almost a year, I wrestled with the decision, but in the end, I just did what anyone else would do: put myself first.

—Nora Lancaster

I brushed my ring-clad knuckle against the key reader by the door, and a second later, it slid open to reveal a well-appointed sitting room. I stepped inside, trying my best not to let the luxury overwhelm my good sense. Even so, as the door slid shut behind me, I couldn't help but be impressed. Everywhere I looked, opulence assailed my eyes. Everything was tasteful enough, but no amount of style could disguise the sheer amount of resources that had gone into furnishing the room.

And that was just the entryway. I kept my expression placid, but inwardly, I gaped at the decor, finally understanding what my uncle had meant when he'd explained the difference between being rich and being wealthy. The first meant that you had the money to do just about whatever you wanted. Often, that meant buying fancy cybernetics, rare furniture, or ostentatious jewelry.

By comparison, true wealth meant spending fortunes on things that most people wouldn't even notice, and doing so just because it was slightly better quality. Or a little rarer than the alternative. They had the overt displays, too, but their money went deeper, infecting everything about their lives. Never was that more apparent than when I first stepped foot inside that hotel room, where everything, right down to the floor tiles, screamed luxury and privilege.

I sighed, stepping through the entryway and into the sitting room. As I did, I cast my {Mistrunner} senses out wide, looking for hidden surveillance devices. And I found precisely what I was looking for; there were two cameras in the sitting room, a listening device in the bedroom, and even a camera in the shower. The last made my blood boil. Likely, the voyeuristic camera had been set up by some enterprising employee who'd eventually turn around and sell the results on Nova's intranet.

Virtual reality was extremely popular when it came to pornography, but there would always be a place—albeit an incredibly creepy one—for voyeurism. With a few shifts of my concentration, I used Misthack to disable each device, but I also left something special on the bathroom camera. I let a malicious grin creep onto my face when I imagined the unknown voyeur finding that his terminal as well as his other cameras had all been fried by the Ghost I'd uploaded.

Any other time, using any other disguise, I probably would have been more circumspect. But I was wearing the identity of a Banshee, which meant that anyone who tried to spy on me deserved whatever they got. It would have been more suspicious if I hadn't disabled the surveillance devices in the suite.

Once I'd done a few more sweeps, I studied my surroundings. It was such a far cry from what I'd grown accustomed to that I didn't even know where to start. The sitting room was home to a set of couches and chairs, all made from natural materials. That was so different from what I usually saw in Nova, where everything was synthetic. Abstract paintings decorated the walls, accenting the room's clean lines and pulling everything together into a unified whole that radiated privilege.

I passed through the sitting room, quickly finding myself in the common area. It was more of the same, though it also boasted a sizable screen that stretched from one wall to the other. Most people preferred the convenience of accessing various entertainment feeds via their personal interfaces—even the most basic of them, which didn't require anything like my [Cybernetic Mastery] skill, could handle that much—but the rich weren't satisfied with that. Instead, many of them watched their movies and live events on giant screens with incredible sound systems.

I remembered seeing quite a few such screens in the homes of various Operators who'd worked for my uncle. They were smaller, cheaper, and far less powerful, but they didn't seem to care. Yet another example of their futile and ultimately pointless efforts to mimic the wealthy.

But who was I to judge? When buying equipment, I'd spent a fortune that would've made most aristocrats green with envy, so I wasn't any better than anyone else. Not in that respect, at least.

The rest of the suite, which even had two bedrooms, followed a similar pattern, with the largest bedroom opening up into a huge window that gave me a view of the open sea. It was somewhat marred by the stationary ships and the latticework of the kelp-farming operation, but it was still a beautiful sight that reminded me of sitting atop the buildings in Mobile and gazing out across the bay. Every now and then, something would brush against the Mist shield, trailing a streak of blue light down its surface, before heading away. The water concealed whatever creature was probing Biloxi's maritime defenses, but I knew it wasn't something to take lightly.

After all, my run-in with the giant man-of-war had taught me a lesson that I'd never forget. There were plenty of dangerous creatures roaming the land, but the true monsters made their homes beneath the waves.

I sighed before heading into the luxurious bathroom, where I undressed. I hadn't spent more than a couple of nights out in the wilderness, but I knew just how dirty I'd become. So, I stepped into the shower—which was a tiled room bigger than my quarters back in the Dew Drop Inn had been. I pressed a few buttons on the control panel, and steaming-hot water fell from the ceiling.

I let myself relax for a few minutes as I just enjoyed the feeling of my tense muscles unkinking. I could've stood there for hours, but I knew I was on a schedule. Or my target was, at least. And if I wanted to intercept him, I'd need to take my place very soon. So, I bent to the task of shaving; out in the wilderness or during training, it was easy to ignore a little leg or armpit hair. But with what I had planned? I needed to hold myself to different standards, even if I didn't necessarily endorse them.

After I'd been denuded to my satisfaction, I finished showering. Once that was done, another press of a button activated the dryer function, and after a few seconds of being buffeted by warm air, I was dry.

The next twenty minutes involved me getting dressed and making sure everything looked perfect. From my outfit to my hair and everything in between. Some of it was a little difficult because of the effects of Mimic, but I managed well enough. By the time I went to leave the suite, the sun had set, and I was ready for the mission.

Still, I couldn't stop myself from taking a good look at my reflection. And I liked what I saw.

I knew it wasn't me. My skin had never been that clear, and my hair had never been so straight. But I wasn't so insecure that I didn't recognize that I could have looked almost as good wearing my own face if I'd ever put in that kind of effort. And besides, the body beneath those expensive clothes was all me.

For my night in Biloxi, I'd chosen a pair of real-leather pants that clung to my body like a second skin, leaving little to the imagination. They weren't comfortable, but they were flexible enough that I could still move in them if I needed to. My top was even less practical. Comprised of a few strips of sparkly cloth and some string, it left my entire back bare. In fact, it left most of my skin bare, covering a lot less than the shirts I was used to wearing. It was stylish, though, glittering silver with blue highlights of infused Mist and suggesting at what little it did cover.

My hair hung loose, and my makeup—created by Mimic—tended toward sultry. Finally, my feet were encased in a pair of four-inch heels. In short, even without the use of Mimic, I would've looked so different that few would have connected me with the scrappy girl from the Garden.

Which was precisely the point.

I had considered a lot of different options, but it had come down to a choice between my current attire and something far more businesslike. And I'll admit that I chose the way I had mostly because the idea frightened me. I'd have never worn such an outfit under normal circumstances, but the fact that it was part of a disguise made it far more palatable.

Even so, as I left the suite, my stomach twisted itself into a thousand knots. My anxiety only got worse when I stepped off the elevator and into the hotel lobby. It felt like everyone in the building was staring at and judging me. And I was sure they'd see right through my disguise and recognize me for the fraud I was. Certainly, Mimic was practically foolproof under such conditions. I'd proven that when I'd come into the town and no one had stopped me. But that wasn't really what worried me. Instead, I was more concerned with people judging the way I was dressed.

Would they see me as a little girl pretending to be an adult?

No. Of course not. Even without Mimic, I didn't look like a child anymore. But the insecurity fostered by years of social isolation wasn't concerned with facts or truth. It was too busy cataloging every glance, every unrelated laugh, and each unconnected whisper. It was a nightmare come to life.

But if I could make it through an entire Rift, if I could will my way through hell month, I could endure a little self-doubt.

My heels clicked as I made my way through the lobby, and I couldn't help but thank my Balance ability. Otherwise, even with my enhanced Constitution attribute, which gave me superhuman coordination, I might've stumbled.

Either way, I made it through the lobby just fine, and when I stepped outside, I took a moment to enjoy the sea air before I crossed the street and made my way toward one of the ships.

That was one of the reasons I'd chosen the Calgary in the first place; sure, it was a luxurious hotel fitting the identity I'd assumed. However, it also boasted close proximity to my real destination—the Palace.

It wasn't the largest of the ships, but it was the most luxurious. With its black-and-gold coloring, it even managed to look regal. And that was with me knowing what it represented as well as the debauchery it hosted on a nightly basis.

I kept a straight face as I strode toward the ramp that would lead out to the ship. As I drew closer, I couldn't help but be impressed by the sheer size of the thing. It was as if someone had taken the concept of a ship and simply blown it out of wild proportion. The result was something more akin to a building than anything used for transportation across the water. Probably a good thing that it had almost assuredly been cemented to the seafloor so it couldn't move.

When I reached the ramp, which was guarded by a couple of mooks whose black-and-gold suits couldn't hide their bulging cybernetics, I paid my entry fee, then swept past them. They didn't even think to stop me, which soothed a little of my anxiety. I must have looked like I belonged.

The ramp was almost a hundred yards long and sloped at a moderate incline, which gave me little trouble. Others weren't so lucky. I passed one corpulent, well-dressed man who hadn't banked on such a trek, and I almost grinned at how hard he was breathing.

Soon enough, I reached the entrance of the actual ship, and I stepped inside to see a place that lived up to its name. The decor wasn't any richer than it had been in the Calgary, but the Palace's wealth was far more overt. The sheer amount of gold and silver pushed well past the point of posturing and into the realm of obscenity. The point of their posturing wasn't lost on me. As a casino, they needed to wear their wealth on their proverbial sleeve, lest people get the impression that they couldn't cover their losses.

Of course, like any casino, I imagined that they would always come out on top. Rigged or not, they were in the business of making money, after all.

I strode forward, projecting as much confidence as I could. As I moved through the lobby, I could feel dozens of pairs of eyes following my every step. I ignored them, quickly covering the ground and passing between a pair of life-size golden lion statues to enter the casino proper.

Once inside, I saw dozens of tables intended for various card games, almost as many roulette tables, and even some screens dedicated to sporting events I'd had no idea even existed. Apparently, being an aristocrat meant being far more aware of the wider world. It was yet another way Nova's elites had kept the lower-class population of the city uninformed, isolated, and under control.

I wove through the crowd as I crossed the gambling hall, eventually finding my way to the bar on the other side. Leaning against the polished wooden surface, I got the attention of the barkeep, who was a young, handsome man with a cybernetic eye.

He gave me a smile, asking, "What can I get for you?"

"Whiskey," I said, returning his smile with one of my own. I wanted to look approachable, after all. I'd already spied my target, and he'd noticed me in turn. But it wouldn't do for me to make the first move. If I wanted to avoid suspicion, he needed to be the aggressor.

Once I'd been served, I took a moment to savor the drink. Or pretend to. It definitely wasn't to my taste, and it didn't even have the added benefit of accomplishing its intended function. Due to a combination of my inflated Constitution attribute and my Regeneration and Resistance abilities, I was functionally immune to the effects of alcohol. Or any other inebriant, if I had to guess. Perhaps somewhere out there in the wider universe, some alien had come up with something that would work, but everything I'd tried back in Mobile had been entirely ineffective.

I turned around as I sipped my drink and watched the gamblers. Most were obviously wealthy and were just using the casino to blow off some steam. Others had the looks of professionals. I didn't know what, precisely, tipped me off, but I got the impression that they were the predators in this jungle, and I resolved to avoid them at all costs.

Eventually, I let my target catch me glancing in his direction. And when we locked eyes, I knew I had him. He grinned at me. I gave him a coy smile, then turned back to the bar. Now, I only had to wait until he took the bait.

People were so much easier when I was playing a role, when I had a defined target and goal. With someone like Patrick, I had to worry about feelings and the future, but with Calvin Kane, I'd only need to think about accomplishing the mission. There was freedom in how uncomplicated it was, and it allowed me to put my best, most confident foot forward.

After another minute or two, during which I continued to sip at my drink, I heard someone approaching me from behind. Without Observation, I never would have been able to separate his footsteps from the din of the crowded gambling hall, but with it, I had no doubt that Calvin had taken the bait.

I felt rather than saw him sidle up to the bar next to me. At first, he pretended that he hadn't made the trip specifically to talk to me, instead getting the bartender's attention. Once he did, he said, "A beer, Monty. And for the lady . . ."

"Whiskey," I repeated my order. I didn't look at him. Not yet.

"So, you're new around here, right?" asked Calvin. I saw him out of the corner of my eye, looming beside me. He was a tall man, with an athletic build. And he was incredibly handsome—but that was probably artificial because I'd seen a photo of his mother, and they looked nothing alike. Even so, I wouldn't begrudge a man his vanity. Not when I was wearing a top that barely even covered my chest, at least.

"I am."

"A woman of few words, then? I like it," Calvin said, almost as if he was having a conversation with himself. The file Salvatore had given me had called him self-absorbed, and he'd given me no reason to label that description false. "What brings you to my little town?"

His town, huh? The statement wasn't exactly inaccurate. Biloxi was owned and operated by Blue Epoch, and he was the highest-ranking executive around. Still, it felt a bit presumptuous to claim ownership of his employer's property.

"Banshee business," I said.

Even though I wasn't looking in his direction, I could almost see his face go white. He really had no idea who I was. Or rather, who I was pretending to be. Enforcers might not be as feared by the elite as they were by the residents of the poorer districts of Nova City, but they weren't to be trifled with, either. And nobody—aristocrats or street urchins—wanted to deal with a Banshee.

"Oh . . . ah . . . s-sorry. I didn't—"

I let out a fake laugh, then turned toward him. I flashed my widest grin before saying, "Oh, your face right now. Priceless. Absolutely priceless."

"W-what? You're not . . . you know . . . one of them?" he asked.

"No, no—I definitely am," I said. "But for tonight? Let's just put that aside, huh? I've never been to this quaint little town, and I'd love a local guide. You up for it?"

It took him a moment to process what I was offering. I couldn't have been clearer without holding up a sign that said, "I'm interested, you mook!"

But Calvin clearly wasn't the sharpest sword in the arsenal, even if he was very good-looking. I got butterflies just looking at his dazzlingly blue eyes; those couldn't be real, could they? No. Nothing about him was real.

Besides, I was just doing a job here. Not getting involved.

"Right. Sure," he said, smiling back at me as he recovered his composure. "I think I could play that role."

"Good," I said, setting down my glass and taking his arm. "I want to see everything Biloxi has to offer."

CHAPTER TWENTY-SEVEN

RUINING A LIFE

I wonder if Mira is still out there. She was the instrument through which Jeremiah showed his disdain for me, but that wasn't her fault. I tried to protect her, but I have no way of knowing if I was successful.

—Nora Lancaster

"Do you have any more?" asked Calvin, looking at me with bloodshot eyes. His whole body twitched, and he shivered in the damp heat of the Biloxi night. Suddenly, he jumped to his feet and wheeled around, hissing, "Who's there?"

Of course, I knew that no one was there. That was just the dust withdrawal causing hallucinations. It would get worse. Much, much worse. But that was the point. Dust wasn't like most drugs. It didn't care about attributes or skills; no—it cut right through every defense, resulting in a euphoric high that I'd heard was unmatched by any other substance. But like most good things, it came with a significant downside: addiction and the degradation of mental faculties. Most dust fiends didn't even notice the latter, but it was there. It didn't just destroy brain cells. Instead, it attacked the attributes directly, focusing on Mind.

I had no idea how quickly it was supposed to work, but after only a week of heavy use, Calvin was already showing the signs. Not only were his reactions much slower, but he'd grown increasingly paranoid. He was convinced that someone was out to get him. He was right, of course, but he didn't suspect me in the slightest.

It hadn't even been that difficult to earn his trust. Once, I'd marveled at how easily Jo could manipulate people into doing what she wanted. She was never malicious, but everyone in her group of friends tripped over themselves to stay on her good side. With Calvin, I'd channeled my inner Jo, and he'd fallen in line. Odd that, after all my training, my friendship with Jo would be so impactful on my mission.

Getting him hooked on dust was even easier. Like many privileged idiots, he'd spent his youth dabbling in every inebriant he could find, so he'd sampled dust a handful of times. And just like everyone else who ended up an addict, he'd thought himself immune to dependence. All it took was a pretty girl with a ready supply, and he'd fallen right into my trap.

"Nobody's there," I said, dumping a bit of pink powder into a glass of water. Then, I downed the resulting concoction.

"You sure I can't—"

"This is my private stash," I said, holding up the bottle. "That stuff you've been taking doesn't do anything for me. I need a stronger compound."

It was a lie, of course. The "dust" I'd been taking to keep pace with him was nothing more than dyed sugar. I wasn't about to test myself against the potent drug, even if I was curious if the combination of my high Constitution, Regeneration, and Resistance might give me immunity. The bottles I'd gotten for him, though, were the real thing.

It was like watching a hover car slamming into a megabuilding in slow motion.

When we'd first met, Calvin was suave, handsome, and self-assured. Now, I could already see the effects of the addiction I'd foisted upon him. His cheeks had grown hollow, his eyes were watery and deeply sunk into his skull, and he'd already lost quite a few pounds. Soon, he'd look just like any other junkie, albeit one who could cover some of it up with the trappings of wealth. It was like looking at an abandoned building, but one with a fresh coat of paint. From a distance, it might look okay, but up close, its real nature would become evident. So it was with Calvin, and this was after only a week. In two, he'd alternate between being a desperate, twitching mess and passing out in alleys and stairwells.

I almost felt bad about what I had done to him.

But I hadn't forced him to take the drugs. I'd just made a suggestion. He was the idiot who'd decided to throw away a life of privilege in favor of being a junkie. Actions, as my uncle had often said, had consequences, and it was almost satisfying to see Calvin dealing with the effects of his own decisions.

Or it would have been if he wasn't so pathetic.

Luckily, I was almost finished. I only needed to ease his path to true addiction by putting him in touch with someone who could satisfy his drug habit. To that end, I said, "I think I can help with your problem, though."

"What? How? You know someone?" he asked.

I nodded. I hadn't spent my days in Biloxi idly twiddling my thumbs. Instead, I had explored most of the town, even venturing into the nearby tenements that housed the men and women who harvested the kelp. There, it hadn't taken long to find a den of dust fiends who, in turn, had directed me toward their dealer. I might not have been comfortable navigating the luxurious environs of the wealthy, but I was completely at home in the slums.

"I do," I said, pushing myself to my feet and looking around the hotel suite. Once, it had been pristine, but now, it looked like the dust den it had become. Furniture had been toppled, the expensive paintings had been destroyed, and there was filth everywhere—all courtesy of Calvin, who reacted to the drug with unrestrained mania followed by long stretches of unconsciousness. I had no interest in constraining him; the more destructive he was, the better. We were establishing habits, after all. When I left, I needed him to be completely incapable of hiding his addiction.

And he was well on his way. I only needed to make sure he had a ready supply, and then I would be in the clear to enact the next part of my plan.

"How?" he asked.

"I'm a Banshee," I said. "I know how to find things I want to find. You think a drug dealer can hide from someone like me?"

"Oh . . ."

He really was pathetic. Even without my influence, Calvin wasn't the most intelligent person around. But under the effects of the dust? It was if his brain was running at half speed. Doubtless, after I left, he would quickly show his incompetence.

Of course, I wasn't going to wait for that. Even if he started making mistakes, it was likely that someone would cover it up. Or just send him away. No—I needed something big; when Blue Epoch investigated, they'd find that they'd left a dust fiend in charge. After that, the blame would soon fall on his mother, who'd gotten him the job in the first place.

Simple.

A bit cruel, but definitely not complicated.

Besides, he was in charge of the kelp-harvesting operation and, as such, complicit in the suffering of the people he used as workers. They weren't slaves, exactly, but they weren't that far off. Even the farmers and factory workers in Nova City were better treated. So, even if he hadn't created the system, he certainly hadn't done anything to change it. Which made him easy to hate, so long as I kept that at the forefront of my mind.

I was well aware that my judgment of him was hypocritical. It wasn't as if I'd gone out of my way to help anyone else. But I studiously ignored that fact, focusing on what made my task easier to stomach.

I stood, running my hand through my straightened hair. I definitely didn't like it very much; instead, against all odds, I preferred my natural hair. I'd complained about it often enough that my preference surprised even me, but

I couldn't deny it. In any case, the straightened hair was still necessary for the disguise.

"Come on," I said. "I have somebody I want you to meet."

All hints of flirtation were gone from my voice. Thankfully, the moment I'd gotten Calvin hooked on dust, the necessity for such an act had been obviated. The reality of it was that even if I could fake it for a while, flirtation and interpersonal relationships just didn't come naturally to me. Sure, he wasn't really perceptive enough to recognize my clumsiness as the red flag it was, but that fact didn't make me any more comfortable with my inadequacies.

That first night, I'd covered it up with sheer promiscuity, and even I can admit that sleeping with him was enjoyable enough. But it had quickly lost its appeal the more he'd become mired in the dust habit I'd thrust upon him. Fortunately, his own interest had lagged as the addiction progressed. Still, I wondered if I could have been so blasé about the whole thing if I hadn't been playing a role.

Probably not.

He quickly agreed to go with me, chattering manically about nothing as he followed me out of the hotel suite. When we made it to the lobby, we both got some strange looks. I'd expected that; Calvin looked like the dust fiend he was, and I'd discarded my fancy clothes in favor of something less conspicuous. After all, looking too rich or prosperous in the slums would paint a target on my back. I had no interest in dealing with that, so I'd made some effort to blend in. To that end, I wore a simple pair of coveralls that I'd stolen from one of the kelp harvesters.

Not appropriate for a luxurious hotel like the Calgary, but it would keep me from standing out in the slums.

In any case, we quickly headed out of the hotel and down the sidewalk that ran along the main street. Biloxi wasn't a huge town—smaller than Mobile, in fact—but it was still large enough that it took us almost half an hour to reach our destination in the slums. A tenement loomed over us, boxy, blocky, and made of unadorned concrete. At ground level, graffiti decorated the walls, and on the floors above that was a grid of narrow windows. It looked like nothing so much as the prison it practically was.

A few men and women, all showing the same signs of addiction Calvin had begun to display, loitered nearby. Fortunately, they'd clearly just come down from a high, and they hadn't recovered enough to start looking for a way to get their next hit. Otherwise, there was every chance that Calvin's expensive clothes would attract all the wrong kinds of trouble. I had a plan for what to do if that happened, but it wasn't quite as buttoned-up as my first option.

So, we pushed by a couple of people who'd perched themselves on either side of the door. One of them asked us for credits, but I ignored her. Calvin took his cues from me, doing the same. Or maybe he just didn't care. Either way, I wouldn't let myself get distracted by a beggar.

The interior of the tenement wasn't much better than the facade, though there was only one man in the lobby. He looked healthy enough, which meant that he wasn't a dust fiend. Instead, judging by his faded blue coveralls and his slightly salty odor, he was a harvester who'd just finished a shift. The kelp had stained his hands a deep red.

Once I saw that he wasn't a threat, I moved past him on my way to the stairwell, which I mounted a moment later. Calvin followed close on my heels until we finally reached the appropriate floor, where I led him into a dingy hall.

At one point, it might have been a decent-looking space. Utilitarian and without frills, but adequate. Now, though? There were stains on the walls, the lighting flickered, and in more than one spot, the carpet had been ripped from the floor. There was also a pervasive smell that clung to the place—like body odor, fish, and vomit, all rolled into one. It wasn't overbearing, as if someone had made some attempt to purge the odor only to find that it had seeped into the very walls.

It was disgusting, and I wondered how anyone could live in such conditions.

Of course, the answer was that they did it because they didn't have any choice. Nobody chose to live in a tenement. It was just the last stop on the way to homelessness.

But I ignored those details; I'd seen them the last time I was there, and I didn't need to focus on them anymore. Instead, I headed confidently down the hall, making a couple of turns before I finally reached the door that was my goal. I banged on the door with the flat of my hand, and a moment later, it slid open.

"You're late," said the man on the other side. He was short, thin, and had a ring of stringy hair falling down to his shoulders. The top of his head was bare, and he had sharp features that gave him a dangerous look. He was clad only in a dirty robe and a pair of once-white underwear. "Come in. And bring your boy toy with you."

Calvin took offense to that characterization, saying, "I am not a—"

I cut him off with a glare. "Just shut up and follow my lead," I said. "Do that and you'll get what you want, okay?"

I could see the fear in his eyes. Not of me. Instead, he was terrified of not getting his dust. That was the thing about the drug; it was so addictive that it only took a couple of hits before someone was hopelessly dedicated to getting their next high. It was possible to go clean, but few people managed it. Some of that was because most people who went down that road had done so for a reason. They just wanted an escape. Dust provided that, even if it ruined what was left of their lives. If you were going to live in squalor, you might as well do so while high on dust.

It was the same desperate hopelessness that drove others to spend all their credits on Bourbon Street. Or to spend their whole lives hooked into one VR chip or another. I didn't blame them, even if I did judge them for their weakness.

"You've got what I ordered?" I asked, following him inside. Calvin did the same. "Or . . ."

"I got it, I got it," the man said as the door slid shut. The interior of the domicile was small and cramped, but it was clean enough. On one side was a narrow bed—little more than a cot—that was built into the wall. On the other, a counter that was covered in glassware. Very little of it was in use, but at the very end, there was a beaker containing the sludge that would eventually become dust. I had no idea how it was made. Nor did I know the ingredients. I just knew that making it was dangerous due to the volatility of the process.

But Marv was the best cook in Biloxi. Everyone I'd spoken to claimed as much, which was why I'd contacted him earlier in the week and contracted a huge batch of dust.

Marv sat on the bed, then opened a drawer that was concealed in its base. He took out a plastic box, which he handed to me. "Just like you ordered," he said. "That's enough to last you and your boyfriend a month. Maybe two if you don't go too crazy."

I could practically feel Calvin's excitement as I took the box and checked the contents. Sure enough, there was a sealed bag full of glittering pink powder, enough to ruin Calvin's life a dozen times over.

I initiated a transfer of credits—just ten thousand—to Marv, who accepted it with a greedy smile that revealed a distinct lack of teeth. There were a few still there, but most had long since succumbed to poor dental hygiene.

With our business done, Calvin and I didn't waste any time leaving the domicile and the tenement. When we left the slums behind, I handed Calvin the box, saying, "There. My gift to you."

"W-what?" he asked, his voice quivering in excitement. It was all he could do not to tear into the dust right there on the street. "You don't want to do it with me? We could have a lot of—"

"Call it a parting gift," I said. "I'm leaving Biloxi."

"Why? You could stay, and—"

"Can't. I have responsibilities," I said. "And I finished my task two nights ago. Staying this long was already pushing it."

A lie, of course. Calvin was my task, and by giving him the dust and showing him where to get more, I'd just finished the first of the plan. I was eager to move on with the second stage. After all, the sooner I finished, the sooner I could get back to Nova and what was truly important.

"I . . . When can I see you again?" he asked, his voice hopeful. That he could focus on me at all when he had a box of dust in his hand was a little disconcerting.

"I'll be by here in a couple of months," I lied, reaching up to caress his cheek. His skin was cold and clammy. "Just don't have too much fun until I get back, okay?"

I didn't waste time waiting on an answer. Instead, I strode ahead and into the hotel. Before long, I was back in my suite. Someone had been inside to clean up. Or perhaps they had drones for that. Either way, the room was spotless, but I knew I'd be charged for it. As much as I didn't want to spend credits unnecessarily, I knew it was all worth it.

Now, I just needed to finish things up by creating a disaster that would bring the Blue Epoch Corporation down on Calvin's head.

So, I stripped my coveralls off and donned my infiltration suit. Once I made sure that I hadn't left anything behind, I left the suite and headed downstairs to check out. As I'd expected, my bill was astronomical. I paid it without question, then went outside where I summoned my Cutter and headed out of the city.

I didn't look back until I was well out of sight. Then, I let Mimic drop, adopted a completely different persona, and turned around. I didn't head for the gate, though. My first trip into Biloxi was aboveboard. But this one? It would be a stealth mission.

CHAPTER TWENTY-EIGHT

DISASTER ARTIST

I'm not looking for a fight, but I can't back down. No one respects our strength anymore, and they think they can take whatever they want from us. The moment I let anything slide is the moment I start losing control of the Specters. And I won't let that happen. Not after everything I've sacrificed.

—Nora Lancaster

Biloxi's defenses weren't nearly as impressive as Nova City's, but they still represented a significant hurdle for my return to the town. It was a good thing that, in the week since I'd first entered the town, I'd spent quite a bit of time on reconnaissance. Fortunately, it didn't look like anything I couldn't handle.

Still, I needed to get in range without being seen before I could worry about that. So, I veered off the cracked but otherwise well-maintained road, dismissing my Cutter before heading into a copse of dense trees. With Observation enhancing my senses and ensuring I wasn't ambushed by some ambitious predator, I made quick time through the woods, reaching the tree line only twenty minutes later.

The wall loomed a few hundred yards away, and even if it was only fifteen feet high, it would still slow me down. A shimmering blue Mist shield encircled the town, and a plethora of cameras studded the wall. Drones and guards patrolled the area, ensuring a third line of defense. To a novice, it might have looked impregnable.

But I was no novice.

I embraced Stealth as I crept forward. Camouflage, which was a passive ability that made me blend into my surroundings, also shrouded my approach. The ability wasn't nearly as effective in the city as it was in the wilderness, and

I often forgot its effects. But all my passive abilities were invaluable, even if I sometimes took them for granted.

The terrain outside of the city was characterized by knee-high grass and a smattering of trees, which I used to full advantage as I moved ever closer to the wall. When I was only twenty yards away, I crouched low to the ground and waited. Soon enough, a pair of guards—both women—strode into view. They were dressed in the dark-blue uniforms that marked them as Blue Epoch's employees, and both held standard-issue assault rifles. Idly, I wondered if they were even powerful enough to penetrate the combination of my Sheath and infiltration suit.

I didn't intend to find out. I already got shot often enough as it was without seeking it out for testing purposes.

Instead, I embraced my Misthack ability, and a menu appeared on my HUD:

Initiate Misthack?
[Yes] or [No]

I chose the affirmative option, resulting in the familiar swarm of numbers and puzzles that represented a person's defenses. In the beginning, my Misthack technique could best be described as blundering forward and overwhelming anything that stood in my way. There was still an element of that present in my current efforts. However, I'd developed a somewhat lighter touch that allowed me to pull back if the defenses looked too extensive. It was a necessary change; otherwise, I'd have run the risk of enduring a significant backlash every time I even peeked at someone's defenses. I'd paid the price for that before, and I'd worked extremely diligently to correct my clumsy approach.

Thankfully, the first guard's defenses didn't look very advanced—few people invested in a proper Mistwall, instead relying on their interface's native defenses—so I immediately pushed into the familiar puzzles, unlocking one node after another until I got access to the guard's system. Once I did, another menu flashed on my HUD:

Misthack successful. Options:
Reboot system
Overcharge
Disable cybernetics
Upload Ghost

If I chose Reboot system, the guard would briefly lose her connection to her interface. In the right situation, that could be an extremely powerful attack that would disrupt any skills and abilities. But it wasn't the right choice in this instance. Neither was Overcharge, which would agitate the Mist in her system, stunning her in the process. Again, it was a very powerful—if situational—ability. I'd used an unrefined version of it to help my uncle defeat the giant that had led the attack on our caravan just outside of Mobile, and that was before I'd had any training at all. Now, it would be absolutely devastating. Of course, it required a second or two to initiate the Misthack and overcome any defenses, but it was still very useful.

Disable Cybernetics was similar and would prove devastating against anyone who'd invested heavily in their cybernetics. Usually, those sorts of people leaned on their mechanical parts, and losing access to them would, at the very least, disrupt them. It also lasted for almost fifteen seconds, and I couldn't suppress a grin as I thought about all the damage I could do in that amount of time.

But it still wasn't right for what I wanted to accomplish. So, I chose the fourth option: Upload Ghost. When I did, another menu appeared on my HUD:

Upload Ghost. Options:
Time Bomb
Seizure
Confusion
Blind

Time Bomb was the best option if I wanted to disable an entire platoon. Or as I had back in Mobile, everyone in a building. But it didn't work very quickly, and it would make it extremely obvious that someone had infiltrated the town. I didn't want to leave any footprints, so I considered the next option, *Seizure*.

Like the name suggested, using it would cause a period of time characterized by uncontrollable spasms. It was somewhat mitigated by an individual's Mist attribute, but when I'd tested it on Patrick—who'd reluctantly agreed to be my guinea pig—it had been extraordinarily difficult to shake off. A nice weapon for my arsenal of Ghosts, but it wasn't appropriate. If the guards suddenly started seizing in the middle of their patrol, it would undoubtedly raise some red flags. The same was true of *Blind*, which was as appropriately named as *Seizure*.

Which was why I had planned to use *Confusion*. So, I selected the appropriate option. The moment it took effect, the guard stopped in her tracks. The other, noticing that her companion had stopped, turned and asked, "What is it? See something?"

The other guard looked around, confused and muttering, "Uh . . ."

That's when I completed the process on the second guard, and even from so faraway, I could see the glassy-eyed expression on her face. Moments later, the pair wandered away in random directions. That was the beauty of *Confusion*. It didn't do anything as overt as causing seizures or blindness, but it did just what its name suggested. In a few minutes, when the two guards recovered from the Ghost, they would be unable to remember what they were doing or why they had chosen to do it. In the meantime, they'd have wandered well off their patrol path.

With that done, I crept forward, targeting the drones and cameras, one by one, until I had disabled them all. The cameras just shut down, but the drones' safety protocols meant that they used their backup power to land safely. That was all the easy part, though. The more difficult part of the plan required me to somehow get past the Mist shield.

But I was prepared for that, too, which was why I had chosen my ingress point very carefully. Once I got within a foot of the wall—and the Mist shield that shimmered only a few inches from it—I cast my awareness out, finding a security terminal in a building just on the other side of the wall. It stretched my range to its very limits, but I quickly initiated a Misthack. This time, the defenses were significant, but because of my advancements in Mind as well as the modifiers that had come with my {Mistrunner} class, I managed to overwhelm the terminal's Mistwall. Then, I shut the system off.

The shield in that sector winked out, and I wasted no time before leaping as high as I could. The wall was only fifteen feet tall, but I still barely managed to catch the edge and haul myself over. Even as my feet hit the ground on the other side, the shield reactivated.

That was the problem with using Misthack. It gave me access, but whatever changes I forced upon the system would be limited in both scope and duration. Even most Ghosts were short-term effects. If I'd used Mistwalk instead, the changes would have been more or less permanent, at least until someone else came along and corrected whatever alterations I'd made. Even so, it took the Mist shield a few seconds to cycle, which had been barely enough time for me to scale the wall.

Anyone without a significantly inflated Constitution attribute would have stood no chance of making it in time. That ruled out people like Helen Stone, my former [Mistwalker] instructor. She was skilled when it came to what she did, but she'd never worked too hard on her physicality.

That was the difference between a real {Mistrunner} and those who'd merely claimed the name. I wasn't nearly as limited.

Once I got my bearings, I rushed along the edge of the building, and I quickly passed into the town's slums. I kept to the shadows, well aware of how much I'd stick out if someone saw through my Stealth. Fortunately, it was a very powerful ability that I'd spent quite a lot of time training, so most people—especially in a backwater town like Biloxi—were woefully incapable of penetrating through it. Still, I kept my wits about me, avoiding people as I slowly made my way across the town.

Night had long since fallen, and Blue Epoch had never invested much money in keeping the slums well lit. So, my way was clear all the way to the coast—or more importantly, the lattice they used to grow and harvest the kelp.

I still wasn't completely sure how it all worked. Calvin had tried to impress me with an explanation, but he'd been manic from ingesting too much dust, so it had been a bit garbled. Even so, I knew the lattice had something to do with concentrating the Mist so that the kelp would grow more quickly. It pulled double duty by acting as a platform from which the workers could harvest the valuable red seaweed.

A little down the coast, I saw the steady lights of the ships. As I suspected, none of them were seaworthy. Instead, they were cemented in place and used just like stationary buildings. People liked the novelty, though. Some, like the Palace where I'd first met Calvin, were completely dedicated to gambling. But others were devoted to hedonistic pursuits not unlike Bourbon Street. There was even a ship that functioned as an arena for prizefighting like the Emporium back in Nova City.

Perhaps Calvin was on one of those ships, high out of his mind and entirely unaware that I was about to ruin his life. Well, more than I already had. Being a drug addicted junkie was one thing. Some people could manage that kind of life well enough to keep their heads above water. I didn't think Calvin had the self-restraint to do that, but I'd been wrong about people before. Nora came to mind, but I suppressed the wave of anger that came with that line of thinking. But in Calvin's case, even if he did manage to live with—or against all odds, overcome—the addiction I'd maneuvered him into, he wouldn't go much further. That was the point of what I was about to do, after all.

Corporations like Blue Epoch would overlook a lot of things, but that was contingent upon a person's usefulness. So, when Calvin proved himself a failure, his fall would be abrupt and swift.

Even for the affluent, life was brutal.

I sighed. I didn't want to think about Calvin. Or what I'd done to him. He wasn't such a bad guy. More blind than anything. But he was between me and my revenge, and I couldn't allow anything to stand in my way. He was but one more sacrifice on the altar of my vengeance. I made it willingly and without hesitation or doubt.

Glancing from right to left, I searched the street for anyone who might see me. Aside from a parked hover car almost a block away, there was no one. That wasn't unsurprising. It was the middle of a shift, which meant that anyone in the area was already focused on their work.

I darted forward, crossing the street in a second before ducking into an alley beside one of the buildings where the kelp was packaged for shipment. It was a huge warehouse, protected by drones and cameras. There was a guard, but during my reconnaissance, I had confirmed that he rarely left his office. From there, he could jack straight into the security terminal and keep an eye on everything.

Unless someone disabled his cameras, of course. Which I did. I also targeted a single drone that was in my way, bringing it down just like I had the ones hovering over the outer wall. So long as I remained focused and paid attention, nothing in Biloxi could bar my way.

Once the automated defenses were down, I continued along the side of the building until I reached another intersection. There were no streets in this area, only narrow paths that were just wide enough to accommodate the exosuits—which were yellow and moved with the stiffness of low-quality cybernetics—they used to move the heavy pallets of kelp. None were in view, so I quickly moved on, maintaining my caution along the way. A few times, I was forced to wait as the heavy, mechanical exosuits stomped by, but the workers manning them were only focused on doing their jobs. Most never even looked my way, and the couple who did were thwarted by my still-active Stealth ability.

I lost count of the number of drones and cameras I disabled, but for the first few minutes, I was wary of a response. After all, if I'd been in charge of that security station, I would certainly have investigated a string of cameras going dark—even if only for a half minute. I had a plan for that, but I never had to use it. Apparently, the guard was either lazy or incompetent. Probably both, judging by the standards I'd observed. Enforcers, they definitely were not.

Eventually, I reached my destination—the beach. From a distance, the lattice looked like a grid of wires. However, up close, I saw that those wires were at least ten feet across, and they loomed a dozen feet over the water, supported by thick metal columns. Workers trudged through the area, lowering giant claw-like apparatuses into the water. When they pulled them up, they were loaded with red kelp, which the workers soon removed from the extractor and piled onto the waiting pallets, where it waited until someone in an exosuit came to retrieve it.

I'd studied the process, and I knew that, for the most part, the workers didn't even look at the water. So, I wasted no more time before wading into the sea. The warm water lapped against my thighs as I continued forward. Eventually, I was forced to swim. Like that, I covered the few dozen yards out to the first pillar. I could feel the density of the ambient Mist increase the farther I went. It wasn't painful, but I couldn't deny that it was at least mildly uncomfortable. It reminded me of the outer edges of the Dead Zone.

I knew that the area was completely protected from the denizens of the sea, but my memories of the man-of-war were still strong. So, my heart raced as I swam from one pillar to the next until, at last, I reached my destination.

This column was a good deal larger than the others, and I knew from my research that it was one of the hubs that controlled the Mist-gathering function associated with the lattice. It only governed a relatively small portion of the overall structure, but it was enough for what I intended. The only problem was that it only had two terminals that could get me into the system. One was atop the lattice, where I would doubtless be seen. The other was underwater.

I took a deep breath, then slipped under the waves. The moment I looked down, I saw a forest of glowing red kelp. Crimson energy danced from one frond to another, arcing between them like electricity. Going down there was out of the question; I still didn't know what exactly would happen if I did, but I'd heard from Calvin that it was dangerous. Thankfully, I didn't have to chance it because I quickly located the panel that was my goal.

I flipped over and kicked down a half dozen yards and grabbed ahold of the handle. When I turned it, the latch released, and the small door swung open to reveal a terminal. I could hold my breath for a while—far longer than most people—but I didn't want to waste any time. So, I quickly extracted the black-and-gold cord of my personal link from my artificial wrist and thrust the end into the terminal's port.

A familiar message flashed on my HUD:

Secure terminal:
[Enter Password] or [Mistwalk]

I chose the latter and was immediately confronted by an elaborate puzzle that was far more complicated than most defenses I had encountered. It didn't matter. I spent most of my spare time training my Mind by completing one puzzle after another. I'd even graduated to creating my own and letting an AI try to break through. I never succeeded in thwarting the artificial intelligence, but it was great training. Whatever the case, the terminal's admittedly stout defenses eventually fell before me, giving me access to the lattice.

It took a few minutes for me to find the appropriate section—after all, it was an unfamiliar system—but once I did find it, I wasted no more time before tripling the Mist-condensing function. Immediately, I felt the Mist stir, which told me that the job was done. Now, I just had to get out without being seen.

The excess Mist would almost assuredly kill the kelp in that section. And even if it didn't, it would mutate. Either way, it would completely ruin an entire crop and shut down harvesting in that section for weeks while they let the Mist normalize. That would cost Blue Epoch hundreds of thousands of credits. Perhaps even millions. But more importantly, it would get their attention. If everything worked properly, they would send someone to investigate, and when they did, they would discover that Calvin was a junkie. The blame would land squarely on his shoulders, and if he was lucky, he would go home in disgrace. If he was unlucky, Blue Epoch might make an example of him.

Regardless of which outcome presented itself, his mother, who'd gotten him the job in the first place, would shoulder some of the blame, as well. Humiliated and brought low in the eyes of her employer, her star would dim, giving Mia Salvatore the chance to rise.

And all it took was ruining one man's life.

I wanted to believe it was worth it, but niggling doubts crept through my mind. As I swam toward the shore, I squashed them mercilessly. I would ruin the lives of a hundred Calvins if it meant I could get my revenge.

CHAPTER TWENTY-NINE

A GRIM REMINDER

The wolves are nipping at my heels. I'm surrounded on all sides by people who want to take what I've worked so hard for. I wonder if Jeremiah ever had to deal with anything like it.

—Nora Lancaster

I left Biloxi much as I'd entered, though I managed to get out without running into any more of Blue Epoch's guards. When I finally left the town behind, I let out a sigh of relief. Performing that kind of a mission wasn't as adrenaline pumping as getting into a firefight, but it was, perhaps, even more stressful. The whole time I'd spent creeping between the buildings, my heart had been beating out of control. But finally, with my task complete, I could relax a little.

Of course, that was when I was attacked.

I was only ten miles or so away from Biloxi when something raced out of the night's shadows and tackled me from my hover bike. Due to the uneven terrain, I hadn't been going that fast, so the impact as I hit the ground wasn't very jarring, but still, I was a bit surprised that I hadn't sensed whatever it was that had attacked me.

I rolled across the ground, using the Hand of God to block the monster's snapping jaws as we skidded to a stop. The cybernetic hand was nearly indestructible, so it served well as a bit until I finally yanked Ferdinand II from his holster and hip fired into the monster's torso.

One shot.

Two.

Then a third.

Each one tore a massive hole through the creature, but it didn't stop fighting until the fourth. I pushed away, and I only had a moment to confirm that my attacker was a wildling. Long, rangy, and naked, the creature even had teeth that had been filed to sharp points. If I'd let it get to the bare skin around my neck, those needle-sharp teeth would have easily torn through my throat. After all, these former humans were strong enough to survive among the wild monsters. Thinking that my Constitution attribute—or even my Sheath—would protect me was folly.

I climbed to my feet and, just to be sure, put another bullet in the monster's head. Then, I holstered Ferdinand II and drew my R-14 from my arsenal implant. It was loaded, and I was ready for whatever came next.

With a flick of my mind, I de-summoned the Cutter. It had kept going for a few dozen feet before sliding from the road and into the woods, so it was at the edge of my range. Any farther, and it would have been too faraway to de-summon.

But I wasn't really worried about that. Instead, I was on the lookout for the wildling's pack. Like the people they'd once been, wildlings were social creatures. I'd only seen individuals a couple of times, and those had been scouts. So, if there was one around, it was almost guaranteed that there would be plenty more to follow.

Flaring Observation to its limits, I swept my gaze around. As dark as it was, that ability represented my only hope of seeing them coming. The wildling had attacked from the north—the right side of the road—so that's where I focused my attention. And sure enough, I saw dark shapes flitting through the trees.

There weren't just a handful of the humanoid monsters. There were dozens. Maybe more than a hundred. I'd never seen a pack so big. More, they had never hesitated before attacking. These wildlings, though, showed some level of intelligence in that they took the time to surround me.

Like wolves.

Or the intelligent human beings they once had been.

It was a terrifying thought.

I brought my weapon to my shoulder and slowly backed away. I could stand and fight, but there was every chance that they'd get through my defenses. Or they'd continue to encircle me. If that happened, I'd end up as food.

One of the wildlings got tired of waiting, and he darted out of the forest, his bare feet kicking up leaves as he dashed toward me. His fingernails had either been filed or transformed into claws. I didn't want to get close enough to find out, so I fired a burst in his direction.

He twitched to the side far more quickly than I thought a human being could move, and though the plasma burst clipped his shoulder, it should have hit him in the chest. How had he moved so quickly? I had no idea. I fired again, this time accounting for his twitchy speed. He tried to dodge, but my aim was true.

His chest exploded.

But he didn't stop. Not immediately, at least. Instead, he leaped across the space between us and swung at me in a sweeping strike, his claws leading the way. I ducked, then used my rifle's stock in an uppercut that sent him flying into the air. He thudded into the ground, still twitching, but he didn't rise.

My panic rose, my heart beating through my chest. That was just one of them. And there were dozens—maybe hundreds—more slowly surrounding me. I couldn't take them. Not in the open, at least. No—I needed a strategic retreat.

So, I turned and ran.

It was as if a dam had burst. The wildlings flooded out of the forest, howling with glee and anticipation. I could practically feel their bloodlust. Their hunger. It spurred me to run even faster.

My Constitution was impressive, and I had the willpower to eke the most out of the attribute. But still, I knew I couldn't escape. The wildlings were faster. Stronger. They were going to catch me. It might take a few minutes, or it could be over in a couple more seconds, but eventually, they would overtake me.

If I stopped to summon my Cutter, they'd overwhelm me before I could even mount it. I had to remain afoot. I needed shelter. A defensive position. So, I ran, my feet thundering against the cracked pavement of the road as I searched for some way to even the odds. The BMAP might do it, but I suspected the wildlings were too fast. One had almost dodged the assault rifle's issue, so doing the same with the BMAP's relatively slow-moving projectile would be comparatively easy.

The scattergun, maybe?

It would slow them down a little, but these wildlings were advanced enough that it would almost assuredly be nonlethal. My nano-sword would cut them. My Pulsar would make easy work of them. But both had problems, too. In the case of the nano-sword, I'd have to get in close. They were faster and stronger than me, so that was a recipe for a quick death. I might take a few of them out, but I'd fall soon enough.

I considered trying to lose them in the woods, but that was a recipe for disaster, as well. After all, they lived there. It would be sheer idiocy to fight them on their home turf. So, I continued to sprint down the road, barely keeping ahead of the howling pack of wildlings. Listening to them—or even seeing them—it was sometimes difficult to believe that they'd once been human. They certainly sounded like animals, and they no longer looked completely human, with their elongated arms and legs, misshapen bodies, and natural weapons.

But I knew that they were just victims, transformed by unrestrained and uncontrolled Mist. The only thing protecting most humans from that fate were the Nexus Implants. Without them, we'd all end up as little more than wild animals driven by instinct and cunning.

I continued to run. I couldn't stop, lest they fall upon me like a pack of starving wolves. Even if I took a few of them out, the rest would finish the job. And they certainly wouldn't flinch at seeing one of their number laid low. Fortunately, with my training and Constitution, I could run flat-out for quite some time. Unfortunately, so could they.

My steps ate up the ground, but I couldn't leave them behind. As I pushed myself to run faster, I did stretch my lead a little, but I knew it was temporary. They would eventually catch me and rip me limb from limb. I tossed out a couple of grenades as I ran, but the creatures were intelligent enough to recognize their danger. Even as the sound of explosions filled the air behind me, the wildlings wove their way through the various blasts, almost as if they possessed some sixth sense.

Still, I kept running. And they followed.

My heart continued to pound, my wind finally started to give out, and still, I saw no way out. I was on the verge of turning and taking the initiative by blanketing my surroundings in the BMAP's issue, but then I finally saw my salvation.

It was just a house.

Or what was left of one, at least. But I knew how to use that kind of terrain to my advantage. So, I quickly veered off course, leaping over a few bushes before I crashed through the doorway. I rolled and twisted, coming up with my R-14 pointed in the direction of the doorway. A second later, the first wildlings poured through, all screeching hunger and wicked claws.

I fired, one three-round burst after another. Each time one of the wildlings fell, another took its place. A couple tried to get through the window, but I drew Ferdinand II with one hand while I continued firing at the door with the other. Dual wielding weapons significantly reduced my accuracy—especially when one of those weapons was a rifle—but with my enemies so close, I couldn't miss.

Soon enough, Ferdinand II ran dry—he only had a nine-shot canister, and I'd already used a few rounds in the first assault—so I slowly backed away and up a set of nearby stairs. They creaked underneath me, and I was prepared to leap if they collapsed. But miraculously, they held true. I continued to fire, stopping only to switch magazines.

Dozens of wildlings went down as they flooded through the front door and up the stairs. A human would have been smart enough to come at me from a different angle. These creatures were too focused on the meal in front of them to even consider that, though. They hunted by instinct, giving them the illusion of cunning, but it was a shallow thing. They just couldn't think.

Or that's what I thought.

Just after the last of the wildlings fell on the stairs, I found out just how dangerous making assumptions about the capabilities of my enemies could be.

A line of fire erupted on my back as a particularly huge wildling swept her claws diagonally from one of my shoulders to my ribs. I let out a scream as I tumbled forward, rolling across dead or dying wildlings. The ones who yet lived swiped feebly at me, but they caught only air.

That didn't mean I was out of the woods, though. As I reached the bottom of the stairs, I rolled to my feet just in time to see a giant female wildling barreling down the stairs like an out-of-control monorail. I dove to the side, narrowly avoiding a swipe of her claws, squeezing the R-14's trigger as I sailed through the air. The assault rifle barked, and superheated balls of plasma hit her in the ribs. However, to my enormous surprise, they only sizzled a bit.

No giant holes. No exploded torso. Just a tight grouping of burn marks.

As I hit the floor, skidding across ancient hardwood, she howled, her every muscle contracting as she swung to face me. But she didn't rush. The shots had hurt her. She was wary.

I fired again.

Over and over until my magazine ran dry. Still, she strode forward, her arms so long that her claws nearly scraped the floor. I didn't have time to exchange the empty magazine for a fresh one, so I dismissed the weapon back into my arsenal implant. I reached over my shoulder, drawing my nano-sword. It had been sharp enough to get through Horace Lafontaine's subdermal armor back during my first test. It should get through this hulking wildling's flesh, too.

I rushed toward her, ducking under a wild swing of her claws, but I didn't lash out with my blade. Not until I'd passed her by. Then, with a backhanded strike, I attacked her hamstrings. Once. Twice. They parted cleanly. She fell to her knees with a howl, and I tried to follow up with a fatal strike to her head, but I had to abort the attack in order to narrowly evade an overhand swipe of her claws.

Even then, I had to whip my blade up to knock it aside. When sword met claw, sparks flew, telling me just how lethal the wildling's natural weapons were. I backed away until my back hit the wall.

She hissed and spat as she tried to track me, but her ruined hamstrings made her clumsy. The movement of the wildlings was jerky in the best of times—almost as if they could scarcely control their own bodies—but the severing of her hamstrings exacerbated the situation.

I was right next to the open door. I could probably run, and she would have little chance of catching me.

But I didn't want to do that.

She had attacked me. Wounded me. She had picked a fight. And I was unwilling to let her get away with nothing but a couple of wounds that would probably heal. So, I sheathed my sword, drawing the BMAP a moment later. Then, I activated Disengage as I kicked into a backward leap. The ability had only one purpose—to put distance between me and a target. It did that by augmenting the force of my next step, which, in this instance, was a leap.

I flew through the door even faster than I could run, and as I sailed through the air, I brought the BMAP to my shoulder. At the same time, I saw the giant wildling step right into the fatal funnel. An all-too-human hatred burned in her eyes as she grasped at the doorframe.

I fired.

The BMAP's round, as big around as my wrist and with a payload that could level an armored personnel carrier, flew with a slight arc. The wildling hadn't tried to dodge my previous shots, and this one was no different.

I was thirty feet away and still in the air when the round went off.

Everything went white, and I was swept even farther away by the concussive blast. I slammed into a tree, which sent me tumbling into another. Then another until I hit the ground, digging a small furrow into the carpet of leaves and dirt. I skidded to a stop a dozen or so feet later, my entire body aching.

I lay there for a long moment before I managed to gather my wits enough to push myself to my feet. I knew I had at least a concussion, but probably a couple of broken ribs, too. And my knee had been twisted in the wrong direction; I didn't feel as if anything was broken or torn, but it certainly didn't feel good.

I rose on unsteady feet and looked back in the direction of the house. I could see the steady glow of flames, but I was too far into the forest to see much more than that. So, I limped forward, using the various trees to steady myself. I kept the BMAP out, but I knew that if the wildling had survived my last shot, I didn't really have anything in my arsenal that could take her out.

A headshot from my Pulsar, so long as I used Empowered Shot, would probably do the trick. But even that wasn't certain. I dismissed the stubby artillery platform, exchanging it for my sniper rifle.

Then, I crept forward, my gait rendered awkward by my left knee's refusal to bend. I pushed through it, eventually finding my way to the tree line.

I gasped at the scene before me.

The house was just gone, replaced by a dimly glowing bonfire. Nothing but the foundation remained, and there were smaller blazes burning in a dozen different places throughout the area. I even saw one a hundred yards away. Hopefully, that wouldn't start a forest fire, but given the wet climate, I thought that an unlikely possibility.

In any case, my eyes were trained on the charred body lying where the house used to be. There were others nearby, but they were little more than blackened skeletons. The other wildlings, I reasoned. But the big one—the alpha—she was more or less intact, if charred beyond all recognition.

Then, I saw her twitch. That twitch turned into a heave. I wasn't sure if she was still alive or if that was just a death rattle, but I wasn't going to take any chances. So, I raised the Pulsar, sighted in, and used Empowered Shot. After waiting two seconds for the ability to charge, I fired.

The moment I did, I started the process anew. Aim. Empowered Shot. Fire.

The first shot took her in the chest. The next, in the legs. Whatever force had allowed her to resist the rounds from my R-14 did nothing against the Pulsar. Her torso exploded. Then, her legs. I was comforted to see that there was no more twitching.

I sagged in exhaustion, pain, and relief.

But it was short-lived. I still had Observation running, and I picked up the telltale hum of Mist engines churning in the distance. Doubtless, someone had seen the explosion. Or heard the gunfire. And now, they were coming to investigate. There was every chance that they were friendly—not everyone was out to kill everyone else—but I couldn't take that chance. Not so close to Biloxi, where I'd just sabotaged Blue Epoch's kelp-harvesting operation. No—I needed to get gone, and fast.

So, I focused my bleary thoughts and summoned my Cutter. The paint was scraped on one side where it had collided with a tree, but it was in otherwise good condition. Not surprising, considering its quality. It would take a lot more than a little wreck like that to affect the hover bike on anything more than a cosmetic level. Still, it was annoying that my beautiful, sleek bike now had a scratch running along its fuselage.

I mounted up, then tore off down the road. The force of the rapid acceleration put even more pressure on my wounds, but I didn't dare slow down. I was in no condition to fight a battle, so all I could do was flee.

I did keep my head on a swivel, though. The last thing I needed was to get ambushed again. The various cities and towns were dangerous, but the wilds were perhaps even more so. And I would do well to remember that.

CHAPTER THIRTY

THE BACK DOOR

I had to kill three upstarts today, two of which I've known for more than a decade. I didn't even give them the chance to explain themselves. I couldn't afford to. Not when doing so would only be interpreted as weakness. Jeremiah never had to deal with that kind of thing. When he spoke, people listened. I don't have that kind of effect on people, so I don't have a choice but to rule with an iron fist.

—Nora Lancaster

I swung around Nova City, taking a wide course that would keep me off the Enforcers' radar. I'd left my pursuers far behind, but I didn't discount the possibility that they were still following. It was unlikely, given the steps I'd taken to obscure my trail, but I wasn't about to discount anything. Instead, I intended to head north for a few days until the commotion died down.

I wasn't even sure anyone had followed me, but with the size of the explosion I'd caused, I thought it was fair to assume that they had. That close to Biloxi, they'd have to be fools not to investigate. And when they did, the degree of firepower I'd brought to bear would be evident. Hopefully, they'd just assume it was an Enforcer drill or something, but I couldn't afford to bank on it. So, I had run.

Eventually, once I'd covered nearly thirty miles, I slowed to a stop in front of an abandoned building. It was a few stories tall, and judging by the clump of other buildings nearby, it had once been part of a town. However, most of the other structures had already surrendered to the effects of time and neglect, so it had become the settlement's lone survivor. Even then, kudzu coated the walls, and it was missing its windows and doors. Still, it was the best shelter I was likely to find.

With a groan, I dismounted my Cutter and hobbled toward the front door. I wasn't so injured that I'd lost all sense, though, and I summoned my R-14 before entering. Stepping through the door, I looked left and right, but I saw no threats. Like that, I cleared the bottom floor before heading to the second. Then, the third. And finally, the fourth. I found nothing dangerous.

There were a few areas that had clearly housed various wild animals, but they were long since abandoned. The building was empty.

So, with that done, I found one of the innermost rooms and settled down to tend to my injuries. Arduously, I stripped down to my underwear to find a body that had been put through a crucible. I didn't have any major lacerations—the combination of the Sheath and my infiltration suit had reduced any potential gashes to surface-level cuts and abrasions. However, they'd done little to combat the blunt-force trauma to which I had been subjected. My entire body was covered in bruises, each with varying degrees of seriousness, my knee was swollen to at least twice its size, and I could feel a sharp jab of agony every time I took a deep breath.

And I couldn't do much about any of it.

The cuts and abrasions weren't bad enough to require anything more than an antiseptic wipe, and there wasn't anything to be done for broken ribs. The same was true for my knee. When I looked at the silhouette on my HUD that was meant to indicate my health, I saw that my knee pulsed a deep orange, while my side was a bright red.

That's when I remembered that, after rearranging my interface, I could check my conditions. I did, letting out a deep sigh at the results:

Conditions:
Broken ribs (R2, R3, L4)
Torn lateral collateral ligament (right)
Strained medial collateral ligament (right)
Concussion (mild)
Abrasions (multiple)
Contusions (multiple)
Minor lacerations (multiple)

It was exactly what I'd expected to see. I'd known my ribs were broken, and finding out that I had a concussion wasn't a surprise. The only thing that really worried me was the torn ligament in my knee. I had no way to tell how bad it was, but I suspected that if it had torn all the way through, I'd have had a lot more trouble walking. As it stood, it was painful, but I could still move well enough if the situation called for it. That, coupled with the fact that it wasn't accompanied by a red indicator on my silhouette, suggested that it wasn't as serious as it could have been.

After summoning a blanket from my arsenal implant, I covered a portion of the floor, then sat down. Leaning against the wall, I considered what had happened to me. For the first time since Mobile, I'd come close to dying. All wildlings were dangerous, but I'd thought their danger lay rooted in their numbers. That clearly wasn't the case. That alpha had been big, fast, and incredibly strong. In addition, even my advanced weaponry wasn't enough to put her down easily.

The BMAP, which had destroyed that entire house, hadn't even been enough. I'd had to finish her with the Pulsar.

It would have been different if the ambush had been the result of a misstep. I could accept that, correct the issue, and move on. But the wildlings had come out of nowhere; even with Observation running, I'd had no indication that I was even being stalked. No—I couldn't have done much differently, aside from maybe bringing the BMAP out a little sooner. However, I'd been concerned about stirring up a commotion. That, plus I'd been worried about using the artillery platform when my enemies were so close.

Judging by how beat up I was, that was a valid concern.

But I had survived, if only barely. I could learn from that, too.

I summoned a med-hypo from my arsenal implant, then pressed it against my bare thigh. I hit the button, and with a pneumatic hiss, it discharged its payload of pain relievers and antibiotics. I was fairly sure that my Regeneration and Resistance would protect me from most infections, but I wasn't willing to take that chance—especially when I wasn't trying to conserve supplies. Soon, I'd be back in Nova City, where I could restock.

After storing the used med-hypo back in my arsenal implant, I let another deep sigh. Relief was already spreading through my body, smothering the pain that had bypassed my Pain Tolerance. As I leaned back against the wall, I knew that I'd gotten incredibly lucky. If that alpha had been the one to initiate the attack, I would have been dead.

That was the difference between the wilds and Nova City. In Nova, I could predict the dangers and prepare for them. Outside, though? That was different. The moment I got comfortable was the moment I'd end up dead.

Not for the first time, I imagined how the world must have felt just after the Initialization. Back then, they'd been wholly unprepared. Millions—perhaps billions—had died. More, I was once again floored by the fact that my uncle had survived. He'd even thrived, and with nothing but old-world weaponry at his disposal.

Of course, he'd lost almost everyone he cared about, too. In that respect, we were remarkably similar.

For a few minutes, I sat there. I had been riding so high off my victory in Biloxi, and now, I'd had that success undercut by a close brush with death. It was a cruel world that seemed intent on keeping me from gaining any sense of equilibrium. It made me anxious for what might happen next, and I couldn't stop myself from clutching the grip of Ferdinand II, just in case something snuck up on me.

Eventually, though, the combination of my fatigue, injuries, and the med-hypo took their toll, and I drifted off into an uneasy sleep. Thankfully, my recent experiences didn't affect my dreams.

The next morning, I awoke to the sound of chirping birds and unrelenting discomfort. My entire body hurt, and badly enough that my Pain Tolerance was helpless against it.

Pushing myself into a sitting position, I winced at the sharp pain in my side. Wryly, I muttered, "Almost like I was in an explosion. Or I was attacked by a giant, superhuman wildling."

That brought a grim chuckle that soon became a pained snarl. Summoning a ration bar and a bottle of water, I choked down my breakfast before consulting my interface. On the positive side, the various abrasions and lacerations had disappeared from the readout. On the negative, the ligament in my knee was still torn, and my ribs were still broken. Fortunately, the concussion was gone; I hadn't meant to fall asleep, which was terrible when under the influence of a concussion, but I hadn't been able to resist.

Settling back down, I resolved to wait. Soon enough, my injuries would be healed by my abilities; I just had to endure. Which was what I did. For three days, I sat in that building, barely moving as my body healed itself. I had plenty of ration bars and enough water to last me another month, so I wasn't in a hurry to head back to Nova until I was completely healed.

To pass the time, I spent hour after hour engaged with my Mind training program or writing various Ghosts, most of which I discarded as soon as they were done. The majority were just variations of what I already had but written completely differently. It was a good exercise that forced me to be creative with how I built them. Not terribly productive, but it didn't need to be.

On the third day, I summoned my status onto my HUD:

NAME	Mirabelle Lisa Braddock
CLASS	MISTRUNNER
LEVEL	12 (19%)
CONSTITUTION	52/94

MIND	56/94		
MIST	43/94		
SKILLS	7/7		
SKILL NAME	Skill Tier	Modifiers	Abilities
CYBERNETIC MASTERY	Tier 1 (62%)	100% Efficiency	6 Cybernetic Slots
COMBAT	Tier 1 (91%)	+50% Damage (All) +50% Speed (Melee) +50% Accuracy (All) +25% Range (Firearms) +50% Reload Speed (Firearms)	Empowered Shot (D) Double Shot (E) Combination Punch (D) Pummel (E) Engage (E) Disengage (F) Mark Target (F) Barrage (F)
INFILTRATION	Tier 1 (38%)	+15% Effectiveness (Stealth)	Stealth (E) Camouflage (E) Deception (E) Mimic (E) Observation (D)
MISTRUNNER	Tier 1 (46%)	+25% Speed (Misthack) +25% Speed (Mistwalk) +50% Strength (Mistwall) +50% Breach Range	Mistwalk (D) Misthack (D) Mistwall (C) System Redirect (F) Disable Cybernetics (F) Overcharge (E)
FIELDCRAFT	Tier 1 (58%)	+25% Combat Effectiveness	Triage (D) Basic Explosives Handling (D) Combat Focus (C) Pain Tolerance (D) Resistance (E) Foraging (E) Improvisation (D) Regeneration (D)

DEMOLITION	Tier 1 (82%)	+15% Explosive Radius +5% Explosive Strength	Blast Shield (E)
ACROBATICS	Tier 1 (66%)	+35% Proprioception	Balance (E)

I usually didn't consult my status very often. When I'd first gotten access to my interface, I couldn't go more than a few minutes without looking at it. However, my constant training had broken that habit, and once I'd gotten my class and the upgraded skills that came with it, the glacial progression had further dissuaded me. So, it had been weeks—perhaps even more than a month—since I'd last looked at it.

However, I was happy with the changes I saw. I hadn't increased the tier of any of my skills, but I had made good progress, especially in [Combat], [Demolition], and [Acrobatics]. [Mistrunner], [Fieldcraft], and [Infiltration] had lagged a little behind, but that wasn't necessarily unexpected. That I'd progressed them at all was a good sign that my training was effective.

But what really drew my eye was the fact that I'd progressed two levels, bringing my potential for each of my attributes up to ninety-four. In addition, my actual attributes had continued to climb, as well, likely due to my constant focus on training. My enhanced Constitution was probably the only reason I'd managed to survive my most recent battle.

It was nice to see that my efforts hadn't been in vain.

Over the next two days, I checked and reloaded the weapons in my arsenal implant, but aside from that, I occupied myself with more mental exercises. Slowly, my injuries healed enough that I could get up and move around. I didn't overdo it, though, and I confined my exercises to light calisthenics. A further three days, and I was back to normal.

So, I donned my infiltration suit, made sure that I hadn't left anything behind, then went back outside to resume my journey back to Nova City. I wasn't that faraway, so I could see the various platforms looming large on the horizon, and I wasted no more time before mounting my hover bike and heading in the appropriate direction.

I didn't head toward the gates, though. As I was, they'd never let me in. And my disguise as a Banshee wasn't credible enough to fool their much more accurate sensors. On top of that, they had access to the Enforcer database, which meant that it would only take a single scan before they recognized me for the impostor I was.

Fortunately, I knew another way in.

Originally, I'd intended to contact Gunther, who'd claimed he could smuggle me in. But I chose not to do that for two reasons. First, I still didn't completely trust him. He'd yet to betray me, but I suspected that was more because he was waiting for a bigger payday. Or maybe I was just being overly paranoid. Either way, I wasn't going to give him the chance to hang me out to dry. Second, I didn't want there to be any record of my comings and goings. That was a good way to get caught.

So, it was a good thing that I had both the skills and the knowledge to take the back door into Nova City, which was why I found myself staring up an enormous concrete pillar. In the shadow of the giant city platform, it was almost like night had fallen, but I could see the steel pitons running along its length easily enough. I'd already climbed down once before, so I didn't see any reason I couldn't climb back up.

Once I'd dismissed my Cutter, I got to work, using the pitons as a ladder to climb the column of concrete. It wasn't pleasant, and I made a point not to look down too much, but at least I wasn't being attacked by a flock of bloodthirsty birds, which made it a lot better than my descent had been.

Even so, it took me hours to climb, and by the time I reached the base of the platform, my forearms were screaming at me. I kept going, though, because I didn't exactly have any alternative. Turning back around, I gripped one piton with both hands while balancing atop another. Then, I spied my goal almost a dozen feet away. Taking a deep breath, I used Balance before flinging myself toward my destination.

Windmilling my arms, I had a brief moment of vertigo as I realized that there was nothing between me and a thousand-foot drop. Then, I grabbed the piton connected to the bottom of the platform. It was L-shaped, so it offered a decent handhold, but still, I almost missed.

My heart jumped into my throat as I felt the piton slip from its anchor. As my stomach twisted into knots, I was showered with tiny bits of concrete as the piton worked free. Without Balance, I would have fallen, but the ability gave me just enough opportunity to swing to the next piton. As I let go of my previous handle, it broke free of the concrete and tumbled into the air.

A single instant more, and I'd have fallen right beside it. I wasn't sure if I could survive such a fall. Maybe. But it wouldn't be pleasant. And given the predators that made the swamp their home, I didn't fancy my chances if I were to be stranded in the marsh, injured and immobile.

Pushing those thoughts aside, I swung from one piton to the next until, finally, I reached the grate. Perching on the ledge, I drew my nano-bladed sword and went to work. The blade cut through the mundane iron with ease, and before long, I pushed into the tunnel and collapsed onto the water-stained concrete, my breath coming in ragged gasps.

That had been too close for comfort.

But now, I was back in Nova, and despite the issues I'd encountered, I'd accomplished my goals. I only had to head back to Lakeview where I could meet with Mia Salvatore. She would hold up her end of the bargain, and the next part of my revenge plan could commence.

I still had some way to go, but I was getting closer and closer by the day. Soon enough, Nora would fall, I'd get my vengeance, and then . . .

I didn't know what would come next. I hadn't thought that far ahead. But that didn't matter; until Nora paid for what she had done, I couldn't spare much thought for anything else.

So, with my mind firmly ensconced in my plans for revenge, I used Mimic to adopt the identity of a middle-aged woman I'd seen during my first trip through the Underground and donned a mundane outfit before setting off to find my way to the surface of the city. My trip went off without a hitch; apparently, nobody expected someone to come from down below, so there was no security barring my way. I used that to my advantage, and within twenty minutes, I was back among the familiar megabuildings of the Garden District.

I sighed in relief.

As much as I hated everything Nova City represented, it was still home, and I would never be quite as comfortable anywhere else. Here, everything made sense. I knew most of the rules. But outside, things were different. One wrong step, one little mistake, and I'd end up in some ridiculously powerful monster's belly.

Shaking my head, I realized it wasn't really so different in Nova. There were plenty of hidden threats in the city, too, and I'd be a fool not to tread lightly, even if I thought I knew what I was getting into.

With that in mind, I climbed out of the drainage trench where the entrance to the Underground was located and quickly found my way to the monorail, which I rode back to my compound. When I finally reached my destination, I felt myself relax for the first time in quite a while.

But I couldn't let it last. Not for more than a day. After that, I needed to get back to it.

CHAPTER THIRTY-ONE

ECHO

I just want respect. Obedience. They all gave it to Jeremiah so willingly; would it be so hard to give me the same? Haven't I earned that much?

—Nora Lancaster

My arrival back at the compound in Algiers came with no fanfare. Patrick didn't even look up from his study materials when I ascended from the basement, and I didn't want to disturb him. Instead, I headed straight for my quarters where I quickly stripped down and hopped in the shower. I'd only been in the wilderness for about a week, but the grime clung to me like a second, horrible-smelling skin. I was eager to remove it, so I wasted no time before cleaning myself thoroughly. After that, I stood beneath the cascade of scalding water as I tried to relax.

I was mostly unsuccessful.

Certainly, reaching the security of my home relieved a noticeable amount of stress. However, it wasn't enough to truly impact my state of mind. From experience, I knew it would take a couple of days for the stress to dissipate, and even then, I wasn't sure if it would ever completely go away. I had too much on my shoulders. I was juggling too many plans. And the danger of Nova City, while more subdued than that of the wilderness, was always present. One wrong move, and everything could come crashing down.

But the hot shower helped. As I stood there, my muscles slowly unkinked, and I let out a long sigh. I had come very close to the edge out there. Even though I knew there wasn't much else I could have done—after all, those wildlings had come out of nowhere, and even my Observation hadn't been up to the task of detecting them—I was woefully aware that I needed to figure out how to do better. I was already cautious, but I needed to steer straight into paranoia if I was going to have any hope of survival.

Was that really the appropriate term, though? In Nova City—indeed, in the post-Initialization world—everyone was out for themselves. Betrayal lurked around every corner, and being ready for it was the height of sensibility. After all, it wasn't really paranoia if everyone truly was out to get you. My uncle's fate had reinforced that lesson, and it wasn't one I could soon forget.

I stayed in the shower for almost thirty minutes after I was clean. I probably would have remained longer if I could have afforded it. For now, though, I needed to stay focused. I couldn't let myself relax too fully, lest I lose my edge. So, I finally stepped out of the shower and wiped my hand across the foggy mirror.

I'd dropped Mimic the moment I'd gotten home, so my reflection was familiar. However, I couldn't help but notice the addition of a few new scars. Thin white lines that told the story of how many times I'd been injured. According to the silhouette in my HUD, I was completely healed, but I still felt some phantom pains in my ribs and knee. I'd have to work those out during training.

After inspecting my body for any wounds that might have been hiding under the grime, I dried myself with a fluffy white towel and wrapped it around my chest. Then, I padded into my room, where I put on a pair of underwear before diving into the bed. After spending a week sleeping on the hard floor of that abandoned building, it was a welcome change, and I fell asleep almost immediately.

The next morning, I awoke refreshed and ready to enact the next piece of my plan. So, I quickly dressed, and after exchanging a curiously tense greeting with Patrick over breakfast, I headed out to Lakeview. The trip was largely uneventful, and I met Mia Salvatore at the café across from her building. There, she confirmed that Calvin had been hung out to dry, and that she'd already been scheduled for a meeting with her boss. It was a prelude to her promotion, she was sure, and as a result, she was more than happy to hold up her end of the bargain. So, with that taken care of, I headed back into the poorer parts of the city.

I knew Mia's sabotage of the bio-enhancers would take a little while to take full effect. Nora was due a shipment in about a week, and even then, it would take a few more weeks for them to affect her. And then a couple more months to get her where I wanted her. It was a good thing that I had plenty of plans for how to use that time. To that end, I headed to the northern part of the Garden.

My destination was a comparatively small megabuilding near the edge of the district. When it came into sight, I quickly ensconced myself on an abandoned floor of the building across the street. I'd chosen it for one reason: it had clear sight lines. The fact that it was sparsely populated was just a bonus.

Settling down beside a window, I surveilled the other building, watching for guards, cameras, and other security. Normally, I wouldn't have had to pay much attention to such things, but this building was different from the rest of the Garden in a number of ways. First, it was half the size of other megabuildings. Still a huge structure, but it looked small against the rest of the district's skyline. It was also more luxurious, and from a distance, it looked almost like the buildings in Lakeview. However, the closer one came, the more it looked like a cheap knockoff. Which it was. But that still put it on a higher tier than almost any other building in the district.

It also had a proper name instead of just a series of numbers. The Estate. A grandiose moniker for a building that housed the sort of people who cared about that kind of thing. It was all a facade. That building as well as the people who called it home were only a little better off than most of the Garden's residents, but they clung to that tiny difference like it was a lifeline to a better life.

My target, Echo, resided within.

It probably would have been easy enough to just kill her. I could've just perched atop one of the buildings and waited for her to step out into the open. I had no doubts that my Pulsar would make quick work of her, even without Empowered Shot. But that wasn't the plan, and for a couple of reasons.

For one, I didn't want Nora to know that someone was hunting her and her people. As far as I knew, she was completely ignorant of my actions, and I wanted to keep it that way. After all, my goal was to tear everything down around her, both to punish the others who were complicit in the betrayal of my uncle and to see her face when she was left with nothing but the crumbling ruins of a once-mighty tribe.

For another, I didn't want to tangle with the Enforcers. With how volatile the Garden was, I knew it would only take a small spark to reignite the war that had only just begun to wane. That would bring the Enforcers back into play, which would make the rest of my plan more difficult. The time would come for the Enforcers to play their part, but that time was still a ways off.

No—there was a better way to bring her down that would serve the overall plan much better.

I continued to watch for a few more hours. Even as night fell, I didn't make a move. The building might've been a sad facsimile of a higher-quality structure, but one area where it hadn't skimped was the security. There were dozens of guards and a plethora of cameras. It was also equipped with quite a few auto-turrets, as well. And those were just the security assets I could observe; I was certain there were others that had flown beneath my radar.

After midnight, I decided to make my move. So, I descended from my perch, crossed the street, and circled around to the back of the megabuilding where I knew I would find the service entrance. All megabuildings—even one as heavily modified as this one—adhered to a similar layout.

As I approached, I used Misthack to deactivate the cameras and autoturrets that guarded the back entrance, then, after connecting to the security terminal in the door, used Mistwalk to gain entrance. Just like that, I was inside. When I had first gotten my [Mistwalker] skill, I'd been surprised to find so few defenses against intrusion. However, my uncle had explained to me that it was an extremely rare skill and that guarding against it was both expensive and usually pointless. Ever since that skill had evolved into [Mistrunner], I'd found that to be doubly true; few of the defenses I'd encountered had been able to hold up under my intrusion, and the building's defenses did nothing to buck that trend.

Still, as I crept through the back door, I kept Observation at the forefront of my mind—and it was a good thing, too. Otherwise, I would have missed the two autoturrets at the end of the hall. I wasn't sure if I could survive such an assault—I suspected that I had a chance, given my infiltration suit and the Sheath beneath my skin—but even if I could, it would still result in horrific injuries. I'd seen autoturrets in action, and the last thing I wanted was to find myself on their bad side.

I stopped just out of range and deactivated the autoturrets with Misthack, then crept forward. Having taken the back entrance, I had access to the service elevator, but I still chose the stairs. Elevators, in my experience, could quickly turn into death traps. Stairs were better, even if I didn't look forward to climbing thirty flights.

Slowly, I made my way up until I reached the tenth level. If this building was laid out like all the other megabuildings, that's where I would find the security terminal that was tied into the rest of the building's defenses. I left the stairs behind, walking through the corridors with purpose. The decor was only a little better than what I'd expect to find in a typical megabuilding. The carpet was unstained, the paint wasn't peeling, and the lights didn't flicker. But it was all still made of bare concrete and steel, with little decoration to disguise the utilitarian nature of the building's interior.

I quickly found the security terminal in an unmanned room in one corner of the building. During the day, it might've had a guard, but after midnight, it was completely empty. So, I wasted no time in disabling the cameras and heading inside, where I used Miswalk to gain access to the terminal.

A few puzzles—and a handful of seconds—later, I was in the system. From there, I had access to all the building's defenses. I deactivated the cameras, put the autoturrets to sleep, and gave myself administrative access to all the building's locked doors. In short, I took it over. Until the system reset in the morning, I would be in complete control.

With that out of the way, I went back to the stairs, passing only one person—a maintenance worker, by the looks of him—along the way. He didn't even look twice at me, and even if he had, all he would see was the persona I'd adopted via Mimic. My infiltration suit was concealed beneath much more normal clothing, and so as far as he could tell, I was just another worker.

Step by step, I climbed until I reached the thirtieth floor. It wasn't the penthouse, but it was high enough that when Echo looked out the window, she could pretend that she was above all the misery in the Garden below.

I approached the door, disabling Echo's private security system before heading inside. The apartment was tastefully decorated, though far less opulently than I would have expected. But that was her—no-nonsense to the very end. It was why my uncle had liked her, and it was one of the traits that made her so effective at managing the tribe's logistics. I could have almost liked her if she hadn't been part of Nora's betrayal.

And I knew she was. Nora could never have taken over without the support of my uncle's other lieutenants. So, in my mind, they were just as culpable as she was.

My anger surged, and I considered just waiting in the apartment for Echo's return. Cutting her up into little pieces would have been just punishment for what she'd done to Jeremiah. But I suppressed my rage and focused on completing the plan.

With Observation, it didn't take long for me to find Echo's hidden terminal. Most people would have missed the tiny, barely visible seam in the concrete, but it was obvious to me. Getting in proved more difficult than expected, though. Even with my skills and abilities, hacking through its lock took a few minutes. But in the end, I succeeded, gaining access to her personal terminal.

Breaking its security protocols was laughable after bypassing the lock, and before I knew it, I was in. That's when I started planting evidence. A few altered lines of code, a few thousand deposited credits, and a couple of glaringly obvious hints, and anyone who cared to look through that terminal's files would come to the conclusion that Echo had been embezzling money from the Specters.

Of course, it was naive to think that she hadn't already been doing just that, but she was skilled enough to hide it from all but the most intense scrutiny. The planted evidence was far more obvious. Even a child could have followed those bread crumbs. Or Nora.

With that done, I made sure that everything was put back into place before leaving the apartment behind. I descended the building, making a quick stop at the security terminal to retract my access before leaving the megabuilding behind. I couldn't help but smile as I walked to the monorail; the seed had been planted. Now, all I needed to do was make sure that Nora knew where to look.

To that end, I took the monorail back to the station closest to Gunther's Guns. Ideally, I wouldn't have to involve him in any of my schemes, but I didn't know a better way to get the information to Nora. Sure, an anonymous tip might have worked, but it would be taken a lot more seriously if it came from someone like Gunther.

Riding the monorail was as depressing as ever. But I did notice that there were a lot fewer passengers than even the late hour could account for. Perhaps the still-simmering war between the various tribes had resulted in far more casualties than I'd expected.

Or maybe the rumors about people leaving the city in droves had been accurate. I hoped they were because things were going to get a lot worse in the coming weeks. If I had my way, the entire city would burn, and I knew I would sleep much better at night if an exodus of civilians kept the collateral damage to a minimum.

In any case, I wouldn't let myself be dissuaded from my path.

Eventually, the monorail reached the appropriate stop, and I jogged across the street as I made my way to Gunther's. Like most businesses in Nova City, it never closed, and there was even a sizable crowd of customers in the lobby when I arrived. But most of the clientele weren't Operators like I might have expected. Instead, I saw more than a few factory workers and farmers among the crowd. Maybe the citizens of the Garden were arming themselves against the unrest.

That was good. If that was the case, they'd only add to the chaos, which would bode well for my plans. And maybe—just maybe—they would be able to take care of themselves and survive, though that was a lesser concern.

As always, Gunther knew when I'd arrived, and he met me in the lobby. Instead of his typical leather suit, he was wearing a broad-brimmed hat studded with some kind of sharp teeth, a pair of jeans, and a long leather duster. A thick cigar was clutched between his teeth.

"Long time no see, girl," he said. "To what do I owe this dubious pleasure?"

"I need a favor," I stated, glancing around the lobby. Most of the customers were in line to head back to the actual store, but there were a couple milling around. I didn't think they were close enough to overhear, but I didn't want to take any chances. After all, there were plenty of other skills and abilities that might echo my Observation ability's effects. "In private."

He nodded. "As you wish, m'lady," he said with a wide grin and a tip of his hat. I could understand his enthusiasm; he always made money when I came around. And profit was the arms dealer's guiding star.

I followed Gunther through his building until we reached his office, where he sat in one of his immense leather chairs. With his hunting trophies staring down at me with lifeless eyes, I explained what I wanted him to do. Once I was finished, he said, "I think I can handle it."

"What's the price?" I asked.

He gave me another grin. "You did so well last time, I figure we can just repeat the process," he explained. Then, he handed me a chip, adding, "Shouldn't be that difficult. Just kill her and I'll spread as much misinformation as you like."

I sighed. It would have been easier if he'd just wanted money, but given my dwindling funds, it was probably better to exchange favors. Besides, I didn't mind killing people for him. At worst, I was just adding to the inevitable chaos that would soon engulf the district, and that suited me just fine.

"Okay," I said. "I'll get it done."

"I have all the confidence in the world," he said, once again tipping his hat at me.

I knew he was probably up to something, but my plan required his participation. When the time came for him to betray me, I'd be ready, though, because I knew it was coming.

CHAPTER THIRTY-TWO

PLANS ON TOP OF PLANS

> *I completely lost it today. Just snapped and killed two of my captains because they had the audacity to question whether we should consolidate our territory. As if I wasn't strong enough to hold what we had. Beat them both to death with my bare hands. Nobody complained much after that.*
>
> —Nora Lancaster

I sat across from Patrick, shoveling Nutty-Oats into my mouth. The cereal could best be described as sugary, which wasn't exactly tasty, but I didn't want to waste my ration bars when I wasn't out in the field. They were far more expensive than the synthetic foods readily available in the Garden, and for the time being, I was on a budget. I had some ideas on how to fix my credit-flow problem, but they were still in their infancy.

Sure, I could steal from Nora and the Specters, but whatever contraband I happened to get ahold of would have to be fenced. And doing that would put the spotlight directly on me. Right now, with my plans starting to bear fruit, I couldn't afford any extra attention, complicating everything unnecessarily. So, while I had the ability to take whatever I needed, I couldn't allow myself to fall into that trap, no matter how easy it might seem.

I glanced at Patrick, who was staring at his own bowl of cereal and just stirring it around with his spoon. Ever since I had gotten back from my mission in Biloxi, he'd been distant and standoffish. Perhaps the strain of staying under the radar was getting to him. Or maybe he was upset with me about something.

If that was the case, it didn't take a genius to figure out what that something might be. I might have had the emotional quotient of a desk chair, but even I knew there would be repercussions for how our trip into the French Quarter had ended. He clearly wanted things to have gone differently, so it was natural that he would be a little upset about my rejection.

Or was that even the right word? In my mind, it wasn't a firm no. Rather, it was more like, "Not right now because I have way too much on my mind to deal with that kind of thing." But did he know that? I'd hoped that it would be obvious, but clearly, it wasn't.

Even though I could recognize the problem, I had no idea—or inclination, really—to fix it. I was in the middle of waging a guerrilla war against the whole district, so Patrick's feelings really weren't at the top of my list of priorities. I just needed him to grow up and focus on the important things.

Of course, that was easy for me to say. I'd just spent a week with Calvin, where I'd let off quite a bit of steam. Sure, I was working. It was all a ruse. But before Calvin descended into addiction, he was more than pleasant company, and I'd let myself get carried away by the setting.

I didn't precisely regret sleeping with him. I was an adult, and so was he. But in retrospect, it did leave me feeling a bit . . . greasy. Or guilty, perhaps. Part of it was that Calvin was exactly the sort of person I'd always hated. The beautiful, wealthy aristocrats who'd had the world handed to them on a silver platter. But it was also because, misguided as it might seem, I felt like I owed Patrick something.

We weren't together. I wasn't even sure if our trip into the French Quarter qualified as a date. But I knew he had started to develop feelings for me; I just wasn't sure if they were reciprocated. In any case, I was in no position to deal with relationship issues. I still needed to keep an eye on him, though, as much to keep him from growing too resentful as to keep from burning a bridge that I might one day want to cross.

I took a deep breath, then said, "Look, Patrick—"

"I've got to go," he said, pushing away from the table. He grabbed his empty bowl, tipping it back and downing the soy milk. "Dr. Montague is expecting me."

"Can we talk for a second?" I asked.

"I've got training," he stated.

"I know, but . . . I just wanted to talk about what happened the other day," I said. "You know, when we got back from . . ."

I trailed off, unsure of how to categorize our night in the French Quarter. A lot had happened since then—I'd ruined a man's life and nearly died on more than one occasion—but it still loomed large in my mind. Before my uncle's death, I might have pursued it. Back in Mobile, I'd had time for that kind of thing. But now? Casual sex was one thing, but a relationship? How could I let something like that happen? I couldn't—not in good conscience.

"It's fine, Mira," he said, shaking his head. Then, he ran one hand through his blond curls and sighed. "Really, it is. I know how to take a hint. That doesn't mean we can't be friends or whatever. I'm a big boy, and I can handle a little rejection."

But I wasn't rejecting him. Not really. In my mind, it was just a pause until I finished what I had to do. Once I had my revenge . . .

I really didn't have any plans for my own success. My entire being had been so dedicated to my quest for vengeance that I'd never even stopped to consider what I would do once I'd gotten it. Would I set myself as some local warlord like my uncle had? Or was there something else out there for me? I had no idea.

But I knew that, whatever awaited in the future, I didn't want to be completely alone. Not forever, at least.

I said, "It wasn't . . . I mean . . . God, why is this so difficult?"

"Just say whatever you want to say," he stated. "No frills."

"Fine. Okay." I breathed, gathering my thoughts. "What happened the other night, I didn't mean it like you think I meant it. I'm not . . . rejecting you, okay? I'm just saying not right now. I have so much going on. I feel like I'm juggling a hundred different plans, and if I . . . I don't know . . ."

I trailed off, not knowing how to proceed. I hoped it would be enough to keep him from hating me.

After a second, Patrick said, "Alright."

"Huh?"

"Alright. Okay," he said. "I understand. You're too wrapped up in your plans to focus on figuring out if there's anything between us, right?"

"Exactly!"

"I can accept that," he said with another sigh. "But there is one thing I want to say, and I hope you'll take it as it's meant." He sat back down, then leaned forward as he continued, "Remy wasn't always the best father figure. Or mentor. Or whatever. But he did give me a lot of good advice. One thing he told me to never forget was when it came to girls, to just say things plainly. So, that's what I'm going to do. I like you, Mira. A lot. You're strong and pretty and driven . . . and I want this to happen. So, I hope that when you're ready to figure it out, you'll remember that. Until then, I'm still your friend."

That just made me feel even guiltier about my dalliance with Calvin, and I had no idea how to respond. After a few seconds of awkward silence, I just nodded and said, "Okay."

He flashed his crooked smile my way, then said, "But as much as I want to continue this awkward conversation, I really do have to head out. Dr. Montague isn't exactly tolerant of tardiness."

I took the conversational out he'd given me, saying, "I don't know how you deal with her."

"She's not so bad," he said. "Once you get past the ice-queen exterior, she's actually a decent person. Mostly."

"I'll have to take your word for it," I said. Dr. Montague was a means to an end, and though she was obviously good at her job as a cybernetic engineer, I'd have been perfectly happy if our paths never crossed again.

"Guess I'll see you later, then," he said, then headed toward the kitchen, where he deposited his bowl before heading for the stairs. And just like that, I was alone once again, which let me turn my mind from frivolous relationship issues to what was really important—my plans for the day.

Mia Salvatore had already assured me that Nora's shipments of bio-enhancers would be contaminated, so I just had to sit back and wait for them to do the job they were meant to do. In the meantime, I had two main objectives. First, I needed to continue my plans to undermine the Specters' lieutenants. I'd already taken the initial steps down that path when I'd planted the evidence of embezzlement on Echo's terminal; Gunther would soon hold up his end of the bargain and give Nora a tip to steer her directly toward the "betrayal." That would stir up the hornet's nest, but I had plans for her other lieutenants, as well.

First, though, I needed to poke the proverbial bear and start down the road to completing my other objective. Finally, it was time to antagonize those untouchable people in the more prosperous districts. After all, I hadn't forgotten their role in my uncle's death. Most of the time, I was focused on Nora's betrayal, but I intended to make everyone pay for Jeremiah's demise.

To do that, I needed conflict, and I knew precisely how to accomplish that.

So, after finishing off my unpleasant meal, I went into my room and got changed into an innocuous set of coveralls that were meant to help me blend in with the crowd. I was unwilling to take any chances, so underneath it all, I wore my infiltration suit. Then, I used Mimic to adopt a new, unremarkable persona and left the building. The entire block was deserted, and I quickly made my way to the monorail, which I took to the Garden.

Ignoring the other sunken-faced, malnourished passengers, I bent my mind to the task before me. It wasn't going to be easy, I knew. I was used to infiltrating megabuildings and poorly guarded outposts like Biloxi. But my target's defenses would be far more elaborate and advanced.

My mind was occupied with my budding plan until the monorail reached my stop, and I disembarked. I looked up, seeing a Silo looming over me, and I couldn't help but feel a little impressed.

The huge cylindrical building before me was at least as big as a megabuilding, but it was far more important to the city's infrastructure. Without the Silos, not only would the earning potential of the elites be devastated, but the population would go unfed. And once people got hungry, they'd get restless, which was precisely what I needed. A war between the various tribes wasn't enough. It was too isolated. It didn't really affect the elites. But a rebellious populace? That would go much further toward creating the chaotic atmosphere I wanted.

I split off from the crowd of workers heading through the massive gate, instead heading down a nearby alley, where I embraced Stealth. Once there, I waited, observing the Silo's defenses. In addition to the huge gate, which was manned by dozens of Enforcers, all of whom were armed with assault rifles, a thirty-foot wall of reinforced concrete circled the building. Atop that wall was coiled razor wire, cameras every twenty feet, and a plethora of autoturrets. Every fifty yards, blocky towers rose far above the wall; they were manned by even more Enforcers, and I'd have been surprised if they weren't equipped with sniper rifles. In short, the Silo was like a combination of prison and fortress, and getting inside was going to be incredibly difficult.

So, it was a good thing I had a plan.

Individually, I could have overcome any of the defenses. I'd done so in the past, and I knew I would do so again going forward. However, when they were all put together, they presented a serious problem that I couldn't hope to defeat. So, instead of trying to go through them, I planned to bypass them altogether.

Enforcers, as a whole, were good at their jobs, but they had plenty of blind spots. First, they struggled to adjust to anything they didn't expect. I'd exploited that a few times. Second, they tended toward overconfidence, largely because they were so rarely challenged. And third, very few of them were true believers. They were mostly just people who were doing a job. As such, they did just enough to satisfy the terms of their employment. Most of the time, that was fine. There were enough redundancies that it almost always worked the way it was supposed to. But sometimes, things slipped through the cracks.

I was going to exploit all three flaws.

After making sure that I understood the Silo's defenses, I crept through the nearby alleys, steadily getting farther and farther away from the huge structure. Most of the surrounding buildings were warehouses and distribution centers intended to shoulder the logistics of handling the massive amount of produce grown within the Silos, but the farther from the massive building I traveled, the more I saw variation in the architecture As I went, I flared Observation as much as I could, noticing every tiny detail of the area.

Most of the information was useless, and I knew that, without my advanced Mind attribute, I likely couldn't have made sense of that much sensory input. However, because I spent hours of each day training it, I had no trouble categorizing everything. And, after a couple of hours, I found exactly what I was looking for.

Located in an alley abutting an abandoned warehouse, the tunnel entrance was twelve feet across and camouflaged by scattered garbage as well as a holographic display. I saw through it immediately; after all, it was never intended to stand up to intense scrutiny, much less my Observation ability. So, noticing that the scene looped every forty-five seconds was child's play.

Still, I planted myself in a secluded corner of the alley and settled down to watch the smuggler's tunnel. I knelt there for hours, unmoving and cloaked by Stealth, as I watched for anything out of the ordinary.

The existence of smuggler's tunnels was an open secret to anyone from the Garden District. In fact, I suspected that even the Enforcers were aware of the smugglers' activities. However, so long as the losses fell into acceptable parameters, it was easier to just let it go than to spend all the time and resources to end the practice. Of course, every now and then, they'd make an example out of someone, but other than that, it was just part of doing business.

Besides, a fed populace is a subdued populace. So long as people had food and distractions, they would put up with almost anything. The moment either ran dry, there would be issues. So, it was in the city's interests to look the other way when people stole a little extra food.

Still, I wasn't going to stake my own safety on that assumption, so I kept an eye on the tunnel entrance for long enough that I felt certain that it didn't pose any dangers. Once I'd satisfied my own caution, I stood up and crossed the alley. When I stepped into the holographic display, it flickered, revealing the pair of double doors beneath the illusory display. I wasted no time before bending down and pulling them open, where I was greeted by a mundane concrete ramp that led deep underground.

Casting my senses down the tunnel, I looked for defenses, both physical and Mist-based, but I found nothing but a string of lights along the tunnel's ceiling. Still, as I descended into the passage, I strained Observation and Misthack to the maximum of their potential, finding nothing.

It made some sense, I supposed. There was little reason to guard such a tunnel. If the Enforcers found it, the smugglers would simply move on and create another before resuming business as usual. Otherwise, they just didn't care if someone else used it, and anything more than the holographic camouflage would've risked notice. So, they had every reason to leave it unguarded.

Even so, it didn't sit well with me, but given that my senses hadn't picked anything up, I could either go forward or abandon my plan. I chose to keep pushing toward my goal. If it turned out to be a mistake, I'd just have to deal with it.

After I descended into the tunnel, I closed the doors behind me. Then, I snuck forward, slowly and with immense caution. But it was all for naught. No threats presented themselves, and after a little more than a quarter of a mile, the tunnel sloped back upward, ending in another pair of doors.

As I approached the doors, my breathing quickened, and my heart thudded in my chest. If something was going to go wrong, it would be here. I focused on Observation and Misthack, but I sensed nothing on the other side of the doors. No cameras. No security terminals. No people. Nothing.

Briefly, I considered going back and rethinking things. After all, it wouldn't be difficult to liaise with the smugglers themselves. Doing so would make everything so much safer—for now. But that came with a couple of issues—one minor and one much more serious. The minor problem was that every time I interacted with someone, I ran the chance of revealing my secrets. I was confident in Mimic, but if someone saw through it, it was possible that my description would eventually get back to Nora. In that event, I trusted that she was intelligent enough to connect the dots. It was an unlikely eventuality, but it was possible.

The real concern, though, was that if the smugglers had any inkling of what I had planned, they would almost assuredly try to stop me. And I couldn't run that risk. So, as far as I could tell, I had no choice but to forge ahead.

After taking a deep, steadying breath, I pushed the door open and stepped into the lowest level of the Silo.

CHAPTER THIRTY-THREE

POKING THE BEAR

Often, I find myself thinking back to Mira. I did what I could to ensure her survival, waiting until she was gone before I revealed Jeremiah's location, but I fear it wasn't enough. Did she die on her training mission? Or was she one of the thousands of casualties? I can't say, and not knowing haunts me.

—Nora Lancaster

As soon as I stepped into the Silo's lowest sublevel, I felt like I was suffocating. The humidity was so thick that it was nearly solid, and a visible fog hung in the air, mingling with the ambient Mist in a way that made me stumble. I quickly caught my balance on a nearby pipe, but I jerked my hand back from the heat. Thankfully, I moved quickly enough to prevent serious burns, but it still hurt, even through the gloves of my infiltration suit.

I ignored it as I gathered my wits and tried to get my bearings. Looking around, I didn't see any workers; in fact, all I saw was the ubiquitous fog and a tangle of pipes that would have put the Underground to shame. Beneath my feet was corrugated metal that hung above a giant cistern of black water. Lights flickered on and off, as if they hadn't been maintained in a while.

After a few seconds, I let out a sigh as my body acclimated to the harsh humidity and heat, but inwardly, I cursed my own stupidity. I should have expected it. I knew how the Silos worked, so I should have been prepared for the environment. The upper levels were little different from the climate-controlled atmosphere of the city, but the lower levels were dedicated to providing the resources to maintain the optimal growing conditions for the crops above, which meant heat and water, both in large amounts.

By the time I got my bearings, sweat was already pouring down the middle of my back; without my infiltration suit, it might have been troubling, but one of its features was hydration conservation. I didn't know how it worked—probably a function of Mist—but it would somehow repurpose the sweat and reintegrate it into my body. Patrick had tried to explain it to me, but he'd lost me after the first minute. In any event, I didn't need to know how things worked; I just needed to be reassured that they did what they were supposed to do. And the infiltration suit worked as advertised, so I had no reason to investigate its inner workings.

I took a deep breath to steady my nerves, but I regretted it only a moment later when my lungs were filled with hot, moist air that almost made me feel like I was drowning. And after my run-in with the man-of-war off the coast of Bayou La Batre, I knew precisely what that felt like. Irrational as it was, I felt my heart start to race as panic gripped my mind. With a force of will, I pushed it aside, focusing on the task at hand.

For this mission, I'd chosen to dress like one of the normal Silo workers, so I was wearing faded blue coveralls I'd gotten in one of the secondhand markets that dotted the Garden. It fit passably well, but it bore plenty of signs of hard use—which was perfect because it lent my role a layer of authenticity that otherwise would have been impossible. After all, nothing makes a person stick out as an impostor among manual laborers quite like perfect cleanliness.

I set out down the corrugated walkway, turning this way and that through the maze of pipes as I kept my senses unfurled, searching for passive defenses. I found none, which made sense; the lack was probably the reason the smuggler's tunnel connected to the sublevel in the first place. Sweat poured down my face, soaking the collar of my coveralls as I sought out the spots I'd marked on the blueprints I'd downloaded from a government terminal. It wasn't found in any of the public repositories, but even the more secure knowledge databases weren't very secure, either. So, it wasn't difficult to break through the meager defenses, take what information I needed, and get out without leaving a trace.

As I traversed the sublevel, I retrieved a series of tiny blocks from my arsenal implant and left them behind in the appropriate locations before moving on to the stairs that would lead me up to the next sublevel. There, I repeated the same pattern before climbing to the Silo's first level. It was there that I started to run into workers.

Like me, they wore blue coveralls and weathered faces as they tended to row after row of crops. Every now and then, a watery mist would fall from the ceiling, keeping the plants hydrated. Meanwhile, a grid not unlike the latticework I'd seen in Biloxi lined the ceiling, concentrating the Mist in such a way that it would accelerate plant growth. I felt certain that there was more to it than that, but that explanation was all I'd been given when my class had taken a field trip to the Silos a few years before I'd gotten my Nexus Implant.

Gradually, I worked my way around the room, planting more of the tiny blocks in out-of-the-way places. I felt certain that my actions would be suspicious to anyone that cared to look, but none of the workers paid any attention to me. Instead, they mindlessly did their jobs, clearly checked out until they were allowed to go home. So long as I made an effort to look like I belonged, nobody would care what I was doing. I'd learned that lesson from Vanna back in Mobile, and it had been reinforced by my recent trip to Biloxi.

Once I'd planted ten of the small cubes throughout the level, I climbed the stairs to the next floor, where I repeated the process. Vaguely, I noted that this level contained a different sort of crop, but I didn't really care about that. Instead, I just continued working toward the completion of my mission.

Over the next few hours, I climbed forty-two levels, leaving hundreds of the cubes behind. And not once did a single person stop me. Even the sparse Enforcer presence was completely blind before my subterfuge.

By the time I reached the top floor, it was well past midnight, and I was exhausted. Not physically—I could keep going for days if necessary. Rather, I was weighed down by the mental fatigue that came from spending hours on the edge of alarm as I infiltrated deep into the Silo. But finally, I had finished my task. All I needed to do was accomplish one last thing, get out, and then enact the last step of the plan.

So, I retraced my steps as I headed back to the smuggler's tunnel that had been my ingress point. The return trip went much more quickly, and before long, I was stepping through the final door and back into that oppressive atmosphere of the lowest sublevel.

But this time, I had company.

Two Enforcers, one of which was kneeling down and inspecting one of the tiny black cubes I'd left behind. The other was staring right at me with a look of surprise on his face. He started to speak, but I was already moving.

In the confines of the narrow corridors, I knew my nano-bladed sword was out of the question. I didn't dare use my firearms for fear of raising the wrong kind of alarm. Fortunately, my nano-bladed dagger was only a thought away. It was small enough that I could still summon it at will without wasting one of my weapon slots, so even as I used Engage to dart forward, it materialized in my hand. Before the Enforcer could even bring his rifle to bear, I'd buried the dagger in his temple.

He was dead before he even knew what had happened.

As I yanked the blade out of his skull, I aimed a kick at the other Enforcer. He had just enough time to react, and he blocked my kick with a lowered forearm. Then, he rolled back, coming to his feet a couple of yards away.

I advanced, but in an instant, I found myself rocked back by a blow that was so fast I never even saw it coming. I stumbled, then another blow found me. And another. I raised my arms, blocking as best I could, but I could barely even perceive the man's attacks, much less defend against them.

I was fast. Very fast. I knew there weren't many people—especially not some random Enforcer—who could boast similar attributes. So, it only made sense that this man's speed wasn't based on that; instead, he was using a skill. Perhaps his entire class was built around speed.

Fortunately, his attacks weren't individually strong, or I never would have lasted against his barrage. Gradually, his furor began to dissipate until he backed away, his breath coming in ragged gasps.

At some point, my dagger had been knocked out of my hand to tumble down into the cistern below. So, I had no choice but to deal with the man with my bare hands.

"Was that it?" I asked, giving him a cocky smile that I didn't really feel. The man was too fast, and his technique was sound. I wasn't even sure if I could beat him without resorting to using my firearms, which would come with all sorts of consequences I didn't want to think about.

But I was willing to try. If worse came to worst, I could always use Ferdinand II.

The Enforcer was clearly thinking along the same lines because, at that very moment, he reached for the pistol holstered at his waist. I jumped forward, slapping his hand aside just as his fingers tightened around the grip. His hand flew wide, and I hit it again, aiming for the nerves in his wrist. His grip loosened, and the pistol went flying, clattering against the pipes before it descended into the watery abyss below.

My strike didn't come without consequences, though, and I soon received a blow to the jaw that left me reeling. I staggered, but quickly recovered enough to connect with a controlled uppercut. Then, I activated Combination Punch, throwing three punches in quick succession before ending with a stomp to his instep. He blocked the first attack but could do nothing to defend against the next three. Each one hit him flush, and I felt bones crunch beneath my boot with my final attack.

He howled in pain, but I didn't let up. Neither did he surrender easily. And over the next forty-five seconds, we exchanged blows. I blocked some. Dodged others. And took more than a few hits. But he got it worse. After the barrage of Combination Punch, he was on his back foot, and he never recovered. I ended the fight with another use of the ability, and again, each attack landed solidly. He fell to the ground, his face already broken and his breath coming in ragged wheezes.

I summoned my nano-bladed sword, put the tip against his head, and pressed down. It went through his skull without a hint of difficulty, ending his life without further delay. I kicked both bodies into the water, where I hoped no one would think to look, then resumed my journey to a security terminal I'd passed on my way in.

I flipped it open, then retrieved my cord of my personal link from the Hand of God before jacking in. In a few seconds, I'd passed the first line of defenses; there were other deeper levels I could have accessed if I wanted to assault the system's Mistwall, but I didn't need to do that. Instead, I navigated to the appropriate command, then sounded the fire alarm.

Immediately, the lights flashed red, and a loud Klaxon resounded through the sublevel. I knew that the same could be heard throughout the Silo. Hopefully, the workers would heed the warning because that was as far as I was willing to go to push them out of harm's way.

With that, I hurried back to the smuggler's tunnel, which I used to leave the building. Fortunately, when I found my way to the alley, it was just as deserted as when I'd entered the tunnel. Nestled in the darkness, I changed out of the coveralls and into something less conspicuous before leaving the alley and quickly hurrying away.

Already, the Silo's workers were pouring out of the building in a great wave of dark blue. The Enforcers were trying to herd them into some semblance of order, but many of the workers had already begun to panic, making things that much more difficult.

I wanted to let them all reach safety, but I wasn't going to hang around to make sure. Already, I could see teams of Enforcers setting up roadblocks. So, using Stealth, I slipped through the cracks in their perimeter and headed to a recent casualty of the tribal wars. The building had once been a low-quality tenement meant for Silo workers—the sort of place whose design had originally been intended for the factory workers in Algiers, but at some point had been integrated into the more prosperous Garden. Even when it had been whole, it had made the megabuildings look high-class.

But it was no longer whole. Instead, it had been gutted by a fire that had been started by one of the tribes. Nearly everyone who called that place home had perished in the flames. No one had even batted an eyelash at the loss.

Not even me.

I didn't care about the building's history. Instead, I was only concerned with two things. First, its location. I needed somewhere within a mile of the Silo. It qualified, if only just. Second, it needed to be deserted, which it certainly was. Even the transient dust fiends avoided the place, and it wasn't difficult to see why.

The air inside the blackened building still hung heavy with the smell of smoke, and I could tell that breathing those fumes would be toxic for anyone without my unique blend of attributes and abilities. But even for me, it was unpleasant. Still, it offered a level of protection nowhere else in the area could boast. The Enforcers wouldn't even look for me inside a building filled with toxic fumes.

Once I made my way to the third floor, I set up near one of the windows facing toward the Silo. I could just see the top peeking over the roof of another building. Then, I settled in to wait.

One minute passed. Then two. And finally, fifteen.

I knew I couldn't wait any longer. If the workers hadn't gotten out by that point, then . . . well, then they were just destined to be collateral damage. So, resolved in my plan, I summoned the detonator from my arsenal implant and wasted no more time before activating it.

At first, I didn't think anything had happened. I'd built those demolition charges myself, and I was sure that they would work. Long seconds passed, and doubt began to creep into my mind. But then, suddenly, a roar filled my ears, and I saw exactly what I was looking for. The top of the Silo had begun to crumble.

Then, a sound unlike any I'd ever heard rolled over me, followed by a cloud of dust that swept through the streets and billowed through the building's open windows. I choked, covering my mouth as chaos erupted outside.

It was done. The Silo had been brought down.

My plan was based on a simple notion: so long as their basic needs are met, any population can be subdued. It didn't matter if they were oppressed and exploited; as long as they had food, shelter, and a few distractions, they could be held in check. But interrupt any of those things, and people got restless. And once that happened, one of three things would happen. Either the oppressors would have to lean even more heavily on the population, the people would revolt, or they would just leave. The exodus had already begun during the tribal war between the Specters and the Cyberdogs. Now, the Enforcers were going to be added to the mix. Soon, people would flee Nova City in droves, which would, in turn, set the stage for the final phase of my plan.

First, though, I needed to finish dealing with Nora. And to do that, I had to continue to pick her organization apart, one strand after another until there was nothing left. Then, I'd take care of her. Once that was finished, I would focus on everyone else that might have had a hand in my uncle's death.

After I was satisfied that the job was done, I gathered myself, refocused on my surroundings, and then headed down to the street below. Panic filled the streets. Enforcers were around, but they seemed just as stunned as the civilians. Meanwhile, I activated Stealth and crept past them like a ghost.

It was almost an hour before I left the dust cloud behind, but even then, most of the people I saw were staring in the direction of the downed Silo with expressions of awe and horror on their faces. In some ways, I was proud of what

I'd accomplished. It felt like a formidable blow against the bastards who'd killed my uncle. But I also knew that it would come with a cost. People would starve. Some would die. Many already had. All because of me.

I threw my empathy aside. In a war—and that was precisely what it was—I couldn't afford to let my feelings get in the way of doing what I needed to do. Instead, I had to stay focused. Compassion had no place in battle.

But still, a bit of lingering regret and persistent doubt clung to the back of my mind. I could only ignore it.

"Patience," I sighed as I turned down a dark alley where I intended to summon my Cutter. "One step at a time. Lieutenants. Then Nora. Then the aristocrats and Enforcers."

I permitted myself a small, grim smile. The war had only just begun. Before I was finished, Nova City would be on its knees.

CHAPTER THIRTY-FOUR

GLADIATOR

When I saw the video, I felt only a brief sense of elation, the result of knowing that I had won. I'd beaten the unbeatable. I had toppled a giant. And the prize was mine for the taking. However, as I watched them rip him apart, piece by piece, the guilt set in. I can still hear his screams. I can still see his decapitated head staring at me with those accusing eyes. I know that image will stick with me for the rest of my life.

—Nora Lancaster

"You know the deal, right?" asked the man behind the counter, his double chin wobbling with each word. He was short, fat, and mostly bald, save for a few wisps of hair he'd tried to arrange in such a way as to cover the shiny crown of his head. He wiped his bulbous red nose on his sleeve, adding, "Ain't no real protection in there. You go in, and there ain't nothin' to stop them from tearin' you a new one."

I leaned forward, my hands on the edge of the counter, and drew to within a few inches of the plasti-steel cage that was supposed to keep him safe. "I'm aware," I said with as much confidence as I could muster. It was a tricky thing, trying to pretend to act a certain way. My character was new, so she was supposed to be nervous and afraid, but she also knew that she wasn't supposed to show that. Layers of deception, all to conceal my identity and put me into a position to accomplish the next part of my plan.

He snorted a laugh, spraying the cage with spittle and little pieces of the pitiful sandwich I saw on the other side of the counter. Fortunately for me, the food particles didn't make it through the second barrier, which was a comparatively weak Mist shield. It wouldn't stop a determined attacker, but it would slow them down. Of course, that was assuming said attacker didn't have access to Misthack and the ability to shut it off without lifting a finger. Still, I chose not to do so because it wouldn't suit my agenda. Even so, it would have felt nice to put the disgusting man in his place. The moment I'd stepped into the Emporium, I'd felt him undressing me with his eyes.

I was used to being ogled. That was just part of being in Nova City, where the very air seemed to have been suffused with sex, violence, and corruption. But in this case, it made me feel more unclean than usual—perhaps because I knew the manager of the fighting arena was a truly detestable human being. He wasn't satisfied with merely profiting off of the often desperate people who'd been driven to fight death matches for the amusement of the more fortunate, but he was also reputed to possess a harem of slaves that he kept hidden in his compound. Men, women, and everything in between—he didn't care. His perversions were reputed to have no bounds. And as such, he was right at the top of my list of loathsome people.

But he was also a means to an end, so I had pushed my personal feelings aside for the moment. He would get his, and soon. For now, though, he was safe from my wrath.

The blubbery man raked a hand through what was left of his greasy hair, then said, "Suit yourself, hot stuff. Weapon of choice?"

"Sword," I said.

"You know how to use it?"

"I do" was my simple response.

He clearly didn't believe that, based on the roll of his watery, red-rimmed eyes. He punched a few buttons on an analog terminal—those weren't that common, but they were also far more secure than the newer versions. I couldn't Misthack into that system; instead, I'd have to jack in manually via Mistwalk.

"Alright, then," he said. "I got you for a bout in about an hour." He pointed to a door on one side of the cage. "Go through there. You can get changed. The more skin, the better, especially for somebody like you. The crowd goes nuts if they see a nice pair of—"

"I'm wearing what I intend to wear," I said. "Do I need to do anything else?"

He shook his head, saying, "Shame. Pretty little thing like you could really get the crowd riled up. More excitement, more credits flyin' around. But suit yourself. So long as the blood's flowin', I don't care. You get ten percent of the take. Nonnegotiable. If you win. If you lose . . . Well, you won't be needin' credits, then."

"I understand the rules."

With that, he typed something else into his terminal, then told me to head back. I didn't hesitate before leaving him behind; one more second in his presence, and I might have forgotten my mission altogether, torn through that flimsy Mist shield, and put him down like the rabid animal he was. But I restrained my murderous instincts and headed through the door.

As I did, I studied my surroundings. The exterior of the Emporium was meant to mimic some ancient arena, complete with a multitude of carved columns and decorative arches with a distinctly unique design I couldn't place. Topped by a massive dome that flashed with different colors based on the whims of the owners, it cut an impressive figure among the austere architecture so common in the Garden.

In a way, it reminded me of Bourbon Street. Not because it bore any similar characteristics—they were completely different in nearly every facet of their appearance. Rather, because of their purpose. Where the clubs and brothels of Bourbon Street were dedicated to sex, lust, and carnal intentions, the Emporium was a giant altar to violence. Both were effective distractions, and I considered them two sides of the same coin.

The interior of the massive building had no decorative touches, and as I traversed the hall leading to the locker room, I was reminded of the same featureless architecture I'd seen in every megabuilding I'd ever entered. Eventually, I found my destination and passed through another door, where I was greeted with the sight of a host of fighters in various states of undress. Judging by the coating of blood, some had just finished battles in the arena, while others were focused on upcoming fights.

I went to a corner and sat on one of the benches, where I leaned forward, my hands on my knees as I mentally prepared myself for the task before me. In many ways, I hated what I was about to do. I didn't want to contribute to the culture of distraction that kept the citizens of Nova City in line. I also had nothing to prove—to myself or to anyone else—so I considered the upcoming contest beneath me. However, that disdain was also tinged with a degree of excitement. I liked fighting, and the Emporium gave me a perfect arena to do just that.

A shadow enveloped me, followed by a smooth voice saying, "Hey there, gorgeous. I haven't seen you here before."

I looked up to see the reason I'd decided to subject myself to the Nova City's most brutal sport. Asheligh, Nora's chief thug, stood over me, naked as the day she was born. In fact, her groin was only a foot away, looming large in my field of vision. I ignored it, pushing my gaze upward across her muscular torso, impressive chest, and to her squarish face.

The rest of her was decidedly less fleshy, with both arms and both legs having been replaced by brutish cybernetics that had obviously been built for strength. Her neck was encased in red-enameled metal, the material covering her jaw and ending just below her ears. But her features were otherwise completely human, without even the addition of cybernetic eyes. Red hair stood up in a stiff mohawk that cut a line down the center of her otherwise smooth head.

"Can I help you?" I asked, keeping my voice emotionless. I knew that, if I wanted to, I could summon my nano-bladed sword and, in only an instant, carve out her heart. Even with most of her body having been replaced with cybernetics, I was certain that would do her in. If not, I could keep on carving until I got to something vital.

Of course, doing so would have caused a ruckus. More, Asheligh wasn't a pushover, and she would surely resist. I felt confident I could win the fight, but I didn't know how quickly I could put her down.

Besides, that wasn't the plan. I'd get to her soon enough.

She gave her hips a slight buck, trying to draw my eyes. "You can help me with all sorts of things," she said with a lascivious grin. "That mouth of yours looks like it could—"

"No, thank you," I said before looking back down at the dirty tile floor.

It took Asheligh a moment to register what I'd said, and clearly it wasn't what she had expected. "You little . . . Do you know who I am?" she demanded.

I didn't answer. Inwardly, though, I regretted wearing the face I'd chosen. Using Mimic, I'd adopted the identity of a very pretty young woman with stark white hair and plump lips. My choice was rooted in a simple fact: the grotesque manager of the Emporium was right. The crowd loved seeing beautiful people fight, which was why I'd also decided to wear a skintight white faux-leather suit that left every curve on full display. I felt a little ridiculous—after all, my normal attire was decidedly more conservative—but it was all just part of the role.

And obviously, it had worked. Otherwise, Asheligh wouldn't have taken notice of me. I wasn't sure if she was really as lustful as her reputation suggested or, like me, she was playing a role that put her more in line with her boss's inclinations. But whether she was merely mimicking Nora or not was irrelevant. She still had to play the part in public, which was why she'd planted herself in front of me.

Even if I hadn't hated the woman for the part she'd played in Nora's betrayal, I wouldn't have been interested. For one, I really wasn't attracted to women. I knew that put me in a bit of a minority among the residents of Nova City, who mostly had a much more fluid view of sexual attraction, but it was just how I felt. For another, even if I did prefer women, the copious use of cybernetics would have been a complete turnoff. The idea of being fondled by those metallic hands was enough to send a shiver up my spine.

There were plenty of people in Nova who felt the opposite way. They loved visible cybernetics. And even among them, there were different subsets. Some liked parts like Asheligh's that looked almost like heavy machinery. Others wanted sleek and shiny. I'd even heard about some people who'd had their skin replaced with chrome. But I didn't belong to those groups. Instead, I preferred flesh and blood.

I looked back up at Asheligh, saying, "No. Should I?"

"I'm—"

"Saint!" came a call from the other corner of the locker room. "You're up!"

"That's my cue," I said, standing and pushing past Asheligh. She tried to grab my arm, but I easily dodged her grasping metallic hand. The mostly cybernetic woman called out again, but I ignored her. Even she wouldn't presume to interrupt the Emporium's schedule, lest she get blacklisted. And she couldn't let that happen. After all, much of her authority was rooted in her combat prowess, and if she couldn't show that off in the arena, she'd end up having to defend her reputation out on the streets, where anything was fair game. At least in the Emporium's fights, she knew things were mostly fair.

When I reached the other side of the room, I stopped in front of a slim man who looked like a former fighter. He had a crooked nose, a cauliflower ear, and a cybernetic that wasn't cleanly attached, as if the decision to replace his arm had been necessity rather than a choice. He wore a white tee-shirt and a pair of baggy pants. A dozen gold chains hung from his neck, partially obscuring the intricate spiderweb tattoo that ran along the contours of his stringy muscles to cover his neck and most of his left shoulder.

"You Saint?" he asked.

I nodded. I'd chosen the name on a whim, but it felt appropriate.

"Good. C'mon," he said. "Your fight's in five minutes."

Had I really been sitting there so long? It hadn't felt like it, but the clock on my HUD told me that he wasn't mistaken. So, after that, I followed him through a maze of tunnels. As I did, I felt more than heard the roar of the crowd, which I knew was directly above me. Something interesting must have happened in the arena, which meant that someone had probably just been killed.

After a couple of minutes, we stopped before a pair of wide double doors, through which a pair of workers were dragging a beheaded corpse. Its blood was still wet, leaving a trail along the floor. But the entirety of my focus was on the arena on the other side of that exit.

The floor was mottled concrete, and it was an entirely open space. The crowd was there to see the action, after all, and no one wanted their view obstructed. Besides, it was a test of personal combat ability, and adding environmental factors was counter to that mission. It took me a couple of seconds to recognize that the concrete wasn't blotchy by design; rather, portions were darker due to the prevalence of dried blood that had seeped into the surface, staining it in the process.

It was a grim reminder of what I faced.

"You said you're a sword user, right? Well, did you forget your blade? If so, we got plenty of—"

I cut him off by summoning my nano-bladed sword from my arsenal implant. Its edge crackled with blue energy, a promise of pain and barely contained violence.

"Right. Sure. Just make a sword appear outa nowhere," he muttered. "In my day . . ."

He trailed off, but I ignored him. He wasn't important. Only the person on the other side of that arena was worthy of my attention. I could just see my enemy—a tall, whipcord-thin man armed with a wicked battle-ax—standing in the other entrance across the battlefield. He raised his axe in salute.

I ignored his gesture.

"Ladies and gentlemen!" crowed a deep voice across the arena's public address system. The crowd quieted at the sound. "We have a treat for you tonight. The Raven needs no introduction, but his opponent is a newcomer who goes by the Sword Saint!"

I ground my teeth together as the crowd erupted into a cacophony of cheers. I knew that a hologram of my image was floating above the arena floor. Doubtless, my looks were the reason for the crowd's dubious support.

"That's your cue, your worshipfulness," said the former fighter that was my guide. "Head in. Don't start until you hear the bell or you'll be gunned down. And no hot weapons, either. You pull a gun outa your ass, the arena's security force will put you down. Understand?"

I nodded.

"Good. Go on in. And good luck."

I took a deep breath, then squared my shoulders before taking a step into the arena. Then, another. And another. As I strode forward, I couldn't help but feel a tinge of awe at my surroundings. The crowd was massive, at least thirty thousand strong, and every single one of them was on their feet and screaming. A huge hologram floated about fifty feet above the arena floor, depicting the so-called Raven, who was walking forward, just like me. But where I remained stoic and stone-faced, he was waving at the crowd, blowing kisses to his admirers, and having an altogether fantastic time.

Was it an act? Or did he truly enjoy the adoration of the sorts of people who got off watching people try to kill one another?

On the other side of the hologram was the depiction of me. Or rather, the version of me that I'd decided to show the crowd. My body was real enough, even if the skin color was far paler than my real complexion. But the face and hair were completely different. Would they have cheered so loudly for the real me? Or was their reaction based on the beautiful visage I had adopted?

I'd had similar questions about my brief relationship with Calvin. He had obviously been attracted to the woman whose identity I'd adopted for my trip to Biloxi, but there was something else there, too. A level of attraction that had nothing to do with my physical appearance. Would he have reacted similarly if he could see the real me? Maybe. I had no way of knowing.

Those distracting thoughts took me to the center of the arena, where I stopped only a dozen feet from the Raven. Up close, I saw the source of his namesake. He wore a long, loose coat, but no shirt beneath it, revealing a huge tattoo of a blackbird that stretched across his bare chest.

"I hate to kill such a beautiful creature," he sneered, a wide grin decorating his thin face. "Surrender and kneel before me, and I'll have you fitted with a slave implant before the night's over. I'll treat you good, too. Real good. Like a real person, even."

I didn't answer. Instead, I stared straight at him, waiting on the bell. Inwardly, though, I seethed. If I'd had any issues with killing him before, they disappeared the moment he opened his mouth. A good thing, really. Now, there was no chance I'd feel even remotely guilty.

"Not gonna take my generous offer? Well, suit yourself," he spat. "Such a waste."

He didn't say anything else, but the announcer did, reciting the Raven's record—he'd won fifteen fights already, which made him a dangerous opponent. Of course, I'd done my own research, and I'd discovered that most of those so-called battles had been against slaves who'd been pushed into the arena against their will. Colloquially, those were known as slaughter matches, and the real warriors were never in any mortal danger, unless, of course, they found themselves facing off against someone who'd hidden their true power. But that almost never happened because few truly powerful people would allow themselves to be taken into slavery. It happened, but so infrequently that a slaughter match was as safe a fight as one could get in the arena.

Finally, the bell rang.

I used Engage, springing forward with my sword held at the ready. The Raven reared back, intending to cut me in two, but I was far too fast for him. In fact, he'd barely raised the great axe when my nano-sword sheared through his neck and out the other side. I skidded to a stop and turned, ready for any retaliation he might offer.

But it was unnecessary. The fight was already over, the end announced when his head toppled from his shoulders and hit the ground with a dull thud. His body followed soon after, crumbling into a heap of dead flesh.

The crowd went silent.

I started walking back to the door, not even stopping as I spit on the Raven's corpse as I passed.

One down. A few more fights to go.

CHAPTER THIRTY-FIVE

THE RED TERROR

Weakness is not to be tolerated. The moment we show anything less than absolute strength, we lose everything. That's just how Nova City works.

—Nora Lancaster

I sat in the private room, massaging my temples with my knuckles. It had been six weeks since I'd begun my conquest of the Emporium, and in that time, everything had changed. Not only had I fought my way through a dozen battles against proven gladiators, but I'd also continued with my plan to bring the city to its knees. And finally, after everything, my efforts were beginning to bear fruit.

The entire Garden had come to a standstill after I brought down the third Silo. There were plenty more—dozens, in fact—and the city's food output was only marginally affected by my direct actions. However, the indirect effects were making things much more difficult. Chiefly, the exodus from Nova City had reached a crescendo; anyone who could get out had, and though there were still more than a million residents who'd remained—either by choice or because they had no other options—the decrease in population had brought production to a screeching halt. Contributing to that was the fact that, upon seeing those monuments to the city's authority crumbling to the ground, people had lost all faith that the government could protect them.

Certainly, I'd made efforts to minimize civilian casualties, but that didn't mean there weren't plenty of deaths waiting to be laid at my feet. And though that collateral damage weighed on me, I refused to let it affect my actions. After all, I'd always known that people were going to die. Some would be killed by my direct actions, but others would fall as a secondary effect. I was prepared for that.

Or so I thought. Still, seeing people starve was almost enough to break my resolve.

To distract myself, I'd chosen to focus on the things I could control. My training, primarily, though even that bore a grim reminder of the cost of my revenge. Every time I looked upon my status, I saw the results of my actions. Almost on instinct, I looked upon it once more:

NAME	Mirabelle Lisa Braddock		
CLASS	MISTRUNNER		
LEVEL	18 (74%)		
CONSTITUTION	85/136		
MIND	93/136		
MIST	76/136		
SKILLS	7/7		
SKILL NAME	Skill Tier	Modifiers	Abilities
CYBERNETIC MASTERY	Tier 1 (98%)	100% Efficiency	6 Cybernetic Slots
COMBAT	Tier 2 (7%)	+60% Damage (All) +90% Speed (Melee) +60% Accuracy (All) +35% Range (Firearms) +60% Reload Speed (Firearms) +25% Damage (Small Arms) +50% Damage (Heavy Weaponry) +5% Movement Speed +25% Jump Height	Empowered Shot (D) Double Shot (E) Combination Punch (D) Pummel (E) Engage (E) Disengage (F) Mark Target (F) Barrage (F)

INFILTRATION	Tier 1 (83%)	+25% Effectiveness (Stealth) +15% Effectiveness (Stealth Abilities) +30% Effectiveness (Deception) +25% Effectiveness (Observation)	Stealth (D) Camouflage (D) Deception (E) Mimic (D) Observation (D)
MISTRUNNER	Tier 1 (91%)	+40% Speed (Misthack) +25% Processing Speed (Mistwalk) +50% Strength (Mistwall) +50% Breach Range +25% Infiltration Stability +15% System Defense +5% Damage (All)	Mistwalk (D) Misthack (D) Mistwall (C) System Redirect (E) Disable Cybernetics (E) Overcharge (E)
FIELDCRAFT	Tier 2 (11%)	+25% Combat Effectiveness +50% Effectiveness (Triage) +25% Less Food/ Water Required +25% Effectiveness (Combat Focus)	Triage (D) Basic Explosives Handling (C) Combat Focus (C) Pain Tolerance (D) Resistance (D) Foraging (E) Improvisation (D) Regeneration (D) Universal Language (E)
DEMOLITION	Tier 2 (14%)	+30% Explosive Radius +25% Explosive Strength	Blast Shield (D)
ACROBATICS	Tier 2 (23%)	+45% Proprioception	Balance (E)

I looked over my status, noting that many of my skills had progressed in strength, with four of the seven even gaining a tier. With those improvements came increasingly powerful modifiers that had made a noticeable difference in every facet of my combat strength. In addition, there were some quality-of-life improvements, like the decrease in the amounts of water and food I needed to survive. In short, I was deadlier and more effective than I'd ever been.

But what really garnered my attention was the sharp increase in levels. Gaining a single level represented dozens of kills, and I'd gained six of them in the past few weeks. Each time I brought down a Silo, I'd gained at least one level. Sometimes two. And on the backs of murder, my power potential continued to climb.

I admit that there was a part of me that felt ashamed of that fact. Sure, the only way to gain levels was by killing things, which resulted in the absorption of a portion of their Mist. However, in the beginning, I'd always imagined that I would primarily progress via killing monsters. Now, though? I knew that every powerful person's strength was built on a mountain of bodies. I was no different.

Of course, the guilt that came from that realization wasn't enough to dissuade me from my quest for vengeance, but it certainly didn't make me feel good about myself. To distract myself, I delved a little more deeply into my status, opening the window for [Combat]:

Tree	**Combat: Tier 2 (7%)** +60% Damage (All) +75% Speed (Melee) +60% Accuracy (All) +35% Range (Firearms) +60% Reload Speed (Firearms)			
Branch	Small Arms: Tier 1 (33%)	Heavy Weaponry: Tier 1 (12%)	Melee: Tier 1 (19%)	Movement: Tier 2 (7%)
Tier 1	+25% Damage	+50% Damage	+15% Speed	+5% Movement
Tier 2	+25% Range	+15% Range	+25% Damage	+25% Jump Height
Tier 3	Ability: Explosive Shot	Ability: Shatter Shot	Ability: Riposte	Ability: Double Jump
Tier 4	+25% Accuracy	+50% Rate of Fire	+25% Accuracy	+15% Movement
Tier 5	Ability: Multishot	Ability: Instant Reload	Ability: Execute	Ability: Teleport

I'd looked at it plenty of times over the past few weeks, but I was still a little disappointed that I wasn't making faster progress. Part of it was because the grade of the skill was higher than the two skills that had fueled its evolution. Unless I was mistaken, that meant it took twice as long to progress, but when it did, it provided much more potent benefits. A necessity, given how limited skill slots were, even for me. Even so, getting the different branches to Tier 1 had resulted in a marked increase in my damage, not to mention the bonuses I'd gotten from pushing the movement branch to the second tier. I moved on to the next skill tree:

Tree	Infiltration: Tier 1 (83%) +25% Effectiveness (Stealth)			
Branch	Spycraft: Tier 1 (22%)	Stealth: Tier 1 (68%)	Deception: Tier 1 (3%)	Sensory Input: Tier 1 (19%)
Tier 1	+15% Effectiveness (Deception)	+15% Effectiveness (Stealth Abilities)	+15% Effectiveness (Deception)	+25% Effectiveness (Observation)
Tier 2	+15% Effectiveness (Deception)	+25% Effectiveness (Stealth Abilities)	+15% Effectiveness (Mimic)	+25% Effectiveness (Observation)
Tier 3	Ability: Charisma	Ability: Distraction	Ability: Bluff	Ability: Sense Deception
Tier 4	+15% Effectiveness (Charisma)	+15% Effectiveness (Stealth Abilities)	+25% Effectiveness (Bluff)	+15% Effectiveness (Sense Deception)
Tier 5	Ability: Interrogate	Ability: Vanish	Ability: Chameleon	Ability: True Sight

Despite my incognito foray into Biloxi and my constant use of Mimic, the various branches of [Infiltration] hadn't seen quite the growth that [Combat] had. Still, I'd managed to bring everything up to Tier 1, which resulted in more powerful modifiers. I was looking forward to some of the abilities that came with the higher tiers of mastery, though. Next, I moved to the skill tree for [Mistrunner]:

Tree	Mistrunner: Tier 1 (91%)			
	+25% Speed (Misthack)			
	+25% Processing Speed (Mistwalk)			
	+50% Strength (Mistwall)			
	+50% Breach Range			
Branch	Misthack: Tier 1 (22%)	Mistwalk: Tier 1 (17%)	Mistwall: Tier 1 (82%)	Combat: Tier 1 (71%)
Tier 1	+15% Speed (Misthack)	+25% Infiltration Stability	+15% System Defense	+5% Damage (All)
Tier 2	+15% Ghost Strength	+25% Processing Speed (Mistwalk)	+25% System Defense	+5% Damage (All)
Tier 3	Ability: Surge	Ability: Rewind	Ability: Backlash	+5% Damage (All)
Tier 4	+25% Ghost Stability	+25% Processing Speed (Mistwalk)	C-Grade System Defense	+5% Damage (All)
Tier 5	Ability: Plague	Ability: Skeleton Key	Ability: Mental Fortress	Ability: Assassinate

Like [Infiltration], my growth in [Mistrunner] had lagged a little behind [Combat]. However, I was still happy with the growth of each branch. Particularly, I found that having a stronger Mistwall gave me peace of mind. Finally, I looked at the skill tree for [Fieldcraft]:

Tree	Fieldcraft: Tier 2 (11%)			
	+30% Combat Effectiveness			
Branch	Medic: Tier 1 (25%)	Survival: Tier 1 (33%)	Communication: Tier 1 (19%)	Utility: Tier 2 (0%)
Tier 1	+50% Effectiveness (Triage)	+25% Less Food/Water Required	Ability: Universal Language	+25% Effectiveness (Combat Focus)

Tier 2	+50% Recovery Speed	+25% Less Sleep Required	Ability: Share Map	+25% Effectiveness (Regeneration)
Tier 3	Ability: Stabilize	Ability: Bastion	Ability: Waypoint	Ability: Ignore Injury
Tier 4	+25% Medication Effectiveness	+50% Endurance	Ability: Combat Map	+25% Explosives Yield
Tier 5	Ability: Mend	Ability: Tinkering	Ability: Secure Connection	Ability: Focused Will

The only branch of [Fieldcraft] that had progressed to Tier 2 was Utility, granting me increased Combat Focus and Regeneration, but I was more excited about the Universal Language ability. Few places would be like the Bazaar, where languages were automatically translated. Having that ability would mean that, once I'd finished with Nova City, I wouldn't be limited by an inability to communicate, which was a comforting thought.

Eventually, I couldn't distract myself any longer, and I started to think about what was coming. I didn't think I'd fail in my current endeavor. None of the other gladiatorial fights in the Emporium had pushed me to the limit of my abilities. However, I knew that Asheligh was a very different breed of opponent than the warriors I'd faced over the past few weeks. Not only was she strong and fast, but she was also an expert melee combatant.

So was I.

But was I good enough to beat her without resorting to my other options? I'd do so if it was the difference between living and dying, but if my plan was going to bear fruit, I needed to not only beat her, but also humiliate her by exposing her ineptitude. The moment I did, it would shine the spotlight on the Specters. Hopefully that would be enough to highlight the weaknesses of the entire tribe and invite the sorts of challenges they weren't equipped to deal with.

After all, with Jeremiah gone, much of their reputation hinged on the personal combat prowess of people like Asheligh and Nora. If they were exposed as weaklings, then it wouldn't take long before the city's other tribes decided to take their territory. Sure, the organization was likely strong enough to defend themselves, but doing so wouldn't come without significant cost.

It was just one more way I was chipping away at them. By the time I was done, it would only take a little push to bring the entire thing crashing down. I couldn't wait to see that happen.

But before that, I needed to beat Asheligh, which was why I was sitting alone in the bowels of the Emporium, waiting as the weaker combatants got the crowd riled up for the main event. Even though I was deep underground, I could still hear their muffled roars as they clamored for more blood. More gruesome deaths. More violence to distract them from the state of their own lives.

I sighed, shaking my head in disgust as I stared at the room's tiled floor. Fortunately, because of how high I'd climbed, I didn't have to use the communal locker room anymore. Now, I had my own dressing area—not that I used it. I always fought in the same white outfit I'd worn upon my arrival.

Others weren't so nonchalant about it, instead choosing to cultivate entire personas based around elaborate costumes. I'd fought against one man who'd been wearing a broad-brimmed hat, jeans so tight I wondered how he could move, and a plaid shirt. He'd fought with his bare hands—a mistake even though they were cybernetic. I severed them at the elbow, then killed him via brutal decapitation.

The next fight had been against a crowd favorite wearing a few strings that were supposed to be lingerie of some sort. She'd flipped around like a gymnast, displaying truly incredible balance. But she also moved in patterns, which made it easy to bisect her at the waist. She didn't look so sexy with her guts decorating the concrete floor of the arena.

My third and fourth opponents had both been far more difficult, though for different reasons. One had been a hulking man who seemed to have just as many mechanical parts as Gunther's cyborg guards. It was high-quality stuff, too, judging by how ineffective my sword was. Of course, everything has weaknesses, and it only took me a few minutes to find the seams. After that, it was child's play to take him apart. When I was done, he was little more than a disembodied head and a pile of scrap metal.

The fourth was probably my most challenging opponent, mostly because he was so hard to pin down. Not because he was fast. He was, but not as fast as me. Instead, he had some sort of skill that made it difficult to focus on him. One second, I was watching him, and the next, he was burying a dagger in my back. Thankfully, once I saw his little trick, I could account for it, but that first strike had been almost enough to do me in.

After that, I hit my stride and acclimated to the sort of combat I could expect in an arena. Once I was in the right mindset, I didn't have any more close calls, and I cut all my opponents down in record time.

And that was how I'd earned the right to challenge Asheligh, the Emporium's champion. She'd fought hundreds of battles in the arena, and she'd never been pushed to her limits. But then again, she'd never fought anyone like me, either. I was looking forward to ripping her apart.

After all, while she might not have been complicit in the actions that had gotten my uncle killed, I found it difficult to believe that she hadn't at least known it was coming. On top of that, she'd fallen into line right behind the woman truly responsible for Jeremiah's death. That was enough to condemn her, at least in my mind.

So, I was going to enjoy killing her.

For the next hour and a half, I sat in that room, awaiting my turn. Then, finally, a woman appeared to escort me to the arena. I didn't say a word, instead choosing to follow her through the twisting maze of tunnels that eventually made their way up to the gate that would lead to the floor of the arena. I was just in time to see a pair of workers dragging a partially dismembered body away. I ignored it, focusing on the task at hand.

Or more importantly, on the gate positioned directly across the arena from where I stood. Behind it was my opponent—a woman I desperately needed to kill. I summoned my nano-bladed sword from my arsenal implant, briefly startling the woman who'd escorted me topside.

At last, once the arena was clear, the announcer's voice echoed through the Emporium, silencing the crowd.

"Ladies and gentlemen!" the announcer thundered. "Tonight, we have a special treat. The Sword Saint has challenged the Red Terror!"

Red Terror. Such an unimaginative name, but the crowd didn't seem to care. They loved her, as much because of her brutality as because she fought completely naked. Originally, she'd claimed that it was a tribute to ancient gladiators who'd done the same, but I knew it was meant to increase her popularity. Like everyone else, she knew that in Nova City, sex was on everyone's minds. I found it disgustingly manipulative, but it was the least of my issues with the woman. Besides, I already hated and intended to kill her. Adding a little more fuel to the fire wasn't going to make much of a difference.

The announcer went on, describing our attributes. He crowed about Asheligh's record of brutality and commitment to her so-called code of honor. As far as I knew, it was all completely made-up. She had no honor, else she wouldn't have let Nora sentence my uncle to death. But the crowd ate it up.

When the announcer described me, he talked about my lack of frills and cold demeanor. He claimed that I was there to punish the debauched, implying some sort of idiotic religious bent. It was nonsense, but I didn't care. The crowd clearly loved it, though. Or at least some of them. Others made their displeasure known by calling out curses and throwing boos in my direction. Clearly, I was not the crowd favorite Asheligh was.

Of course, I considered that a good thing. Attaining the approval of the bloodthirsty masses would have given me pause. That I hadn't was something of a badge of honor. Or perhaps I was merely making excuses to assuage my ego. Either way, the announcer soon finished his introductions, and the gate slid open.

I walked out, barely noticing the holographic display hanging above the arena. It would give the crowd an unimpeded view of the fight, even for those with the cheapest seats.

My attention was on Asheligh, who was striding into the arena, waving at her adoring fans as if she'd already won. When we were only fifteen feet apart, Asheligh grinned at me, saying, "Get on your knees right now, little girl. Do that, beg me to spare you, and maybe I'll just take you into my harem. You're a bit too ugly—even my boys are prettier than you—but I'll make an exception."

I remained silent, staring her in the eyes, focusing on the war paint she'd donned. If I looked anywhere else, I'd have to see her naked body—or what was left of it. Her arms and legs were cybernetic, but her torso, groin, and head remained largely unmarred by the red-enameled mechanical parts.

She rolled her metallic shoulders, then said, "Suit yourself, then."

After that, she hefted the massive hammer that was her weapon and adopted a fighting stance. I raised my sword, angling my body so as to present a slimmer profile. Then, the announcer roared, "Begin!"

CHAPTER THIRTY-SIX

CHAMPIONSHIP FIGHT

The entire world is open to me now. My future is brighter than it's ever been. So, why can't I stop thinking of the past?

—Nora Lancaster

The hammer whistled through the air, barely missing me by an inch. The so-called Red Terror's swing was so violent that its momentum sent her spinning around. I could have ended the fight right there; in only an instant, I saw a dozen vulnerable spots. But I restrained myself, dancing backward.

"Is that it?" I taunted. "All that talk, and that's the best you can come up with?"

As Ashleigh recovered from the miss, she roared, then bounded in my direction. Her steps rattled the floor, and I was a little surprised that she didn't leave cracked concrete in her wake. Her muscles bunched, and her cybernetic parts hissed with mechanical strength before she aimed a much more controlled strike at my torso. I leaped over it, then twisted in midair to dodge the follow-up attack, landing a few more feet away.

"Too slow, lady," I said, smirking at her. "Maybe I should offer to let you join my harem, huh? We could get you some new, more appropriate parts. Something sleek and sexy, maybe."

Her face turned red—not in embarrassment, but rather in unrestrained fury—telling me that I was pushing all the right buttons. She attacked again, this time with a short jab, before following up with a more powerful swing that should have crushed my shoulder. The crowd gasped as I dismissed my sword, dodging the attack by only a hair's breadth.

Dancing backward, I said, "You know what? I don't even need my sword to beat you. For a little girl like you? I might not even need to make a fist. A good openhanded slap might be enough to put you down."

Of course, I knew precisely how to needle her to the greatest effect because I could remember when she'd joined my uncle's organization. Back then, she'd been a prostitute fresh off of murdering her pimp. I wasn't sure how she'd gotten to the Specters, but back then, she had been nothing more than a slip of a girl. Since, she'd managed to completely remake herself into a fearsome warrior, but she'd never forgotten her past.

Neither had I.

It wasn't enough just to beat Asheligh. That would hurt Nora and the Specters, sure. But I didn't only want to hurt them. I needed to humiliate them. And there was no better way to do that than to toy with their top thug before putting her down. Doing so wouldn't just deprive Nora of an asset; it would go a long way toward ruining the tribe's reputation. It was difficult to fear a group whose most powerful Operator was just embarrassed and beaten to death in the arena for everyone to see.

In theory, that was easy enough. But in practice, Asheligh was still a dangerous fighter who could beat me if I didn't take her seriously. Fortunately, she was notoriously hot-tempered and easily enraged; it would have gotten her killed sooner, but she truly was a talented combatant—even when she wasn't in her right mind.

Luckily, I was better.

Barely. I could probably dodge her attacks for hours, which would eventually wear her out. But if I made one mistake, the power behind her hammer would pound me into paste. However, I didn't want to drag the fight out and turn it into a battle of attrition. Instead, I intended to make a statement.

So, the first thing I did after dodging her initial barrage was to use Mark Target. Often, I forgot the ability even existed, mostly because, to date, it hadn't really been necessary. Rare was the occasion when a few well-placed shots from my powerful weapons proved insufficient to kill my enemies. And when that had been the case in the past—like with the wildling alpha that had nearly killed me—I'd been so panicked that I'd completely forgotten about the ability.

But I'd been working on adding it to my repertoire, and while it hadn't quite reached the point where it was second nature, I was well on my way to reaching that mark.

The ability itself wasn't complicated:

Mark Target (F)—Wreathe a target in Mist, preventing the activation of obfuscation abilities and increasing all damage done to the target by 15%.

A straight fifteen percent increase to all damage was an incredible modifier, which only proved how much of an idiot I'd been to ignore the ability. But the past was the past, and if I continuously dwelled on my mistakes, I'd lose sight of the present. Or the future. And I couldn't allow that. Instead, I could only correct what I could correct and keep pushing forward. Any other strategy was doomed to failure.

When I used Mark Target, a cloud of blue Mist enveloped Asheligh's form, making her appear as if she was glowing. However, after testing it a few times, I knew that the Mist was only visible to me; almost assuredly, it was the anti-stealth portion of the ability. A useful utility, but not the one I cared most about at that moment.

I kicked off the ground, using Engage at the same time; the combined effect was almost as effective as true teleportation, and I covered the distance to Asheligh so quickly that she couldn't hope to react in time to stop me. Then, I used Combination Punch. One punch. Two. Then, a third and a fourth strike—all in rapid succession. Each punch doubled the damage of the previous, so by the fourth attack, it hit with exponentially more force than the first.

I was sorely tempted to activate the ability again, but there were two problems with that. First, I knew that standing still for any longer would almost assuredly get me killed. The woman's skill with that hammer was nothing to underestimate, and if she managed to connect, it would almost certainly spell my doom, my various defenses be damned.

Second, she staggered out of range, coughing up blood.

And that presented a perfect opportunity to taunt her again.

"Such weak defenses," I said, bouncing on the balls of my feet as she struggled to straighten to her full height. The fans of the barbaric blood sport loved the banter between combatants, so my words were broadcast to the entire arena. "So disappointing for someone of your reputation. Perhaps you earned it in other ways. Like on your back."

I hated the words even as they came out of my mouth. I knew Asheligh hadn't chosen her past. And even if she had, who was I to judge her choices? Still, it was a means to an end. Sowing the seeds of doubt and making everyone question whether or not her strength was real was as important as killing her.

I went on. "How much did it cost to fix your previous matches? Surely, that's the only way you could hope to win. I don't—"

With an enraged and wordless scream, she charged, her mechanical legs pumping. I leaped over her, spinning as I sailed a foot over her head. She tried to grab me, but her agility left a lot to be desired, so she came up empty-handed, stumbling as we crossed paths. I landed lightly, then pivoted to face her. I could have attacked again. I knew it. The crowd knew it. And when Asheligh turned back in my direction, I could see that she knew it, as well.

Tears of anger streamed down her face. Blood coated her chin. And her side bulged in all the wrong places, evidence of her shattered ribs. Judging by her wheezing breaths, her lung was punctured, as well. With an obviously high Constitution attribute, it probably wasn't fatal, but it would definitely slow her down.

In any case, I had no intention of dragging it out any longer. I'd proven my point. Anyone who'd watched the fight so far had to know that I'd been toying with the once-fearsome woman. Now, it was time to end it with a flourish.

I took a deep, steadying breath, but I kept my expression placid. Then, I erupted into an Engage, and I was on her in an instant. My sword reappeared in my hand, and I sliced out, aiming for the joint where the metal of her mechanical leg ended and her flesh began. My first attack bit deep, stopping only when it reached her bone. Then, as I rushed past, I aimed a backhanded strike at the opposite side. The two wounds met, and though my impossibly sharp blade cut into her pelvic bone, it didn't slice completely through.

However, as I stopped and turned, she tried to follow. But when she put weight on that leg, it collapsed under her. As she fell, I repeated the strike on her other leg, this time severing it completely.

She went to the ground, collapsing in a legless heap.

I wasn't finished, though.

My nano-bladed sword dripping blood, I stepped toward her. Without her legs, she was mostly immobile, but Asheligh wasn't one to give up without a fight. She scratched and clawed, trying to swing at me, but her efforts were ineffectual. I kicked her in the face, splattering more blood across the concrete. Then, stamping down on her arm, I raised my sword high into the air. It fell with inevitable speed, severing her arm at the shoulder.

She cried out, but I ignored it, kicking her again.

The crowd went silent as I stepped over her. Again, my sword fell. Again, her mechanical arm flopped to the ground, a lifeless hunk of metal.

Without arms and legs, Asheligh was just a pitiful, naked torso. For a long second, I stood over her, looking down at the pitiable sight. Such a proud, powerful warrior, reduced to nothing. It was a brutal world, and her easy defeat just proved that no matter how strong you thought you were, there was always someone more powerful.

And it was only a matter of time before your number came up.

I knelt beside her. Predictably, she tried to squirm away, but her efforts were useless.

"Just finish me, you little cunt," she growled through gritted teeth.

"Not yet," I said. Then, I gripped her chin before leaning close to her ear. Once I was only a few inches away, I whispered, "This is what you get for your betrayal. Did you think I would forget? Did you think I would just let it stand?"

"Betrayal?" she hissed. "I don't even know you!"

"Oh, but you do," I said, my voice too low for the arena's recorders to pick it up. "I remember when you joined my uncle's organization. You were even more pitiful, then. All flesh and bone, not this mechanical monstrosity. But I liked you better back then. Do you know why?"

She stared at me in horror. "Mirabelle," she muttered. "H-how did—"

"I liked you better because, back then, you were loyal," I stated. Then, before she could respond, I dismissed my sword, reactivated Combination Punch, then, using the Hand of God, aimed a barrage of strikes at her face. The first didn't do much more than break her nose. The second shattered the bones in her cheek. The third collapsed half her face. And the fourth went completely through her skull, ending with my cybernetic fist mashing her brain to pulp.

Then, I stood, shook the brain matter from my hand, and calmly walked back toward my gate. For my first few steps, the crowd was completely silent, stunned as they were by the sudden and brutal end of the fight.

But that didn't last long.

After a few seconds, they erupted into roaring applause. As the crowd went wild, the announcer declared my victory, driving them to greater heights of excitement.

I barely heard any of it. Dismissing my sword, I kept my back straight and my shoulders square—at least until I passed through the gate and into the arena's staging area. I was just about to relax when I saw that there were dozens of people inside. A few were medical attendants, and some were the staff dedicated to cleaning the arena, but the ones that really drew my eye were the media people.

That's when it hit me that beating the longtime champion of the Emporium was a big deal. Everyone was clamoring for my attention, personal recording devices hovering above their owners' shoulders as they provided narration.

"The Sword Saint is once again victorious . . ."

"She handled the Red Terror without even batting an eyelash!"

"Miss Saint—this seemed personal . . ."

I ignored them all, pushing through the crowd. The sea of people parted after an angry glare, and I disappeared into the tunnel. After a few twists and turns, I left everyone behind. That's when I activated Stealth and ducked into a janitorial closet.

There, surrounded by various cleaning supplies, I sank to my knees and finally let my emotions out. Tears traced lines down my cheeks, and my shoulders trembled with heavy sobs.

Killing people was one thing, but what I'd just done to Asheligh was a complete deconstruction of who she was as a person and fighter. I'd left her nothing; even her accomplishments in the arena would now be tainted. Perhaps they wouldn't be completely forgotten, but I'd cast enough doubt that it would be impossible for the people of Nova City to ignore.

And what's more, there was a time—not that long ago, really—when I had liked Asheligh. Just like I'd liked Nora. Both had been kind to me, once upon a time, and while I hadn't been nearly as close to the so-called Red Terror as I had been to Nora, I wasn't so coldhearted that I could be unaffected by what I'd just done to her.

It also forced me to question my path. Up until that point, I hadn't killed people I knew—not in my old life, at least. Instead, my kill count was populated by a bunch of nameless mooks. But not anymore. And killing someone just hit differently when it wasn't shrouded by anonymity.

Was it a hint of what I could expect when I finally killed Nora?

Maybe. But where Nora had actively betrayed my uncle, Asheligh and the others had only stood aside as it had happened. Did that make them less guilty? Did that make them less worthy of my ire? Of my vengeance?

I wasn't sure.

But killing Asheligh had been one of the most difficult things I'd ever done. Not physically—that had been easy enough. With my recent gains, few could match the combination of my raw attributes, skills, and abilities. Certainly, there were plenty of people who could—my uncle wasn't the only old monster to have survived to thrive in the post-Initialization world—but that number didn't include Asheligh. Instead, the difficulty lay in the emotional effects of what I'd done.

I hadn't been ready for that.

I don't know how long I remained in that closet, crying over something that didn't really deserve my tears. Maybe it wasn't even about Asheligh. For weeks—probably even months—I'd been pushing my emotions to the back of my mind as I focused on taking the next step in my plan. And it had obviously taken its toll on my emotional health.

Any reasonable person would have taken a step back, perhaps thought of a different way. But the path of vengeance wasn't reasonable. It required unnatural dedication, even through the emotional turmoil that came with exacting revenge.

I did wonder if there would be anything left of me when I was finally finished.

Probably not. But I couldn't let that stop me. Not until it was done. My uncle's memory demanded as much.

So, after a while, I stood, wiped my eyes, then changed into a different set of clothes I had nestled in my arsenal implant. With that done, I changed my face via Mimic and set out from the bowels of the Emporium, content that I'd accomplished one more task on the way to completing my plan of vengeance.

No one paid attention to me as I made my way out of the Emporium. Once I found a shadowy alley where no one would see me, I summoned my Cutter, made sure that it was disguised by Mimic, and set off back to Algiers. It was the middle of the night, which meant that traffic was predictably light; however, with the mass exodus from the city, it was even more sparse than the time would indicate. So, I made good time, arriving back at my compound in only thirty minutes.

As I stepped out of the elevator and into the living quarters, I was confronted by nothing but emptiness. It was only then that I realized how much I'd been looking forward to seeing Patrick. Of late, he'd spent less and less time at home, which meant that I rarely saw him. Part of that was my fault, given that I didn't even always sleep there. But I couldn't help but feel a little resentment that he wasn't there when I wanted him around.

Was my annoyance reasonable? No. He didn't live according to my whims. But it still rankled all the same.

Sighing, I settled down to eat a ration bar and go over the plan for my next steps. Eventually, even that couldn't hold my attention, and I headed to my room where I quickly showered and went to bed. As I drifted off to sleep, I found myself hoping that I'd feel a little more stable in the morning.

It was probably a dim hope, but I clung to it all the same.

CHAPTER THIRTY-SEVEN

THE FRAME JOB

They're all idiots. Echo, for stealing from me. Asheligh for tempting fate in the Emporium. The morons who thought they could get a quick payday by killing those Cyberdogs. I feel like I'm the only one trying to keep everything together.

—Nora Lancaster

I stood atop one of the most central megabuildings, looking down on the Garden. I was almost high enough to see into the more affluent districts. Almost. But I knew they'd never allow that to happen. They didn't just stand above us on the social ladder; they did so literally, as well. And it made me want to scream. For now, though, I focused on the fruits of my labor, a grim smile playing across my face as I beheld the results of my actions.

Pillars of thick black smoke curled into the sky as hundreds of fires roared out of control in the streets below. Even as high as I was, I could hear the steady staccato of gunfire that heralded the escalation of the tribal war, and I knew that Nora and the Specters were being pushed from all sides. Blood was in the water. The sharks were circling. It would only take one push before it all started to fall.

The first blow had been the frame-up I'd staged in Elysium, which had been far more successful than I could have hoped. It hadn't resulted in a war, but there'd been plenty of fighting on the streets as the Cyberdogs tried to collect their pound of flesh. But the Specters were strong, and they could endure the smaller tribe nipping at their heels. After all, they'd been built by my uncle. How could they be anything but one of the most powerful tribes in the Garden?

But without him, that power was tenuous, and the foundation upon which it had been built had crumbled into nothing. Nora and her lieutenants were trying to keep it from falling down around their heads, but they could only do so much, especially when my every action was calculated to undermine them.

The second blow had come when I'd framed Echo for embezzling. In better times, it might have been easy to sweep under the rug. But Nora's grip on the Specters was too new; she had no choice but to make an example. When I watched Nora give the order to execute her, I was reminded of how my uncle had killed those mooks who had attacked me so long ago. Nora had always been capable enough, in the right circumstances, but she was just a shallow reflection of Jeremiah. The only difference was that Nora had been unsuccessful—so far. Echo had escaped her judgment, though I suspected that situation wouldn't last much longer.

When I'd killed Asheligh—or the Red Terror, as she was known in the Emporium—it had sent shock waves through the Garden District. To that point, her reputation had been unassailable. The fear she instilled in her enemies had been palpable. Now that she'd been so thoroughly defeated, everyone had begun to wonder if it had all been for show. Had she really been as strong as everyone claimed? Or was it all a ruse? The mere question had been a blow to the Specters' reputation. After all, if the Red Terror had been weak all along, how sturdy could the Specters' standing really be?

It had only been a week since I'd killed her, and already, the conflict on the streets of the Garden that had previously begun to wane had bloomed anew. The Specters couldn't even leave their territory without being assaulted by other tribes who wanted the reputation of unseating the kings of the Garden.

It was glorious.

But it wasn't quite war. Not yet. To push them over the edge, I'd need to incite outrage. So, for that, I had chosen to target the closest thing the Specters had to an ally—the Coyotes. Once, my uncle had told me that if I ever needed to smuggle anything into or out of the city, they were the ones to contact. In fact, it was their tunnels that I'd used to infiltrate the Silos, so they were already on high alert and looking at nearly everyone else with at least a modicum of suspicion.

More than normal, at least.

Which would make my task a lot more difficult, but it also meant that they were a powder keg on the verge of ignition. One small spark, and they'd explode, taking half of Nova City with them.

Metaphorically speaking. More literally, if I managed what I intended, they'd throw the Garden into open warfare and push the Specters—and Nora—even further against the wall. For me, it was the perfect chance to enact the penultimate portion of my plan.

To that end, I stepped away from the edge of the roof and made my way through the megabuilding and down to the street. As I went, I saw just how twitchy the Operators were. If I hadn't been wearing the blue armband of the Specters, they might have attacked me on sight. As it was, they only looked at me with suspicion.

Heading into the Specters' territory, even if it was only one of the buildings on the edge of their turf, was risky, but I'd had no choice if I wanted to accomplish my goals. For now, though, I pushed that out of mind and focused on the task at hand: framing Wash, who was the man in charge of the Specters' thieves.

A proficient burglar in his own right, he'd been a legend even before I was born. There was nowhere he couldn't infiltrate, nothing he couldn't steal, and on occasion, nobody he couldn't assassinate. But more than that, he was a detestable man who was too smart not to have known what Nora had planned for my uncle. He knew, and yet, he'd done nothing. So, now he needed to pay.

So, after I left the megabuilding, I ducked into an alley and summoned my hover bike. Once I'd mounted up, I sped away, eventually crossing over to Algiers. Unlike most of Nova's tribes, the Coyotes had established their headquarters in the poorest district of the city, and for one simple reason—that was where all the warehouses were. From there, they could stretch their influence across the city's entire shipping industry. So long as they didn't take too much, and they paid off all the right people, the Enforcers looked the other way.

Of course, they had plenty of other routes to get things in and out of the city. Some were aboveboard, but others were akin to my own route. Though unlike the Nats, their paths required no death-defying stunts or killer birds. They had the art of smuggling things in and out of Nova down to a science.

And they guarded that ability jealously; they looked the other way when it came to groups like the Nats, mostly because they paid tribute to the more powerful tribe. Rare was the organization that would go up against the Coyotes, and for one simple reason: nobody else could do what they did.

So, when I was looking for a group to enrage, they had been the obvious choice, if for no other reason than because I knew precisely how to do it. After all, the secret to their success was, in actuality, no secret at all. They had a map of Nova City's entire infrastructure, right down to the access and drainage tunnels—an invaluable resource for people who made their money by moving things in and out of the city.

And I was going to steal it.

Once I got to the right block, I pulled into a shadowy alley and dismissed my Cutter. Once it had dissipated into Mist, I engaged Mimic and adopted a new persona: that of Wash, the Specters' famous thief. Of course, being a famous burglar was kind of idiotic, so far as I was concerned, but he'd always liked the attention. For my part, I always thought a good thief would have been invisible, but his ego wouldn't allow for that. In fact, as far back as I could remember, Wash had made a habit of boasting about all the things he'd stolen. I only believed about half of it.

More than that, though, if he'd been that talented, he would have been involved in my training. However, Jeremiah had hired an outsider to handle my infiltration instruction. That said plenty about what my uncle thought of Wash's skills.

Once I was wearing the man's face—and his body—I settled down to wait for nightfall. No self-respecting thief operated in the bright light of day, after all. Fortunately, I'd timed my arrival fairly well, and I only had to wait for an hour until the sun set. Another hour after that, and I was heading toward my target. Using Stealth and Camouflage, I stuck to the shadows as I approached the Coyotes' compound.

Like most of the warehouses in Algiers, it was protected by a high wall, cameras, and autoturrets. There were even Operators on patrol, proving the compound's value. I'd done my research, though, so I already knew the location of my prize.

After watching the pattern for half an hour, I made my move. First, I used Misthack on the cameras, briefly deactivating them. As soon as I did, a sixty-second timer appeared on my HUD. That was how long I had to get over the wall and get into cover. To that end, I repeated the process on the autoturrets before taking a running leap and grabbing ahold of the top of the wall before heaving myself over. I landed lightly and raced toward the building itself, where I crouched in the shadows as I waited for the timer to run down.

Things would have been different if the cameras had been equipped with thermal sensing, but that kind of tech was expensive. And besides, I still wasn't completely sure if even thermal sensing could see through my skills. Maybe. But given that it was all Mist based, there was no certainty that the concealment was limited to the visual spectrum.

Either way, I was already past the first line of defense. Now, I just had to get inside the building.

So, moving as quickly as I dared, I crept along the side of the concrete building, dodging various plasti-steel crates along the way. I had no notion as to their contents—perhaps they were even empty—but they weren't my goal, so I didn't stop to check. All I cared about was that they provided decent cover for my activities. After all, Stealth and Camouflage always worked better when they were helped along by the environment.

Soon enough, I reached the backside of the building, where I found a huge loading dock and a crowd of people. Most were workers who'd been tasked with unloading a truck that, judging by the mud caked on its sides and tires, looked like it'd just arrived in the city from the wilderness. But there were Operators there, too, armed and armored with tech that would have been intimidating to most people. But I recognized the cheap nature of their knockoff cybernetics and the mundanity of their weapons. Even if I got into a shoot-out with these mooks, they wouldn't pose much of a threat to me.

Still, I didn't want to be seen just yet. So, I circled around, keeping to the edges of the property as I searched for an ingress point. However, I didn't find anything in the back, so I continued around to the other side of the compound, which mirrored where I'd come in. Still nothing. Finally, I found myself at the front of the building, which was guarded by a trio of Operators who were engaged in casual conversation.

I scanned the area. The front of the building was nothing special—just a plain concrete facade like every other warehouse in Algiers. However, there was quite a bit more security. There were cameras, autoturrets, and even a couple of drones flitting around the area. The entrance to the compound was a gate manned by another few Operators. None looked very threatening, but that wasn't the point. Sure, I could kill them all if I chose—probably—but that would ruin my plan. So, I continued to search for a way in, but I was sorely disappointed by the fact that the whole building was completely buttoned up.

Finally, I was forced to admit that I only had two options—brave the loading dock and try to sneak past the dozen or so men and women working in the area, or head through the front door. The three mooks who were supposed to be guarding it almost never even looked in that direction, so my choice was easy enough.

There were a few hover cars out front—probably some of the guards' personal vehicles, judging by the garish colors and shiny trim—and I used them as cover as I drew closer to the door. And then, when the mooks burst into laughter at something one of them said, I darted forward and slipped inside.

I slid the door closed and pressed my back against the inside of the wall, my heart beating out of my chest. Even though I knew I wasn't in any grave danger—after all, I felt confident even if things broke into a firefight—it was still a nerve-racking experience. Fortunately, there was no one in the immediate area, so I took a moment to compose myself before heading deeper into the compound.

The entryway was mostly empty—just an unmanned desk, a few ratty couches, and a dark screen on one wall. As far as I knew, their headquarters was also a functional shipping business. It was a front, but they still did legitimate jobs, and the entryway was their point of contact with potential customers.

I ignored most of the decor as I crept into the first hall, making a beeline toward the stairs. Nothing important would be on the first floor. Instead, I needed to go to the third level, where I knew the leader's office was located. That information had cost me a few thousand credits, but I hoped it would be money well spent.

There were a few Coyotes around, but none of them were terribly alert. Why would they be in their own compound, which was protected by multiple guards, a bevy of cameras, and a multitude of autoturrets? If they couldn't feel safe there, they wouldn't feel safe anywhere.

As a result, I didn't have much difficulty reaching my destination, though to get into the office in question, I was forced to use Misthack to unlock the door. The office itself was nothing special—just a desk, a few filing cabinets, and a security terminal. But with Observation running, I couldn't help but notice the false wall that turned out to be concealing a safe.

This one was a real doozy, and when I connected to it, I realized that it was far outside my ability to unlock. Thankfully, I didn't need to because that safe was just a decoy. Instead, the real prize was behind the bulky metal container. To get to it, I had to draw my nano-bladed knife and use it as a lever. After that, I slowly inched the safe forward, bit by bit, until it reached a tipping point. Then, I let gravity do the bulk of the work as I gently lowered it to the floor.

That's when I found my prize, which was a simple plastic tube.

Most people would have dismissed it out of hand due to its mundanity. Besides, who used hard copies anymore anyway? Paper wasn't exactly a scarce commodity, but it was rare enough that almost everyone stored information on chips or security terminals. But the Coyotes knew those were vulnerable to people with the right skill set—people like me, in fact. So, they'd chosen a different route.

"You'd better put that down, friend," came a scratchy voice from behind me. I slowly turned around and saw the very person I'd expected to see.

Roberto King. The leader of the Coyotes and one of the more powerful men in Nova City. Or at least among the lower class confined to the Garden and Algiers. I didn't think his personal strength could compare to my uncle's, but he'd definitely been one of Jeremiah's contemporaries.

I held up my hands, saying, "You got me."

I knew that I had no chance of copying Wash's voice, so I chose to use a voice modulator instead. It was a simple program I'd installed into my interface, but it did the job fairly well. He had no idea that I wasn't a man, even if he might have suspected I wasn't the person I was imitating—which wasn't certain.

Roberto was a tall, thin man with narrow shoulders and the smooth movements of a person who knew exactly who he was and what he could do. He wore a broad-brimmed hat, a red tee-shirt, and jeans. Around his waist was a thick leather belt held together by a giant jewel-encrusted buckle, and his feet were clad in a pair of snakeskin boots. Holstered on one of his hips was a revolver that his reputation suggested he knew how to use. His only visible cybernetics were his eyes, which glowed green.

I didn't know his class, but I suspected it was something akin to Patrick's, which meant that he probably had skills and modifiers associated with using pistols.

So, he was a dangerous man, even to me.

"Wash?" the man asked, squinting at me. "What the hell?"

I shrugged, unwilling to say anything else. At the same time, I initiated Misthack, and a message appeared on my HUD:

Misthack successful. Options:
Reboot system
Overcharge
Disable cybernetics
Upload Ghost

I selected the third option. In the same instant, I mimed tossing something at him. He reached for his gun, but I dove to the side. That's when his eyes went dark. I darted past him, dragging my nano-bladed dagger out of a sheath at my waist before raking it across the backs of his ankles. He cried out and fell forward as his Achilles tendons gave out, but by that point, I was already sprinting down the hall.

I didn't bother with Stealth. Nor did I disable the cameras. I needed them to see me. I needed them to know that they'd been victimized by Wash. So, clutching the plastic tube that contained the tribe's greatest treasure, I made no effort to conceal my identity.

Other than Mimic, of course. But they didn't know about that.

I was down the stairs and through the door before any of the mooks on guard even knew I was there, and the moment I leaped over the gate, I knew I was home free.

A few seconds later, I dipped into an alley and activated Stealth before storing the tube in my arsenal implant. Then, I changed my disguise, using Mimic to adopt an entirely new persona before following the alley to the other end. Once I was there, I took a turn. Then another at the next intersection. And another after that. Before long, I was completely out of the Coyotes' limited territory.

And more importantly, I'd gotten exactly what I'd intended to get. Not the map, though I expected that would be valuable enough. Instead, I had accomplished my goal of framing Wash. Soon enough, the Coyotes would turn on the Specters, and as a result, they'd be even closer to complete collapse.

And I hadn't even had to kill anyone.

That would change, and soon.

CHAPTER THIRTY-EIGHT

LONG OVERDUE

I lost a fight today. First time that's happened in years. I don't know what's gotten into me. It's like I feel less and less like myself every day. Thankfully, it was just a spar, but I can't help but wonder what'll happen next time I get into a real fight.

—Nora Lancaster

"We need to get out of here," Patrick said, pacing back and forth across the compound's common room. "It's not safe."

"This was always the plan," I pointed out. "Besides, nowhere is safe. Not really. I thought you understood that."

"Don't patronize me," he muttered.

I shook my head. It had been a week since I'd framed Wash, and in that time, the Specters had become further enmeshed in a war on multiple fronts. Not only were they still in a feud with the Cyberdogs, but the Coyotes had joined the fray, as well. Neither of those clans were martially specialized—not like the Specters—but they had allies who were. As a result, the Specters had their backs against a wall, and war had truly come to the Garden. Add the Enforcers that had been assigned to the Silos to the mix, and it was only a matter of time before everything truly exploded.

When that happened, it would make the petty battles that had so far embroiled the district look like a series of fistfights. I couldn't wait.

But in the meantime, that war had spilled over into Algiers, and more than once, battles had been fought practically on our doorstep. The compound that was supposed to be our safe haven had become anything but that, which was why Patrick was begging me to relocate. And even though I'd argued against it, I was beginning to think that he was right. But instead of just moving to a different part of Nova, I was beginning to wonder if we wouldn't be better off leaving the city altogether.

After all, I had the means. With the map, we could get out anytime we wanted. No one could stop us. The question was what we would do while we waited on the conflict to escalate. It was too early to move on Nora. She needed to suffer more before I finally put her out of her misery. I wanted her whole organization to crumble down around her; only once it had would I even consider killing her.

Otherwise, what was the point of everything else I had done?

No—I needed to let things simmer a bit before I finished her off. But if I left Nova, I didn't want to waste all that time. That's when I remembered that I still had one more task to accomplish. Something I had been putting off for quite a while.

I needed to rescue Heather.

I'd been by Heaven and Hell on Bourbon Street more than a few times since I first saw her dancing in that window, so I knew she was still alive. But I'd yet to pull the trigger on rescuing her, partially because I didn't want to alert Nora that I was back. After all, who else would bother rescuing someone like her? She didn't have any family. Nor did she have friends. Like me, she'd lived a life sequestered in Jeremiah's penthouse, cut off from everyone else. I was likely the only connection she had left.

However, that was probably more of a justification than a real reason. Instead, my reticence to rescue her was rooted in my reluctance to confront her enslavement. That kind of thing made me incredibly uncomfortable, and I had no idea what it might have done to her psyche. And if it had destroyed her like it had so many others, there was no escaping the reality that she'd only been enslaved because of her relationship with my uncle. To some, that would be enough to assign blame.

"Fine. We'll go," I said. "But there's something I need to do first."

"What?" asked Patrick, stopping and turning toward me.

"There's somebody I need to rescue. Hopefully, I'll be in and out," I said. Then, I retrieved the plastic tube containing the Coyotes' map from my arsenal implant. After handing it to him, I said, "In the meantime, I need you to map a route out of the city. Can you do that?"

"Who are you going to rescue?" he asked.

I told him, adding, "Heather was never my favorite person or anything, but I feel responsible for her. She always tried to be good to me, and truthfully, I should have done this a while back. I'll go in, get her, and then we'll get out of the city for a while. I don't know where we'll go, but—"

"There's another town west of here," he said. "I can't remember what it's called, but Remy and me, we stopped there once. Can't be more than a couple hundred miles away. Probably less."

I nodded. "Alright, so that's a plan, then," I said. But I knew I didn't want to just lie low in some random town. I needed to work toward accomplishing something. Figuring out what would have to wait, though.

With that, I went into my bedroom and donned an outfit appropriate for a trip into Bourbon Street. It wasn't quite as risqué as the outfit I'd worn during my first foray into Biloxi nightlife, but it wasn't that far off, either. Red leather pants, boots with a chunky heel, and a black tank top emblazoned with the Leviathan logo; I let my hair go wild and curly, teased out for maximum size, and adopted an identity with similar ethnicity to my own. It was an effective disguise—nobody would look at the person I was pretending to be and think of Mirabelle Braddock—but it was close enough that I didn't feel like I was pretending to be someone else.

I'd considered wearing my infiltration suit, but I'd chosen discretion over protection. Hopefully, I wouldn't end up regretting it.

Once I was dressed, I left my bedroom and headed downstairs to where I could leave the compound unseen via a tunnel that led off-site. As I walked through the common area, I could feel Patrick's eyes on me, though. He didn't say anything, but then again, he'd kept his obvious attraction to himself ever since I'd rejected him after our pseudodate.

Did he resent me? Or had he simply given up? I didn't know. Nor was I sure if I liked either notion. I didn't want him to chase me or anything, but I wouldn't have been upset to find out that he was pining for me, at least a little.

Of course, I didn't really have time to think about that kind of thing. So, I just gave him a wave and headed out. In a few minutes, I was driving my disguised Cutter through the streets of Algiers.

Normally, I would've preferred to take the monorail, but with the two districts so firmly embroiled in unrest, the elevated train had become far less reliable. Once or twice, it had even been the scene of brutal attacks that had to be suppressed by the Enforcers. Of course, their version of law enforcement meant killing everyone in the area, which only served to increase the tension even more.

Either way, I wasn't going to trust the monorail for transportation. The Cutter might draw a little attention—mostly the wrong kind—but I was far more comfortable using it than relying on anyone else. At least astride it, I was the one in control.

As I traversed the district, I couldn't help but notice the signs of recent battles. More than one building was crumbling, and those that weren't falling down had walls marred by cracks and scorch marks. Everywhere I looked, I saw armed civilians. Even the normally withdrawn factory workers were wary, which was expressed in the form of furtive eyes and twitchy movements reminiscent of rats.

Or maybe that was just my imagination making that connection. After all, the people of Algiers had a lot in common with the rodents that infested every corner of Nova City's poorer districts. They were dirty, often diseased, and more than willing to eat whatever garbage fell in their general direction. But more than anything, they were survivors who'd managed to carve out a place even when everything was set against them. They were also looked upon as a nuisance by those who thought themselves their betters.

Was I one of those people? Sometimes. It was difficult to see some of those homeless wretches as actual people. It was even worse when I had to smell them, and I often found myself cringing away in disgust. Even though I knew it wasn't really their fault—most of the time, at least—I found myself looking at them with a mixture of disdain, pity, and annoyance. When I thought about it, I managed to shove some compassion in there, but it definitely wasn't my first instinct.

In a lot of ways, I was ashamed of that. I wanted to be better. I just wasn't sure if I was up to that task.

I had to make a few detours along the way, mostly because of fighting in the street or fallen buildings blocking the roads. But I knew the area well enough that it didn't take too much longer than normal for me to reach the spiraling ramp that would lead to the Garden District. I kept a keen eye on my surroundings as I mounted the ramp, but I didn't run into anything before reaching the next platform. In fact, it went a lot faster than it usually did, probably because traffic was a lot lighter. I wasn't sure if that result could be laid at the feet of the increasingly dangerous streets or the continuing exodus from the city, but I appreciated it all the same.

The Garden was even more volatile than Algiers had been, and on a couple of occasions, I had to resist the urge to stir the pot. If I got too caught up in forcing the situation to escalate, I'd run the risk of losing my focus. Still, it was difficult not to pose as a member of one of the tribes and pick off an Operator here or there. I managed to resist the call to battle, though, and eventually, I found my way to Bourbon Street.

Surprisingly, the area seemed completely immune to the chaos in the rest of the city, and it was just as packed as ever. If anything, the patrons seemed even wilder than they had the other times I'd visited, which was quite an accomplishment, given the things I'd seen. Perhaps with death regularly knocking on their door, the Operators had lost the few inhibitions they had once harbored.

Whatever the case, I wasn't there for a good time, so I had little interest in the crowd, save to make certain that they didn't pose any threat to me. They didn't. In fact, even dressed as I was, I barely got a second glance. After all, Bourbon Street didn't lack for beautiful men and women, and few of them were dressed nearly as conservatively as the outfit I'd chosen for my foray into the den of iniquity.

I took a meandering path toward Heaven and Hell; I didn't want to alert anyone by looking out of place. But I also didn't want to linger too much. It was a balancing act, and one I found completely tiresome. It would have been different if I'd been there for the place's intended purpose, but as it was, I found the entire scene somewhat exhausting.

Soon enough, I found myself entering the club itself. Immediately, I was confronted by a tall, broad-shouldered doorman dressed in black pants and a black tee-shirt. In a curiously high-pitched voice, he said, "No weapons allowed. If you have any, surrender them now."

As he spoke, he pointed to a line of lockers on the other side of the foyer. I wasn't about to give up the weapons, and I didn't think I'd need to, either. I couldn't imagine anyone seeing inside my arsenal implant, after all. So, I just told him I wasn't armed, which he didn't believe at all. So, I had to submit to being frisked, which, given that he paid extra-special attention to some of my most private parts, made me feel more than a little violated. I wanted nothing more than to pull out my infrequently used tetsubo and break a few bones, but I restrained my violent impulses.

Either way, I wasn't in the best of moods after he gave me the go-ahead to step up to the counter, where I paid a nominal entry fee before stepping past the bored-looking attendant and into the club itself. When I did, I saw that it was exactly what I had expected: alternatingly seedy and gaudy. The prevailing color scheme was red and gold, with the former tending toward a velveteen texture and the latter toward a shimmering facade that clearly went no deeper than the surface.

Throughout the room, there were various tables and booths populated by a multitude of faceless mooks. And then there were the entertainers. In the manipulative illumination of the club, they all looked distractingly perfect. Whatever flaws they had—and with Observation, I could see that there were plenty—were covered up by makeup, clever lighting, or distracting sensuality.

But it was all hollow.

Like the club's ubiquitous gold-plated trim, it was just a facade. It wasn't real. The services on offer were nothing more than diluted versions of real connections. Sure, it would feel good for a little while, but it was a poor substitute for a genuine relationship. Not that I would know, of course. I'd had some experiences, but nothing that would make me an expert on human connection.

But as ignorant as I was, I knew that there was no real happiness to be found in a club like Heaven and Hell. Just distraction and a fleeting sense of euphoria.

The theme of the club was obvious. On one side, the entertainers wore angel wings and halos and little else, while on the other, they had black horns, red body paint, and swishing tails. I had no interest in investigating how those tails were attached.

I pushed forward to the bar, where I was greeted by a lithe man with cheekbones that could cut glass. He was shirtless, wearing nothing but a pair of skimpy underwear that did little to hide his assets.

And he was just the bartender.

"What can I get for you, baby?" he asked, his voice sultry and suggestive.

"Information," I said. Before he could object, I went on, "I'm looking for a woman. She's blonde, in her mid- to late-twenties, and named Heather. Sound familiar?"

I knew I'd hit a mark, but judging by his expression, I could tell that it wasn't the one I'd intended to target.

"I'll make it worth your while if you can point me in her direction," I said. Then, I initiated a transfer of a thousand credits, but I didn't finalize the transaction. Neither did the scantily clad bartender. "All yours if you just tell me where to find her."

His eyes flicked back and forth, but he didn't say anything. It was only when he focused on something behind me that I realized we had company. I stepped aside just in time to avoid a grasping hand. I took another step, then aimed a jab at a stout man's ribs. I felt them break beneath my fist before I grabbed his shirt and slammed his head into the bar.

His face shattered in an explosion of blood.

People screamed.

And I leaned forward, dragging his face away from the remnants of the cracked surface of the bar as I hissed, "I think you better tell me what the hell's going on before I really start breaking things, yeah?"

As I dragged him upright, I noticed that many of the patrons had already scattered. The dancers were the same way, but even then, I didn't see Heather. I knew better than to think that she was simply off for the day. People with slave implants didn't get breaks. That was the whole point. To their masters, they weren't people. Just commodities to be used.

In a lot of ways, it was more straightforward than the roundabout oppression propagated by the city's aristocratic caste. But it was also far more restrictive and infinitely worse, if for no other reason than that they weren't afforded even a semblance of free will.

As I looked around, I saw a dozen Operators. Not just thugs like the doorman or the guy whose face I'd just shattered. No—these people were the real deal, with midgrade cybernetics and weapons that could prove lethal, even to me.

"So, this is how you all want to play it?" I asked, my voice hard. Even as I waited for an answer, I was breaking through whatever defenses their systems featured. It was child's play, and by the time someone chose to answer, I'd already infiltrated three of the mooks' systems. A couple more seconds, and it would have been all of them.

"You made a big mistake, little lady," spat one of the men.

I supposed he'd have to be my first example. I disabled the cybernetics of the three Operators whose systems I'd bypassed. As the effect took hold, I summoned my assault rifle and tossed the man with the broken face aside. I had plans for him after I dealt with his friends.

At the same time, the nine other mooks opened fire, and I dove behind the bar. Bullets tore into the structure, but it was made of higher-quality material than I'd originally expected, so none of them made it through.

"Knew I should've worn my infiltration suit," I muttered to myself. Then, I poked my head out, took aim, and put one burst through a mook's head. The superheated plasma erased his skull, leaving only a stump of charred flesh behind.

That's when they buried me beneath a hail of gunfire.

CHAPTER THIRTY-NINE

CAGES

Loose ends can't be left hanging. As terrible as it can sometimes be, they must be trimmed, or else the whole thing will unravel. Heather was one of those loose ends, and though I wanted to keep her around, I knew it wouldn't work out well. So, I did what I had to do. Still, it keeps me up at night.

—Nora Lancaster

I crawled across the floor until I reached the end of the bar. Then, I poked my head out, took aim, and fired. My R-14 spat three bursts of superheated plasma that tore through the group of mooks who were still shooting at the last place they saw me. The others reacted quickly to my reappearance, but they weren't fast enough to keep me from decimating their ranks. Before long, the sound of gunfire ceased, and there was nothing left but a series of corpses, all smoking from where my assault rifle's plasma rounds had burned holes in their chests.

That was the advantage of the R-14. It didn't matter if they were wearing protective gear or had subdermal armor. Nothing readily available in the Garden could stand up to the weapon's power. Sure, there were elites that could take a shot and keep on coming, but they were rare enough that I had yet to run into any of them. I was certain that the Enforcers' better gear could handle it, too—especially the higher-ranked Banshees—but it had been some time since I'd picked a fight with any of them.

The weapon was far from infallible, but it was more than enough to deal with a group of random mooks. And that's precisely what I'd done, laying waste to the men and women who'd attacked me for the simple sin of asking a question.

And that didn't bode well for Heather's fate.

After all, if she was just another dancer, they wouldn't have attacked. The fact that they had was troubling, and I couldn't stop myself from wondering what I would find if I kept searching. Not that I considered giving up. Now that I'd committed to rescuing her, I wouldn't stop until I found the woman. Even if that meant confronting something I'd have preferred not to see.

With that in mind, I pushed myself back to my feet and searched the club for any survivors. There weren't any. The club's dancers, servers, and other entertainers had all fled, and my attackers were all dead. The hail of gunfire that had been intended for me had ripped the bar to shreds, and the man I'd left alive in hopes of interrogating him had caught a few strays from the mooks' poorly aimed barrage. My own shots were unerring, which meant that the rest of the club had survived intact.

Devoid of dancers as well as patrons, it made for an eerie sight, though. The lights were still flashing. The music was still thumping. And the holographic displays featuring impossibly beautiful—and wholly naked—people showed nary a flicker. But without real flesh and blood, the club was a depressing sight.

I swept my weapon around as I searched for any stragglers, but I found nothing of note. So, I headed toward a door in the back of the club. When I reached it, it slid open to reveal a hallway. With slow, confident steps, I pushed forward, sweeping my weapon back and forth as I searched for anyone left in the building. Like that, I cleared the first level, which contained a storage room, an office, and a dressing area for the entertainers. No one was present, so I kept moving until I reached a stairwell.

One set of stairs led up, presumably to a set of apartments for the workers. After all, they all had slave implants, and I was fairly certain that none of them would be allowed off the premises. That meant the owner—whoever they were—would be forced to house them. Some slave owners treated their property well, looking at them as investments. Or expensive commodities. Others saw them as disposable pieces of equipment—or worse, as toys—that would require frequent replacement. The latter was far more common.

What I found after mounting the stairs suggested that the owner of Heaven and Hell belonged to that second group. The apartments were cramped, and I could tell that each of them housed three or four people. Moreover, I found plenty of evidence of drug use, as well, which tracked with everything I expected to see. After all, for someone with a slave implant, the only way to get through the days was if they'd been rendered insensate by various inebriants. Some used dust. Others used glitter. Alcohol was common, too. And there were a half dozen other popular drugs in evidence.

But there were no people.

It looked as if they'd all just left without even gathering their things. Given the time, most had probably been working downstairs. However, there were almost assuredly some that weren't. Or there should have been.

My stomach twisted as I continued my search, but I found nothing noteworthy. Nothing to suggest where the people had gone. And certainly nothing to hint at where Heather was. I cleared the apartments before heading back downstairs.

I knew I didn't have much time left. None of the Garden's various tribes had claimed Bourbon Street, but they would all protect it. It wouldn't be long before someone responded to what I'd done in the club, and I needed to be gone when the swarm of Operators started to arrive. But first, I needed to check the basement.

Gradually, I crept down the steps, keeping my assault rifle ready just in case. It was a good thing, too, because the moment I reached the bottom of the stairs and the door to the cellar slid open, someone took a shot at me. A gunshot rang out, echoing through the enclosed space before the sound of a shattered concrete wall came from behind me. The shooter had missed, and badly, but I wasn't going to give them the chance to try again. So, I slipped into the room, identified that the target was crouched behind some sort of cage, then fired.

Only their foot was sticking out, so that's where I'd aimed. The R-14's superheated plasma round completely destroyed the appendage, burning and ripping through it with a combination of intense heat and kinetic force. The owner of that foot cried out, flailing as they screamed in agony. I was on the figure—a man, I noted—in an instant, kicking his pistol away.

I aimed down the barrel of my own weapon, saying, "Shut up or the next one's taking your head off. You got me?"

The man nodded, tears leaking down his pudgy cheeks as I got a better look at him. And I was unimpressed. He was short, stubby, and round, with an ill-fitting but expensive-looking suit, shoes that shined like polished glass, and earrings in both ears. His hair—what was left of it, at least—had been slicked back and held in place by some unknown substance, giving him an altogether shifty appearance.

"You're the owner, I guess," I said, noticing that he wore a series of gold chains around his neck, as well. He wore his collared shirt unbuttoned down to reveal a mat of chest hair.

"I . . . I don't . . . Y-you shot me . . ."

"And I'll shoot you again if you don't answer my questions," I spat. Before I'd even laid eyes on the man, I'd hated everything he stood for. Even if it had become fairly common practice, the idea of enslaving people was abhorrent, and he'd taken advantage of it as much as anyone else in Nova City. But looking at him, my disdain rose to new heights. I knew it was unfair to judge people based on their appearance, but I couldn't help but think that his greasy look was appropriate for the sort of man he'd proved himself to be.

Tears streamed down his face—and rightly so; losing a foot couldn't have been pleasant—as he sobbed uncontrollably. I stepped forward and kicked him in the stomach, growling, "Focus, asshole!"

"W-what do you want?" he managed between the tears.

"You had a woman here," I said. "Name of Heather. Where is she?"

"I . . . I don't know . . . anybody by that name . . ."

"Wrong answer," I said, taking aim at his other foot. He screamed, but I paid it no mind. Instead, I shot him again, obliterating another appendage. "Heather. Blonde. Pretty. Probably came here around . . ."

That's when I noticed the room's contents. I'd been so hyperfocused on the man beneath me that I hadn't even paid attention to anything else. I'd just cataloged that there were no other threats, then moved on. But now, I saw it.

Or them.

Cages. Rows of them, lining the walls, and stacked one atop the other. There must've been thirty of them. And some of them had occupants, though none of them moved. That told me all I needed to know about their status. Dead or comatose, every single one of them. I focused on Observation, looking closer.

There, a rising chest. A twitch. A shift. Most were alive, but they were unconscious. Probably drugged, considering the noise I'd made. If they'd just been sleeping, the gunshots would've doubtless woken them up. But there were a few that looked like they might've been dead, too.

"What the . . . What's going on here?" I demanded, stepping forward and pressing the barrel of my rifle against the man's forehead.

"I . . . I remember . . . the one you're talking about . . ."

"And?" I spat.

"She's . . . she's gone," he said. "I . . . uh . . . I sold her. To Edgar . . . Edgar Russo."

My insides twisted into a knot. Edgar Russo was widely known throughout the district for his reputation as something of a mad scientist. Sometimes, that worked out—I had heard about him eking quite a bit of power out of some pretty low-quality cybernetics—but other times, it was less successful, resulting in death or . . . worse. There were skeletons in his closet, and everyone knew it. The only reason nobody had done anything about it was because he'd done plenty of favors for various tribes. In return, they'd protected him.

"What was he planning on doing?" I asked.

"I . . . I don't know," he whined. I shifted, and he screamed, "I swear! I don't know! I just couldn't move everyone, so I needed to liquidate!"

"What are you talking about? Why are all these people in cages?"

"I . . . I can't take them with me," he said. "So, I've been selling them, a little at a time. Stocking up on credits before . . . before I get out. You m-must have seen . . . You have to know everybody's leaving . . ."

That's when I shot him in the face.

Rationally, I knew that enslaving people often involved buying and selling human beings, but for some reason, hearing him talking about liquidating his assets—which were people—still set me off. And I was unable to stop myself from ending him.

In any case, I'd gotten the information I needed. Heather had been sold to Edgar Russo. I knew where he was, too, so it wouldn't be difficult for me to find him. But in the meantime, I needed to figure out what to do with the people in the cages.

That's when I realized there wasn't anything I could do. They were either dead or drugged into unconsciousness. If I could wake them up, maybe I could lead them to freedom. But even that was a dicey prospect, largely because I knew I'd probably have to fight my way out. With how long I'd been in the building, there was almost no chance the place wasn't at least surrounded. Likely, someone with ill intentions was already upstairs, and it was only a matter of time before I had to deal with them.

"Fuck," I muttered, looking around.

I couldn't take them with me, so I had no choice but to leave them behind to whatever future fate had in store for them. More slavery, no doubt. It made me sick. But there wasn't anything else to be done, unless I wanted to put them out of their misery, and I wasn't so far gone that I could force myself down that road.

With a sigh and a shake of my head, I tore my eyes from the caged people—presumably, they were packaged for transport, like animals—and turned back to the exit. Soon enough, I found myself numbly climbing the stairs until I reached the ground floor. Predictably, there were two Operators standing on the other side of the stairwell's door.

Immediately, I cast my senses out, latching on to the first presence.

Initiate Misthack?
[Yes] or [No]

I chose the affirmative option, then read the resulting notification that appeared on my HUD:

Misthack successful. Options:
Reboot system
Overcharge

Disable cybernetics
Upload Ghost

I chose the fourth option, which in turn brought up another menu:

Upload Ghost. Options:
Time Bomb
Seizure
Confusion
Blind
Chain Stun

The fifth Ghost available to me was one I'd been working on for quite a while. It had started out as a less powerful variation of *Time Bomb*, but it had quickly evolved into something more expansive. I'd kept the spreading effect, but I'd removed the incubation period. That required me to dial the lethality down, but that was okay—that had always been my intention.

In any case, the Ghost had been far more complicated than I'd expected, and it had taken months to get it just right. However, I couldn't have been happier with the result. I selected it, then charged through the door, my last remaining nano-bladed knife at the ready. I'd lost the other during my first trip into a Silo, and I hadn't had the chance to go to the Bazaar to replace it.

The first mook had already locked up, his every muscle contracting under the effect of *Chain Stun*, and I wasted no time before burying my knife in his temple. The Ghost jumped to the man on the other side of the door, and I watched as *Chain Stun* took hold, shocking him with charged Mist even as he reached for the pistol at his hip. His muscles locked up, and I ended him much the same way I'd taken out the first. Then, I moved on, tracking the Ghost as it jumped from one Operator to the next, killing them as they were rendered helpless.

Chain Stun didn't care about walls or other barriers. Perhaps it might've been stopped by a Mist shield, but there were none of those in Heaven and Hell. So, the Operators who'd infested the club while I'd searched for Heather were completely incapable of resisting it. And as a result, they couldn't even put up a fight as I swept through the building.

Anyone else might've had difficulty keeping up with the Ghost—after all, it only stunned someone for a second or two—but with my heightened Constitution and Engage, I had no problem. Before long, I had torn a bloody path through the club, not stopping until the leader—a Tier 4, though a weak one—fell before my blade. She was only stunned for a fraction of a second, but that was all I'd needed.

It was a massacre, but after what I had seen, I wasn't in a merciful mood. Rationally, I knew the Operators weren't responsible for what the club's owner had done to those people. But that didn't matter. All I really cared about was that I was angry and frustrated at my inability to help them, and those Operators made for convenient targets to quell my anger.

Of course, the threat didn't end inside the club. There were more Operators outside. But after killing fourteen men and women—not even counting the owner, who was more like a greasy cockroach than an actual person—I was tired of killing helpless people. So, I activated Stealth and waited until someone opened the door before slipping out behind them. In seconds, I was gone.

But my search wasn't finished. I still hadn't accomplished my goal. Heather was still out there, enslaved by one of the worst people in the city. And I needed to rescue her.

Thankfully, I knew precisely where she was. Unfortunately, getting to the so-called Mad Scientist was going to be a lot more difficult than infiltrating an unguarded club like Heaven and Hell. He would have active and passive defenses—probably dozens of dangerous Operators—and that wasn't even considering Russo himself. I'd never met him, but I knew the stories. He might've had no qualms about experimenting on other people, but he was just as free with testing things out on himself.

It would be a challenge, but I felt I was up to it. I just had to keep my anger in check, lest I make costly mistakes.

And with Heather's life on the line, I couldn't afford that. So, with those things in mind, I set off through the crowd of Bourbon Street, heading toward the edge of the Garden where I knew Russo's compound was located. Once I got there, I'd get in, kill everyone who got in my way, and rescue Heather.

It would be sloppy, but it was the best I could do on such short notice.

CHAPTER FORTY

MAD SCIENTIST

I hate some of the things I've had to do. But that's how the world works. There's only so much room at the top, and if you want to be the one in charge, someone has to fall.

—Nora Lancaster

As soon as I was out of Bourbon Street, I stepped into a corner convenience store—deactivating the surveillance camera inside—and headed straight for the bathroom. Upon my entry, the attendant didn't even look up from her handheld screen. I didn't blame her. The pay was minimal, and whoever owned the shop got exactly what they paid for.

When I reached the bathroom, the door slid open to reveal a cesspool of filth. In the wilderness, I'd been in all sorts of terrible situations, but that bathroom had to rank at the top of my list. Not only did it look as if it hadn't been cleaned in months—no excuse for that, considering it could be done with the press of a button—but the level of filth far exceeded the bounds of normality. Why anyone would smear human waste across one of the walls was a mystery.

Thankfully, I wasn't there to use the facilities. Instead, after throwing down a towel I'd kept in my arsenal implant, I stripped down and changed into my infiltration suit, adding some mundane clothing on top of it. Then, I changed my appearance with Mimic before leaving the bathroom—and the towel I'd thrown onto the floor—behind. As I moved through the small store, I reactivated the camera and left, looking entirely different from when I entered. The clerk still never looked up.

As I moved through the sparse crowd of pedestrians walking along the side of the street, I dwelled on what I'd discovered beneath Heaven and Hell. All those people, caged like animals, all because the owner—I still didn't know his name—wanted to liquidate his assets before fleeing the city. Did that make it my fault? After all, I'd spent months feeding the fires of war between the tribes, which had, in turn, driven the citizens to flee Nova City. So, in a way, I was to blame for everything that happened after that, wasn't I?

No.

I refused to shoulder that burden. Even if I believed I was at fault, I couldn't be held accountable for the evil actions of others. Ultimately, it was the system of oppression itself—and the people who supported it—that was to blame. The city had been built on a foundation of corruption and enslavement, so it had only ever been a matter of time before it all crumbled. I'd just given the situation a little push.

Of course, that didn't completely exonerate me of my actions. I knew that, without the things I'd done, those people would still be alive. But I also suspected that it would only be a temporary stay of execution. They'd died because they were weak and keeping them alive was inconvenient for their master. They weren't even worth delaying his escape so he could sell them.

I shook my head, seething at the injustice of it all.

At least the owner was dead now. That was comforting, as were his screams of pain after I had removed his legs with a couple of well-placed shots.

My path took me toward the edge of the Garden. I didn't dare ride the monorail, and my hover bike would attract far too much attention. So, I walked. Fortunately, I only had to travel for a few miles before I found myself standing before what was colloquially known as the Laboratory. The name was drawn from its owner, the Mad Scientist, Edgar Russo. I hated using the nickname—it felt like I was giving his reputation too much power—but as far as I knew, he'd earned it.

The area around the building was almost completely deserted, aside from a few dustheads and other addicts who'd taken up residence in the abandoned buildings. Being on the edge of the district, the area looked more like Algiers than the rest of the Garden. The structures were only a dozen stories tall, and they bore the signs of gross neglect. Everywhere I looked, I saw crumbling concrete covered in inartful graffiti. People, thin, bruised, and insensate, huddled in the shadowy corners or gathered around burning barrels cooking unidentifiable meat. If the people of Algiers were dead eyed and apathetic, then these fringe dwellers were almost all wild-eyed, dirty, and pitiful.

It was a fine distinction between one and the other, but it was plain enough that I immediately noticed the differences.

I slipped into an abandoned building that had a clear sight line of the Laboratory and started my climb to the roof. Inside was more of the same—dirty, damaged, and devoid of anything that might be mistaken for hope—and the denizens didn't even look up at my passing. Before long, I made it to the roof and settled down to study my target.

Almost immediately, I saw that this building would be a tough nut to crack. The Mad Scientist hadn't skimped on the security, with cameras, drones, and robotic guards in abundance. And there were some people, too, though I hesitated to think of them as such. Most were equipped with copious cybernetics—not an uncommon sight in Nova City—but they all seemed misshapen and lacked any symmetry at all. One guard had a mechanical arm that looked bigger than the rest of his body, while another had a dozen cybernetic legs in place of the normal two. I even saw one whose entire head seemed to have been replaced by a cybernetic with nine glowing red eyes and a tangle of exposed wires.

That was how the Mad Scientist worked. He didn't care about aesthetics or preserving a person's humanity. For him, the only thing that mattered was functionality. Or the pursuit of it, at least. According to rumor, he'd try just about anything at least once, regardless of how insane or horrifying the result might be.

And now he had Heather.

There was no telling what he might have done with her—or to her—and I suspected that I didn't have the time for proper surveillance. According to the owner of Heaven and Hell, she'd been sold only a few days before, which meant that I had a limited window before Russo started experimenting on her. In fact, there was every chance that I was already too late.

I needed to act, and subtlety wasn't really in the cards.

And if I was honest, I didn't mind that so much. For some reason, the Mad Scientist's actions had evoked a deep sense of disgust that exceeded what I felt about most of the injustices that ran so rampant within Nova City. It wasn't enough to just rescue Heather. I wanted him to die. To suffer. And I wanted to destroy everything he'd worked for.

With that in mind, I summoned my Pulsar and, kneeling on that roof in the middle of the night, took aim at the lopsided cyborg with the huge mechanical arm. I activated Empowered Shot, waited two seconds, then fired. His chest exploded in a shower of charred flesh, melted metal, and boiling blood.

Even as I aimed at the spider-legged mook, the compound erupted in activity. The drones swarmed, and the cameras swiveled in my direction. I fired again, tearing a hole in the woman's chest just like I had with her partner. Like that, I continued my assault, killing each of the guards with a single shot apiece.

But they didn't stand idle. Four were dead before they homed in on my location, and when they did, a hail of gunfire came in my direction. I ducked behind the lip of the roof, banking on their weapons' inability to go through solid concrete. I was right. But my location was blown, so I crawled toward the middle of the roof before rising and taking off at a sprint that took me to the other side of the building.

I leaped, clearing thirty feet with ease before crashing through the neighboring building's window. I hit shoulder first, protecting my exposed face with my arms. The glass would have ripped a normal person to shreds, but it was completely incapable of getting through my infiltration suit, much less my Sheath. When I hit the floor, I did so with a roll that that brought me back to my feet, and I continued my sprint, regaining my speed in only a couple of steps.

I practically flew down the hall until I reached my next destination. I reared back and aimed a front kick at the door of an apartment, caving it in. But it took another two kicks before I completely dislodged it. Expected, considering that it was obviously reinforced, but still annoying. Predictably, the room was empty; the buildings in the area around the Laboratory were almost completely abandoned, and this one was no different. So, I moved to the window and, after seeing that my calculations had been spot-on, took aim at the compound once again.

The view wasn't as pristine as it had been on the roof, but it was still good enough that I had a clear shot at seven guards. I took aim at the biggest of the bunch—a mook with enormous claws in place of hands—activated my ability, and after the requisite two seconds, fired. My Pulsar was a top-of-the-line weapon, and it was backed up by the significant modifiers that came with my skills and class. So, the results were predictable.

I tore through them like they were nothing, and it wasn't long before the rest of the guards retreated into the main building. It was six stories tall, so it looked squat compared to the rest of the district. But it still had a sizable footprint.

With a grimace, I stowed my Pulsar in my arsenal implant. I'd hoped to kill a few more of the guards before I went in, but they'd reacted more quickly than I had expected. It was fine, though. If nothing else, I was confident in my abilities. So, I quickly exited the room and climbed down to the ground floor before leaving the building behind. As I stepped into the street, I summoned my R-14 assault rifle and brought it to my shoulder.

The area had gone completely quiet. Even the addicts and bums had fled at the sound of my sniper rifle, so the street was eerily deserted. Good. At least they wouldn't get caught in the cross fire, though I couldn't help but wonder if getting gunned down was preferable to the sad excuse they called a life.

Of course, I knew the answer to that. I didn't know them, and as such, I couldn't comprehend their struggles. For all I knew, they'd consciously chosen intransience and addiction. Perhaps they preferred that to living in a city hellbent on beating them down and enslaving them.

Or maybe they were just as pitiful as they seemed.

In any case, who was I to judge? Their lives were their own, and it wasn't as if they were hurting anyone but themselves. On that count, I could certainly sympathize; after all, I'd made a few self-destructive choices of my own.

In any case, I flared Observation as I crossed the street and approached the compound. When I got close enough, I got to work on the cameras. Using Misthack, I overwhelmed their meager defenses and shut them off. It was a temporary measure, but it was enough. For the drones, I didn't even bother with Misthack. Instead I just shot them. They were meant to be durable, but they couldn't stand against a burst of superheated plasma rounds from my R-14. Soon enough, the exterior of the building was clear, and I found myself approaching the front door.

When I got there, I saw that it was made from some durable alloy I couldn't identify, and it had been reinforced to the point that I knew I couldn't quickly breach it. So, I tried to use Misthack, and for the first time in quite a while, I was rebuffed. The Mad Scientist, it seemed, took security seriously enough that he'd invested in quite a Mistwall. Given enough time, perhaps I could have bypassed it, but I could recognize it as the work of hours rather than minutes, and I didn't think I had that much time.

So, I went with my backup plan.

When my [Mistrunner] abilities didn't work, explosives would pick up the slack. To that end, I retrieved a few shaped charges from my arsenal implant and carefully positioned them on the edge of the door. Then, I retreated a dozen or so yards, where I crouched behind the big-armed mook's corpse before pressing a button on the detonator. The explosion was somewhat muted—a characteristic of the compound I'd used—but it did its job remarkably well, blowing a series of holes in the door.

The moment the explosion went off, I charged forward, aiming a front kick at the door. It flew inward, and I heard a cry of pain as the door flattened someone, but I didn't stop moving forward. My R-14 spat superheated plasma, burning holes in the other two cyborg guards in the hall. Once they were dead, I kicked the door away to reveal a third, killing her with a well-placed plasma round to the head.

Looking around, I saw that the building's lobby was otherwise deserted, but there was a camera focused in my direction. I raised my weapon and shot it, disdaining subtlety entirely as I stalked forward. As I progressed through the compound, I saw that it was mostly deserted, aside from a cyborg here or there. But when I reached the second floor, I found that it was populated with horrors.

Everywhere I looked, I saw the misshapen humanoid forms of wildlings. Naked, thin to the point of malnutrition, and with elongated limbs, the creatures would have been intimidating if it weren't for the fact that they were all unconscious. And most of them had been dismembered, at least to some degree. A missing hand here. A stub of a leg there. There was even one that looked like he'd had his face peeled off.

I felt bile rise in my throat, and I barely suppressed the need to vomit.

I had seen a lot of death and destruction in my short life, but nothing really compared to what I saw laid out before me.

Russo's moniker seemed even more appropriate than ever before. Mad Scientist, indeed.

For a moment, I considered leaving them as they were. Some had been butchered so thoroughly that even if they woke up, they would pose little threat to me. However, my training pushed me into a different decision, and I began the arduous process of exterminating them. As I stowed my rifle in my arsenal implant and summoned my nano-bladed sword, I told myself that my actions were merciful.

I almost even believed it.

But with every throat I cut, I hated myself a little more. These people—or what had once been people—had done nothing wrong. They were victims, albeit a different sort than was usual for Nova City. Instead of being preyed on by other human beings—or even aliens—they'd been victimized by the Mist itself. And rather than try to help them, we, as a species, had chosen to simply ignore the problem and look at them as something lesser.

It was right there in the name.

They weren't human beings. They were wildlings.

My blade flashed, and one after another, their suffering ended. And that distinction didn't make it any easier to stomach.

By the time I'd finished that detestable task, my anger had mounted, and my hatred of the so-called Mad Scientist had reached new heights. So, I continued to the next floor, which had clearly been the living quarters for the cyborgs. There was even one room that was a bit larger than the others that I figured was where Russo himself slept. But I found no other people, though there were cameras aplenty.

I destroyed them all, mostly out of pique rather than because I wanted to conceal my movements. He already knew I was coming for him, after all.

The fourth floor was used for storage, and it contained crate after crate of medical equipment, cybernetics, and weapons. I left them where they were, intending to come back for them once I'd dealt with Russo and found Heather. The other two levels were more of the same, leaving only the sublevels to worry about.

So, that's where I went, keeping my R-14 at the ready as I descended one floor after another until I finally reached a blast door.

I didn't have any explosives that were powerful enough to take it down but limited enough not to bring the building down with it. So, I used Misthack instead. The defenses were substantial, but I now had time to overcome them. So, I set about doing just that, conquering one puzzle after the next until, an hour later, I'd gained access. With that done, I unlocked the door and pulled it open.

When I did, I heard a sound I never expected to hear.

Applause.

"Oh, that was impressive!" came a mild voice. "Very, very impressive! The way you just went through my toys . . . Bravo!"

CHAPTER FORTY-ONE

THE PRICE OF PROCRASTINATION

Echo is gone, fled to my enemies for sanctuary. Wash is dead, turned over to the Coyotes in order to maintain the peace. And Asheligh got herself killed by some upstart in the Emporium. As a result, I've begun to lose my grip on the Specters. They are only a hair's breadth from mutiny, and war is the only thing keeping them in line. I don't know what to do.

—Nora Lancaster

The sublevel was not what I had expected. Upon stepping through the door, I found myself in a long corridor, on either side of which were a series of rooms with heavy glass security doors. And what I saw on the other side of those doors was enough to give me nightmares.

I'd thought the cages beneath Heaven and Hell were horrific. But the contents of these cells made them seem practically mundane. Each chamber housed a naked person, though they were all in various stages of transformation. The first was the least affected, with the only evidence of her transformation being that one of her arms had grown by about six inches.

More troubling were her eyes, which were completely devoid of anything approaching sapience. I'd seen their like before, though not inside the city. They were wildling's eyes.

My gaze traced a path along one side of the hall, finding that each subsequent cell held a progressively more devolved human being. If the first only showed a few signs of becoming a wildling, then the final cell held the genuine thing, with elongated arms and legs, sharpened teeth and claws, and a demeanor more suited to a wild animal than a human being.

And it was clear that those changes had occurred rapidly, as well. Skin that was incapable of keeping up with the transformation had split apart, revealing raw muscle beneath, and a few bore signs of distress, with claw marks across their naked skin, as if they'd known what they were becoming and had tried to tear the transformation out with their bare hands.

On the other side of the hall, and only two cells down, I saw Heather.

Or what was left of her, at least.

She was no longer beautiful. Her blonde hair had been torn out in clumps, and what remained was stringy and wet. Her face bore self-inflicted claw marks, and her body had been twisted all out of shape. Upon noticing that I was looking her way, she went crazy, launching herself against the plasti-glass door, her claws tracing grooves in the durable material as she tried to tear her way through.

The others were in a similarly agitated state, and seeing Heather, it didn't take me long to come to the conclusion that they weren't natural wildlings, if there even was such a thing. They weren't native to the forests outside the city; instead, they'd been deliberately transformed.

And the man responsible stood at the end of the hall.

I didn't hesitate any longer, raising my assault rifle and bracing it against my shoulder in one smooth motion. I fired before the so-called Mad Scientist had a chance to object. The superheated plasma rounds tore through the hall, leaving heat distortions in their wake. My aim was true, but just before they reached the despicable man I'd come to kill, a blue barrier shimmered only a few feet in front of him. A trio of small explosions, one on top of the other, echoed through the corridor, but when the smoke cleared, the man was entirely unharmed, protected as he was by the Mist shield in front of him.

I fired again. And again, hoping to overwhelm the shield, but even after I emptied my entire magazine, it remained completely intact. That suggested that it had a potent power source—likely a supply of Rift Shards.

As I reloaded, I felt another shield slide into place behind me, preventing retreat. As if that had ever even crossed my mind.

"I've been keeping an eye on you," said the man I knew to be Russo. His voice was distorted by the Mist shield, carrying with it a slight buzzing sound. The man himself was unremarkable, save for the fact that one side of his head was metallic. The cybernetic extended over his eye, cutting across his cheek to cover his ear. The eye blinked with green light. His figure was average, though his narrow shoulders suggested a life devoid of physical labor. That was expected, given what I knew about him. He smiled as he continued, "Your exploits are impressive. The way you've escalated the situation between the tribes—truly an accomplishment. But then again, great things can be expected from anyone who achieves the {Mistrunner} class."

"What are you talking about?" I demanded, mentally checking that Mimic was still active. It was.

As if reading my mind, he said, "Oh, your disguises are impressive. But you've left a trail a mile wide, so long as one knows where to look. And I pride myself on knowing those sorts of things."

"What do you want?" I spat, wondering just how well his Mist shield would hold up to the BMAP. But using that would bring the building down on me, and while I hoped I would survive, there were no guarantees I wouldn't be crushed. And even if I did, I'd still be buried under tons of concrete.

"Straight to the point," Russo said, running his hand through the hair on the side of his head. "Call it a test."

"Of what?"

"Your combat ability," he said. "These unfortunates are the only ones to survive the transformation. Out of hundreds, only sixteen made it. I'd hoped that they would retain their awareness after I removed their Nexus Implants and flooded them with Mist, but alas—they have become true wildlings. It really is remarkable."

I didn't need him to continue his explanation to guess what he had planned. And it wasn't good. Wildlings were dangerous, and not just because they possessed outsize physical traits. They were stronger and faster than most people, but they threatened me especially because they weren't susceptible to my [Mistrunner] abilities. Without Nexus Implants—or any other cybernetics—they may as well be ghosts, for all I could affect them with my most potent tools. That left only pure force.

I'd managed to deal with a few of them in the past, but if any of the ones in the cells displayed the sort of strength I'd seen from the alpha outside of Biloxi, I didn't stand a chance of survival.

"What can a fabled {Mistrunner} do against such odds?" he asked, grinning broadly. Then, he clapped his hands, declaring, "Let's find out."

As one, the plasti-glass doors slid open, and the wildlings flooded out, howling for my blood. I reacted immediately, turning and firing at the closest. The plasma rounds hit the nearest creature's chest in a tight grouping, but the attack was only moderately effective. I'd hoped that the shots would carve deep craters into the creature, but the true effect was much less impressive. Clearly, the balls of superheated plasma did damage, but it only amounted to a little more than a flesh wound. If I really wanted to punch through its tough hide, I would need an entire magazine.

But I didn't have time for that because the wildling that had been confined to the cell on my left was bearing down on me. I whipped around, using

Disengage at the same time, and as I sailed through the air, I fired again. The wildling stumbled backward, but her skin proved just as durable as the first creature's. I fired another burst before I landed in a crouch at the back of the cell of my first enemy.

He'd barely managed to recover before I hit him with another burst, this one targeted at his knee. That proved a little more effective than aiming for center mass, and it only took one more burst before the joint exploded in a shower of charred bone and gore. But he still dragged his way forward, clearly intending to rip me to shreds with his clawed hands. I fired again, this time targeting his head.

He was only a few feet away, so there was no possibility of a miss.

His head rocked back with the initial burst of fire, but even though the skin blistered and cracked, he showed no signs of slowing down. I fired again. And again. Finally, on the next burst, his skull shattered, and he fell limp, thudding to the dingy tile floor.

I had no time to savor my victory, though, because the female wildling from across the way had recovered. She tore across the hall, covering the ground between us in an instant. I fired again and again, using the same tactic that had worked against the male, but she was slightly more durable, and by the time I destroyed her skull, I had emptied my entire magazine.

And more troubling, the other fourteen wildlings had arrived, with what was left of Heather leading the way. There was no recognition in her eyes. None of the kind, caring woman I knew. Heather was dead. Something else was just using her body. And I couldn't afford to let sentimentality slow my reactions. So, I pushed my emotions aside and acted.

Rather than take the time to reload, I summoned my scattergun and let loose. The weapon wasn't intended to be used with only one hand, so it bucked and threw off my aim. However, the wildlings were so close and packed together so tightly that I couldn't miss. Lightning arced out, hitting Heather in her naked chest. Her body convulsed as electrical burns spread across her torso. The lightning jumped to the next wildling. And then the next after that.

They shook and trembled, their muscles contracting involuntarily, but I knew from experience that the weapon wouldn't kill them. That was its largest weakness; it had been designed for nonlethality, and though it had exceeded that mark with weaker targets, against creatures like the wildlings, it worked as it was originally intended to function, slowing them down but coming up short in terms of its ability to kill.

That was expected, though.

Stowing the scattergun, I reached down to my hip and drew Ferdinand II from his holster. He'd been loaded with antipersonnel rounds designed to penetrate deep, then spall, tearing through comparatively soft internal organs.

I fired, putting a round just below Heather's breastbone. It penetrated and did its job, but a wildling could still function without intestines. And I'd just discovered how hard those bones really were, so attacking something vital like the heart was out of the question. I changed tactics, firing at legs.

The wildlings were insanely durable, but their joints were still mechanical in nature. So, if I managed to sufficiently destroy the muscles responsible for locomotion, their combat capability would be significantly reduced.

But Ferdinand II was only the beginning. For one, he only had nine rounds, and reloading the pistol took longer than any of my other weapons. Once I'd discharged the entirety of his payload, I holstered the weapon and re-summoned my R-14. By the time I'd jammed a new magazine into place, the wildlings had recovered from the electrical assault of my scattergun.

I'd gained some time, though. More, the first few wildlings in line—Heather included—moved on unsteady legs, their muscles and joints having been mutilated by Ferdinand II's issue. I aimed to exacerbate that problem.

I fired again, my rounds tearing through the already injured legs. The moment they stepped, their limbs buckled, and they fell. But their fellows bounded over them, unharmed and ready to join the fight.

I kept shooting until my magazine ran empty. The superheated plasma was insufficient to leave more than superficial damage—not without concentrated fire, which, on moving targets, wasn't the easiest thing in the world. However, the kinetic force behind each shot sent them stumbling a half step backward.

So, their advance slowed to a crawl before the barrage.

But it was a losing battle. I just couldn't do enough damage. Not with my firearms. I needed to switch things up.

The issue was that I couldn't do so without significant danger. At the rate I was going, though, it was even more dangerous to keep doing what I was doing. I'd probably kill a few more of them, but then I'd just be swarmed by the remainder. I just didn't have enough rounds in my arsenal implant to deal with all of them.

As I saw it, I had two choices. One was almost assuredly suicidal. The other was only slightly better.

If I pulled out the BMAP, I knew I could kill the wildlings. With the combination of my modifiers and the sheer power of its rounds, the damage I could bring to bear was truly impressive. However, that destructive power was a double-edged sword that would cut me just as keenly as it did my enemies. If I let the weapon loose, I would soon find myself buried under tons of concrete.

The other, slightly better plan involved me getting in close and hacking the wildlings apart via melee combat. My nano-bladed sword was one of my longest-tenured weapons, but its sharpness was unparalleled, and it had proven a match for even the hardest materials. So long as I hit my target enough times, at least.

And it had one advantage none of my other weapons had: it didn't run out of ammunition.

But getting in close came with obvious disadvantages.

I just had to make the best of a bad set of circumstances.

So, just as the wildlings got within a few feet, I dismissed my assault rifle and once again summoned my scattergun. By the time it materialized in my hands, the lead wildling, after climbing over his fallen fellows, had gotten close enough that I could smell his fetid breath.

Using Double Shot, I fired a double dose of lightning, and as the wildlings' muscles locked up, I focused on the creature still in the doorway and activated Engage. Even as the lightning arced from one wildling to another, I sailed through the air with unprecedented speed. Claws darted out, driven more by instinct than any conscious intention, and I was forced to activate Balance in order to contort my body to avoid those wickedly sharp talons. Even so, one managed to trace a long line down my ribs. It would have gutted me if it weren't for the protection afforded by my infiltration suit and Sheath. Even with them, my skin parted before the claw, and one of my ribs was shattered.

I ignored the pain, and the moment I got a look at the wildling bringing up the rear of the group, I planted a foot on one of the creatures and activated Engage once again. With my already substantial momentum augmented by the second use of my ability, I rocketed through the air, outrunning even the lightning until I finally crashed into the final creature. We went sprawling in a tangle of limbs, and I summoned my nano-bladed sword as I rolled free.

I pushed myself to my feet, then kicked off. The lightning from my now-dismissed scattergun finally caught up, and the wildling's muscles spasmed. I hacked into its neck with as heavy a blow as I could manage, rending its flesh and exposing the white bones of its neck. I attacked again, the sword biting deep and severing its spine.

Even as the creature flopped to the ground—still alive, but incapable of moving—I darted forward, swinging my sword with brutal efficiency. I only had a short time before the wildlings recovered from the scattergun attack, and I used that brief span to the fullest extent of my abilities. In the space of three seconds, I'd incapacitated nine of the remaining eleven wildlings. A few were dead, proving that the creatures weren't all equally durable, but most were still alive, even if they weren't much of a danger anymore.

But that left two more, and both of them had been hobbled by my previous strategy.

Still, they were dangerous enough that I didn't dare underestimate them. So, maintaining my focus, I pushed past the creature whose head I'd just severed and attacked the penultimate wildling of the bunch. He went down only a few seconds later, leaving only one.

The wildling that had once been Heather.

She was barely standing, but her fury was still as potent as ever. I knew I imagined it, but there was also a glint of accusation in her eyes. As if she knew that my procrastination was the reason she'd found herself afflicted with such a fate. And I couldn't argue with it, either. I had known where she was for months, but I'd put off saving her in favor of accomplishing my own goals.

Heather was just another victim of my quest for revenge.

I wasn't directly responsible for what had happened to her. Like so much else, the blame for that could be laid at Nora's feet. However, I had played my part, too. Just like with the handful of Silo workers who hadn't escaped before I demolished the buildings. Just like all the people who'd probably starved as a direct result of the disruption of the food supply. Or the ones who'd been caught in the cross fire of the war I'd started.

How many deaths could be traced back to my actions? Dozens? Hundreds? Maybe even thousands?

All varying degrees of innocent.

But I couldn't stop. Not until I finished what I'd started.

So, with grim determination, I stepped forward and engaged in combat with a woman who'd always treated me with unconditional kindness and respect. Who only ever wanted to be my friend. Even as I felt my blade bite into her neck and sever her spine, I felt tears tracing lines down my bloody cheeks.

Silence reigned, broken only by a pair of thumps—one for her head, and the other for her body—and the heavy sound of my panting breaths.

CHAPTER FORTY-TWO

A PUBLIC SERVICE

Loyalty means nothing to these people. I've given them everything they could ever want, and yet, they still dare to disagree. I will have to make some examples.

—Nora Lancaster

I stared down at Heather's mutated corpse, wondering how things had come to this. Even when I looked at her misshapen form, all I could see was the woman who'd tried so hard to be my friend. To support me. To help me. And I had abandoned her just as I'd abandoned everything else that wasn't my quest for revenge. I'd accepted that as the necessary cost of my vengeance, but for the first time since I'd begun my journey, I found myself wondering if I'd made the right choices.

I could have done things differently. I could have turned the other cheek, to borrow a colloquialism popular among those who still clung to the notion that there was a God and that he actually cared about them. Such a belief seemed silly to me, given the state of the world, but the fervor of their belief was unassailable. But were they right about leaving the past where it belonged? It felt so counterintuitive. If someone wronged you, you didn't just ignore it. That was how you ended up dead or enslaved. Instead, you fought back. You took from them what they intended to take from you. Corpses posed no threat, after all.

But looking down at Heather, I knew that wasn't true. She was dead, and before that, she'd lost whatever made her the person she'd been. But even so, my inability to protect her, my refusal to save her—it haunted me like nothing had since my uncle's death. Because of my choices, she was gone.

I felt tears falling down my cheeks and a lump building in my throat.

More than that, though, rage had begun to wrap itself around my heart, burning everything else away. I knew it was dangerous, leaving it to spread unchecked, but in that moment, I just didn't care. I hated the world. I hated the man who'd experimented on Heather. I hated Nora, for sentencing her to enslavement in the first place. But most of all, I hated Nova City for setting the stage where such things were possible.

I slung my blade to the side, sending a splatter of blood against the wall, then turned my attention to the man who'd sequestered himself behind the Mist shield. He thought he was safe, the idiot. He didn't know that nowhere was safe from my wrath.

I stalked down the hall, my sword held in a death grip as I glared at the closest object of my ire. I couldn't kill Nora. Not yet. And I couldn't destroy the city any more than I could change the world. Perhaps one day, but those goals were so far-off as to be nonexistent.

But I could kill the detestable man behind the curtain of blue energy.

He thought he was safe.

Against my monumental anger, the very concept of safety was laughably weak. And I was grimly eager to show him the error of his ways.

One step. Then two. My feet barely made a sound, but they left bloody imprints with every footfall.

The lights flickered as the Mist swirled around me. The man said something, grinning like a moron. He had no idea how vulnerable he was.

He thought he was safe.

I intended to show him otherwise.

The distance between us shrank with every bloody step, but my eyes never wavered. I reached out, searching for the controls of the Mist shield, and I found them only a moment later. How could I not, with them blazing in my senses? I dove in, unsurprised to find substantial defenses before me. Mist shields were usually like that, and this one was even better protected than most.

It didn't matter.

I'd spent years honing my mind. Countless hours developing the ability to overwhelm such defenses. Hundreds of nodes bloomed before my mind's eye, each one glittering with the potential to stop me. But potential is not reality, and I fell upon them like an avalanche, unstoppable and undeterred.

He thought he was safe.

My will would not be denied as I sought to show him how wrong he was.

In moments, the first few fell. A few seconds more, and I'd begun to carve a path through those defenses, solving puzzles and equations with unprecedented rapidity. I had never been so focused. I had never worked so quickly. Seconds turned into almost a minute, and then, as the last node was crushed beneath my will, the system was laid bare before me.

He thought he was safe.

He was not.

I deactivated the Mist shield. He screamed. I was undeterred by his terror.

Using Engage, I covered the distance between us. My sword flashed, a blur of silver and blue followed by a red mist, and his arm fell to the ground. I didn't hear the impact over his screams of pain and fear. My sword flashed again, and the other arm fell, as well.

I was reminded of how I'd dismantled Asheligh, the Red Terror of the Emporium. But she had been a warrior and worthy of at least a modicum of respect. The man before me was neither, and I swung my sword again, slicing through his left leg at the knee.

He fell with an agonized screech.

Only minutes before, he'd thought he was safe.

Now, he knew that death was coming.

But it wouldn't come quickly.

No—he needed to suffer. Once, I might have hesitated to torture someone. It was useless as an information-gathering tool, often resulting in the victim telling the torturer whatever it took to get them to stop. Truth was irrelevant, and so, whatever information that came as a result was useless. No—torture didn't work for that.

But what it did do was make me feel like justice was being done. It wasn't. I was self-aware enough to know that it was a barbaric practice. I just didn't care. Not in that moment, at least. I wanted him to suffer, so suffer he did.

I took him apart, one inch at a time, slicing bits and pieces off with grim determination. It wasn't satisfying. I knew I'd end up regretting it. I should have just killed him and been done with it. But I needed to make him hurt. I wanted him to feel what I'd felt. That hopelessness that had suffused my very being when I realized what had happened to Heather. What I had let happen to her.

I thought she was safe. I thought she would be fine until I got around to helping her. She hadn't been.

I hacked and slashed, each cut precise and well measured. It wasn't a conscious choice, but rather the result of years of practice and untold hours of training.

By the time I'd finished, there was nothing left of the man. Just a pile of bloody flesh.

It made me want to vomit.

I wasn't proud of what I'd done. Nor was I ashamed, which was probably what my actions warranted. Instead, I just felt numb in a way I'd never really felt before.

I stood there for a long time, just staring down at the pile of meat I'd created. Then, without further deliberation, I planted one of my demolition charges inside the room. It was the same sort I'd used to such great effect in the Silos, and I placed a half dozen of them throughout the sublevel before moving up to the ground floor and repeating my actions. I didn't bother with the other floors. There was no point, and somewhere in the back of my mind, past the numb fury, I acknowledged that the demolition charges were expensive to make.

Once I was sure I had planted enough explosives to bring the structure down, I left the building and retreated a few hundred yards down the street. Thankfully, there were no pedestrians about. Even the addicts avoided the area, lest they find themselves captured and used as one of Russo's experiments, so it was as deserted as any place I could have hoped to find.

Then, without further ado, I retrieved the detonator from my arsenal implant and pressed the appropriate button. I watched as a massive explosion rocked the building. Fire erupted from the first-floor windows, and the ground shook. Even as the building crumbled in on itself, sending billowing dust out into the street, I never looked away.

Not until it had become a pile of broken rubble, at least. In a way, it reminded me of the building's owner, only instead of bits of flesh and pools of blood, the building had become a collection of shattered bricks, cement, and dust, broken down to its base components.

Satisfied but far from happy, I summoned, then mounted my Cutter and left it all behind me. As I sped through the Garden's streets, I couldn't help but remember the part I'd played in all of it. Not only had I put off saving Heather, which resulted in her being sold to the Mad Scientist, but I couldn't forget that everything had started the moment my uncle had given me the Tier 7 Nexus Implant. If I'd never taken it, would he still be alive? Would Heather? I didn't know, but my deluded state of self-pity suggested as much.

I rejected it, of course. How could I not? Rationally, I knew I shouldn't hold myself accountable for the actions of others. But sometimes, reason doesn't really fit the way we want it to. As a result, my guilt lingered in the back of my mind. It wasn't enough to derail my plans. I was too committed for that. But I couldn't dismiss it outright, either.

Perhaps it would drive me to make better choices in the future.

The trip back to my compound went by in a blur. Vaguely, I noticed the fighting in the streets, but I avoided it easily. Otherwise, I didn't pay much attention to any of it. Instead, my mind remained mired in the day's events, images of Heather's naked and mutated corpse dominating my thoughts.

So it happened that I pulled up to the back of the lot, disabled the holographic display that camouflaged the entrance to the tunnel, and slipped inside. Once I was safely ensconced in the basement, I dismounted and dismissed my hover bike before heading upstairs.

I didn't stop at the apartment I shared with Patrick. Instead, I kept going until I reached the roof, where I sat staring up at the Garden. Hands on my knees as I leaned against an air-conditioning duct, I lost myself in thought for the next few hours. I would've sat there for longer, except Patrick interrupted my introspection by sitting next to me.

For a long few minutes, he didn't say anything. I knew he wanted to ask questions, but I appreciated his restraint. He knew me well enough to understand that I'd talk about it when I was good and ready.

Which I did, almost an hour later when I said, "You were right before. We need to get out of Nova for a little while."

"What happened?" he asked.

"I . . . I went to rescue Heather," I said. "Just like I said I was going to do."

"Once or twice," Patrick said. "She was your uncle's . . . partner, wasn't she?"

I nodded, wiping my eyes. I hadn't even realized that the tears had started again. Then, I told him exactly what had happened. When I started explaining the situation, I'd intended to keep some things to myself, but before I knew it, I was telling him the whole story. I didn't hold anything back, and in some ways, it felt right. In others, it made me feel more vulnerable than I'd ever felt before.

But I knew I needed to tell someone, and Patrick was all I had.

At some point, I found myself leaning into him. His arm wrapped around my shoulders, and he pulled me closer. There, I wept—truly and deeply, without trying to hold it back. It didn't make me feel better, but it was necessary all the same.

"I didn't . . . She wasn't my favorite person," I muttered. "For the longest time, I resented her because she . . . because she had my uncle's attention. It was only right before I left that I realized just how petty I'd been. She just wanted what was best for me. She wanted to be my friend. And . . . and I rejected her, thoroughly and without any real reason for it."

"It's not your fault," he said, holding me close.

"But it is. It is my fault because I could have saved her," I said. "If I'd have gone after her the day I found out where she was, she would be here right now. You . . . you would have liked her, I think. She was nice, just like you."

"You couldn't have predicted what happened," he said.

"I know that. But knowing it doesn't really help" was my response. Then, I pulled away, wiping my eyes. I sniffed loudly before saying, "Sorry. I didn't mean to . . . This isn't something you should have to worry about."

"It's not—"

"I just need to not be in this city right now," I stated, changing the subject. "And I think I know where we can go. If you want to, I mean. You might want to stay here."

"Where do you want to go?" he asked.

"While I've been snooping around, I found out that there's another Dead Zone a few hundred miles north of here," I said. "Maybe a little farther. I've got coordinates, so we should be able to find it pretty easily."

"And what are we going to do with a Dead Zone?"

"I figure there's probably a Rift somewhere inside," I explained. "We could go in, gather some Shards, and then come back. By then, some of the heat will have died down, and it'll be time to finish this thing off."

In truth, I could have probably done that at any moment. I'd already destroyed the pillars that were keeping the Specters aloft, so it wouldn't be difficult to bring them crashing down. However, the spiked shipments of bio-enhancers hadn't had a chance to truly do their work. I wasn't afraid of Nora—not really. Rather, it was about taking from her the one thing she valued above all else—her strength. And that required time.

With all my other tasks finished, I didn't want to just sit around and train. So, running a Rift was just the sort of thing I needed to keep me occupied. Of course, part of it was that I didn't want to stick around the city—not after what I'd just experienced. I needed to get away, and this was the perfect excuse.

"I don't know if that's a good idea," Patrick said. "I'm not . . . I don't do as well out there as you do. And a Rift . . ."

"Is incredibly dangerous, I know," I said. "But if you want to gain levels, it's the best you're going to find. Besides, you haven't heard the best part."

"Uh . . . what?"

I grinned at him—an expression I really didn't feel—and said, "Well, Rifts means Rift Shards, which means tons of credits. And I was thinking, once we're done here in Nova, there's nothing keeping us here. We could go up to the Bazaar and get a ship. It'll probably cost everything we loot, but I'm sure Gala can point us toward something we can afford. Think about it—you and me, going from town to town and seeing what the world has to offer."

"And you would . . . be happy with that?"

I shrugged. "I have no idea, honestly," I said. "I just know there's nothing left for me here in Nova. Not after I take care of Nora. Too many bad memories, maybe. I don't know. I just think there has to be somewhere better, right? It can't all be like this."

"I . . . I don't know . . ."

"But that's for later," I said, trying to sound upbeat. I wiped more tears away. "For now, we just need to get out of here for a little while. I don't care where we go, but I think the Rift is as good a place as any to lie low for a little while."

I knew that I'd pushed things too far too quickly, and as a result, even the Mad Scientist had been paying attention. I hadn't forgotten that he'd known who I was and what I was doing. So, getting out of Nova City for a little while seemed like the smart choice.

Plus, I just didn't want to look at the place anymore. Not for a while, at least. "Please."

Patrick didn't answer for a few seconds, then sighed before saying, "Fine. I'll go. But we play it safe, okay?"

"Always," I said, knowing I would do no such thing. Sure, I'd probably take fewer chances if I had Patrick tagging along, but I still wasn't the type to flee from danger. Not without good reason.

"Good," I said, throwing my arms around him. "That's good. I didn't want to go without you."

"Would you have?"

I shrugged. "Maybe. I don't know," I said. "But it doesn't matter because you've already agreed. But for now . . . there's something I've been wanting to do . . ."

"What are—"

I interrupted him with a kiss. I wasn't sure how I felt about Patrick, but I knew that, for at least one night, I didn't want to be alone. And judging by his response, I felt positive that we were on the same page.

CHAPTER FORTY-THREE

NORTHBOUND

He knows something. I could see it in his smug little face. But nobody messes with Gunther and comes out the better for it. If they manage to live through it at all. He's reasonable, though. I just need to figure out what he wants and make a deal for the information I need.

—Nora Lancaster

Getting out of Nova City was a lot easier, now that everyone in the city was trying to leave. The flood of refugees was so constant that the Enforcers couldn't check everyone. As a result, our flight was a simple matter of blending into the crowd. I had plenty of experience with that, and with my skills and abilities, I knew there was no chance the Enforcers would look twice in my direction.

For Patrick, I expected things to be different. Apparently, though, his [Smuggler] skill was good for more than just negotiation, flying, and gun fighting. It was also equipped with an ability that allowed him to blend into his surroundings. It was different from Stealth or Camouflage in that it didn't conceal his presence. Instead, it just made him seem unremarkable. The only limiter seemed to be his own Mist attribute, which was high enough that even I had difficulty focusing on him. And that was with me knowing what was going on. So, it seemed fair to assume that the Enforcers that guarded the gates wouldn't notice him.

And even if they did, who cared? He wasn't really all that remarkable, being only Tier 3. Sure, most of the other refugees would be Tier 1 or Tier 2, but people with his potential weren't uncommon enough to garner extra attention. In any case, I didn't think anyone was looking for him anyway.

After all, Remy had kept a low profile, so it would have been extremely surprising to find that Patrick was even on anyone's radar.

So that was how we found ourselves standing amid a crowd of refugees as we waited to exit the city. The line—more like a blob of people, really—was slow-moving, so I guessed it would be midday before we reached the lift that would take us down to the swamp below. I'd overheard that a temporary settlement had sprung up around the lift. From there, huge caravans going in every direction would depart. For the right price, a person could reserve a spot.

Some of those caravans were almost certainly fronts for slavers. I wouldn't have been surprised to find that most were, in fact. But these refugees weren't like the ones I'd accompanied into the city before; most were armed, and many sported cybernetics. Having lived in Nova City, they knew how to protect themselves. So, trying to enslave them, while not even close to impossible, would carry with it a heavy cost.

Or maybe I was just being optimistic.

It wasn't like the hardened residents of Nova City weren't already enslaved in droves. Why would the refugees be any better off? Maybe they'd be better protected because they were on guard, but their desperation to leave the city probably negated that advantage. There was every chance that the only thing protecting these people was the fact that there were so many of them. With that many options, the vast majority would be ignored in favor of the real gems. The beautiful ones. The useful people. The valuable commodities.

I spat on the concrete street in disgust, which drew a few angry glares from the refugees surrounding me.

I was just fed up with Nova City, and I couldn't wait to leave it behind. When I looked at the place—when I beheld the desperate faces all around me—all I could see was oppression and enslavement. I wanted to help them, but I wasn't even sure if they were worthy of my assistance. Most wouldn't even accept it, they were so conditioned to look at the world through a lens of suspicion. And the few who would take my help would probably do so with an eye on betraying me the moment I had my back turned.

Nova City was a cesspool of human misery, selfishness, and despair.

I saw that now. Beneath the glitz and glamour of those flashing holograms, daring fashion, and impressive technological advances, it was everything that was wrong with the world.

No wonder my uncle had said that the aliens were destined to take over. Even if humanity somehow developed the ability to properly resist, we were too selfish to come together and work for the common good. Divide and conquer was a basic tenant of warfare, but in this case, the aliens didn't even have to worry about dividing us. We did that to ourselves, driven by our very nature to discard the greater good in favor of our own personal enrichment.

Or survival, I supposed.

I was no better than anyone else, either. That was the worst part of it. I knew I should've done things differently. I'd been given great power, and I knew I could make a difference. A small one, sure, but a difference all the same. But I'd chosen a different path. I was just as selfish as anyone else, picking revenge over the common good.

And what's worse, I knew it was the wrong choice. I knew that I should've tried to help people. But in the face of everything I'd seen in Nova City, I knew it wouldn't do much good. One person, regardless of how powerful, couldn't fight an entire system.

Not without tearing it all down.

I shook my head and turned my attention to the coming journey. Before leaving the compound, I'd had Patrick store all our ammunition and enough supplies to last us for a few months within his own storage space. We'd even brought a few creature comforts, like cots and tents, as well as a couple of portable autoturrets. They weren't terribly high-quality—I expected that they couldn't even get through the infiltration suit, much less my skin or my subdermal Sheath. But that was fine. They wouldn't be used for defense; rather, they were an early-warning system combined with a distraction for any monsters that might come upon us in the night.

There were better options to secure a location, but they were expensive, both in terms of credits and upkeep. And I just couldn't afford the cost, which was one of the reasons I'd chosen to get out of Nova City for a while.

I could have probably stolen what I needed, but not without leaving a trail. With the ongoing tribal war, everyone was on high alert, which meant that stealing from them would probably result in me being exposed. I wasn't ready to put my plans at risk just for a few credits. Not yet.

Couple that with my disgust with the city, as well as the potential payday that would come with completing another Rift, and leaving Nova seemed like the best option. Of course, it wouldn't be without its own dangers. Not only would we have to traverse the wilderness—avoiding all the dangers it presented—but clearing the Rift was no trivial matter. Even finding it wasn't altogether guaranteed, even if I'd managed to acquire a little information that I hoped would point me toward the Dead Zone itself.

But we had a lot of ground to cover before we got to that point. More importantly, we had to take the first step of our trip, which was to get out of Nova City. To that end, we stood in line, shuffling forward every few minutes as people were allowed onto the lift. It was a long, arduous process, and judging by the number of people behind us, it wasn't going to end anytime soon. Probably not ever.

The worse things got in Nova, the more people would try to leave. And the lifts acted as bottlenecks, slowing everything down. Great for security, but not so good for efficiency.

Eventually, we reached the front of the line, where we were eyed by a pair of Enforcers. Dressed in their black-and-white uniforms, they looked just like every other Enforcer I'd ever seen. However, what set them apart was the sense of bored apathy that hung from their shoulders like a cloak. They'd been at it for too long to care anymore—much to my benefit, given that they weren't alone. There were eight other Enforcers nearby, and they were all armed with assault rifles. Given half an excuse, they'd cut the vulnerable crowd to pieces.

After another ten minutes, the lift rose into view and locked into place. Only then were we allowed forward, crowding onto the metal surface right up to the edge. There were guardrails there, but they looked flimsy, like they would collapse at the slightest application of pressure. I didn't want to be anywhere near the edge, so Patrick and I planted ourselves a few rows back.

And then, once it was full, one of the Enforcers flipped a huge lever, and the lift began its descent. Creaking and screeching, it sounded like it was only a hair's breadth from falling apart. But thankfully, we made the trip unscathed, and after we disembarked from the lift, it rose once again.

I took that opportunity to look around, and I saw exactly what I'd expected to see. The area around the base of the lift was occupied by a series of storage containers made of plasti-steel. Those would be the temporary bases of operation for the leaders of the convoys. Beyond, there were tents, in which I expected to find a rudimentary market where refugees could buy basic supplies. And just past that, I saw the convoys themselves.

Mostly, the convoys were comprised of rugged trucks that were originally meant to transport goods. I pitied the people who would be confined to those miserably cramped quarters, but it was also probably the most efficient way to move as many people as possible. It wouldn't be comfortable, but that didn't count for much next to the opportunity for a little more profit.

There were also a fair few military-esque vehicles that were probably supposed to act as escorts for the convoys. I was skeptical that they could do the job, given that each one of them was just a converted transport truck. Sure, they had some extra armor that had been crudely welded to the sides, and each one sported at least one cannon, but I knew just how ineffective that kind of thing could be against some of the more dangerous denizens of the wilds.

Of course, none of that mattered to the refugees. Even if they knew how poorly prepared those convoys were, they didn't have much of a choice in the matter. Staying in Nova City was even worse than braving the dangers of the natural world. At least that was what they thought. I couldn't help but wonder if they'd come to regret their decision to leave the familiar dangers of the city in favor of the unknown threats they would undoubtedly encounter in the wilderness.

Not to mention that I felt confident that none of the other cities were much better. Nova was a representation of the way the world was, and I couldn't imagine that any other major city would have escaped that reality unscathed. These refugees were just trading one set of terrible circumstances for something that was probably just as bad.

But I couldn't save them.

Nor did I really want to. I did pity them, though.

In any case, I grabbed Patrick's wrist and pulled him aside. Once we'd moved outside the flow of traffic exiting the lift, he asked, "Where do you think they're going?"

"I don't care," I said. "Most of them won't even make it, and those that do aren't going to be much better off. If at all."

"That's a cynical way of looking at it," he said, shaking his head.

"I've earned my cynicism a thousand times over," I stated. "Here, let's hole up for a few hours until it gets dark. Then, we can slip out without anyone seeing us."

Patrick looked around, and with a lowered voice, he asked, "You think people are looking for us?"

"No. Not us specifically, at least. But if we're seen going off on our own, it'll probably get people asking questions," I said. If I'd been alone, I could have gotten away using Stealth and Camouflage, but with Patrick tagging along, that was impossible. Perhaps his abilities would help, but they were untested, and I didn't want to depend on them. It was much better to slip out under the cover of darkness.

For the next few hours, we visited the various tents, buying a few things here and there. We already had supplies, but we were playing the role of refugees. So, it would have been noteworthy if we didn't buy some supplies. We also spoke to a few caravan leaders, and the situation turned out just as I'd expected. Some of them were better than others, but all of them were in it for profit. A few even offered spots in their caravans in exchange for indenture, which I knew would almost assuredly become true slavery.

Because that was how people worked. The moment these people were any significant distance from the city, they would be vulnerable. Some caravan leaders were honest, and they'd stick to the deals they'd made. However, just as many would probably shake their passengers down. Some might even just kill them, take whatever they had, and return to the camp for another batch.

Thankfully, I had no intention of dealing with any of them. Not really. But Patrick and I did speak to a few, playing our parts as well as we could manage.

Like that, we spent the hours until nightfall, and when the sun finally set, we slipped through the shadows and fled the camp. Once we were a few miles away, I summoned my Cutter, and we set off to the north, using the crumbling highways to speed us on our way.

For the rest of that night, I kept Observation flared. I didn't want a repeat of what had happened outside of Biloxi, when I'd been ambushed by a horde of wildlings. But nothing assaulted us, and we made decent time.

More than once, we encountered fallen bridges and were forced to backtrack in order to find intact routes across streams, lakes, and marshes. And the roads were overgrown enough that we couldn't travel at much more than an idle. But even with that, that first night saw us leaving Nova City far behind.

We stayed in an abandoned house that I thought had probably been old, even before the Initialization. Beneath all the grime and the vines covering the building's facade, it had been painted white. At a couple of stories tall, with thick columns and a peaked roof, it was easy to imagine that it had once been a majestic structure—especially surrounded as it was by ancient oak trees.

But that image was ruined by the fact that half of the building had been crushed by a fallen aircraft. The vehicle was very different than what I'd come to expect, with broad wings and a sleek fuselage.

"It's an airplane," said Patrick. "Remy tried to explain how they worked. Something about lift, air pressure, and speed. I didn't really understand it, if I'm honest. Modern ships are a lot less complicated, what with Mist and all."

I shrugged. "They had to work with what they had available, I guess," I said.

Then, we headed inside, where we found a secure room to make camp. That night, Patrick tried to make a move, but I shut him down. Despite the night we'd shared, I didn't want to complicate the trip with romance. In fact, I regretted my moment of weakness for that very reason. Perhaps it was silly of me—there was part of my mind that was screaming at me to stop being an idiot and to take whatever pleasure I could get out of the world—but I resisted. Even if I did want to let it progress, it wouldn't have been in the center of a steadily rotting house. I had more respect for intimacy than that.

Or maybe I was just scared of letting myself get too close. After all, when I'd gone down that road in the past, everyone had either died or betrayed me. And given the nature of my life, it wasn't a leap to expect it to happen again. I could protect myself well enough—and if I failed, then I wouldn't be around to regret it—but with others? That was different. The burden of keeping someone like Patrick safe would run the risk of derailing my plans.

And that wasn't the worst that could happen.

How would I react if he ended up dead because of me? I didn't want to consider it.

So, I focused on my mental exercises, less for the training itself and more for the distraction it represented. Fortunately, Patrick took the hint and, after setting up his cot, went to sleep.

I might've imagined it, but it felt a little like he was sulking. Or maybe he was just confused. I don't know, and right then, I didn't want to explore it any further.

The rest of the night passed without incident, and the next morning, we resumed our journey north. The next few days passed in similar fashion, and though we were making progress through the wilderness, it wasn't nearly as much as I'd hoped. However, midway through the morning of our fifth day outside of Nova City, we encountered something that took my breath away.

The road cut off only twenty feet ahead of us, giving way to a huge crater that was absolutely filled with abandoned and rusted tanks. But that wasn't what drew my eye. Instead, I couldn't tear my gaze away from the skeleton at the center of the crater. It was at least fifty yards long—probably bigger—and it reminded me of the alligator I'd fought during my first trip outside of Nova City.

But it was subtly different. More sinuous. And far bigger.

I couldn't be sure, but that skeleton brought to mind a mythical creature. Certainly, I knew it was probably just some grossly mutated reptile, but looking at the size of the skeleton and taking in its imposing nature, I couldn't think of it as anything but a dragon.

Thankfully, it was dead.

But the question remained—if one of them had existed, who was to say that there weren't more out there?

CHAPTER FORTY-FOUR

BATTLEFIELD

In an effort to placate the Coyotes, I had to kill Wash. Executed him in front of half the tribe. It was so easy; the man wasn't exactly friendly, so nobody was willing to speak up for him. Not against me, at least. I just hope it's enough to show Roberto that Wash's actions weren't endorsed by the Specters.

—Nora Lancaster

I stood at the edge of the clearing, clutching my assault rifle in a white-knuckled grip as I beheld the destroyed landscape before me. The crater was at least a hundred feet deep, with sharply sloped sides that were miles apart. It took me a few minutes to realize why I found the scene so disturbing, but when I finally understood why, it took my breath away.

"There's nothing alive down there," I muttered.

Upon closer inspection, I saw that the tanks weren't just rusted out. Some were almost completely destroyed, with bits and pieces having been ripped away by some incredible force. Most were still intact, though because of their obvious age, they were completely inoperable, and many had been overturned and flipped onto their sides.

Other vehicles were in evidence, as well. I recognized the remains of a few armored personnel carriers and dozens of downed ancient aircraft. Their wings were broken, and their fuselages bore dozens of holes, making it difficult to even recognize what they had once been. I also saw the remains of heavy artillery, but they were scattered across the battlefield, suggesting that they'd been thrown aside by some unknown force.

Even among the other odd sights, the huge skeleton drew the bulk of my attention. In addition to the expected white of bone on the skeleton, there was a good deal of metal, as well. I'd seen something similar in a few monsters I'd fought, so that wasn't such a surprise. What was shocking was its size, though. To date, the biggest monster I had seen was the alligator I'd fought while traveling from Nova City to Mobile, but this skeleton's size made that huge creature look like a mundane gecko. It had once been as big as a building—a frightening prospect.

"Remy told me about this," Patrick spoke up from beside me.

"He did?" I asked, glancing at my companion. His face reflected my own emotions, with shock, awe, and fear dancing across his features.

He swallowed hard, nodding as he said, "Before the Initialization, people had developed some very damaging weapons. Bombs that could destroy everything for miles. So, when it became clear that their other weapons weren't useful for fighting the mutated creatures, that's where they turned. This . . . this is the result."

My jaw dropped. With my skills and abilities, I could create a truly fearsome explosion. What would I be capable of with such a destructive bomb? If it could destroy so much even before the Initialization took full root, what could it do with my modifiers?

"What happened to them?" I asked.

"Some of them were used," he answered. "Others were confiscated by the aliens. But at some point, what was left just stopped working. Something about the Mist interfering with that kind of thing. The way Remy described it, it was a good thing, too. Otherwise, they'd have killed everyone and everything. These bombs, they don't just explode and kill everything. They poison the earth until nothing can even grow there."

"How?"

He shrugged. "Remy called it something, but honestly, I didn't really believe him about any of it. It sounded so . . . unreal. I mean, if someone told me they had a bomb that could do that much damage now, I might believe it. But pre-Initialization?"

"I know. It . . . it doesn't seem possible," I said. Then, I gestured to the old battlefield, adding, "But I guess that kind of speaks for itself, huh? I don't know anything else that could do that."

Indeed, if there was one thing I'd learned about the local flora, it was that it was indomitable. Even keeping a place like Mobile from becoming overgrown was a constant battle, so seeing a completely bare patch of ground out in the wilderness was a particularly eerie sight. Perhaps pre-Initialization humanity was more dangerous than I'd given them credit for.

"This poison, does it stick around?" I asked.

Patrick shrugged. "I have no idea," he said.

I glanced at the huge crater. I could scarcely see the edge on the other side, and I didn't know how wide it really was. So, we had a choice: either we went around, which could potentially add weeks to our journey—after all, the road we'd been following ended at the crater, which meant that we would have to go ahead on foot, at least for a while until we found another road. Or we could cut across and brave whatever poison had been left behind.

It didn't take a genius to come to the right choice.

"We should go around," I said.

"I . . . I agree," Patrick stated. His Constitution was much lower than mine, and he didn't have the advantage of abilities like Regeneration or Resistance to protect him. So, it wasn't a surprise that he wanted nothing to do with whatever had kept the vegetation from growing within the crater.

"But I want to look around for a bit," I said. "Just on the edges, and not for long. Maybe thirty minutes or—"

"What is that?" he asked, pointing into the crater.

I whipped my attention in that direction, but for a moment, I didn't see what he meant. Then, I did.

And I desperately wished I hadn't.

The ground a hundred or so yards into the crater had begun to shift.

"Uh . . ."

"Run!" I shouted, seeing something humanoid erupt from the earth. I only had a moment to see that it looked like a wildling, but even more deformed than normal. It had the same unnaturally long arms and legs, but its stomach was distended, and its skin had a sickly yellow hue. But more than anything, I saw that, unlike most of the wildlings I'd seen so far, it was wearing clothes.

Or rags, really. Rotted and barely hanging on in strips, the clothing was coated in the same red dirt that covered the crater. However, with Observation running at full blast, I could see that the clothing had a camouflage pattern. And on its head was a green helmet—after a second glance, I realized that no, it wasn't on its head. Rather, it was attached, with bits and pieces of the creature's distorted skull having grown through it.

If the wildlings were disturbing, then this new creature was horrifying on an entirely different level that instantly made me feel like vomiting. But warring with that nausea was palpable fear that froze me in place, if only for a split second.

And then I reacted, shoving Patrick toward the hover bike and taking aim at the creature. As I let out burst of gunfire, I screamed, "Take the bike! Just get away from here!"

My aim was true, but at the last moment, the mutated wildling twitched to the side, avoiding my attack. The way it moved reminded me of the alpha I'd killed outside Biloxi.

"What about you?!" Patrick yelled.

"I'll be fine!" I spat, squeezing the trigger again as I quickly navigated through my HUD and gave him permission to operate the bike. Meanwhile,

I'd already begun to shift away from the road; I hoped the enemy would keep its attention on me. Patrick was another story, though, so I shouted, "Just go! I can't kill them and worry about you at the same time!"

That much was true. Patrick might be able to take care of himself against the normal threats found in the wilderness, but despite his dedication to training over the last few months, he still wasn't up to fighting something like the monster before us.

Thankfully, he didn't argue anymore and hopped onto the hover bike before speeding away. I'd have done so, too, but I had already seen how fast a wildling alpha could run. And I didn't want to chance the thing catching up to us. Instead, I aimed to take it out before it could pose that kind of threat. I'll admit that my hubris played a part, too. I had plenty of room, a whole arsenal implant full of potent weapons, and the skills to back them up. I truly believed the danger to me—if not to someone like Patrick—was minimal.

Unfortunately, the wildling wasn't alone.

Even as it broke into a shambling run that was far faster than seemed possible, a dozen more of the things burst from the ground and joined their fellow.

"Shit," I muttered, immediately second-guessing my decision to stay and fight.

But it was already done. Given how fast they were moving, I didn't have much time for regret. And besides, it was for the best. I was far better off without having to watch out for Patrick.

Aiming down my sights, I continued to fire a stream of three-round bursts, but the wildling easily avoided my attacks. It was almost as if it had a preternatural instinct and was moving before I even squeezed the trigger. But as it drew closer, the time it had to react was greatly reduced. And as it came within fifteen yards, my rounds finally connected in a spray of blood.

Or that's what I thought it was. However, it was green and glowing, so I couldn't be completely sure.

Besides, I didn't have much time to think about it before it was on top of me. Its claws flashed, and I was forced to duck, firing another burst at point-blank range. My shots took it in the bulbous stomach, and the moment they hit, it burst like a punctured cyst, showering me with green goo.

That's when the burning started.

It was like I'd just been submerged in boiling poison, and I instantly knew that if it weren't for my inflated Constitution as well as my Resistance, I would have died, then and there.

But I didn't.

I was just in agonizing pain that cut through my Pain Tolerance like nothing ever had. The only thing that had come even remotely close was when I'd been assaulted by the falling lights back in the Rift. But even that wasn't quite at the same level because I could feel bits and pieces of my skin sloughing off.

Which was all sorts of disconcerting.

Still, I kicked out, taking the monster in its spindly legs before barrel rolling away. I left a good bit of skin behind, but I didn't have time to think about it. Instead, as soon as I was a few feet away, I pushed myself to one knee and fired another few shots into the wildling.

Thankfully, that was enough to put it down, which told me a couple of things.

First, these wildlings weren't as durable as the alpha I'd fought. She'd taken the best I had to offer and kept kicking. Sure, I was a bit stronger now, but not so much that it should have made that much difference. No—the more appropriate conclusion was that these wildlings were fundamentally different than any I'd fought before.

Supporting that deduction was the fact that it seemed to have been filled with acidic poison strong enough to erode my skin and set my stomach to twisting into knots. Even as I turned on the other mutated wildlings, I felt my entire body shaking uncontrollably.

I was done playing around, though. If I was going to live through this, I needed something with a little more oomph than my assault rifle. So, I dismissed it and summoned my BMAP.

Then, I fired.

With a thump, the weapon discharged a huge explosive round. Then another. And another. I kept firing, putting six of the things in the air before the first one made contact.

When my first round hit, it did so with an enormous conflagration that, even thirty yards away, sent me flying backward until I hit the trunk of an enormous oak tree. That first explosion was followed by a second. Then a third. A fourth, fifth, and sixth—each one sending out a shock wave that battered my already injured body. My insides felt like they'd been liquified, and a handful of metal debris—presumably from the remains of a tank or some other armament—sliced into me.

Then, I fell forward onto my hands and knees, my ears ringing from the explosions, and vomited blood and whatever was left of that morning's breakfast. That definitely wasn't good.

Even so, after a shake of my head, I pushed myself to my feet and cast my gaze toward the dust cloud that had been kicked up by the series of explosions. For a few seconds, nothing moved.

But then I saw them.

Hundreds of wildlings. No—thousands.

All running forward with the shambling gait of creatures whose legs are different lengths. It seemed that the crater wasn't as devoid of life as I'd first thought. It was just that the life was of a different sort than I'd expected.

There was no way I could fight against so many. A dozen, sure. Maybe. But hundreds? Thousands? I'd run out of ammunition before I finished them off.

But what else was I going to do? In my battered state, I couldn't outrun them. Perhaps I could make it a few miles on adrenaline and attributes alone, but my injuries would soon catch up to me. As much as I'd advanced, I wasn't completely immune to internal injuries or blood loss.

Just mostly. And I felt that my wounds were pressed right up against what I could handle.

No—I had no choice but to fight, even if that fight was doomed from the very start.

The horde of mutated wildlings advanced with reckless abandon, vaulting over the debris all across the battlefield as I reloaded the BMAP. Once I'd replaced the ammunition, I slapped the cannister shut, then took aim, starting on the right and firing one round every second as I raked the weapon across the battlefield in a wide arc.

Even as explosions echoed across the battlefield, enveloping the wildlings and ripping them apart, I reloaded and repeated. It was an impressive expression of firepower—any other time, I'd have been grinning ear to ear at the mayhem—but it wasn't nearly enough. I continued my cycle until I'd run out of the valuable ordinance, then dismissed the weapon and switched to grenades.

My throwing arm wasn't quite as powerful as the BMAP, and my homemade explosives couldn't compare to the rounds I'd bought in the Bazaar. But with the surging horde of wildlings packed so closely together, it was still better than trying to pick them off with my assault rifle.

More explosions filled the air. Incendiary grenades burned the mutated wildlings to a crisp even as fragmentation grenades ripped others apart. But as many as I killed, there always seemed to be more to take their place. I'd killed dozens with my initial BMAP volley—and about half as many with my grenades—but it was barely a drop in the bucket.

I couldn't stop, though.

Re-summoning my assault rifle, I peppered the mutated soldiers with one burst after another, but it proved wildly ineffective. Certainly, I put a few of them down, but my efforts didn't even make a dent in their numbers.

I couldn't even take a breath, though. Any chance I had at escaping—slim though it was, even in the beginning—was gone. I had no choice but to fight it out.

So, I kept going until the first wave reached me.

I dodged a grotesquely mutated arm, dismissing my assault rifle and exchanging it for my nano-bladed sword. In melee, it was just a better option.

Then, I went to work, slicing through that arm with an upward strike before darting forward and aiming a sweeping attack at another creature's spindly leg. Both attacks went off without a hitch, and I went to follow up with another.

But that's when one of them landed a kick to my side.

I felt my ribs crack as I went flying into the arms of another wildling. With a quick pulse of Balance, I righted myself in midair, then sprang off of the wildling's shoulder. As I went, I brought my sword down in a wicked hack that nearly severed its neck, but I knew it wouldn't finish the mutated creature off. I couldn't stop moving, though. Any hesitation, and I would be a goner. I'd already learned that lesson, and I didn't intend to forget it.

So, I kept going, leaping, dodging, and ducking as I became a whirlwind of sword strikes. Each attack severed a limb, but even as I fought, I knew it wouldn't be enough. It couldn't be. There were too many, and I was incapable of killing them with a single strike. Even the ones whose limbs had fallen victim to my blade weren't out of the fight.

But it wasn't like I had a choice. My fate had been sealed the moment I'd erroneously decided to stand my ground.

I was in more pain than I'd ever experienced. In places, my skin had been melted from my very body. And my insides were twisting and turning, both from that poisonous green goo that had been in the first wildling's belly as well as from the internal injuries I had sustained. In short, I wasn't going to last much longer.

But I refused to give up.

After everything I had been through—the hellish training, the numerous fights for my life, and my quest for revenge, to name a few—I couldn't even consider the idea of surrender.

Instead, I fought.

I knew it was useless. I knew I was destined to die. But I didn't care. If that was how it was, then there was nothing I could do to change it. So, I resolved to take as many of the mutated monsters with me before I finally succumbed.

And succumb I would. It was only a matter of time.

CHAPTER FORTY-FIVE

END OF THE LINE

I hate people. They're all so ambitious, as if each of them thinks they can do what I do. I'm of half a mind to let them, just so I can watch as everything burns down around them.

—Nora Lancaster

My nano-bladed sword swept through the unprotected neck of a mutated wildling, biting deep and coming to a halt only after it hit the spine. One more strike, and it would have been decapitated entirely. But I couldn't spare the few seconds it would take to complete the kill; instead, I was forced to continue moving, lest I take even more wounds.

I'd lost track of how long I'd been fighting. An hour? A few minutes? It was all the same to me. I couldn't afford to think about time. Or how many more of the mutated creatures there were. Neither could I acknowledge how much my injuries had slowed me. I just had to keep fighting.

Standing and fighting had been a mistake born of arrogance. I knew the odds had been stacked against me from the very beginning, but my recent victories had given me too much confidence in my abilities. That confidence was misplaced. As powerful as I had become, the wilderness had already proven it was stronger. And if by some miracle I survived, I would do well to remember that.

In Nova City, I was a big fish in a small pond. But in the wilds? I was barely a guppy.

But I couldn't give up. I didn't have that capacity—not anymore. So, I kept going, dodging and ducking as I swept through the sea of wildlings. I was only moderately successful. Most of my attacks were shallow and wouldn't pose more than a minor inconvenience for the kill-crazed creatures.

On the other side of the coin, I made a good show of avoiding their raking claws and biting teeth. However, I was still human, and as good of a combatant as I had become, I was incapable of perfection. As a result, I took quite a few injuries along the way. Within minutes, my arm was hanging limp after nearly being ripped off by a particularly strong wildling, and I bore a hundred festering cuts all over my body. Most of their attacks didn't get through the combination of the Sheath and the infiltration suit, but the sheer volume of wounds left my skin hanging from my body in ragged strips.

Where it hadn't been melted off by that acidic concoction in the first mutated wildling's bulbous belly, I mean.

Even so, I kept going, ignoring the increasingly drastic state of my injuries. At some point, I lost my nano-sword when it got lodged in a creature's torso. I wasted no time in switching to my scattergun and filling my surroundings with lightning. As had been the case with most strong opponents, the weapon was only good for a brief stun. To finish any of them off, I was forced to yank Ferdinand II from the holster at my waist.

He was effective, and each shot exploded one of the stunned wildlings' heads. But it wasn't enough. What were nine kills amid a horde numbering in the thousands?

I didn't have time to reload, so I holstered the weapon and resorted to pugilism. My hand-to-hand abilities weren't complicated, and I wasn't the sort to leap around with spin kicks and the like, but what I lacked in grace, I made up for in sheer brutality. One Combination Punch after another, and dozens of wildlings fell before me, their limbs and bodies broken beyond mobility.

But there were always more.

I lost myself in the fight, and time grew even more muddled. I didn't have space to reload my firearms, my nano-bladed sword was lost, and my wounds continued to mount. I was going to die. I knew that, and as I fought, I made peace with my own mortality. There were a hundred things I could have done differently, a thousand little mistakes that might have made all the difference, and a few huge errors that had thrown me into such a terrible situation.

Even those thoughts fell by the wayside as the battle continued to rage.

Amid all the carnage, the Hand of God really showed its worth. As seemingly indestructible as it was, I began to favor it with my attacks. Even as the faux skin was ripped away, leaving the black-and-gold cybernetic bare, the structure of the hand was completely unharmed. And I used that to my advantage, putting every point of my Constitution attribute behind each blow. It proved an effective attack, especially powered by Combination Punch, but against the tide of mutated wildlings, my efforts were useless. At some point, fatigue would catch up to me. My injuries would continue to slow me down, and soon, I'd pass the point where I could reliably dodge the wildlings' attacks. But more than anything, I feared the moment when my Mist would run dry.

I'd rarely exhausted the Mist collected within my body, partly because I used most of my abilities sparingly. The ones I did activate more often—like Stealth and Mimic—were cheap, and the cost was barely noticeable. However, martial abilities like Combination Punch and Empowered Shot were incredibly hungry. Without my inflated Mist attribute, I'd have never been able to use them so frequently. Even my innate abilities, like Resistance, Pain Tolerance, and Regeneration took a comparatively small but constant stream of Mist to work properly.

All of that added up to mean that, in a protracted battle, I'd eventually run dry of Mist. When that happened, not only would I lose access to Combination Punch, but the passive abilities I depended on so heavily would deactivate. Even my arsenal implant would go dark until I regenerated enough Mist to power it.

In short, even if I was able to avoid a lethal attack—a tall order, under the circumstances, but possible—I would eventually exhaust the limits of my power. When that happened, I would be defenseless. When that moment came, I would die.

But as inevitable as it was, I couldn't let myself surrender to the circumstances. So, I fought as hard as I'd ever fought before. It hearkened back to hell month. Even though I'd grown much more powerful since those grueling few weeks, the single lesson it was intended to teach remained just as applicable as the day I'd learned it.

Persist.

Endure.

And outlast.

That was the whole point—to teach me my limits and show me that I could push past them. Back then, it was summed up by the simple act of continuing to put one foot in front of the other. But now? It was one more punch. One more kick. One more incapacitated wildling.

I lost myself to the rhythm of combat, completely and without reservation. I might have been fighting a losing battle, but there was still a certain beauty in the all-important theme of kill or be killed. It was simple survival boiled down to its most basic ingredient.

But willpower, though I had it in abundance, wasn't always enough, and gradually, my condition deteriorated until I was barely capable of standing on my own two feet, much less fighting a horde of monstrous mutants.

All around me there were dead wildlings, their bodies pummeled beyond recognition. Their green blood pooled on the uneven ground and coated my whole body. My fleshy hand was mangled, with acid burns and broken bones.

The Hand of God had fared much better, and it looked the same as it had when I'd first seen it in the box back in the Bazaar. Its artificial skin had been completely stripped away, though.

The rest of my body hadn't gotten off any lighter, and I knew that, even if the fight ended right then and there, I probably wouldn't survive without significant medical treatment. In more than one spot, my subdermal Sheath was completely exposed or had been ripped apart.

I was barely standing, but my brief moment of respite was enough to tell me that I wouldn't last much longer.

And I was furious.

After everything I had done, after all my careful plotting, my desire for vengeance would go unfulfilled. All because of a chance encounter. It was galling.

I glanced around, looking for some method of escape. I knew they'd run me down. The mutated wildlings were well adapted to the wilderness, and even if I was completely healthy—which I most assuredly was not—my flight would be cut short by their dogged pursuit. In any case, they had surrounded me, and my way was blocked.

But just when I was on the verge of giving up all hope of survival, my eyes alighted on my salvation.

A tank loomed only thirty yards away, and it looked to be mostly intact. If I could figure out how to get inside, perhaps it would protect me long enough for . . . something. I wasn't sure what I hoped for. The wildlings weren't likely to lose interest; despite their appearance and demeanor, they weren't animals. Their intelligence had obviously been affected by their transformation, but they were still equipped with cunning and an ability to reason that no mere animal possessed.

As a result, they wouldn't just forget where I was and move on.

Still, I was going to die if I kept going the way I was going. I knew it down to my bones. So, while hiding within a tank wasn't the solution I'd hoped for, it was probably the best option I was likely to find.

I darted forward, my injuries turning my smooth gait into more of a pained shamble. But I was still fast, and my sudden move took the wall of wildlings by surprise. I tore through them with a series of vicious attacks powered by Combination Punch and sheer momentum. Each strike broke a bone, and more than a few put already wounded mutants out of commission. I forged ahead, using my injured arms and legs like the weapons they'd become, and with glacial progress, I gradually made my way to the tank.

If I'd been healthy, I could have leaped upon the vehicle with ease. But wounded and fatigued as I was, I was forced into a scrambling climb that took far too long. Wildlings scratched and bit at my legs, but I ignored the attacks as I pulled myself up. Once there, I climbed to my feet and looked around, only to gasp at what I saw.

There weren't just hundreds of the mutated wildlings. There were thousands. Perhaps tens of thousands. Most were similar to the ones I'd fought so far, but across that ancient battlefield, I saw a few enormous creatures that towered over all the rest. They still looked humanoid, but their bodies were densely packed with muscle. They were still afflicted with the same bulbous and bloated stomachs that seemed common to the other mutated wildlings, but to my absolute horror, I could see that something writhed beneath the skin.

Even as numb as I'd become to such sights, nausea still twisted my stomach into knots.

But I didn't have time for disgust. I kicked a climbing wildling in the face, shattering its misshapen jaw and sending it to tumble from the tank. Then another. And another. Each falling creature took another with it, but despite my success, I knew it couldn't last long.

And even if it could, I knew my Mist wouldn't. Neither would my body, given how much punishment it had endured. The blood loss alone would soon be enough to push me into unconsciousness. When that happened, I needed to be somewhere safe. Or whatever passed for safety amid a horde of mutated wildlings.

With that in mind, I took a second to look down, searching for the access hatch. It didn't take long to find what I was looking for, but in that moment, another couple of wildlings had swarmed to the top of the tank. I went on the offensive, aiming not to disable them, but instead, to knock them off the tank. Once that was done, I reached down, grabbed the latch, and pulled.

If I'd had normal human strength, it would have been impossible to get the latch to budge. Fortunately, I was many times stronger than a mundane human, and after only a little effort, the latch broke free. I pulled with all my might, and with a great screech of protesting metal, it gave way. With that done, I yanked the hatch open and jumped inside, closing it behind me. With another twist of the latch, the tank's entry was sealed.

But I knew that wouldn't be enough.

The wildlings were animalistic, but I wasn't so naive as to think they couldn't turn that lever. So, flaring Observation, I found the simple lock. I flipped it, and a bar fell into place. It was a good thing, too, because only a moment later, something tried to turn the lever. With that bar in place, it was useless, though.

I sagged to the ground, the last of my Mist having been used to find the lock. One by one, my passive abilities deactivated, and with that, I felt the full extent of my injuries. Without Pain Tolerance blunting my perception of pain, I had no defense against the agony of so many wounds.

I whimpered, tears falling down my cheeks as I collapsed in on myself.

I had experienced quite a few injuries since my Awakening, but nothing on the scale of what I'd just endured. And making matters worse, I didn't have the comfort of my abilities to shield me from it. Finally, without Regeneration or Resistance, I knew my death was only a matter of time.

So, after waiting a few agonizing minutes for the tiniest bit of my Mist to recover, I activated my arsenal implant and found a simple-looking med-hypo. But instead of antibiotics and pain killers, this one was loaded with concentrated Mist.

It was colloquially known as a booster, and though it was extraordinarily expensive, I'd acquired it for just such a situation. Without hesitation, I jabbed it into my thigh, ignoring the pain as it discharged its payload.

Instantly, I was beset by a surge of adrenaline and euphoria that briefly overwhelmed the agony coursing through my body. It only lasted a few seconds until it faded, but even that was so overbearing that I very nearly blacked out. Fortunately, the moment it ceased, the agony returned in full force, almost sending me into a state of shock.

The booster did its job, though, and I recovered enough of my Mist that my passive abilities once again reactivated. Pain Tolerance cut through my agony, diminishing it just enough that I could think clearly. I used that clarity to take full stock of my body.

And it wasn't good.

In addition to my broken and mangled arm, my body had become a collection of ragged lacerations, contusions, and acid burns. My infiltration suit was in tatters, and only bits and pieces of my outer clothing had survived. Even my hair had been burned off.

After glancing at my acid burns, I had no intention of looking at my face.

Without my abilities, I knew I wouldn't have even been conscious. Even with them, I was barely holding on. Knowing that it wouldn't last for much longer, I got to work.

My first step was to retrieve another med-hypo—this one loaded with a blend of antibiotics and anesthetics—which immediately began to take effect. With that relief coursing through my veins, I began the arduous process of stripping down. Removing the infiltration suit took quite a bit of skin with it, but I gritted my teeth as I endured the pain. Even cut by the anesthetic and my ability, it was very nearly enough to send me into shock.

But I persisted, and eventually, I was naked and sitting on a blanket I'd laid out.

With trembling hands, I upended a jug of water I'd had stored in my implant, washing away whatever remained of the acidic green substance as well as the blood and bits of flesh that had coated my body. Tears streamed down my cheeks as the water flowed over my damaged skin, but I couldn't do anything but endure.

I was forced to use another pain-relieving med-hypo, though.

Once I was reasonably clean, I coated my body in foam bandages. I knew it wasn't ideal, but I also knew that burns—from either acid or fire—were notorious for getting infected. And while I hoped my Regeneration and Resistance would prevent that, I wasn't ready to trust it just yet.

Meanwhile, the wildlings continued to assault the tank, filling the air with the screeching sound of claws against metal. But it had been built to last—after all, it had survived the explosion that had left the huge crater—so their efforts were in vain. I was safe for now.

After spending a good deal of time treating my wounds, I took the time to reload my weapons. Then, I let myself relax. With two doses of powerful anesthetic flowing through me, it was all I could do to keep my eyes open. And with my immediate survival assured, I finally let unconsciousness overtake me.

I don't know how long I slept. Minutes. Maybe hours. But I jerked awake some undetermined amount of time later when an ear-splitting screech of metal on metal filled my ears. I was awake and aware in an instant, summoning my rifle and aiming it at the hatch.

Because I saw a sliver of daylight peeking through, which shouldn't have been possible in the sealed space.

But more than anything, I noticed that the wildlings had gone silent. Before I could react further, the metal hatch flew open. I wasted no time on pointless thought, instead bringing my weapon to my shoulder.

Then, something appeared in the opening.

I fired before I took the time to gauge the threat. Metal flashed, and my mind caught up with the situation. That's when I saw that my attacker wasn't one of the mutated wildlings. Instead, it was a bald man wearing a bemused expression.

"Ah, you might want to put some clothes on," he said, his cheeks turning red.

I was so shocked that it took me a second to realize what he'd said. Still, I didn't have the energy to be embarrassed. In fact, I was still in so much pain that I could scarcely think. And now that the danger seemed to have passed, the spike of adrenaline that had awakened me faded, and unconsciousness overtook me once again.

CHAPTER FORTY-SIX

MIRACLES NEVER CEASE

When I drove through the Garden today, it felt so empty. I feel so alone. No friends. No family. Just a bunch of people who've latched on to me like leeches. All they care about is whether or not I can help them with their own goals. None of them care about me. Not as a person, at least. Instead, I'm just a means to an end.

—Nora Lancaster

By the time my eyes fluttered open, night had fallen. I was lying on my back, with my arms at my sides, held in place by some sort of flimsy straps. I could've easily broken them, which told me they weren't really there for the purpose of imprisonment. Rather, they were just meant to keep me from flailing about too much.

For a long moment, I stared up at the night sky, appreciating the silvery light of the moon and stars. However, that only lasted a few seconds before my mind truly caught up with my situation. In a flood, my memory came back, washing away any sense of peace or contentment, and I bolted upright.

I gasped in surprise at what I found.

For one, Patrick, whom I expected to be halfway back to Nova City by that point, was sitting by my side like a protective puppy. Not that I'd ever had a pet of any sort—nobody in the Garden did—but I'd seen them on various entertainment feeds growing up. Apparently, the rich elites weren't under the same kinds of restrictions that kept the poor from owning pets.

In any case, Patrick's presence was only the first of many surprises. When I turned my head, I saw nothing but people clothed in all white. Most wore simple tunics with loose pants, but there were a few wearing curious robes. All were stark white, though, which marked them as Templars. It didn't take me long to recognize the area as a temporary camp, what with the tents, campfires, and the general atmosphere.

Patrick reached out, gripping my arm as he said, "Take it easy. They only finished healing you a few hours ago."

"Huh?" was my confused response. Unless I'd been in a coma, there was no way I could have been healed so quickly. No matter how much time had passed, those acid burns hadn't been simple. A few had gone down to the very bone. It would have taken months to recover from something like that, even with Regeneration speeding my convalescence.

Which meant that something was wrong.

I pulled my hands out of the straps and sat up. As I did so, the blanket that had covered me fell away, revealing my naked torso. By reflex, my arm found its way across my chest, but maintaining my modesty was quickly forgotten when I saw my arm.

It was in pristine condition. No burns. No bandages. I didn't even see any scars, which was so shocking that I could scarcely even think. During the fight with the mutated wildlings, I'd been too busy trying to stay alive to take stock of my injuries, but even then, I knew that, even if I managed to survive, I wouldn't do so without significant scarring. Once I was safe inside the tank, I'd tried to ignore that reality, but the thought had remained nestled in the back of my mind nonetheless.

But now? Now, I saw that I'd somehow avoided that fate, and as best I could without a mirror—or without exposing myself even further—I inspected my body. And what I saw was more of the same. Perfect, unmarred skin. Even the Realskin that hid the Hand of God had been replaced.

"What the . . ."

"The patient awakens, huh?" came a feminine voice that broke through my turbulent thoughts. I looked up to see a short, compact figure standing over me. From her voice, I guessed that she was a woman, and she stood with the kind of easy confidence that came from knowing you're the most capable person in any room. Or any city. She knelt beside me, asking, "How are you doing?"

Like everyone else in the area—aside from Patrick and me, at least—she was wearing all white, marking her as a Templar. Once she'd lowered herself to my level, I saw that her face was pretty enough, though her prominent nose probably kept her from being beautiful. If I was forced to describe her in one word, I would have labeled her striking.

"Mira," said Patrick. "This is the healer, Isla."

"Battle healer," said the woman, as if the distinction was the most important thing in the world. "But whatever. How are you feeling?"

"Uh . . . good? Maybe. I don't know," I said, blushing as I pulled the blanket up to cover my chest. "I . . . I shouldn't . . . I don't understand what's going on."

She let out a hearty laugh. "Fair enough," Isla said, running a hand through her long auburn hair. "I'd be a bit confused, too, if I were you. So, here's the thing. One of our scouts ran into your boyfriend, who was screaming through the woods on the sweetest hover bike I've ever seen. He was going on and on about a horde of mutants. Well, we know the area pretty well, so we figured somebody had stumbled onto that old battlefield. So, Zachariah ran off to rescue you."

"Zachariah?"

"Bald guy. Uses a giant axe. Constantly muttering about fractals or some such?" Isla said.

It took me a moment to remember my rescuer. Almost as if summoned by my thoughts, the man himself appeared. My first thought was that he wasn't as physically impressive as I might have expected from the kind of guy who could deal with a horde of those mutated wildlings. But my second thought was that he seemed incredibly powerful. It was almost as if the Mist itself had congealed around him. Other than that, he seemed like an average—if completely bald—guy.

"You were a decimeter away from kicking the bucket," he said, kneeling next to Isla. "I was afraid you wouldn't make it, even after I crammed a few healing pills into your mouth. My Dao heart can rest easy now that you are well."

Isla rolled her eyes and backhanded Zachariah on the arm. "Those things aren't healing pills, you meathead! You're lucky they didn't kill her!"

He shrugged his shoulders, saying, "They work for me."

"Because you're too stupid to let something like poisonous, Mist-infused mushrooms and the like kill you," she muttered.

Zachariah replied, "If it isn't broken . . ."

"You're broken," Isla mumbled.

"Uh . . . guys . . . Where are my clothes?" I asked.

"Huh? Oh. Clothes," Isla said. "Yeah, I could see why you might want those. That suit you had is top quality. Shame it's ruined, though."

"What?! Ruined?" I half screamed, getting the attention of everyone in the area. I took a breath, then lowered my voice. "It self-repairs. I just need to feed it some Mist."

"Really? Wish we had something like that," Isla said, shaking her head. "Stupid Templars and their stupid rules. What I wouldn't give for some actual freaking armor. Like, a mech suit or something. With huge fists and—"

"You know that won't work with us," interjected Zachariah. He ran his hand over his bald head, saying, "We tread a different path. The Dao won't—"

"Oh, shut up about the stupid Dao," Isla said, obviously annoyed. She'd clearly had the same conversation before. "That's how it always is with you. Dao this. Dao that."

"It's my path."

"It's cultural appropriation is what it is," Isla countered.

"Guys, can you just tell me what's going on?" I asked. "I mean, after that, you can argue all you want. But I don't know where I am. I don't know who you are. And I have no idea what you're going to do with me."

I felt fairly certain that they didn't intend me harm. After all, they'd saved my life. Besides, I hadn't forgotten Frederick, the Templar I'd met on my way back from my first Rift. He'd been kind to me, and I was predisposed toward thinking that these people would follow that pattern, despite their curious idiosyncrasies. And their obvious tendency toward bickering.

"At least I don't go around punching things," Zachariah said under his breath. Without Observation, I probably wouldn't have been able to hear him.

Meanwhile, Isla spoke up. "Okay, so here's the deal. You're about twenty miles north of where Zachariah found you. So, that puts us about fifty miles from the Dead Zone. That's where your friend said you were going, right? You wanted to challenge the Rift."

"Uh . . ."

I didn't really know how to respond to that. Certainly, I had no interest in revealing my plans to complete strangers, but it seemed that Patrick had already beaten me to the punch. I didn't want to blame him—after all, he'd probably saved my life, or at least my looks, by finding help—but I couldn't help but feel a little annoyed.

But then I considered things from his perspective. He'd probably been scared out of his mind—both for me and for his own life—and he'd let his mouth run a little. I wasn't so callous that I couldn't understand the effect fear could have on a person. On top of that, there was every chance he'd been coerced. Or maybe these Templars had the ability to read minds. They were a complete mystery, but the stories had always agreed about one thing: they were powerful.

"Well, you had the misfortune of coming across that horrible place," Isla went on. "Most of us know to avoid that battlefield. I'm not sure how it happened, but those things are extremely strong."

"Immortal, too," interjected Zachariah.

"They're not immortal," Isla said. "They just don't age while they're hibernating underground."

"Same difference."

"I'm not going to argue with you," she said with a long-suffering sigh. "My point is that you had no way of knowing that you were walking into a death trap."

"Did you kill them all?" I asked.

Isla chuckled. "Oh, no. Even all of us together couldn't handle that," she stated. "After Zachariah snatched you up, we cut and run. Thankfully, they won't go more than a mile from the crater."

My heart skipped a beat. "So, if I'd have just gotten on the bike with Patrick..."

"They would've given up the chase," provided Zachariah.

Isla rolled her eyes and slapped him on the shoulder. "Don't be like that," she said. "She didn't know."

"I feel like I'm going to be sick," I muttered, my stomach twisting into knots.

"That would be Zachariah's healing pills," Isla said. "I cleansed most of the impurities, but... Well, some remained."

"Makes you stronger," he said. "Natural treasures open your mind to the Dao, and—"

"It might make you stronger, but you're a freaking unkillable tank who..."

I stopped listening. I'd almost gotten killed—no, I should have been killed—all because of my own ignorance. And arrogance. It was galling, really. I'd thought I had learned my lesson after the encounter with the wildling alpha outside of Biloxi, but clearly, it hadn't really sunk in. The problem was that, in Nova City, I felt almost invincible. There were so few people in the Garden who could really threaten me, and they were easy enough to avoid that I'd not really been challenged for a while. The wilderness was different, though. Not only were there the dangers I knew about—like the wildlings and the wildlife—but there were clearly plenty of which I was completely ignorant. And if I kept charging ahead as if I was invincible, I would end up in some monster's belly.

But I also couldn't afford to be too cautious. My plans depended on me getting stronger. Sure, I could probably get my revenge in my current state, but what then? The aliens were still coming sooner rather than later. And I knew they weren't going to be pushovers. If I became complacent, I would end up enslaved or dead. And I couldn't stomach that.

Still, I knew that, while I couldn't afford to stop taking risks, I needed to be smarter about how far I pushed. It was a fine line, and one I knew would be difficult to walk.

"So, what now?" I asked, still clutching the blanket around me. It was thin protection, and I was keenly aware of my nudity. Still, no one else seemed to care; curiously, I didn't feel any leering gazes like so often followed me around in Nova. So, I pushed my discomfort to the back of my mind. "Are we prisoners or something?"

"Gods, no," Isla said. "That would mean we had to take care of you. Most of these people can barely take care of themselves, much less guests."

"Speak for yourself," grumbled Zachariah. "I'm fine surviving on my own. Did I ever tell you about the time I dove into a pool of liquified Mist and—"

"Yes. I know all your stories," Isla interrupted. Then, she looked at me, adding, "Look—Templars are weird. It's the Mist. Each and every one of us has been affected in some way, and it makes us... I don't know... Some people would call us crazy, I guess. My point is that, aside from the mandates of our order, most of us aren't too concerned with people like you. Sure, we'll fight to protect you, but actually managing things? Or gods forbid, taking care of anyone? It's just not in our nature."

"You talk about it like you're a different species or something," said Patrick, finally finding his voice.

Isla shrugged. "In a way, we are," she said. "Templars aren't that different from the wildlings. Sure, we maintain our sense of self, and we don't show external mutations. But we're also not completely human. The Mist changes everything. Your Nexus Implants slow things down and make it less dangerous, but you're still being changed. Most people on this planet won't ever get the chance to see how much, but that's kind of why we're here. To give people that opportunity."

"Too much, Isla," Zachariah said.

Isla shrugged her shoulders. "Whatever. It's not like anyone's paying attention to us right now," she said, rolling her eyes. "But fine." Then, to me, she added, "Just know that you're on the right track. The Mist already clings to you. It won't be long before you start to manifest an aura."

"What's an aura?" asked Patrick, giving voice the question on the tip of my tongue.

"A manifestation of your willpower," Isla answered. She glanced up at the sky. "I . . . I don't think I should say more."

"But—"

"Drop it, Patrick," I said. "She's under some sort of restrictions. Kind of like getting any meaningful information about the rest of the universe from Gala and the rest of them up in the Bazaar is almost impossible. They'll sell us stuff, and they'll give us a few tidbits here and there, but nothing that really matters." I looked at Isla and asked, "That about right?"

"Close enough," she said with a small smile.

Zachariah asked, "Do you still intend to challenge the Rift?"

I nodded. "Probably," I said. "Why? Want to come?"

"Can't."

"Huh?"

"We can't," he said. "It's one of our tenets. No Rifts unless specifically authorized by our parent organization."

"I don't understand," I admitted.

He shrugged but didn't elaborate. But Isla said, "Part of the support we get from the Templars—the real ones that aren't allowed on this planet yet—is contingent on noninterference. Sure, we can help people here and there, but if we make too big of a splash, bad things are going to happen. And us going into Rifts without their approval will definitely make a splash."

"Oh," I said. I didn't really understand galactic—or universal, maybe—politics, but I didn't really need to. I'd gotten the information I needed. As strong as they were, they had rules. And those rules said the help they could give us was limited. They were probably already pushing it by healing me.

"You can stay with us for a couple of days," Isla said. "We're taking some new recruits into the Dead Zone."

They had no way of knowing it, but Frederick had already told me the dangers of exposing the new recruits to enough Mist to spark their development. Some would be successful. Others would be lost, many of which would become wildlings just like everyone else who didn't have a Nexus Implant. Even if I wanted to see the process, I had no desire to see the unlucky ones who failed.

My memories of Heather—yet another failure on my part—were too fresh.

"No, thanks," I said. "I . . . I think it's best if we leave in the morning."

"Fair enough," Isla replied. Then, she hiked her thumb in the direction of the tent behind her, saying, "Your stuff's in there. I'm sure you want to get dressed. Zachariah even managed to find your sword."

"Yeah. Thanks," I said. "Anything you can tell us about the Rift?"

"It's being mined by Octavangians," she said. "Eight appendages with these moving claws that rip everything to shreds. Faces like mutated squid. They spit poison, too. Nasty stuff, if it gets on you. Not as bad as the fluid from those mutated wildlings' gut sacs, but not something you want on you. Probably only five or six of them there that could pose a threat to you, so if I were you, I'd hang back a bit, get the lay of the land, and pick your first targets carefully. Once the big ones are out of commission, the rest will go down without much difficulty."

"Do they use slaves?" I asked.

She shook her head. "No. Octavangians don't trust any other race enough for that," she stated. "Just . . . when you hit 'em, you better hit 'em hard. They're fast and strong and can be a pain in the ass to take down. So, make the first attacks count."

"I think I can do that," I said with a small smile. "Anything else? What's the Rift like?"

"Not a clue," she said. "I've only ever been allowed inside two Rifts, and neither of 'em are around here."

"Fair enough," I said. "Anything else I should know?"

"Not off the top of my head."

Patrick, who'd remained silent for a while, asked, "Is she healed, though? I . . . I don't want her to . . . you know, push it too far."

"She's in perfect health," Isla stated. "You've got the battle-healer stamp of approval."

Zachariah chuckled at that. "You and your battle-healer nonsense," he said, shaking his head. "You'd be way more valuable just staying on the back lines and healing the other warriors."

"But what's the fun in that?" she asked.

"You got me there," he agreed. "Can't imagine anything worse than standing back and not fighting."

I just shook my own head, wondering just how crazy these people were. Sure, I was reckless, but my own attitude was nothing compared to these two battle maniacs. But perhaps there was something to it. They certainly seemed freer than anyone else I'd met.

As the pair continued their good-natured bickering, I gathered the blanket around me and retreated into the tent they'd set aside for me. There, I found what was left of my tattered clothing as well as the infiltration suit. As I picked it up, noticing the huge gashes in the garment, I sighed. Hopefully, it was still salvageable. Whatever the case, even as compromised as it was, it could provide some protection. So, after putting on some underwear I had in my arsenal implant, I slipped the suit on. After that, I donned some black fatigues and a matching tee-shirt.

I let out another breath as I sat on the ground inside the tent. Hopefully, the next fight would go better than the one in that crater. I needed to make better decisions, or I'd end up dead before I had the chance to see my plans to fruition.

CHAPTER FORTY-SEVEN

MOVING ON

Someone is behind it all. I can feel it in my bones. I don't know whom, and I don't know how, but someone is trying to push Nova City into chaos. And it's working, at least in the lower districts. Algiers is on the verge of collapse. The Garden is a war zone. And it's even spilled over into Bywater. It's only a matter of time before everything comes crashing down.

—Nora Lancaster

The next morning, I awoke feeling healthier and better rested than I had in months, perhaps since leaving Mobile on the final test that saw me assaulting my first Rift. Like everyone else who grew up in Nova City, I was aware of the rumors surrounding the Templars. According to the stories, they were supposed to wield incredible and unexplainable powers. And ever since I'd gotten my Nexus Implant, I'd been inclined to believe those rumors. However, I'd expected them to function like everyone else, channeling Mist through various skills to create results that seemed like magic.

But the experience with Isla had made me rethink that. At the end of my fight against the mutated wildlings, I'd been on the precipice of death. With most of my body covered in acid burns, multiple broken bones, and more wounds than I could count, even my enhanced Constitution, Regeneration ability, and the high-quality med-hypos I'd used were incapable of fully healing me. At best, I'd have survived, but with huge swaths of my skin deformed by scarring from the acid burns.

That wasn't what had happened, though.

When I rose from the cot and gathered a mirror from my arsenal implant, I found that my skin was absolutely pristine. No scarring. No bruises. No half-healed wounds. It was as if I'd never fought at all. Even a few old scars from previous battles were gone. My complexion looked healthier than it had in some time, too. In short, I was in pristine condition, and only a day after I'd sustained enough injuries to kill most people a dozen times over.

That told me all I needed to know about Isla—and by extension, the Templars in general. The ones that survived being inundated with Mist without the benefit of Nexus Implants were capable of shocking things, and I would do well to remember that going forward. It did make me curious about their martial abilities, though. If Isla could heal so thoroughly, then what about the more battle-focused Templars?

That brought to mind Zachariah, the bald man who'd saved me. As far as I knew, he'd done so alone. He'd cut through that horde of mutated wildlings—the same one that had overwhelmed and forced me to retreat—to rescue me. That was arguably just as impressive as Isla's healing.

I suppressed a shudder. No—the Templars were not to be trifled with.

However, it did beg the question of why, with all their power, they hadn't done more. They'd mentioned that they weren't allowed to exert undue influence, but where was the line? Surely, they could have done something to combat the rampant oppression and enslavement of their people. Then again, I didn't have any room to judge. I'd actively chosen not to help plenty of people. Certainly, I had an excuse in the form my vendetta against Nora, but it was flimsy in the face of all the human suffering I had seen.

All the pain I had personally caused.

I shook my head and pushed those thoughts from my mind. They weren't useful, and it wasn't as if I was going to abandon my quest for revenge now. Not after spending so much time and expending so much effort in its pursuit. There was nowhere for me to go but straight ahead. Anything else, and I don't know if I could survive the lack of forward momentum.

With a sigh, I retrieved a few sanitary wipes I had stored in my arsenal implant and cleaned myself as best as the situation would allow. It wasn't as good as taking an actual shower, but it still helped. At least someone had bathed me during my first bout of unconsciousness; otherwise, the wipes wouldn't have been up to the task of removing all the filth of my ill-fated battle against the mutated wildlings.

Once I had achieved some semblance of cleanliness, I addressed the issue of the integrity of my Sheath. It had assuredly regenerated a little in the time since the battle, but according to its listing I pulled up on my HUD, it was down to forty-three percent effectiveness. That wouldn't do, so I grabbed one of my limited stock of Mist boosters from my arsenal implant and injected the hypo into my hip. Twin hisses—one from the hypo as it discharged its payload and one that escaped from between my lips—filled the air. It wasn't painful—not really—but the cold numbness that spread from the point of injection was decidedly uncomfortable. Thankfully, it would soon fade.

I nodded as I saw the integrity of my Sheath tick up a few percentage points. The booster wouldn't immediately restore the subdermal armor to perfect condition; instead, it would take at least twenty-four hours before it was repaired. Hopefully, I wouldn't need it before then.

Next, I turned my attention to my infiltration suit. I'd put it on the night before, hoping that it would repair more quickly if I was wearing it, but when I gave it an inspection, I was sorely disappointed. The thing was in tatters, and that was after a full night's worth of its self-repair feature going to work. If I wanted it restored, I'd need to use another one of my Mist boosters.

Which posed a problem.

I'd only acquired five of them, so if I used another, it would only leave two for the Rift. And after my first experience in a Rift, I suspected that would be insufficient. Even five would be pushing it.

So, I had a choice to make. Either I could use the booster immediately and have the protection of the infiltration suit for the journey to the Rift, or I could wait and let the suit's self-repair work as intended. The first would be safer, but it would cost one of my precious boosters. The second would be riskier, but having that extra booster available for the Rift might make all the difference.

In the end, though, I chose to use the booster. I'd already made the mistake of underestimating the wilderness's ability to put me in the ground, and I had no interest in making that mistake again. Certainly, I hoped that the journey to and through the Dead Zone would be uneventful, but I had no guarantees of that. If I was attacked by a truly powerful enemy, I needed to be at full strength. That meant having the infiltration suit at full integrity.

Still, as I hooked the pistol-shaped booster to the appropriate port and pressed the button that would feed the concentrated Mist to the suit, I felt an almost tangible sense of pain at the loss. Dismissing that feeling, I could only hope that I hadn't just wasted the valuable resource.

Hopefully, it would be back to at least minimal effectiveness within the next hour, so I settled down on the tent's cot and distracted myself with mental puzzles. Over the past few months, my efforts in that arena had been effective, and my Mind attribute had risen considerably. Still, the latest version of the puzzle program was challenging enough that I really had to concentrate if I was going to solve the various number problems. So, it was great for when I wanted to kill a little time while still making an effort at productivity.

Even so, I found it difficult to concentrate, so after thirty minutes, I decided to take a look at my status:

NAME	Mirabelle Lisa Braddock		
CLASS	MISTRUNNER		
LEVEL	20 (12%)		
CONSTITUTION	98/150		
MIND	103/150		
MIST	91/150		
SKILLS	7/7		
SKILL NAME	Skill Tier	Modifiers	Abilities
CYBERNETIC MASTERY	Tier 2 (1%)	150% Efficiency	7 Cybernetic Slots
COMBAT	Tier 2 (47%)	+60% Damage (All) +90% Speed (Melee) +60% Accuracy (All) +35% Range (Firearms) +60% Reload Speed (Firearms) +25% Damage (Small Arms) +50% Damage (Heavy Weaponry) +5% Movement Speed +25% Jump Height	Empowered Shot (D) Double Shot (E) Combination Punch (D) Pummel (E) Engage (E) Disengage (F) Mark Target (F) Barrage (F)
INFILTRATION	Tier 2 (14%)	+25% Effectiveness (Stealth) +15% Effectiveness (Stealth Abilities) +30% Effectiveness (Deception) +25% Effectiveness (Observation)	Stealth (D) Camouflage (D) Deception (E) Mimic (D) Observation (D)

MISTRUNNER	Tier 2 (21%)	+40% Speed (Misthack) +25% Processing Speed (Mistwalk) +50% Strength (Mistwall) +50% Breach Range +25% Infiltration Stability +15% System Defense +5% Damage (All)	Mistwalk (D) Misthack (D) Mistwall (C) System Redirect (E) Disable Cybernetics (E) Overcharge (E)
FIELDCRAFT	Tier 2 (18%)	+25% Combat Effectiveness +50% Effectiveness (Triage) +25% Less Food/Water Required +25% Effectiveness (Combat Focus)	Triage (D) Basic Explosives Handling (C) Combat Focus (C) Pain Tolerance (D) Resistance (D) Foraging (E) Improvisation (D) Regeneration (D) Universal Language (E)
DEMOLITION	Tier 2 (18%)	+30% Explosive Radius +25% Explosive Strength	Blast Shield (D)
ACROBATICS	Tier 2 (93%)	+45% Proprioception	Balance (E)

I was of two minds about my progress. On the one hand, attaining Tier 2 in any of my higher-grade skills meant that my progress had been significantly slowed. On the other, my attributes and modifiers had seen quite a boost. I'd even gained a couple of levels—not surprising, given how much had happened since the last time I had checked my status. Since then, I'd killed dozens of wildlings—mutated and otherwise, the Mad Scientist and his mooks, and the Operators who'd responded to my assault on Heaven and Hell. And that wasn't even considering my fights in the Emporium. In fact, thinking back on it, my progress seemed a little slow.

Of course, I had no idea how leveling really worked. Sometimes, I'd kill something, and it wouldn't noticeably affect my progress. Other times, it would jump by a couple of percentage points. I suspected that it had something to do with how much Mist my enemies had gathered, so there was a correlation between the strength of my opponents and how much Mist I managed to absorb after killing them. But that didn't always seem to be the case; for instance, those bandits who had the dubious honor of being my first human kills had awarded me enough Mist that I gained a couple of levels. However, I had no illusions about their actual power. They'd relied on surprise and a single combatant with a powerful weapon to take out the convoy. Since then, I'd killed much more powerful people—and creatures—but I'd never gotten quite that same boost to my level before.

In the end, it didn't really matter, though. I wasn't killing people in hopes of advancement. I was doing it to achieve a goal. So, the ins and outs of leveling weren't really all that important.

With that in mind, I checked my skills, and I saw that, while I'd made some advancements in the individual branches, it wasn't enough to push me into a new tier. So, with that done, I decided to check my infiltration suit. To my surprise, the influx of Mist had worked wonders, and most of the major lacerations had been mended. There were still a few cuts here and there, but the suit had recovered enough that I could wear it without risking further damage.

I'd worn it so often that it had begun to feel like a part of me, and seeing it so damaged had been like losing a part of my body. Now, though, with it hugging my body, I suddenly felt whole. To that point, I hadn't even realized how attached I was to the suit.

With that done, I slipped on some black fatigues and a matching tee-shirt before topping it off with a pair of unassuming boots. I wouldn't be winning any fashion awards, but trekking through the wilderness wasn't really conducive to that kind of thing. I could've just worn my infiltration suit and nothing else, but given that it fit me like a second skin, I wasn't really ready for that kind of exposure.

Perhaps one day, I'd have that kind of confidence. It was a bit strange that I could go into battle without a hint of hesitation, but the moment I thought about putting myself in a position to be ogled, I retreated back into my shell. Especially if it was the real me on display and not some disguise conjured by the combination of Mimic and my acting skills. If I was playing a role, like I had back in Biloxi, it was so much easier. But in my own skin? That was much more difficult for me to accept.

After getting dressed, I scanned the small tent to make certain that I hadn't left anything behind. I hadn't, so I wasted no more time before emerging into the morning sunlight. The Templars were already up and about, and I quickly spotted Patrick sitting next to Zachariah. The two of them were deep in conversation while they ate something from tin bowls.

It would have been so easy to join them. To laugh and joke like everything was normal. But the reality of it was that I just couldn't force myself to take that first step. For months, I'd held myself apart from Patrick, and now, I was paying the price. It would've just felt so awkward, forcing myself into their conversation like that.

"You hesitate too much," came Isla's voice from behind me. I turned my head to see her standing next to the tent, her arms crossed. Her white ensemble was spotless—just like was the case with all the other Templars—and I took a second to wonder how they maintained such pristine cleanliness. I didn't know about the others, but at the very least, Zachariah's robes should have been covered in gore. Isla's, too—healing wasn't really conducive to cleanliness, after all. But neither of their outfits bore even a speck of dirt, much less blood.

"What was that?" I asked.

"I said that you're thinking way too much," she said. "If you want something, go for it. That's what I do, and I've never regretted it."

"What are you talking about?"

"You and the boy," she stated, stepping up to stand next to me. She put her hand on my shoulder. "I'm not trying to get in your business or anything, but that kid definitely has some strong feelings for you. He tries to hide it when you're looking, but when he saw how close you were to dying, he couldn't hide his panic."

"That's because he depends on me."

She shook her head. "You're not stupid enough to believe that" was her response. "And I don't know you all that well, but I get the feeling that you care about him, too. I don't know what's holding you back, but if you want my advice, here it is: Just go for it. Don't think. Don't convince yourself that it's a bad idea. Just do it. Maybe it doesn't work out. Maybe it does. But you'll regret it for the rest of your life if you don't give it a go."

For a moment, I didn't say anything. Then, I felt a wave of resentment. Isla wasn't much older than me, and she'd only engaged me in a single conversation. So, why did she think she had the right—or the ability—to give me advice?

"You're right. You don't know me," I said. Then, I changed the subject. "Thank you for the healing. If I'm ever in a position to help you, I will. But it's time for us to go."

"I never even got your name," she said. Nodding toward Patrick, she added, "Or his."

I shrugged. "Life's full of disappointments," I stated.

Without another word, I crossed the short distance to where Patrick was sitting next to Zachariah. When I reached him, I asked, "Are you done with breakfast? We need to hit the road."

"Huh? Why? Are we in a hurry?" he asked. "I mean, is it smart to leave just yet? It was only a day ago that you were—"

"I'm fine. Good as new," I said, cutting him off. "And I don't want to overstay our welcome."

For a moment, he looked as if he wanted to argue, but with a sigh, he shook his head and said, "Fine. Guess we're going, then."

As he said goodbye to Zachariah, I looked around and asked, "Where's my bike, by the way?"

Zachariah pointed to the other side of the camp. "Left it over there," he said.

"Thanks. Not just for the bike. For rescuing me, too."

"Not a problem," he said with a smile. "Gave me a chance to stretch my legs."

"Right. Sure. But thanks again," I said. "I told . . . Isla, but if I can ever help, I will."

After that, I extricated myself from the awkward conversation by heading toward my bike, which I found in the same condition as the last time I'd seen it. Still, I took a minute to inspect every inch of it until I was certain that it hadn't picked up so much as a scratch. By then, Patrick had joined me, and after I mounted the bike, he hopped on the seat behind me. With that, we took off, quickly finding our way to a nearby road that took us north.

As we went, I considered what Isla had said. If nothing else, the experience in that crater had hammered home how vulnerable we all were. All it took was for us to wander into the wrong area, and our lives would be cut short. It didn't matter how powerful I'd become; there was always something else out there that could kill me.

So, did it make sense for me to continue my stubborn refusal to acknowledge the relationship Patrick so plainly wanted to advance? We'd only traveled a few miles before I realized the answer: no, it didn't make any sense at all.

That's when I decided to take that next step with Patrick as soon as we got the chance.

CHAPTER FORTY-EIGHT

THICK OR THIN

When I was young, I blamed my parents for putting me in such a horrible situation where I had no choice but to do terrible things in service of my own freedom. As I grew older, it was Jeremiah keeping me down. Now, I look around and see nothing but ineptitude preventing me from achieving my goals. Sometimes, though, I wonder if I'm the problem.

—Nora Lancaster

Patrick and I sat inside what was left of a building, an awkward silence stretching between us. To distract myself, I once again studied the shelter I'd chosen, and I couldn't help but suppress a sigh. It really didn't offer much in the way of protection, largely because it was comprised of a few crumbling walls that looked on the verge of falling apart. As far as I could tell, they would hold for at least a little while longer—I'd tested their structural integrity before committing to depending on them for the night—but beyond that, I knew it wouldn't be long before they surrendered to the creeping vines that coated their surface.

Despite its lack of a roof—and one of its four walls—it was the best shelter I'd found. A few buildings we'd passed were already home to beasts or wildlings, which eliminated them from contention, but the vast majority were in even worse shape than our current temporary abode. It was as if the farther north we went, the more committed nature seemed to destroying any evidence of human civilization. And it was doing a good job, too. In a few more years, there would be nothing left but scattered debris and half-buried foundations.

It was a poignant reminder of how far humanity had fallen.

The blue-tinted light of a Mist lamp cast our surroundings in deep shadow, mingling with the slivery rays of a full moon to produce an eerie sort of ambiance. I'd experienced it many times before—after all, I'd spent quite a bit of time traveling the wilds—but I'd rarely shared it with anyone else.

And I hated it.

Not because I didn't want Patrick's company. I did, though despite my previous resolution to take the next steps in our relationship, I had done no such thing. For that all-important moment, everything had to be perfect. And a crumbling building in the middle of the wilderness, with both of us smelling and looking like we'd been traveling all day, certainly didn't reach that lofty standard.

Still, I couldn't deny that his presence was, in a lot of ways, comforting. Even so, I hated that he was there because I knew how vulnerable it made me. Back in Nova, he could take care of himself well enough. His pistol was top-of-the-line, and he had a skill that augmented it. However, what was good enough in Nova City was woefully inadequate in the wild places of the world. If I hadn't already known that before my encounter with the horde of mutated wildlings, almost dying had hammered home the point in a way that made it impossible to forget just how exposed we both were. I was confident that I could survive most things the wilderness could throw at me—my own arrogance and stupidity notwithstanding—but I couldn't do so and protect Patrick at the same time.

The war between those two emotions—relief that he was with me and fear that I couldn't protect him—created an awkward situation, and the silence between us continued to stretch until, at last, he asked, "Do you want to talk about what happened?"

I glanced his way to see his brows furrowed in concern. For me. How long had it been since I had anyone look at me like that? My uncle had never let his emotions show, and I hadn't really let anyone close since his death. Nobody but Patrick, who always seemed like he put my emotional needs before his own. It was such a strange feeling, knowing that he actually cared about me. Jeremiah had, but even that had been tempered by his taciturn personality. At one point, I'd thought the same of Nora, but she'd proven that lie when she'd sold us all out to the Enforcers.

Besides, everyone who'd ever seemed to care about me had done so with an ulterior motive. Jeremiah had been filled with so much regret that he'd latched on to helping me survive as some sort of penance. Or to right the wrongs of his past, like when he'd let my mother refuse the Tier 7 Nexus Implant. Nora had only cared insomuch as it allowed her to enact her own plans. Being a surrogate big sister—or aunt, maybe—had given her the chance to take my uncle down, and I didn't think it went much further than that.

But Patrick—he was different. He didn't really want anything from me, save for my company. Even when I'd turned him down, it hadn't affected his ability to care about me and my well-being. Perhaps that was why I found his presence so comforting. It didn't matter if we never got together; he'd still be there when I needed him.

I wanted to say that I would return that favor, that I cared about him as much as he seemed to care about me, but I knew that wasn't true. Next to my quest for revenge, whatever relationship we'd managed to cultivate was only of minor importance.

Still, I'd have to have been stupid not to see that the potential between us, and I didn't want to lose that.

"What do you mean?" I asked, already knowing the answer to the question.

"You almost died, Mira," he said quietly. "Like, your skin was melting off. That stuff, it went right through your subdermal armor, too. I saw bones. I . . . I thought I was going to lose you."

"I'm fine," I insisted.

"Because we got lucky," he said.

"Didn't feel all that lucky when I was fighting those things." I said it with a slight smile and a slightly amused tone. A mistake, I soon found.

He shook his head. "This isn't something to joke about," he said. "I didn't make a big deal about it back there, but this whole thing—it's insane. You know I'm not against taking risks. Remy and me, we did it all the time. But there's taking a risk, and then there's throwing your life away for nothing."

"This isn't about what happened back there, is it?" I guessed.

He ran his fingers through his blond curls, then said, "Not entirely."

"Then say what you really want to say," I muttered, already getting frustrated and annoyed. I really wasn't great at talking to people, especially when it came to feelings. Sure, I could confront a gang leader and dictate terms with the best of them, but the moment I needed to discuss emotions with someone that mattered, I couldn't help but get defensive. One of my many character flaws, I suppose.

"Fine. Okay—you want me to say what needs to be said? I can do that," he responded, pushing himself to his feet. "This whole vendetta is crazy. I don't know half of what you've done, and even that much is enough to keep me up at night. I have no problem with you killing the woman who betrayed your uncle. She deserves it. But you've gone so much further than that, Mira! I don't know what the city was like before we got there, but I do know that it's on the verge of an explosion."

He sighed and shook his head before continuing. "It's rough out here. Super dangerous even for us. But half of Nova's population would rather take their chances with the monsters than stay in the city. There are more leaving every day, too. And the ones that stay are dead set on fighting a war that none of them even know why they're fighting. And you . . . You're in the middle of all of it. For all I know, you instigated it. I don't ask you about your plans because—"

"You could."

"What?"

"You could ask," I said. "I'll tell you everything. But . . . but I know you're not going to like it."

"How many people have died because of the things you've done?" he asked.

I shrugged. "Directly? Thousands," I said without hesitation or remorse. "Indirectly? A lot more."

"H-how do you live with that?" he asked.

"Because most of them are barely even living, Patrick," I stated. "Men and women who spend every waking hour in virtual reality. The addicts. The ones who've just given up on everything. The people who trudge back and forth to the factories or the Silos, working shifts so long they can't do anything but spend their off time sleeping, all so they can get up and do it again the next day. The Enforcers who think that just because they have a little power, they matter. The Operators who don't even know they're part of the system of oppression that hangs over everything in the city. And then there are the ones at the top. The aristocrats. The rich. The powerful. The ones who could make a difference if they wanted to but choose to keep their thumbs on everyone else. I'm willing to let them all die because they just don't matter. In most cases, when they die, it's a mercy."

"You don't believe that, do you?" he asked.

"I do," I said. "And do you want to know the worst part? Even if everyone somehow came together for the common good, if everything was magically fixed, it would all still be pointless."

"How so?"

"Because in a few years, the aliens are going to come and enslave us all," I stated. "They've already started. All those people who look down on us from Lakeview or whatever, they're slaves just like all the rest of us. They've just deluded themselves into believing the little bit of slack they've been given is actual freedom. Instead, they're wearing leashes, just like everyone else."

I sighed. "You don't see it because you don't want to," I said. "My uncle did. He knew what was coming, and everything he did was so I'd have a chance to escape the aliens' grasp. So I could be free."

"And how is that working out for you?" he asked.

I didn't answer because, deep down, I knew it was all a lie. A justification for my single-minded pursuit of vengeance. Sure, things were bad, but that wasn't new. If I looked closely enough and twisted the facts the way I wanted, I suspected that I'd see the same sort of problems. Oppression was just a part of human nature. Perhaps it was part of being sapient, to exploit other people for your own gain.

It wasn't everyone. It probably wasn't even most. But there would always be people—or aliens—who were willing to enslave and oppress the population in the pursuit of power.

I'd just chosen to latch on to all the worst parts of human—and alien—nature so that I didn't have to confront the high cost of my revenge. If I thought everyone was terrible, doomed, or enslaved, what did it matter if a few thousand innocents were killed? It was easier to think of it as a mercy than to admit that I was just as selfish as anyone else. Maybe more, considering the lengths to which I would go just to feel marginally better.

"I don't know," I admitted quietly.

"Then why? Why do it?" he asked, kneeling beside me when I didn't immediately answer. He reached out, putting a comforting hand on my shoulder. "Listen—I'm not going to tell you to stop. If this is what you think you need to do, I'll support you every step of the way. If I'm being honest, I don't care so much about all those other people. But I do care about you, about what this is doing to you."

"I'm fine."

He cupped my chin and gently raised my face so that we were looking each other in the eye. "No. You're not," he said, his voice clear and strong. "Once, when I was really young. Before my mom died, we had a house. A real home. Remy had set it all up, you know? It was on the edge of a cliff overlooking the ocean. It was . . . It was nice. Cozy. I don't remember a lot about it, but I do remember the garden. Mom loved working in it, digging and planting and all that. I don't know if she had a skill or whatever, but it didn't really matter. I don't think it was about results. It was about the act itself."

"That . . . That sounds nice . . ."

"It was," he agreed, pulling away. "What I can remember of it, I mean. But then, one day when Remy was making a run, some men found us. They . . . They did . . . horrible things. I hid in a closet, so I didn't . . . I didn't see everything. But when I got out, Mom was . . . She was different. The whole house was trashed, and her garden had been destroyed. I can't know for sure, and at the time, it never even crossed my mind—but looking back, it's obvious what they did to her. Especially after how Remy reacted.

"He just went cold. Like . . . It was like all the happiness or joy or whatever just got sucked out of him," Patrick explained, his eyes welling up with tears. "I could see it in his eyes. Even as young as I was, I knew what it was, too. Murder. And after he got Mom settled . . . That night, after she was finally asleep, he left the house. I couldn't sleep, and I stayed up all night. When he got home just before dawn, he was covered in blood.

"It took me a while to work up the courage to go to him, to ask what he'd done," he went on, turning away so I couldn't see the wetness of his cheeks. "I found him in the kitchen, patching himself up. He still had blood all over his face. I'll never forget what he said when I asked him what had happened."

Patrick sighed. "He told me, 'This is something you're gonna have to learn sooner or later, kid. Some people deserve to die. Ain't nothin' else to it, either. The world is a better place without 'em. Those men, they deserved to die. Worse, really. But I'll tell you right now—that's a dark road, killin' everyone who deserves it. It stains your soul. Do it enough, and killin' starts to look like the answer to every problem. Most of the time, it is. That's the problem with it, boy. Killin' is effective. But even when it's right, it ain't. One day, you'll have to do it, too. That's the way the world is now. But it always has a price. Sometimes, it's as simple as pissin' off the wrong person. Other times, it's up here.' He tapped his head, then. 'But no matter what, the biggest effect is here.' He slapped a bloody hand on his chest, leaving a red handprint."

Shaking his head, Patrick went on. "Despite what happened on that battlefield, I'm not really worried about you dying. It was shocking, but I've always known that it was a possibility. And if it happens, I probably won't take it that well. But what I'm really worried about is here," he said, reaching out and tapping a finger against my chest. "I think what Remy was talking about was that every time you kill somebody, it gets a little bit easier. And Mira, you've killed a lot of people. I just don't want it to get too easy for you."

Even though my first impulse was to react defensively, it only took me a moment to recognize what he was trying to say. Ever since I'd begun walking the path of revenge, killing had become progressively easier. Before my uncle's death, I would have blanched at the thought of killing even one innocent person. But now? Hundreds had died in my attacks on the Silos, and exponentially more had been killed during the war I'd started.

Certainly, I truly believed everything I had said. Most of the people in Nova City were living hollow existences that barely even qualified as lives. I felt that right down to the very core of who I was. However, claiming that their deaths were acts of mercy was an absolute falsehood. It was just an excuse so I wouldn't have to take responsibility for all the collateral damage I had left in my wake.

And it was effective, too.

It wasn't that surprising, though. For months, I'd looked at my revenge as the most important facet of my existence. In the throes of righteous vengeance, I had pushed everything else aside. Not only had I looked the other way when it came to all those people who'd died, but I had also pushed Heather's fate to the back of mind, and in doing so, I'd condemned her to something worse than death.

Finally, I had to ask the question that had been marinating in the back of my mind for weeks. Maybe even months. I looked up and into Patrick's eyes, asking, "Am I the bad guy?"

It was a valid question, even the potential answer terrified me. My actions weren't those of a hero. I didn't save people. I didn't make the world a better place. Instead, the only things I'd left in my wake were death and destruction.

"No," Patrick said, though that wasn't unexpected. After all, he cared about me, and the way I saw it, his bias was always going to shine through. Plus, even if he did think I was the sum of my evil actions, it would be the height of idiocy to admit it. Telling that kind of truth to someone with my track record was a good way to get killed.

Of course, I wasn't the type of person who would do that, even if the facts of my actions suggested otherwise. I hoped Patrick knew that.

"You're just a little lost right now," he said. "We all go through it. What happened to you . . . It . . . Conventional ideas of good and evil don't really apply. I'm not telling you to stop doing what you've been doing. I know how much you need it. But I just think you need to be cognizant of the cost. And more than anything, I want you to know that I'm here for you. No matter what you do or how you choose to do it, I'll be here to support you. Because we're in this together, Mira."

"And if it turns out that I end up being the bad guy?" I couldn't help but ask.

"Then we'll be bad guys together," he said without a moment's hesitation. "I trust you. You kill somebody, I believe they probably deserved it."

It was a vote of confidence I sorely needed, and not for the first time, I found myself thankful that our paths had crossed.

"Don't think I won't tell you when I think you're making a mistake, though," he said. "I will. So, I might not always tell you what you want to hear. But at the end of the day, I'll be right there with you, through thick or thin."

I let out a sigh. "Thanks," I said. "That . . . That means a lot to me."

CHAPTER FORTY-NINE

PURPOSE

Money. Power. I wonder what any of it even means when I'm surrounded by so much hate.

—Nora Lancaster

The next day, Patrick and I continued our trek through the wilderness. Thankfully, we weren't assaulted by any new threats, and we even shared a pleasant meal on a cliff overlooking a series of wide ravines that looked like some enormous giant had raked its claws across the landscape. Perhaps they had, but if that was the case, it had happened long ago, considering the thick vines snaking down the edges of the cliffs. Flitting around the small ponds that had formed at the bottom of the ravines were flashing blue lights that I recognized as Mistflies. Overcast as it was, the sight was strangely comforting, and it reminded me of the advice Jorge had given me what felt like a lifetime before.

Back then, when faced with a similar scene, he'd told me to enjoy what beauty I could find in the world. At the time, he'd probably meant it to counterbalance all the horrors I would see, but after everything I'd been through, it served a different purpose. It was so easy to look at the Mist as evil, but the reality wasn't quite so simple. Certainly, the onset of the Mist had resulted in billions of deaths, and it had irrevocably changed the world. However, it wasn't malicious. It was more like a force of nature, and blaming it for the transformation of the Earth and its inhabitants was akin to hating a hurricane for flooding a city.

That wasn't to say that the situation wasn't frustrating. It was. But it wasn't evil.

Never was that more obvious than when confronted by the beauty that came with it. Like the Mistflies. Or the skills I'd been given. Even the more daunting wildlife had a certain allure.

Thinking about it did beg the question of what I would have been doing if the world hadn't been upended. What would I have become if I'd lived in a world like the one my uncle had known? The few stories he'd shared told me just how different things were back then, so it was difficult to know. However, one thing he'd made clear was that it was a far safer and more peaceful place, so I probably wouldn't have been a fighter.

Without that, what was I? I'd once cultivated a variety of interests, but ever since my training had begun, I'd steadily left them behind. And then, when my world was torn into a million pieces, I hadn't even considered focusing on anything else. When I wasn't actively working toward achieving my goals, I was training. Or sleeping. There really wasn't anything else in my life.

Except Patrick, but that was complicated enough without it becoming some kind of defining characteristic. I liked him well enough, and our relationship had grown closer than ever before. He was there for me in a way nobody else ever had been—except maybe Jo, but the two situations were so different that it was hard to even compare them.

That night, Patrick and I were forced to make camp under an old bridge. It seemed structurally sound, and below it, I saw evidence of old train tracks. It wasn't perfect, but given the distinct lack of standing buildings in the area, it was the best we could hope to find. And I wasn't willing to camp out in the open, mostly because, before night fell, I had seen dark clouds on the horizon.

Sure enough, only twenty minutes after we'd made camp, a thunderstorm began. The rain fell in sheets even as furious bolts of lightning filled the air, followed by deafening claps of thunder.

Growing up in Nova, I didn't experience a real thunderstorm until I'd left the city. Certainly, Nova had its share of rain, but it wasn't a natural phenomenon. Instead, it was a product of the city's climate-control system, and the rain was intended to wash the streets clean. Outside, though, things were very different and much more dangerous.

Once, after seeing a bolt of lightning leave a melted crater almost five yards wide, I'd asked my uncle how people had survived such storms before the Initialization. That's when I'd discovered that, like most everything else, thunderstorms fed off of ambient Mist, which made them far more potent. In the first few months after the Initialization, such storms had killed almost as many people as the mutating wildlife. However, the discovery of Mist shields had served to cut those numbers down considerably; still, in some of the less-protected settlements, the dangers of such storms were still very real.

Thankfully, hiding under a bridge or in a fallen building was often enough protection. That wasn't always the case, though.

"Storms are much worse south of here," Patrick said, unwrapping a ration bar as he sat on his portable cot. The pair we'd brought weren't that comfortable, but sleeping on even a thin mattress was much better than doing so on the hard ground.

His statement drew me from my thoughts, and I asked, "How so?"

"More common," he said. "If you don't have a decent Mist shield, you're probably going to die, too. I asked Remy about it once, and he said it was because of ambient Mist levels. The more there is, the worse things get."

"Kind of like a Dead Zone," I said.

He shrugged. "A few hundred miles south, and everything's a Dead Zone," he said. "There are still areas that are even worse, too. Apparently, that's why there are more cities up here. The Mist is mostly tame. But in other parts of the world, things start getting really weird. There's an area across the ocean where nobody lives. Like, it's a whole continent of wildlings and mutated beasts."

"Really?" I asked.

"A lot of Rifts there, too," he stated. "Remy only went there once, and it was to transport some heavy hitters as close to the Rift as he could. He said these were the best of the best. As strong as your uncle, from what he told me. But they never came out. After that, he came back here and settled down with my mom. Said it was a lot safer to do local runs."

"Interesting," I said.

And it was. An entire continent of unexplored Rifts? It sounded incredibly dangerous, but it also sounded kind of exciting. What else was out there? I often thought about the wider galaxy, but I rarely even considered the fact that I'd only explored the tiniest portion of my own world.

It was such a shame, too. Sure, there was plenty of danger out there, but it was also exciting. And that danger was often accompanied by commensurate beauty. I thought back to the dragon's skeleton I'd seen in the center of the battlefield where I'd faced off against the onslaught of mutated wildlings. What would it be like to face something like that? To see it in all its glory?

And maybe to fight it?

I wasn't some unrepentant battle junkie, but I couldn't deny that there was a certain joy in facing a terribly strong opponent and coming out on top. I'd felt it after fighting my first beast, even if it had been nestled in heart-pounding terror, and I'd felt it during the battle against the mutated wildlings, as well. Perhaps I was going insane. Or maybe I'd just latched on to the one thing I could point to as a defining characteristic.

After all, being good at something tended to bring a joy all its own. And I was very good at fighting. Not the best, mind you, but very good nonetheless.

"What do you like to do?" I asked.

"Huh?"

"I mean, like, for fun," I said, the addendum to the previous question punctuated by another flash of lightning followed by a thunderclap.

He shrugged, saying, "I don't know. Not much room for fun lately."

"Before, then," I prompted, leaning forward. Our cots were arranged parallel to each other, with the Mist lamp between us.

For a moment, he didn't respond, but after a couple of seconds, he said, "I used to like to draw. My mom used to get me real sketchbooks. Like, with paper and everything. I would draw birds and other animals around the house. But that was before she . . . before she died. I kept a couple of those sketchbooks, but they were destroyed along with *The Jitterbug*. I . . . I didn't bother trying to replace them."

"Oh."

I knew I'd brought up a sensitive subject. Not surprising, considering his past. But wasn't that the case with everyone? I had my issues, and so did he. So did everybody. Either way, I was a little surprised that his mother would give him something as valuable as a sketchbook with real paper. Such things weren't common, not only because the materials were expensive to come by, but also because they just didn't serve much purpose. Anything that could be done on paper could be accomplished on a tablet or a screen. Using actual paper was a luxury that most people neither wanted nor could afford.

"What about you?" he asked.

I shook my head. "That's a good question," I stated. "I used to like reading. And there are a couple of bands I follow."

"Like Leviathan."

"Right. Like Leviathan," I said. "But the older I get, the less any of that seems to matter."

"You say that like you're some old lady," he said with a slight chuckle. "You're not even twenty yet."

"I feel a lot older," I replied. And that was true. The weight of my own expectations and the mission I'd taken upon my shoulders were heavy enough to make me feel like a cynical old crone.

"What else?" he asked.

"Nothing," I said.

"Oh, come on—there's got to be something," he said. "Let's say you finish all of this. Like, tomorrow, you wake up, and all your goals have been accomplished. What do you do?"

"I . . . I don't know."

But I did. His mention of the unexplored and inhospitable wilderness had sparked a fire in my imagination, and the only answer that made any sense was to say that I wanted to explore and discover new things. I wanted to fight new and dangerous enemies. And most of all, I wanted to see things nobody else got to see.

I'd taken those things for granted, but in my short life, I'd already experienced a lot more than most, and that set me apart. It made me feel special.

"I want to explore, I guess," I said. "Go out and see everything this world has to offer. I'm strong enough to survive most places. And once I'm done on Earth, I want to see the rest of the universe."

Perhaps in doing so, I would discover some new civilization that had managed to avoid the rot that pervaded Nova City. Probably not, which was why I preferred the wilderness. Sure, it was dangerous, but it was also straightforward. A monster might try to kill me, but it would never attempt to capture and enslave anyone. That made all the difference, at least as far as I was concerned.

"Is there room for a partner in all that?" he asked, casting a sly grin in my direction.

"I don't know. Maybe," I said. "So long as you can keep up."

After that, the storm's fury increased to the point where we couldn't even hear each other, so it wasn't long before I went to sleep. However, it was difficult to keep a smile from creeping across my face as I thought about the conversation. It proved that Patrick wanted to stick with me, and that was a comforting thought.

The next morning, the rain had slowed to a drizzle, and as I ate another ration bar, I groaned, "Ugh. This is going to be miserable."

"We could just stay here for the day," Patrick suggested. "It's not like we're on a schedule."

But we were. I'd wanted to get out of Nova for a while, but I still had my plans. And now, I was even more eager to finish what I'd started so Patrick and I could start planning for what came next. Already, my imagination was running wild with all the adventures we would experience, all the new and exciting things we might find.

As those thoughts raced through my mind, I was well aware that they would prove inaccurate. It wouldn't be easy, and I felt certain that there would be plenty of days laced with complaints. More, I knew just how alien some of those thoughts were. Since the fall of Mobile, optimism and excitement had been left behind, so it felt a little strange to be looking forward to something that wasn't related to my quest for revenge.

But I liked it.

"Better to just go," I said. "The sooner we hit that Rift, the sooner we can start exploring the world, right?"

He gave me another one of his winning smiles before he ran his hand through his curly blond hair. Then, he said, "You're serious about that?"

"You weren't?"

"Oh, I definitely am—it's just a little surprising coming from you," he said. "Haven't seen you really smile in a long time. It's nice."

"Uh . . ."

"It's also adorable how you have no idea how to respond to a compliment."

"Shut up," I said, turning away. I heard a light chuckle, but I ignored it as I folded my cot in on itself and stored it away. It was on the edge of what my arsenal implant could handle, but it fit alright. Soon enough, Patrick had done the same, and we set off once again.

The trip continued to be uneventful until I felt the Mist levels begin to rise. Soon enough, we'd reached the edge of the Dead Zone, which happened to coincide with our arrival at an abandoned and ruined city. Or town, really. None of the buildings were more than seven or eight stories tall, and there were only a couple of them that even managed that feat. The rest were fairly short and squat, suggesting that it had never been a metropolis.

It didn't take Observation to tell that none of the buildings were architecturally sound, either. Everywhere I looked, walls had fallen into piles of rubble, and none of the structures I could see were remotely close to maintaining even a semblance of structural integrity.

Not that it mattered. In the event we were forced to stay inside the Dead Zone, I'd make a more thorough search. For now, I was more interested in the wildlife.

Curiously, though, the entire area was dead silent. There were no animals in sight. No birds chirping. No insects flying around. Nothing.

And that definitely put my guard up.

"Follow me but try not to make any noise," I whispered. "Use your skill if you can."

Patrick nodded, and I summoned my assault rifle while dismissing the hover bike. Using it in the Dead Zone was possible, if only barely, but I wasn't comfortable with the noise. The thing wasn't loud, but in that desolate area, I knew the sound would carry. No—it was better to go on foot.

So, hefting my rifle, I advanced, passing into the Dead Zone proper. Immediately, the familiar tingles I'd felt in the last Dead Zone returned, telling me that the ambient Mist levels had skyrocketed. Following behind me, Patrick let out a subdued gasp, which drew my glare. He held his hands up and mouthed an apology. I just shook my head. Apparently, his version of quiet meant gasping at every little change in Mist levels.

I stepped forward, quickly crossing the rubble-strewn street to hug one of the crumbling buildings. Like that, we crossed the town, using the buildings for cover when we could and moving as quickly as the terrain allowed. Over the next few hours, we made decent time, but I came to a sudden halt when I finally heard a noise that didn't originate from us.

It was a slight buzzing sound, barely perceptible, even with Observation. But it was definitely there. Curious, I pushed forward until the sound became clearer. Then, I pointed to a nearby pile of rubble, then at Patrick. The meaning was clear. I wanted him to stay behind while I scouted it out.

For a moment, I thought he was going to argue or refuse, but he surprised me by doing precisely what I'd asked. I did notice that he'd drawn his sleek black-and-gold pistol, though. Hopefully he was ready to use it.

Pushing Patrick out of mind, I focused on the task at hand. Darting forward on silent feet as I engaged Stealth, I turned down a narrow alley that I hoped would lead me to my quarry. To my dismay, a collapsing wall had piled the rubble high, blocking my path. Undeterred, I retreated and found another route. I could have climbed over that first obstruction, and probably easily, but I didn't want to take the chance of falling rocks alerting whatever was making that noise.

It took me a few more tries to find an unblocked path, but I didn't allow the mounting frustration to push me into a mistake. I'd already made plenty of those, and I knew I needed to change that pattern if I hoped to survive. Eventually, my search bore fruit, and I found a mostly unobstructed path. It required me to get on my hands and knees and crawl, but that wasn't so onerous.

Gradually, I crept forward, careful to maintain my silence, and after a few more turns, I found myself approaching the head of an alley. Beyond, I could see an open space, and in the distance, I saw an enormous structure that reminded me of the Emporium back in Nova. It wasn't really a match—the details were all wrong—but the general style remained the same. An arena of some sort, I reasoned.

However, its sheer size beggared belief. The Emporium was huge, but this was a true monument to excess. And what's more, it didn't seem to match the town itself. I reasoned that even if the entire population of such a town were to pile into that arena, there would still be room left over.

In any case, the sight of that enormous building could only occupy my mind for so long, and soon enough, I turned my attention back to the buzzing sound. Or rather, the originator of said noise.

Channeling my inner Patrick, I couldn't suppress a gasp of my own.

CHAPTER FIFTY

OCTAVANGIANS

Sometimes, I wonder if I did the right thing. Jeremiah was running the Specters into the ground. I knew it. He knew it. Everyone did. Hundreds of thousands of credits gone, just for one little girl. I couldn't let him do it. Someone had to remember that there were thousands of people depending on us.

—Nora Lancaster

For a long moment, I wasn't even sure what I was looking at. At first, I thought it was just a man standing next to an animal of some sort. But then I saw the tentacles—or more importantly, what they were doing at that moment.

Clearly, it was one of the aliens who'd claimed the Rift, but this creature was unlike anything I'd ever seen before. It was as if someone had mashed together a man and an octopus, the combination being far more monstrous than the description suggested. With purple skin, a half dozen thick, ropy tentacles instead of arms, and a head with what looked like a sea anemone instead of hair, the Octavangian was a truly horrifying sight. And that was before I flared Observation and saw what he was doing with the creature whose body had been wrapped in the alien's muscular tendrils.

The Octavangian's black-furred prey was some sort of huge canine, but with oversize jaws and overdeveloped musculature. In addition, it had an extra pair of legs in the center of its torso. It was intimidating enough that even I wasn't certain if I'd come out on top if I had to tangle with the creature in a melee. However, the Octavangian that had wrapped its tentacles around the creature seemed to have no trouble at all. Sure, the canine fought back, and fiercely, but its struggle was pointless. With Observation flared, I could hear its bones cracking under the massive force of those six muscular appendages.

But it was the buzzing that truly unnerved me—or rather the source of the sound. With Observation running at full blast, I could see the bladed claws extending from the undersides of the alien's tentacles, but with how fast they were moving, I had some difficulty making out the details. What I saw was enough, though.

The claws had a metallic gleam, though I had no idea if they were organic or artificial. What I did know was that they were moving so fast that they blurred together. Like a chain saw, they ripped into the unfortunate canine, sending blood and bits of meat spraying into the air. All the while, the Octavangian let out what sounded like a burbling laugh.

It was nauseating.

I had seen some grotesque things in my short life, but nothing really matched up to the sight of an octopus man gleefully tearing a canine to shreds.

But I didn't look away. If I wanted to assault the Rift, I needed to get past the Octavangian guards. And given what I saw, the odds that I could do so peacefully were almost nonexistent.

It wasn't so much the act itself that I found so objectionable. I had no issues with killing the wildlife. Few were the animals that weren't aggressive, and anyone who didn't approach life in the wilderness with the same mindset was a naive idiot. Killing the animals that had been mutated by the Mist was just part of life in the wild.

Rather, I was disgusted by the obvious glee the Octavangian took in the slaughter. Of course, I knew that the alien's appearance played some part in my revulsion; I could admit that much, at least in my own mind. If I'd seen the creature in more peaceful circumstances, I might have overlooked my own bias, but watching it tear that canine apart removed any filter I might have tried to maintain.

Or perhaps my prejudice was just that strong against the aliens. But in my defense, my uncle had instilled in me a healthy disdain for our would-be overlords. So, was it really that surprising that I would latch on to any negative trait—even if it was only their looks—and hold it up as evidence of their monstrosity?

Whatever the case, despite the overwhelming desire to look away, I continued to watch as the canine surrendered to its wounds. The Octavangian kept going well after the creature was dead, and that same burbling laugh combined with the buzz of its moving claws continued to fill the air. Eventually, though, there was nothing left to shred, and the alien retracted its six tentacles. When the alien had finished its gruesome act, the bulk of the appendages seemed to pull into its torso—how, I didn't know—leaving it with six arm-length tendrils poking out of a red jumpsuit.

It stood there for a long moment, the wavy anemone-like protrusions on its head wiggling in the air until, finally, it just turned and walked away. I followed it with my eyes until it reached a building and turned left, taking it out of my line of sight. Only then did I let out a sigh of relief.

As much as I wanted to kill the thing—and every instinct was screaming at me to do just that—I knew that would have been a mistake. I needed to gather information first; otherwise, I stood the risk of bringing the whole operation down on my head. Maybe I could win in such a situation, but then again, maybe not. The first aliens I'd fought—the Castorix I'd encountered before delving my first Rift—weren't that powerful, but I also knew that I'd cheated a little in that fight by disabling their robot guards. If I hadn't, I had no doubt that things would have been much more difficult.

So, it stood to reason that these Octavangians would prove even more troubling. And if I was going to get past them, I needed a good plan.

To that end, once I was sure the coast was clear, I crept out from the alley in which I'd been hiding and followed the alien's path. I tried not to pay attention to the pile of gore that represented all that was left of the canine as I passed it by. Instead, my every sense was tuned into my surroundings; the last thing I wanted was to walk into an ambush. I still had Stealth wrapped around me, but who knew whether or not the aliens could see through it? For all I knew, there were machines or cybernetics that could do just that, not to mention the existence of skills that could pierce through the concealment.

Not taking any chances, I hugged the wall of a ruined building as I followed in the Octavangian's footsteps until I reached the first corner. I stopped, then leaned out to check that the way was clear, and when I saw no evidence of the alien, I slipped out of my hiding spot and kept going.

Though I was certain that there were plenty of skills and abilities that could do so, I had no way to easily track the alien. Sure, if we'd been in the forest, I could've made a better showing—Jorge had taught me the basics—but in a ruined city where most of the surfaces were concrete? I just didn't have the talent for that kind of thing.

Even so, I could make some educated guesses as to where the alien was heading. For one, the rubble-strewn street it had chosen made a beeline toward the huge stadium, suggesting that was its destination. For another, I could feel the rising levels of ambient Mist with every step I took in that direction. I'd felt the same around my first Rift, so it didn't take a leap of logic to assume that's where the alien was probably going.

As I slowly made my way in that direction, I kept my senses trained on the environment. Keeping Observation flared gave me a bit of a headache, but it had proved its worth often enough that I couldn't imagine going into unknown territory without it. And sure enough, after only a hundred feet, the strategy bore fruit when I saw a three-inch circular plate attached to one of the walls.

I stopped in my tracks, sinking down to a crouch as I studied the oddity. Other than a few puddles of water from the rainstorm the night before, nothing else within the ruined city had been shiny, so the plate looked immediately out of place. Couple that with the fact that it didn't seem to serve any discernible purpose, and it wasn't long before I reached the conclusion that it was integral to the Octavangians' defense.

I knew there was every chance that I was being too cautious and that the round plaque was some curiously well-preserved remnant of a dead society, but if that proved to be the case, my caution wouldn't have been an issue. I lost nothing by being careful. So, I settled down a few dozen feet away from the object and began my study.

After staring at it with Observation flared for ten minutes netted no results, I switched to the sense that had come with my {Mistrunner} class. Before I'd attained the class, those senses were faint and hard to read; now, though, that sense had become an integral part of my tool kit.

I shifted my focus, finding that it was indeed ripe for a Misthack. So, I sank my awareness into it, resulting in a familiar menu:

Initiate Misthack?
[Yes] or [No]

I chose the affirmative option, prompting another menu:

Misthack successful. Options:
Reboot system
Hijack system
Deactivate system
Upload Ghost

Craving more information, I chose to hijack the system. As soon as I did, an incredibly complex Mistwall bloomed before me. It contained a hundred nodes, all arranged in a cluster around the system, and the moment I sank my mind into the first, I knew I was in trouble.

Usually, the first few nodes were the easiest to crack and almost always consisted of eminently solvable equations. They weren't exactly two plus two, but to my advanced Mind, they might as well have been. However, this Mistwall started with logic puzzles that would have been at home at the end of any other chain of defenses. But after plunging headlong into the system, I didn't have much choice but to keep going.

Sure, I could pull back and only suffer a minor backlash, but in a system as advanced as the one I'd found, I knew it was almost guaranteed that the

Octavangians would know that someone had tampered with their equipment. The only way to skate in under the radar and avoid discovery was to keep pushing forward.

So, that's what I did, bending every ounce of brainpower toward that goal. The first node fell fairly quickly; though it was much more difficult than what I was used to seeing, it still wasn't enough to keep me out. However, the complexity of the puzzles and equations continued to mount with every fallen node, and by the time I'd pushed past the halfway mark, the mental fatigue had started to get to me.

That was the problem with attacking unknown systems. Taken in isolation, even the most difficult-to-conquer nodes weren't that hard to overcome. All it took was time, focus, and care. However, solving a single equation or puzzle was very different than tearing through a hundred progressively more difficult problems in a row. It was enough to strain even the most formidable mind, so the real deciding factor was a person's willpower. Lots of people had the skills. Few had the stubborn refusal to quit required to make full use of them.

I liked to think I was one of those few.

But confidence could only take me so far, and by the time I toppled the seventy-fifth node, I felt like someone was repeatedly jabbing an ice pick into my brain. I knew it was going to be a close call, and I needed to make a choice. If I kept going, I might conquer the defenses. But I also had a good chance of failing, too. And if that happened, the backlash would be immense.

By comparison, if I pulled out now, it would be much easier to endure, and I would stand a much better chance of escaping.

So, I needed to pick a path. Either I could chance it and, should I fail, run the risk of knocking myself out with the backlash. Or I could choose to give up, suffer a much slighter backlash, and escape on my own terms.

But that came with its own issues—chiefly that it would alert the aliens to my presence. If they knew someone like me was around, they would take steps to counter my skills. And that would make delving the Rift that much more difficult. In fact, if I pulled out now, it was probably a good idea to abandon the idea of delving the Rift altogether.

And I wasn't going to do that.

Perhaps it was stupid. Or maybe I was just letting my stubbornness push me into foolishness. But I really did think keeping going was my best option. So, that's what I did.

Immediately after making that decision, I began to regret it. Still, I pushed on, and one node after another fell before me. I couldn't enjoy it, though. The headache continued to intensify, and soon enough, my focus began to waver.

I kept going, harnessing every ounce of concentration I could muster. Even so, I wasn't certain if it was going to be enough. The eightieth node was a struggle. The eight-fifth was a labor the likes of which I'd never experienced. The ninetieth and ninety-fifth depleted my reserves of willpower like nothing else ever had. And finally, the hundredth node was a knock-down, drag-out war of attrition, the result of which was uncertain until the very last second.

And then, suddenly, it was over.

I let out a deep breath and wiped the sweat from my brow before diving into the system. And what I saw was more than a little surprising. In some ways, it resembled the cameras I'd hacked so frequently back in Nova City. However, instead of using visual means for detection, it used aural input. The slightest noise would trip the sensors, and I assumed it would prompt a response from the Octavangians.

Fortunately, by Misthacking one, I had inadvertently gained access to all of them—which made sense, given the difficulty involved. I'd effectively hacked thirty-four devices all at once. Obviously, with that kind of infrastructure backing it up, it was never going to be easy. In fact, I knew just how lucky I was to have made it through that Mistwall.

Pushing that from my exhausted mind, I focused on what information I could glean from the system. And it wasn't much. Aside from its basic purpose—an early-warning system—I could only surmise that the thirty-four sensors had been laid out in a loose web around the stadium. Beyond their purview, there were no other defenses.

Which I found odd, but I wasn't going to complain.

So, I shut them down and ran forward, hoping to bypass the web before they had a chance to reboot. I sprinted down the street, maintaining Stealth even though I knew the sound of my steps was probably enough to expose me. I couldn't worry about that, though. I needed to get inside the defenses.

And I barely made it, too. By the time they rebooted, I'd ensconced myself in one of the crumbling buildings, where I intended to rest my mind for a few minutes. As I did so, I chastised myself for taking such a huge chance. At the time, using Misthack on the sensor hadn't seemed like a big risk, but that was because I'd assumed the aliens' technology was on par with what I'd seen back in Nova. Obviously, that wasn't the case, and I was incredibly lucky that I hadn't gotten myself killed.

Sighing, I sank to my backside as I closed my eyes. I kept Observation going, but without flaring it to its maximum capability, the mental strain was negligible. Like that, I settled down to await my recovery.

It took almost an hour before my headache began to fade, and another hour until it was gone completely—a testament to how close to the edge I'd gotten. If there'd been even one more node, I would have failed.

But I hadn't, and all I could do now was resolve to do better in the future.

Sighing, I pushed myself back to my feet and resumed my trek toward the stadium. Fortunately, I didn't find any other defenses in my way, but the journey actually took a lot longer than I'd expected. The sheer size of the structure had thrown off my perception, and I'd assumed it was a lot closer than it actually was. By the time I reached it, I could only stare in awe at the building.

It rose more than a hundred feet into the air and was shaped like an enormous bowl, albeit with one open end. I couldn't see inside, but I suspected that was where the Octavangians had set up shop.

Once again, I settled down in an out-of-the-way alley to gather information. However, my reconnaissance wasn't very effective, and all I saw were a few other aliens coming and going. Using all my senses, I at least felt reasonably sure that there were no other automated defenses. So, the way was open for me to explore further.

Knowing that if I went back, I'd have to disable the aural sensors two more times—one on the way out and another time when I came back—I decided that I needed to take care of the Octavangians before going back for Patrick. I'm self-aware enough to realize that my reticence to return was also tied up in the fact that bringing him along for the ride would only make things more difficult. I was better off working alone rather than trying to protect him—which begged the question of why I'd agreed to let him accompany me in the first place.

I didn't want to answer that at the moment, so I pushed the query to the back of my mind where it belonged. Instead, I focused on doing what I needed to do.

CHAPTER FIFTY-ONE

THE SMARTER PLAN

It all comes down to power. Sometimes, the means of that power is money. Other times, it's about fear. Or threats. Gunther built his empire on knowledge. He knows who's been targeting us, and I just have to figure out how to make him tell me.

—Nora Lancaster

Under the cover of deepening night, I retreated from the stadium, stealthily making my way back to the metal plaque of the aural sensor. Once there, I set upon it, leveraging my abilities and attributes to slowly overcome the Mistwall. It wasn't easy, but then again, I knew it was never going to be. Still, I couldn't allow myself to be dissuaded from the proper course of action just because of a little discomfort or difficulty. Instead, I simply needed to put my head down and forge ahead with the only plan that might result in my survival.

It took a little more than an hour, but eventually, I tore through the Mistwall and deactivated the net of aural sensors. Seconds after that, I was already on my way. As I trekked through the crumbling city, I flared Observation, hoping it would be enough to warn me of any dangers that might present themselves. I needn't have worried, though; the Octavangians had been thorough in exterminating any threats, so the entire city was as quiet as a tomb.

Unnatural as that silence was, I was grateful. After two battles against that Mistwall, my head felt like it had been split in two, and I desperately needed to simply close my eyes and rest. The result of my mental fatigue was that if I was attacked, I would be beset by slowed reactions that would leave me far below a hundred percent effectiveness. I could still defeat most of the native creatures, but if I found myself assaulted by the Octavangians or a pack of wildlings, things could quickly become overwhelming. So, as much as I just wanted to rest and let my mind go blank, I forced myself to focus as I made my way back to Patrick.

Fortunately, the combination of the dilapidated town's lack of wildlife and the shadows of the overcast night gave me all the leeway I needed to remain undetected. So it was that, after only another hour, I dragged myself to the outskirts and the building where I'd left Patrick. Before leaving, I had told him to keep a low profile, and true to my instructions, he'd foregone the light of a Mist lamp, which meant he was huddled in a dark corner, his eyes shining with anxiety.

When I finally revealed myself, I found that I was facing down the barrel of his pistol. His alarm only lasted as long as it took him to recognize me, and when he did, he sagged in relief, dropping the weapon to his lap like it weighed a thousand pounds.

"Good job," I said. "Way to stay alert."

"I hate this," he muttered. "I wish I could deploy the autoturrets we brought along."

"Can't," I responded, sitting next to him. He hadn't even brought out the cots, which was probably for the best. Discomfort, as unpleasant as it was, often became fuel for remaining alert. "Told you that before I left. These aliens, they're too strong, and those turrets are way too weak. They can't even reliably take care of the wildlife."

Indeed, I'd only insisted on bringing them along so we could use them as an early-warning system and distraction in the event something attacked us in the wild.

"They're too loud, too," I added. "The Octavangians would be here in a second if they heard gunfire."

"I know that," he mumbled half to himself. He truly seemed miserable, which made me feel a bit guilty for not bringing him along. My own day had been difficult, but I knew I shouldn't discount how horrible his had been. Stranded next to an enemy encampment, terrified of making even the slightest noise—it must have been exhausting as well as nerve-racking. Then, he sighed, "So, what's going on? Did you . . . you know . . ."

"I didn't kill anyone yet," I said. His hesitation to even talk about it was a little annoying; these aliens didn't deserve his empathy. Instead, they'd earned every bit of punishment I could dish out. After all, their presence was part of why Nova City—and the rest of the world—was so screwed up.

"But you are, right?"

"You know I am. They won't just let us stroll into the Rift."

"We don't have to go, though," he said. "I mean, there are easier ways of making money."

"Not the kind of money we can make in a Rift. It took me a couple of weeks to get through the last one, and the Shards I mined in there were enough to buy my whole arsenal. Even if all I did was steal from people like Nora, it would take me years to build up that much money," I explained. "And if I'm going to do the things I need to do—after Nora's dead, I mean—I'm going to need a ton of credits. Ships aren't cheap."

"I'm aware," he said. "*The Jitterbug* wasn't the highest-class ship, but Remy always complained about how much it cost. Even the parts were expensive."

"See? This is the best way," I said.

Even if the Rift turned out to be a carbon copy of the last one, the earnings would go a long way toward buying a ship. I'm not sure when I'd decided that was going to be my next step after I got my revenge, but now that I'd latched on to it, I wasn't keen to let it go. Besides, without a ship of our own, there was no way we were going to cross the ocean and visit that other continent.

And for whatever reason, that was precisely what I wanted to do. I'd never really felt the call of adventure before, mostly because I hadn't had the opportunity. From the moment I'd absorbed that Tier 7 Nexus Implant, my life had been carefully curated—at least up until Mobile was destroyed and everything went off the rails. Since then, I had been almost entirely focused on making Nora pay for what she'd done.

But now that I was out of the city with Patrick, I felt like I could see a light at the end of the tunnel. Soon enough, I'd be finished with Nova City, and I could move on with the rest of my life. I knew I'd never be inclined to build an organization like Jeremiah had. I had neither the patience nor the desire for something like that, and even if I was suited for leadership, I'd already seen the end of that road. My uncle might not have been the best man for the job, but he'd given almost everything to the Specters. His efforts had been rewarded with betrayal.

No—I'd never be able to follow his path, which meant I needed to find my own. And given my skill set, nothing really suited me better than a life spent delving the Rifts.

No responsibilities to other people. No one to betray me. No restrictions. Just me and Patrick, exploring and adventuring. It was a nice dream, and one I was increasingly more convinced I could turn into a reality.

But first, we needed to take out the Octavangians and dive into the Rift only a few miles away. To that end, I'd come up with a plan.

It would have been easy enough to set up within the stadium and start picking the aliens off, one by one, until they were all dead. However, given that I'd counted a couple dozen enemies, each capable of bringing an unknown degree of power to bear, that seemed like the height of carelessness. And I was convinced that, while I could probably kill quite a few of them, that strategy would eventually lead to me being overwhelmed by sheer numbers and likely killed.

Not precisely an optimal result, so as I'd continued my reconnaissance, I'd come up with a different sort of plan. The only problem with it was that it required me to take a step back, leave the area around the stadium, overcome the aural sensors' heinous Mistwall, and take things slower than I normally would.

"So, what's the plan?" asked Patrick.

"Nothing complicated," I answered. "We wait for them to come outside, then I ambush the first group. Then the second. And I'll keep going until I'm finished. It'll probably break out into a firefight before that, but it'll have to do."

"Couldn't you just break out that bomb gun you have?"

I narrowed my eyes. "Bomb gun? You mean my BMAP?" I asked.

"That's the one," he said. "You could explode their whole camp, right?"

I shrugged, saying, "Probably. Maybe. I don't know. I'm sure they have some kind of defense against it, though." I really wasn't sure that was the case. It wasn't like there were a bunch of towns in the general area, and even if there were, the Octavangians usually wouldn't have to worry about someone breaking out a mobile artillery platform. I wasn't the only one on the planet with such weaponry, I was certain, but I was just as sure it wasn't commonplace. "Doesn't matter, though. The Rift is in the center of the camp, which means that I'd probably damage the apparatus that allows for passage in and out if I started lobbing bombs in there. And it's not a bomb gun. It's a mobile artillery platform."

"Sounds like a bomb gun to me," he reiterated with a grin.

I rolled my eyes. "My point is that blowing stuff up kind of ruins the whole thing," I said. Though it was true, I didn't particularly like the fact that I couldn't use what was rapidly becoming my favorite weapon. Sure, the R-14 was steady, and I liked the idea of sniping enemies from afar with the Pulsar, but there was nothing quite as climactic as an enormous explosion. The only problem was that bringing that kind of heavy ordinance to bear almost always brought with it complications. Like when I'd used the weapon in that crater and alerted thousands of mutated wildlings to my presence. The BMAP was amazing, and I loved what it could do, but I still needed to employ caution before deciding to use it.

Much to my chagrin.

"Point taken," he said. "So, you're just going to assassinate them?"

"Something like that," I stated. "Hopefully, I can kill a good portion of them before they realize what's happening."

"Wish it wasn't necessary at all," he mused. "I don't know why we can't all just get along. I mean, it's not like we couldn't work together or something."

"Not the universe we live in," I said. "Maybe that's how it works elsewhere. I don't know. But on a newly Initiated planet like Earth, these aliens don't even look at us as people. We're just resources to be exploited or annoyances to be exterminated, and with nothing in between."

"Cynical way of looking at it," he said.

I shrugged. "I'm just calling it like I see it."

He didn't really have an answer for that, so our conversation soon petered out. I was well aware that my own views had probably been tainted by my uncle's experiences. He hadn't lived an easy life, and he'd been forced to watch almost everyone he cared about die, many at the hands of the aliens. His hatred of them was both justified and utterly understandable.

For my part, I'd only seen a fraction of what he had. In fact, it was arguable that human beings were just as bad as any alien—even the ones who'd created a cycle of enslavement around the site of my first Rift. Were they any worse than people like Russo, who'd not only killed and enslaved people, but experimented on them, as well? No. But it was far easier to peg the aliens as the enemy, if only because they were so different.

I was aware of that bias, but I just didn't care. Besides, I had enough hate for both groups.

As the silence stretched between us, I forced myself to eat a ration bar before leaning against the wall so I could get some rest. It wasn't the most comfortable position in which to sleep, but I wanted to be as mobile as possible. That meant we couldn't afford to risk bringing out the cots. Fortunately, I was well versed in sleeping in less-than-perfect conditions, so it wasn't long before I dozed off.

Sleep came, but it was a shallow thing, and far less restful than I might have hoped. However, it was enough to soothe my fatigue, and by the time I woke up a few hours later, my headache had dissipated. That I could function on so little rest was an advantage of my high Constitution; I couldn't go indefinitely, but I could keep pushing well past the point when a baseline human would have collapsed from total exhaustion.

Rested and ready, I took a few minutes to take care of some necessities before I woke Patrick and told him that I was going to get started with my plan. He nodded, and though I knew he wanted to go back to sleep, he rose.

I'd considered bringing him with me, but I knew he'd just get in the way. As much as I liked Patrick, he was not a frontline combatant, and I knew that if he ever wanted to be effective, he'd have to be kitted out with powerful gear. I was fine with that—after all, it was one of the reasons I was so keen to delve the Rift in the first place—but we weren't quite at that point yet.

So, with Patrick up, about, and aware, I left the building in which we'd made camp and stalked toward the stadium. I didn't go as far as the aural sensors, though. Instead, I positioned myself in a three-story building that gave me a decent line of sight to the stadium. Once there, I summoned my Pulsar and watched for movement.

It was just before dawn when my efforts were finally rewarded. I watched as a group of three Octavangians exited the stadium. One waved its tentacles as if gesturing while the other two walked by its side. It was easy to imagine that they were engaged in idle conversation, just like the members of a human patrol might be, but I cautioned myself against assigning human characteristics to the aliens. For all I knew, the tendrils doubled as sensory organs. It was a far-fetched idea, but it was a strange universe out there.

I continued to watch for a few minutes as the trio of tentacled aliens left the stadium behind. As I did so, I noted that they all had different skin colors. One was purple, another was blue, and the last was a dingy yellow. I didn't know what any of that signified—if anything—so I merely filed the information in the back of my mind.

Once I was certain that the trio weren't going to be followed, I activated Stealth and set off to stalk them. And it was ridiculously easy, too. They never looked in my direction, not even when I drew to within fifteen feet. Apparently, Stealth was plenty powerful to mask my presence from them. Still, I didn't lose focus or grow overconfident. That was how people got killed, after all.

After a couple of hours, one of the Octavangians stopped dead in its tracks and whipped its anemone-covered head to the left. Without waiting more than a second, the alien took off at a sprint, its tentacles waving wildly all the way. The others didn't hesitate to follow, and so, I was forced into a run, lest I lose them.

Fortunately, my Stealth remained up to the task of keeping me mostly concealed. Not that it mattered, of course—the Octavangians weren't paying any attention to anything but their prey, which turned out to be a giant spider. The thing was at least as big as a person, with eight spindly legs. However, there was no web nearby, which I found curious. Perhaps it was a species of spider that didn't rely on such traps.

Either way, the Octavangians fell on it with obvious glee, their elongating tentacles shooting out so quickly that the spider had no chance to dodge. In only a couple of seconds, it was entirely wrapped in three sets of tentacles. It bucked and screeched, but its efforts were to no avail.

That's when the buzzing started.

I had no idea how those claws worked, but they ripped into the spider's carapace with enviable ease. As flesh, ichor, and chitin sprayed into the air, the aliens' sea-anemone-like appendages quivered in the air, and I got the sense that they represented the Octavangians' emotions in some way.

Or perhaps I was simply imagining things.

Either way, that's when I struck.

In the space of a second, my nano-bladed sword was in my hand. I moved like lightning, my first stroke falling with such celerity that none of the aliens even knew what had happened before my first victim's head hit the cracked pavement. My first attack—a horizontal strike—flowed into a backhanded swing that decapitated the second alien. By that point, the third had begun to react, but it couldn't hope to move fast enough.

So, I was a little surprised when, just before my blade bit into its thick, rubbery neck, a blue Mist shield sprang into being. Sparks flew and a cracking sound filled the air as my sword was turned aside, and I couldn't help but notice the shield's telltale waver.

But I couldn't take advantage of it right away because the Octavangian reacted much more quickly than I'd expected, retracting its tentacles with such rapidity that I couldn't even track them. Before I could strike again, I felt thick tentacles wrap themselves around my torso. Then, that buzzing resumed, and I could feel the claws bite into me. Thankfully, they didn't immediately shred my infiltration suit, but I knew it wouldn't be long before those sharp claws ripped through my first layer of defenses.

So, even as the tentacles writhed and ripped, I aimed another blow at the Octavangian. The shield held, so I struck again. And again. Three times, each one causing a longer shimmer. I knew it was failing, but I was against the clock—already, the claws had begun to accomplish their task, not to mention the constricting nature of the tentacles, which threatened to break my ribs.

I kept going, knowing that my life depended on success. I struck again, and the shield flickered. It was on its last legs—even I could tell that much. So, with all my might, I brought my sword down in a two-handed attack. The shield collapsed, and my blade bit deep, slicing through the Octavangian's head.

The tentacles went limp, instantly falling away as the alien collapsed.

For a long moment, I stood there, panting as I tried to catch my breath. But then, I muttered, "Three down. Lots more to go."

CHAPTER FIFTY-TWO

PROGRESS AND CHOICES

> *I thought things would get better when I took over. I cared more about the tribe than Jeremiah ever did, but it doesn't seem to make a difference. He was willing to abandon everyone, all for the sake of one little girl. And I've given them everything. Why can't they see it?*
>
> —Nora Lancaster

The next two days went better than I could have hoped, and I killed quite a few more groups before the Octavangians realized they were being hunted. When that happened, the rest retreated into their stadium stronghold, leaving me a little unsure of how to proceed. When my assault began, I'd chosen to eschew directly attacking their base for a couple of reasons, chief among them that I didn't want to damage the mechanism that allowed access to the Rift. I'd learned firsthand just how fragile the machines could be, and I didn't want to chance rendering the whole trip pointless.

So, as I watched the stadium from just outside the influence of the aural sensor, I contemplated my next moves. Obviously, I could just wait. Eventually, the aliens would relax and resume their normal habits. However, that option wasn't without danger. There was every chance that these aliens could call in reinforcements; perhaps they already had. And while I knew getting to the surface wasn't easy for the aliens—after all, the planet was still in quarantine for a few more years until the Integration—I wasn't so naive that I thought it was impossible. No—if I pushed them too far, they would absolutely bring more aliens to the surface. Once that happened, I would be forced to flee.

The other option was to take the fight to them. That came with its own issues. Not only would I have to take them all on at once, but I'd also be forced to limit myself. At the very least, explosives were off the table, save for in very controlled circumstances. Given that the BMAP was my trump card, I knew that removing it from the deck would leave me vulnerable.

Finally, I could just turn around and go back to Nova City. Perhaps I could find another Dead Zone—and a Rift—sometime in the future. No guarantees on that front, but at least I would live to fight another day. Survival would have to be a reward all its own.

In the end, it came down to three choices: caution, aggression, or retreat. All three had detriments as well as merits. Even when I weighed them against one another, I couldn't decide which route offered the most advantages.

My every instinct told me to take retreat off the table. Certainly, despite nearly dying, I'd made great progress during the trip. Killing hundreds of those mutated wildlings had come with significant advancements in my skills as well as my level. Even Patrick had managed to make some gains, mostly from killing wildlife we'd encountered during the trip. By all rights, I should have been happy with that.

But I wasn't.

Not even close.

The problem was that I had quite a bit of difficulty admitting defeat. Sure, I knew I couldn't always win. That was a given, and during my training, I'd become intimately acquainted with losing. Sometimes, that was even the point. Learning to cope with defeat was a necessary skill, after all.

But quitting before I'd even gotten started? That just rubbed me the wrong way.

I would run if I found myself facing off against an opponent I couldn't beat. I didn't have a death wish. However, running away from the Octavangians felt so wrong, primarily because I knew I could win. Perhaps not without cost, but victory was within my grasp. Quitting now wouldn't just see me leaving resources behind, but it would be a blow to my pride I wasn't sure I could endure.

To distract myself from the sour taste of even thinking about retreat, I opened my status:

NAME	Mirabelle Lisa Braddock
CLASS	MISTRUNNER
LEVEL	24 (91%)
CONSTITUTION	102/178
MIND	121/178
MIST	101/178

SKILLS	7/7		
SKILL NAME	Skill Tier	Modifiers	Abilities
CYBERNETIC MASTERY	Tier 2 (27%)	150% Efficiency	7 Cybernetic Slots
COMBAT	Tier 2 (67%)	+60% Damage (All) +90% Speed (Melee) +60% Accuracy (All) +35% Range (Firearms) +60% Reload Speed (Firearms) +25% Damage (Small Arms) +50% Damage (Heavy Weaponry) +5% Movement Speed +25% Jump Height	Empowered Shot (D) Double Shot (E) Combination Punch (D) Pummel (E) Engage (E) Disengage (F) Mark Target (F) Barrage (F)
INFILTRATION	Tier 2 (56%)	+25% Effectiveness (Stealth) +15% Effectiveness (Stealth Abilities) +30% Effectiveness (Deception) +25% Effectiveness (Observation)	Stealth (D) Camouflage (D) Deception (E) Mimic (D) Observation (D)

MISTRUNNER	Tier 2 (41%)	+40% Speed (Misthack) +25% Processing Speed (Mistwalk) +50% Strength (Mistwall) +50% Breach Range +25% Infiltration Stability +15% System Defense +5% Damage (All)	Mistwalk (D) Misthack (D) Mistwall (C) System Redirect (E) Disable Cybernetics (E) Overcharge (E)
FIELDCRAFT	Tier 2 (69%)	+25% Combat Effectiveness +50% Effectiveness (Triage) +25% Less Food/Water Required +25% Effectiveness (Combat Focus)	Triage (D) Basic Explosives Handling (C) Combat Focus (C) Pain Tolerance (D) Resistance (D) Foraging (E) Improvisation (D) Regeneration (D) Universal Language (E)
DEMOLITION	Tier 2 (31%)	+30% Explosive Radius +25% Explosive Strength	Blast Shield (D)
ACROBATICS	Tier 3 (11%)	+60% Proprioception	Balance (E)

The biggest change had to do with my attributes. Killing the Octavangians had proven to be extremely valuable, at least in terms of gathering Mist. I could only think that, while they weren't overwhelmingly powerful, that was probably due to possessing low-tiered Nexus Implants. It made sense that they'd spent their time on Earth killing anything that moved, and so, they'd probably gained quite a few levels. So, they were walking bags of progress, as far as I was concerned.

After gaining four levels since the last time I'd studied my status, my potential had crept ever closer to two hundred. A few more levels, and it would surge past that line. And while I hadn't really come close to realizing that potential, I was still extremely proud of the achievement.

More importantly, my actual attributes had experienced a huge surge, and all three categories now exceeded a hundred points. That was no small matter, either.

Ever since my Awakening, each point of improvement had represented an incremental increase in power. The difference between reaching ten and eleven points in Constitution was barely measurable. Even a gain of a dozen points, especially when it came so gradually, was difficult to notice. However, if I were to compare the current version of me to the one right after my Awakening, the difference was downright scary.

Put in easier-to-understand terms, before I'd have struggled to lift more than a hundred pounds. But now? I could deadlift a thousand pounds without missing a beat, and that was just one facet of Constitution. My body was far more durable than it had been even a few months before. I could think faster, parse more information, and draw on a truly huge pool of Mist to power my skills and abilities.

But the biggest jump in my relative power came from passing the one-hundred-point mark in each of the categories. It was as if my effective power doubled almost overnight, and I was still trying to get used to it. Still, I knew it was only the beginning; my uncle had been fighting for almost a century, and his strength reflected that. I'd never asked him about his attributes—he probably wouldn't have told me even if I had—but from what I'd seen, his numbers were probably at least double mine. Maybe far more than that, given that I'd never really seen him go all out.

That was what I had to look forward to.

As far as the progress of my skills, I'd made incredible strides. They'd all reached at least Tier 2, with [Acrobatics] passing into the third tier. I could only explain its rapid improvement by remembering that my other skills had evolved when I'd attained my class. As such, it—as well as [Demolition]—progressed much more quickly. Eventually, they would catch up and probably evolve, but for now, rapid growth was the name of the game.

Thinking of my skills, I opened the appropriate menu and continued my inspection:

Tree	**Combat: Tier 2 (67%)** +60% Damage (All) +75% Speed (Melee) +60% Accuracy (All) +35% Range (Firearms) +60% Reload Speed (Firearms)			
Branch	Small Arms: Tier 1 (63%)	Heavy Weaponry: Tier 1 (49%)	Melee: Tier 1 (54%)	Movement: Tier 2 (16%)
Tier 1	+25% Damage	+50% Damage	+15% Speed	+5% Movement
Tier 2	+25% Range	+15% Range	+25% Damage	+25% Jump Height
Tier 3	Ability: Explosive Shot	Ability: Shatter Shot	Ability: Riposte	Ability: Double Jump
Tier 4	+25% Accuracy	+50% Rate of Fire	+25% Accuracy	+15% Movement
Tier 5	Ability: Multishot	Ability: Instant Reload	Ability: Execute	Ability: Teleport

I had to admit I was a little disappointed with the slow progress of [Combat]. Certainly, it was a powerful skill. I knew that, just as I knew that without its modifiers I would have been a lot less effective. Still, after reaching Tier 2, its progress had slowed to a crawl. Even now, the individual branches hadn't experienced nearly the improvement I would have expected, with none of them—save for the Movement branch—reaching the second tier.

It wouldn't have been so bad if those third-tier abilities didn't seem so powerful. But anything with a name like Explosive Shot had to be strong. Or perhaps that was just my predilection toward blowing things up making itself known.

In any case, I moved on to the [Infiltration] tree:

Tree	**Infiltration: Tier 2 (56%)** +30% Effectiveness (Stealth)			
Branch	Spycraft: Tier 1 (82%)	Stealth: Tier 1 (99%)	Deception: Tier 1 (63%)	Sensory Input: Tier 1 (40%)

Tier 1	+15% Effectiveness (Deception)	+15% Effectiveness (Stealth Abilities)	+15% Effectiveness (Deception)	+25% Effectiveness (Observation)
Tier 2	+15% Effectiveness (Deception)	+25% Effectiveness (Stealth Abilities)	+15% Effectiveness (Mimic)	+25% Effectiveness (Observation)
Tier 3	Ability: Charisma	Ability: Distraction	Ability: Bluff	Ability: Sense Deception
Tier 4	+15% Effectiveness (Charisma)	+15% Effectiveness (Stealth Abilities)	+25% Effectiveness (Bluff)	+15% Effectiveness (Sense Deception)
Tier 5	Ability: Interrogate	Ability: Vanish	Ability: Chameleon	Ability: True Sight

[Infiltration] had seen more improvement than [Combat], but the progress was still maddeningly slow. That slow development was made even more annoying because the Stealth branch was only one percent from rolling over into the second tier. The reward—a modifier to the effectiveness of the Stealth ability—wasn't a huge deal, especially considering that I had yet to run into anything that could easily see through the ability, but that single percentage point still taunted me.

I was less interested in the abilities associated with reaching the third tier of the individual branches, but perhaps those new abilities would prove just as vital as any of the others I regularly used.

Next, I looked at the [Mistrunner] tree:

Tree	Mistrunner :Tier 2 (41%) +30% Speed (Misthack) +30% Processing Speed (Mistwalk) +55% Strength (Mistwall) +55% Breach Range			
Branch	Misthack: Tier 1 (51%)	Mistwalk: Tier 1 (36%)	Mistwall: Tier 1 (94%)	Combat: Tier 1 (91%)

Tier 1	+15% Speed (Misthack)	+25% Infiltration Stability	+15% System Defense	+5% Damage (All)
Tier 2	+15% Ghost Strength	+25% Processing Speed (Mistwalk)	+25% System Defense	+5% Damage (All)
Tier 3	Ability: Surge	Ability: Rewind	Ability: Backlash	+5% Damage (All)
Tier 4	+25% Ghost Stability	+25% Processing Speed (Mistwalk)	C-Grade System Defense	+5% Damage (All)
Tier 5	Ability: Plague	Ability: Skeleton Key	Ability: Mental Fortress	Ability: Assassinate

As was the case with [Combat], the progress had been glacially slow. However, that had always been the case with both [Mistrunner] and its predecessor, so I was inured to its slow progression. Still, I was eager to reach Tier 2 in the Combat and Mistwall branches. Gaining more damage as well as a stronger Mistwall was never a bad thing, after all.

Finally, I took a look at the tree for [Fieldcraft]:

Tree	Fieldcraft: Tier 2 (69%) +30% Combat Effectiveness			
Branch	Medic: Tier 1 (61%)	Survival: Tier 1 (41%)	Communication: Tier 1 (29%)	Utility: Tier 2 (11%)
Tier 1	+50% Effectiveness (Triage)	+25% Less Food/Water Required	Ability: Universal Language	+25% Effectiveness (Combat Focus)
Tier 2	+50% Recovery Speed	+25% Less Sleep Required	Ability: Share Map	+25% Effectiveness (Regeneration)

Tier 3	Ability: Stabilize	Ability: Bastion	Ability: Waypoint	Ability: Ignore Injury
Tier 4	+25% Medication Effectiveness	+50% Endurance	Ability: Combat Map	+25% Explosives Yield
Tier 5	Ability: Mend	Ability: Tinkering	Ability: Secure Connection	Ability: Focused Will

It played host to one of the few branches I'd progressed to the second tier, but the pace of its progress was just as slow as all the rest. As much as I liked the idea of my Universal Language ability, it had yet to be put to the test, so my feelings about its utility were more than a little mixed. What good was an ability if you never got to use it?

More useful were the modifiers that came with the other branches. Already, my high attributes meant that I needed less sleep, food, or water than other people, but every time I ate a ration bar, I found myself looking forward to the day when I wouldn't need them. The other Tier 2 modifiers, both of which would almost assuredly enhance my ability to recover from injuries, would be a welcome addition, as well.

But as happy as I was with my progress—and I was, despite how slowly my individual skills had grown in power—I knew I was just delaying the inevitable choice laid before me. Did I retreat? Did I attack? Or did I wait?

Oh—who was I kidding? I hadn't come so far and braved the dangerous wilderness just to turn tail and run the moment I ran into difficulty, had I? No. Of course not. That was the easiest option to dismiss.

Waiting was a little more difficult, mostly because I knew it was the smarter choice. The chances that the Octavangians would seek reinforcement at this point were unlikely. My uncle had been adamant that, to the aliens, the only thing that mattered was profit. Because of that, I felt certain that the Octavangians wouldn't waste the time and effort necessary to bolster their ranks, if only due to the reduction in profit such a choice would represent. Besides, if they were going to request backup, they would have already done so.

No—I was safe from reinforcements, I expected.

Unless my uncle's assessment of the aliens' priorities was wrong, at least. But I'd already come too far to start questioning his judgment, especially after building my own philosophy around it.

So, the last remaining option was probably my best.

But just because I'd decided on all-out assault didn't mean I had to run in there, guns blazing and asking to be cut down. Instead, I could be smart about it. Sneaky. To that end, I would take a page out of my uncle's playbook.

Before that, though, I needed to take care of something I often overlooked: establishing a secure connection with Patrick. My oversight wasn't that surprising, considering that I often worked completely alone. Patrick was my companion, but I'd never really considered him all that useful. If my plans came to fruition, that would change, and soon, but for now, he was more of an afterthought when it came to actual combat.

Still, when I'd returned from my latest hunt to find that he'd devolved into a bundle of raw nerves, I had begun to see things from his perspective. Often, I just left him to his own devices, never looping him into my plans. How would I have felt if we were forced to trade places? To me, the ignorance would have been the worst part, so I had decided to remedy that with a secure connection.

Of course, *secure* was a relative term, which was why I had yet to do it. My uncle had once warned me how easily someone could hijack a connection—with the right skills, my enemies could discover all my secrets, and with the proper equipment, someone could use the connection to track me. No—according to Jeremiah, it was better to limit important communication to face-to-face meetings.

And he was probably right, too. My own [Mistrunner] abilities didn't go down that road, but they were close enough to suggest that people with the right abilities or equipment could hijack even the most secure communication lines.

Even so, I felt it was worth it just to maintain Patrick's sanity. So, I initiated the secure connection, helped along by the KIOI, which served to augment the security, as well. Patrick's end was still a source of weakness, but I tried to ignore that as I asked, "Can you hear me?"

"I'm right next to you," he said. "Of course I can hear you."

"No—through the connection, I mean," I said, rolling my eyes.

"Oh. Yeah. Loud and clear," he said. "Are you sure I can't help? I know I'm not the fighter you are, but—"

"I'll be fine," I said. "Just . . . It's better if you hang back unless I need you, okay? Maybe you can swoop in and save the day like you did back in Mobile."

He gave me a slight smile. "Maybe," he admitted. "Just . . . When you go in there, just be careful. This isn't worth dying over."

That was where he was wrong. Certainly, I didn't intend it to be some sort of suicide mission, but the moment I stopped putting myself in danger, that was when I'd fall behind. I was well aware that I'd grown addicted to my own progression, but I didn't think that was a bad thing. Instead, I felt that it was a great motivator to keep me from committing the sin of weakness and falling under the thumb of someone more powerful. After all, I hadn't forgotten that, aside from the threat posed by the dawning of the Integration, there were still plenty of people out there who could've given my uncle a run for his money. If I came up against one of them, I wouldn't last more than a few seconds. The only solution was to keep moving forward, and for that, I needed to acknowledge that mortal danger would forever be a part of my life.

Even so, I placated Patrick by throwing a grin right back at him and asking, "When am I not careful?"

"Uh . . . you're never careful," he said. "You see that, don't you? I can't even count how many times you've almost died."

"Oh, c'mon—it hasn't happened that often," I argued.

"It really has," he said. "And that's just the times you've told me about. I bet the real number is way higher."

Well, he wasn't wrong about that, but I wasn't about to admit as much. Instead, I changed the subject, saying, "Just keep your head on a swivel, okay? I don't think they'll call in reinforcements or anything, but if you notice anything out of the ordinary, let me know. In the meantime, just wait for me to finish clearing them out, and we can hit that Rift. Before you know it, we'll be swimming in credits."

I liked the idea of having access to so much money; after all, better equipment usually equaled an easier time with survival. But I couldn't even convince myself that was why I was doing it. In the end, I just liked challenging myself. My time in Nova had thrown a blanket over that enjoyment, but now that I was out of the city, it had returned with a vengeance.

"Just be careful."

"I will," I said. Then, without further delay, I left the building where we'd made our camp and headed toward the stadium. There was a nest of aliens I needed to exterminate.

CHAPTER FIFTY-THREE

ASSAULT

I've come to realize that the tribe feeds off of conflict. They need it. Without war, they'll realize just how bad things have gotten. Often, I wonder what Jeremiah would have done in my place. Because so many have left the city, times have gotten lean. A good fight and an enemy to hate is a perfect distraction.

—Nora Lancaster

I crept into the stadium, whispering through the secure connection, "Approaching the entrance. No contact."

"Acknowledged," came Patrick's voice through my interface. I wasn't a stranger to communicating in such a way, but doing so with a battle looming over me was a little disconcerting. What if the Octavangians hijacked the connection? What if they knew I was coming? It would ruin my whole plan.

As I went, I deposited a number of demolition charges along the way. They were small enough that I hoped they wouldn't be noticed, and if push came to shove, they might be enough to secure my escape. Hopefully it wouldn't come to that; after all, I still didn't want to risk damaging the mechanism that made the Rift passable. But I'd rather chance that and survive than the alternative.

Still, I hoped I wouldn't have to make that choice..

And if everything went according to plan—or even close to it—I wouldn't have to worry about making that kind of decision. Even if I did end up detonating the charges, there was no guarantee that it would damage the machinery. It was a risk, but a calculated one that I hoped would ensure my survival.

I progressed slowly, not only because I took the time to deposit the charges, but also because I leveraged Observation to its maximum effect in an attempt to see any threats before they presented themselves. To my surprise, though, the stadium's corridors were entirely devoid of anything that might derail my plan. No aliens. No traps. No sensors. It was just empty.

Still, even as focused as I was, I couldn't help but note just how impressive the structure was. It was at least twice the size of the Emporium back in Nova City. Perhaps not in seating capacity, but in sheer volume. The corridors were wide, and I could see the ruined remnants of booths lining the outside wall. Every now and then, I saw faded, decayed, or otherwise deteriorated signs. Most of which were unreadable, but some were legible enough to give me hints as to the purpose of these booths.

A few had obviously been food stalls, a supposition that was supported by the rusted steel ovens and other cooking apparatuses. However, others sold clothing and trinkets, a few of which had actually survived. I even found one rubber trinket that depicted some sort of red boar as well as a leather sack that took me a moment recognize as a deflated, oblong ball of some sort.

It felt like a window into the past, and though I was incredibly interested, I didn't allow myself to become too distracted. Instead, I traversed those corridors until I found a ramp that would take me to the stadium's peak. At least twenty feet wide, the ramp followed a winding spiral until it led me to my destination.

Once there, I carefully found my way to a corridor that would lead me to the interior of the stadium. I stalked forward, keeping my assault rifle at the ready as I continued to push Observation to its limits. I saw nothing out of the ordinary, save for the fact that the curious lack of wildlife—even down to the insects—persisted. Clearly, the Octavangians didn't like to share their space, a conclusion supported by the absence of wildlife as well as the zeal with which I'd seen their hunting parties operate.

Not that it was surprising. Even back in Mobile, the Amigos as well as the town's militia had fought a constant battle against the encroaching fauna. Anything else, and they'd have run the risk of being overwhelmed. And that was with a whole town backing them up; obviously, with their lack of numbers, the Octavangians had taken a far more proactive approach.

It was also a good opportunity for them to gain levels.

In any case, I appreciated their efforts, if only because of the lack of complications as I approached the corridor's exit. As I did, I reaffirmed that Stealth had remained active; the ability had become almost reflexive, and I rarely went into any dangerous situation without it draped around me.

Still, the ability wasn't foolproof; it was difficult for most people to see through it, but it did little to negate other senses. So, I kept my footsteps light and my breathing even. Even so, as disciplined as I was, I couldn't help but gasp when I reached the exit and beheld the scene before me.

The stadium was shaped like a giant oval, but with one end open. That end wasn't empty, though; rather, it played host to a giant screen that must have been at least a hundred and fifty feet across and half as tall. Such a thing was completely unnecessary in the modern world—we had holographic displays that would serve the same purpose, but without the necessary infrastructure of an enormous screen—but it was still impressive, nonetheless. It made me contemplate what other wonders my forebears might have created, but it also made me realize just how much we took our technological advances for granted.

The Initialization had devastated humanity, but it had ushered in a period of rapid advancement, as well. It was such a shame that so many were never afforded the opportunity to see how far Earth had come. I did sometimes wonder what Earth would have been like had the aliens followed the system's rules. Certainly, millions—perhaps even billions—would still have died. That was inevitable in the wake of such a momentous change. However, there was every possibility that the exploitation that was so prevalent in a city like Nova could have been avoided.

Or maybe that was a pipe dream. Human nature would have remained, and that dictated that people were ultimately self-interested. My uncle claimed that the world was a fairer place before the Initialization, but he also tended to look at those days through the lens of nostalgia. For my part, I expected that things were just as unfair back then, only the oppression was better hidden.

Perhaps that was just my cynicism bleeding through, though. I had no way of knowing for sure, one way or the other.

I pushed those thoughts out of my mind as I scanned the rest of the stadium. Most of the plastic seating had survived, though, judging by the rusted brackets, fasteners, and supports, I suspected that if I sat in one of them, it would collapse under me. Still, the stadium must have accommodated a hundred thousand people during its heyday—an impressive number by anyone's measure.

On the ground in the center of the stadium was a clear space, longer than it was wide, and at one end, there was a curious statue made of slim tubes. It rose from the ground as a single trunk, but about ten feet up, it diverged into horizontal branches that soon became vertical spires. I had no idea what it was supposed to be—perhaps an abstract of a tree—but given its position of prominence, I suspected that it had once been important.

Despite how interested I was in conjecture, I couldn't afford to study the thing for very long because the real goal of my infiltration lay directly in the center of the open space. There was only one building, and from its size, I expected that it could house around twenty Octavangians. At present, the aliens were setting up a series of pillars that I suspected would be useful in the defense of the camp. The Rift lay nearby, held open by an apparatus that looked similar to the one I'd seen in the Castorix camp—meaning that it reminded me of an overturned metallic spider, in the center of which was a shimmering and formless prism.

As I watched, I counted the aliens. There were nine of them out and about the camp, but I had no idea how many were within the lone prefabricated building.

It didn't really matter, though. Nine was enough, and unless there were fifty of them huddled in that structure—unlikely, given its size—my plan wouldn't change. I did find it curious that their defenses were so underwhelming, though. Perhaps that was a result of breaking the rules to get a jump on their competition. Maybe they couldn't bring anything along that would stand out too much, lest they be sanctioned by the system.

I shook my head. That was just a guess. For all I knew, these Octavangians were the equivalent of minor bandits, and they were equipped as such. While it was easy to imagine that every alien who'd infiltrated the planet was well funded and well equipped, it didn't make sense that that would be the case. More likely, they were desperate people with extremely thin margins; otherwise, they wouldn't have chanced it.

Whatever the case, I couldn't concern myself with those sorts of things. Having seen my enemies and established that their numbers were within acceptable parameters, I set out to scout my immediate surroundings. Fortunately, the exits that led down into the corridors that circled the stadium were sufficient to provide adequate cover, so it didn't take long before I set up at the very top of the structure.

After all, I wanted to establish as much distance as I could. Perhaps the Octavangians had a sniper, but the chances that they were all marksmen were extremely slim. That lack would hopefully even the odds a bit.

After a few more minutes, during which I waited for the sun to descend a little farther toward the horizon, I settled down into a shadow, retrieved my Pulsar from my arsenal implant, and took aim. As I'd been taught to do when fighting multiple targets, I settled my sights on the first—and biggest—Octavangian. Then, I moved to the next. And the next after that. One, two, three. Over and over, I practiced the motion; the situation wasn't ideal, but I hoped to down at least a couple of them before they managed a response.

For ten minutes, I went through the cycle until, at last, I felt as prepared as I could be. With that done, I once again settled my sights on the biggest alien, activated Empowered Shot, and waited the necessary two seconds before I squeezed the trigger. The gunshot had barely even registered before my sights found my second target. This time, I didn't bother with an ability, instead opting for speed over power. I fired again, then moved to the third victim before firing the final shot.

By that point, the first Octavangian was on the ground, half its torso destroyed by my initial salvo. I didn't need medical expertise to know that it was dead. The other two had fared a little better, but my second target had also been slain. The third was only wounded, though. It had moved at the last possible second, so my shot had only destroyed a couple of its tentacles.

An acceptable result, either way.

I sprang to my feet, once again embracing Stealth as I dashed away. It wouldn't be as useful now that they knew I was there, but that was why I'd waited until dusk. I had no idea how dependent the Octavangians were on their vision, but a little caution never hurt.

"Two down. One wounded. At least six more to go," I said, sprinting down the narrow walkway between seats. A moment later, I descended back into the corridor only to reemerge at the next entrance. When I looked down, I saw that the camp had erupted into motion. One of the Octavangians was kneeling next to the lone survivor of my first volley, but the rest were taking up defensive positions as they raised curious-looking weapons.

I recognized them as firearms, but beyond that, they couldn't have looked more different from what I typically used. In fact, they had more in common with tridents than rifles, but by the way they were pointing the weapons around, it didn't take a genius to figure out that they were ranged weapons. And probably powerful ones at that.

So, it was a good thing they clearly had no idea where I was.

That was just fine by me.

I once again took aim, this time at the kneeling Octavangian I expected was a medic of some sort. I activated Empowered Shot, then squeezed the trigger. The alien exploded in a shower of gore, and a second later, a hail of gunfire fell upon my position. But I was already gone, descending back into the corridor where I had some cover.

I sprinted down the walkway for almost thirty yards, passing two more entrances before reemerging into the seating area. By that point, the Octavangians were in full-on panic mode as they tried to take cover behind the building. It would have been a viable strategy if I'd remained at my previous position, but given that I'd already relocated, my new angle rendered their cover moot.

I took aim once again, used my ability, and was rewarded by another exploded torso. This time, I took an extra second to shoot at another alien, but to its credit, it reacted too quickly. The ball of superheated plasma splashed harmlessly against the wall of the building, and a familiar rain of gunfire destroyed the area where, only a second before, I'd been crouched.

They were getting faster.

Not a surprise, given that they had almost assuredly gotten over their panic. Too bad it wouldn't do any good with their current tactics.

No sooner had that thought crossed my mind than I saw a series of drones—sleeker and faster than any I'd seen before—rise into the sky. In the space of an instant, they'd closed the distance between us and opened fire. A buzzing sound of rapid gunfire filled the air even as the concrete erupted into rubble in my wake, and I ducked into another corridor just in time to avoid the worst of an explosion.

Still, the shock wave blew me forward almost ten feet. Activating Balance, I managed to twist my landing into a roll that ended with me back on my feet and running. As I did so, I embraced Stealth and ducked into one of the booths as I crouched behind the counter.

It was just in time, too, because the drones were hot on my trail. My heart was beating out of control as they stopped. There were three of them, all with white fuselages and sleek designs that reminded me of my Cutter. I wouldn't have been surprised if they'd been manufactured by the same company.

Fortunately, hidden as I was, I had the benefit of the stacked effects of both Camouflage and Stealth, which meant the drones had little chance of finding me, save by accident. So, with a couple of seconds to act, I used Misthack and, after spending a tense thirty seconds overcoming the thing's defenses, deactivated one of the drones. I almost flinched as it clattered to the ground, but I narrowly managed to maintain control long enough to initiate and execute another Misthack. Half a minute later, another drone fell to the ground.

With the third one, though, I took a different tactic. Instead of simply deactivating it, I took it over. It took a little longer, but given that it was the last one, I thought it was a valid risk. And it paid off because, a little more than a minute later, a new window opened in my HUD, and I piloted the drone back through the corridor and to the Octavangian camp.

It was still abuzz with activity, but the aliens seemed to relax when they saw the reappearance of the drone. Clearly, they thought that it had killed me.

So, I can only imagine their surprise when I directed the drone to close in and open fire. Before they could react, I'd peppered another three aliens with holes; the drone's ordinance wasn't nearly as damaging as what I could bring to bear, but it was sufficient to at least wound the Octavangians.

After a few seconds, they gathered their wits and fired on the drone. I tried to dodge, strafing them with gunfire at the same time, but I was no expert drone pilot, so my efforts came up short. To my surprise, though, the drone proved incredibly durable, and it took a veritable hail of gunfire to bring it down.

And given the effect their weaponry had had on the stadium's concrete, I knew they didn't lack firepower. Instead, the drones were obviously equipped with advanced armor. So, it was a good thing I'd used the Misthack strategy rather than try to bring them down with more conventional weapons.

By the time the Octavangians downed the drone, another three aliens were dead or so injured they wouldn't be able to fight. Counting the couple who were injured, that meant there were only three left from the original nine. However, as I'd expected, there were a handful—four, to be precise—more in the building that had come flooding out as reinforcements.

To my annoyance, when I poked my head back out, I saw that they'd retreated into the building, dragging their wounded inside.

I was more than a little tempted to just bring out the BMAP and demolish the structure, but the Rift apparatus was far too close for me to guarantee that it wouldn't be affected. No—if I wanted to clear them out, I'd have to go down there and get them.

Grinding my teeth in frustration, I said, "Seven left uninjured. At least two are wounded and probably out of the fight, but they've taken shelter inside their building. I'm going in."

"Be careful," came Patrick's voice over my interface. "I don't . . ."

I stopped listening because I was too busy diving forward as I narrowly avoided a clawed tentacle. I rolled to my feet just in time to dodge another. And another after that, raking across my arm and sending my Pulsar clattering to the ground. I could hardly even see them, they were moving so quickly, but their owner loomed over me like a specter of death.

Its skin rippled and changed color with every step, matching up with whatever was behind it. It was no wonder that I had missed it because, if it had stood still, there was no way I would have noticed. But now that it had made its move, I felt a little better about my chances.

I drew Ferdinand II from the holster at my waist, but I didn't fire. Not immediately. I could already tell that the alien was incredibly fast, so it wasn't out of the question that it would dodge, given the chance. So, I needed to wait for an opening.

To that end, I twisted and turned, avoiding the storm of striking tentacles; it wasn't easy, and I took a couple of shallow cuts from its claws, but I managed to endure its barrage mostly intact. It quivered with frustration, then slowed.

To my surprise, it asked, "Why?"

I could tell that its voice didn't really match up with what I heard, which was a strange gargling noise that sounded more like an underwater growl than anything else. But my Universal Language ability had finally shown its worth.

"We did nothing to you!" it burbled.

"You invaded my planet," I spat. "That's enough."

And then I shot it. It tried to dodge, but it couldn't move quite fast enough. Still, my shot didn't find center mass like I'd hoped, clipping one of its shoulders instead. But that was okay—I had eight more rounds in the cylinder, and I used every last one of them. It made a valiant effort at avoiding my shots, but each one tore a chunk of its rubbery skin from its body. By the time I'd emptied the cylinder, its arms were barely hanging on, and there were no less than three holes in its chest. Still, it hadn't died, even if it was mostly immobile now.

So, I calmly emptied the cylinder and reloaded before once again taking aim. Two shots later, it was dead. But I kept going until it was filled with another seven holes.

Finally, with that out of the way, I turned my attention back to the Octavangians who'd holed up in their building. I had a plan for them, too.

CHAPTER FIFTY-FOUR

ADRIFT

In the beginning, I thought I knew what I wanted. Money. Power. Respect. It seemed so simple. But now? I'd settle for a companion who isn't looking to leverage my friendship into some advantage.

—Nora Lancaster

I pressed myself against the wall of the prefabricated building, clutching a grenade as I focused on the readout on my HUD. Only one node remained before I gained access, but I didn't immediately tear through it. Instead, I took a moment to ensure I was ready for what I'd find when I forced the door open. I shifted, the fingers of one hand tightening around the grip of my R-14.

The plan was simple enough, but simplicity didn't always mean it would be easy to pull off. In fact, I knew there were dozens of things that could go wrong. But in my situation, there weren't a lot of other options—not ones that would get me what I wanted, at least. So, after taking a deep, calming breath, I plunged my awareness into the final node, solving it after only a few more seconds. Once that last line of defense fell before me, I took control of the door and immediately commanded it to open.

It slid to the side, exposing the interior—or more importantly, the Octavangians who'd sheltered inside. Ignoring them, I tossed my grenade through the door, and a second later, it exploded in a wave of light and sound.

I didn't hesitate before leaning out and squeezing the trigger. The R-14 barked in a series of three-round bursts that tore through the stunned aliens with surprising ease. But they didn't go down easily. That rubbery skin was tough, and it had some sort of passive regeneration that made them incredibly difficult to put down.

But it was nothing that couldn't be solved by a copious cascade of plasma rounds. Before they had a chance to recover from the flash-bang-induced stun, I'd already peppered them with bullets. As I exchanged the weapon's empty magazine for a fresh one, they continued to struggle, a few even begging for mercy. It made me regret my Universal Language ability.

It was easy to slaughter the Octavangians so long as I could look at them as the aliens they were. Easier still when I couldn't understand their burbling language. However, it grew much more difficult to put them down when the act was accompanied by their urgent pleas for mercy. Still, I hardened my heart by reminding myself that they were invaders. Sure, I hadn't seen them enslaving or killing people—not like the Castorix I'd encountered at the other Rift—but I wasn't so naive as to think their tentacles were clean.

But then again, neither were mine.

I wasn't ready for that kind of introspection, though, so I pushed those thoughts to the back of my mind and finished what I'd started. Before long, the aliens had twitched their last tentacles, and silence reigned through the area. I broke it by using the secure connection to contact Patrick, saying, "Threats neutralized. Come on over."

After he acknowledged, I set about inspecting the camp. It was surprisingly bare-bones, but I did find the trident-like weapons the Octavangians had carried to be interesting. I even fired one, but I soon discovered that my physiology didn't quite match up with the weapon's grip. I could easily see how tentacles would fare better.

I also found some supplies and a metallic crate half-full of Lesser Rift Shards, though there was nothing else of value. The Shards were of the smallest variety, suggesting that the aliens hadn't dared delve too deeply into the Rift. I set the crate aside before settling in to loot the aliens' bodies.

There wasn't much aside from a few credits, which I had to initiate a one-sided transfer to retrieve, the clothes on their backs, and the aforementioned weapons. All in all, it was a poor haul, but I hoped that the Rift would prove a better source of income. It did beg the question of why they seemed so destitute, though. I knew firsthand how much money could be made delving the Rifts, so why, then, were they not better equipped?

But it didn't take me long to answer my own question. Obviously, I couldn't be sure, but from what I'd learned, it wasn't cheap for the aliens to smuggle people onto the planet. So, it made sense that they would cut costs in order to maximize their profit. On top of that, I couldn't imagine that mining a Rift was a prestigious job. More likely, the aliens in charge had sent minimally qualified underlings. And finally, it wasn't as if the area was that dangerous. They'd already cleared out all the wildlife, and humans avoided Dead Zones. So, the reality was that they just didn't need to be well equipped or highly capable warriors. Instead, they needed a bunch of hapless mooks who'd accept whatever low pay they were probably given.

Suddenly, I wasn't so proud of my easy victory.

Fortunately, by that point, I only had to wait a few more minutes before Patrick joined me. I could see that he was a little disturbed by all the bodies, but I wasn't certain if that was due to the aliens' macabre appearance or if he just wasn't comfortable with my massacre. Probably some combination of the two.

Over the next few minutes, I directed him to store the loot in his own skill-based storage. It was much larger than my arsenal implant, but storing anything cost a significant amount of Mist. Retrieving his stored goods was even more expensive. He could get around that requirement by using a specialized Node, but those were fairly rare. There were a couple in Nova, most notably in the Dome, but other than that, the only one I knew of was owned by Gunther. Of course, the rich elites in the more affluent districts assuredly possessed their own access points, but that didn't matter much to me.

In any case, it only took Patrick a few minutes to store everything away. Once he'd finished, I asked, "You ready?"

He nodded, though his anxiety was written plainly across his face. Understandable. I'd been nervous the first time I'd encountered a Rift, as well. Even now, with that experience behind me, I was still a little apprehensive. After all, Rifts could take almost any form, which meant my experience was less valuable than it probably should have been. However, I had gained a significant amount of power since my last foray into an unknown Rift, so I hoped it would be a little easier.

Regardless, I was committed, and I wasn't going to waste the opportunity. That didn't mean Patrick had to go, though. So, I said, "If you don't want to do this, it's fine. I won't look down on you for it. You can stay out here and keep an eye out for—"

"No. I'm going," he said, his voice laced with steel. That's one of the things I had always liked about him. He might've been frightened, but he wasn't going to let that steer him off course.

"I thought so" was my response. "But I wanted to give you a chance to back out. Anyway—let's do it, then."

So, with that, we headed toward the nearby Rift, which presented itself as a formless and multicolored prism, around which the arms of the stabilizer curled. In some ways, the Rift was a beautiful sight, but it was also wholly disturbing, considering it just hung in midair, unsupported by anything and looking like nothing so much as a shapeless window into another unknowable dimension.

For his part, Patrick was far more interested in the stabilizer, which made sense. He was much more mechanically inclined than I was, so his fascination with the advanced machinery was unsurprising. Still, we were on a schedule. I didn't think the aliens had had an opportunity—or the inclination, really—to call in reinforcements from on high, but if they had, I didn't want to be around when the newcomers landed. The only reason I was willing to chance it at all was because I knew just how difficult it was for the aliens to infiltrate a planet still under the influence of the Initialization. If we didn't have the security of the quarantine, I would never have attempted it.

Even so, I had no intention of lingering, so I said, "C'mon. Let's do this. Remember, whatever happens in there, keep your head on a swivel and follow my lead. It's dangerous, so don't hesitate for even a second."

"I got it," he said.

"Good."

With that out of the way, I stepped forward and into the Rift. Patrick followed, though the moment I touched that blue prism, I lost all awareness of him—at least until, a second later, I stumbled into a strange situation. Patrick followed, almost tripping over me, but he managed to keep his feet. I wasn't paying much attention to him, though.

My previous experience within a Rift had conditioned me to expect something fantastical, but what I found was surprisingly familiar.

"Is this . . . the Bazaar?" asked Patrick.

My initial thought was that it was indeed the familiar space station orbiting Earth. However, there were a couple of key differences, chief among them that there was no crowd. The other major discrepancy was that the place looked like it had been abandoned for decades. The metallic walls, many of which bore huge rents that looked like claw marks, were rusted and stained with blood, and the floors hadn't fared any better.

"I don't think so," I said. "I think . . . I think this is . . . I don't know. A copy or something, maybe."

To the people of Earth, the Bazaar was a unique setting, but as far as I knew, there were dozens—perhaps even hundreds—of worlds in various stages of Integration in the wider universe. As such, it made sense that each one would play host to its own space station. It didn't take a leap of logic to assume that they were all similar.

In a way, that thought made me feel smaller than ever before. Humanity wasn't even close to unique. We weren't special. We were just a speck when compared to the rest of the universe.

"It doesn't matter," I said, hefting my R-14, which I'd summoned the moment we'd passed through the Rift. I scanned the giant entryway—it was at least five hundred yards long and perhaps twice as wide, with ceilings more than a hundred feet above the floor—but I found no threats. The place was entirely empty.

And creepy.

The Bazaar was an intimidating place, largely because of its incomprehensible size and the technology on display. However, it had also felt surprisingly mundane, mostly due to the crowds of humans that frequented the space station. This, though . . . This was different. Seeing its abandonment and the state of decay sent a shiver up my spine.

"Was the other Rift like this?" Patrick asked, his voice quivering a bit. I noticed that he at least had his pistol out, but he was clutching it so hard his knuckles had turned white. Not surprising, given the ominous atmosphere.

"No. No, it wasn't," I replied. "But it doesn't matter. They're all different. This is just another scenario. Let's move. I'm not sure what we're going to have to fight here, but it'll probably be something horrible."

Indeed, the creatures in my first Rift had been terrifying tentacle monsters and ratlike creatures. I didn't know if that was normal, but I suspected that each Rift would play host to something terrible.

With that, we started forward—gradually and with great caution—but it proved unnecessary. Nothing attacked us. There weren't even any obstacles. Still, I didn't relax. Even if the disturbing environment allowed for such a shift in my demeanor, I knew just how quickly things could turn. So, with my weapon up, we progressed into the first corridor.

For a while, we didn't encounter anything, and I began to think that the space station truly was completely abandoned. However, after about an hour, I saw something that put my hackles up.

One side of the wall was completely missing, and it was entirely open to space. The only thing keeping the atmosphere from escaping was a thin, blue Mist shield, though I knew from experience just how flimsy those could be. One little Misthack, and the thing would come down. If that happened, Patrick and I would be sucked out into the void of space.

But for now, even though it flickered with every passing second, it still held, which allowed me to focus on the planet looming in the distance. Or it had once been a planet.

"It . . . It looks like something took a bite out of it," muttered Patrick.

I could only nod in agreement. There was a sizable portion missing from the sphere, and though a few pieces lingered, slowly orbiting the planet, there wasn't enough material to account for the absent pieces.

I was just about to say something when I noticed the blackness of space move.

"Oh . . . Oh, God . . ."

Whatever it was, it was enormous beyond all comprehension. I could barely see more than the outline, but even that was enough to twist my insides into a thousand knots. It had the shape of a giant serpent. Or perhaps a worm. I couldn't make out any more than that.

But it was enough.

In the past, I'd wondered about the nature of the universe. I had only been Awakened a few years before, and already, I'd developed superhuman abilities and traits. And I knew that Mist extended life spans significantly. My uncle had been over a hundred years old, and he hadn't even looked like he'd reached middle age. So, extrapolating from that, what kind of power could someone twice his age achieve? What if they had the benefit of a fully Integrated world and all the technology and information that came with it? What about someone a thousand years old? Two thousand? What was the limit? Did one even exist?

More, I had seen extremely powerful creatures, as well. I also knew that, while they didn't progress in the same way that someone with a Nexus Implant might, they could still grow stronger. I'd sometimes wondered what would happen if something like that dragon had survived the bomb that had been meant to kill it. What if it had continued to grow more and more powerful?

Perhaps the thing hovering near the planet was the answer to that question. It didn't take a lot of guesswork to wonder if it had been the cause of that planet's woes. After all, it was large enough that it wasn't difficult to imagine that it had taken a bite.

Fortunately, it hadn't noticed us. Even if it had, would it even care? We weren't even ants to that monster.

Taking a deep breath, I stepped back from the huge rent in the wall, retreating until I couldn't see the scene outside the space station. That's when the lights started flickering.

I flinched, but with a force of will, I focused on the things I could affect. If that monster decided it wanted to eat the space station, then that's what it was going to do. I couldn't stop it. I couldn't even make it think twice. When it came to that creature, I was entirely powerless.

And I hated it.

Not because I thought I had reached the pinnacle or anything. I knew I hadn't. In fact, I knew I wasn't even close. But I'd somehow convinced myself that I could stand up to whatever monster happened to cross my path. After all, I'd spent a relative fortune on an arsenal of weapons that would take care of most threats on Earth. Maybe I wouldn't be able to stand up to enemies from other parts of the universe, but I could at least give them pause.

Seeing that planet-sized monster put the lie to that expectation.

"Are you okay?" asked Patrick, his voice trembling. He was just as terrified as I was. I knew that. But still, he was worried about me.

"No. Not really," I said. "I . . . I don't . . ."

I took another deep breath. Seeing that creature didn't change anything. I didn't need to be the most powerful person around, did I? No. I just needed enough strength to dissuade anyone from taking advantage of me.

"I'm fine," I lied. "I'm fine. Let's . . . Let's keep going . . ."

"But—"

"I said I'm fine, Patrick," I reiterated. Then, I took another deep breath before adding, "Nothing's changed. We still need to finish this Rift."

"I . . . Shouldn't we just turn back?" he asked.

I shook my head. "Did you see an exit? Because I didn't," I said. I'd looked for it, too. During my first Rift experience, I'd been stupid enough to keep going well after I should have turned back. Back then, I'd had my reasons—mostly that I wanted to prove myself to my uncle, and I thought that retreating from the Rift would have counted as a failure of the test he'd given me—but they didn't matter in the face of how foolish the decision had been. So, I'd vowed not to repeat it.

The Rift seemed to have other ideas, though, and it didn't offer a convenient exit. If I had to guess, we weren't getting out unless we found our way to the end. I did wonder how the Octavangians, who I'd assumed had never progressed far into the Rift, had gotten out. Perhaps they had some specialized equipment or something. Or maybe they just knew what they were doing. I had no way of knowing and little opportunity to research possible explanations.

With that, I started forward, pointedly ignoring the giant hole in the space station's fuselage—or more importantly, the shadowy creature that had taken a bite out of planet. Patrick followed, probably because he had no idea what else to do.

For the next hour, we saw nothing else of note, save that the state of the station was more of the same. So, when we finally stumbled upon a change, I almost didn't notice it.

"Stop!" Patrick said, reaching out and grabbing my arm.

In most cases, he wouldn't have been capable of stopping me, but the moment he'd spoken, my awareness snapped back to reality, and I saw precisely what had alarmed him. Before us was a metal wire stretched across the hall at chest height, so thin that it was barely even visible.

"What the . . ."

"I only saw it because the lights flashed," he muttered. "What do you think it is?"

"I don't know," I admitted. "It almost looks like a . . ."

A series of clicks sounded from up ahead, and I looked up just in time to see one more horror to add to my nightmares.

". . . A spider's web."

CHAPTER FIFTY-FIVE

ARACHNOPHOBIA

Finally, I know the truth. At first, I couldn't believe it. How did she survive so long? Why didn't she come back? All Jeremiah ever did was torture her. She should have thanked me. Instead, she chose to set herself up as my enemy.

—Nora Lancaster

I swept my arm, pushing Patrick behind me as I took aim at the abomination skittering down the corridor in my direction. It was a spider, but unlike any I had ever seen before. For one, it was at least as big as a person, though it was hard to be sure because the legs made it seem much larger than it really was. For another, it seemed to have been constructed almost entirely of silvery metal, with the most notable exception being its head, which was completely organic and just as horrible as the giant-spider label would suggest.

But by far the most horrifying aspect of the arachnid's appearance was the bulbous abdomen in the back. Completely transparent, save for a frame of the same gleaming metal so prevalent in the rest of its body, the abdomen's primary purpose seemed to be to show off the giant brain floating in the green-tinted liquid within.

Which had all sorts of disturbing implications.

Was it just a spider with an extra, abnormally large brain? Was it some creation of a mad scientist? A fusion of a sentient creature and a heavily modified giant spider? I had no idea, and I wasn't eager to find out.

All those—and a hundred other—thoughts rampaged through my mind for only a second before I ruthlessly shoved them aside and focused on survival. After all, my experience with Rifts told me that the monster bearing down on us wasn't interested in a peaceful exchange of ideas. No—as far as

I knew, the monsters in Rifts were universally aggressive. And this spider didn't seem keen on bucking that trend, given the way it had screeched and charged upon seeing us.

I opened fire.

From behind me, so did Patrick.

The spider skittered to the left, avoiding the initial salvo. My rounds hit the floor, caroming toward the ceiling, where the plasma melted through to the next level. But by then, the monster had closed on us, and I felt something wrap around my stomach and drag me in its direction.

Panicked—after all, I'd seen nothing to explain what was happening—I continued to fire on the spider. But I was off-balance, and the monster was more than capable of dodging. The result was that my shots went wide as it yanked me toward its clacking mandibles, which looked more like they belonged on a giant beetle than a spider. And given that they were serrated, it wasn't difficult to figure out that they were intended to tear the spider's prey into more manageable pieces.

Even as I flew through the air, I made a split-second decision, dismissing my R-14 and drawing my nano-bladed sword. Just before I came into range of the spider's horrifying jaws, I lowered the sword like a lance.

The monster tried to react, and I felt the invisible pressure around my waist dissipate. But it could do nothing about my momentum, and I crashed into the monster, blade first. My sword slid into that organic head with frightening ease, all the way up to the hilt. As we collided, the creature went wild, bucking and stabbing at me with its metallic legs. The subdermal Sheath, which, courtesy of the Mist boosters, had repaired itself over the past few days, held up.

But despite having two feet of nano-blade buried in its head, the creature didn't die. As I was thrown to the side, I maintained my grip, wrenching the nano-bladed sword free in a shower of black ichor. The spider's bloodcurdling screech echoed off the walls as I skidded across the floor. Activating Balance, I turned my clumsy tumble into a roll and came to my feet a few feet later.

I didn't stop, though. Instead, I drew Ferdinand II from the holster at my hip and, one-handed, fired. The spider was still stunned from the hole I'd left in its head, so its attempt at a dodge was more like a drunken stumble. My aim was true, and Ferdinand II's issue collided with its thorax. It did little good, though, bouncing off without leaving so much as a scuff mark.

I was about to exchange Ferdinand II for my assault rifle when the monster erupted into vibration so violent that it took the form of a high-pitched buzz that assaulted my ears. A second later, something hit me in the chest. A moment after that, something else punched me in the ribs with the force of a battering ram. Then, yet another unseen pillar of force sent me flying through the air until I collided with the ceiling.

Over the next few seconds, I endured a half dozen more blows. All I could do was protect my most vital asset by curling up and wrapping my arms around my head. My body was durable, and I could endure quite a bit of punishment. However, if something started rattling my brain, I'd be done for.

In something of a panic, I activated Misthack while in midair. I shouldn't have been surprised when the option to hack into whatever passed for the monster's interface flashed on my HUD. I thudded into the wall before I could confirm the infiltration. My head crashed against the metallic surface, and for a second, I was stunned.

That was all the spider needed.

It rushed forward on its spindly legs, and in that moment, I felt some indefinable pressure clamp down on me. I couldn't move. I couldn't really think. I could barely even breathe. But the spider was unaffected.

It loomed over me, rearing up for a strike I knew would be fatal.

And then a series of shots rang through the corridor. The sound of metal on metal filled the air, and out of the corner of my eye, I saw Patrick standing in a classic shooting stance—feet shoulder width apart and both hands on the black-and-gold pistol he'd gotten from Gala—as he repeatedly squeezed the trigger.

When Gala had sold it to us, I'd known that the Tergan Tactical Energy Pistol was a powerful weapon. After what it'd cost, it should have been. And the fact that it required a specific certification supported that assessment. I also knew that Patrick had a skill that modified the damage he could do with pistols. And he'd been practicing, too, so it was probably reasonably advanced.

Still, I'd underestimated him because he rarely fought.

That had been a mistake.

The sheer kinetic force of the rounds sent the monster stumbling away. As surprising as it was, it didn't really do much damage. But that brief stumble gave me the opportunity to confirm my Misthack and dive into the creature's Mistwall. Fortunately, it wasn't difficult to bypass; I'd encountered more robust defenses back in Nova City, and after spending the last few days repeatedly hacking into that aural sensor, getting through the spider's Mistwall was practically a breeze.

However, I got a bit of a shock when I burst through only to see that there was a distinct lack of options. In fact, there was only one: Overcharge. Annoyed, I selected it before the spider could regain its balance.

The moment I felt the Mist agitate at my command, the creature locked up and let out an unholy screech that echoed through the whole corridor. I ignored it, yelling, "Aim for the brain!"

Even as I shouted the order, I summoned my Pulsar, and trusting the Misthack to keep the creature busy for a few seconds, used Empowered Shot. By the time the requisite charging period had passed, the spider had begun to recover, but it wasn't enough.

I squeezed the trigger.

The Pulsar roared.

And less than an instant later, the monster's abdomen exploded in a ball of liquid-hot plasma. The force of the shot threw the creature against the wall, denting the decayed metal surface. But when the smoke cleared, I saw that the glass abdomen only bore a slight crack. The green-tinted liquid inside boiled, and the monster twitched in obvious pain, but that single shot, powerful though it was, wasn't nearly enough to put it out of commission.

So, I fired again, this time without the benefit of my ability. I knew it wouldn't do that much good; I could only hope that the crack would provide a point of weakness I could exploit.

But before I could find out, my shot was joined by Patrick's. Neither of us stopped. He fired two shots for each one I could coax from the Pulsar—its slower fire rate on obvious display—but the rifle's rounds were clearly more powerful. Either way, we filled the corridor with the sound of a veritable cascade of gunfire.

Still, by the time I'd emptied my magazine, the monster was still alive. Barely.

I pushed myself to my feet and repeated my Misthack, stunning it with Overcharge once again. And again. I kept it locked up as I calmly took in the state of the creature. Its abdomen bore huge cracks that leaked green liquid that had already puddled on the floor, and its legs twitched out of control.

Clearly, it wasn't long for the world.

But still, I wasn't going to take any chances. So, once I had replaced the spent magazine with a fresh one, I calmly took aim, used Empowered Shot, and squeezed the trigger. It was more than the abdomen could bear, and it shattered into a million pieces. A hissing sound greeted my ears as the superheated plasma round boiled and evaporated a good portion of the green liquid. But even that didn't finish the spider off.

So, I did it again; this time, my shot was accompanied by Patrick's.

The brain exploded in a shower of gore and what was left of the green-tinted water.

Finally, the spider collapsed under its own weight, and I let out a sigh of relief. I didn't relax, though. Where there was one, there might be others, and I refused to be taken by surprise again.

"I think it was telekinetic," Patrick muttered, his voice quivering from adrenaline and fear.

"You think?"

He shrugged, and replied, "I mean, it's the only thing that really makes sense, right? And with that big brain . . ."

I wanted to disagree, but all the evidence pointed in the direction he suggested. In fact, I was a little embarrassed that I hadn't come to the same conclusion earlier. I was busy being pummeled by an unseen force, so I guess I had an excuse, but it still irked me a little. I'd have to pay better attention from now on.

"And this is what you want to do . . . for fun and relaxation?" he asked, obviously referring to my tentative plans for the future. At the time I'd given them voice, I hadn't really given it much thought, but in the interim, I'd made up for it with plenty of contemplation. And what I'd found was that there was a certain appeal to spending my days challenging Rifts. Obviously, that wouldn't be my entire life—nobody could keep up that pace—but I could easily see that becoming my focus.

"I don't know if I'd put it like that," I said, kneeling next to the spider's corpse. In death, it seemed a bit smaller than it had in life—likely because the legs had curled under it—but I was still horrified by its size. As I began my inspection, I continued, "It'd be more like a job. Or a purpose. I don't know. I just can't imagine myself settling down and . . . I don't know . . . gardening for the rest of my life."

He took a knee beside me, and as he started his own inspection, he asked, "What about kids? A family?"

"Maybe," I said, shrugging. I'd never given that much thought. I certainly wasn't celibate or anything, so I suppose pregnancy was always a possibility. But there were plenty of ways to prevent that sort of thing. And besides, the whole idea terrified me in a way a giant spider never could. Not only was the notion of growing another life inside my body difficult for me to wrap my brain around, but the idea of raising an actual child was even more horrifying. I could barely take care of myself, much less another human being, and I had no interest in that kind of responsibility. "I don't know. That's a question for another day, though."

"Yeah. You're probably right," he admitted. "So, is this what it's always like?"

"How should I know?" I replied. "I've only been inside one other Rift, and it was nothing like this."

"How so?"

"Well, it was more like a series of rooms," I said. "Each one was more difficult than the last. And the connecting corridors each had . . . restrictions."

"Like what?"

I told him about the hall filled with the falling motes of light that, when they had touched me, sent agonizing pain throughout my body. Or the one filled with gelatinous ooze that tried to melt my feet off.

"That's . . . horrifying . . ."

I shrugged. "I made it through okay," I said. "I ended up having to spend weeks healing, though. Hopefully, this one will be easier."

"Pretty sure it's going to be the opposite," he said.

"Why do you say that?" I asked. Sure, it was different, but that spider hadn't been that much more difficult than those furry tentacle monsters. But then again, my own power had grown considerably since that first Rift, which might have skewed my perception a little.

He shrugged. "I don't know," he said. "I didn't go through the last one, so I can't say for sure. But what we saw . . . with that planet and everything . . . It suggests that this is . . . I don't know . . ."

I understood the sentiment. It was easy to think of that giant, planet-sized creature as mere window dressing, but even from hundreds of miles away—or more; perception of distance was difficult in space—the thing's power had almost overwhelmed me. It was probably worse for Patrick, too. But what inclined me to agree with his assessment was largely unrelated to that.

"It does seem a lot more elaborate," I stated. "That might mean it's a higher level of difficulty. Maybe it had more Mist to work with or something."

Not for the first time, I wished there was more information on Rifts. My uncle had explained the basics, but he'd clearly held quite a lot of information back, probably intending to educate me at a later date. He'd never had a chance, though, which left me dangerously ignorant.

But I refused to believe that those Octavangians could successfully mine the Rift if I couldn't. Of course, they'd probably taken the time to scout it out, and there was no telling what kinds of specialized equipment they'd possessed. For all I knew, they had an easy way of dealing with monsters like the spider we'd just brute forced.

I sighed.

"What?" he asked.

I shook my head. "It's nothing," I answered. "Sometimes, I just feel like I'm fighting an uphill battle, you know? Things would be so much easier if I wasn't just blindly feeling my way through all of this."

I didn't think there was an easy solution, though. For whatever reason, people guarded any valuable information extremely jealously, which meant that I wasn't going to solve my ignorance with mere research. Instead, I had little choice but to do so via experience, which was incredibly dangerous.

But that was kind of the point, wasn't it? I wasn't so blind to my own personality that I couldn't see that the danger was what made overcoming a Rift so satisfying. If it was easy, like many of my operations in Nova City had been, I wouldn't have found it so psychologically rewarding.

Besides, that very danger was what made the Rift Shards so valuable.

Speaking of which, I said, "Keep your eyes peeled, okay? In the last Rift, every time I overcame an obstacle, I was rewarded with a bunch of Shards."

Patrick nodded, and after we continued our inspection of the dead spider—which yielded no new information—we continued along. We didn't get far before we were confronted with a series of cocoons made of metallic webs.

"Wish I had a flamethrower," I muttered to myself as I picked my way through. I didn't need to unravel the cocoons to guess what they contained. Basic knowledge of spiders and the vaguely humanoid shapes on display were enough to make that abundantly clear. After all, Earth's spiders had a habit of wrapping their still-living prey in webs and saving them for a later meal. I had no reason to suspect the weird alien spider had different habits.

Or rather, I had no interest in inspecting it further. The things creeped me out, and I just wanted to find the Shards, complete the Rift, and be on my way. Even the furry tentacle monsters from my first Rift couldn't really compare to how unsettling the spider had been.

Slowly, we continued along, keeping an eye out for stray webs. We needn't have bothered because, over the next few hundred yards, we encountered nothing. Then, finally, there was an open door. And inside was a huge crate. I didn't need to open it to know what was inside; my Mist sense told me enough that I could guess that the crate held a cache of Rift Shards.

The only problem was that it was draped in metallic webs and absolutely covered in fist-sized spiders that looked like miniature versions of the creature we had just killed.

"Definitely wish I had a flamethrower," I whispered.

We were more than twenty feet away, and my voice had been barely loud enough for Patrick to hear. But even that was enough to alert the little monsters.

"Uh . . . Mira . . ."

A shiver ran up my spine as the creatures flowed toward us in a wave of clicking metallic legs, collective hissing, and clacking mandibles. I did my best to ignore it as I readied myself to greet them.

CHAPTER FIFTY-SIX

INFESTATION AND EXTERMINATION

I thought she would understand. I hoped she would see that what happened was necessary. And I tried—I truly tried—to keep her out of it. But how does she repay me? With betrayal. The apple clearly didn't fall very far from the tree.

—Nora Lancaster

The horde of spiders raced toward me in a grotesque wave of legs, clacking mandibles, and metallic chitin. Seeing that, it was so difficult not to panic. Lots of people are afraid of spiders, but I'd never been afflicted with arachnophobia. Not until I saw hundreds of them skittering toward me, at least. It's almost impossible to maintain composure in the face of such a sight.

With an urgent sweep of my arm, I shoved Patrick behind me. Notably, he didn't protest, and for a split second, I wondered if he had the right of it. After all, he didn't really have to get away. He just had to keep me between him and the wave of spiders. Still, I didn't dwell on it for long. Instead, at the same time as I was pushing him out of harm's way, I was dismissing my assault rifle and summoning my scattergun.

Because, for all its faults when it came to lethality, it did one thing remarkably well. When the little monsters drew within five feet, I let loose with a Double Shot–empowered cone of condensed lightning, bathing the area in twin waves of electricity. It hit them with an audible hiss—their metallic bodies turned out to be excellently conductive—and I was surprised when a cascade of shattering glass assaulted my ears, followed by the acrid smell of burning meat. It didn't take me long to notice that the little brains suspended in the green liquid within their abdomens were sizzling. As one, the still-twitching arachnids skidded to the floor, their limbs spasming out of control.

I fired again.

And again after that. I kept going until the cannister was empty, and even then, I switched it out for a fresh one and kept going. The first spider had been so durable that I had no intentions of taking any chances with these much-smaller creatures. So, I didn't stop until I'd emptied two full cannisters into the horde of many-legged monsters, and by that point, even their metallic chitin had begun to melt and deform. Of their brains, only a series of thumb-sized charred husks remained.

"I . . . I think you got 'em," said Patrick, his voice trembling a little.

I stepped forward and prodded one of the things with my foot. It didn't react, so I simply said, "Yeah."

It was a bit anticlimactic, but in a good way. The mere thought of those little spiders crawling all over me was enough to send a shiver of discomfort up my spine.

"What do you think's in those cocoons?" my companion asked, pointing to the bundles of spun metal wire attached to the walls and ceiling.

I shrugged. "Prey, probably," I stated. "If I had to guess? Octavangians who didn't make it."

But in reality, I had no real idea, and I wasn't going to try to pick those metal webs apart to find out. So, it would remain a mystery. However, as unconcerned as I was with the contents of those cocoons, I was equally interested in the crate at the center of the room. After all, I'd already felt the condensation of Mist that suggested it contained Rift Shards. The only question was how big they were.

So, Patrick and I entered the room, and after making sure there were no other spiders hiding in the shadows, we stepped up to the crate. It took me a moment to figure out how to open it, but once I puzzled out the latching mechanism, the lid sprang upright, revealing the contents.

"Jackpot," I said, grinning. Inside were hundreds of Rift Shards, and a quick mental calculation told me that it was roughly equal to the number I'd gotten from the first two nodes in the other Rift. That suggested that it was a much richer Rift.

After all, if the past version of me had been attacked by that first spider, I would've been easily killed. The only reason I'd managed to come out on top this time was because of a combination of my escalating power and Patrick's presence. So, given the increased danger, it stood to reason that the rewards would be commensurate.

Or perhaps I was entirely wrong.

I had no way of knowing until I progressed farther into the Rift. To that end, I had Patrick store the entire crate away.

"That's convenient," I said.

"Takes a ton of Mist, though," he said, obviously feeling the strain. "Thankfully, it's pretty thick here, but it'll still take me a few minutes to get back to normal."

"A break, then."

"Is that safe?" he asked.

I shrugged. "I spent weeks in the first Rift," I explained. "Most of it was spent healing, but I spent time training, too. If this follows the same structure, we should be fine."

"And if it doesn't?" was his next question.

"Then we'll deal with it," I stated. Despite being home to a bunch of dead arachnids, the room was actually a great place to rest, mostly due to the fact that we had only seen a single entrance. If push came to shove, I could defend that for hours. Of course, I had no intention of staying any longer than necessary. Once Patrick regenerated enough, we'd move on to the next challenge.

As it turned out, it only took Patrick half an hour before he announced he was back to normal. With that out of the way, we left the room and continued to delve the Rift. For a couple of hours, we encountered nothing but empty corridors, but soon enough, we nearly stumbled over another strand of metallic webbing stretched across the hall.

"Probably another one of those big spiders," I guessed, keeping my voice low.

"Should we go back and try to find another way?"

I shook my head. "No. That's not how this works," I stated. We'd passed plenty of offshoots as we traversed the derelict space station, but the few we'd explored were blocked off. Therefore, I'd come to the conclusion that the Rift wanted us to follow a specific route and overcome whatever threats it put in our path. In that way, it was similar to the first Rift I'd delved. So, I added, "I'm pretty sure there's only one viable route. But I do think we should retreat a bit."

"Why?" he asked.

"Spiders aren't the only ones who can make traps," I answered.

Then, we headed back a few hundred feet. Luckily, this part of the hall was fairly straight, so we maintained a good sight line on the web. It wasn't visible from so far away—even with Observation—but I knew it was there. And somewhere nearby, its creator doubtless lurked.

Once Patrick and I were set up, I summoned the Pulsar and aimed down the hall. Then, I whispered, "Now."

Patrick took aim and fired his pistol. It wasn't as noisy as any of my firearms, but it was loud enough to send the report echoing down the corridor. As soon as he fired, I started charging Empowered Shot. The requisite two seconds passed, but the spider still hadn't responded, so I held it at the edge of release.

Gritting my teeth at the strain, I muttered, "C'mon, you stupid bug. Come and get us."

I didn't have to wait much longer before I heard the sound of metal clacking against metal echoing down the corridor. Only a second later, I saw another huge arachnid skitter into view a few hundred feet away. Finally, I squeezed the Pulsar's trigger, sending a ball of superheated plasma rocketing down the hall. Immediately, I used Mark Target on the creature, more for the modifier to my damage than to keep it from slipping away.

The spider tried to throw itself to the side in order to dodge, but its momentum was too great, and the Empowered Shot took it in the thorax. It wasn't precisely where I'd aimed, but it would have to do. The force of the shot slammed the enormous creature into the wall, but it only took a second for it to gather itself and shoot forward.

By then, I'd already charged another Empowered Shot.

I let loose once again, and to similar results. Over and over, I fired, and with each Empowered Shot, I felt my reserves of Mist drain away. Meanwhile, the monster doggedly persisted in its charge, gaining a few dozen feet between one shot and the next. By the time my magazine ran dry, its carapace glowed red, and it was peppered with gaping holes. Unfortunately, its dodges had not been random. Instead, they were calculated moves meant to protect its vulnerable abdomen. As such, I'd only managed to land one shot on the transparent casing that held its huge brain.

Still, my efforts were not in vain. One of the monster's legs had been severed by a particularly lucky shot, and half its mandibled face was missing. Even so, it maintained its lethal viability as a dangerous predator.

That's when Patrick enacted the second part of the plan, tossing a pair of conflagration grenades in the monster's vicinity. The blast radius of those grenades was such that precision was inconsequential, and when they exploded, they bathed the arachnid in twin rings of liquid flame that could melt steel in a few seconds. The spider's carapace was made of some stronger alloy, though, because it emerged from that fiery inferno still intact.

But it clearly wasn't unscathed.

In that time, I'd exchanged my Pulsar for my R-14, and the moment it skittered out of that wall of flame, I opened fire in a series of three-round bursts. Not to be outdone, Patrick yanked his pistol from the holster at his hip and let loose, as well. Like that, we both emptied our magazines into the unfortunate monster, each round tearing a new hole in the spider's half-melted carapace.

Still, it dragged itself forward one skittering step at a time.

By the time it closed to within ten feet, it was barely recognizable. I exchanged my empty magazine for fresh one and continued the barrage as I backed away. Patrick did the same, following my lead as we kept up the pressure. Like that, we continued on until we'd retreated another hundred feet.

The spider surged forward in a final, twitching attempt. But it came up predictably short. Finally, it collapsed to the ground. Miraculously, it was still alive, though. Half-melted and riddled with holes, with half of its legs missing or twisted into slag—it refused to surrender. Calmly, I exchanged my assault rifle for the Pulsar and reloaded.

Then, at last, I raised my weapon, used the last of my Mist to activate a final Empowered Shot, and fired a round at the monstrous, bulbous backside. It tried to twitch out of the way, but our assault had rendered it completely incapable of moving much more than a few inches. And that wasn't nearly enough to take it out of harm's way.

The Pulsar's issue shattered the glass-like abdomen and tore through the monster's hind brain. With that, it finally collapsed and surrendered to death.

And I let out a sigh of relief.

"Those things are way too durable," Patrick said.

"Yeah," I agreed. I had some thoughts about other ways to attack the thing, but I was too afraid of its telekinetic abilities to implement them. I didn't want to tangle with something I didn't understand, and that invisible force definitely fell under the umbrella of things that evaded my comprehension.

But it did once again suggest that this Rift was much more advanced than the one I'd tackled before. Or perhaps I just didn't know the trick to dealing with the arachnids. I refused to think that those Octavangians were strong enough to do something with which I struggled. I'd already beaten them, after all.

"Well, on a good note, if it follows the same pattern, we should expect to find another cache somewhere around here," I said.

"What if the difficulty increases?" he asked.

It was a valid question. In fact, I fully expected to encounter something stronger, and soon. Considering that the spiders were already stretching the limits of our capabilities, the idea that we might find something more powerful barring our way was a bit intimidating. As such, it was probably a good idea to just head back and search out an exit. One had to exist; we simply hadn't found it yet.

The problem was that the single crate we'd recovered wasn't enough to accomplish my goals. So, sure—it was dangerous to keep going. But that was the appeal, wasn't it? Or at least part of it.

Besides, I knew I would regret it if I retreated.

"We'll deal with it," I said. "I haven't really stretched myself yet."

That, at least, was true. And as dangerous and difficult a foe as those spiders were, they hadn't pushed me to the absolute limit of my abilities. For instance, the most recent fight hadn't even required me to use my {Mistrunner} skills.

"Let's get moving."

With that, Patrick and I continued down the corridor, soon leaving the spider's corpse—as well as its webs—behind. After a while, we found another cache that was, predictably, guarded by another horde of smaller arachnids. I dealt with them much as I'd killed the first group, and we were rewarded with yet another crate of Rift Shards.

But by that point, we'd been in the Rift for almost ten hours, so I said, "This is a good spot to rest, I think. Let's set things up."

We spent the next hour engaged in spider-corpse removal, and after we'd relocated the mound of arachnid bodies outside, we took a few minutes to set up the autoturrets we'd brought along. I had no illusions about whether or not they'd be sufficient in any sort of defense, but they could function as an early-warning system and a distraction. Hopefully, that would be enough to give us time to respond, should we be attacked.

After that, Patrick and I set up our cots. I insisted on taking the first watch, and soon enough, he was asleep. After all, he wasn't used to fighting for his life, so it had probably been a very trying day for him. Even my nerves were a bit frayed, and I was accustomed to such struggle. I could only imagine how he felt.

For the following six hours, I kept watch, but it proved completely unnecessary. Nothing attacked us during that time. Nor were we subjected to an assault while I took my turn sleeping. So it was that we shared a breakfast of ration bars before we set off to explore the rest of the Rift.

And for a while, it was just more of the same. We fought one more giant spider and the subsequent horde of smaller spiders guarding a third crate of Rift Shards, but by that point, we had the process down to a science. The giant spider never even got close, and the smaller arachnids were dispatched with ease.

So, it was somewhat understandable that, when things did change, we were taken completely by surprise.

It was a few hours after our second night—subjectively speaking; outside the Rift, it was midday—when we entered one of the cavernous spaces that, in our version of the Bazaar, had been reserved for the various merchants. Row upon row of stacked cubes that served as the premises for the resident businesses stretched beyond my perception, but I wasn't focused on these structures.

Instead, my attention was squarely on the people who, the moment we stepped into the space, turned to face us. A shiver ran up my spine as I realized that they did so in unison, almost as if they were a single entity.

"Not good," I muttered, noticing that the entire area was draped in metallic cobwebs.

And then there were the spiders.

Hundreds of them, each the size of a small child, perched in the densest parts of the webbing.

As one, the people let out a collective scream of outrage. Hundreds of races were represented, but it didn't seem to matter. They were clearly all connected, as if they were only one piece of a greater whole.

Before I reacted, I couldn't help but notice that the spiders didn't move. Nor did they look like the ones we'd encountered before. No metal carapaces. No giant floating brains. In fact, they looked much like normal, mundane arachnids, save that they were comparatively enormous.

The crowd of humanoids surged forward, and I screamed, "No holding back!"

That's when I brought out the big gun. My BMAP roared, and one explosion after another rocked the ship.

And so the battle began.

I could only hope that we would survive.

CHAPTER FIFTY-SEVEN

SOUL SPIKE

Sometimes, a purge is necessary. I didn't want to, but it was my only option when dealing with those ungrateful wretches. Luckily, their entitlement never had a chance to spread before I nipped it in the bud. Still, I regret that it was necessary.

—Nora Lancaster

Until that point, I'd eschewed the use of my most powerful weapon, mostly because I wasn't sure how well the walls would hold up under the weight of its ordinance. However, with a horde of humanoid thralls bearing down on me, I had little choice but to go all out. If the hull was breached, I could only hope that the Mist shields would keep the atmosphere contained. Otherwise, it wouldn't matter if I was ripped apart by the mob.

Before the BMAP's rounds landed, I couldn't help but notice that a multitude of species were present within the surging horde. I saw scales, multiple arms and legs attached to curiously shaped torsos, and fur-covered bodies in abundance. There were humans, too. And plenty of creatures I couldn't really categorize as anything but monsters. One and all, though, they continued their screeching charge.

Explosions rocked the space, sending dozens of the creatures flying through the air—often in more than one piece—but I continued firing until the drum was empty. As I reloaded, I was beset by déjà vu, my mind immediately latching on to the similarity of the surging horde of mindless aliens and the mass of mutated wildlings I'd fought less than a week before.

But the situations were dissimilar enough that the illusion shattered under even the lightest scrutiny. For one, while the aliens came in all sorts of shapes, they weren't deformed like the wildlings had been. For another, they didn't seem as feral. Instead, aside from their screeching, they were remarkably devoid of any expression. No anger. No fear. Just immutable placidity.

Finally, the aliens all moved in perfect unison, as if they were being controlled by a hive mind. Considering the presence of the smaller spiders and my previous experience with the others spiders' telekinetic prowess, it didn't take a leap of logic to stumble upon the possibility that the horde was being telepathically controlled by the spiders.

Which was horrifying.

Not least because I had no real defense against such an assault. Hammering that home was a sudden spike of pain that felt like it sliced right through my brain. Or my thoughts. I let out a grunt, knowing full well that I'd only retained consciousness because of Pain Tolerance. Or perhaps my high Mind attribute. Either way, it was enough to keep me from blacking out, but not nearly enough to keep me from experiencing untold agony.

Behind me, Patrick got it worse, letting out a full-fledged scream as he clutched at his temples. I couldn't spare him any thought, though, because my barrage had only slowed the horde down. It would take far more than a single cannister of explosive rounds to completely stop them.

It was a good thing that I'd brought plenty of ammunition, then.

In a move I'd practiced a thousand times before, I exchanged the spent drum for a fresh one and resumed my bombardment. The thump of the BMAP's discharge filled the air, followed by the soothing sound of explosions. But the aliens' numbers seemed endless. If I had to guess, I would've said that the horde was populated by each and every one of the space station's previous occupants—an assumption supported by the numbers as well as their disparate attire.

Some were dressed casually, looking remarkably similar to what I might see in Nova City. Others wore military uniforms. Still others wore rich, flowing robes that suggested wealth and influence. None of the clothing was in good shape, but it was still easily categorized.

Of course, not every thrall was completely intact. Plenty sported grievous and rotting wounds. More than one looked as if it should've been in a grave. But they maintained enough mobility to contribute to the charge.

Dozens—then hundreds—fell before my barrage, but I knew it wouldn't be enough. There were too many, and I had too little ammunition. It was a similar problem to what I'd encountered against the mutated wildlings. I could kill them well enough, but one person could only do so much. And with every passing second, the horde of thralls pushed closer, ensuring that it would eventually devolve into a melee. Like had been the case with the wildlings, I would doubtless defeat many more, but at some point, the weight of their numbers would bear me to the ground. When that happened, I would be ripped to pieces.

I could see it all so clearly. I was destined to lose.

So, I needed to change the game.

Retreat was a possibility, but not an attractive one. Perhaps the thralls would give up the chase, but I suspected their pursuit would doggedly continue. And given that I knew the Rift would eventually repopulate—perhaps it already had—there was every chance that retreat would see us running headlong into more danger. With the thralls still in pursuit, we'd be stuck between two hostile forces.

No—retreat wasn't really an option.

Nor was fighting the horde head-on.

It wasn't until I noticed that the spiders still hadn't moved that I stumbled upon a potential solution. If the aliens were being controlled by these stationary spiders, then what would happen if I started killing them off? Perhaps they'd lose control altogether. At the very least, it might buy us some time.

The only problem was that, with the thralls bearing down on us, I couldn't spare the time it would take to target them. Fortunately, I wasn't alone.

"Patrick!" I screamed as I loaded my third cannister. "Target the spiders!"

I had no idea if he even heard me. In fact, I felt certain that he hadn't, considering that he was still screaming in agony. But in that moment, I chose to trust him. Perhaps it would prove a fatal mistake, but I wanted to wait until the last instant before I adjusted the plan.

I continued firing, but the surging horde clamored over the still-smoking bodies of their brethren as they closed the distance between us. All the while, their screeches continued to fill the air; Patrick's own screaming had died down, and I dared to hope that he'd managed to find a way to focus through the pain.

For my part, the agony was distracting, but I had plenty of experience and an ability on my side. He didn't, as far as I knew.

Fifty yards away, the aliens came into focus. At first, it was difficult to notice, largely because of their alien physiology, but after only a second or two, I could confidently say that they were, one and all, malnourished. How long had the spiders kept them captive? Weeks, at least. Probably longer, considering that higher Constitution meant a reduced need for sustenance. In my case, I could easily survive for a couple of months without food. It wouldn't be pleasant, but I could do it.

The enthralled aliens continued their shambling charge, and I maintained my bombardment, eventually emptying yet another cannister. I exchanged it quickly, but even that small delay meant that the aliens gained a few extra yards.

When they closed to within twenty yards, I started mapping out a plan for retreat. It would be close, especially if I had to carry Patrick, but I felt confident that I could outrun the horde. They weren't the real issue, though. Instead, that designation belonged to whatever we'd left in our wake.

Rifts didn't follow normal rules. Instead, they were just manifestations of densely concentrated Mist. As such, the conjured spaces—and the creatures within—functioned on a timer. Eventually, the monsters we had killed, as well as the Rift Shards we'd gathered, would repopulate. I had no idea how long that would take, but my intuition told me it wouldn't be long.

Perhaps the spiders had already reformed.

There was no way I intended to run headlong into that kind of danger if I had any other option. But it was quickly becoming apparent that I wouldn't be afforded much choice in the matter.

Finally, just as I was on the verge of using grenades to cover my retreat, I heard the distinct sound of Patrick's pistol going off. Once. Twice. Three times, all in quick succession. Out of the corner of my eye, I saw one of the spiders fall from the wall, its body torn to pieces by Patrick's handheld rail gun.

The horde went wild, screaming in despair as they tore at their own faces. I wasn't going to let that opportunity go, and I quickly filled the air with another cannister's worth of ordinance. Meanwhile, Patrick targeted another spider, taking it down with a few well-placed shots.

Unfortunately, there were no others in range, but the damage had been done.

The thralls had completely stopped, many of them sinking to their knees as they clawed at their own bodies, dragging chunks of flesh away with every passing second. It would have been the perfect opportunity to retreat and regroup.

But I had another idea.

Maybe it would have been smarter to take the safer option and come back to fight the horde as well as the spiders on our own terms, but I suspected that was the point of the Rift. I was no expert, but it seemed to me that Rifts were more than just a collection of progressively more powerful opponents to overcome. Instead, there was a pattern to it. It wasn't a puzzle—not precisely—but the design wasn't completely benign, either.

To me, it seemed that the situation had been set up to force us into a retreat. And if that was what the Rift wanted, I was experienced enough to know that it was probably smart to avoid it at all costs. So, if it wanted us to go back—probably to spring some kind of trap—I reasoned that the best course of action was to move forward.

So, I yelled, "Follow me! Don't lag behind!"

With that, I lobbed a few more rounds from my BMAP at the horde of enthralled aliens, then raced forward. Even as the explosives tore a hole in the crowd, I exchanged the mobile artillery platform for my R-14. I'd have preferred the more potent firearm, but it would pose almost as much danger to me as it would to the thralls. And even more to Patrick, who didn't have my unnatural durability or the benefit of my [Demolition] skill to protect him.

So, if I was to punch a hole through the horde, I had to do so with a more mundane gun.

Not that the R-14 was incapable of doing the job.

We advanced, a storm of superheated plasma rounds leading the way as I carved a path through the mass of mind-controlled aliens. Most didn't even resist, they were so distraught by the loss of their arachnid overlords, but a few managed to regain their aggression at the last second. It was too late, though, and they were cut down just like the rest.

Like that, we moved forward until we'd progressed deep within the horde. When we drew within range of one of the spiders, Patrick went to work, tearing through the stationary targets. It was all too easy.

Over the next half hour, we continued on, ruthlessly exterminating the telepathic spiders, and slowly, the horde's cohesion began to degrade. Before long, the aliens were fighting one another almost as much as they tried to reach us.

At one point, they were probably civilized and sapient, but the spiders' influence had stripped them of anything but feral fury. Before, they'd moved with a curious union of mind, but with the spiders' numbers gradually declining, so too did the arachnids' influence. As a result, the aliens came to resemble the wildlings with which I'd grown so familiar. The only difference was that they didn't have the physicality to back up their savage instincts.

As such, the danger slowly decreased until, at last, Patrick put the last spider down.

Suddenly, every single member of the horde collapsed.

"What the . . ."

I swept my rifle around, searching for some surprise attack. But nothing came. So, I knelt down and touched one of the aliens. It was some reptilian variant, but the moment my fingers grazed its scaly skin, I knew it was dead.

"Are they . . ."

I nodded, saying, "Dead. All of them, unless I miss my guess."

"How?" Patrick wondered.

I shook my head and told him that I had no idea. Then, I guessed, "The spiders seemed to be keeping them alive. I mean, look at these people. Even before they collapsed, they were barely holding together."

"That's . . . disturbing," he said.

"You're not wrong," I agreed. "But we need to—"

Just then, the ground trembled as something incredibly heavy dropped from the ceiling and hit the floor. In truth, I'd been expecting something like that. The mind-control spiders were dangerous, but defeating them had been too easy. It only stood to reason that there would be some other guardian.

But when I jerked my gaze to the right and beheld the new threat, I had to admit that I was more than a little surprised at what I saw.

I guess it could accurately be called a spider, just like the rest of the creatures I'd encountered in the Rift. However, this one looked nothing like any of the others I'd killed. For one, it was the size of a tank, with spindly legs and a slim body that, despite its enormous size, looked like it was built for speed.

For another, it was entirely crystalline. Gleaming black, the spider also had a dozen quivering tendrils extending from its abdomen. To call its undulating movements unsettling would have been vastly underselling just how creepy the scene was.

And that was before I saw it whip out and slice into some nearby alien corpses, splitting them with ease.

"Run," I croaked. When Patrick didn't move, I screamed, "Run! This is not a fight for you!"

To his credit—or perhaps he was driven by his fear rather than an impulse to obey my directive—Patrick wasted no more time before turning and sprinting back the way we'd come. That left me facing the spider alone.

Which was probably appropriate. Patrick's previous contributions notwithstanding, I usually worked better when I didn't have to worry about anyone else.

With that, I exchanged my R-14 for my Pulsar, took aim, and embraced Empowered Shot. After two seconds—during which the spider remained curiously stationary—I squeezed the trigger and fired. The sniper rifle thundered, sending a round blistering through the air at supersonic speeds. It tore into the spider's multifaceted eye with a booming explosion that sent shards of crystalline flesh misting into the air.

But the spider didn't move.

Not at first, at least. Instead, I felt it the moment the creature's attention settled on me, and when it did, my knees went weak and my will shattered as I stumbled forward and fell to all fours.

My mind raced to fill in the gaps, but I could feel some integral part of me splintering into a million pieces. Tears flowed down my cheeks. My every muscle twitched, stiffening as I fought for my very survival.

No—it was more than that.

I could feel the very essence of who I was being ripped asunder. It wasn't an attack on my mind. Rather, it was an assault on my soul. Mentally and metaphysically, I flailed, but I had no defense against such an intrusion. Suddenly, everything that made me an individual was laid bare.

And I hated what I saw.

I was a weak, pitiful thing. My actions had never been about justice. They weren't even about vengeance. Under that assault on my soul, I saw that everything was an attempt to exert some measure of control. That was why I'd dragged it out so long. Within the familiar confines of Nova City, cloaked in constant

Stealth and other identities, I didn't have to confront the reality of the situation. I didn't have to acknowledge that I was no different from any of the other poor people I saw every day. I was just a product of outside circumstances.

But I knew I could be better. That's what my uncle had worked so hard for.

He could have easily created an assassin; if he had, he would have just made me in his image. Instead, he'd always wanted more for me. Time and time again, Jeremiah had said as much. I just hadn't listened.

Or perhaps I had forgotten.

Suddenly, I realized that he would never have approved of my quest for revenge. Certainly, he wouldn't have had any issues with killing Nora, but he would have seen my monthslong quest to make her suffer as she watched everything crumble around her as entirely misguided.

I knew that.

But I'd done it anyway because I'd convinced myself that it would somehow make me feel better. It wouldn't, though. Deep down, I had always known that. But it was so much easier to focus on that than to plan for a future I was ill-equipped to contemplate. My instruction had been cut short, meaning that I'd only ever been trained to kill. I had no doubts he would have taught me how to live, had he not died.

As it stood, I'd have to figure it out for myself.

But first, I needed to kill a spider. To that end, I focused inward, leveraging every point of my Mind and Mist attributes into gathering the shattering pieces of my soul and dragging them back into place. I really didn't know what I was doing. There was no structure to it. Instead, I could only brute force it.

Fortunately, I was well equipped to do just that, and gradually, it worked.

At some point, my awareness of the surroundings returned, and I realized that the spider had begun to advance. With a monumental effort of will, I flexed my Mind, and the Mist followed suit. With that, I wrenched my soul from the crystalline spider's grasp. It stumbled back, but I couldn't take advantage. I was too busy gathering my wits.

So, by the time I pushed myself back to my feet, the creature had recovered. However, it seemed much more wary than before.

Good. For now, it was wariness. Soon, it would be fear.

CHAPTER FIFTY-EIGHT

BOIL

Usually, I am a straightforward person. I don't like traps or convoluted plans. But for Mira, I need to step out of my comfort zone.

—Nora Lancaster

I could feel the spider's searching tendrils scraping against the back of my mind, but so long as I maintained concentration, its efforts remained futile. Or so I hoped. I had no way of knowing for sure—in fact, I was certain that this creature was something wholly unique to the Rift. And that surety led me to believe that the Octavangians had never ventured this far into the space station.

Or perhaps I was underestimating their technological advantage. Maybe they had some way to cut the giant spider's mental attacks down to nothing, and I was just doing things the hard way. Certainly, it wouldn't be the first time, and I knew it wouldn't be the last, either. For all my strength—and I felt confident in my power—I still didn't know enough about the universe to prepare myself for every eventuality. Usually, I just blundered my way through, trusting my high attributes and the power of my skills to see me through to the other side.

Eventually, that wouldn't be enough, though. I needed to be better. I needed to learn more. Otherwise, I'd run up on something too strong to fully resist.

But that day had yet to come.

Staggering to my feet, I took aim with my R-14 and let loose with a hail of three-round bursts. Most thudded home without even leaving a mark, but it only took me a few seconds to realize that the area around its joints was far more brittle than the rest of its crystalline carapace. So, I focused my fire, sending an entire magazine of rounds to tear through the middle joint of its frontmost right leg.

It let out a screech that was accompanied by a mental sledgehammer of thought that shook me to the very core of my soul, but I'd already tasted its best attack, so I was well prepared to endure its latest efforts. Still, it wasn't pleasant, and the shock threw my aim wide. With that small opening, the gargantuan spider skittered forward, its sharp legs piercing through the carpet of bodies at its feet as it closed in on me.

I grunted as I regained my composure and, marshaling my own courage, raced forward to meet it head-on. Not the best tactic when my lone advantage seemed to be range, but I'd already determined that I could empty a hundred magazines into that creature, and it would still keep coming. No—I needed a different plan, and I thought I had a good idea what to do.

I just had to survive long enough to make it work.

As I sprinted toward the huge thing, I was taken aback by just how large it was. If it was smaller than a tank, I would have been surprised. But fighting a huge monster wasn't really a change of pace for me, so I ruthlessly shoved the blooming fear into the back of my mind where it couldn't affect me. Things had begun to get crowded back there.

I raced forward, firing one three-round burst after another. As powerful as the R-14 was, it proved an ineffectual weapon against such a formidable foe. It had happened before, and I knew it would happen again. The reality was that it was too versatile a weapon to really pack the punch I needed. Even with my modifiers, which were significant, it could still only do so much.

The Pulsar was better, but its fire rate, especially slowed down by Empowered Shot, was incredibly slow. My pistol, Ferdinand II, was even more versatile than the assault rifle, but it didn't lack stopping power. Instead, its trade-off came in the form of ease of use. If I wanted to get the most out of it, I needed the proper ammunition; couple that with the fact that it was slow to reload, and it was only as good as my preparation dictated.

And I was woefully unprepared for something like the spider.

So, while I vowed not to repeat that mistake going forward, future me couldn't help with my current situation.

The scattergun wouldn't do much good, either. Sure, it might stun the monster for a second or two, but by itself, it just wasn't powerful enough to make much of a difference. That was something I'd need to change, and soon. I couldn't afford to carry weak weaponry meant for incapacitation anymore.

With that, I was down to my nano-bladed sword. The weapon had proven extremely effective at cutting through even the most durable materials, and it had the advantage of never running out of ammunition. Certainly, the blade required a small trickle of Mist to maintain, but for me, it was negligible to the point I often forgot about the slight drain.

But like each of my other weapons, it came with a downside—chiefly, it required that I get in close. With the spider, that would mean getting in range of those sharp legs and whatever other natural weapons it could bring to bear. I wasn't so naive as to think that its physical tools would be any weaker than the mental attack to which I had already been subjected.

No—it was a monster, and monsters were built to kill.

All that had coalesced into a series of strengths and weaknesses that drove me into what probably looked like a reckless charge. It wasn't. I had a plan. I could only hope that it would work.

I covered the ground in the space of a second or two, and when I drew close enough, I dropped into a slide that took me under the monster's crystalline carapace. Clearly, it hadn't expected as much—probably because most of the area was covered in the corpses of the alien thralls—but there was just enough open space for me to enact my plan.

As I slid forward, I retrieved a demolition charge from my arsenal implant and slapped it against the spider's black carapace. It stuck, and I let my momentum carry me along the creature's length; in the process, I narrowly avoided the slashing tendrils attached to its thorax. When I reached its backside, I used one of the corpses to halt my momentum so I could pop up and continue running. By the time the spider managed to skitter around to face me, I was twenty feet away and sprinting for all I was worth.

That's when I snatched the detonator from my arsenal implant and pressed the appropriate button. A cacophony of sound erupted behind me, followed by a wave of force, and even from more than twenty feet away, I was thrown from my feet by the shock wave that followed the explosion. I flipped through the air, adjusting my trajectory after activating Balance, but even so, when I landed, I couldn't stop myself from tumbling over a mound of corpses.

It took me a moment to get my bearings, but when I did, I felt something wet hit my head. A second later, I was showered with raining blood and viscera—the remnants of exploded corpses.

I couldn't help but gag a little.

But I knew the job wasn't finished, so I summoned my BMAP and, when the rain of gore ceased, I sighted in on the spider—noting that it was still very much alive, if a bit dazed—and let loose with a bombardment of artillery.

In seconds, the chamber was filled with the sound of one explosion erupting after another, but I didn't stop. I didn't dare. I kept going until I'd emptied the first cannister, exchanged it for another, and spent that one, as well. However, when I reached into my arsenal implant, I was horrified to see that I'd used every bit of the BMAP's ammunition I had in my arsenal implant. There was still a bit more in Patrick's storage, but that wouldn't do me much good.

"Crap," I muttered, hesitating for only a second before I exchanged the weapon for my Pulsar. It wasn't long, but it was just enough that the proverbial dust settled and revealed that the spider was still on its feet.

I took aim and cycled through the familiar steps of using a series of Empowered Shots. Each time I fired, the resulting shot took a chunk of black crystal out of the monster's extraordinarily durable carapace, but the battle had taught it a lesson concerning the necessity of protecting its most vulnerable spots. So, it twisted and turned, preventing me from affecting any lasting damage.

As I emptied that first magazine, I knew my plan had failed. My demolition charges could bring a building down, but apparently, the explosion had done little more than stagger the creature.

Well—that wasn't completely true. A web of cracks had spread across the thing's glittering black carapace, but it was still a long way from defeat. I knew that because, with a sudden burst of speed, it darted into range. It was all I could do to avoid its slashing mandibles as I leaped to the side. But it had no intention of letting up. Instead, it stabbed down with its spear-like legs, forcing me to roll this way and that, lest I end up impaled.

It was a losing tactic, though. I couldn't remain on the defensive.

So, after dodging one stabbing leg, I rolled forward, exchanging my Pulsar for my scattergun, which I quickly used to send a Double Shot–enhanced cone of lightning to envelop the spider in its entirety. It screeched as the electrical current raced through its body, locking it up for the critical few seconds I needed to extricate myself from its grasp.

But I didn't run away. Instead, I gathered my legs under me and jumped, once again exchanging one weapon for another—this time, the scattergun for my nano-bladed sword. When I landed, I had to activate Balance just to keep from tumbling from the sleek surface. Doing so drained a significant portion of my Mist, but I couldn't worry about that right now. Instead, I took the sword in a reversed two-handed grip and jabbed the blade into the creature's cracked carapace.

It didn't go as I expected it to, and the blade skipped off the surface, barely chipping it. But I wasn't going to give up at the first failure, so I flared Balance and struck again. And again. My Mist drained at an accelerated rate, but after the fourth attack, the strategy bore fruit as the blade finally sank deep into the monster's thorax. It was just in time, too, because it had finally recovered from the scattergun attack.

It bucked, trying to throw me free, but my grip was like iron.

When I'd first leaped atop the thing, I'd intended to plant a series of demolition charges. If one didn't do the trick, then a few had to, right? When one explosion wasn't sufficient, increase the number until the target goes down. But as I hung there, I thought better of that plan.

The demolition charge had done almost nothing. It just wasn't strong enough. So, expecting a few charges to pick up the slack was too optimistic for my taste. Instead, I chose to use the one skill I had yet to employ.

When I had first obtained the [Mistwalker] skill, I'd thought it was limited to infiltrating various systems. However, I'd soon learned that it was quite a bit more versatile than that. When I'd discovered Ghosts, I'd come to realize that I'd only scratched the surface of what was possible. The only limitation was that it didn't really work on any living thing that lacked a Nexus Implant or cybernetics.

So, why did it work on that first spider I'd encountered in the Rift? That it had suggested that these creatures were not natural. Perhaps they were some form of advanced robotics. Or maybe a sentient race of super spiders who'd gained access to Nexus Implants. I had no idea. But what I did know was that if one spider was vulnerable, then it stood to reason that they all were.

So, clinging to that bucking spider's back, I embraced Misthack, and to my eternal relief, the familiar prompt bloomed on my HUD:

Initiate Misthack?
[Yes] or [No]

Frantically, I chose the affirmative option, and the prompt changed:

Misthack successful. Options:
Reboot system
Overcharge
Disable cybernetics
Upload Ghost

I chose Overcharge, and once the ability took hold, the monster locked up, giving me a few extra seconds to repeat the process. This time, I chose to upload a Ghost, prompting the appearance of another menu:

Upload Ghost. Options:
Time Bomb **(Mark 2)**
Seizure
Confusion
Boil

I spent a good portion of my free time working on expanding my repertoire of Ghosts, and that effort had paid off in the form of a continuously evolving arsenal I could employ in a wide variety of situations. However, until recently,

I'd ignored one very important option: lethality. It wasn't an oversight—not exactly. Instead, I'd simply fallen into the rut of seeing the [Mistrunner] skill as one devoted to utility. It was great for information gathering, incapacitating enemies, and infiltration, so I'd gotten into the habit of narrowing my focus to those facets of the skill. After all, I already had plenty of ways to kill; why would I need to explore lethal options with [Mistrunner]?

Lately, though, I'd begun to see that as the mistake it was.

To rectify the issue, I'd been spending much of my downtime working on a very special series of Ghosts, and I'd only managed a couple of successes right before we'd entered the Rift. In this case, one seemed very appropriate for the situation. Called *Boil*, its purpose was just what that name suggested—it was supposed to take hold of the Mist in someone's body and agitate it to such a degree that it would literally boil them from the inside.

Like most Ghosts, it had limitations that I'd had to balance against the strength of its effects, and in the case of *Boil*, I'd chosen to limit the range to only a couple of feet while ratcheting up the lethality to an absurd degree.

I hadn't had the opportunity to test it yet, but if it worked, I hoped it would cut the fight against the spider short. So, I selected that Ghost, and as it uploaded, I held my breath.

At first, the effect was unnoticeable. However, after only a few seconds, the spider's furious bucking ceased, and the shock caused by the sudden cessation of movement nearly sent me toppling from its back.

That's when I felt the carapace start to heat up.

Until that moment, the smooth surface had been cool to the touch, but over the next few seconds, it slowly grew warmer until I had no choice but to fling myself away, lest I be burned to a crisp.

When I landed, I did so in a roll that took me across a carpet of bodies, and I quickly found my feet, fully expecting the creature to attack. But it remained completely rooted in place, its only movement coming in the form of a subtle shudder. That tremble became more pronounced with every passing second, eventually turning into a vibration so rapid that the edges of the spider looked blurred.

Then, a series of high-pitched whistles filled the air, and I saw billowing steam erupting from the cracks in the spider's carapace.

That's when it exploded.

I barely had time to register what was happening before the carapace shattered into a million pieces of black crystal. I was close enough that the shock wave swept me from my feet—a good thing, too, because an instant later the air was filled with flying shrapnel. Even on the ground, I caught more than my fair share, but if I'd have been on my feet, I would have been shredded.

I probably would have survived, but it wouldn't have been pleasant. And besides, I didn't want to spend another booster to repair my infiltration suit.

It took another moment before I was bathed in a second shower of gore—this time stark-white meat and milky blood—but I barely cared. I was too relieved that the fight was over.

I sat up and took a deep breath. The smell of burned meat assaulted my nostrils, but I welcomed it as the herald of victory it was. Once I managed to gather my thoughts, I turned around to look for Patrick. I didn't immediately see him in the flickering lights of the ruined space station, but when I did catch sight of him more than a hundred yards away, I let out another sigh of relief.

He seemed okay.

Obviously rattled, and more than a little frightened, but okay nonetheless.

My bones creaked as I pushed myself to my feet, and I ran my hand through my gore-slick hair in disgust. "Ugh," I muttered. "Gross."

But as nasty as it was, at least I'd survived. The spider couldn't say as much, that was for sure. Arduously, I climbed over the carpet of corpses as I made my way to Patrick. He was clearly too stunned to move from where he'd been crouching behind a mound of bodies that had fallen next to one of the walls of cubicles. When he caught sight of me, though, I could see him relax.

It took me a little while to cover the distance between us, and when I did, I asked, "Are you okay?"

"No."

"What? Are you hurt?" I asked.

"No."

"Uh . . . can you use a different word?" I asked.

He fixed me with a glare of disbelief before saying, "No."

I rolled my eyes and said, "Don't be like that. It wasn't so bad. You should've seen the tentacle monster I had to fight at the end of my first Rift. Now that was—"

He interrupted me by saying, "Mira."

"What?" I asked.

"Just shut up for a second, okay?" he pleaded. "That thing was horrifying, and not just because it was a spider bigger than a hover car. Do you have any idea how close I came to losing it?"

That's when I realized that the soul attack hadn't just been directed at me. It had hit Patrick, too. And he clearly hadn't fared any better than I had. Perhaps he would have succumbed altogether if I hadn't pushed through it and fought back. If that had happened, his mind—or soul, maybe—would have been shattered.

"Right," I said, not really knowing how to respond. "We should probably find somewhere else to rest, though. Because this . . . probably isn't the best place to relax."

He let out a shuddering sigh. "Fine. Let's go, then," he muttered, obviously still rattled. I didn't blame him. He didn't have my advantages, and so, he would obviously be affected to a much greater degree.

Maybe it had been a mistake to bring him along after all.

I reached out, offering him my hand. He took it, and I hauled him to his feet. Then, we set off toward the edge of the huge room, looking for somewhere that wasn't covered in corpses so we could rest and recover. However, when we reached the other side of the chamber from where we'd entered, I saw an enormous crate that agitated the surrounding Mist to such a degree that I knew we'd found a jackpot of Rift Shards.

More importantly, I saw a formless prism directly behind the crate. It seemed we had completed the Rift after all.

CHAPTER FIFTY-NINE

THE BEST WE CAN DO

Jeremiah never went far enough. He held back when he could have given us everything. I won't make that mistake. I will drag the Specters to the top even if it kills every last one of them.

—Nora Lancaster

After Patrick and I took a few minutes to rest, we set about gathering the contents of the enormous crate that had appeared once the giant spider had died. I'd already felt the strength of the agitated Mist surrounding it, so I knew the metallic crate held incredible wealth, but when we finally cracked it open, I couldn't contain the gasp that forced itself out of my mouth.

I flashed a grin toward Patrick, asking, "Think that's enough for a ship?"

"I . . . I have no idea," he answered, his eyes wide as he looked at the pile of sparkling crystals. Each one looked as if it contained a galaxy all its own, and there were hundreds of them, each big enough to bring in tens of thousands of credits. "If we're looking for something like *The Jitterbug*, then . . . definitely. But I'm guessing you want something better."

Indeed, I did. That little ship had been fine for traveling between the local towns and cities, but for what I envisioned, we needed something far more robust. After all, *The Jitterbug* had nearly fallen to an overgrown bird, and I suspected that more Mist-rich regions would play host to much more powerful creatures. To survive on that other continent, we'd need a flying tank of a ship.

"Definitely," I said. "But I don't really have any context for what that might cost."

Still staring at the crate of crystals, Patrick shrugged. "*The Jitterbug* was built here on Earth," he stated. "Remy got it years ago from some place called Ohio. He always said that's where the best shipyards were, but he never got around to taking me. He kept saying he would, but . . . Well . . . you know . . ."

I shook my head and looked away. The carpet of corpses wasn't a pleasant sight, but it was still preferable to seeing so much grief painted across Patrick's face. It had been months since Remy's death, but it still weighed heavily on him. Usually, he kept it bottled up where it couldn't affect him, so it was easy to think he'd adjusted to his loss. However, there were times when it came bubbling to the surface, and when that happened, it was clear that it would be a long time before Patrick felt whole.

In that respect, we were similar, though in my case, Jeremiah's death rarely strayed far from the surface of my thoughts. I wasn't sure which was healthier. Perhaps neither. Maybe that's why we clung to each other the way we did.

"How much do you think it's all worth?" Patrick asked.

"I don't know," I said. I had no interest in counting the Shards, and even if I did, there was no guarantee that my estimates would be accurate. After all, prices tended to fluctuate, not to mention that the sizes of these individual Shards didn't really line up with the categories I'd established in my first Rift. Back then, there were three distinct tiers. But these? They were larger than all but the biggest I'd seen before. So, the value was almost impossible to estimate. I chose not to even try, simply telling myself that it was almost assuredly enough that it would allow me to accomplish my goals.

The crate was too big for Patrick's storage ability to accommodate without help from an access point—a fact for which he apologized profusely. It wasn't a big deal, but he seemed to take it pretty hard. Perhaps he thought that was the only reason I'd brought him along. In a way, that was accurate. His ability to store a huge amount of mass was extremely valuable. But even if he didn't have that on his side, I would have brought him with me anyway.

Maybe.

I did enjoy his company, and I felt that something special might be growing between us. However, the fact that he could be useful aside from his meager skills with a pistol had definitely tipped the balance in his favor.

"It's fine," I said. "We'll just divide it into two separate crates. I'll carry a couple of small ones, and you can bring the others along."

"That's going to push my capacity," he said.

"Then we make room by discarding some of the supplies," I said. "I need to reload on ammo anyway. And we're heading back to Nova and straight to the Bazaar. We can survive without the camping supplies and most of the rations. Getting these Shards back to the city is priority number one."

With that, Patrick started dumping supplies out of his storage space. Fortunately, it was all small enough that he could do so without the benefit of an access point; the crates of Shards wouldn't have that advantage, but that was expected. Soon enough, the cots, a few boxes of ration bars, the useless autoturrets, and our tents had been piled on the floor. For my part, I delved into my own supplies, discarding anything that wasn't immediately useful before having him transfer a few boxes of ammunition to me.

Curiously, when we were done making room, Patrick's pile was fairly neat and organized while mine looked like a haphazard pile of junk.

The process only took a few minutes, and when we'd cleared enough space, we started to divide the Shards into something more manageable. I ended up getting three small crates—one for each of my storage slots—while Patrick took the rest. With that done, we gathered a few of the discarded items until both of our storage spaces were filled to the brim.

For Patrick, whose space was tied to an ability, it created an uncomfortable drain on his pool of available Mist. For me, the only issue was the blinking light in the corner of my HUD that told me I'd reached the extent of my storage capacity. Annoying and potentially distracting, but nothing I couldn't handle. Patrick would be incapable of using any of his abilities until he emptied his space, though.

"What is that ability called, anyway?" I asked.

"It's dumb," he muttered.

"Oh, c'mon. Now you have to tell me," I said.

After a second, he seemed to realize I wasn't going to let it drop, and he let out a sigh before saying, "Fine. It's called Pack Mule, okay?"

"Mule?"

"That's what I said."

"Like the animal?" I asked.

"Like the animal," he confirmed.

"But aren't they known for being . . . I don't know . . . difficult?" I asked. Obviously, I'd never seen a mule outside of a video, and even that had been an artist's representation. Still, we'd learned about the beasts in school, and though the creatures had been considered useful, once upon a time, they also had a reputation of stubbornness and had spawned a number of less-than-flattering phrases meant to describe undesirable traits. Some of those insults still survived, lending some weight to the creatures' poor reputation.

"Yes," Patrick stated. "But they could carry lots of stuff. I asked Remy about it when I first got the ability—I mean, what kind of sense does it make for a skill to reference an Earth animal?"

"Jeremiah said that the skill and ability names are just translations," I provided. "Like, that ability is called Pack Mule, right? But maybe in its original language, it referred to some famous beast of burden from whatever planet created the system."

"Remy just said the names were created by our brains," he said. "But I guess they both could be true."

"Or neither."

"Or neither," he agreed. "But I thought the Mist was just . . . I don't know . . . a naturally occurring thing."

"It's not," I said. "It was created by someone. When I asked Jeremiah about it, he said that it was probably just some kind of experiment or something that got out of control. Nobody he ever talked to knew for sure. But the system—that's different. That was definitely created by some aliens who wanted to help people survive the Mist. They built the first Nexus Implants and somehow tied the system to the swarm of nanites that constitute the Mist."

"So, there's some super-advanced alien civilization out there that's responsible for all of this?" he asked.

I shrugged. "No idea," I admitted. "And I don't think anybody else knows, either. Not on Earth, at least. Personally, I think it's more likely that whoever created the Mist died out."

"And the ones who made the system?" he asked.

"Maybe they're still around," I stated, though I had no evidence to support that idea. It was just that if any civilization was advanced enough to have harnessed the Mist and created a system by which to utilize it without the negative consequences associated with Mist exposure, I had a difficult time believing that anything could kill them off.

Of course, the memory of that giant, shadowy creature that looked like it had taken a bite out of a planet injected plenty of doubt into that supposition. Sure, it had been in a Rift, which meant that it probably wasn't entirely real—I still wasn't sure how it all worked—but the setting had felt too solid to have been created out of nothing. Instead, it was easy to imagine that the Mist had used some past event as fuel for the scenario. And if that was the case, there very well could have been something that terrifying floating around out there in space, just waiting to eat any planet that got on its bad side.

"Either way, I think we should table this discussion and get out of here," I said.

"How?" he asked. "Just walk through that prism like we did to get in here?"

"Yeah" was my confident response. "But I should go first, just in case there's something out there waiting on us."

I was still very much aware that the Octavangians had had plenty of time to call for reinforcements. None had arrived when I'd escalated the attack, but that didn't mean they weren't on their way. If they'd arrived while we were in the Rift, they were probably waiting to ambush us as soon as we stepped back into the real world.

And if that was the case, I needed to be the one to take the brunt of that attack. Part of it was so that I could protect Patrick, who just seemed so incredibly fragile, but I also knew that I was far better equipped to survive such an ambush.

Still, there was an insistent voice in the back of my mind that told me that sending him out there first would provide a viable distraction. Sure, it'd probably end up with him dead, but it would increase my chances of coming out on top.

I mercilessly squashed that line of pragmatic thought. The last thing I wanted was to become the sort of person who'd sacrifice her allies—or worse, her friends—just for a slightly better chance at survival. If anything, I wanted to be the person who did the opposite. But I knew, at least in the back of my mind, that I probably would never be the sort of girl who engaged in noble sacrifice. I just wasn't built that way, and nothing I'd experienced had pushed me even a smidgen in that direction.

But I still wished I could make that kind of choice.

After what I'd experienced under the mental thumb of that giant spider, I felt compelled to make some changes in my life. For a long time, I had known that my pursuit of vengeance, while justified, would leave me scarred. It would drive me to do things I never would've done otherwise. And it had. Not only was I responsible for the deaths of thousands of innocents, but I'd also chosen a course of action that had ended up with Heather—someone who'd never wanted anything more than to be a friend to me—as a mindless wildling. At the time, I'd pushed much of the resulting pain aside, but the spider had stripped my mind of its defenses, laying my choices bare.

And I hated what I saw.

"Do you think we are what we've done?" I asked as I stood before the Rift's gate. "Or do you think intent matters? Can people change? Or are we always going to be the sum of our past sins?"

"I . . . I don't know."

"Me neither," I agreed.

But I hoped I could move past my selfish choices. I hoped they wouldn't define me for the rest of my life. That was what had happened with my uncle. I don't know how I'd never seen it before, but the reason he'd never seemed concerned with saving himself was because he didn't think he was worthy. Sure, he was strong. Stronger than anyone else, I was sure. But just like me, he'd done horrible things. In some cases, he'd been forced. But in others, he'd made a conscious choice of brutality.

I had left thousands of bodies in my wake, but Jeremiah's kill count could well have been in the millions. After all, I'd only had a few years to bolster my total, while he'd had decades. Even if his number didn't reach seven figures, it almost certainly came close. And it had taken its toll on his psyche.

So, he'd latched on to ensuring my survival because he just didn't care about his own, save that it would help him in that goal. Dozens of times, he'd cautioned me not to follow his lead. He'd taught me his skills, but he'd made it abundantly clear that he never intended me to become a killer.

And yet, that's precisely what I had become. He would have been ashamed of me.

Sure, he probably wouldn't have minded if I'd killed Nora as well as whoever had sent those Enforcers, but he'd have looked upon the meticulous deconstruction of the Specters as unnecessary. And the innocents I'd killed?

I shuddered to think what he would have said about that. I felt certain that he wouldn't have berated me. Nor would he have been overly critical. Instead, he'd have just been disappointed that I fell so far short of his expectations.

I had plenty of excuses on my side. My training had been cut short, and though I'd become a proficient warrior, a decent thief, and a passable tactician, I still lacked a host of skills. I still wasn't entirely comfortable in social situations—a remnant of my upbringing, no doubt—and my mind tended to work in straight lines. Surely, he'd intended to extend my training to shore up those weaknesses.

That had obviously never happened.

But I knew he wouldn't accept any of those excuses, especially when it came to my actions since returning to Nova City. He'd always held me to an impossible standard, and as such, it was absolute folly to imagine he would have made an exception in this case.

"What's wrong?" asked Patrick, interrupting my thoughts. I'd only been standing there for a few seconds, but with my Mind attribute having reached such heights, my thoughts raced along at unprecedented speeds. Then, before I could respond, he added, "I don't think you're a bad person."

"Really?" I asked, turning to face him. "Because I've been thinking about some of the things I've done, and . . . and it's not pretty, Pick." I ran my hand through my tangled hair in disgust, both at the things I'd done as well as the splatters of gore the mass of hair had managed to accumulate. "You know some of it. But not all. The other day, I cut a woman apart one little piece at a time. And I enjoyed it. She'd never really done anything to me, and yet . . . I felt justified, you know? Because she was one of Nora's people. And that's not even considering what happened to Heather . . ."

"That wasn't your fault."

I resisted the urge to roll my eyes in derision. "Then whose fault was it?" I demanded, my voice rising. Before he could answer, I went on, "I knew she was there, Pick. For weeks. Months. I knew where she was. I could have gone in and rescued her. I mean, I could've just bought her. I could've gotten the money. But do you know what I did? I actually forgot about her for a while! I mean, who the hell does that, Pick? Who does that?!"

He didn't bother answering. Not at first. Instead, he just stepped forward and wrapped me in his arms, embracing me in a tight hug. Until that moment,

I hadn't even realized that tears were flowing down my cheeks. I was just so angry. Not at the people who'd enslaved Heather. Not at the system of oppression that made it possible. Not even at Nora. Not really. Instead, I was furious with myself. At every turn, I'd made the selfish decision, and innocent people had paid the price of my actions.

"I feel like a monster," I sobbed, burying my face in his shoulder.

"You're not."

"I am. I know that. It's exactly what my uncle didn't want, but I did it anyway," I said, my words coming out muffled.

For a long few moments, he didn't say anything. To me, that was all the confirmation I needed. Even Patrick could see what I had become.

But then, he pushed me to arm's length and said, "Okay. You've done bad things. Who hasn't? One time, just a few weeks after I started riding with Remy, a woman tried to break into the ship. Do you know what I did? I killed her. Shot her right in the head, just like it was target practice. It wasn't until later that I found out that she had four kids she was trying to feed. She was desperate. Her kids were starving. And here we were, a couple of strangers who came to town with all kinds of things everyone needed. We'd practically painted a target on our backs.

"When it happened, I felt good," he admitted. "It all went down so fast, I didn't even see her. Not really. I just reacted. And it felt like I'd finally made myself useful. I was thirteen years old, small and scrawny. Until that day, I hadn't done anything to help Remy. But then it finally happened, and I was *proud*. Of killing a starving woman who was trying to feed her kids. Once I recognized the situation for what it was, I had no idea what to do. I didn't know how to act. I didn't know whether to feel guilty, to hate myself, or to just be a man and move past it."

He shook his head. "But in the end, I didn't do any of those things," he said. "I just . . . I just sort of lived with it. I cried a few nights. I beat myself up. I vowed to do better. But at the end of the day, nothing I could do would change what had happened. A few weeks later, once we'd left that town behind, Remy took me aside and told me something I can never forget.

"He said, 'Look, kid. Ain't nothin' you did wrong. You did what you were taught to do. That's it. You saw a threat, and you reacted. If anybody's to blame, it's me. But it ain't that simple, is it? You pulled that trigger, so you get a piece of the guilt. She was the aggressor, so she gets some blame, too. Even if her reasons were understandable, she still made her choice. If she'd just come to us and asked, we'd have picked her up. You seen it in other towns, right? That's how we work. Help the needy, charge the ones who can afford it. But she didn't think. She just acted. And she ended up dead. Her kids are orphans now—poor things. My point is that if you go around takin' all the blame, you'll never survive. So, do your best to move on—easier said than done, don't I know it. Try to do better. Try to be better. That's all any of us can do.'

"And then he just left me to it," Patrick concluded. "We never talked about it again, but any time I make a bad choice, I think about that. I'll never forget what happened, but I don't think we're supposed to, either. Forget, I mean. I think we're supposed to remember it and use that to help us make better choices going forward."

I wiped my cheeks and said, "You've got one. I've got thousands. I don't know if that'll work for me."

"It has to, Mira," he said. "And I believe you can do it."

"I . . . I hope you're right," I said. Then, I added, "Thanks."

He gave me a crooked grin, responding, "Anytime."

Then, I turned around, wiped my eyes, and stepped through the prism and back into the real world.

CHAPTER SIXTY

THAT MOMENT

I hate traps. They're so underhanded and dishonest. Instead, I prefer to tackle my issues head-on. But sometimes, the situation demands that we step out of our comfort zones. And never let it be said that Nora Lancaster backed away from a challenge.

—Nora Lancaster

To my surprise, stepping out of the Rift was entirely anticlimactic. After gearing myself up for a fight, seeing that nothing about the Octavangian camp had changed was almost eerie. I was so shocked that I spent quite a bit of time searching for traps or other surprises, but I found nothing of the sort.

So, through our secure connection, I told Patrick to come on through. I was so off-balance that I'd never even considered the possibility that the connection wouldn't persist across whatever gap existed between the real world and the Rift, so it was a good thing that the connection worked as intended. Patrick stepped through only a few minutes after I did, and he was just as surprised at the lack of an alien threat as I was.

Neither of us were going to argue with good fortune, though, and free from immediate danger, we set about on a thorough exploration of the camp. After all, we'd been a bit rushed during our first pass, and I was eager to learn more about the aliens who'd infiltrated our world. Fortunately, this was where my Universal Language ability came in handy.

After jacking into a security terminal in the camp's lone building, I discovered why the Octavangians hadn't sent any reinforcements. In short, the aliens had never put out a distress call. And after reading through a few messages, it wasn't difficult for me to figure out why that was the case.

Basically, the Octavangians operated on a shoestring budget. The Rift was profitable, but they'd never gone past the first crate before retreating to the real world and waiting for the Rift to repopulate, which took about a week. Even that had been pushing their abilities to the limit, supporting the idea that they were far from the best the aliens could offer. Instead, I got the sense that they were akin to the factory workers back in Nova City. Skilled enough to get the job done, but anything outside of that would prove an insurmountable obstruction on their path to profitability.

The real warriors wouldn't be deployed unless they were threatened, and even then, the miners were incentivized to wait until the last moment. If they put up a distress call, the cost of sending those warriors down to the surface would be held against their budget. And if they went into the red, they would be replaced.

Suddenly, I didn't feel so mighty. If the Octavangians I'd fought were effectively civilians, I had no interest in meeting the real fighters.

I also learned a little bit about the Rifts themselves. First, they were described as extradimensional pocket worlds created from excess Mist. Sometimes, they used real-world events to create the scenarios, but other times, they were completely fabricated from nothing. I suspected that had been the case with my first Rift. It had felt far more contrived than the ruined space station.

Finally, I discovered that the scenario I'd just seen was based on a verifiable event from the real world. The creature I had seen was called a galactic wyrm, and it existed by literally consuming Integrated planets, asteroids, and moons.

"You look like you just saw a ghost," remarked Patrick, who'd been standing guard as I perused the information in the terminal. No one had been waiting for us, but that didn't necessarily mean the area was safe. For all I knew, the aliens would send someone down after a certain amount of time had passed with no communication. Or the wildlife would begin to reclaim their once-abandoned territory. Letting down our guard would be an absolute mistake.

But I wasn't really thinking about that.

I shook my head. "Just realized that we're a lot smaller than I thought we were," I admitted. Then, I told him about the galactic wyrm, likening it to a dragon from popular programs on the entertainment feeds. He'd seen it in the Rift, same as me, but learning that it was a real creature came with the sobering realization that, no matter how powerful we became, there was always something out there that could squash us like bugs.

"I feel like that most of the time, honestly," Patrick admitted. "Doesn't matter if I get killed by some meathead with a gravity hammer or a giant space monster, really. Dead's dead, and I have just as much chance of surviving in both cases."

"That's not even close to true," I pointed out. "I mean, you can run from a mook with a hammer. But you can't really run from a giant space dragon that eats planets."

"See—that's where you're wrong," he said. "We get a ship, and we can probably get away."

"From a giant space dragon?" I asked. "Yeah—I think you're underestimating what something like that would be capable of. But it doesn't really matter. According to the files in this security terminal, that wyrm was killed by some kind of intergalactic fleet. And most of its species never get big enough to really threaten anything more than a small asteroid."

"Comforting."

"I know, right?" I said, giving him a grin. "So, we just have to worry about aliens, terrestrial monsters, and humans."

"Don't forget birds. I've seen some terrifying raptors out there," Patrick pointed out.

"Right. Birds, too," I agreed.

After being reminded that we weren't invincible, I cut off my research, opting to simply download the relevant files. Just as I had been taught, I sequestered the packet into an isolated part of my interface where the effects of any hostile files would be limited. Then, I disengaged and asked Patrick how he was doing on Mist.

"It's a strain," he said. "But I should be fine. I think it'll be close once we leave the Dead Zone, but I'm pretty sure I can handle it long enough to get back to Nova. So long as we head straight to the Dome where I can unload everything."

"That's the plan," I said. "Let's get out of here."

With that, we exited the building and made our way out of the stadium. Once again, I wondered what the thing's purpose had been. Was it intended for live performances of some sort? Or perhaps a sport? I had no idea, and I questioned whether or not I would ever discover the truth. Few were the people who'd managed to survive long enough to have seen such things firsthand; my uncle had, but like most, he'd always been a bit cagey about the past. Likely, he just wanted to forget. I could sympathize with that.

We trekked through the surrounding town on foot. Using the Cutter would have been faster, but only marginally so due to the copious amounts of rubble obstructing the roads. Even on foot, there were some routes that were completely impassable, so it took us a few hours to leave the ruins behind. Once we did, I wasted no time before summoning my hover bike and speeding to the south.

We covered quite a bit of ground before the sun began to set, but we were still a long way from civilization. As such, I kept an eye out for a suitable spot to camp, eventually settling for a half-buried culvert. Due to a mudslide, it only had one opening, which made it very defensible, if not particularly comfortable.

That night, while we were eating a supper of ration bars, Patrick said, "When we get a ship, we won't have to rough it like this anymore. I think that's what I miss the most about *The Jitterbug*. It wasn't perfect or anything. It was way too cramped, and it had a . . . smell that took a while to get used to, but it felt like home. I definitely miss that."

I sat next to him on one of the cots and leaned against him. The whole time, my heart felt like it was beating out of my chest. Curious that I could face off against giant spiders, octopus men, and mutated wildlings without skipping a beat, but rubbing shoulders with a boy pushed me to the verge of a panic attack.

"What kind of ship do you think we'll be able to afford?" I asked. It was a repeat of a previous question, and inwardly, I cursed myself for such a stupid line of conversation. I knew Patrick liked me. He'd told me so, and everything he'd done since had supported the claim. However, my insecurity refused to rescind the dominion it held over my thoughts.

Staring ahead at the Mist lamp, he answered, "She'll be big. Like, really big. Lots of room for you to train. She'll be slow in Earth's atmosphere, but that's fine. We don't need to be the fastest thing around. Not here, at least. Once we can leave the planet, though . . . That's when she'll shine."

"Thinking ahead, huh?" I asked, nudging him with my shoulder.

"Oh, yeah. Definitely," he answered, grinning at me. "It's going to be awesome. I mean, we can't leave yet, but that won't always be the case. And I don't think there's anything really keeping us here, right? We could put together a crew and just . . . explore. Like, no restrictions. Just us and the vastness of the galaxy."

"And whatever trouble we could get into," I added.

He laughed. "Probably. I guess. But what's life without a little adventure?" Patrick asked.

"I could do with a little peace and quiet," I admitted, which drew an even heartier laugh from my companion. I demanded, "What? I can do peace and quiet."

"Wait—do you really believe that?" he asked. "Mira—ever since I've known you, it's been one crisis after another." He held up his hands, continuing, "Nothing wrong with that. Obviously. I'm here with you, right? But I just don't know that you'll ever be okay with settling down. That's one of the things I like about you. Never a dull moment, you know? You've always got something going on. It forces me to be . . . I don't know . . . more than what I would be otherwise."

"You make it sound like I'm your trainer or something."

"That's not what I meant, and you know it," Patrick said with a shake of his head. "I'm just saying that I'm better when I'm with you. By necessity. For instance, I never would have gotten training for [Cybernetic Engineer] without you. Sure, that's what I wanted. That's what Remy and I talked about. But chances are, even if Remy would've lived, I'd have just done enough to help us do what we were already doing. You're a catalyst, though. Everything goes through you, at least when it comes to my life. And I'm fine with that. Better than fine. I like that trying to keep up with you makes me better." Then, he added, "Even if it can be really frustrating sometimes."

I was taken aback, and for a few moments, I didn't respond. In some ways, I found his confession incredibly flattering. Everyone wants to be someone's inspiration, right? But from another perspective, it made me extremely uncomfortable. I already had plenty of pressure on me without knowing that he held me up as his life's muse.

That was a heavy burden, and I wasn't certain I could ever live up to it.

So, I changed the subject by saying, "We could just leave as soon as we get the ship, right? What's stopping us?"

"The system," he stated, thankfully allowing the shift in conversation go unremarked.

"What do you mean?"

"Just that it won't let us leave," he said. "I mean, aliens getting down here is one thing. Any decent smuggler could do that—at least according to Remy. But getting out? That's something else altogether. Even the aliens who've come down are basically stranded here. Remy told me that they have to use humans and the Bazaar to send anything off planet. So, we're stuck here until the Integration."

I shook my head, muttering, "Guess that ends that idea."

After that, the conversation petered out, and a pregnant silence stretched between us. I knew he probably wanted things to take the next step. Sure, I'd gotten most of the gore and blood out of my hair when we'd chanced upon a stream earlier in the day, but we were both still filthy. That wouldn't change until we were afforded the opportunity to take proper showers. So, despite our growing closeness and the intimacy of our previous topic of conversation, I was in no mood for romance. So, even though I was aware of his intentions—and on the surface, I didn't find them objectionable—I refused to go down that road when my hair still held bits of dead alien.

Perhaps I was crazy, but even the tiniest bit of gore tended to suck the romance out of the air. At least for me. I felt certain that, in Nova City, there was probably someone into that sort of thing, though.

Eventually, we retired to our separate cots. I didn't immediately go to sleep; instead, I just lay there keeping Observation running as I kept an eye on the culvert's lone entrance. We'd left the autoturrets behind in the Rift, so we didn't even have them as an early-warning system. Still, my diligence proved pointless, and after seven hours, I woke Patrick and forced myself to rest while he took watch.

I only slept a couple of hours, but when the sun rose, I was well-rested enough that I didn't think my performance would be impacted. Too many nights of that sort, and that would no longer be the case, though. With my high Constitution attribute, I could keep going for quite some time without sleep, but even I had limits. And I needed to keep those in mind, lest I pay the price.

After Patrick and I took care of our morning needs, we got back on the hover bike and continued south toward Nova City. The journey was almost entirely uneventful, save for the wide detour we took around the crater where I'd fought the mutated wildlings. I had no interest in revisiting that hellhole, so we made sure to keep well away. As it turned out, the crater was even larger than we'd first anticipated, and it took most of the day to skirt around it.

That night was more of the same, though I managed to sleep for a few hours. It wasn't very restful—largely because of the nightmares filled with giant mind spiders who forced me to relive some of my worst memories—but it was better than nothing. Or that's what I told myself. In the back of my mind, I thought it would've been better if I'd simply remained awake.

Even so, we continued on our journey the next day, and after finding the crumbling road we'd followed from Nova City, we made exceptional time. Before nightfall, I could see the city on the horizon, but we didn't immediately approach. Instead, we found an abandoned building in which to make camp so we could enter the city by the light of day.

The next morning found us at the base of the pillar I'd once used as a back door to the city. Patrick wasn't up to climbing nearly a thousand feet straight up, so he was forced to swallow his pride and clip himself to my back. He usually wasn't afflicted with misplaced masculine vanity, but he clearly wasn't happy with the situation. Still, I was tempted to tease him a bit, but in the end, I thought better of it and kept my mouth shut.

The climb was surprisingly easy, even with Patrick strapped to my back. I could only suppose that my recent gains regarding my Constitution were responsible. I'd already noticed it, but eclipsing the hundred-point mark had resulted in a huge jump in the attribute's effectiveness. That increase showed its worth as I ascended the pillar, climbing from one piton to the next. Even the once-precarious crossing from the column to the grate proved a weak adversary, and I defeated it without issue. In no time at all, we were stepping into the city's Underground.

However, it only took me a moment after Patrick and I uncoupled to realize that something was wrong. Before, the various chambers and tunnels had been packed with people. The Nats, a small tribe devoted to a lack of cybernetics, lived there, after all. But now, there was no one around.

I summoned my assault rifle and held it to my shoulder, whispering, "Be on your guard. Something's off."

Patrick, for his part, had already drawn his sleek black-and-gold pistol. He had clearly picked up on what I'd noticed, so my warning was unnecessary. Perhaps he was learning after all.

Gradually, we advanced through the tunnels. I kept Observation flared as strongly as I could manage as I meticulously searched for any traps. I found none. In fact, even when we found our way to the main chamber, we'd yet to run into any of the tribe who called it home.

In the end, it was the smell that gave it away.

At first, I thought it was just the ubiquitous stink that came from living in old drainage tunnels, many of which were directly tied into the city's sewer system. Various Mist-powered machines took care of the worst of the human waste, but nothing could rid the Underground of that ever-present smell. However, I soon came to recognize it for what it was.

Rotting meat.

It wasn't long after that before I followed the scent to a chamber that was absolutely filled with naked corpses, each one in a reasonably advanced state of decay. Giant rats and other native scavengers skittered across the bodies as I stared in horror. There were hundreds of them. Thousands, maybe. Clearly, I'd found what was left of the Nats.

"Why?" muttered Patrick, his voice constricted by a tightening throat.

"I . . . I don't know," I answered in a hoarse whisper. But that wasn't true. Certainly, there were any number of potential explanations that could account for the scene laid out before me. Perhaps the Nats had run afoul of one of the stronger tribes. Or maybe they'd offended the Enforcers. They'd never been the most powerful or popular tribe in the city, so it wasn't really a stretch to think that they'd been massacred by a rival.

However, in the back of my mind, another explanation clamored for my attention. Someone had discovered my route in and out of the city, and the Nats had paid the price for the role they'd played.

CHAPTER SIXTY-ONE

DISCOVERY

I didn't want to do it. My hand was forced. I can't let defiance stand. They helped her—knowingly or unknowingly—and they refused to make it right. Now, everyone knows the price of standing against me. Sometimes, examples must be made in order to show others the consequences of making the wrong choices.

—Nora Lancaster

"What . . . What do you think happened here?" asked Patrick, his hand covering the lower part of his face. Maybe it was an attempt to cover the smell, but it just as easily could've been an expression of shock. After all, the pile of bodies before us warranted either reaction.

I'd seen a lot of death since my Awakening. I had even killed quite a few and was responsible for even more. But nothing could compare to the pile of rotting meat that had once been a group of living, breathing human beings. The visceral nature of it shook me right down to the core of who I was, and even if I hadn't recently experienced an epiphany about my own actions, seeing the mound of corpses would have been a wake-up call. It was impossible to look upon it and remain blind to the human suffering I'd caused.

At one point, I'd toyed with the idea that I'd acted evilly in the past. But this display of casual murder represented a clear distinction between what I'd done and true wickedness. It made me want to vomit.

But even more, it reaffirmed my resolution to be better in the future, lest I somehow descend to a level where callously killing hundreds—or probably thousands—of people seemed like a valid path. It seemed impossible that I might one day go down that road, but whoever had killed all those people had probably thought the same thing. It wasn't just one step. It was a descent of inches. Hundreds of little decisions. Thousands of tiny moments. Each driving you further toward depravity until you look around and recognize that you've reached hell. And that you have become a monster meant for that setting.

"I don't know," I admitted in a whisper. But I intended to find out. To that end, I turned and began an exploration of the tunnel. It took a couple of minutes, but I eventually found a security terminal. When I jacked in, I had no difficulty using Mistwalk to bypass the defenses and infiltrate the system. It was so much easier when I had a hardwired connection than when I was forced to use Misthack, and it wasn't long before a web of security cameras, inactive autoturrets, and other various defenses were exposed to my mind.

I ignored the defenses—most had been damaged to the point of inoperability—zeroing in on the security logs. In seconds, I gathered the appropriate video feeds and set about perusing them. With my Mind attribute, the Hand of God, and my [Mistrunner] skill, I could process the information extremely quickly, so it didn't take more than a few minutes before I had a good picture of what had happened.

Predictably, it was the Specters.

I had been betrayed. I wasn't sure exactly what had passed between Nora and Gunther, but from the few stray bits of conversation I heard on the security feeds, it was clear that he'd revealed many of my secrets. Chief among them was that I'd cooperated with the Nats, and Nora had chosen to make an example of them.

It wasn't really targeted at me. She likely didn't think I'd use the same route back into the city. Perhaps she didn't think I'd ever return. Either way, that wasn't the point. Instead, she'd approached the Nats expecting some sort of compensation.

It made sense, too. After all, she couldn't really attack Gunther. He was too powerful. And I hadn't associated with any other organizations. Besides, the Nats were loners. They'd never cultivated alliances with the other tribes. Finally, they were weak enough that the Specters could easily defeat them.

I watched as the fight broke out, and it was a massacre. After the Specters killed Gavin Paulson—the tribe's leader—as well as his warriors, they spread out through the Underground, murdering anyone they saw. A few escaped, but not as many as I might've hoped. In the end, the Specters stripped the bodies and area of anything valuable, piled the corpses into the heap I'd just seen, and left.

Some of the Operators were clearly disgusted, but a disturbing number took glee in their abhorrent actions. For her part, Nora only participated in the first stage, leaving the extermination of the rest of the tribe to her underlings.

Before, I'd had trouble connecting the woman I thought I knew with the sort of person who could betray my uncle. But watching her on those security feeds, any doubts I might've harbored dissipated into nothing. She wasn't just the enemy. She was actively evil.

Of course, I wasn't so blind that I believed she was alone in her nature. I was certain that my uncle had done similar things in the past. But there was a difference between ephemeral suggestions masquerading as knowledge and visual evidence. The former fostered doubt. The latter engendered certainty.

"What do you see?" asked Patrick. "Who did this?"

"Nora" was my dispassionate answer. "She killed them all."

"W-what? Why?"

I shook my head. "She needed to make an example," I explained. "The tribes, they exist in a delicate balance. I . . . I upset that balance by weakening the Specters, and they needed to make a big splash if they were going to maintain their place and keep the others from pouncing on a perceived weakness."

"I . . . I don't . . . Why these people, though?"

"Because I passed through," I said. "I used this route out of and back into the city. But that was just an excuse. She probably didn't even think I'd return this way. This wasn't for me. It was for everyone else."

"So . . . What do we do?" Patrick asked.

"I don't think there's anything we can do," I answered. "I mean, most of those people would have just been dumped into the swamp anyway. That's probably what'll happen regardless. Once people figure out that the Nats are gone, another group will move in here. They'll toss the bodies, and . . . and I don't know, Patrick. I don't think it matters."

"You don't think what matters?"

"Anything? I don't know," I said, loosening my grip on some of the emotions rampaging through my mind. I was angry. Disappointed. Horrified. And a hundred other variations of the same feelings. "I just don't know, Patrick. This wasn't my fault. I know it wasn't. I didn't kill those people. But they wouldn't be dead without me. It's . . . it's a heavy feeling, and I don't know . . . I don't have a clue how to deal with it."

Patrick looked away, but he didn't say anything. For some reason, that made me even angrier.

"What? No stories this time? No sage advice? Nothing from Remy?" I demanded.

"No."

"Seriously? Nothing?" I spat.

"I don't think Remy ever saw anything like this," he said, his voice barely audible. If it weren't for the passive component of Observation boosting my senses, I wasn't sure if I'd have even heard him.

"No. He didn't," I said, some of the fire dissipating from my tone. I knew it wasn't Patrick's fault. I was just so angry. At Nora. At the situation. At Nova City in general. It just wasn't fair that these people had paid for my sins. For something they had nothing to do with. "I don't think many people have."

After that, the conversation lapsed into silence. Neither of us really knew how to confront our emotions or the scene we'd just witnessed, so it was easier to simply move on. The journey through the Underground tunnels was accompanied by an oppressive silence, and to distract myself from my roiling thoughts, I focused intently on Observation. Nora might not have considered the former Nats' base to be terribly important, but I found it unlikely that she would have left it completely abandoned.

For a while, I found nothing. However, as I followed the path to the exit, I stumbled upon a simple motion sensor. When I dove into its underlying system, I discovered that it would only trip if it sensed something larger than a child. It didn't take much effort for me to follow the threads of its connection to other similar systems throughout the tunnels and chambers that made up the Underground.

I deactivated them all, though I looped the connection so that the receiver wouldn't be alerted to a problem. More, that tether allowed me to pinpoint the location of whoever was monitoring the web of sensors. I marked them on my map, fully intending to take ruthless revenge on the people who'd killed the men, women, and children in the corpse pile I'd encountered.

But then I thought better of it.

Right now, we needed to get to the Bazaar, unload the haul of Rift Shards we'd mined, and use the resulting funds to buy a ship. Everything else would come later.

I still intended to kill Nora. Not even the personal growth that had been forced upon me in the Rift could do anything to derail that mission. But in my mind, it felt almost like an afterthought. An item on my to-do list that needed to be checked off before I could move on with my life.

A marked change from when my revenge was the driving force behind every decision, but as difficult as it was to keep myself from returning to bad habits, I knew it was necessary. I had seen the person I could become, and I wanted to avoid that fate at all costs.

So, not wanting to alert anyone to our presence, I donned a disguise by embracing Mimic and led Patrick, who was cloaked in his own camouflaging skill, out of the tunnels and to the huge concrete aqueduct that cut through the Garden. I didn't see the monitors, but I knew they were nearby, likely beneath a holographic display that masked their presence. Still, I trusted my disguise as well as Stealth to keep me hidden, largely because it had never failed me before.

It also helped that I figured the watchers were dependent on their web of sensors to alert them to any activity. It would have been so easy to just pop into their midst and kill them all. But I restrained my murderous impulses, focusing on what was really important.

And as we climbed the sloped sides of the aqueduct to the ladder that would lead us to the street above, we remained undetected. It was possible that they were merely putting on a show of ignorance, but I was familiar enough with the Specters to know how unlikely that strategy was. They were the strong, and if they did manage to see through our stealthy abilities, we would appear weak. Doubtless, they would have attacked, intending to add a couple of fresh bodies to the corpse pile.

That didn't happen, though, and we reached the street without issue. Once there, I took a moment to look around, taking in the familiar confines of the city. Structurally, it was the same as ever, with giant megabuildings dominating the skyline. However, for the first time in my memory, I found myself feeling completely alone on the streets of Nova City.

There were no pedestrians in evidence. No homeless men or women begging for loose credits. No addicts sprawled in the alleys. And certainly no exhausted people trudging to and from dead-end jobs that expected them to sacrifice everything while giving them next to nothing.

"Eerie," said Patrick, noticing the same thing.

For months, the citizens of Nova City had been in the midst of a mass exodus. And it seemed that, while we were gone, it had finally reached that critical point where the city felt empty. I knew that, in some of the busier parts of the city, people would be in greater evidence—the Nats had chosen their base specifically because it was less populated and didn't infringe on anyone else's territory. But it had never been so abandoned.

I wasn't sure how I felt about it, either.

On the one hand, I hated Nova City and its oppressive policies that forced the bulk of its citizenry to scramble for whatever scraps happened to fall from the higher platforms. That part of me applauded the people for breaking their chains and fleeing the city. But the more realistic part of me couldn't escape the reality that most of those people had fled right into the jaws of the wilderness. The vast majority probably never reached their destinations. Instead, they were almost assuredly consumed by the various threats so ubiquitous in the wild places of the world.

I wasn't certain which fate was preferable.

It didn't really matter, though. The die had been cast, and nothing I could do would change the course of events. I could only do what I'd come to do and go on with my life.

To that end, Patrick and I found an abandoned alley, where I summoned my Cutter. Once mounted, we set off through the city. As we did, I couldn't help but note that the tribal conflict hadn't abated during our time outside the city. If anything, its intensity had only increased, and it was rare that we passed a side street that didn't show the evidence of a city at war.

Operators swaggered around, looking like they were itching for a fight. Roadblocks abounded, forcing us to take alternate routes. Fires burned, sending thick, dark clouds of smoke billowing into the atmosphere. And the sound of gunfire and explosions—some distant, but others disturbingly close—filled the air.

A few times, groups of Operators tried to stop us, but the Cutter was quick and maneuverable enough that such attempts were destined for failure. Still, some of the angry gunmen tried to take potshots at us. A few came distressingly close to hitting the mark. They probably wouldn't been more than an inconvenience for me, but for Patrick, they would have been far more impactful.

Eventually, we reached the ramp connecting the Garden to Bywater, and after reaching the other platform, we saw the other consequence of the tribal war. The Enforcers were out in great numbers. Ostensibly, they seemed intent on leveraging their presence toward keeping the peace, but I saw the truth. They were just another tribe, and more than once, I saw their brutality on blatant display.

Nobody stopped a group of Enforcers when they gunned down a young girl who'd been running down the street. Perhaps she'd robbed someone. Or maybe she just liked to run. Either way, the Enforcers took it as an opportunity to exercise their more murderous tendencies. My bias could have been showing, but I thought they looked like they were playing a game to see who could shoot her first.

I didn't see how it ended, but I couldn't imagine it would be a good outcome for the young girl. More, I couldn't help but see the parallels between her path and my own life. It wasn't that long ago that I'd been that girl, sprinting through the streets after stealing a pair of boots.

I saw more than a few such scenes as we raced through the streets, but at some point, I just stopped paying attention. I couldn't save them. And I knew that dwelling on such things would send me down a dark path. So, I closed myself off to it.

Patrick clearly didn't have the ability to ignore his nature, and I felt his arms tighten each time he saw injustice playing out in front of him. I felt sorry for him, but I was also proud that my companion still had the capacity for empathy. So many people who'd seen the things he had seen would have long since descended into cold cynicism. I had, at least to some degree, so I knew how easy it could be.

At some point, the Dome came into view, and we pulled to a stop before the plaza depicting statues of humanity's various deities, all with their gazes cast skyward as they worshipped the incoming aliens. It was disgusting.

But I couldn't allow myself to dwell on it.

So, we dismounted the Cutter and hurried through the square and into the huge domed building that housed the access point for the Bazaar. The area was mostly deserted, but there were still enough people around that it almost felt normal. I knew it wasn't.

"Don't look, but we've picked up a tail," I whispered to Patrick, keeping my eyes trained forward. "Six Operators, dressed in cheap knockoff suits. All armed with pistols."

When I had first noticed the group, I'd thought they were just normal civilians. However, those cheap suits couldn't disguise the bulky cybernetics that eschewed sleek, compact design, exchanging it for raw power. Once they got my attention, I flared Observation and saw their shifting eyes and constant attention for what it was. They were following us.

And there was only one reason that would be the case: we'd been recognized somehow.

"What do we do?" Patrick asked, his voice quivering slightly with fear.

"Keep going. Get into the Bazaar," I said. "Hopefully, you have enough Shards to buy a ship."

"What about you?" he asked.

"I'll deal with the situation."

That's when I noticed three other groups closing in on us. I recognized a few of them, too. How could I not? I'd seen them often enough.

But one, in particular, caught my eye. Real leather suit. A wide-brimmed hat. Ridiculous boots. Suddenly, I didn't question how I'd been recognized. Gunther had always been able to see through my various skills, after all.

"Go. Now," I spat.

To his credit, Patrick didn't hesitate. Instead, he immediately accelerated into a flat-out sprint. Meanwhile, I wheeled around, summoning my R-14 and sending a few bursts of fire at the closest groups. At the same time, I sprinted to the side, taking cover behind a bulky bench.

Glancing in Patrick's direction, I saw him turn a corner, and I breathed a sigh of relief. So long as they hadn't stationed anyone at the Bazaar Node itself, he would be fine. I just had to take care of the threats so they couldn't attack his body while his awareness was in the space station miles above the surface.

"Nice to see you again, Gunther!" I yelled. "I always knew you'd turn on me."

Gunther shouted back, "Nothing personal. It's just business, girl. Now, surrender and we'll leave your little friend alone. If you fight back, Dierdre here will tear him apart one limb at a time."

CHAPTER SIXTY-TWO

BATTLE OF THE DOME

As always, Gunther has to be difficult. He wants her for himself. Not because of any vendetta—no, he wanted her stuff. The incredibly expensive weapons. The hover bike that cost more than many buildings. And whatever else she has tucked away. It's disgusting, but I can't afford to add another side to the war I've been forced to fight.

—Nora Lancaster

Everything erupted into chaos. Behind me, a pair of autoturrets descended from the ceiling and opened fire even as thick metal shutters slid shut over the exposed windows. I dove away, exposing my position to Gunther and his goons, but they couldn't take advantage because they were just as subject to the Dome's defenses as I was. Down the corridor, I could see that they were taking fire from another set of autoturrets. Hopefully, that would keep them busy.

As I crawled behind one of the thick concrete columns that supported the ceiling, I cast my {Mistrunner} senses out, and I quickly found the autoturrets that had targeted me. Without hesitation, I dove into the first's system, tearing through the meager defenses as I took control of the automated weapon. Then, I directed it to ignore me and target Gunther and his mooks.

It seemed almost too eager to comply.

Of course, I knew it was just a mindless machine, so I was probably just anthropomorphizing the thing. But I was in no position to question it. So, I moved on to the next, repeating the process before tackling the three that were already firing on my enemies. I didn't want them out of the fight—not if I could just exclude myself from the list of targets. The turrets weren't that powerful, and I didn't think they'd kill any of the others, much less me, but they were more than capable of creating confusion and slowing my enemies down.

And that was all I really needed.

In the few seconds it took me to subjugate the machines, Gunther and his mooks had recovered from their surprise. I knew I didn't have long. I needed to turn the tables. And I knew precisely how.

It only took a moment for me to find my target. She—if gender even applied to someone whose entire body was mechanical—stood out like a sore thumb. Dierdre had barely even made an attempt at ducking under cover, and the bulk of her metal body was exposed. The turrets fired upon her, but the bullets were rendered useless by her thick armor. I suspected that it would be similarly effective against my weaponry.

So, I didn't even bother shooting.

Instead, I once again embraced my {Mistrunner} senses. Like the moon among starry sky, she blazed in my awareness, so she wasn't difficult to find. With Misthack, I thrust into her system, finding predictably upgraded defenses. However, after going through those aural sensors around the Octavangians' camp multiple times, I was barely fazed by the effort required to batter my way through one node after another until, after only a handful of seconds, her system was laid bare before me.

I didn't have the access I would've if I'd jacked into the system via a hard connection, but I didn't really need it, either. Instead, I initiated the Misthack, which brought up the familiar menu on my HUD:

Misthack successful. Options:
Reboot system
Overcharge
Disable cybernetics
Upload Ghost

I already knew the route to victory, so I merely had to select it. I didn't bother with a Ghost. Nor did I choose to restart her system. And Overcharge would've been little more than a slap. Besides, it wasn't about defeating her. Nothing in my arsenal could do that on its own. No—I wanted to scare her. I wanted to tear into the morale of her comrades. To that end, I chose the disable-cybernetics option. But I held off from activating right away.

Then, I moved on to the next.

There were six cyborgs—men and women who'd given up the majority of their flesh in favor of mechanical parts—and I repeated the action. With each victim, the strain on my Mind increased, but I was well versed in pushing through such things, so the burden wasn't nearly as heavy as I might have expected.

After thirty seconds—during which Gunther and his goons managed to destroy two of the three autoturrets—I finally toppled the last of the cyborgs' defenses and initiated the ability. Instantly, the hail of gunfire dissipated as one loud metallic thump sounded after another as the cyborgs hit the floor.

That's when I made my move.

With my R-14 still in hand, I summoned a stun grenade from my arsenal implant. With practiced movement, I tossed it in the direction of my enemies. Even as it arced through the air, I closed my eyes and forcibly cut Observation short.

Then, it exploded in a cacophony of sound and light that, even from fifty feet away, was enough to send me reeling. I could only imagine how badly it had affected my attackers.

There was definitely something to be said for homemade grenades. Sure, I could've bought a huge stock, and fairly inexpensively. However, that convenience came at the cost of effectiveness. The store-bought ones would be plenty for most situations, but my grenades were far more potent. For instance, the handmade stun grenades like the one I'd just tossed were powerful enough to kill a civilian outright. Sure, it couldn't end a real Operator, but their higher attributes meant that, to stun them, a little extra oomph was needed.

Couple those more powerful grenades with the modifiers from my [Demolition] skill, and I had an extremely powerful tool.

Finally, the cyborgs had already been stripped of their defenses, so they were even more affected.

Which meant it was time for me to make my move.

I leaned out of cover, looking for an appropriate target, but my attackers were no amateurs, so they'd ensconced themselves behind cover provided by benches, a few fake plants, and a couple of statues lining the hall.

In a perfect world, I would have just waited them out. Only an idiot would leave cover in a firefight. But I had a couple of things working against me—most notably, that my previous efforts wouldn't last forever. The cyborgs would recover control of their cybernetics after a little more than a minute, and the stun grenade's effects wouldn't even last that long. Perhaps just as importantly, there was no telling how many mooks Gunther could bring to the battle. Sure, he'd only attacked me with a couple of handfuls, but who was to say he didn't have a hundred more in reserve? He was a man of means, after all. And as an arms dealer, he would have made certain that his goons were well armed.

No—I needed to end the ones in front of me, and soon. Otherwise, I would be forced to continue fighting a battle where Gunther had all the advantages.

So, as much as my learned instincts were screaming at me to stay where I was, I gritted my teeth and dashed out of cover. In only a second, I'd covered the fifty feet between us, and I leaped over a bench, exposing the two mooks who had the misfortune of being my first victims.

The R-14 barked, sending a pair of three-round bursts of molten plasma to tear through their chests. Before the shots had even landed, I was already making a break for another cluster of Operators who'd taken shelter behind a statue of some unknown leader from the distant past.

But I only had eyes for the two cyborgs in their midst. They had been rendered helpless by my {Mistrunner} exploits, but I knew that wouldn't remain the case for very long. So, I took aim at the only unprotected portions of their bodies and sent a tight grouping of shots at their exposed faces.

The result wasn't pretty. Charred flesh, shattered skull bones, and the smell of burned synapses filled the air as I ended the lives of the other mooks who'd surrounded the cyborgs. They were helpless, as well, and they fell even more easily than the cyborgs.

I darted toward the next group, but that was when the various impediments I'd thrown my attackers' way faded into uselessness, and I was suddenly exposed to a cascade of gunfire. Luckily, my aggression—or perhaps, the sight of their heavy hitters falling helpless—had rattled them, and so, most of their shots went wide. Still, quite a few landed, though none made it through the combination of my infiltration suit and subdermal Sheath.

Each shot still hurt, though.

I refused to let it derail my momentum, and even as I was peppered with gunfire, I swept through another two groups. My training paid off, and none of my shots were wasted. Still, as impressed as I was with my own steady aim, I couldn't even begin to kill the entire group before my defenses inevitably gave out. My equipment was top-notch, but it had limits, and I was quickly approaching the point where I'd have to make some tough decisions.

With the ticking time bomb of my armor's eventual failure steadily counting down, I changed tactics. I didn't need to immediately kill them all, did I? I just needed to thin the herd. And I was convinced that a little concentrated lightning would do the trick.

In a blink, I exchanged my R-14 for the scattergun. At the same time, I hadn't stopped moving. [Acrobatics] came in extremely handy as I maintained my balance even under the constant thuds of so much gunfire. Trying to maintain my armor's integrity for as long as possible, I dipped, dodged, and ducked, avoiding more shots than actually found their mark, but the wave of gunfire was dense and unceasing. I couldn't avert damage entirely. I could only avoid what I could and endure what I couldn't.

A familiar trade-off with which I was well acquainted.

When I reached the next group, I found myself faced with a shimmering blue shield. Without skipping a beat, I activated Misthack and tore through its defenses in the blink of an eye; I'd never gone so quickly, but with the adrenaline of battle pumping through my veins, it didn't even seem difficult. Either way, the seven Operators who expected safety were soon disabused of that notion when a cone of dense lightning enveloped them.

As I fell upon them, I didn't bother exchanging weapons. Instead, I hefted the Hand of God and went to work as I pummeled their convulsing bodies with one Combination Punch after another. In a matter of seconds, the once-healthy Operators had become a pile of twitching muscles and broken bones. Some survived. Most did not.

But even the ones who yet lived were out of the fight. It would take a skilled doctor to undo the damage I'd wrought, and even then, I expected full recovery would be impossible. At the very least, they were no longer a threat to me, so I didn't take the few precious seconds required to finish them off.

Because the next group had fully recovered, and it included Dierdre and three other cyborgs. Even with my attributes, engaging them in a melee was an absurdly bad idea.

So, I threw a fragmentation grenade at them.

I didn't expect it to kill anyone. Their armor was too thick, their defenses too stout. I just wanted a few extra seconds to enact the next part of my plan. Or to repeat the first one.

After all, if it worked once, it would probably work again.

That's when I got one big surprise and a much smaller one.

The smaller one should have been predictable. Every system had some innate defenses against my efforts. Some were practically impregnable. Others went down in the face of a virtual stiff breeze. And there were hundreds of others in between those two extremes. However, I was mildly shocked to discover that personal interfaces were adaptable, and when I used Misthack to infiltrate Dierdre's system, I got an alert I had neither expected nor wanted to see.

Warning! Repeated attempts to Misthack a personal interface will result in suboptimal results!

"Great," I muttered to myself as I deactivated Dierdre's system. Before, it had only lasted a minute, but I got the sense that this latest attempt would be far less effective. If I got more than a few seconds out of it, I would've been surprised.

But there was nothing for it but to adapt.

I leaped forward, drawing Ferdinand II from the holster at my side with one hand while retrieving the sword from my back with the other. My first shot thundered into Dierdre's head, the armor-piercing ammunition I'd loaded into my weapon's cannister tearing through the thick metal plate covering her temple.

That's when the big surprise hit me.

Or rather, tore into my side, piercing through my infiltration suit and subdermal Sheath like they were no more impenetrable than mundane skin. I screamed, more in surprise than pain, and wrenched myself free of what I would soon find was the blade of a spear.

I tumbled forward in an awkward roll that allowed me to barely avoid another strike. Somehow, I found my feet and faced off against my new attacker, and I saw Gunther standing only ten feet away and holding the spear he'd used to stab me in the back. He'd obviously been targeting my kidney, but my status readout told me that he'd missed my vital organs.

He didn't know that, though.

"You're almost as hard to kill as your uncle," he spat, twirling his weapon with expert precision. Constructed of solid metal, it must have weighed a hundred pounds, and it sported a blade that could have doubled as a shortsword. "He didn't know his place, either."

I raised Ferdinand II and shot him.

The look of shock on his face was worth more than whatever minor damage I might've done. Clearly, he'd expected me to banter. Or respond in some way. Instead, I'd taken the spare second to snatch the momentum from him.

The resulting round did little damage—as expected—but Ferdinand II was a powerful weapon, and he sent Gunther staggering back a few steps. Still, it was obvious that he was equipped with top-tier armor, so putting him down would likely prove incredibly difficult. It was a good thing that I intended to save him for last.

With Gunther on his back foot, I darted toward Dierdre and her squad. Surprisingly, the shot to the head hadn't killed her, and she'd started dragging herself to her feet. However, even as she swung a huge machine gun around, I noticed that she was unsteady. I was on her in a moment, taking advantage and letting Ferdinand II lead the way.

I fired one round at her, but the remaining six found their way to her companions. They didn't have the benefit of her high-quality armor, and Ferdinand II was perfectly equipped to tear through what protections they did have. None were killed in that opening salvo, and I didn't have the opportunity to finish them off.

Because Gunther had recovered and made another move.

This time, I was ready for him. The moment he'd appeared out of nowhere, I'd come to the conclusion that he was using some sort of stealth variant to mask his approach. So, ever since that first stab, I'd been flaring Observation. It wasn't easy, sorting through the mass of stimuli assaulting my senses—especially in the middle of a fight—but my Mind attribute wasn't just for show, and I quickly took control.

And the results were better than expected.

Gunther's ability, like my own stealth-focused abilities, was almost entirely focused on the visual element. As such, his footsteps still made sound, and with Observation doing the heavy lifting, I knew precisely when he was going to make his move.

Even then, countering wasn't easy. It happened so quickly that I was barely able to twist out of the way. Still, I managed it, and when his spear found nothing but air, I clamped my arm down, pinning it to my side.

That's when I discovered that Gunther hadn't put much effort into raising his Constitution. My grip, awkward though it was, was like iron, and even though he put every ounce of his weight behind his efforts to pull it free, he made no progress.

So, I whipped my arm around in a backhanded blow that found the side of his surprised face. Ferdinand II was empty, so I couldn't shoot him again. That was fine, though; I didn't think he could get through whatever armor Gunther was wearing. But the same couldn't be said for the nano-bladed sword suddenly clutched in my other hand.

I struck with lightning speed, the blade tracing a line across his throat before he even finished his fall. It was a shallow wound, and I heard the metallic clank of metal on metal, telling me what sort of subdermal armor he'd chosen. The heavy kind that traded mobility for virtual impenetrability.

Emphasis on the virtual part.

But I didn't get the chance to follow that attack with another before Dierdre recovered and, like an out-of-control train, tackled me. I didn't fall to the ground. The sheer momentum of her monumental weight forced the breath from my body, then slammed me into the nearest wall. I felt bones crack, and my head whipped into the concrete with enough force to give me a hundred concussions.

Through an effort of will, I maintained consciousness, but only just. My various abilities went into overdrive, helped along by my inflated attributes. But that thin thread wasn't enough to let me dodge the barrage of body blows Dierdre aimed at my sides. At first, it was just a handful, but each punch came faster than the last, and before I knew it, her arms blurred with speed.

Agony tore through my body as I felt like my organs had ruptured anew with each rapid punch, but somehow, I managed to embrace Misthack before I was completely overwhelmed. The familiar menu blossomed in my HUD, and I selected the first option I saw. It was the right choice because, a second later, Overcharge tore through Dierdre's artificial body. It was even more effective than I might have expected—if I'd had the ability to think properly amid the pain—and Dierdre's attacks suddenly ceased as she fell to the ground, twitching like she'd been electrocuted.

The reality wasn't far from appearance, but instead of an electrical current, she was beset by agitated Mist. Whatever the case, it gave me the opening I needed. In the best of times, Overcharge wouldn't last long, but diluted by her system's evolving defenses, the effect would fade in only a second or two. So, I couldn't afford to waste time.

When she'd collapsed, I'd fallen to my knees, but I couldn't allow myself to rest. Instead, I pushed myself to my feet and struck. My blade, crackling with blue energy, fell upon the helpless cyborg's neck. Once. Twice. Three times—all in the space of a second.

The twitching faded.

Her head fell free.

And like that, only Gunther was left.

Or that's what I thought before another barrage of bullets tore into me, forcing me to stagger behind the scant cover provided by a nearby bench.

I had no idea how many people the gunrunner had brought with him, but it felt like an army. It was a good thing that I had a weapon perfectly suited to assault such a force.

To that point, I hadn't used the BMAP because I was afraid of the collateral damage. But as wounded as I was—the entire health readout was blaring red—I knew I couldn't hold back. So, I holstered Ferdinand II and slid the nano-bladed sword into the sheath on my back. Then, I summoned the BMAP from my arsenal implant, took aim, and let loose.

CHAPTER SIXTY-THREE

DEMOLITION

Gunther never took her seriously. He just thought she was a silly girl with some expensive toys. I knew better. I had seen parts of her training. But more, I knew the depths of Jeremiah's desire to prepare her for the harsh realities of the world. Even half-trained, Mira was a grave threat. Gunther couldn't see that.

—Nora Lancaster

Six identical thumps, all in quick succession, resounded, and a sextet of explosive rounds flew through the air. I was already reloading before they found their mark, and when they finally hit, they did so with what felt like a singular explosion that blanketed the entire area in fire and concussive force. I was thrown backward by the shock wave, but because of Blast Shield, which reduced the severity of the effects on me from my own explosions, I was otherwise unharmed.

The same couldn't be said for Gunther's small army of mooks. The two dozen or so Operators who were unlucky enough to find themselves at the epicenter died instantly. However, there were plenty of others who were less affected. A cloud of dust born of shattered concrete billowed into the air, and when the sound of the explosion faded, it was replaced by the creaks of the Dome's unstable foundation.

After all, when I'd first acquired the BMAP, Gala had described its capability as being sufficient to tear down buildings, and it definitely lived up to that description. But the Dome wasn't just any building, and I felt certain that, reinforced as it was, it would continue to stand. Otherwise, I would never have risked using the BMAP indoors.

Still, I knew that plenty of danger remained from the damage wrought by the mobile artillery platform. The Dome's overall structure might've remained sound, but the same couldn't be said for the building's other parts and pieces. Punctuating that thought, a giant chunk of cracked concrete fell from the ceiling, sending a wave of force to ripple through the dust cloud.

I dragged myself to my feet, my ears still ringing from the explosion and my body protesting its ill treatment. I still had broken ribs. My organs were, at the very least, bruised. At worst, I was bleeding internally.

But I was alive, and given my Pain Tolerance as well as my Regeneration ability, I felt confident that I could still fight.

It was a good thing, too, because the moment I found my feet, a clatter of cascading concrete sounded in front of me. A moment later, a battered and bruised Gunther stepped out of the cloud of dust. And he looked even worse than I felt. His leather suit was torn to shreds, one of his arms hung limp by his side, and each step came with a pronounced limp. Half his face had been pulverized into a mass of bruises, broken bones, and lacerated flesh, and his eye was entirely missing, leaving a gaping hole in its wake.

But he was alive.

And he was angry.

Still twenty feet away, he thrust his spear at me with one hand, growling, "You little bitch! Do you have any idea what this is going to cost me? Dierdre was a masterpiece of modern technology and—"

I leaped, using Engage to cover the distance in an instant. As I did so, I dropped the BMAP into my arsenal implant; I didn't have time to summon another weapon. Nor would I get my pistol or nano-bladed sword out before I reached him. But that didn't matter. I still had the Hand of God at my side.

Gunther tried to react as I closed on him, but to the naked eye, Engage was so quick that it seemed almost a teleport, and I was on top of him before he could bring his spear to bear. Without his stealth ability or his army of goons to back him up, he was practically powerless before my charge.

I landed with a mighty, if unimaginative, punch that took him directly in the ruined half of his face. To my surprise, I didn't feel bones shattering beneath the blow. I'd put everything into it—the entirety of my Constitution as well as the momentum of Engage—but the result only staggered him back by a couple of feet.

It was a good thing I'd activated Combination Punch, then.

The next blow—an uppercut with my other hand—took him in the stomach, bending him double. The one after that was a hammer blow that hit him in the back of the head. And the fourth was a knee to his descending face that forced him upright so he could receive the final attack—a simple hook with the

Hand of God that hit with enough force to send him rocketing into a wall ten feet away.

A spiderweb of cracks spread from the point of impact, but when Gunther dropped to the ground, he was still moving, albeit with the sort of drunken lack of coordination that came from a severe concussion.

I stepped forward, my fists clenched in anger.

I'd always expected Gunther to betray me. That was who he was. The moment betrayal became more profitable than cooperation, he was always going to turn on me. Even so, he'd managed to surprise me. After all, he'd made thousands of credits off of me, and as far as he knew, thousands more were still to come. I thought it would've been some time before the balance tipped out of my favor.

Clearly, I was wrong.

Unfortunately, when I reached Gunther and kicked him over to lay on his back, I saw the damage I probably should have expected. The flesh on one side of his face had been ripped away by the sheer force of my final blow, exposing the layer of metal armor beneath. However, it bore an imprint of my fist, which dented the subdermal layer out of shape. I was certain that the skull beneath it had been completely shattered, and his brain had followed suit.

He was still alive, but his one remaining eye stared forward sightlessly. He twitched a few times, but even if I left him as he was, there was little chance he'd ever regain full consciousness.

Which put a bit of a damper on my plan for interrogation.

So, it was fortunate that I didn't need to verbalize questions in order to get information out of him. With my foot, I turned Gunther's head to the side, exposing his information port. Then, I knelt beside him and dragged the braided black-and-gold cord out of the Hand of God, inserting the exposed end into the small slot.

I kept part of my awareness trained on my surroundings; with Observation flared, I could tell that the Operators who hadn't been killed were still out of the fight, but that wouldn't always remain the case. So, I'd need to extract Gunther's information as quickly as I could.

But the moment I connected, I found a problem.

Gunther's system sported what was easily the most robust set of defenses I had ever encountered. There weren't just hundreds of nodes; there were thousands, each as complex as the ones I'd found in the aural sensors around the Octavangian camp. I was sorely tempted to chance it and dive into those defenses—I hated admitting defeat, after all—but my better judgement won out, and I disconnected. I experienced a slight backlash, but the spike of mental pain was easily ignored. If I'd done so after diving into the defenses, it would have been much, much worse.

Either way, Gunther's secrets would remain his own.

Not that it mattered so much. I could guess the high points of his betrayal. But I'd hoped to find some information I could use to rob him blind. With the Shards Patrick and I had mined in the Rift, we were very wealthy, but one could never have too much funding. And I had a sense that, once he bought a ship, our riches would be sorely depleted.

With a sigh of disappointment, I retracted the cord back into my artificial hand and turned my attention to the survivors. In the Rift, I had resolved to be a better person who wasn't solely driven by a quest for revenge. However, that resolution didn't include mercy toward those who had directly attacked me, if only because leaving an enemy alive in your wake was a terrible idea.

Nora had made that unwitting mistake, and I'd spent the past months steadily weakening her entire organization. So, who was to say that the same vow of revenge couldn't be aimed at me? No—it was better if I ended any potential threats before they had a chance to blossom into anything serious.

So, over the next few minutes, I engaged in the unsavory task of finishing off my enemies. As I did so, I took the extra time to snatch any credits they might have accumulated, but because my arsenal implant was still full of Rift Shards, I couldn't loot anything but the virtual currency. And even that wasn't possible with each of them; some had secured their credits by locking them behind a set of impregnable defenses, and I had neither the time nor the inclination to spend hours solving equations and puzzles just to get a few thousand extra credits.

Once I'd finished my task and taken what I could, I used the secure connection I'd created to contact Patrick.

"You okay?" I asked.

"Me? What about you? I didn't—"

"I'm fine," I said. "The bad guys are dead, so I'm coming to you."

"Uh . . . Probably not a great idea," he said. "If it's even possible . . ."

Then, he proceeded to explain that, once the attack had commenced, the Dome's security protocols had engaged, locking him behind a set of steel doors. There were dozens of autoturrets, a few drones, and a couple of advanced robots guarding the area around the Bazaar's access point. However, the good news was that he was completely safe, even if he was basically a temporary prisoner.

After administering a couple of med-hypos to help me deal with the pain of my injuries, I hurried down the hall in his direction. Soon enough, though, I found the defenses he'd described. The exterior was only guarded by a couple of autoturrets, both of which opened fire the moment I came into view. I was ready, though, and I avoided injury by quickly ducking behind a corner.

I spent the next few minutes deactivating the autoturrets. They were more advanced than anything I'd seen before, but my {Mistrunner} abilities had progressed far enough that tearing through their defenses wasn't more than an inconvenience.

The doors were a different story altogether.

If I wanted to get through them, I had two options. I could either spend hours dismantling their defenses, or I could use force—which might've actually taken even longer. Neither option seemed attractive to me.

But then I realized that I didn't need to get through at all. Patrick was safe for the moment, and what's more, he was precisely where we wanted him. Nothing about his mission had to change. In fact, the situation was probably better than anything we could've hoped to encounter. With the strength of the defenses surrounding him, Patrick could head up to the Bazaar and buy our ship without having to worry about his own safety.

Of course, when I told him to do just that, he wasn't happy about it, but he eventually saw reason and agreed to do his job.

Meanwhile, he dropped another information bomb on me.

"She says the whole city's after you now," Patrick said, referring to Cirilla Montague, his [Cybernetic Engineer] mentor. "She's in hiding, but she wanted to . . . Ah . . . She wanted me to . . ."

"What? Spit it out, Pick."

"She wanted me to leave you," he admitted. "She's leaving the city, and she wants me to go with her to somewhere called Indiana."

Suddenly, I realized that Patrick and Montague had grown far closer than I had previously thought. Not surprising, given how much time he'd spent with the woman. Still, I had to wonder about the nature of their involvement. Did she look at him as a valuable assistant? That made sense. I knew just how capable Patrick could be. Or did she see him as a friend? A little brother, perhaps?

Or maybe she liked younger men.

Certainly, she wouldn't be the first with such tastes. Even Heather had been a mere fraction of my uncle's age.

"And? What are you going to do?" I asked.

"What? We're in this together, Mira!" he answered. The vehemence in his voice was all the assurance I needed. Or that's what I wanted to believe, at least. Still, the fact that Montague had tried to steal Patrick away from me left a sour taste in my mouth. In the past, I might've killed her for it. But now, I just wanted to have a conversation—one that might end with her face swollen beyond recognition.

Yeah—that would definitely make me feel a little better.

But I didn't have time for any of that, so I said, "Just get the ship. You know better than I do what we need, so I trust your judgment."

We'd already discussed the parameters of the ship we wanted to buy, but we both knew that our options would be limited, both by our funds as well as availability. I could only imagine that the Bazaar's stock was finite, so Patrick would have to use his discretion to determine what kind of trade-offs we were willing to make. But considering he'd be the one flying the ship, that was probably appropriate.

"Good to know," he said, a hint of irritation in his voice, probably because he thought I was patronizing him. I hadn't intended it that way, but I could see how it might seem a bit condescending.

"Alright," I said. "I don't think the secure connection will persist when you head to the Bazaar, so good luck."

"What are you going to do?" he asked.

"I think it's time I ended this," I stated. "Nora's not going to stop, and now that she knows I'm still alive, I'm not convinced my abilities will be enough to keep me under the radar. I need to take her out now, or she'll have even more time to set up her defenses."

"You're going by yourself?"

Even though I knew he couldn't see me, I couldn't keep myself from shrugging. "What choice do I have? I don't have an army, Patrick," I said. "Besides, I work best alone."

"We could wait. I could get the ship and come with you."

"No. You'll just slow me down," I stated. "If what Montague told you is true, the whole city's going to be gunning for me. I'm going to have to move fast. I can't do that and worry about whether or not you'll be safe."

"I can take care of myself," he argued.

"I know you can. This isn't about you or your abilities," I countered. "This is about me. I can't . . . I can't lose you, too, Patrick."

Silence reigned for a few moments before he said, "Fine. But . . . but take care of yourself. You get reckless sometimes. Just get to Nora, kill her, and get out. Nobody else matters. Once she's dead, we leave the city and go on our adventures. Deal?"

"Deal."

"Okay—I'm leaving for the Bazaar. Stay safe, Mira. I can't lose you, either."

And with that, the connection severed.

For a few seconds, I considered just holing up in the Dome and waiting it out. Once Patrick emerged, we could collect our ship and leave the city. It would have been the safer option.

It would have been the smart choice.

But as much as I thought I'd grown as a person, I couldn't even consider abandoning my quest for vengeance without nausea twisting my insides into knots. I might have decided to abstain from the revenge-at-all-costs mentality that had driven me to kill thousands of innocent people, but I knew I could never live with myself if I left Nora alive.

And even if I could, I didn't want to live in a world where Nora kept on breathing.

It wasn't about vengeance. Not anymore. It was justice. She'd betrayed and killed my uncle, sentencing the entirety of Mobile to death in the process. And for that, she deserved to die. It was such a simple equation, but it was a profound declaration nonetheless. More importantly, I didn't need to clutter it up with any further plans to make her suffer. I just needed to act.

So, with that in mind, I turned from the great metal doors and headed toward the Dome's exit. As I did, I saw quite a few cowering people, but I'd embraced Stealth before setting out, so they had no idea I was in their midst. When I finally reached the exit, I was unsurprised to find that it had been barred and was guarded by more autoturrets. Apparently, that was part of the security protocol.

Hidden as I was, I took my time dismantling the defenses. The last thing I wanted was a failure caused by impatience. I needn't have worried, though. I tore through the various Mistwalls without much difficulty, then deactivated the autoturrets before commanding the doors to open.

When they did, I saw an army of Operators amassed before me.

CHAPTER SIXTY-FOUR

UNIQUE ADVANTAGES

If there's one thing the powerful leaders of Nova City hate, it's being made to look like fools. For months, Mira has done just that, and now that the cat's out of the bag, my peers have reacted predictably. They're out for blood, one and all, and they won't be satisfied until she's dead.

—Nora Lancaster

Under so much scrutiny, my grip on Stealth wavered. The Mist quivered, threatening to unmask me, and I was forced to leverage the entirety of my Mind toward keeping it within my grasp. Still, it felt like trying to wrangle a mass of greasy noodles, and I struggled to keep the ability active. I knew that, in only a few seconds, I would fail.

So, I ran.

From copious experimentation, I knew that the ability didn't react well to rapid movement. The best I could manage without creating telltale ripples in the air was a light jog, but I could tell that wouldn't be enough. Already, my grip was slipping, and it would only be a few more moments before the ability shattered altogether. When that happened, I needed as much distance between me and the amassed Operators as possible.

There were hundreds of them. Maybe more than a thousand. A veritable army of armed, armored, and experienced warriors, all howling for my blood. Even bringing the BMAP to the party would be insufficient in the face of such a force. My only option was to escape and lose them in the streets of Nova City. Perhaps once I was hidden, I could wage a guerrilla war. Or, better yet, I could just hit Nora and leave the city behind. After all, I had no real quarrel with most of them.

Of course, they probably didn't see it that way, which was why they'd come. I didn't know how they'd discovered my presence or evidence of my previous actions. But it was clear that they knew enough to recognize me as an enemy.

Not that it really mattered in the grand scheme of things. I had enough to worry about concerning my escape without trying to puzzle out the reasons for their attack. Instead, I needed to focus on staying alive because, after only a few sprinting steps, the first Operators noticed the ripples in the air that denoted my ability falling apart around me.

I didn't stop, pouring every ounce of my inflated Constitution attribute into my legs as I dashed to the right. Someone shouted, and a moment later, a hail of gunfire erupted, falling in my wake. By that point, I was moving far too quickly for most of them to take proper aim; at one point, I'd clocked myself at almost forty miles an hour, and I'd only grown stronger since establishing that benchmark. Still, a few of the more talented marksmen adjusted beautifully, and only a second later, I felt the familiar sensation of multiple bullets thudding into my back and side. Fortunately, my infiltration suit held up, keeping them from testing my subdermal Sheath.

But I knew it wouldn't last.

A few bullets from these relatively weak Operators didn't pose much of a threat, but each one tore into the integrity of my suit. And if enough of them found their mark, it would fall apart. Then, I'd only have my Sheath to protect me, and powerful though it was, the subdermal armor wasn't infallible.

Quantity, when it came to gunfire, was a quality all its own. And there were hundreds of guns pointed in my direction.

I stumbled from each landed shot, turning my sprint into more of a stagger. I was still moving with incredible quickness, but I would never win any awards for style. It didn't matter. I only needed to reach cover for a few seconds so I could summon my Cutter. When I managed that, I could be a mile away before they had a chance to react.

To that end, I circled the exterior of the Dome, leaping over a few scattered benches and dodging around a statue of a bearded man holding a lightning bolt. Zeus, perhaps. Or maybe some other deity from Earth's mythology. I continued along in a zigzag pattern as I wove between the various statues until I broke free of the plaza. With each step, I left all but the physically strongest Operators behind, and I eventually found my way to the Bywater markets.

If I'd had any ideas that the Operators would hold their fire in order to spare the civilian shoppers or storefronts, I would have been sorely mistaken. They didn't let up, and as I burst through one crowd after another, their assault continued unabated. More than a few unlucky bystanders were torn to pieces by errant gunfire, and even more had limbs shattered by the Operators' powerful weapons.

I hated thinking it, but I was actually somewhat grateful for the fact that, unlike was the case in most parts of Nova City, Bywater was mostly unaffected by the mass exodus. As such, they provided a good distraction and a potent obstruction. Even as that thought crossed my mind, I felt horrible. But that didn't make it any less true, and soon enough, I burst through the edge of the crowd and turned down a side street. With the resulting few seconds of space, I summoned my hover bike.

It materialized out of the Mist, and just as I hopped on, a trio of Operators shouldered their way through the panicked crowd and took aim. I twisted the accelerator in my grip, but in the brief second it took for the engine to spin up, a half dozen bullets thudded into my back. I grunted in pain as my already broken ribs felt the brunt of the impacts, but I refused to acknowledge it further. Instead, I leaned forward and shot down the street, leaving the angry horde behind.

I sighed in relief as I turned a corner, removing myself from their view. For a few moments, I raced down the street and, using my map, put myself on a direct course to the Garden, where I hoped to end my quest for vengeance. Once that was done, I intended to leave Nova City behind for good.

It might've been better to simply go to ground and hide until the heat died down. However, there were a couple of issues with that plan. First, I wasn't sure that the Operators would ever give up their pursuit. I'd angered a lot of people, and it seemed the price of my actions had come due. Second—and perhaps more importantly—I had no idea how exposed I was. Surely, Nora and Gunther had discovered my base in Algiers, and I would've been a fool to believe that they were ignorant of the other safe houses I'd scattered throughout the city. After all, Gunther had helped me set most of them up. He'd only acted as an intermediary between other contractors, but I wasn't so naïve as to believe he wasn't aware of their locations. Surely, he'd informed Nora as to their existence.

If Nova hadn't been mostly abandoned, I might've been able to melt into the wider population. Using Mimic, maybe I could have hidden in plain sight. But as empty as the city had become, that strategy seemed destined for failure. Sure, I probably could have hidden away in the Underground or in the abandoned buildings of Algiers, but I'd eventually have to come up for air. When I did, the Specters—as well as the other tribes—would be there to ambush me.

Even as I raced through Bywater, I couldn't be sure I wasn't being watched. With every corner sporting a security camera, it wasn't outside the realm of possibility that the entire city was under Nora's watchful eye. Maybe she'd made a deal with the Enforcers. Or perhaps she had access to someone who specialized in infiltrating those kinds of systems. I had no idea what kind of pressure she could bring to bear when her back was against a wall.

And I had no interest in giving her time to explore her options.

Instead, I intended to end the fight—one way or another—as soon as possible. Sure, it would be difficult. Maybe impossible. But I was tired of stretching it out. I wanted to finish it and move on, and I couldn't stomach the notion of spending months trying to formulate the best plan possible.

Impulsive? Probably.

Reckless? Assuredly.

But for my mental state, it was necessary.

First, though, I needed to find somewhere I could get a few minutes to administer some first aid and initiate the repair of my equipment. To that end, as soon as I'd gone a few dozen blocks, I pulled into a deserted alley and dismounted the Cutter. As I did, I dismissed it into the dedicated spatial storage device in the bracelet on my wrist. With that done, I ducked behind a dumpster and embraced both Stealth and Camouflage.

It wasn't perfect. Someone like Gunther could probably see through it. But for the run-of-the-mill Operators, it would be fine. Once that was done, I took one of my last remaining boosters and injected it into the infiltration suit's port. The subdermal Sheath was almost entirely intact, so it didn't require repair. My body, on the other hand, did.

Consulting the appropriate menu on my HUD, I found that I had six broken ribs, multiple bruised organs, and a minute crack in one of my vertebrae. None were life-threatening, and the less severe injuries had already begun to heal, courtesy of Regeneration. However, the last med-hypo I'd used had begun to wear off, and my Pain Tolerance had reached the edge of its effectiveness. Soon enough, I'd be awash in agony unless I administered another pain suppressant.

It probably wasn't healthy, using them so flippantly, and it certainly wasn't inexpensive. But I pushed my concerns aside and did what I had to do.

When I'd suffered serious injuries in the past, I'd had plenty of time to retreat and heal. However, I had no such options this time. Sure, that was due to my own stubborn refusal to hide and convalesce, but it was a reality all the same. In any case, I was convinced that if I did try to hole up, my instincts screamed it would be a mistake.

I stayed there for fifteen minutes, letting the booster, med-hypo, and my abilities work on getting me back to fighting shape. But eventually, my convalescence was cut short when a trio of Operators—big, bulky figures with powerful cybernetics—stepped into the alley.

"I'm tellin' you, Brick—I feel somethin' down this way," said the smallest of the three. She was barely recognizable as a woman, her proportions were so blocky. She also sported a masculine haircut, heavily muscled shoulders, and a square jaw that would make any man proud. The other two were plainly men because they both sported thick, braided beards.

The one I assumed was named Brick said, "You said that 'bout the last two alleys. What makes this one any different?"

"We shoulda just went to the ramp," said the final member of the group, his voice whiny and annoying, even to me. I could only imagine what his companions must've thought. "That's where she's goin'. Everyone said so."

"Shut up, Roach."

"I told you I don't like that name!" growled the whiny-voiced Operator.

"It's a compliment," said the woman, slapping him on the shoulder. "You're hard to kill."

"Still don't like it," he muttered.

"Both of you—shut your traps," Brick spat, clearly irritated by their banter.

All three members of the group were predictably armed. Brick carried a double-barrel shotgun that looked like it would fire shells as big around as my wrist. Roach had a pair of submachine guns, and the unnamed woman carried an actual crossbow. In most cases, that would've been the least intimidating of all the weapons on display, but I could feel the Mist swirling around it, suggesting that the ammunition was incredibly powerful. Likely, it had some sort of elemental effect like my scattergun.

That, more than anything else, took underestimating them off the table.

The three continued to bicker as they made their way down the alley. I didn't move, lest even the slightest ripple alert them to my presence. The woman—whose name I learned was Barbie, of all ridiculous monikers—clearly had some means of detecting me, but given that they'd made a few stops along the way, it seemed safe to assume that it was limited.

As I waited, I slowly drew Ferdinand II from the holster at my hip.

A slight twitch of Barbie's eyebrow was all the warning I got, but it was enough that, when she brought the crossbow up, I had plenty of time to spring into action.

Or that's what I thought before the weapon flashed, and in only an instant, the dumpster behind which I'd been hiding erupted into an explosion of molten slag. Even as the concussive force of the blast threw me a dozen feet in the wrong direction, I was pelted by molten metal. More distressingly, the spot I'd vacated only a second before was turned into a crater of melted concrete.

Any slower to react, and I'd have ended up in that same condition.

As I flew through the air, I activated Balance so I could twist into a firing position. Three times, Ferdinand II barked, and three heads exploded before I hit a wall with enough force to shatter bones. My Constitution was up to the task of enduring the force, but only just. And it did nothing for the burst of agony that came from having one of my shoulders wrenched out of its socket.

I fell to the ground, splashing into a puddle, the contents of which I didn't want to contemplate. I took only a second to gather my wits before I realized that, though I'd killed the trio of Operators, the explosion and gunfire would surely bring more running. I needed to move.

As I climbed unsteadily to my feet, I realized that whatever healing I'd managed to promote during my brief respite had been completely undone. Pain lanced through my torso with every breath, and I had a dislocated shoulder to add to my agony. Tears in my eyes, I repositioned myself and slammed my side against the wall, wrenching it back into place. After a brief spike of pain, relief flooded through me.

I took a second to test it. Thankfully, the ligaments and tendons seemed to have held together. If they hadn't, my arm would have been useless. Even with them still intact, I couldn't count on full range of motion. The only solace came from the fact that it wasn't my dominant arm.

With the weight of an impending response from any Operators in the area bearing down on me, I summoned my Cutter, mounted, and tore down the alley. Thankfully, no enemies barred my way, though, with Observation, I could hear them coming. I vacated the area just in time to avoid being buried under an avalanche of gunfire.

It just reaffirmed my intention to take the fight to Nora as soon as possible. Barbie's skill might not have been developed enough to completely nullify my own ability to hide, but it had pointed her in the right direction. Going to ground seemed like an even worse idea.

No—I needed to get to the Garden, head to the Specters' megabuilding, and kill Nora. After that . . . After that, I could reevaluate my options.

But it didn't look good. I didn't think the other tribes would just give up the hunt, and I wasn't so arrogant that I thought I could kill them all. I'd deal with that when the time came, though.

Either way, the first step was clear, so I raced toward the Garden. However, when I came within sight of the ramp, I pulled to a stop. The mass of Operators—even more multitudinous than the horde outside the Dome—loomed before me, barring my way. They hadn't seen me yet—I had the advantage of Observation on my side, while they didn't—but I knew it would only be a matter of time.

So, I dismissed the Cutter and dashed behind cover.

There was no way I could kill so many. The BMAP could take out quite a few, but I'd run out of ammunition before I made an appreciable dent in their numbers. So, if I was going to get through them, I had only two options.

First, I could try to infiltrate their ranks with Mimic. If it worked, I could get through and into the Garden without any trouble. The problem was that I had no idea what kinds of skills or tech they might have at their disposal. For all I knew, they had the ability to see through my disguise. Gunther had, and I wasn't so naive as to believe he was the only person who'd gained such a skill. So, that route was rife with hidden danger.

The second option seemed more attractive.

But it would take a lot of concentration as well as Mist, and I'd have to get close if I was going to make it work.

Still, it seemed the better of the two options, so I took a deep breath to steady my nerves, embraced Stealth and Mimic, and crept forward. I moved incredibly slowly, lest I give away my position, and I did everything I could to use whatever cover I could find. Whether it was a parked hover car, the base of a monorail platform, or a pile of refuse, it didn't matter. I used everything I could, and gradually, I closed in on the mass of Operators.

The closer I drew, the more my heart felt like it was going to beat out of my chest. The group was huge. At least a couple of thousand. Maybe more. It was as if the tribes had put aside their many differences to focus on a common threat. And they'd pulled out all the stops, committing everything they had.

Sure, there were quite a few Operators who hadn't shown up. Some were independents. Others were doubtless held in reserve. And still others were out and about on different tasks. Still, it was an intimidating and unprecedented show of force as well as cooperation.

Thankfully, the tribes hadn't completely forgotten their previous enmities, and as I crept closer, I could see that it wasn't a cohesive unit arrayed before me. Instead, tensions were high, and in more than one case, I saw that the situation was on the very edge of boiling over. I was thankful for that because, otherwise, I'd have never gotten close enough to enact my plan.

When I was only a few dozen feet away from the mismatched army of Operators, which was the edge of my range, I used Misthack. The moment I did, the familiar menu appeared on my HUD:

Initiate Misthack?
[Yes] or [No]

I chose the first option, and that menu was predictably replaced with the next step of the process:

Misthack successful. Options:
Reboot system
Overcharge
Disable cybernetics
Upload Ghost

I didn't hesitate to choose the fourth option, sending me to the final menu:

Upload Ghost. Options:
Time Bomb (Mark 2)
Seizure
Confusion
Blind

I chose *Time Bomb* (Mark 2).

Then, with nothing else to do, I retreated to my previous position and settled in to wait. It would take a while for the Ghost to spread, but once the wave started, there would be no stopping it. And the closely packed mass of Operators had presented an absolutely perfect environment for the infectious Ghost.

It was then that I realized what an advantage I had as a {Mistrunner}. To even get the class as an option required a multitude of skills, including ones dedicated to combat, infiltration, and of course, Mist manipulation. By contrast, most people with that last ability—like my one-time mentor Helen Stone—were specialized and ill-suited for combat. I had no such limitations, and because of that, I could employ my {Mistrunner} skills to much greater effect.

Never was that more obvious than when I used a single Ghost to take down an army.

CHAPTER SIXTY-FIVE

MARK TWO

Mira had no idea what she was doing. The leaders of the tribes of Nova City are all proud people, and they don't take too kindly to being manipulated. Even I didn't realize how angry they would be when Gunther laid everything bare. I wish I could deal with her myself, but there's no way they'll let her escape alive. If I just had a chance to explain, to reason with her, we could take the whole city for ourselves. Pity that the others will never leave her alive long enough for that conversation to happen.

—Nora Lancaster

I knelt in a shadow, waiting impatiently for *Time Bomb* to take hold and begin its spread. Since creating the Ghost, I'd made a few adjustments to its lethality—before, it was limited to incapacitation—but the trade-off was that it took even longer to ramp up. The problem was that the fuel—my pool of Mist—was finite, and though it could be stretched quite a bit by my skills, it would always eventually run dry. That was the great limiter of my Ghosts.

The first time I had used *Time Bomb*, I'd knocked dozens—maybe as many as a hundred—Enforcers out. Since then, my power had grown immensely, and so, I'd adjusted the Ghost to utilize the resources at my disposal. It was difficult getting everything to stabilize, but I'd had plenty of downtime over the past few months. The result was the perfect tool for my situation, and I was eager to see it sweep through the army of Operators arrayed between me and the ramp down to the Garden.

Aside from increasing the power consumption, ramping up the damage required that I adjust the incubation time, as well. Otherwise, the Ghost would unravel into uselessness. So, even if my every cell was screaming at me to act, I had no choice but to sit back and wait for *Time Bomb* to do its thing.

The minutes ticked by, one after another, and by the time an hour had passed, I could tell that the Operators were getting just as restless as I felt. Already, they were sending small groups out to search for me; likely, the surety in my chosen direction had begun to waver, and they'd started to consider the possibility that I'd opted to go to ground and wait them out.

But by that point, the damage was done.

They didn't know it, but after an hour, *Time Bomb* had already become widespread. If there was a single Operator who hadn't become infected, I would have been surprised. At best, a few of the stronger members of the mismatched army might've possessed defenses sufficient to resist infection, but even that seemed unlikely. I'd seen what Nova City's Operators called defenses, and they were woefully insufficient to the task of rebuffing the efforts of a true {Mistrunner}. Even Helen Stone, as limited as she was, could've torn through most of what passed for a Mistwall in Nova City, and she didn't have some of my most potent advantages.

No—I didn't think anyone would escape my *Time Bomb* unscathed.

If the city hadn't been so deserted, I might've worried that it would infect civilians, too. But the range wasn't wide enough for that when two-thirds of the population had already fled the city.

Still, I needed to remember how dangerous such a Ghost could be in a densely populated settlement. If the deaths of a few Silo workers had left me grief-stricken, what would I feel if I accidently killed an entire city? I wasn't sure I could handle something like that, so as I knelt in the shadowy alley, I vowed to keep *Time Bomb* on a tight leash.

I pushed those thoughts from my mind as I focused on the situation at hand. I felt confident in my ability to hide, especially when my potential pursuers had no idea I was around, but there was always the possibility that someone could see through Stealth and Camouflage. And I needed to remain vigilant so that I could combat such an unlikely occurrence. Still, a person can quickly grow accustomed to even the most stressful situations, and I was no different. As the first hour spread into the second, I found my mind wandering even further afield. When I noticed it, I took great pains to wrangle my thoughts into some semblance of control, but it wasn't easy, and it certainly never lasted long.

With the absence of any impactful stimuli, my mind automatically settled on the future. Or more importantly, what I would do after my mission was complete.

Before my most recent foray into the wilderness—and the subsequent fight against the soul-spiking spider—my every thought was dominated by plans for revenge. I rarely thought of what might come after, mostly because I'd somewhat assumed I'd end up dead in the attempt to bring Nora and the Specters to their knees. I certainly wasn't suicidal, but I also wasn't anything close to perfect. At some point, I would mess up, and it was only a matter of time before one of my many mistakes bore lethal consequences.

But against all odds, I'd survived, and so long as I could get through the thousands of Operators between me and my goal, I felt confident that I would make it through mostly intact. So, I was increasingly cognizant of the fact that I had no real, concrete plans for what might come after that. Sure, there were vague notions of adventure, of a life spent delving one Rift after another, but that wasn't a plan. Not really. It was more like a child's fantasy—heavy on intent, but light on meaningful details.

I'd have probably kept going along that train of thought if, at that very moment, my Ghost hadn't completed its incubation. In its first incarnation—which was the product of months of work on its own—*Time Bomb* was meant to glitch out a person's cybernetics to such a degree that it would incapacitate them. And in that endeavor, it had been incredibly effective, even killing a couple of the Enforcers who'd been its first victims. And that had given me the idea of ramping up the lethality.

So, over the following months, I'd spent countless hours combining the underlying structure of Overcharge with the potent Ghost. The simple goal was to ramp up the lethality of the Ghost, but as uncomplicated as the idea might have been, the implementation had proved to be an absolute pain. Sometimes literally because creating an uncooperative Ghost often resulted in a blinding headache. In fact, those headaches were as responsible for the progression of Pain Tolerance as my more gruesome injuries. But I had persisted, creating one incarnation after another until, at last, I'd built something that worked, albeit not in a way I had expected.

Overcharge was built to harness the ambient Mist in order to create a sudden, sharp surge of energy that could incapacitate or kill its victims. Doing so was incredibly Mist hungry but commensurately effective. However, doing that on the massive scale that came with *Time Bomb* was problematic in that it would completely drain the ambient Mist before the effect had spread past a few people. So, I'd had to get creative with how the effect was applied, and I'd stumbled upon a tiered approach.

During the lengthy incubation period, the Ghost would steadily drain a small amount of the ambient Mist, fueling the initial leap from one host to another as well as banking a good portion for the upcoming surge. However, instead of a single shock, *Time Bomb* would create an escalating series of miniature charges that would detonate once everything had reached maturity. That way, the Mist requirement was spread out over hours, rather than a singular instant.

Even so, balancing the time requirement with Mist consumption and the necessary delay needed to maximize the number of people affected was insanely difficult. Still, after doing the math, I knew it would all work out, so I kept at it until, at last, I'd created a masterpiece of mass death.

As I watched, my first victim began to convulse. The men and women around her reacted quickly; some backed away while others scrambled to help. But there was nothing any of them could do; most had long since been infected, and it was only a matter of time before they shared her fate.

Sure enough, only twenty seconds later, the second victim was beset by a Mist-induced seizure. Then, a few seconds after that, a third. Then a fourth. Exponentially, the effects of *Time Bomb* spread until whole swaths of the mismatched army fell into violent convulsions. Some managed to resist, but the escalating nature of the Ghost's effects rendered their resistance moot, and they soon fell before its might.

The first victim died after five minutes, but that event set off a chain reaction as waves of Operators were overcome, their systems overloaded with Mist until their bodies gave out. Before long, the kill count had reached into the dozens. Then the hundreds. Finally, more than a thousand had fallen.

It took almost an hour, and only about half of the Operators outright died. However, the survivors might have been worse off than the slain warriors. Most were comatose. Others were crippled, their cybernetic enhancements smoking, their circuitry destroyed by the overload of Mist.

Barely a dozen had completely resisted the effects.

That was a manageable number.

In other circumstances, I might have felt guilty. After all, I was far from comfortable with mass murder, especially when my opponents were entirely incapable of fighting back. What I'd just set in motion was a mass execution. Or an extermination. But any notions of guilt I might've harbored were cut off by the simple fact that they'd positioned themselves to kill me. They didn't care that they'd amassed thousands to kill a single person. They weren't concerned with fighting fair. And because of that, I couldn't be bothered to do so either.

No—my conscience, in this instance, was clear.

I summoned and raised the Pulsar, used Empowered Shot, and squeezed the trigger. My target—a massive man that must've been seven feet tall, who had the aura of a leader—took the round directly in the chest. However, I was shocked to see that, although he was sent sprawling to the ground, he rose only a second later, completely unharmed, save for a bit of burned flesh I could see through the resulting hole in his combat vest.

So, I fired again, hitting him in the head as he pushed himself to his feet. The round slammed into his face, charring the flesh and tearing the skin away. The momentum of the shot sent him flipping backward, but when he rose again, I could see the gleam of subdermal armor that had been exposed by the latest attack.

By that point, the other eleven Operators had set their shock aside and stirred themselves to action. Two shots weren't enough for them to pinpoint my location, but I knew a third would probably do the trick. So, I retreated down the alley and leaped up to grab ahold of a low-hanging ridge in the building's facade. Hauling myself up, I repeated the action. Once. Twice. Three times until I reached the roof. Then, I sprinted across the expanse and, once I reached the edge, harnessed the entirety of my Constitution attribute to leap across another alley to land on the roof of a neighboring building.

I repeated this tactic four times until I had relocated almost a hundred yards away. Then, I focused on the Operators stranded in the midst of a thousand still-twitching corpses. They hadn't been idle, but with no means of locating me, they could only do so much. Still, the Operators were well-equipped professionals, and they'd erected a portable Mist shield.

However, after *Time Bomb* had sucked the area dry of ambient Mist, the shield was much weaker than it normally would have been. Even from more than a hundred yards away, I could see the telltale flicker of a Mist shield on the verge of collapse.

Hefting my Pulsar, I took aim, used Empowered Shot, and two seconds later, sent a round directly into the center of the shield. It shattered into shards of Mist that soon dissipated into nothing, exposing the men and women who'd huddled behind the flimsy barrier. Their reactions were predictable—shock, followed by disbelief, and then replaced by panic—but by the time they reached that third stage, I'd already exchanged my sniper rifle for the BMAP.

They were at the edge of my effective range—the artillery platform could lob its ordinance up to half a mile away, but my accuracy experienced a precipitous drop after the first hundred yards—but they were close enough that I could make it work.

And I did.

The weapon discharged its shells with a series of audible thumps that, only a second or so later, fell upon the scrambling Operators, and to predictable effect.

The BMAP was an incredibly powerful weapon that could topple buildings. In addition, my [Demolition] skill had grown considerably since I'd acquired it, and so too had my modifiers. The combination of the two, as Gala had predicted what felt like a lifetime ago, was devastating.

A series of explosions erupted, bathing the area in rolling waves of flame and overwhelming force that could pulverize concrete. The Operators might have been powerful, and they were clearly well equipped. However, the BMAP rendered those advantages pointless. Even the giant leader's high-quality subdermal armor would be useless in the face of six rounds from the BMAP.

But for good measure, I exchanged the spent cannister for a fresh one—noting that it was my second-to-last one—and sent another volley to finish them all off for good. In the back of my mind, it might have seemed like a pointless waste of resources, but I had no interest in giving those dangerous Operators any chance to regroup. It was better to end them the best way I knew how and deal with the lack of ammunition for my most powerful weapon if and when the time came.

When the dust settled, only charred corpses and a deep crater in the concrete remained of the elite Operators.

More importantly, the way was clear, and nothing barred my descent into the Garden. That wouldn't be the case for long; more Operators were scattered throughout Bywater, and I knew they would soon converge on the scene of the explosions. Sure, some might see it as a sign to cut off their pursuit—hopefully, at least—but I knew the mentality it took for someone to embrace the lifestyle of an Operator. Most were half convinced they were immortal, and few were the sort to run from danger.

With my path clear, I descended from my perch, opting to take the stairs rather than climb down the facade. The building was predictably abandoned; anyone who might've persisted through Nova City's exodus had probably vacated the area the moment they saw the Operators amassing.

Over the next couple of minutes, I traversed the killing field I'd created. I left the Operators who'd fallen but managed to survive the effects of *Time Bomb* alone. They were out of the fight, and although I could harvest a little extra Mist from killing them, I found the idea incredibly distasteful. Of course, there was a part of me that couldn't help but point out that death might have been preferable to living out their lives as cripples or in a coma.

I silenced that part of my mind, pushing forward with grim determination, and once I'd reached the ramp that descended into the Garden, I summoned my hover bike and sped away. However, I did periodically stop to throw out demolition charges at planned intervals along the way. I hoped that the massive graveyard I'd created would deter any pursuit, but I wasn't going to put all my trust in optimism. Instead, I intended to destroy the spiraling ramp behind me.

So, with those stops slowing me down, it took quite a bit longer than normal to reach the Garden. Fortunately, there wasn't another army in my way, and I quickly sped along, stopping only to detonate the charges I'd set.

With the press of a button, the sound of a series of muted explosions filled the air, and a moment later, huge chunks of concrete began to fall toward the swamp far below. To my surprise, the ramp remained mostly intact, albeit with a few sizable gaps created by the demolition charges. Hopefully, the Operators who'd been scouring Bywater didn't possess the means to bridge those expanses. Even if they did, it would slow them down.

Like that, all pursuit was cut off, and I had leave to continue on with my mission. Looking up, I noticed that night had begun to fall. Hopefully, by the dawn of the next day, I would have finished with Nova City.

Strangely, I no longer looked upon my mission with fiery determination. Instead, it felt like an obligation. An item to be checked off a list. My resolve to see it through was no weaker, but it was less of a goal and more of a chore to be completed.

And I hated that.

I'd spent months working toward this moment, and I desperately wanted—no, I needed—to enjoy it. Otherwise, everything would feel so pointless.

Perhaps it was.

What did any of it really matter? Sure, Nora would be punished, but that wouldn't change anything, would it? Not really. Even my own life would go on.

I shook my head and accelerated. I couldn't let myself get too distracted by errant thoughts. I needed focus. I needed to kill Nora, or else everything I'd done would truly be for nothing. Even if I had become a little disenchanted with my quest for revenge, I fully intended to see it through.

With that in mind, I sped away, hopefully to end things once and for all.

CHAPTER SIXTY-SIX

A MILE OF SHIT

> *At this point, fear feels like a constant companion. I've never been so afraid. Not when I decided to get rid of Jeremiah. Not when the tribal wars broke out all over Nova City. And not when facing down the Enforcers who conveniently insisted that I take their protection. I think I created a monster.*
>
> —Nora Lancaster

I sped through the streets of Nova City, the scheduled rainstorm coming down in a steady pour. Night had fully taken hold of the city, and it was awash in the familiar glow of a million holographic signs. A few pedestrians remained, all hefting neon-rimmed umbrellas or wearing slick ponchos, but the mass exodus had hit the Garden harder than anywhere but Algiers. So, the crowd was much thinner than it should have been. Still, traffic clogged the streets, and I was forced to weave between the slow-moving hover cars as I made my way toward the megabuilding that doubled as the Specters' headquarters.

I saw a couple of Operators here and there, but if they recognized me as a high-value target, they didn't give any indication. Instead, they were engaged in petty crime, mugging the few civilians who happened to wander down the wrong alley or boosting a hover car whose owner forgot to engage the vehicle's defenses. Such scenes had once been ubiquitous, but now, the incidents were scattered and diffuse—a symptom of the war I'd started. With most of the civilians having fled the city, the independent Operators had no one left to victimize.

Overall, the falling rate of petty crime was probably a good thing, but the lack of such a familiar part of Nova City's atmosphere left me feeling curiously regretful. Odd, how quickly people could adapt to even the worst situations and how wrong things felt when the familiar faded away.

In any case, the eerily empty city sent a chill up my spine that had nothing to do with the cold water trickling down my back.

The trip through the Garden wasn't a long one. Not at the speeds my hover bike could reach, at least. However, it did afford me an opportunity to take full stock of my condition. And it wasn't good.

My ribs were still broken, and the healing had been constantly interrupted by my acrobatic antics. One or two might even have to be replaced, once everything was said and done. At some point, I'd picked up a severely sprained ankle that, despite my Regeneration and Pain Tolerance, as well my copious use of med-hypos, sent throbbing spikes of agony up my leg with every movement. My once-dislocated shoulder had swollen enough to become almost completely immobile, and a few of my bruised internal organs seemed on the verge of rupture. Finally, I felt positive that I had a slight concussion that, without my prodigious Mind attribute, would have probably rendered me completely loopy. As it was, it barely slowed down my cognitive abilities.

In short, I needed a couple of weeks' worth of downtime before I would even approach full strength. Once again, I considered retreating to one of the safe houses I'd told no one about, so I could rest, heal, and plan, but I rejected that idea without giving it much more than a cursory examination.

The fact was that if I gave Nora time to prepare, there was every chance she'd use that to shore up her defenses. Or worse, she might flee. Once that happened, it could very well be years before I found her, if at all. The world was a huge, disconnected place, and trying to find a single person—even one as recognizable as Nora—would be an exercise in futility and frustration.

But even more, I just wanted it to be over. I wanted it finished. I needed to kill Nora and put Nova City—and my past—behind me where it all belonged. Until I did that, I knew I'd never be able to move on with my life.

However, that plan took a bit of a hit when the Specters' megabuilding came into view. I was still almost a mile away, but even then, I could see enough defenses that I had little choice but to pull to a stop and rethink my approach. Before, I'd intended to sneak in, much as I had a handful of times while doing my reconnaissance over the past few months, but after seeing the forces arrayed just on the lowest level, I had no choice but to discard that plan.

Hundreds of Enforcers, with plenty of Banshees among them. A barricade. A full-power Mist shield. A mobile camp with a full-fledged command center, complete with a mobile bunker from which the specialized Enforcers could pilot their drones and robots. In short, the building had become a fortress.

And that was just the ground floor.

I could only imagine what else I would have to go through to get to Nora.

I slipped down a side street before any of them could see me and then turned into an alley, where I dismissed the Cutter. I was already wearing a new face courtesy of Mimic, but I didn't want to tempt fate by remaining out in the open. Who knew what kind of abilities the Enforcers might bring to bear? They weren't the elite fighting force I'd always thought them to be—my encounters with them had cemented that knowledge in my mind—but they were still capable enough. And the Banshees counted plenty of truly powerful warriors among their number.

If I was hesitant to engage the mismatched army of Operators that had planted themselves between Bywater and the Garden District, then I would've had to have been an absolute idiot to directly assault the fortress the Enforcers had established.

The key word there was *directly*.

It was a good thing, then, that I'd spent years living in that very building, and I knew its layout like the back of my hand. More importantly, I knew a way in that I was sure they had overlooked. Even Nora had probably forgotten it simply because few people would choose such a route.

When I was younger and I'd stepped out of line, one of my uncle's favorite punishments was to send me down to the subbasement to work on the megabuilding's filtration systems. In truth, I got in the way of the legitimate maintenance workers more than I helped, but that wasn't the point. Instead, it was meant as negative reinforcement. Do bad things, get sent down to fiddle with the foul-smelling muck.

Of course, its effectiveness was always short-lived, so I was forced to endure repeated visits. However, even if it didn't always accomplish the goal of keeping me in line, it did provide me an opportunity to inoculate myself against all things disgusting. Without that dubious training, my life since would have been much more difficult.

But that wasn't the benefit that prompted the memory. Instead, that distinction belonged to the fact that I'd always been a curious girl, and once I'd gotten over my disgust, I'd aimed that curiosity at the filtration system itself. To date, I still had no idea how it really worked, but I did know the ins and outs of the system's layout. Or more importantly, I knew that it emptied into the city's sewer system.

That knowledge did come with a couple of caveats—one minor and the other far more important.

First, the access point I intended to use was absolutely tiny. My shoulders were fairly narrow, but I knew it would still be a tight fit. Exacerbating that was my recently dislocated shoulder, which meant that even if I did fit, it wouldn't be without significant pain. Still, pain I could endure; after all, I was well versed in doing just that.

The bigger issue—at least in my mind—was that the access point was, by its very nature, disgusting. I could flush it out before climbing through it, but that would do nothing for any residual filth. And there was always the smell to contend with. As used to it as I was, there was still a point where any strong odor exceeded a person's ability to ignore it.

Whatever the case, I would forcefully cancel Observation if I chose that route.

First, though, I wanted to test the Enforcers' defenses. After all, I'd just killed one army—who was to say I couldn't repeat that feat by infecting the Enforcers with *Time Bomb*? To do that, though, I needed to get close, which meant that I had to spend an hour gradually creeping from one shadow to another. Still, I'd been forced to develop quite a relationship with patience, so even if it was tedious, it wasn't nearly as frustrating as I might have expected.

Eventually, I drew close enough to touch the Mist shield and attempted a Misthack.

Almost immediately, I jerked my consciousness back. The shield was equipped with a Mistwall that made the one guarding the aural sensors outside the Rift look like the product of a talented child. Hundreds of security nodes, each a complex tangle of equations and logic puzzles, barred my way. I knew the defenses weren't actually solvable equations or puzzles; instead, they were strings of alien code that, in their raw form, were incomprehensible. My [Mistrunner] skill, combined with my interface, did quite a lot of heavy lifting by turning the defenses into something I could understand. But even then, my tech and abilities could only go so far, which meant that overcoming the higher-grade Mistwalls required a lot more user input. In this case, it would take a lot more skill than I possessed, and even then, breaking through would take hours of work.

No—bringing down that Mist shield was a fool's errand.

So, I moved on to the closest Enforcer, hoping to repeat the massacre over which I'd recently presided. To my shock, though, the moment I tried to access his system, two things happened. First, I was entirely rebuffed. I never even saw his Mistwall, which told me that they either possessed some sort of jammer or had employed someone with a skill designed to counter my abilities.

That was troubling enough, but the second issue was even more distressing.

Because a second after I'd tried to Misthack the Enforcer, the door to the mobile bunker flew open, and a Banshee came sprinting out, screaming, "She's here! I just got a hit!"

That was my cue to leave.

As I backed away, taking great pains to corral my panic and take it slow, the camp erupted into motion. Enforcers and Banshees darted around, establishing a perimeter as impenetrable as the ridiculously durable Mist shield. But none ventured out into the open, which was both a source of annoyance and appreciation.

Annoyance because I wanted to discover whether or not the shield was what had prevented me from Misthacking the Enforcer. Appreciation because I really didn't want to engage in a fighting retreat. If that happened, I'd be forced to abandon my plan of attack.

Thankfully, they remained hunkered down behind their defenses, which allowed me to slowly retreat out of sight. Once I was safe from scrutiny, I took a deep breath, steeling myself for what was to come. If I committed to my plan, there would be no turning back. I had to see it through.

But there really wasn't any other option, so far as I could see. Perhaps some great strategist, with the benefit of seeing things from afar, could come up with some foolproof plan, but with my time constraints and, more importantly, my priorities, I only saw one way forward.

With that surety in mind, I made a wide circle around the megabuilding, and I discovered that the Enforcers' cordon extended all the way around the huge structure. I couldn't imagine the resources needed for such an endeavor, and it was easy to imagine that the bulk of the city's so-called peacekeeping force had been committed to guarding Nora.

Or more likely, they were meant to deal with the threat I represented.

After all, I had brought the city to its knees. I'd shown the aristocrats that they weren't quite as insulated from the lower platforms as they thought they were. By assaulting the Silos and fostering war between the tribes, I'd not only directly disrupted productivity—an unforgivable sin for people who basically worshipped wealth—but the city's mass exodus had created a shortage of workers to exploit. In short, I'd thrown a spanner into the gears of their well-oiled machine of oppression, and they were desperate to return to the status quo. Likely, they thought I was the only thing standing in their way.

Naivete, as far as I was concerned. The people were gone, and it would take years to get them back. By the time they managed it, the Integration would've arrived, and with that, everything would change.

No—I might not have set out to end their reign, but I'd definitely started the ball rolling. And I didn't think it would stop anytime soon.

In any case, there were hundreds—perhaps thousands—of Enforcers between me and my goal, and I had no choice but to go around. Fortunately, I already had a plan for that.

To that end, I set out to one of the entry points for the Underground. I'd never known there were so many of them, but the map I'd stolen from the Coyotes was a cure for that ignorance. I had to wonder if my uncle had known how exposed his megabuilding had been.

Probably.

Jeremiah had never been infallible. That much was clear. But he took security very seriously, so it was hard to imagine that he hadn't known the building's every point of weakness. Perhaps he'd even sent me down to work on the filtration systems with the express purpose of exposing those weaknesses to my young mind.

Or maybe not. There was every possibility that I had chosen to remember him as far more capable and forward-thinking than he'd ever actually been.

Whatever the case, once I found the entrance to the Underground—which was disguised via a holographic display—I descended into the depths. The tunnel bore all the signs of disuse. The lights were inoperable, and there were no footprints in the muck that had begun to accumulate on the floor.

I ignored it.

Stalking forward slowly, I kept Observation flared to the point where the smells made my eyes water, but even then, I didn't dare let up. There was every chance that Nora or the Enforcers knew about the Underground passages, and if that was the case, they would've placed some sort of defenses. But as I kept going, I found nothing. No cameras. No autoturrets. And certainly no Operators or Enforcers. It was as empty as a disgusting drainage tunnel should've been.

After a while, I reached my destination.

The pipe was only about thirty inches wide, which meant that it would be just as tight of a fit as I expected. Countering that negative point was a bit of a bright side in that it was clear that it had been quite some time since the pipe had seen use. What little waste clung to its interior was completely dry, aside from the results of the ambient humidity so prevalent in the tunnels.

It made sense, though. Most of the Specters' Operators had remained in the city, but their support personnel—not to mention the civilians who lived in the megabuilding's lower levels—had clearly experienced significant attrition. As such, there was nobody to work the filtration systems. Some of the buildings functions were automated, but every mechanical system required maintenance and oversight. Without it, things just didn't work properly.

Nora had never really cared about the civilians who supported the tribe, though. She was only ever concerned with the fighters. Jeremiah had always known better, but his attitude clearly wasn't the one prevalent among most warriors. Clearly, Nora hadn't learned from the man she had betrayed, and now, she was going to pay the price for that oversight.

First, though, I needed to prepare.

The last thing I wanted was to traipse through the megabuilding in muck-covered clothing. I had no intention of confronting Nora looking like I'd just climbed through a sewer pipe, either. So, I quickly stripped down, storing my clothes in my arsenal implant along the way. When I did so, I ignored my battered and bruised body; with the readout on my HUD, I knew precisely how bad of shape I was in, so a visual inspection was unnecessary.

Or maybe I just didn't want to see it.

In either case, it only took a couple of minutes for me to undress, and once I was naked, I took a deep breath that I instantly regretted—as much because of the smell as the pain in my ribs—and climbed up the wall and pushed myself into the pipe.

As I'd expected, it was a tight fit. My injured shoulder screamed at me to back away, but I was far too committed to give that any credence. Instead, I fortified my mind and slithered forward, one disgusting inch at a time. As I did so, I tried not to give much thought to the composition of the muck. I also had to force myself not to think about the tight fit. Or more accurately, what would happen if the pipe narrowed.

I wasn't claustrophobic, but the idea of getting stuck was horrifying enough to prompt a racing heart.

Even so, I endured. I persisted. And inch by inch, I dragged myself through the pipe. Soon enough, the inches turned into feet, and the feet turned into yards. I lost track of the passing time, and my mind shut itself off from unnecessary thoughts. It was the same tactic I'd learned during hell month.

One foot in front of the other.

Or in this case, one slithering inch after the last. There was nothing else. Just moving forward.

Like that, time passed. It might have been minutes. It could have been hours. I neither knew nor cared. In the depths of my stubborn refusal to acknowledge my own discomfort, I knew only persistence.

And finally, there was a light at the end of the pipe.

Desperately, I dragged myself forward until, at last, I tumbled free. And into a half-full vat of . . .

No—never mind. I refused to acknowledge what it was. Instead, after a brief moment of surprise, I managed to scramble to my feet. The muck was only about calf high, and it was mostly solid, but there was no mistaking what it was.

After all, I'd worked the system often enough to recognize where I was.

I had to suppress the urge to wretch as I climbed to freedom. Fortunately, the chamber was completely empty, confirming my suspicions that all the workers had fled the city. Even more thankfully, I knew that the chambers were equipped with a series of showers meant for the workers' use. So, I padded barefoot across the corrugated-metal platform surrounding the vat and descended to the concrete floor before finding my way to the showers.

Over the next thirty minutes, I scrubbed every inch of my body, slathering myself with disinfectant soap as well as administering a few med-hypos loaded with antibiotics and antiparasitic medication. However, as thorough as I was, even when I'd taken the equivalent of three showers, I still felt dirty.

So I kept going until a few minor abrasions had joined the multitude of bruises I'd acquired. Only when I knew I was doing more harm than good did I stop.

Finally, I stepped out of the shower, dried off with a towel I kept in my arsenal implant, and then got dressed. Thankfully, it seemed as if the combined efforts of Nora's Specters and the Enforcers were focused outward, so I remained completely undetected the whole time.

After tying my hair back, I summoned my R-14 and began my climb to the penthouse apartment Nora had taken as her own. She had usurped my uncle. She had engineered his death. And she had stolen our home. There were thousands of deaths to lay at her feet, and finally, at long last, she was going to pay the price for her sins.

CHAPTER SIXTY-SEVEN

CLIMBING THE TOWER

I never meant for things to get so out of control. I just wanted what was owed me. Is that a sin? Is that wrong? No. I refuse to believe that. I just wish everyone else could see the truth.

—Nora Lancaster

The subbasement might've been completely abandoned, but I soon discovered that the same couldn't be said for the rest of the megabuilding. The place was huge, spanning multiple city blocks, and normally housed more than a hundred thousand people. Only a fraction of that number remained after the mass exodus Nova City had experienced, but it seemed that every combat-capable member of the Specters had chosen to remain. Or perhaps they'd had that decision forced upon them. Either way, after seeing so many Operators stationed on the first floor, I realized that I hadn't seen any familiar faces among those I'd killed with *Time Bomb*.

It made some sense. Nora knew I was coming for her. She had to. So, she had clearly chosen to keep her people close while she let the other tribes—and the Enforcers outside—run interference.

Which presented yet another problem for me.

When I saw the first clump of would-be warriors, I tried to take care of them in the safest and most efficient way possible. That meant using Misthack again to infect them with *Time Bomb*. However, that strategy soon hit the same wall I'd encountered outside, and something—I still wasn't sure what—prevented me from using my most potent ability. I couldn't even hack into the security cameras dotting the building.

No—if I was going to reach Nora, I'd have to go through the Specters the hard way, and what's more, I needed to do so quietly, lest I bring the entirety of the tribe's Operators down on my head.

At one point, I might have blanched at the task laid out before me. After all, the Specters were one of the three biggest tribes and arguably the most powerful tribe in Nova City. My uncle's guidance had thrust them to the top, and his absence—as well as my efforts—had only begun to weaken them. Eventually, the entire organization would crumble, but that would take years.

It really put my monthslong campaign to sabotage their operations into perspective. Sure, I'd been annoying. I had struck a few key blows that would eventually bring the behemoth down, but truly making a difference would have taken far longer than my patience could support.

It hadn't been completely pointless—in fact, I'd been far more successful than I had any right to expect—but it veered far closer to that extreme than I wanted to admit. Killing a few lieutenants and fostering conflict between the tribes was a good first step, but if I'd really wanted to bring the Specters down, it would have taken years. They were just too big for anything else.

So, it was a good thing that I'd abandoned that path.

Because although I might not have been capable of quickly ending them through subterfuge, there was nothing to say that I couldn't do so via a more direct approach. In short, I expected that having all the Specters gathered in one place might make my task much, much easier to complete. And on top of that, I didn't even have to worry about civilians getting caught in the cross fire.

Not that that had ever really stopped me before.

But I'd changed. I couldn't deny it. And I really wasn't sure if I could justify the deaths of even a few innocents. Not anymore.

Luckily, I didn't have to confront that conundrum. The city's virtual abandonment had freed me in a way nothing else could have.

But just because the situation was set up so I didn't have to make difficult moral decisions, that didn't mean my path would be easy. The megabuilding was absolutely infested with Specters, and that was saying nothing of the thousand or so Enforcers just outside. The first hint of conflict would bring them running to intervene. So, I needed to find a way up to the top floor without being seen.

Once again, my previous knowledge of the building came in handy, and I knew precisely what route would serve me best. So, after checking to make sure that my weapons had been reloaded and Stealth was active, I exited the stairs that I'd climbed from the subbasement. Immediately, I saw a clump of Operators stationed nearby. But they weren't really paying attention, probably because they reasoned that someone would have to go through an army of Enforcers to reach them. That, combined with Stealth, was plenty to keep me hidden.

But that wouldn't remain the case for long. I wasn't sure how the ability actually worked, but I did know that Stealth was far from perfect. It was great so long as it was bolstered by Camouflage or if nobody was looking for me, but the more attention my enemies paid, the less effective Stealth would be. So, I didn't waste any time before backing away and out of sight.

Turning a corner, I almost ran into another group.

The collection of mooks was only a few feet away, but they were so preoccupied with their own conversation that they didn't even notice me as I skirted past.

"I flat out don't believe it, Stick."

"That's 'cause you're an idiot, Lesa."

"She's just a little girl."

"A little girl who happens to have the Wraith's blood."

"And she's not so little no more," added the third member of the group. "She's gotta be eighteen now? Nineteen? When I was that age, I'd already killed three folks."

"That's 'cause you're a murderous psychopath, Bob."

"I don't know why . . ."

I passed out of range, leaving them to their conversation. Over the next hour, I slowly crept through the megabuilding's halls as I made my way to my destination. And over that time, I overheard a dozen such conversations, making it clear that Nora hadn't been secretive about whom, exactly, they were supposed to be guarding against.

Fortunately, most of the Operators lacked urgency and were only barely paying attention to their surroundings. They didn't really believe in the threat, and even if they had, they were protected by an army of Enforcers. As far as they were concerned, they were just backup in case I chose to attack the Enforcers outside.

It brought a certain satisfaction, creeping among them undetected. Certainly, it was nerve-racking, and the entire time, my heart felt like it was going to explode from overuse. But it brought with it a feeling of power unlike any other. One little flick of my blade, and I could end any of them I chose. That knowledge, that I held their lives in the palm of my hand, gave me a heady rush I can scarcely describe.

Not that I would exercise that power. If I did, I knew I couldn't keep it quiet. And soon enough, a wave of armed and armored mooks would descend upon me. I'd had my fill of fighting hordes of enemies, and I had little desire to test myself against such odds. Not again. So, I remained hidden as I crept through the corridors.

There were a couple of close calls, and I was forced to stop and wait out a particularly diligent Operator or two, but eventually, I found my way to the first floor's security terminal. In most cases, each floor featured a closed security system. However, I knew from personal experience that there was still a nominal connection. There had to be so that, if the building went on lockdown, it wasn't just on one floor.

For most would-be hackers, that would be an insurmountable issue. But for a {Mistrunner} like me? I was willing to bet that I could use that connection to access the entire building's security. If not, I would have to adjust my plan—avoiding the cameras on the sparsely protected first floor hadn't been that difficult, but I knew that getting to the penthouse undetected would be impossible unless I managed to deactivate the cameras, at the very least. Hopefully, I could manage a bit more than that, though.

First, though, I needed to take care of the two mooks who'd been stationed outside the hub.

Usually, I'd just Misthack them and knock them out of the fight via a Ghost. However, with whatever protections blocked my abilities, that was impossible. So, I had no choice but to do things the hard way.

So, I crept closer, slowly pulling my nano-bladed sword from its sheath on my back along the way. As I closed in, I could see the two mooks' body language shift. They knew something was wrong, even if they couldn't completely see through my Stealth. Soon enough, they would start paying more attention, and once that happened, the indicator on my HUD would flash red, and I would be discovered.

I couldn't let that happen.

I pounced, my blade slicing into the first mook's neck with a horizontal strike. An instant later, I reversed my momentum and sent the mirror image of the first cut into the other one's neck. In less than a second, the pair were dead. A pair of heads—one studded with actual metal spikes—fell to the concrete floor.

Before the blood could pool, I grabbed the pair of bodies and dragged them into the room containing the security hub. Then, I did the same with their heads before taking a moment to wipe the worst of the blood away with a towel I kept in my arsenal implant. It wasn't perfect, but bloodstains weren't so uncommon in the megabuilding that new ones would be remarkable. And if it came down to that level of scrutiny, the absence of the mooks meant to guard the hub would probably be more impactful.

In either case, I expected to be gone by that point.

With my tracks covered as best as I could manage, I sealed the door behind me and turned my attention to the security hub. In most buildings within Nova City, a simple security terminal would have sufficed. However, my uncle had taken it upon himself to upgrade his base's defenses. So, instead of a single security terminal, there were three of them, all hardwired together. In addition, there was a large screen where someone could monitor the feeds from the various cameras.

It was the same sort of security system employed on the higher platforms, and like them, it relied on hardwired connections. That was the only reason I thought my plan would work. So, without further ado, I retrieved my personal link from the slot on my wrist and stretched it to the appropriate port in the dominant security terminal.

Finally, I used Mistwalk.

And to my enormous relief, I found no restrictions on the ability. There was a Mistwall, of course. Even the least secure terminals were equipped with basic defenses. But that mysterious force that had prevented activation of Misthack had no effect on Mistwalk.

It took a while to overcome the defenses, but one node after another fell before my practiced skills, and after about twenty minutes, I had full access. The first thing I did was deactivate the first floor's cameras. Then, I sealed the exterior doors; I hoped to remain undetected, but in the event that I failed, I didn't want a thousand Enforcers on my tail. Finally, I deactivated the autoturrets that protected the various elevators and stairwells.

With that done, I began my search for the virtual bridge that connected the ascending floors, and after a little more than half an hour—during which my heart continued to thud against the confines of my chest—I found it. Once I overcame yet another Mistwall, another hour had passed, but it was time well spent.

Because the entire building's functions were laid bare before me.

With that access in hand, I quickly climbed one floor after another, repeating the steps I'd taken with the first level. And soon enough, the building was entirely unprotected.

But that wasn't enough.

So, after retracting my personal link back into the Hand of God, I took one final step before setting off toward the elevator. Along the way, I set a series of demolition charges in out-of-the-way places; I had no intention of bringing the building down while I was still inside, but once I was finished and on my way, I fully intended to destroy whatever Specters remained.

I might've abandoned the idea of revenge at all costs, but leaving a bunch of potentially powerful enemies at my back just seemed like suicide with a couple of extra steps. And I certainly didn't have a death wish, so I took appropriate caution.

Traversing the corridors of the first floor was just as anxiety inducing as it had been the first time, and added to that was the mental fatigue that came with already having spent hours at full readiness. I was a durable person with what I thought was a well-honed ability to focus, but even I had my limits.

I couldn't even think about stopping, though.

Nor could I employ my normal one-foot-in-front-of-the-other strategy. That was great for repetitive tasks that required minimal input, but for something like infiltrating an enemy base, I needed to maintain a sharp focus.

Adding it all up, by the time I reached the elevator, I was a bundle of frayed nerves. But I avoided detection, even managing to plant a few extra demolition charges along the way. So, I was prepared to consider that a success.

I was tempted to simply take the elevator up to the top floor, but I knew that would be a recipe for disaster. There was no guarantee anyone was paying attention, but I had to assume the worst. Nora wasn't an idiot, after all. Surely, she'd guard the most obvious point of ingress.

So, I chose to forgo riding the elevator. I didn't intend to take the stairs, either. No—I was going the hard way.

With the autoturrets having been disabled, nothing barred my entry into the elevator car, and once I was inside, I leaped to the hatch at the ceiling, opened it, and climbed through.

A sense of vertigo washed over me as I looked up the seemingly endless vertical shaft. The megabuilding was more than a hundred stories tall, which meant that it stretched over a thousand feet straight up. The pillars that held the city aloft were even taller, and I'd already climbed those multiple times—once with Patrick on my back—but for some reason, the elevator shaft looked more daunting.

It didn't matter, though.

I knew I could do it, and even if it further aggravated my already frayed nerves, I wasn't one to stray from my chosen path.

I got to climbing.

It was a little easier than I expected, especially considering that I didn't need to rely on pitons for handholds. As effective as those spikes driven into the concrete pillars were, using them to climb more than a thousand feet had always been an exercise in torture. By comparison, the elevator sported quite a few convenient ledges, facilitating the climb to a large degree.

Even so, I forced myself to stop every three floors, partially to rest my battered body, but mostly to plant a few extra demolition charges. In some ways, they were superfluous—after all, if the ground floor went down, the rest of the building would go, too—but I didn't want to take any chances. Thankfully, the higher floors were more sparsely populated than the ground floor—it seemed that most of the Operators had been concentrated down there—so sneaking through those levels wasn't as nerve-racking as it could have been. Still, even though I was careful in my approach and I kept my wits about me, I still had a couple of close calls—one of which ended with me having to strike down a particularly observant Operator before she could call for help. Aside from that, my path was unimpeded.

Like that, I climbed to the top of the towering megabuilding, leaving dozens of demolition charges in my wake. They were homemade from relatively easily obtained materials, so I'd come equipped with quite a few of them, but by the time I reached my destination, my supply had dwindled to nothing.

Not unlike my stores of ammunition. I still had enough to do what I needed to do—probably—but I'd definitely have to resupply when everything was finished.

If I survived.

Which wasn't even close to guaranteed. I was self-aware enough to recognize that my chances of making it out alive were slim. After all, even my uncle hadn't been invincible, and as strong as I'd become, I was nowhere near his level. But if it came down to a choice between my life and Nora's, I knew which path I would take. And I would do so without even a hint of regret. In fact, if I had to trade my life for hers, I'd consider it well spent.

In the meantime, though, I had one more floor to conquer. And I knew it wouldn't be easy, because even if Nora had sent the bulk of her people down to the ground floor, she would have kept the most powerful around her as a ring of protection.

That was fine, though. I just needed to go through them.

So, perched on the slim ledge beside the exit to the last floor, I took a steadying breath, then reached over to pry the elevator doors open. Without skipping a beat, I raced through the opening, my R-14 at the ready.

CHAPTER SIXTY-EIGHT

TERROR

I know she's coming. And after what she did to those people—more than a thousand dead, most without so much as a scratch—the terror has reached a fever pitch. I know I'm safe. I know she won't kill me. But still . . . The fear remains.

—Nora Lancaster

The R-14 spat fire as I kicked off the ground and flew through the air. I landed half a dozen feet away in a roll that ended with me behind one of the concrete columns that supported the roof. An instant later, a hundred bullets followed in my wake, thudding into the ground and sending puffs of dust and shattered concrete spewing into the air. My own shots hit a blue Mist shield that was so well powered that it had become almost solid.

I peeked out from behind cover, hoping to see that my most recent salvo had had some effect, but as powerful as the R-14 could be, it still suffered from the limitations inherent in its design. As an assault rifle meant for versatility, it was good at a lot of things. It had solid range, good damage, and a decent rate of fire. However, being good at all those facets of combat meant it couldn't excel at any one thing.

So, the Mist shield—which was sturdier than any I'd seen so far—remained annoyingly intact and frustratingly unwavering. To make matters worse, it did nothing to prevent the Operators it was protecting from throwing out one barrage of gunfire after another. Sort of like a two-way mirror, it was permeable from their side while being completely impenetrable from mine.

Fortunately, it didn't form a complete circle. Instead, it took the form of a convex semicircle, which meant that, while I couldn't simply go through it, going around might be possible. Of course, that brought with it a host of other problems, not least that doing so would force me to cross forty feet of open ground while they tried to pepper me with bullets.

I could take a few hits. I knew that because I'd experienced it. However, neither my subdermal Sheath nor my infiltration suit had really had enough time for complete repair, and my defenses would unravel very quickly under a hail of gunfire. To make matters even worse, my Misthack ability was still blocked, meaning that I couldn't simply deactivate the Mist shield or let one of my Ghosts do the heavy lifting.

No—if I was going to get to Nora, which seemed increasingly less likely, I needed to get around the Mist shield, kill the Operators the hard way, and then move on to whatever other defenses Nora had set up.

Because I knew this was just the first layer. If I knew her at all—and I thought I did, by now—she would throw every Operator at her disposal at me. That way, even if I did make it through, I'd be exhausted and probably injured, which would make me that much easier to defeat.

Hiding behind that pillar, for the very first time, I seriously considered retreat. I'd already set enough demolition charges to bring the building down. So, I could accomplish my goal from more than a mile away, if it came down to it. All I had to do was head back the way I'd come, and there was nothing Nora could do to stop me.

Sure, getting through the Operators on the first floor would be difficult now that they'd doubtless been alerted to my intrusion, but I felt confident that I could make it through, even if I probably couldn't do so unscathed. I would survive, though. I didn't doubt that for a second.

But I dismissed that plan before it even had a chance to take root. Not because it was doomed to failure. Rather because it wouldn't give me what I needed.

I wanted to watch Nora die by my hand. I wanted to see the life leave her eyes. But more than anything else, I needed to ask her why she had thrown everything away. I wanted to demand an explanation.

And then, I needed to put her down like the traitorous dog she'd proven herself to be.

Anything else, and I wouldn't get the closure necessary for me to move on. I was often beset by self-delusion, and I knew good and well that I was a very different person than my innermost thoughts might indicate. But I did know myself well enough to recognize that I'd never be able to live my life with any sort of peace of mind if I didn't see Nora die.

So, even if retreat was probably the smartest option, I couldn't stomach the idea for more than a second.

That didn't mean I had to attack the problem like an idiot, though. And I knew precisely how to get around the issue.

Unsurprisingly, it came down to one word: explosions.

No—I didn't intend to bring the building down prematurely. Instead, I reached into my arsenal implant and retrieved a pair of rough orbs. One was a fragmentation grenade, while the other was a flash-bang, which was the first one I sent sailing through the air. However, the fragmentation grenade followed only a moment later, though on a different trajectory.

The flash-bang hit the Mist shield and exploded in a cacophony of sound and light; the shield was great at stopping projectiles of all sorts, but it did nothing to stop the wave of sensory input that came from the flash-bang. I didn't even need to look to know that the Operators behind the shield had been stunned.

So, they never saw the fragmentation grenade fly up and over the Mist shield, carom off the ceiling, and land directly behind them.

It exploded a moment later, sending an eruption of fire, force, and shrapnel to shred through them. That's when I darted out of cover and raced down the corridor in their direction. Using every point of my Constitution to speed me on my way, I covered the forty feet in less than a second. Then, I leaped, kicked off the side wall, and vaulted over the Mist shield. Twisting in midair so I landed facing the Operators, I opened fire.

My fragmentation grenade had wrought havoc in their ranks, but these were Nora's elite underlings, so none of them were mortally wounded. That had never been the point. Instead, I just wanted to shock and distract them, and the combination of the two grenades had done that job with aplomb.

The R-14 barked, sending a half dozen bursts of fire at the grouped Operators. A couple reacted to the gunfire by throwing themselves to the concrete floor, but it only required a minute adjustment of my aim to take them out. In only a few seconds, the entire group were riddled with burning holes. Most were already dead, but a couple managed to survive. Calmly, I reloaded, then finished the job.

The entire process had taken less than thirty seconds.

Once again jamming a fresh magazine into the R-14, I moved on. I didn't have room in my arsenal implant to accommodate any loot I might acquire from the Operators, so I left their bodies alone. This wasn't about gaining equipment or wealth. I only had one intention—kill Nora and get my revenge. With my goal so close, every other impulse was easily ignored.

The top floor of the megabuilding had once played host to an entire village worth of people. Thousands of them, all bearing some level of loyalty to my uncle. If somebody wanted to, they could live their entire lives without ever leaving the floor. Only the virtual reality addicts ever took it that far, but most ordinary people's lives revolved around the community they'd built.

Sure, those who held down jobs outside of the megabuilding went to work—usually at one of the factories in Algiers or the Silos from which the

Garden District had derived its name—but otherwise, they only left on special occasions. I'd been like that, only venturing into the city in order to attend classes at the city-mandated school.

But now? The stalls in the central market were empty, both of goods as well as their proprietors. Most of the apartments, once playing host to thousands of people, were vacant and had been stripped of anything valuable. The megabuilding had become a ghost town.

And it was my fault.

I'd set the stage for all those people to pick up anything they could carry with them and flee into the wilderness. Perhaps some had made it to other settlements. A few might've even gotten so far as one of the major cities. But most had either died or were enslaved by their unscrupulous escorts.

Could all of that be laid at my feet? Was I at fault? No. Not really. But I'd put it all into motion, so some of the blame had to fall on my shoulders.

Even so, I couldn't help but wonder if they were better off. A life lived in the isolation of a megabuilding didn't seem like much of a life to me. And to make matters worse, Nova City itself had intentionally been cut off from the rest of the world. Sure, the elites up in the higher districts were far less isolated, but as far as I was concerned, they didn't really count. They were practically a different species, and I couldn't be bothered thinking about their fates.

Gradually, I crept down the corridor, and along the way, I encountered a half dozen other Mist-shield-protected choke points. In each case, I attacked them the same way I'd taken down the first, which worked well enough. However, I encountered a bit of a snag on the seventh instance of my implementation of the strategy.

The first difference I noticed was that my adversaries were far more powerful than the mooks I'd killed so far. Part of that was because I recognized a couple of them as once belonging to my uncle's elite inner circle. None were suited for leadership, but they were some of the best warriors the Specters could put on the field—which meant that Jeremiah had subsidized their development to the point where he'd made sure they were equipped with expensive weapons and powerful cybernetics.

This extended to the Mist shield they were using as cover because, unlike the others, its protection reached the ceiling. Perhaps one or more of them had some sort of skill to augment it. Or maybe it was just higher-quality. I had no idea, but it presented a problem in that my previously established strategy was suddenly useless.

I needed to adjust.

Fortunately, my progression through the floor's corridors meant that I had a few extra options at my disposal. I'd yet to use any of them because there was no point in fixing a strategy that was working, but now that necessity had forced my hand, I was eager to mix things up.

Or maybe I was just excited because I was getting close to the penthouse where I hoped to find Nora.

Thankfully, I'd continued to make copious use of Stealth, so the mooks behind the shield never noticed me before I ducked behind a corner to figure out exactly how I wanted to approach them. They obviously knew I was coming, but without specifics, that information was mostly useless except to put them on guard. As far as I could see, I had two options.

First, I could go through the air ducts. When I took a moment to inspect them, I found that they were only barely wide enough to accommodate the width of my shoulders. It only took the memory of my recent foray into the waste pipes before I firmly established that as plan B.

Plan A was more attractive anyway, if only because it satisfied a childish need for a dramatic entrance.

So, with that in mind, I checked to make sure that Stealth was still active, crouched, and stepped into the hall. I kept close to the wall, my form partially hidden by a couple of vending machines stocked with cheap, minimally nutritious foods as I crept forward. The whole time, I kept my eyes trained on the mooks barring my way, but even though they were alert, none of them seemed capable of seeing through my Stealth—so long as I didn't make any mistakes.

Or move too quickly.

Or linger in the open.

These were elites. Men and women who'd earned their positions via a mountain of bodies. If anyone was going to see through Stealth, they were the best candidates. But I had little choice but to trust the ability that had yet to really fail me. Like that, I slipped ever closer to the Mist shield, but when I got close enough that I could hear the mooks' panicked conversation, I slowed to a stop.

". . . Should've left when I had the chance. Cece offered me a spot in her crew. Good pay, too. And all the boys I could handle . . ."

"Keep it in your pants, Tate. This ain't the time."

"Just sayin'," the woman muttered, her voice a bit petulant. She had one cybernetic hand and metal plate around one fake eye. Carrying an automatic shotgun sporting an enormous cannister of ammunition, she would be deadly in close quarters. "This whole thing should never've happened."

"The boss—"

"Is a fucking idiot," Tate spat. I could hear the tremble in her voice. She was terrified. I could see the telltale signs that she wasn't the only one, either. All her companions were afraid, too. And who could blame them? I knew they had the ability to communicate with one another, so this group was well aware that I'd been picking off their fellows, one group after another. Soon enough, I'd add them to the list. "Everything was fine when the Wraith was in charge. You know it. I know it. Even Nora knows it. She's just too stubborn to admit a goddamn mistake."

"Don't let her hear you say that," mumbled one of the others.

Tate shook her head. "She ain't so tough. Not no more. I don't know what happened, but I've seen her," she said. "She ain't the woman she used to be."

That was definitely good to know. Clearly, the sabotage of Nora's bio-enhancers had borne some fruit. Not that it mattered. Not now, so late in the game. Even if she was at full strength, it couldn't change my plan. I'd come too far. I had sacrificed too many. If she'd somehow resisted my manipulation and maintained the full scope of her power, then so be it. I'd just have to figure something out.

In any case, using the resulting conversation to mask my passage, I covered that last couple of feet before entering one of the apartments. The moment the door opened and closed, the mooks reacted with predictable gunfire. However, by that point, I was already safe within the apartment. Eventually, they'd make it through, but not before I had moved on to the next part of my plan.

Even as they bombarded the door with various forms of gunfire, I couldn't help but shake my head at the fact that they could've simply opened it the same way I had. But that would require them to leave the safety of their Mist shield, which none of them seemed eager to do.

I moved through the apartment, entering the bathroom. Then, I stepped into the shower. The domicile was unoccupied, so there wasn't enough power to provoke a response from the automated system. That felt odd to me—as did stepping into a shower fully clothed—but I put the abnormality out of my mind as I reached into my arsenal implant and retrieved a series of shaped demolition charges.

Unlike the ones I'd scattered throughout the building, this was a new design I'd only recently developed. Instead of a simple black cube packed full of a powerfully explosive compound, the shaped charge took the form of a simple and incredibly narrow tube that was filled with a comparatively weak explosive.

It would never bring down a building, no matter how much I used. But it could do wonders on a door. Or, in this case, a concrete wall.

I stretched the string out, unraveling it from a spool I'd built to ease the charge's application. The pattern I chose was a simple rectangle about the size of a closet door. Then, I made an X pattern in the center of the rectangle.

With that done, I retreated just outside the bathroom door. Meanwhile, the gunfire still hadn't ceased, and as a result, the apartment's main door teetered on the verge of collapse. It didn't matter, though.

Because I was ready.

Holding the detonator I'd paired with the shaped charges, I flipped a switch to arm the explosives, then pressed a button. A muffled boom shook the walls, and dust filled the air. But I didn't hesitate or let myself be distracted. Instead, I raced through the bathroom doorway, R-14 at the ready, and dashed past the destroyed shower to dive through the opening I'd just created.

Suddenly, I was among the Operators, firing my assault rifle in controlled bursts that tore through their defenses. My first salvo only killed two—mostly because I managed head shots—while the rest remained in the fight. But they were surprised, most were injured in one way or another, and they were ill prepared for the fury I brought with me.

Still, it wasn't long before someone knocked the R-14 from my hands. I didn't let that deter me as I yanked Ferdinand II from his holster and fired every round in his cannister. Each shot found a home somewhere in an enemy's body, but these Operators were all incredibly durable.

It would take far more than a few armor-piercing rounds to put them down for good.

Luckily, I had brought plenty of other weapons to the party.

But I only needed one.

With Ferdinand II spent, I drew my nano-bladed sword and went to work. My technique wasn't flashy. In fact, my usually precise strikes were little more than brutal hacks as I dismantled the wounded and still-shocked Operators. In the process, I took a couple of shots to my torso. One—from Tate, unsurprisingly—tore through my defenses to take a chunk out of my side while another bullet went through my infiltration suit as well as my subdermal Sheath, only stopping when it hit my femur. Fortunately, its velocity had dissipated enough that it didn't break the bone, but by the time I'd finished putting them down, every step sent a jolt of agony up my leg.

But I was still operable, even if I was a little worse for wear. The shotgun blast hadn't hit anything vital, at least. In that respect, I was lucky.

The same couldn't be said for my enemies, who had all been steadily dismembered—that was the only way to be sure the threat was ended—and I was covered in enough viscera that I felt like I'd just stepped out of a furious rainstorm. Of blood.

I'd made it, though. Now, I just had another fifty yards of corridor before I could finally get my revenge. Or as I kept telling myself, before I could check that box and move on with my life.

Again, my self-awareness wouldn't let me believe that, though. Not completely. Sure, I wanted to move on. But I needed to kill Nora. There was a marked difference between those two things.

As I limped forward, having retrieved my R-14 and reloaded my weapons, I encountered no more resistance. The way was completely clear to the penthouse. And what's more, I soon discovered that the door was open, inviting me in.

At first, I suspected a trap, but no matter how I looked at it, I found nothing.

So, after exhausting my ability to detect any deterrents, I stepped into the penthouse.

"So. You're here. At last," said Nora, who was sitting on the couch, completely at ease. Or that was how she seemed. However, I knew her well enough to recognize that she was terrified. Anxious. But confident. She gestured to the other couch, saying, "Have a seat. It's time you and I came to an understanding."

CHAPTER SIXTY-NINE

IT ALL FALLS DOWN

I had always hoped she had survived. I took solace in the idea that she might be out there somewhere, living her life to the fullest. Free of Jeremiah and his insanity. But now? I just wish she'd been there with him when he fell. It would have been kinder.

—Nora Lancaster

I hefted my assault rifle, aiming it at Nora as I said, "Or I could just do what I came to do. My way seems easier."

"How did you do it?" she asked, ignoring my statement. I hated myself for it, but I couldn't bring myself to just squeeze the trigger. I wanted answers. I wanted the satisfaction of hearing her explain why she had betrayed my uncle.

And she clearly knew it.

"Do what?" I asked, my weapon never wavering. I wouldn't immediately kill her, but if she made one wrong move, I would do what I had to do. It wouldn't be nearly as satisfying, but that was just how things worked out sometimes.

"The people you killed," she said. "The ones guarding the ramp. Most of them weren't even wounded."

"As if I would tell you" was my response. I had no interest in revealing any of my secrets. Obviously, Nora had some sort of plan; otherwise, she would have reacted very differently. I'd seen how she confronted threats, and talking it out really wasn't her go-to move. So, if she was willing to engage in conversation, there had to be a reason.

Of course, that reason might've just been that she was backed into a corner, and she had no clue how she was going to survive. For some reason, the notion of her cowering in fear brought with it a spark of joy.

"I think it's some special class ability," she went on, leaning forward. When she did, I saw a bit of wiring leading to a metal plate at the base of her neck. Perhaps she'd gotten a new, powerful cybernetic, and that was why she seemed so relaxed. "With that Tier 7 implant and the training you went through, I'm sure you were offered some special options. What was it? Did you follow in Jeremiah's footsteps? You do seem to favor your rifles. But then again, I saw recordings of your fights in the Emporium. Jeremiah never would've bothered letting any of those people close. But you . . . You enjoy slicing them up, don't you?"

"Do you have a point?" I asked, cutting in before she could start in on another thought. The last thing I wanted was to reveal my class—clearly, Gunther had kept a few of my secrets to himself—and I didn't like being interrogated by a woman I intended to kill.

"Not really," she said, leaning back and throwing her arm over the back of the couch. I noticed that her limbs were much thinner than I remembered. "Just catching up with an old friend."

"We're not friends."

"Aren't we? Or maybe our connection goes deeper," she said with a slight smirk. "Like sisters. Or maybe cousins. I was there for you when nobody else was. Do you remember that, Mira? All those days I was assigned to protect you? Those times I was your shoulder to cry on? The hours I spent listening to you whine about how unfair your uncle was? And we got even closer during your training. You can't deny that."

"And then you got Jeremiah killed. You sacrificed an entire town, and—"

"As if you haven't done much worse," she spat, finally showing something other than feigned friendliness. "How big of a number is your body count? Thousands, surely. Maybe tens of thousands. So, you don't get to take the moral high ground here. Your hands are just as bloody as mine. Probably more."

I had no response for that.

What's more, I was tired of talking it out. So, I did what I had come to do, and I shot her in the face.

The kinetic force of the burst of gunfire sent her flipping backward over the couch, and she skidded backward a couple of extra feet. I fired again at her prone form. And again. Over and over until the magazine was spent. I had no intention of failing due to lack of gunfire, that was for sure.

I reloaded, intending to add a few more rounds to the barrage. However, as the dust settled, I couldn't help but notice a shimmering blue film hovering an inch above her body. Then, she twitched.

So, I fired again, emptying another magazine into her.

It wasn't until I reloaded for a second time that she growled, "Are you done yet? None of that's going to kill me, but it sure doesn't feel great."

As she spoke, Nora pushed herself upright and, once she'd reached her hands and knees, twisted around to sneer at me, adding, "You really are like him, aren't you?"

"What..."

"Top-quality personal shield," she said. "Cost more than this building, but I'd say it's worth it, considering you don't have anything strong enough to get through it."

"I...I don't...I don't understand..."

"Look—you got your equipment from some small-time arms dealer," she said, finally climbing to her feet. "And it's good gear. Better than most. But you have no idea what else is out there just waiting for anyone willing to go the extra mile. This shield, it runs on raw Rift Shards. Costs a damn fortune, even when it's idling, but there's nothing that comes even close when it comes to defense."

It was true. She'd basically taken a shield powerful enough to guard an entire city and tasked it with personal protection. By contrast, the shields I'd considered before buying my Sheath ran off of a combination of ambient Mist and a person's natural stores. It was the same with my subdermal Sheath as well as any other widely available armor.

But I knew that the cost wasn't the only issue. I could feel the density of the Mist around her; it was like having a personal Dead Zone the size of her body, and I suspected that the concentration of that much Mist was enough to slowly poison her body. I wondered if she realized that her shield was killing her.

Probably not.

"Had to empty the coffers for this bad boy," she said, making a dramatic show of dusting herself off. Pointedly, her hands never actually reached her body. Instead, her fingers skated along the surface of the shimmering blue shield. "But it's totally worth it."

"What do you want?"

"You came here, remember? I should be asking you the same question," she answered.

"You know why I'm here," I said, slamming a magazine into the R-14's well. It slid home with a satisfying click. "And if you think that little shield's going to protect you, you've got another thing coming. Everything has limits. And I'll keep going until it shatters. You had to know that."

"Ah, but that's the thing—if you kill me, you're killing everyone else in Nova City, too," she said, a smug expression on her face. "Didn't expect that, did you? Of course not. Because you're just an automaton who's been programmed to be what Jeremiah wanted you to be. Don't you see that? He was a monster, and he created you in his image."

"He...He wanted me to be better. He said so—"

"You're not that naive," Nora said. "You and I both know that actions speak far louder than words. Look at it objectively. He said he wanted you to be better, sure. I heard it, too. But then he turned you into a killer. That was his priority because he just wanted another weapon to control. He did the same to me. Pumped me full of bio-enhancers and aimed me at his enemies."

"You chose to put that trash in your own system," I said. "He never—"

"I had no choice!" Nora screamed, slamming the palm of her hand against the back of the couch. "He pushed me into it! I had to do something—anything—to make myself stand out. He could have given me that implant, but he made me take a different . . . He forced me down this path, Mira. Can't you see that? He pushed and he pushed, always expecting more. And the only way to satisfy his ridiculous standards was to make bad choices. I won't live past sixty. You know that, right? Everyone else is going to end up living for centuries. But me? That poison . . .

"But that was before. That was when Jeremiah was in charge," she said. "Now, though? The aliens are going to help me. They've already promised that when they come down, I can use their facilities to undergo treatments that will undo all the negative aspects of the bio-enhancers. I'll be . . . I'll be whole again."

That's when everything clicked into place. I'd always wondered why Nora had betrayed my uncle. Part of me was satisfied with thinking that she'd done so for power, to gain control of the Specters, but that had never really felt like it was enough to prompt her actions.

But the combination of shifting the blame for her bad choices onto Jeremiah and the aliens' promise to fix the damage she had done to herself? That fit almost perfectly with Nora's personality.

"You're pathetic," I said.

And I meant it. I might've been responsible for the deaths of thousands of innocent people, but at least I'd never blamed anyone else for making me do it. My choices had led me down my path. Nobody else's. The mere idea of foisting that responsibility onto someone else left me nauseated.

But Nora, she'd always looked for someone else to take responsibility for her failures. And in the end, it had gotten my uncle killed. No matter what happened, there would always be someone else for her to blame.

It was almost enough to make me feel sorry for her, but that line of emotions barely even got started before it was smothered by the reality of all the pain she'd caused.

"Pathetic?! I took hold of my own fate, and—"

"I'm not here to debate, Nora," I said, shaking my head in resignation and interrupting what would likely be a tirade of specious justification. "I'm here to kill you. Plain and simple. Once I'm done, I'm going to move on."

"And you think you can?" she demanded. "With my shield—"

"Shields take energy," I said. "That's a fact. So, unless you've got a backpack full of Rift Shards, I think I can get through that shield."

"And how would you do that?"

"A copious application of firepower," I stated. "And I think you know it. So, cut the crap and just tell me what else you've got hidden away."

"Maybe I'll just beat you to death, same as I have with—"

I laughed. "If you could have done that, you already would've," I said. "Do you know what I think? You've been getting weaker for a while, haven't you? Suddenly, all that strength has faded. You're a shadow of what you once were."

"There's no—"

"I poisoned your bio-enhancers, Nora," I cut in. "For months now, you've been shoving a useless chemical into your body. It might've even been detrimental. I don't know. You feel it, don't you? That weakness. You always hated it. I doubt you could hurt me even if I gave you a free shot or two."

Anyone else, and I'd have been worried about firearms. But Nora had always disdained their use, famously preferring her own two hands when it came to combat. As a result, she had no modifiers for ranged combat or certifications. So, her options for powerful weapons were limited, and even if she'd managed to acquire one, I suspected that, without modifiers backing her up, she would be incapable of quickly finishing me off. By the time she managed to get through my defenses, I could turn the tables.

No—I was in no danger. Not from her, at least.

No sooner had that thought crossed my mind than she started to laugh. It lasted only a few seconds, and she cut off just as quickly as it had started—meaning it was probably feigned. When she finished, she said, "You are so like him. He was sure of his own power, too. He thought he was invincible."

"To you, he was."

I could hear her teeth grinding before she hissed, "And who's dead, huh? If he was so invincible, how come I'm the one still standing tall?"

"You call this tall?" I asked, gesturing all around. "How long do you think it'll be before they all turn on you? Not long, after all this. Even your own people are on the verge of abandoning you, and that's not even counting the pound of flesh the other tribes will demand. Even if I walk away right now, you're done, Nora. And you're the only one who can't see that."

She shook her head, then, in a quiet voice, said, "You're right. And do you know what, Mira? That just means I have nothing to lose."

I didn't like her tone of voice. "What does that mean?" I demanded.

She smiled, and for a moment, I wondered how things had gone so wrong. In that smile, I saw hundreds of previous conversations. I saw all the advice she had given me. All the comfort she had provided. I saw my friend.

I saw family.

"It means if I can't be on top, I might as well tear the whole thing down" was her response. She tapped the metal plate on the back of her neck, continuing, "Called a kill switch. Had it made special a few weeks ago. I didn't think I'd use it for this, but . . . Well, let's just call it a happy accident. I got the idea from you, you know. At the time, I didn't know it was you, but you were definitely the inspiration. Seeing those Silos destroyed, it opened my eyes to the power of a good explosion. So, I had this thing made."

"So, if you die, the building goes down," I guessed.

"The building? God no. I'm going to bring down the whole city."

For a moment, I couldn't respond. Instead, my mind raced as I tried to process her claim. Was it possible? I had no idea. But in my experience, if you used enough explosives, you could blow just about anything up.

"The pillars are the point of weakness," she said. "Relatively speaking, of course. The whole thing is reinforced by Mist, but that can be overcome. The point, Mira, is that if you kill me, you'll be killing everyone else in Nova City. The aristocrats up in King's Row. The shopkeepers in Bywater. The poor addicts in Algiers. The few holdouts in the Garden. All of them."

At its height, Nova City had been home to millions of people, so even now that so many had left, there were at least hundreds of thousands left. The city only felt empty because it had been built to accommodate a much larger population.

"What's your revenge worth, Mira?" she asked, a smirk playing across her smug face.

She thought she had won. I could see that much. The Mira she knew would never have made the kind of sacrifice she'd suggested.

But that wasn't the person standing in front of her.

I sighed, letting my weapon fall to my side. "I thought I'd be allowed to change," I said. "I thought I had turned a corner." I shook my head. "But this world, it's not built like that, is it? It keeps pushing and pushing until we're buried in nothing but bad decisions," I said. "That's the secret, isn't it? You have to . . . I don't know . . . just make the best of one bad situation after another."

"Sucks, doesn't it?"

I shrugged. "It is what it is," I stated, looking up and into her eyes. "You know, I kept thinking that this would be like a fairy tale. Or like one of those parables Jeremiah used to tell me when I was little. Like the one with the Good Samaritan. As if every situation would resolve itself with some moral lesson. But that's not real life. Not in this world, at least."

Then, without another word, I hefted my rifle and fired. Over and over, one burst after another, I assaulted her shield. It easily stopped the superheated plasma, but the sheer kinetic force of each shot sent Nora tumbling to the floor. I kept going, squeezing the trigger with metronomic precision until the magazine was spent. Then, in a swift and practiced motion, I exchanged it for another and continued the bombardment.

Like that, I kept going. I didn't expect the shield to easily fall, but in the absence of any resistance—Nora was kept off-balance by the constant barrage, and even if she wasn't, she had become a paper tiger; she looked tough, but there wasn't much real strength backing it up—I had the leisure to steadily wear the shield down.

Which I did.

One magazine after another until my entire stock of R-14 ammunition was spent. Then, I stowed the weapon for Ferdinand II and continued my assault. The sound of constant gunfire filled the air as I emptied my arsenal implant of pistol ammunition. Then, I switched to the scattergun. It was less effective than the others but more impactful than I might have expected. Still, when the last canister was spent, the shield remained intact.

For her part, Nora tried to resist. She tried to run. Seeing that I didn't care about her contingency plan had frightened her; I could see that much painted across her face, and she had no option but to try to flee. But under my barrage, that was impossible. She was pinned down and incapable of resistance.

Still, her shield was high-quality and vastly overpowered for its purpose, and I couldn't help but wonder if I'd have to veer away from brute-force tactics.

That in mind, I exchanged the scattergun for the Pulsar and started using Empowered Shot every two seconds. That had more of an impact, and each shot sent ripples of Mist to dance across the shield's surface. But even after I'd used every last round in my arsenal implant, it still remained intact.

So, I pounced, intending to take a more direct approach.

I preferred it that way.

When I fell upon her, Nora attempted to throw me aside in a practiced motion, but my sabotage of her bio-enhancers had done its job well. A good thing. An innocent man's life had been ruined so I could foist weakness upon her. If it hadn't worked . . .

No matter. It had.

I repositioned myself atop her, activated Combination Punch, and went to work with the Hand of God. One punch after another, each one stronger than the last, fell upon that shield with monumental force. Four punches, reactivate my ability, and continue—for almost a minute, that was the pattern of my entire existence. I grunted with each strike, putting every ounce of my Constitution behind every punch.

Then, suddenly, my supply of Mist guttered out.

For a long moment, I just stared down at her. I'd thrown everything I had at Nora—or more accurately her shield—but it wasn't enough. The shield flickered and quivered, clearly on the verge of destruction, but it remained strong enough to protect Nora from my measly attacks.

For her part, Nora had long since lost consciousness. Even though my attacks had been blocked, some of the force had gone through, rattling her brain enough to knock her out. Maybe she'd go into a coma. Or experience brain damage. Perhaps that would have to be enough for now.

Plus, it would keep the kill switch from going off. It seemed like a win-win. For all intents and purposes, Nora would be gone, and Nova City would survive.

It was a deal I should've been elated to take.

But I couldn't do it. I refused to let her continue to draw breath. Living the rest of her life as a comatose vegetable was letting her off light.

In the end, it was a decision I'd already made multiple times before. My need for revenge would not be satisfied by mere incapacitation. Nora had to die, and despite the character growth I'd thought I had experienced, I hadn't come so far, I hadn't sacrificed so much or so many just to stop short of my goal. I couldn't live in a world where Nora continued to live—not if I could do something about it.

So, for the last time, I made my choice.

Standing, I drew my blade from the sheath at my back. I took a moment to watch the blue energy dancing along its edge; for such an efficient weapon, it certainly was beautiful. Perhaps in another world, I could have appreciated that. But in my world, in a reality where fables and parables were just silly stories meant to keep children in line, the sword was just a weapon.

And I used it for its intended purpose.

Hefting it in a two-handed grip, I brought it down with furious speed. There were no abilities augmenting its damage, but even so, it cut into the weakened shield with predictable results. I could feel the Mist flicker as it drew more power from the Rift Shards that fueled its function.

Another strike, and the flickers became a persistent shimmer. Still another, and the shimmers became miniature tidal waves of pure Mist. Another followed. Again and again. I put every ounce of my fury behind each strike. I was fueled by frustration, loss, and sheer determination, and unlike the Mist, my emotions were inexhaustible.

Finally, after what felt like my hundredth attack, the shield fell, winking out of existence as if it had never been. And at last, my revenge was at hand.

I'd imagined that moment a hundred times. In my mind, I'd always been an avenging angel, reaping justice as I struck down my hated foe. But the reality was very different. I was just an angry girl standing over an unconscious woman.

My sword fell one final time, biting into her neck with the precision born of a thousand hours' worth of practice. It didn't stop until it hit the concrete floor.

Nora's head fell free, rolling ever so slightly to the right.

Blood pooled, vibrant and red.

Tears fell down my cheeks as I felt overwhelmed by emptiness.

I was finished. I had gotten my revenge. Nora was dead. I should have been elated. I should have felt some sense of satisfaction. But I didn't. Instead, I was just . . . empty.

Just as I was beginning to come to grips with my quest's end, the ground rumbled. Once. Twice. Three and then four tremors shook the megabuilding.

It was an important number because I knew precisely what it signified. After all, the platform that held the Garden thousands of feet above the swamp was supported by precisely four enormous pillars.

The kill switch, it seemed, had activated.

CHAPTER SEVENTY

A NEW TOMORROW

To my ruin, I overestimated Mira's capacity for empathy. Or maybe she did care about all those people. I don't know. But she refused to veer off her chosen path just because a few innocent people were going to die. It was only in the moments before my death that it became clear that she truly had become Jeremiah's successor.

—Nora Lancaster

Panic gripped my mind as tremors shook the city. I'd never been in an earthquake, but I suspect that what I felt in that moment was something similar. It was only due to the increased proprioception that came with [Acrobatics] that I was able to maintain my footing. Still, I took a brief moment to look down at Nora's corpse. In death, she looked much smaller than she had in life.

Was that the effect of the sabotaged bio-enhancers? Or just the lack of her big personality? I would never know.

I should have been elated. Happy. Or at least satisfied. But I wasn't. Looking down on Nora's body, all I felt was a mountain of regret. Not that I'd killed her—that was always inevitable and necessary. Instead, I regretted that she'd chosen such a doomed path. If she'd simply maintained her loyalty to my uncle, she might have had decades more to live. But now, her life had ended before she'd managed to accomplish anything of note.

Another tremor put the lie to that thought. Bringing down a city the size of Nova had to count as noteworthy, right? Perhaps that was the point. Even in death, she'd chosen the selfish route.

But was I any different? I'd wrapped my actions in pretty justifications, but at the end of the day, I'd chosen my needs over the lives of everyone left in the city. I couldn't rightly call that anything but selfish.

That wasn't anything new. Not for me, and not for the rest of humanity. That was the one lesson I'd learned better than any other. Nobody ever really worked for the greater good. They don't want to make the world a better place. Instead, everyone just wants to progress—whether it was in the realm of wealth, power, or influence—so that the injustices inherent in any society no longer applied to them.

And I was a shining example of that philosophy.

I hadn't set out to achieve that dubious distinction. It was just a by-product of human nature. At the end of the day, I just didn't care about anyone else the way I cared about myself or my goals. I wanted to be different. I wanted to choose a different path. But when the time came, I made the only decision that made sense to me.

My goals versus the lives of everyone in Nova City.

I hadn't even hesitated before killing Nora. Not really. And that said more about me than anything else I'd ever done. If my mind had been laid bare by that spider's mental attack, then killing Nora had stripped my soul of any pretenses.

I was not a good person.

Perhaps I wasn't evil. Not really—because I'd never set out to cause needless harm. But in the back of my mind, crowded by all the other thoughts I didn't want to acknowledge, I had to wonder if that distinction really mattered. After all, how many people really set out to become villains? There were bound to be a few, but the vast majority of evil boiled down to simple selfishness. They wanted something so much that they just didn't care about the cost. In that way, maybe I really had willingly descended into that realm.

Of course, I didn't think I'd live to regret it. After all, with every passing second, the intensity of the tremors increased. Soon enough, whatever reinforcement the Mist provided would be overcome, and everything would tumble down to the ground.

It really was fitting. I'd worked so hard, I'd sacrificed so many—it only made sense that my moment of triumph, as grim as the cost was, would turn out to be a double-edged sword that cut both ways.

For a moment, I considered simply surrendering. I'd gotten what I wanted, and no matter what plans I'd made, I really had no idea what I wanted to do with the rest of my life. And besides, I hadn't forgotten about the impending doom that rode on the shoulders of the aliens' upcoming arrival. Once they landed, everything would change, and not for the better. Perhaps it was better if I simply gave in and let the consequences of my actions sweep over me.

Maybe that would be the noble thing to do. The selfless thing. Wherever I went, chaos and destruction followed. I was a walking calamity, and I had no doubts that the world would be a safer place without me in it.

But then, the selfishness reared its ugly head once again, and I realized that I could no more wait for my death than I could simply choose to stop breathing. It was antithetical to everything I was.

So, I started in on a plan.

First, get out of the megabuilding. Second, get to the edge of the platform. Third, jump.

As far as plans went, it was a simple one, but I didn't have time to come up with anything more complicated. Once, I'd survived a fall of a few hundred feet, so I had some hope of making it out alive. Of course, there was a marked difference between a plunge of a few hundred feet and one of a couple thousand, and I'd have to somehow avoid the falling platforms, but I wasn't exactly bursting with options.

Not if I wanted to survive.

With that in mind, I started moving. I covered the distance to the door of the penthouse in a few short steps, and by the time I hit the corridor, I'd accelerated to a limping sprint that took me all the way to the elevator. Without hesitation, I leaped into the shaft, slowing my fall by periodically gripping the ledges I'd used during my climb. I never paused for more than an instant, but it was enough to keep me from splatting against the roof of the elevator car.

I slipped into the elevator car, surprising a couple of Operators. I stopped only long enough to end their lives with two quick strokes from my nano-bladed sword, and then I was once again on my way.

I dashed through the halls and to the front door, pushing myself to run ever faster. My passage didn't go unnoticed, and a hail of gunfire—first, from the Operators who'd been stationed on the ground floor of the megabuilding, then from the Enforcers who'd gathered outside—followed in my wake. However, I was moving so quickly, and I'd arrived so suddenly, that I broke free completely unscathed.

Perhaps the increasingly powerful tremors helped a little, too.

I had no idea what all the others thought was happening, but I didn't think they knew that the entire city would soon fall. If they had, they wouldn't have been worried about me at all. Instead, they'd have been running right alongside me, desperate to find some way of preserving their lives.

I couldn't be bothered with thoughts of their fates, though.

Instead, I continued my sprint until I had enough space to summon my Cutter. Once I'd straddled my hover bike, I felt marginally better about my chances. I was fast, but even I couldn't sprint quickly enough to reach the edge of the platform before everything fell. But with the hover bike, I had a chance, which was all I could hope for.

I raced through the streets, taking the quickest path to the ramp that would lead down to Algiers. I'd considered simply going to the edge of the Garden, but in an attempt at safety, the platform was ringed by tall buildings, without a gap in sight. In the past, I'd considered it a good thing, keeping people from inadvertently falling to their deaths, but as I sped through the Garden, I couldn't help but wish the city's founders were a little less cognizant of their citizens' safety.

In any case, it severely limited my options, and I had no choice but to head to one of Algiers's gates. That had the unexpected bonus of helping me avoid the other falling platforms.

I glanced back the way I'd come, and what I saw nearly made me lose control of the hover bike. In the distance and far above me, the King's Row platform loomed. But even without flaring Observation, I could see the thick fissures spreading across the pillars that supported it. In addition, a cloud of small ships, looking like a swarm of insects because of the distance, had erupted from the surface and into the air.

The aristocrats had begun their evacuation.

Pity, that. I might've lamented the deaths of the remaining citizens of the Garden, Algiers, or even Bywater, but I'd never be caught shedding a tear for the fates of the rich and powerful who called the higher platforms home. I could only hope that the majority didn't possess the means to escape the upcoming catastrophe. If so, then maybe there would be a silver lining to my selfish choice to sacrifice the city on the altar of my vengeance.

After that quick glance, I refocused on keeping the bike under control and at top speed. As I tore through the Garden, I passed more than a few groups of Operators. Some saw me coming and took that opportunity to take potshots at me; universally, they underestimated my speed, but I still picked up a couple of flesh wounds to add to my tally of injuries.

There was a part of me that desperately wanted to stop and make them pay for attacking me, but it wasn't difficult to suppress that urge with the knowledge that I was running out of time.

Almost as soon as that thought flitted across my mind, a huge shudder rocked the platform. I could barely keep the bike under control as a second tremor followed. And then another. Before I could go more than a few feet, the entire platform had begun to tilt to the side.

Even as I kept going, buildings started to fall apart. The megabuildings were reinforced, so they remained intact, but the others—they weren't so lucky. All around me the city began to crumble. I dodged back and forth as I continued to pour on the speed, but I knew it wouldn't be enough. The city's pillars were failing far sooner than I'd hoped.

But I had no choice but to keep going. Even if there'd been other options, I'd gone well past the point of turning back and trying something else. I was committed, and I could only do my best to avoid the obstacles in my way.

A three-story building near the edge of the platform teetered, then fell across the street in front of me. With my Mind attribute, I was able to make the minute adjustments necessary to take me down a side street where I could avoid the worst of falling rubble, but the same couldn't be said for a group of Operators who'd set up a checkpoint directly in its path.

I didn't see them crushed, but I didn't need to, either.

Like everyone else in the city, they'd been doomed the moment I'd chosen to kill Nora.

I turned again, putting myself back on the proper path, and soon enough, I reached my destination—only to find that the spiraling ramp that led down to Algiers had already started to fall.

I kept going.

However, the moment I started circling the spiral ramp, I began to regret it. Above me, the concrete had already begun to crumble, and by the third revolution of the spiral, a couple of huge chunks fell free. I jerked the bike to the side, narrowly avoiding the first, then put on a little additional speed to outrun the second. Both thudded into the ramp, sending huge cracks arcing from the points of impact.

But it held.

Barely.

I leaned forward, eking every ounce of speed I could out of the bike. The centrifugal force pressed against me, making my already injured organs feel like they'd been mashed into jelly, but I had no choice but to go faster. So, I did.

My body did not thank me for it, but I managed to shoot out the other side of the ramp just in time to avoid falling along with the entire structure. Behind me, the sound of the failing structure filled my ears, followed by a deep rumble that could only have been one of the pillars finally giving out.

I couldn't spare the attention to check for sure.

Instead, I raced through the familiar streets of Algiers. Thankfully, it was almost entirely deserted, but there was still a sizable population of homeless people, addicts, and the poorest of the poor. None of them could afford to leave the city. Likely, some of them hadn't even climbed out of their stupors long enough to know that everyone else had fled.

Was it a mercy that they would soon die? That they would be spared a slow death?

Maybe.

Probably not.

Either way, I could do nothing to change their fates. Even without the city falling all around them, most would have died within a few months anyway. Transience and drug addiction made for a short life.

I raced along, barely outpacing the destruction.

And then, suddenly, the street in front of me fell away, replaced by a yawning abyss I could never hope to bridge. I skidded to a stop, barely maintaining my seat. A hundred yards of open air stood before me, followed by the rest of the district. I hadn't even gotten close to the gate that had been my destination.

I didn't remain stationary for long. I didn't have that luxury. Instead, I turned around and found a side street, hoping to take a different route. However, I soon discovered that the way was blocked on all sides.

Except back the way I'd come, but that wasn't an option.

Sitting on my Cutter, I sighed. So close, and yet, so far away. I'd almost escaped. All around me, the city continued to rumble and rock, but I paid it little attention. I'd reached the end of my rope. I was out of options. The only way I could hope to survive was to jump now and hope I somehow avoided the thousands—or maybe millions—of tons of falling concrete that had once been Algiers.

A slim hope indeed.

But who was I kidding? My chances of survival had always been slim. I wasn't going to live through a fall of thousands of feet. I'd progressed a long way, but there were limits to everything. And I'd reached mine.

Still, I couldn't surrender.

I couldn't just give up.

If there was one characteristic that I could point to as integral to the very core of who I was, it was my stubbornness. At times, I'd thought of it as endurance. Other times, I'd dressed it up with prettier words. But at the end of the day, I was just too stubborn to stop.

So, with a deep breath, I dismissed my Cutter and stepped up to the huge rent in the platform and peeked over the edge. The swamp was down there. It barely looked real from so far away. I knew I didn't have a choice but to leap, but still, my insides twisted into painful knots as I thought about doing just that.

As I had done so often in the past, I put one foot in front of the other. Then another. And on the third step, my foot found nothing but air.

I fell.

To my likely death.

And as I tumbled into the open air, my thoughts didn't settle on selfish desires. I didn't think about my future or my goals. Instead, I thought about Patrick. I hoped he'd gotten out. I'd sent him a message before my assault on the megabuilding, telling him to get out of the city as soon as he got back from the Bazaar, but I wasn't even sure it had gone through.

Still, I hoped it had. I hoped he could find a way to survive and make a life for himself. It was probably better this way.

In that moment, I closed my eyes and accepted my inevitable death. If I was lucky, I'd die on impact, but I suspected that wouldn't be the case. No—I'd survive, at least for a few minutes, but I'd probably be broken to the point of incapacitation. Then, unable to move, I'd be incapable of escaping the falling rubble of the city.

That's when I would die, buried under tons of rock and—

I jerked to a sudden stop as I smacked into something. I didn't even have a chance to open my eyes before I heard Patrick's voice over our secure connection say, "Hold on! It's going to be close!"

I opened my eyes to see that I'd landed on a sleek piece of metal, and it took an embarrassingly long couple of seconds before I realized that I was on top of a ship. "W-what . . . How . . ."

"Kind of busy!" he shouted. "Explain in a minute!"

Then, the ship accelerated, and it was all I could do to grab hold of a ridge to keep from falling off. A moment later, we had found open air. It was just in time, too. I looked back the way we'd come, and I saw that the pillars had finally given in to inevitability, and their crumbling announced the beginning of Nova City's fall.

The ship continued to speed along until we were miles away. Without the extra grip strength of the Hand of God, I probably couldn't have managed to stay in place, but with it, I barely maintained my position until, at last, we began our descent. Finally, we landed in a clearing.

As we settled down, I looked back and saw the giant platforms of Nova City plummet into the swamp. Even miles away, the ground shook. I couldn't look away until, minutes later, the entire city had fallen.

"Uh . . . You want to come inside? I don't want to be here much longer," Patrick said through our connection. "I can stay under the radar for a while, but there are a lot of ships in the air right now."

Numbly, I pushed myself to my feet and looked down at the surface of the ship. Its hull was black with gold trim, reminding me of Patrick's pistol, but I couldn't really see much more than the general color scheme. Not that I was in any sort of state to appreciate it anyway.

After all, I was wrung out, both mentally and physically exhausted, and more injured than I'd been at any time other than when I'd fought the mutated wildlings. And I didn't have a friendly Templar around to heal me this time.

Awkwardly, I slid down from my perch to see that Patrick had already exited the ship and was looking up at me. I could tell from his wince that I didn't look great. And no matter my appearance, I was sure I felt even worse.

"You don't look so great," he said, helping me down.

"Don't feel so hot, either," I admitted. "How did you find me?"

"The secure connection," he said. "Kind of a misnomer, honestly, because that thing isn't even close to secure. I used the equipment in the ship to home in on your location. When I saw your altitude decreasing, I kind of figured you jumped. Because of course you would jump."

"Why didn't you contact me?" I asked.

"Believe me, I tried," he said. "But with all those explosions, the Mist went wild. Too much interference for communication until I got close."

"You saved me."

"I did."

"Again."

"And I always will, Mira," he said. "I know you hate not being in control, but—"

I didn't let him finish. Instead, I threw my arms around him and buried my face in his chest. That's when the tears came—from both of us. He muttered something about not being able to lose me. I tried to muster a response, but I couldn't get anything out between the sobs. But neither of us really needed to say anything.

Actions spoke louder than any words could ever hope to match. And when it came down to it, Patrick had proven that he would always be there for me.

After far too long, I pulled away and looked up into his eyes. Then, I said, "Come on. Let's . . . Let's get out of here."

"Where to?" he asked.

"I don't care. Just away from here," I answered. "I've had enough of this place."

ABOUT THE AUTHOR

Nicholas Searcy is the author of Death: Genesis, a fantasy series originally released on Royal Road. He enjoys writing, reading, spending time with family, sports, and, of course, a good cup of coffee.

DISCOVER
STORIES UNBOUND

PodiumAudio.com

www.ingramcontent.com/pod-product-compliance
Ingram Content Group UK Ltd.
Pitfield, Milton Keynes, MK11 3LW, UK
UKHW041433180426
11947UKWH00007B/407